THE FURYCK SAGA

WINTER'S FURY

THE BURNING SEA

NIGHT OF THE SHADOW MOON

HALLOW WOOD

THE RAVEN'S WARNING

VALE OF THE GODS

KINGS OF FATE
A Prequel Novella

THE LORDS OF ALEKKA

EYE OF THE WOLF

MARK OF THE HUNTER

BLOOD OF THE RAVEN

HEART OF THE KING

FURY OF THE QUEEN

WRATH OF THE SUN

FATE OF THE FURYCKS

THE SHADOW ISLE

TOWER OF BLOOD AND FLAME

Sign up to my newsletter, so you don't miss out
on new release information!

http://www.aerayne.com/sign-up

WINTER'S FURY

THE FURYCK SAGA: BOOK ONE

A.E. RAYNE

For Cass

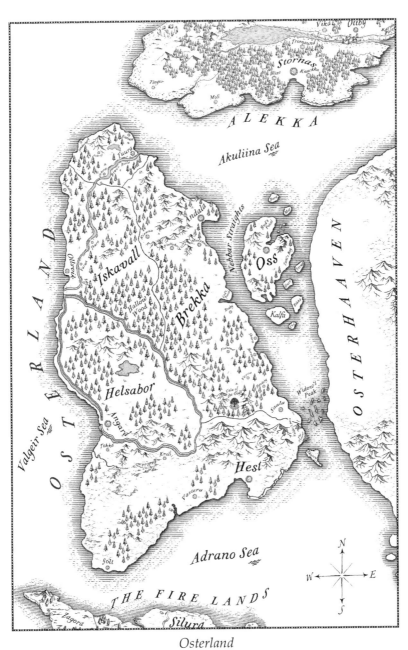

Osterland

CHARACTERS

THE SLAVE ISLANDS

In Oss
Eirik Skalleson, King of Oss
Eadmund Skalleson
Eydis Skalleson
Morac Gallas
Runa Gallas
Fyn Gallas
Evaine Gallas
Thorgils Svanter
Odda Svanter
Torstan Berg
Tarak Soren
Entorp Bray

In Kalfa
Ivaar Skalleson, Lord of Kalfa
Isaura Skalleson, Lady of Kalfa
Selene Skalleson
Annet Skalleson
Leya Skalleson
Mads Skalleson
Ayla Adea

In Rikka
Morana Gallas

CHARACTERS

THE KINGDOM OF BREKKA

In Andala

Lothar Furyck, King of Brekka

Gisila Furyck

Jael Furyck

Axl Furyck

Osbert Furyck

Amma Furyck

Aleksander Lehr

Edela Saeveld

Gant Olborn

Brynna 'Biddy' Halvor

* * *

TUURA

Branwyn Byrn

Kormac Byrn

Aedan Byrn

Kayla Byrn

Aron Byrn

Neva Elgard

Marcus Volsen, Elderman of Tuura

Alaric Fraed

Hanna Boelens

PROLOGUE

You tried to take my head, as my sisters went before,
but in the dark you slept and let the wolf slip out your door.

You tried to take the book, the one that Taegus stole for me,
but I have it with me still, and its magic set me free.

You tried to take my home, but I will begin again;
I will make myself an army of one hundred thousand men.

And when my name has faded from your memories and
your lips,
I will crawl out of my grave, and I will ready all my ships.

And when you're at your strongest, when your happiness
is full,
I will take my sweet revenge and destroy the Furyck's rule.
And when the night is blackest, and your lands are
burned by war...

Your eyes will blind.
Your blood will flow.
Your hearts will beat no more.

Edela woke with a gasp, her heart hammering loudly in her ears.

She tried to hold on to the fading dream; to cling to the warning before it slipped away again; before she fell asleep. But it was too late. She couldn't stop her eyes closing, closing, closing... and once again, the warning fell back, into the abyss of her forgotten memories.

PART ONE

Destiny

CHAPTER ONE

Jael Furyck's feet were freezing in wet socks that clung to numb toes, sitting in damp boots, which, although new, were already leaking. She tried to focus on her cold feet, pressing them harder into the wet wool; into the soft, damp leather of her boots; into the reeds that lined the hard mud floor. She imagined them twisting and strong, like the roots of Furia's Tree; buried deep in the earth, solid and unwavering. If she could just focus on her feet, then maybe she wouldn't say anything. Maybe there was a chance she could control the urgent, angry fire coursing up through her body and into her mouth.

No! Not her mouth, her feet, her feet!

She had to think of her feet.

She had to ignore the anger throbbing at the base of her throat, demanding to be released.

She couldn't let him, them, all of them, watch as she lost control.

Lothar Furyck perched impatiently on the edge of his ornately carved throne, glowering at his niece. His announcement moments earlier had all but guaranteed an explosive reaction from her, but where was it? Jael had a fierce temper, and this was to be the ultimate humiliation of her, and, by extension, her whole family, but so far, she would not play his carefully constructed game. Her face remained impassive, and although he was certain she was seething, she said nothing, which caused an uncomfortable silence to creep around them both. But Lothar had to say something or the moment would be lost to him. The Andalans sitting on their cold benches, looking up at their king would soon start to wonder what power he truly had over any of them. So biting down on his annoyance, Lothar cleared his throat and smiled as though there had been no awkward silence at all. 'And so, the wedding feast will take place on Oss in fifteen days. Plenty of time for you to find a dress!' He waved a chubby hand at Jael's well-worn trousers and cloak, nostrils flaring with distaste. 'And enough time for the rest of us to return to Andala before the Freeze sets in!'

Lothar leaned forward, his bulging eyes demanding a reply, and this time Jael knew that she had to say something. She couldn't just continue to ignore him. 'Will I be able to take my horse?' she asked dully, lips barely moving.

Lothar lifted an eyebrow, remembering how much trouble that horse had caused recently. It was better to be rid of them both. 'You may, but you will give up your sword. You won't be needing it where you're going.'

A surprised murmur echoed around the hall, sending another bolt of fury through Jael's rigid body. 'It was my father's sword,' she muttered haltingly, her devastation revealing itself at last.

'It was *my* father's sword,' Lothar growled, running a jewelled hand through his dark beard. 'The Furyck sword. Handed down from king to king. How or why you received it when my brother died, I do not know, you being neither his heir or a king.'

Jael wanted to launch herself at her uncle.

She wanted to rip out his vile throat, lying hidden beneath the rolls of fat gathering around his sagging chin. To watch his life-blood course down his bloated belly until he was white with death.

Take her sword?

She stood on the edge, ready to abandon all reason, but then, remembering her feet, Jael dug her toes deep into her boots, clenching her jaw. Lothar wasn't going to humiliate her any further. She wouldn't give him that. 'As you wish, Uncle.'

Lothar frowned, his shoulders sagging with disappointment. He'd watched his niece desperately trying to keep hold of her temper, and it appeared that she had succeeded. Though, he had hit his mark at least.

She was badly, if not fatally wounded.

Lothar could feel the growl of his dead brother at his back. Here he was, sitting on his brother's throne, selling his beloved daughter off to his enemy.

Just the thought of Ranuf's indignant face imbued Lothar with confidence, and the smile that curled his wet lips was wide and brimming with satisfaction. 'Good,' he said coolly, glancing at his son, Osbert, who was struggling to contain his own annoyance at Jael's oddly calm reaction. 'We will speak more of this tomorrow. Alp!' he barked, turning to his servant, who was hovering anxiously behind him, waiting to be called on. 'Have the next course brought out! And wine!' Lothar yelled as Alp turned and scurried towards the kitchen. 'I need more wine!'

Jael was rooted to the spot as the hall burst into life around her. The servants started moving again, ferrying trays of sizzling roast boar and pork sausages to the tables, filling cups with wine and ale as conversations sparked around them. It felt as though every pair of eyes was focused on her, and she was desperate to escape. Glancing around the hall, she spotted her mother, Gisila, lurking near one of the large fire pits, the shock of Lothar's announcement still on her pale face.

Jael made straight for her.

Gisila could feel the sting of tears in her eyes as she stared at the high table, watching Lothar and his vile son banging their cups together. It was sometimes hard to remember what it had felt like to sit up there with her husband, but she had, for thirty years, as his wife, the Queen of Brekka. Until Ranuf had died, and Lothar had returned to destroy all their lives.

Gisila felt a sudden pull from behind as Jael grabbed her by the arm and hurried her outside.

Dark clouds rushed across the moon. A storm was brewing, but Jael barely noticed as she stalked across the square, her hood pulled down to avoid the latecomers heading for the hall. Gisila walked quickly beside her, struggling to keep up with her daughter, conscious of the panic that was tightening her shoulders.

When they reached Gisila's small cottage, Jael ushered her mother inside, slamming the door behind them. Gisila's servant, Gunni, jumped in surprise, quickly making herself scarce, merging into the shadows at the back of the sparsely furnished hovel.

Dropping her hood, Jael turned to her mother, narrowing her intense green eyes until her eyebrows almost met in the middle of her face.

'I, I didn't know,' Gisila spluttered, sensing the angry fire that was coming. 'I didn't know!'

Jael was too wild to speak, her eyes sweeping the cottage with its hard mud floor, three low beds, a small fire for warmth and light, another for meals. There was a small kitchen area with a few shelves too, an old barrel for a table, five tree stumps for stools. It was windowless and dank, and utterly miserable, all of which likely delighted Lothar who appeared to take great pleasure in the demotion of his dead brother's family.

After stealing the throne from Ranuf's son, Lothar had kicked Gisila and her children out of the comfortable hall, moving his own family in. And now he presided over them like a tyrant, determined to squeeze every last bit of joy out of their lives.

Letting them live, but on his terms alone.

'What is Lothar thinking? You can't marry that man!' Gisila muttered crossly behind her. 'He is nothing. His family is nothing! His father was a slave. Ranuf's enemy and a slave! It's an insult. The worst Lothar has done to us for sure!'

That was just like her mother, Jael thought. Always making everything about herself.

'Where is Axl?' Gisila turned and directed this at Gunni who had started turning down the beds.

'I don't know, my lady.'

Gisila glanced at her daughter. 'Your brother will have something to say about this, I'm sure.'

Jael said nothing. Her head was a mess of hot fury and building sorrow. She couldn't keep up with her thoughts as they tumbled over one another, desperately seeking a way out of the hole that Lothar had so happily trapped her in. Running her hands through her long dark hair, mostly tied up in messy braids, Jael frowned. Surely she was too old for marriage? And why would Eirik Skalleson of all people want her for his son?

Why now?

Jael turned to the door. 'I'll go and see Edela. She'll know what to do.' And ducking her head, she slipped outside before her mother had even looked up.

The wind whipped the door shut with such a bang that Gisila jumped, and folding her arms across her chest to ward off the chill, she returned her gaze to the fire. There was nothing her mother could say that would stop this, she was certain. Lothar had finally found a way to remove Jael, and with her gone, they would all be exposed, for Jael was their protector, and Lothar knew it. Without her, they were weak and vulnerable.

Just as he intended.

Gisila shivered, eyes lost in the twisting flames, tears running down her cold cheeks.

***

Jael strode up the path to her grandmother's old cottage which sat up a small rise, slippery with patches of ice. A line of bones and stones strung about the porch chimed chaotically to announce her arrival.

Axl opened the door, smiling in surprise to see his sister, although the look on her face quickly soured his. 'Jael? Are you alright?' he frowned. She didn't reply, staring past his gangly frame into the dull glow of Edela's cottage. Axl knew well enough not to prod any further. 'I was just leaving,' he mumbled, squeezing past his tall sister and out into the night. Wrapping his cloak around a pair of broad shoulders, he walked carefully down the path, wondering if his mother knew what was wrong with Jael.

Edela Saeveld sat in her fur-thick chair, just to the right of a low-burning fire. She studied her granddaughter with one raised eyebrow, patting the stool in front of her. 'Well, come on, then, you may as well tell me what your storm is about tonight,' she smiled, her weathered face creasing with an easy humour, which, she noticed, did little to change the fierceness of the face considering her.

Jael didn't sit down.

Edela frowned, her smile disappearing. 'What has happened, Jael? Tell me.'

'Well, you're the dreamer, Grandmother,' Jael grumbled. 'Why don't you tell me? Why *didn't* you tell me? You see everything that's going to happen. Why didn't you see this?' She clenched her jaw, trying to calm herself down, knowing that Lothar was the one she was truly angry at.

Edela blinked, small blue eyes full of confusion before they suddenly cleared. 'Ahhh, so Lothar is marrying you off, then?'

'You knew?' Jael's eyes bulged. 'Of course you knew!'

Edela stood, grimacing at the familiar ache in her right hip as she hobbled towards her granddaughter. 'I will make you some tea, and you will sit down, and we will talk. If you wish to yell, Jael, go and yell at the moon. It is full enough out there to hear you, I'm sure, even over that screeching wind.' And with that, she bustled away to her kitchen corner, rummaging around the overfilled shelves, heaving with pots and cups, fresh and dried herbs, and all sorts of strange items that no one dared ask about. Edela was more than a dreamer, gifted with visions of the future, she was Andala's healer, called upon to cure all manner of ailments. And, after twenty-seven years of looking after Jael, she had grown quite used to easing red-hot tempers.

Jael sighed. Experience told her that there was no shifting her grandmother, so moving the stool closer to the fire, she sat down, her body humming with an urgency to run out into the night and stab her sword through one of Lothar's bulbous eyes.

If he wanted the Furyck sword so much, he could have it.

Marry her to an Islander? Send her away from Brekka?

And what about Aleksander?

Edela came back with a cup and handed it to Jael before lifting her cauldron from its hook, carefully pouring hot water over the fragrant herbs she had sprinkled inside. 'Here, let this sit a while, then have a good drink. It will help with all that fire in there.' She waved at Jael's creased forehead as she replaced the small cauldron, and slunk back into her chair.

'Thank you,' Jael mumbled. 'Now, tell me everything.'

Edela laughed, leaning back, feeling the comforting warmth of fur beneath her bones. 'Everything?' She smiled, rubbing her cold hands together. 'Well, I knew you would be married one day. Yes, I did see that.'

'And you didn't think to *tell* me?' Jael was incredulous, almost spilling the hot tea. 'Grandmother! Why didn't you tell me? I could have done something! Aleksander and I could have made plans to leave! Years ago! We could have done something! Anything but this!'

Edela inhaled the sweet scents of skullcap and chamomile as they steeped in Jael's cup. 'Yes, I could have told you,' she said calmly. 'But being a dreamer is not about revealing everything you see. It's not as simple as that,' she sighed. 'And yes, of course, you could have run away. But in my dreams, I saw you with this man. I saw that it was meant to be. There is something about you and him together that is important somehow. I know it's not what you wanted, but it was clear to me that this marriage was fated. I had no choice but to stay quiet.'

'*What*?' Jael shook her head. 'No. No! You should have told me! You should have given *me* a choice. You should have left it up to *me* to decide!'

Edela sat, untroubled by Jael's bellowing. 'Perhaps. Perhaps you would have found your way to him anyway? But who am I to take that risk? To interfere with the plans the gods have made for you? And not your gods either, Jael, but mine. The Tuuran gods show me my dreams, and I am bound to do their bidding. They believe that you belong with this man, so who am I to argue?'

Jael scowled. Her grandmother had guided and advised her throughout her life. Her visions had always come true – well, those that she had told her about, at least – so there was no reason to doubt her now. 'But Eadmund Skalleson? Eadmund the Drunkard?' she snorted. '*That's* the husband your gods see me with? Are you sure you have the right man?'

'Well...' Edela admitted with a twinkle in her eye, 'that part of my dream is a little hazy, but yes, Eadmund Skalleson. He is the one I have always seen.'

'The one?' Jael wanted to vomit. She absentmindedly sipped the hot tea, grimacing as it scalded the tip of her tongue.

'Well, he hasn't always been known by that name, has he? He was Eadmund the Bold when you fought him all those years ago.'

Jael tried to recall the fleeting moment she had trapped him beneath her sword, but it was too long ago, and she didn't remember him at all. She gritted her teeth, overcome by another burst of rage. 'No! I'm not going to do it! I'm not going to leave Andala! What about Axl? Who will look after him? Or you, or Mother? And what about Aleksander...' Her angry eyes softened suddenly, and she sighed.

Edela reached out and took Jael's hand, her eyes full of sympathy.

Jael snatched it back. 'You never thought Aleksander and I were meant to be together. I know that,' she said harshly.

'No,' Edela admitted. 'That is true, as much as I love you

both. But you and Eadmund, I believe, *are* meant to be. I have dreamed about this since you were born.' She stared earnestly at her granddaughter. 'I know it for certain, Jael. He is the father of the child you will have.'

Edela's words were delivered so quietly that Jael almost didn't hear her, but shock quickly flooded her face. '*Child*?' she breathed, as realisation dawned. 'And you see *that* as my future? A mother? A wife?'

'Yes, there is that, but you will have your sword also, of that I have no doubt.'

'Well, not according to Lothar.'

Edela raised her eyebrows. 'Things are not always as they seem. Our lives shift and change like the clouds. Nothing stands still,' she smiled. 'I see you with a sword. Do not worry.'

Jael felt confused, if not slightly heartened by that news.

But a child? With Eadmund the Drunkard?

How was she going to tell Aleksander?

***

Osbert was drunk.

Drunk and pissing against the side of the blacksmith's shed, when he saw Jael heading in his direction. Blinking to try and clear his blurry vision, he shook off his dripping cock, resetting his fur cloak. Sucking in his bloated belly, he stepped out into the street, snatching his cousin's arm as she flew by.

Jael jerked around in surprise, wrenching her arm out of his grip. Seeing that it was Osbert, she was eager to be gone, but he reached out and grabbed her again, his sharp fingernails pinching her skin. She glared down at him, her face betraying no sign of the discomfort he was causing. 'What do you want, Osbert?' she fumed as the wind screamed between them.

He almost stumbled then, his footing uncertain in the thick mud, but righting himself quickly, he narrowed his eyes. 'This could all have been so different, Jael,' he slurred through freezing lips. 'You need not have become a pawn in my father's game. You could have stayed here in Andala, as you always wanted to. As Queen of Brekka. As my wife.' He was leaning closer now, his sour spittle blowing over her.

Jael curled away from him, yanking her arm free. 'You think *you'd* make a better husband than Eadmund the Drunkard? That I'd rather have Osbert the Coward in my bed?' she snorted. 'No, Cousin, your father has made me a much better match than you would ever have been.'

Her words slapped Osbert across the face, and colour rose in his cheeks as he tried to contain his anger. 'If you say so, Jael,' he sneered, eyeing her threateningly. 'But just remember that while you're on Oss with your new husband, your fat belly, and your runt litter of slave princes, I'll be here watching over *your* family.' His satisfaction bloomed as he watched fear spark in Jael's eyes. 'You never know what accident may befall them if you're not careful. I'd hate for you to lose another member of your dwindling family.' His threat delivered, Osbert stumbled away from his cousin, heading for the hall, where he planned to warm his bones and drown the miserable bitch out of his head once and for all.

***

Aleksander was waiting when Jael arrived back at Gisila's cottage, his dark eyes troubled. He wasn't easy to anger and even now, when faced with losing her, he managed to retain an unnatural level of calm. They had been inseparable for seventeen years, lovers for the past twelve. He wouldn't accept that this was the end.

He couldn't lose her.

'Jael.' Aleksander came towards her as she entered the cottage, but Jael's arms remained firmly by her sides as she stopped before him.

She could barely look at Aleksander's face. His thick eyebrows twitched above a pair of hooded deep-brown eyes, almost black, and so full of concern. Dropping her head, she hurried to warm her hands by the fire, where she waited, trying to think of what to say to any of them. Eventually, shivering as some feeling returned to her body, Jael turned around.

'What did Edela have to say?' Gisila wondered anxiously. She'd been talking about nothing else since Axl and Aleksander had arrived.

Jael ignored her. 'Where were you?' she asked, staring accusingly at Aleksander.

He was surprised by that.

'Hunting. I told you before I left,' he answered defensively, coming to join Jael by the fire. 'I went to the hall to find you. Gant told me what had happened, so I came straight here.'

'You're back late.'

'The weather's closing in. I could barely see. I wasn't going to risk Ren by pushing him too hard.' He shook his head, feeling confused. Worried. 'I'm sorry I wasn't there when Lothar made his... announcement.'

Jael swallowed at the reminder, dismissing his words. She felt angry at Aleksander. Unfairly so. What could he have done to make anything different?

What could any of them have done?

'Jael.' Gisila was insistent now. 'What did your grandmother say?'

Jael sighed, walking a treacherous path in her mind. 'She... she thought it was... the right thing to happen. She'd seen it in her dreams, that it was the... right thing.' Jael couldn't say any more. She looked into a dark corner of the cottage, her head swirling with confusion.

Aleksander's face fell.

Jael had always been an impossibly stubborn woman; always working on a plan. If she believed in a cause, she would fight and never give in. He'd witnessed that enough times. But now, as she hung her head and hid her face from him, he knew.

And turning for the door, Aleksander headed out of the cottage.

Jael spun around to see the door hanging open in his wake.

Her shoulders drooped.

This was not going to be easy, whichever path she decided to take.

'The right thing?' Axl looked confused as he strode over to face his sister, who was almost as tall as he was. Almost as tall as their father had been. 'How is this the right thing for any of us? You'll be lost to Brekka forever! There'll be no hope of me taking the throne from Lothar without you, which, of course, he knows.' He felt angry and frustrated. He'd imagined that Jael would do anything to stay in Andala. That she would never give up the chance to reclaim their father's throne.

To defeat Lothar and Osbert, and get them out of Brekka for good.

He didn't understand her lack of reaction at all.

Jael rounded on her brother. 'How will my staying here change anything?' Heated now by the warmth of the cottage and her own discomfort, she removed her cloak and threw it over a stool, leaving the fire to stand further away, uncertain how or where to be. 'What have *we* been able to do to weaken Lothar's position since he arrived?' she whispered hoarsely. Lothar's spies were everywhere, and she didn't want the wind carrying her words out into the night. 'He has the army behind him. He turned all of Father's men against us. There's nothing here for us. No future. No hope. It's gone, Axl!' She gestured around the tiny cottage. 'Does this look like the home of Brekka's royal family anymore?'

'Well, we won't know now, will we?' Axl spat, his temper

rising to match hers.

Jael stepped towards her brother, glaring into his simmering hazel eyes. 'You think there's something I could do to change this?' she demanded. 'Kill Lothar? And then, what? Kill Osbert? And how would his men respond to that? Happily? I don't think so. Or, we could run, but where would we go? Lothar has allies in nearly every kingdom, and those he isn't allied with would still turn us in. No one wants Brekka for an enemy. We would never be safe! Is that what you want? For our family to run until we're hunted down and slaughtered? Can you see Edela living like that? Mother? Biddy?'

'Stop!' Gisila implored, coming between her two children. 'Come and sit down, both of you. This is no night to be on different sides. We must stay united if we're to stay alive.' She sighed deeply. The sudden change in their circumstances had left her feeling so much older than her fifty-two years. Her long dark hair was thick with silver strands. Her once much-admired figure was frail and thin. She had been the Queen of Brekka for thirty years. Married to Ranuf, a man she had fought and argued with, loved and despised in equal measure. The shame of being reduced to this lesser existence had damaged her pride, and the loss of her husband had broken her spirit. But she had hope still, and that hope was living within Jael and Axl. And she knew that the way back to her rightful place in Brekka was through them.

If only she could keep them believing that.

'And what about you, Mother?' Jael wondered sharply. 'Why didn't you know that any of this was coming?'

Gisila looked surprised. 'Why would I?'

'You and Lothar are very friendly,' Axl said, joining his sister. 'Especially since Rinda died.'

'Not like that, we're not! Nor have we ever been! Lothar may wish for things, but I am no slave, and he won't get anything from me that I do not wish to give. And I do not wish to give *that*!'

'Still, you've always been close to him, Mother.' Jael wasn't letting go that easily.

'And if I am?' Gisila whispered crossly. 'I need to keep us all safe. It's not just the two of you who are thinking of our future.' She shook her head, tears leaking into the heavy creases around her swollen eyes. 'I'm trying to keep us all alive! Do you think I want to do that? Placate the man who stole the throne from you, Axl? No, I do what I must to protect us all. It isn't easy, but what choice do I have? What choice do any of us have?'

Tears slid down Gisila's face, and Axl, who hated seeing his mother cry, put an arm around her shoulder.

Jael stared blankly at the door, wondering where Aleksander had gone; wanting to be with him but at the same time desperate to grab her horse and ride until she couldn't be found. Inside her head, she could hear herself screaming to find a way out, but Edela's words echoed too, imploring her to keep to the path before her. The path that only Edela and her gods could see.

Beside her, Gisila sobbed, and Axl simmered.

And Aleksander had gone.

CHAPTER TWO

The King's Hall was humming with urgent voices, interrupted now and then by the bang and clatter of the tables being cleared. There was only one topic of conversation that passed from open mouth to eager ear, and that was Lothar's surprising plan for Jael.

Most of the men in the hall had been born in Brekka. They'd served loyally under Ranuf, and fought alongside Jael for years. None of them had had much confidence in Axl as a worthy successor to his father, so they'd reluctantly supported Lothar's claim to the throne. Axl had no battle experience and none of the fire of his sister. If Ranuf had made Jael his heir, their loyalty wouldn't have wavered, but she had been put aside just before his death and had made no move to change her position. Therefore, sensibly, or so they thought at the time, Ranuf's men had put their swords behind Lothar. But, in two short years, Lothar Furyck had reminded everyone of why he'd been banished from Brekka by his brother, who had never wanted to see him step foot in his kingdom again.

Lothar could feel the tension simmering before him. The two fires in the centre of the hall burned high, but their hungry flames were not enough to lift the murkiness that hung about the room. The tables and beds that lined the walls were filled with shadows; faces masked in a dark-orange glow.

From his place at the high table, Lothar studied the closely inclined heads, taking note of how many of his men kept glancing towards him. His plan for Jael had not been well received, that was obvious. It was hardly unrest, but still, his sharp eyes raked over the unsettled mood of his people, wondering what his next move should be.

He needed the Andalans to remain compliant, at least until Jael had gone.

Osbert sat next to his father, hunched over, hungrily shovelling dumplings into his mouth. He chewed with an angry impatience, still disturbed by his conversation with Jael.

'They're not happy,' Lothar murmured.

Osbert looked up, wiping gravy from his short brown beard. He took a sip of wine, frowning at the men before him. 'Fuck them,' he spat, loud enough for a few heads to spin in his direction. 'You're the king. You can make any alliance you wish. And besides, she's no use to us, or them anymore. Best she's gone.'

Osbert returned to his meal, but Lothar had no appetite as he continued to survey the hall. Noticing his father's tense mood, Osbert pushed his plate away and picked up his cup. 'Do you trust her?'

'Jael? Of course I don't trust her. Do you?'

'Well, no, but if we can't trust her, why send her to Oss where she could plot with Eirik to destroy us?'

Lothar scoffed. 'You think she'd plot with Eirik Skalleson? Ha! She's more likely to kill him. Ranuf hated the man. Hated him and his stinking Slave Islands. Jael won't betray her precious father's memory, I promise you that.'

'Even if it means she can destroy us by doing so?' Osbert frowned, doubting his father's confidence.

'Eirik's getting old. He wants heirs. And for some reason, he thinks Jael will make the perfect mother!' Lothar snorted. 'I'd assumed at her age there was no hope for her dried-up old cunt, but it seems that Eirik knows something I don't. And the good news for us is that we remove our biggest problem here, and, by doing so, we create an alliance with Oss. So between Brekka and the islands, we'll finally have the ships to conquer Hest!'

Lothar could be a bold and decisive king, but he was often given to arrogance, and Osbert worried that his plan was too simple, too reliant upon what Jael would choose to do.

And Osbert didn't trust Jael.

Nor did he trust Eirik Skalleson.

His father's obsession with claiming Hest was clouding his every move these days. Eirik Skalleson had been Brekka's enemy since he'd proclaimed himself King of the Slave Islands over forty years ago, so why was he suddenly to be trusted now? Why wouldn't he use Jael's skill with a sword against them?

The tables were almost clean now, the ale cups refilled, and Lothar sensed an opportunity. He stood, holding his silver cup aloft in a signal to quell the noise. The men and women of the hall were intrigued once more, ceasing their conversations quickly. Even Osbert was curious as he lifted his cup with one hand, picking his teeth with the other.

'Jael is no longer with us this evening,' Lothar began solemnly in his quest to reclaim the hearts of his people. 'But if she were, I know she would agree with me that this is a good marriage for Brekka.' He saw a few eyebrows rise at that, but he continued, unperturbed. 'It is not what Jael would choose. Of course not! It is certainly not what I would choose for her, as her uncle, but she understands the importance of keeping Brekka safe and strong, and, to achieve that aim, sacrifices must be made. And this sacrifice, on Jael's part, and on ours, will reap bounteous rewards for us all. We do not want to lose her, but in making this alliance with Eirik Skalleson, we now have the opportunity to take Hest together!' His words piqued everyone's interest. Heads lifted higher now, and Lothar smiled as he continued, his confidence surging. 'Eirik will bring his ships to join us in the spring, and together we will destroy Haaron Dragos and his sons! Their land will, at last, be ours! But not just their land, for in conquering Hest, we will claim the greatest prize of all...' He let that hang in the silence, watching as some started to salivate expectantly. 'We will have the key to the South! Hest's harbour will be ours, their ships will be ours, and our opportunities for trading with the Fire Lands will be unlimited. We will be wealthy beyond our wildest dreams! The gods will applaud our endeavours, and our names will be sung in the farthest reaches of the Northern Realm and beyond! We will make Brekka the most powerful kingdom in all of Osterland!' Lothar raised his cup to the smoke-stained rafters, enthused by his poetry. 'To Brekka! And to Jael, for making this great alliance possible!'

His last dampened his earlier words somewhat, leaving a tarnished edge on the glittering prize he had offered up. But still, the men and women around the hall stood in slightly awkward unison, and, raising their cups, they echoed Lothar's words with a small show of enthusiasm. It was not wholly convincing, and he could see that, but when they sat down and started to discuss it amongst themselves, Lothar watched their eyes widen, and their lips moisten with the thought of such riches and fame. Now he just had to deliver on his promise. He needed to ensure that Jael would go through with the marriage ceremony, to solidify the alliance and bring Eirik into his fight.

Leaning forward, he sought out the sunken eyes of the hooded man in the shadows and smiled.

***

The rain was pelting down as Jael eased open the door to the small cottage she shared with Aleksander. Peering into the darkness, she was relieved to see a large fur-covered lump in their bed. She sighed, shaking the rain from her hair as she dropped her wet cloak over a stool to dry.

Sitting on the edge of the creaking bed, Jael yanked off her wet boots, half-smiling at their servant, Biddy, whose eyes were just visible from her own fur-covered bed. Embers from the banked fire burned low; a tiny orange glow in the middle of the cottage.

Jael slipped off her trousers and quickly shivered her way into bed. Aleksander hadn't stirred, but she knew him. He'd always been a light sleeper. They'd both been trained to sleep with a knife under their pillow and one eye open. It wasn't the way that most girls were sent off to bed, but ten-year-old Jael had never been like most girls. Once she had finally convinced her father to train her as a warrior, everything in her life had been a lesson in how to survive. And now, all that she had learned from him was about to be put to the test.

Jael wriggled her way towards Aleksander as the wind raced through holes in the crumbling wattle-and-daub walls. His back was to her, and he remained motionless and silent as she desperately sought the warmth of his body. Her feet were numb as she pressed her legs up against the backs of his, pushing her pelvis into the curve of his arse, resting the weight of her chest on his scarred back.

He didn't stir.

He didn't speak.

And so they lay there like that for some time; Jael burying her head into his back, welcoming the heat of his body as it fused with hers. They had slept like that since they were children and now she couldn't imagine sleeping any other way.

Aleksander rolled over, a dull ache in his chest at the thought of never feeling those frozen legs on his again. Grabbing her face with his large calloused hands, he kissed her roughly. Jael could feel his wet cheeks and the damp bristles of his beard on her lips as she kissed him back. She wanted to lose herself and disappear into him then, but he pulled back and stared at her, tracing the dark shadows on her face with his finger.

Jael was the most beautiful woman he had ever seen.

Not girlish or pretty with soft, agreeable features. She was far too fierce for that; tall and strong, with a determined nose, and a small scar under her right eye which lent her face a threatening edge. Her dark brown hair was long and wild, and a constant irritation, so Biddy braided it for her regularly, keeping it out of her eyes. And those deep green eyes of hers revealed more than everything combined. They were both warm and sharp and, depending on the weather, or how long it had been since Jael had last eaten, you would either get the hint of a smile or a warning that you were about to receive the lash of her unforgiving tongue.

'You can't do this,' Aleksander whispered, his face almost touching hers.

'I... I think I have to,' Jael sighed, feeling the soft crunching of straw as she wriggled uncomfortably on the mattress.

'Why? Why *have* to? I don't understand. What did Edela really say to you?'

Despite the near-total darkness, Jael could sense his eyes searching hers for answers. She had answers, of course, but did she want to share them? Taking a deep breath, Jael realised that she had no choice. 'She saw me... with him... that my future was with him, away from Brekka.'

'Away from me,' Aleksander sighed despondently, his head drooping.

Jael lifted his chin with her finger. 'I don't want this, you know that, but what choice is there? Lothar has arranged it. Edela has seen that it's meant to be. The only way we can stop it happening is to run. But we can't live like that. Even if we managed to escape, Lothar wouldn't stop hunting us until we were all dead. Can you imagine him just letting us go?'

'But that's not something you even want to try. You've made up your mind already,' Aleksander insisted. 'I can tell.'

'I suppose I have. I don't see another way.' Jael paused. 'If I don't go through with it, Lothar will kill us all. I don't have a choice. Not really.'

'And you think we'll be safe here when you go?'

'I hope so. As long as I do what he asks. As long as his alliance with Eirik holds. As long as Axl doesn't cause any trouble.'

'Ha,' Aleksander scoffed. 'Axl not causing any trouble will be difficult. He wants that throne.'

'Well, I can't blame him for that. He *was* Father's heir,' Jael muttered. 'You'll need to look after him for me. Please.'

'Of course I will,' he said, smiling as she rubbed her cold feet against his. 'If only we'd married years ago. Lothar wouldn't be able to send you away like this. He wouldn't be able to take you away from me.'

'Well, that was all my fault,' Jael admitted. 'I wouldn't even let you ask me.'

'I could have tried,' Aleksander said sadly. 'But you were happy, so was I, the way things were.'

There was silence.

A quiet acceptance of the end that was coming.

Jael leaned in until their lips were almost touching. 'It doesn't mean forever,' she insisted hoarsely. 'It doesn't mean that we'll never be together again. Can you imagine me as the Queen of Oss, with that drunk for a husband?' She shuddered. 'Things can change, alliances can break, people can die. Who knows, me on Oss might mean a way back to Brekka for all of us?'

That was something Jael hadn't thought of before, and nor had Aleksander, so they considered that for a moment, but just for a moment, as Jael's hand started to slowly stroke away the tears from Aleksander's face, and their minds and bodies turned to other needs.

Jael closed her eyes, feeling Aleksander's lips on hers, wanting to disappear, to escape the reality they would both have to face tomorrow.

***

The next morning hung about Andala like a foul mood. It was calmer, though, the storm having eased before dawn, leaving behind a twisted mess of debris, and houses in need of repair.

As the Andalans roused themselves out into the wintry cold and started clearing up, Jael headed to the stables. She knew she couldn't escape the looks and the gossip, or her uncle, forever, but she was desperate to find a place to think, at least for a while. There had been no sign of Aleksander when she'd woken, and she could only assume that he was searching for the same thing.

Her horse, Tig, snorted crossly as she slipped a bridle over his twitching head. He hated being stabled and was keen to remind her that she hadn't ridden him for two days; skittering about in the straw, nostrils flaring as Jael tightened the saddle under his smooth black belly. She stroked his mane, and he stilled briefly, just long enough for her to slip one foot in a stirrup and throw herself up into the saddle.

Nudging Tig out of the stables, she navigated him around a squawking gaggle of geese who were in no hurry as they waddled across Andala's busy square.

Andala was Brekka's largest town, home of the Furycks. It had a wide, well-protected harbour, and a bustling market that drew traders from all around Osterland, Alekka too, even during the frigid winter months. The town was fortified on all sides by a deep ditch and high stone walls topped with newly reinforced ramparts. Four guard towers overlooked the harbour to the south and the fields and hills to the north. The main gates, on the northwestern side of the fort, were already open as the local farmers slowly shepherded their livestock inside to set up their stalls for another day's trading.

Once free of the gates and the cumbersome traffic, Jael took a sharp breath of cool air deep into her lungs and tapped her boots lightly against Tig's flanks. He had been anticipating her signal, and quickly finding some purchase in the thick mud, he took off with speed. Wrapping the reins around her hands, Jael leaned over his neck, hanging on as the wind swept her hair and her worries far behind her.

They rode up over the undulating hills to the north, and down, deep into a thick forest. The dense canopy of entwining trees created a private, hushed world around them, and she felt herself relax in the welcome silence. Tig knew this path so well that he barely broke stride as Jael guided him effortlessly through the tree maze, over a slippery bed of needles and out into the dim light.

She turned him gently, and they headed west, more slowly now, towards a cluster of trees hiding a small clearing at the bottom of a craggy hill. A stream ran through it, and in the summer months, Tig would stand in the water and cool off while Jael lay on the grass, enjoying being far away from Lothar and Osbert and all their plotting.

Entering the clearing, Tig's ears flicked around, and Jael could sense someone nearby. She rested her hand on the familiar hilt of her father's sword, waiting, her body tense and ready.

She was surprised to see a familiar face emerge from the trees to her right.

Gant Olborn.

Once her father's man, but, like everyone else, he had taken an oath to Lothar.

Jael scowled at him, not wanting his company at all. Gant had trained her. They had fought together countless times, working to protect Ranuf and keep him safe during battle, but now there was an awkward distance between them, and she didn't know what to say.

Gant nudged his enormous white horse towards her. He was a gaunt man with a serious, scarred face. The weight of his years and his choices rested heavily upon his broad shoulders. He had grown up with Ranuf Furyck. They had been like brothers, and he was still struggling to cope with the gaping hole left by his death.

'What do you want?' Jael asked coldly, her mouth set in an unforgiving line.

Gant wasn't surprised by her tone. They had barely spoken since he'd helped Lothar take the throne. 'I came to warn you. About Lothar.' He spoke quietly, not wanting his voice to carry to unbidden ears.

'What? That he's marrying me to the Drunkard?' Jael scoffed, trying to keep control of a skittish Tig who appeared just as cross at Gant as she was. 'Your warning comes too late, old *friend*.'

Gant dropped his head briefly. 'He wants you dead, all of you,' he warned, eyes up on Jael again.

'Ha! Of course he wants us dead. We're a constant reminder of how he betrayed his brother.'

Gant edged his snorting horse closer to Jael, his iron-grey hair falling lightly over his worried eyes. 'Lothar saw his chance, and he took it. If your father had named you instead of Axl...' He let that hang in the frosty air, but Jael refused to take it up, so he continued. 'He's sending Tiras with you.'

'What?' Jael was shocked. 'Tiras? That shit worm. Why?'

'He's to watch you for any sign of disloyalty. Any sign that you're betraying Lothar and creating your own alliance with the Skallesons.'

'*Me?*' Jael spluttered. 'Make an alliance with the Skallesons? Why would I do that?'

'I don't imagine you would,' Gant smiled, remembering all the years he had spent training her with Ranuf. He knew her, better than she remembered. 'But Lothar wants to ensure that it doesn't happen. As he should, if he's to protect his throne. He won't hesitate to have you all killed.'

Jael felt the weight of his words, heavy on her shoulders. 'You should go,' she warned. 'Tiras is probably hiding amongst the trees, watching me already.'

'He might well be, but I hardly think he wants to make an enemy of me,' Gant remarked coolly. 'He wouldn't like what that would mean for him.'

Jael smiled, relaxing slightly. She had felt so isolated from her father's men since they had gone over to Lothar, especially Gant. He had been like an uncle to her. It was surprisingly enjoyable to have a conversation with him again. It made her feel closer to her father, and, for a moment, less alone.

Gant turned his horse's head away and made to leave. The sky was darkening around them, flooding the clearing with the cold, grey warning that snow was on its way.

'It would have been different,' he said softly over his shoulder, 'if Ranuf had named you. But we just had no choice. Axl wasn't ready. Brekka needed a leader.' He looked sadly at Jael, then spun back around, kicking his horse off into the trees.

CHAPTER THREE

Eirik Skalleson stood, tapping his foot impatiently as he watched his son snoring.

Eadmund had a serene smile on his face as he lay on his back in a pile of mud and other liquids, which may have included vomit, which definitely included ale, perhaps some urine, and Eirik didn't want to imagine the rest. Eventually, the stink made him retch, and he kicked Eadmund in annoyance. His son didn't budge, but his smile disappeared, replaced with a sleepy frown, so Eirik kicked harder, and this time Eadmund sat bolt upright, shocked, surprised, and gasping for air.

'What? What is it?' he panted, wide-eyed, glancing around. He grabbed his head as everything started to ring and spin, sharp pains darting in from all sides.

'What is it?' Eirik rasped crossly, adjusting his thick bear-fur cloak. 'What is it?! It's midday, is what it is, and you're sitting in a pile of your own shit!' Eirik sighed loudly, despairingly, stalking away from the stench of his son and the fishy stink of the drying shed that Eadmund had made his second home of late. Apparently, it was far easier to sleep in a place where you didn't need to go outside to piss, shit, and vomit.

His last chance, Eirik told himself.

This was most definitely his last chance.

Eadmund struggled to his feet, stumbling after his father. He could barely keep his eyes open, but he could certainly hear how wild Eirik was. 'You wanted to speak to me, Father?' he croaked, blinking in the grim morning light, the sound of his voice clanging in his ears.

'I did, but I doubt you can even hear me in that state!'

Eadmund felt himself swaying. He reached out a hand, steadying himself against the side of the shed. 'Perhaps we could find somewhere to sit?'

Eirik nodded curtly, and they walked until they came to a row of moss-covered benches set up just before the seagrass merged into a black-stone beach. Snow was coming, and light flurries drifted down from smoke-coloured clouds, sprinkling the stones.

Eadmund glanced at his father as they sat down. Eirik Skalleson's leathery face looked cold in the gloom. There was nothing good-humoured about him at all. Eadmund could feel a chill settle over his pallid skin, and he glanced around, wondering where he'd left his cloak.

'I've made an alliance with Lothar,' Eirik delivered bluntly.

Eadmund shook his head in surprise, wondering if he'd heard him correctly. 'I'm sorry? Lothar... Furyck?'

'Yes, I'm running out of time to secure our kingdom's future, and Lothar has just what I need to do so.' Eirik smiled at his son, feeling a swell of pride at this, his masterstroke.

Eadmund just looked confused, partly because his senses were so dulled, but also because an alliance with Brekka was an unexpectedly strange move. 'What does he have that you need?' he wondered slowly, feeling himself walking into a trap.

'His niece. Jael.'

That hit Eadmund like a bucket of cold water. 'No!'

'Yes! It's what I need. It's what *you* need,' Eirik insisted firmly.

'No, Father! No, I can't!' Eadmund stood up, panic rising in his chest as he staggered down to the water's edge. He stared into the distance, his eyes trying to focus on the giant shards of stone rising out of the dark sea, his stomach swirling with last night's ale. 'Not again!'

Eirik came to join his son, his footsteps cautious on the slick stones. 'You *will* marry her, Eadmund. If you want to be my heir, heir to all of this...' He motioned to the hill in the distance; to the old stone walls of the fort at its very peak. 'You will marry Jael Furyck and get her with child, quickly. And many times over.' He frowned, fingering his long white beard. 'This family, our family, must not disappear into the Nothing. I didn't conquer these islands to watch them turn back into a slaver's paradise. And when I'm gone, and you drink yourself to death, or die without an heir, what will happen to our people? Who will protect them? I chose you, Eadmund. You, over your brother. And so far you have done nothing but make me regret that decision!'

Eirik's words landed a hefty blow to the tiny remnants of Eadmund's pride, and he couldn't speak. It was something Eirik had been threatening for years, but he hadn't been prepared for the way it would make him feel. Eadmund was a calm, reasonable man. He could see the merits of his father's argument and hear the passion in his words, but still, it was him who would have to marry.

Her.

'I'm not ready.'

Eirik snorted unsympathetically. 'Of course you are! It's been seven years! That's more than enough time for anyone to grieve. You *are* ready, my son. You have no choice but to *be* ready. I am giving you no choice!'

Eadmund tried to think, but his head was a jumble of half-formed words, none of which made any sense. He hadn't seen his father this angry since the Alekkans had left; the hopes of another marriage dashed much to Eirik's annoyance. 'But Jael Furyck? Couldn't you have found someone else? Someone less likely to kill me?'

Eirik laughed, and the tension between them eased slightly. 'She may be a better warrior than you, my son, but she has exactly what we need,' Eirik said confidently.

'And what's that? An extra cock?'

Eirik rolled his eyes. 'The Furycks have the oldest line in all of Osterland. Bringing Jael into our family will give our name the respect it needs. Uniting our line with Brekka's will ensure that my legacy has a future. That you will rule as a legitimate king. Besides, it was your sister's idea.'

'Eydis? Eydis told you I should marry her?' Eadmund was stunned. His sister was only twelve-years-old and blind, but she had been having visions for the past few years. Her mother had been a Tuuran dreamer, and Eirik already relied heavily on her guidance.

'Yes. She insisted that Jael would save you. Save our people too,' Eirik said thoughtfully. 'It surprised me too, but I believe her. So, if Jael Furyck is meant to save you, then I doubt she'll end up killing you. I could be wrong, of course. She won't be happy being forced into a marriage, especially one with you. You are not the prize you once were, my son,' he smiled wryly, running his eyes over Eadmund's chubby face and ever-expanding girth; so far removed from the lean warrior he had once been. 'I imagine you'll have a hard time keeping her sword out of your marriage bed!'

Eadmund looked morosely at his grinning father. The stark reality of Eirik's words, the ruthless look in his eye, and the sinking clouds all conspired to spin his head with thoughts of marriage and wives, both old and new.

And turning away from his father, he bent towards the stones and vomited.

***

Evaine Gallas swung around in a fit of madness and raced towards her father. 'No! No! No!' she screamed, pounding her small hands onto his hollow chest. 'This cannot happen! You cannot let this happen, Father! Eadmund is mine! He is supposed to marry *me*! You are supposed to have been arranging *our* marriage, not helping Eirik marry him to... to... that Brekkan bitch! How could you let this happen? After all that I've done to make Eadmund mine! To make him free!'

'Keep your voice down,' Morac hissed, but Evaine was just getting started. Looking frantically around their lavish house, she grabbed a nearby storage pot, throwing it onto the wooden floorboards, smashing it to pieces. Her mother, Runa, who had been sitting on a bed in the corner of the room, jumped in fright, eager to leave.

Evaine in this sort of mood was to be avoided at all costs.

'Evaine!' Morac growled, grabbing her arm with his long thin fingers, demanding her attention. 'Evaine, this will not help things. If Eirik hears –'

'If Eirik hears?' his daughter screeched. 'Then what? He'll send me away? What difference will *that* make, since he's marrying Eadmund to someone else? Someone who isn't me!'

Her small, lithe body shook with a fury that was at odds with her ethereal appearance. She was usually a vision of breathtaking loveliness but not today. Her long golden hair whipped fiercely around her face, and her blue eyes darted about maniacally. Even the smattering of freckles across her tiny nose glowed red with anger.

Inhaling sharply, Evaine tried to still her trembling body. Despite the heat of her temper, she could hear the sense in her father's words. Eadmund wasn't married yet. There would still be time to change the outcome, as long as she didn't cause Eirik any problems. Her fury cooled slightly, simmering now at a steady heat, her mind flitting desperately from thought to thought.

'A marriage between you and Eadmund made no sense to Eirik. I told you that,' Morac said delicately, dropping his daughter's arm, watching her cautiously. She seemed to have calmed down, but still, with Evaine, it was best to stay alert. 'To marry a slave's son to a slave's daughter does little to legitimise his rule. He doesn't want you to mother his heirs. He was never going to agree to a marriage between you and Eadmund.'

'But what does Eadmund want?' Evaine scowled. 'He won't want to marry her, not when he loves me!'

Morac frowned. His daughter had certainly obsessed over Eadmund since she was a child, but as to Eadmund's feelings for her...

'He loves me, Father. He loves me!' Evaine insisted. 'You'll see. He'll fight Eirik. He won't allow this to happen!' She frantically smoothed down the front of her blue woollen dress, blinking at her father. 'You'll see. Eadmund won't leave me! He'll fight for me, Father. He'll find a way to change Eirik's mind.'

'Alright, alright,' Morac soothed, taking Evaine's shaking hands, leading her towards a chair.

Evaine sat down, her mind humming with panic. She would not lose Eadmund. She would do anything to stop that from happening.

***

By mid-morning Eadmund was almost feeling only terrible as he trudged slowly through the fort on his way to the hall. His father's news had left him in a daze, and the dense fog creeping around his head wasn't helping that sensation clear. He didn't know what was more shocking: a prospective new wife, or Jael Furyck as his wife?

Could there not have been another option?

It was a bitter day, but he had started to perspire heavily. His round cheeks were flushed pink, his armpits damp caves of anxiety. He screwed up his usually cheerful face in annoyance, pawing at his unkempt sandy hair which kept sticking to his forehead. 'Ahhh, there you are, Little Thing!' he smiled triumphantly as Eydis crossed his path. 'I think you and I need to have a word, don't you?' And grabbing her hand, he pulled her gently along with him, slipping down a narrow alleyway, searching for a private place to speak.

Eydis smiled happily as she hurried after him. She was small for her age, with long raven hair and eyes that, if not for their milky blindness, would have sparkled a clear cornflower blue. Eadmund was her favourite person in all of Oss and she relished any time she got to spend with him. He was usually not awake until much later in the day, though, so Eydis knew very well what he wanted her for.

After much winding and creeping about, Eadmund found his friend Thorgils' cottage, and, checking that no one was inside, he guided his sister through the door. Thorgils shared the cottage with his mother, Odda, a frightening shrew of a woman, who Eadmund was eager to avoid. He took the risk that they would be in and out before she returned.

The room was dark, its tiny smoke hole providing only a hint of morning light. Eadmund resisted the urge to light a candle, though. It would mean nothing to Eydis, and he welcomed the cold darkness.

'I know what this is about,' Eydis giggled, making herself comfortable on the creaking stool that Eadmund had deposited her on. 'Jael Furyck.'

'Yes... her,' Eadmund muttered, twitching with irritation. 'Why her? If you're going to keep on trying to find me a wife, Eydis, why couldn't you have come up with a better choice? Evaine, for one.'

Eydis stilled, her sweet round face suddenly serious. 'Not Evaine. You don't love her.'

'Well, I certainly don't love Jael Furyck, and at least Evaine won't cut me to pieces in the night!' Eadmund huffed, peering around the room, wondering if Odda had any ale.

Eydis could sense Eadmund's anxiety as he wobbled on his stool. Her blindness intensified her other senses, and every part of her could feel her brother's emotions twisting and turning.

'Jael will save you,' she insisted quietly, leaning forward, wishing she could see his face. Eydis had been blind since birth; the only images she saw were in the vivid dreams she had every night. And though they were useful, she would have given anything to see her brother sitting before her.

'So I hear,' Eadmund frowned. 'But what do you think I need saving from?'

'Yourself, of course. You are unhappy and lost and lonely –'

'I'm not unhappy! I have Evaine. I'm not unhappy, Eydis. I have good friends. I have fun...'

'Drinking.' She glared disapprovingly in Eadmund's direction. 'That's not what you'd be doing if you were truly happy. None of that makes you happy, Eadmund. You're sad. Sad because of losing Melaena, but she would want you to live. She wouldn't want you to be like this.'

Eadmund's face dropped, and his shoulders sagged, heavy with the weight of his memories. He felt sick and tired. He had only just turned thirty-years-old, but he'd given up on himself entirely when his wife had died. He had been happy with her, excited about their future, but it was so long ago that he couldn't even remember the shadow of that life now. His body had turned to fat and plenty of it. His once handsome face had rounded with drink. He felt ill most of the time, had not carried a sword in years, and could only look on in embarrassment when his friends left the island in their battle gear, prepared for war.

He had loved Melaena so deeply.

The scars left by her death may have healed over, but the wounds they marked still felt raw and painful. Eadmund's grief had taken him into a hole of complete darkness, and he was still lost there, seven years later. He knew that Eirik and Eydis were right. He was an embarrassment of a man. His was a waste of a life, and he was most certainly a disappointment, but that was his choice, surely?

He didn't have to marry Jael.

He could choose another way.

'You could run away, of course,' Eydis whispered, jolting him out of his sad memories. 'But you would only be running away from a chance at happiness. If you don't want to live, Eadmund, you may as well just give up and die.'

Those were harsh words coming from a child, and they cut Eadmund deeply.

And... could she read minds now?

The room was silent as they sat, keeping company with their own thoughts. The sounds of the fort came stealing in from outside: arguing in the alley, low, murmuring clucks from Odda's chicken coop, hammering from the smithy. The rich smell of meat cooking in the square wafted down the smoke hole, stirring Eadmund's empty stomach. He sighed. 'You're only twelve, Eydis. You can't know what it feels like, what it felt like to lose her.'

Eydis looked cross. 'I'm thirteen, Eadmund!'

'You are? Really?' Eadmund was genuinely shocked. 'I'm sure you're only twelve. I don't remember your birthday at all. Did I give you a gift?'

'No,' Eydis said sadly. 'You didn't remember.'

Enough light had seeped into the cottage now for Eadmund to see the genuine disappointment etched onto his sister's face. 'Oh, well then, I am a shit. A useless turd of a brother, aren't I?'

'No!' Eydis' milky eyes were bright again. 'You are so good and kind, but you just need to start living again. Then you would feel things, and maybe even remember my birthday sometimes.'

'Well, I think you're asking a lot there,' he grinned, all the weariness vanishing beneath an easy smile; his soft hazel eyes mischievous for a moment. 'Happiness won't necessarily cure my troublesome memory.'

'No, but it will stop you from drinking yourself to sleep every day,' Eydis insisted. 'And Jael can help you with that. You must give her a chance. I see her in my dreams so clearly. She will save you.'

Eadmund didn't know what to make of that but heavy

footsteps outside had him stumbling off his stool. 'We should go. I don't want to bump into Odda. That would really make me want a drink!' He grabbed Eydis' hand, and they hurried outside, just in time to thump straight into Thorgils, who was standing outside his front door, wondering who was lurking inside.

'What?!' Thorgils exclaimed as Eadmund crashed into his chest, then, seeing that it was only his friend and not some random thief, he smiled. 'Are you lost?'

Thorgils Svanter was a red-headed giant of a man who towered over most people on Oss. Big-hearted and fiercely loyal, he'd been Eadmund's best friend since they were wrapped in swaddling cloths. His mother, Odda, had been Eadmund's first nursemaid. She had frightened Eadmund since birth, and he'd been relieved when his mother had put her aside for a woman with a gentler hand and a kinder tongue.

'Ahhh, no,' Eadmund murmured awkwardly. 'No, we were just looking for somewhere private to speak.'

'We?' Thorgils raised a suggestive eyebrow, then smiled as Eydis popped her head around Eadmund's waist. 'Ahhh, now I understand. I just heard the news from Morac. I'm not surprised you tackled that one there.'

Eydis slipped back behind Eadmund, who kept a firm grip on her hand. She was painfully shy and barely spoke to anyone, apart from Eadmund and their father. Even though Thorgils was like a brother to her, she still felt awkward around him most of the time.

Thorgils joined them as they walked back to the hall, where Eadmund planned to leave his sister. She could get about ably enough by herself, despite her blindness, but he was overprotective and wanted to ensure that she was safely returned to their father. He needed to go somewhere to think, alone. He was already visualising his first drink of the day, desperate to take the edge off all this talk of marriage and his many failings as a man.

'So, have you heard Evaine sobbing, then?' Thorgils grinned as they ambled down the narrow alley. 'I imagine she's crying and raging somewhere nearby.'

'Do you think she knows?' Eadmund wondered, his eyes darting about. The thought of having to face Evaine didn't improve his mood at all.

'Morac would have told her, for sure,' Thorgils said. 'I imagine he helped bring about the alliance with Lothar Furyck. You know Morac, always looking for Eirik's favour... the arse-licking ballsack that he is.'

Having escaped the maze of alleys, they emerged into the busy square. Oss' weather, usually grim and wet, had been getting even grimmer and wetter for weeks. The Freeze was coming, and the ground alternated between hazardously frozen and unpleasantly boggy. Today was a challenging combination of both. A hard frost overnight, following a week of near-constant rain, had the Osslanders on their toes, avoiding muddy sinkholes and icy patches.

The hall stood astride the square. It had been an ongoing project for over forty years now, and despite Eirik's countless improvements, it was nowhere near as impressive as Andala's King's Hall, and that rankled. More square than long, it was topped with a curved roof, made to look like an upturned ship; two fire-breathing dragons fighting at its peak. Its towering doors were carved with interlacing motifs of the sea: waves, whales, and monsters, all flowing together in an endless cycle of life and gruesome death.

Eadmund's attention was quickly consumed by the mouthwatering aromas wafting towards him from Ketil's fire pit. It was the most popular spot in the square, where frozen hands and empty bellies sought salvation in the hot and spicy food that Ketil and his sister offered daily. 'Would you like something to eat, Eydis?' he asked, winking at Ketil's sister, Una, as he rummaged hopefully inside the empty pouch attached to his belt.

'Yes, please,' she answered eagerly, producing a silver coin from her small embroidered purse. 'One for each of us.'

Thorgils' stomach growled gratefully and Eadmund grinned,

ordering three servings of pork wrapped in warm flatbreads. The charred meat was hot and juicy, soft and moist, and the hungry trio sat down at an empty table to devour it immediately.

'So, what will you do with Evaine?' Thorgils wondered, pausing between mouthfuls to blow on his steaming meat.

'*Do*? With Evaine? She's not the problem. It's Jael Furyck I need to worry about. Can you imagine having her as a wife?'

'She'll slice up your balls and serve them to you for breakfast, for sure!' Thorgils laughed, then looking at Eydis, he paused, reminding himself that although she couldn't see, her hearing worked perfectly well. 'Although you never know, perhaps she'll surprise you and be as gentle as sweet Eydis here?'

Eydis rolled her eyes and Eadmund scoffed loudly. 'Ha! Not likely. Have you ever seen her?'

'Of course, you fool!' Thorgils snorted, and gulping down the last of his meat, he wiped a hand through his bushy red beard, eyes back on Ketil's grill. 'I was with you at the Battle of Ligga, when she almost killed you. I saved your life, remember? What was that, eight years ago? One of the countless times I saved you back then.'

Eadmund laughed. 'Saved my life? I may be a drunkard, but I remember very clearly that *you* were the one who needed saving from her that day. You were one stroke away from being a one-armed man until I arrived and cut her down.'

Thorgils shook his head. 'My deluded friend! I like your story very much. *You* cut her down? Ha! Perhaps we should ask Jael Furyck what she remembers when she arrives? Your father said the wedding would happen quickly. Before the Freeze. Maybe next week?'

Eadmund, having just swallowed the last of his meat, dropped his head onto the table. 'Perhaps I should do what Eydis suggested and kill myself before then?'

'What?' Thorgils frowned, staring at Eydis in horror. 'You said he should do *that*?'

Eydis, who was barely halfway through her own flatbread,

shook her head, her mouth too full to speak.

'No, but she may as well have,' Eadmund mumbled, his head still on the table. 'It's either Jael Furyck or death apparently.'

'Hmmm, hard choice, my friend, very hard,' Thorgils grinned. 'But then, as heir to the king, you'll have to get used to making such hard decisions one day.'

Eadmund put his hands over his ears, closed his eyes and focused on the image of that first cup of ale tumbling down his eager throat, dulling his senses, making him smile.

'Evaine,' he heard Thorgils murmur. 'How pleasant to see you. We were just leaving, weren't we, Eydis?'

If he could have, Eadmund would have banged his head on the table then.

He couldn't face Evaine now.

Sighing in resignation, he looked up, just in time to see Thorgils dragging his annoyed sister away, her mouth still full.

Having seen off Thorgils, Evaine smiled sweetly down at Eadmund, pulling the collar of her white fur cloak more closely around her neck. Her unhappiness and anger mingled nervously as she waited for Eadmund to speak, but when he finally looked up at her, he didn't say a word.

Evaine rushed to fill the silence before it became awkward. 'I heard about your father's plan to marry you to that woman. Well, if you can call her a woman...' She did her very best to look suitably upset, masking her barely-concealed anger beneath lowered eyelashes that fluttered continuously.

Eadmund sighed, wondering how to navigate the sensitive waters ahead; unsure that he possessed the clarity to do so. 'Ahhh yes, Eirik and his grand plan. He's finally grown tired of waiting for grandsons, it seems. I suppose I can't blame him. It's been seven years and many failed attempts at finding me a wife.'

Reluctantly getting up from the table, he took Evaine's hand and started to walk across the square, not sure where he was heading.

Hopefully, somewhere his father couldn't find him.

'But why her? Surely he'd rather marry you to someone more suitable? Someone you loved? *Could* love?' Evaine said almost shyly, glancing up at Eadmund, who was looking anywhere but at her. Despite her confident display, she was still not sure how Eadmund felt about her. He had never revealed his feelings since they had become lovers a year ago. Not once.

It made her anxious.

'Well, no,' Eadmund smiled awkwardly. 'No, it's not that simple to a king. Kings make alliances to gain land and riches, trade agreements, support in war. Not many kings make marriages for love.'

'Well, I don't suppose a marriage to me offers any of those things,' Evaine said simply. 'I can't blame your father for preferring a princess to the daughter of a slave. But what about you? Do *you* want to marry her?' She stopped, turning her eyes up to Eadmund, her small mittened hand firm on his arm.

Eadmund sighed, overcome with the need to be alone; he was still reeling from his father's news himself. Old, long-buried emotions were stirring, and he felt aggravated and uncomfortable. He cared for Evaine, and he sympathised with her distress, but at the same time, he wished she would go away so he could find some ale.

'No, no, of course I don't want to marry her,' he muttered distractedly. 'But there are just some things you have to do as the son of a king. And I understand that. Eirik's mind will not be changed. Not this time. He's made his alliance with Lothar Furyck, so I have to make the best of it. *We* will make the best of it.' The words tumbled out of his mouth in a rush, but Eadmund wasn't sure if he was saying them solely for Evaine's benefit, or whether he actually believed them himself.

Evaine stared up at him, frosty breath clouds swirling around her face. 'We will make the best of it, then.'

Relief coursed through Eadmund's tense limbs. 'Yes, we will,' he sighed. 'And marriage to Jael Furyck doesn't mean an end to us. I doubt she'll want to cuddle with me every night!' he laughed, cringing at the thought.

Evaine looked horrified. 'No, I hope not!'

'So there'll be plenty of opportunities for us to be together,' Eadmund insisted. 'I promise.' He regretted that instantly, but Evaine was being so supportive, and besides, he thought pragmatically, why should he put her to one side? When he felt lonely, it was comforting to feel the warmth of her wrapped around him. He didn't imagine that his new wife would want to have anything to do with him, so why not keep Evaine happy?

For now, at least.

Evaine's face shone with pleasure. She had wanted more, of course; to be a wife, rather than just a lover, but knowing that Eadmund still wanted her gave her hope and somewhere to begin. Now she just needed to find a way to deal with Jael Furyck, though she doubted that woman would be more difficult than anything she'd dealt with before.

She reached up, throwing her arms around Eadmund's neck, pressing her body into his. He was hers. He would always be hers. No one would take him from her. And standing on her tiptoes, she kissed him, softly at first, then deeply, curling her tongue around his.

Eadmund, who told himself that he was far too tired and weary to be seduced by Evaine, quickly found himself forgetting everything but those beautifully demanding lips of hers. His desperate need for solitude and ale dissipated as she wound him slowly and passionately around her little finger.

And before he knew it, Eadmund found himself being led off to his cottage for whatever Evaine had in mind.

CHAPTER FOUR

Aleksander hadn't come back.

Jael knew that he was likely trying to find a way to cope with the situation, and she couldn't blame him for that, but she wanted him to return before she left for Oss. She'd been riding for hours each day, hoping to stumble across him at one of his favourite hunting grounds, but without any luck.

He obviously didn't want to be found.

Leaving the stables, Jael headed into the rain, walking back to their cottage, miserable at the thought of spending another night without him.

'Jael! Come, come!' Gisila gestured impatiently from the doorway of the tailor's cottage.

Jael rolled her eyes, wanting to turn around.

She'd allowed herself to be measured a few days ago and now it was no doubt time to be pinned and squeezed into her stupid wedding dress. Her shoulders sagged in resignation as she trudged through the mud towards her mother with sodden boots and a mood to match.

Jael blinked in surprise as she entered the modest little cottage. Arnna, the tailor, was renowned for her rare skill with a needle, but the years and the intricate nature of her work had almost robbed her of her eyesight, so she required more light than most to see by. Lamps and candles dripped fishy-smelling wax and oil over every surface, creating an intense glow brighter than anything Jael was used to.

Arnna had sewn many outfits for her since she was a girl. Most had been beautifully made tunics and cloaks for ceremony and battle, but it had been seventeen years since Jael had worn an actual dress. She remembered the day as a ten-year-old when, to her mother's horror, she'd built a pyre with Aleksander and thrown every one of her dresses onto it. They'd danced around the high flames, banishing 'Princess Jael' into the past, invoking Furia, Goddess of War, to bless the birth of 'Jael the Warrior'. Dressed in her dead brother's tunic and trousers, Jael had walked away, hand in hand with Aleksander as the flames died down, leaving behind all that had gone before in a pile of smouldering ash. And now, here she was, about to be reunited with her long-abandoned femininity and all of its restrictions.

'Hello, Arnna,' she called half-heartedly to the stooped claw of a woman shuffling towards her, carrying the cursed dress. Surprisingly, it was black, and that brought a smile to Jael's sullen face. She was pleased to see that Arnna still possessed a wicked sense of humour.

'I thought that would make you happy,' Arnna cackled slyly, handing the dress to Gisila, who didn't share in the joke.

'Black?' Gisila looked horrified as she held up the long silken garment, her nostrils flaring with distaste. There hadn't been time for much needlework, but Arnna had managed to embroider a series of gold knotted patterns around the sleeves, and a pair of fighting wolves on either side of the neckline. It looked elegant, but Gisila was not impressed. 'Black for a wedding? Lothar will be furious!'

'Why furious?' Jael snorted. 'What does he care?'

Gisila gave the dress to Jael with a look of disdain, unimpressed by Arnna's sense of humour, and Jael's delight in it. 'Try it on to see if it fits you at least. I don't believe there is time to come up with something else, is there?' She frowned at Arnna, who shook her almost hairless head. 'No, so this will have to do, black or not.'

Jael unpinned her damp cloak, happy to irritate her mother,

and hopefully, Lothar too. Gisila prided herself on her highborn ways, and despite Jael being far more highborn, she looked down on her daughter's choice to be a warrior, and she particularly detested the old clothes Jael persisted in wearing.

Jael untied her swordbelt, placing it on Arnna's table before squeezing out of her blue woollen tunic. The chill of the cottage raised the hairs on her arms, and shivering in just her linen undertunic and trousers, she reached out to grab the dress.

'You'll need to take it all off to fit into this,' Gisila grumbled.

Jael bent down, sighing, slipping out of her boots and trousers. 'I'm not taking my undertunic off,' she insisted firmly. 'I'll freeze on that fucking island if I can't wear something underneath that dress!'

Gisila couldn't help but smile, amused that her otherwise impenetrable daughter had such a weakness when it came to the cold. 'I'm sure Arnna can make you a shift to wear underneath it, but for now, that baggy old thing will not fit, so take it off!'

For once, Jael did as she was told.

She stood there, naked in the harsh brightness of the room, glowing white apart from her dark hair which fell damply over a pair of broad shoulders, and a tiny pair of bronze axes, which hung between her small breasts. Her exposed flesh was a mass of bruises, cuts, and scars scattered across lean muscle. Gisila gasped. She hadn't seen her daughter naked since she was a girl, but this was no longer the body of a girl, nor was it the body of a woman.

Jael looked like a battered warrior.

Like Ranuf used to.

Arnna barely blinked. She had watched Jael collect her scars over the years, so there was nothing to surprise her. She took the dress from a stunned Gisila, helping Jael navigate its perfectly tailored seams.

It was similar to Jael's tunic in style, though tight-fitting, flaring out from her waist to sit near the ground in a feminine way. It was an attractive enough dress, and it appeared to fit her well, but Jael quickly felt imprisoned by its clinging fabric.

Arnna creaked and fussed around her, smoothing, adjusting, and turning her reluctant model with a deep rasping hum as Jael wriggled, unable to stand still, desperate to return to the comfort of her crumpled pile of clothes.

'It is good, I think,' Arnna declared, at last, straightening her bony frame with a loud crack. 'I shall make a matching cloak, and with a few brooches and arm-rings... perfect.' She smiled at Jael, showing off an almost-toothless set of gums.

'It may fit,' Gisila muttered, 'but it is no dress for a wedding. It would be better worn to a funeral.'

'Well, it does sound perfect then!' Jael laughed as she hurried to yank the dress up and over her head.

Gisila looked unimpressed and made to leave, wrapping her thick grey cloak around her shoulders. 'I suggest you hide that dress away so Lothar doesn't catch a glimpse of it before we leave. He's likely to rip it up and make you wear a bedsheet!' And grumbling to herself, she slipped out of the cottage without looking back.

Jael watched the door close with a frown.

'Your mother is scared,' Arnna said, laying the dress across the long table that took up most of the main room.

'Scared of what?' Jael wondered, wrapping her leather belt around her waist.

'Of what will happen when you're gone. Of Lothar. Of what he will do.'

'Well, if everyone behaves themselves he won't do anything, will he? Besides, Axl will be here to take care of her.' That didn't sound convincing, though, even to her own ears.

'Axl... hmmm... no, I don't think he'll be able to save your mother from what Lothar has in mind, do you?'

Jael hadn't realised that Lothar's interest in Gisila was widely known, nor that serious.

'It is no easy thing to refuse a king, as you have found out yourself,' Arnna said, taking Jael's cold hands in her tiny gnarled ones. 'Your mother can only do what is possible, and the rest... well, that is for the gods to decide.' She dropped Jael's hands and pushed her towards the door. 'Now begone, so I can think about your new cloak. There is not much left in these old eyes today, especially when I must be working with black wool. I shall be blind by the time you leave for Oss!' And Arnna shooed Jael outside, quickly shutting the door behind her.

Jael couldn't help but smile as she stood on the porch, pinning her cloak to her shoulder. She almost felt like herself again, despite the dress and her mother's mood, but then she frowned, wondering if her new husband would insist upon her wearing dresses, or, more to the point, her new father-in-law, the King of Oss.

That was a fight she wasn't prepared to lose.

'Jael!' Axl ambled towards her, looking cheerful. He was a tall boy-man, with a thick brush of dark brown hair on his head, none on his youthful face, and the look of an unstable foal about him. He skittered towards her in a rush, his cheeks red, his nose too. 'Where have you been?'

Jael motioned with her hand towards Arnna's door.

'Oh.'

'What do you want?' she asked, suddenly irritable as she headed off to her cottage again. Jael didn't know why she always felt cross with Axl.

She did. She did know.

But still, he was her younger brother. Her only brother.

She had to let the past go.

'Edela's looking for you,' Axl replied evenly, ignoring her sullen face.

'Is she?' Edela lived in the opposite corner of the fort, so Jael changed course, Axl trotting alongside her. 'Did she want to see you too?'

'No.'

'So why are you following me, then?'

'I'm not following you. I'm keeping you company.'

'*Company*? Why do I need your company?' Jael wondered, sidestepping a large dog who barked at her.

'Well, I thought with Aleksander missing –'

'He's not missing!' Jael snapped. 'He's gone off hunting, that's all. That's not missing. He's coming back.' She stopped, glaring at her brother. 'He'll come back in time. I know him.'

'Alright, alright.' Axl bravely reached out and placed a hand on his sister's arm.

Jael stilled uncomfortably. 'He'll come back,' she sighed, finally releasing some tension. 'He will.'

Axl nodded, knowing that Aleksander loved Jael more than anyone.

If he could come back from wherever he'd disappeared to, he would.

Jael noticed a few Andalans gawking in their direction, and, grabbing Axl's arm, they started walking again. 'What does Edela want?' she wondered.

'I don't know, she wouldn't say, but she didn't look like herself. She seemed strange, as though she had just woken up. Messy and ill, with her hair all...' Axl waved his hands wildly about his head. 'She told me to bring you urgently.'

***

Edela creaked open the door before Jael had even walked through her gate. Axl was right, Jael thought, peering up the path: she definitely looked out of sorts.

Hurrying Jael inside, Edela closed the door, not wanting to lose any more warmth from her fire. The cottage felt even dimmer than usual, with only scant light beams straining down the smoke hole, and although a lamp was burning, Jael found herself squinting around the room.

'Sit down. Please.' Edela wasn't wasting any time.

'What's happened?' Jael wondered, finding her favourite stool waiting by the fire.

'I've had a dream. Many dreams these last few nights,' Edela murmured, coming to sit in front of her granddaughter. 'Long, dark, endlessly confusing dreams.' She frowned at the bright flames of her fire, desperately seeking the clarity which had so far eluded her. 'When I talked to you about Eadmund, when I saw you together, it always gave me a feeling of light and happiness.' She stopped, considering things. 'I still see that, but there is... something new now.'

Edela looked so confused that Jael felt unsettled. 'What sort of something?'

Edela hesitated. 'It is hard to explain. It's... a darkness. A thick cloud of suffocating darkness. And I see it on Oss, around you and Eadmund. On more than Oss really. On the other islands too. It is an evil thing, this darkness. An old, evil thing that has not been seen or felt for so long that I think we may have forgotten that it ever existed.'

Jael was intrigued. 'A bad omen, you mean?'

Edela shook her head. 'No, no, I think it is magic, dark magic. The type of magic that was banished to the farthest reaches of the land, locked and hidden away...' She stopped, a fearful realisation freezing her face as a long-forgotten memory returned. Edela quickly wrapped her mind around it, willing herself to hold on, lest it slip away.

Jael held her breath, watching rain dripping down the smoke hole, sizzling the flames into an angry protest. *Magic? Who's using this magic? And why?'*

Edela was starting to see more clearly; she could feel a growing understanding pulsing in her veins. 'The Tuuran gods are not spoken about here, not anymore. I used to tell you their stories when you were small, but you grew bored listening because I didn't speak of swords and battles, and bloody deaths.'

Jael smiled, remembering.

'But if you'd listened closely, you would have heard tales that were just as bloodthirsty as you wanted. You would have heard about Raemus, who was the God of Darkness, the Father of Time. He grew so lonely in the empty void that existed before there was life, that he made a wife called Daala. She hated the Darkness, though, and her heart was heavy to be with him in such a desolate place. And so, to make Daala happy, they had a child together, and that child was named Aurea, and she was the Goddess of Light. And now it was Raemus' turn to be unhappy, for he did not wish to exist in such a world. But he loved Daala, so he remained loyally by her side, suffering, while she created a world of sun and water, and living creatures, and all those things that grew in the light. Life flourished all around them in the Realm of the Gods and here on Earth.' Edela paused to catch her breath. 'Raemus grew jealous of all the love and attention his wife gave to the humans, and the animals, and the other gods. And he hid away in the darkest corners he could find, plotting to return to that time when Daala belonged only to him. He wanted it to be the way it was when they had existed alone in the Darkness together.' Edela grabbed her iron poker, prodding the logs in her fire, wanting more flames.

'And what happened?'

'You don't remember?' Edela chided with half a smile. 'Well, Raemus created the Book of Darkness, and in it, he wrote down all the ways in which he could bring about the end of light. He wanted to end life on Earth, to destroy everything that had come between him and Daala. He couldn't ask any of the other gods to join him as they were loyal to her, so he shared the secrets of the book with like-minded humans whose hearts were as black as his. He found many broken souls willing to return to the Darkness with him. To become part of the secret army he forged.' Edela shook her head. 'What those people imagined a world of pure darkness would bring, I will never understand. His followers used his spells and his teachings, helping Raemus to kill, destroying homes and lives with their evil ways. Eventually, it came to Daala's attention that this dark magic was being used, and she knew that she must act to protect her people. So, as much as it broke her heart to do so, she killed Raemus, but she could not recover the book. He had concealed its presence with intricate spells, so Daala would never be able to find it.'

Jael frowned. 'Do you think that's what you're dreaming about, then? That someone has found this book? But surely it's just a story?'

'Not in Tuura, it's not,' Edela snapped. 'Our gods were the ones who made Tuura. The land your father's people took from us and turned into their Osterland. In Tuura, the stories of the gods are taught to our children. Not as tales or fantasy but as lessons in our history. Of how our people came to be. Of how our land was formed and then stolen.'

Jael chewed on that for a moment. 'If this book *did* exist, and if someone has found it, what could they do with it?'

'I don't know. The book is not something that is spoken of, not anymore, except as a warning to those wishing to pursue a dark path.' She paused, considering things. 'Raemus was also the first God of Magic, so that book would have been filled with every spell he knew of, every spell he conceived. And Raemus imagined magic in a dark, dark way.'

'But if he hid the book that carefully, then surely no one could ever find it? And if they did, he must have protected it as well. It seems like an impossible theory, Grandmother.'

Edela looked back to the flames, her mind wandering again. It was one line of thought; a direct line towards the darkness that her dreams were warning her about. But perhaps Jael was right? Perhaps it was a step too far? She certainly didn't want to envision the destruction the book could cause if it were found.

'Grandmother?' Jael was talking to herself, though. Edela had slipped quietly away, trying to piece together the remnants of her long-forgotten memories into an answer, an explanation... afraid of what she would find.

CHAPTER FIVE

'There is hope!' Eirik snorted.

Eadmund staggered across the frost-powdered stones towards his father, shielding his eyes from the only moderately bright sun. Dawn had barely broken, and Eadmund wasn't sure that he'd been awake this early in years. 'You may call it hope, Father, but it feels like a punishment from the gods to me!' He grimaced wishing the birds would stop screeching so loudly; even the noise of the waves rushing up onto the foreshore was giving him a headache.

'Yes, well they should be angry with a waste like you! How many battles have you avoided these past few years? Enough to know that the only place being saved for you in Vidar's Hall is as one of his servants!'

'True, though likely I'll just be sent to the Nothing with the rest of the useless pieces of shit. Perhaps Grandfather will be there to keep me company?' Eadmund spat on the stones, wiping the back of his hand across his mouth.

He needed a drink.

Eirik clapped Eadmund on the back. 'You may have lost your appetite for battle, my son, but you've still got your sense of humour!' He felt genuinely happy as he stood on the beach next to Eadmund, inhaling the brisk morning air, enjoying the clear view of pale sky and dark sea, admiring all that he was king of. It felt good. He felt good. And after his recent setback with the

Alekkans, he was finally close to achieving all that he had hoped for. One step away from formalising his alliance with Brekka. One step from getting a wife into Eadmund's bed at long last.

The Furycks would arrive tomorrow, and, to Eirik's surprise, everything was ready; almost ready, he reminded himself. He still had to check on the bridal bed – his gift to the couple. The bed had been under construction for years in the hope that Eirik would eventually find Eadmund a new wife, and he wanted it to be the most luxurious bed his daughter-in-law had ever slept in; a gift worthy of a queen. So far, nobody had managed to achieve his high standards, but he was determined not to settle for anything less than perfection.

Eirik may have been a king, but he was a self-made one. His royal line extended back as far as himself, and beyond that lay the blood-smeared stain his tyrant father had left behind when he'd beheaded him. So he never fooled himself into thinking that he knew how to act like a real king. Not like Lothar Furyck, whose ancestors stretched back to Furia, the Goddess of War. Her son had been the first Furyck king, and now, two thousand years later, her descendant was marrying his son, the first of his line.

For Eirik, it was perfect. It was a beginning.

For Eadmund it felt like an ending, and as he watched his father vibrating with excitement, he could feel the weight of what was to come pushing him down into the thick bed of stones they stood on. He sighed. 'What did you want me for, Father? I'm sure you've got better things to be doing than talking to me.'

Eirik blinked, suddenly anxious. 'Tomorrow. The Furycks will arrive tomorrow. I need you to understand what is going to happen, Eadmund. What I expect from you.'

'I hardly think it needs a conversation,' Eadmund yawned. 'You want me able to stand on my own, clothes on preferably. Just enough ale to make me merry, not enough to have me vomiting on my new bride.' He winked at his father, eager to be gone.

'Well yes, that's all true,' Eirik agreed. 'But you need to do it. *Actually*, do it. I don't want Lothar to change his mind when he gets a look at the state of you. That would ruin everything. And I've had quite enough of you ruining everything lately!'

'Lothar's not going to change his mind if he sees me flat out on the ground, pissing my trousers. He's going to be even happier that he's giving his niece away to a drunkard like me. He's marrying her off to Ranuf's sworn enemy!' Eadmund laughed. 'I think Lothar will enjoy it all the more if he knows he's making her miserable.'

'That may be true, of course, but I don't care. You will be Eadmund the Very Sober and Not Going to Humiliate His Father while they're here. Or I shall kill you. Or worse, I'll bring back your brother,' Eirik threatened, all humour gone now.

That brought an end to Eadmund's light-hearted mood too. He turned to Eirik, hand on his arm. 'Not that, Father. Promise me you won't do that.'

Eirik took a deep breath, staring out across the harbour, to the tall stone spires in the distance, listening as the waves crashed on the shore. He knew what Eadmund thought about his brother – what Eadmund believed to be true – but he had to put Oss and all of the islands before any personal grievance, no matter how serious. 'I won't promise you that!' he growled. 'Oss needs a king when I die. I want to leave a legacy behind. I don't want to be the only king these islands ever had. To know that all I achieved meant nothing. Just a murmur on the wind. Forgotten. I want to leave something behind of me, and if it can't be you, then it will have to be Ivaar.'

'But –'

'But nothing! You've one more chance. I've arranged this marriage for you. Show me that you can be the next king, Eadmund,' Eirik implored, turning to his son. 'Whatever your brother has done in the past, I won't hesitate to call on him if you let me down again.'

Eirik was in no mood to tiptoe around his youngest son's ego.

He wouldn't let Eadmund ruin this.

He'd been endlessly patient, but there would be an end to it and that end was coming quickly.

***

They were leaving in the morning, and there was still no Aleksander.

Jael nibbled her bottom lip as she sat in front of the fire, watching the flames shrink. Biddy was fussing about in a corner of the cottage, preparing for tomorrow's sailing. Preparing for bed. They would leave Andala early, aiming to arrive in time for an evening feast on Oss. The following day would be the marriage ceremony and then more feasting.

Too much feasting, Jael thought miserably.

And no Aleksander.

She kept alternating between being unreasonably furious and desperately worried that something had happened to him.

But which one was it and where was he?

'Goodnight, Jael,' Biddy whispered, crawling into her small bed. There really wasn't room for three people inside the tiny cottage, but Biddy had taken care of Jael since she was a baby, and Aleksander since he was ten, so when they had moved in, they'd insisted on squeezing Biddy into a corner.

'Sleep well,' Jael replied, grateful that Lothar had allowed Biddy to stay with her on Oss.

She blew out the lamp burning on the table by her bed, but though she had resigned herself to the new day coming and there being no Aleksander to say goodbye to, she just couldn't bring herself to get into their bed alone. So, snatching up her cloak and swordbelt, she slipped out of the cottage, into the night.

Jael saw no one as she walked through the square, just a few cats hunting for scraps and rats. It was bitterly cold, most people likely warming themselves by a fire or buried under furs, sharing their body heat with eager companions. Snow flurries drifted across her path, and for a moment, she thought about going to see Tig, just to feel his warm breath as he nuzzled her face, but she didn't want to wake him. He hated sailing and would need as much sleep as possible for his journey across the Nebbar Straights in the morning.

Sensing movement behind her, Jael turned, her attention on the ramparts where the guards were calling down to someone outside the main gates. Their voices were muffled, but Jael was immediately on edge, slipping a hand inside her cloak, adjusting her belt, assuring herself that her sword was within reach.

Walking towards the gates now, she could hear her boots crunching softly across the settling snow. The beam had been lifted, and the gates were being eased open.

Someone they knew, then?

Jael quickened her pace, her heartbeat skipping as she watched a tall, hooded figure step tentatively inside. She stilled, her breathing shallow. The figure raised one arm towards the guards in thanks. His left arm. And then she knew, and she rushed towards the man, who, looking up, saw her and dropped his hood.

Aleksander.

Jael threw her body into his, nearly knocking him over.

Aleksander clung to her, exhausted, a smile creasing his frozen face.

She was still here.

Stepping back, he cupped Jael's face with his hands, kissing her cold nose, her eyes, her lips, before holding her tightly to him again.

She was still here!

'What happened to you? Where have you been?' Jael peered at his weary face, then frowned, realising that he'd arrived alone. On foot. She looked behind him, confused. 'Where's Ren?'

Aleksander's face fell.

His horse, Ren, had been given to him by Ranuf when he was

thirteen; the brother of Tig; his most beloved friend. And he was gone. 'Wolves.' Snow was falling thickly between them now, and Aleksander brushed the snowflakes out of his eyes, feeling tears coming. 'Fucking wolves. It's all my fault. I should have sensed them, heard them, something. Ren was acting strangely, but I was so... preoccupied... I thought he was just spooked by the storm. I didn't see them until it was too late. It's all my fault!'

'Wolves?' Jael reached out, touching his face; snow and tears in her own eyes. 'I'm sorry, so sorry.' The shock left her numb. She had loved that beautiful, gentle horse almost as much as Aleksander.

Tears ran down Aleksander's face as he shivered before her. He wanted to run back through the gates, back to where he'd last seen Ren. To where he'd had to abandon him. He didn't want to imagine what had become of his horse, though his mind kept wandering to dark places.

Unable to even speak, Jael grabbed Aleksander's frozen hand, leading him through the square, back to their miserable little cottage.

For the last time.

***

In Oss' hall, bodies were falling about in a happy state of ale-induced slumber. The night had been a long one, everyone making an effort to toast Eadmund on his last night of freedom before the she-witch from Brekka arrived.

Well, if they wanted to call her that, Eirik supposed, they could. He couldn't say that she wasn't, but he trusted Eydis and Eydis believed that Jael Furyck would save her brother. And Eirik didn't imagine that a she-witch could be capable of such a gentle thing. So, they made fun of Eadmund's future wife with Eirik's blessing; drunk more than most could handle; engaged in a few half-hearted fights; poked fun at couples humping in darkened corners; badly sang a lot of songs.

And now, finally, a rumbling, snoring peace had descended upon the hall, and Eirik was ready for bed.

He smiled wistfully, manoeuvring his way through the maze of bodies littered about the floor; the lucky ones curled up on rows of fur-covered beds lining the walls; the rest making do with whatever bench they could find. His youth had been filled with nights like these. Nights that deepened the bonds of friendship forged on battlefields. Nights where problems and fears were shut outside, behind heavy wooden doors, so that all that existed was this happy, drunken brotherhood.

In his sentimental state, Eirik stumbled, tripping over a discarded plate, slipping on a puddle of ale. He shook himself awake, cross at his carelessness, not wanting to appear as old and clumsy as he feared he was becoming.

The fires were burning down now, but he could still make out the bloated mound of Eadmund, lying on a bench as though he'd been felled by a hefty axe. Snoring. His mouth open wide enough to swallow an apple. Eirik was surprised that the bench hadn't collapsed beneath his weight. He frowned, wondering what state his son would be in tomorrow. But then, they had a whole day to sober him up, which would surely be enough time?

'Thorgils,' Eirik whispered hoarsely to the tall man who sat at a table, swaying from side to side, either sleeping or trying to stand.

Eirik couldn't tell.

Thorgils looked up, half-drunk, half asleep. 'I thought you'd have been tucked up in your bed long ago.'

'Ahhh, but I'm not that old yet,' Eirik laughed. 'I've a few more nights to come, I think. Just a few. Unlike Eadmund here, who probably has hundreds, if not thousands of nights like this to snore through. Although, if he ruins tomorrow, this will definitely be his last!'

Thorgils grinned sleepily, placing both hands on the table to stop himself moving. 'You needn't worry, Torstan and I will keep him in our sights tomorrow. He won't get near any ale until the guests arrive. We won't let him.'

'I'd believe that, Thorgils, if only I didn't know my son so well,' Eirik sighed, his eyes on the green curtain that led to the bedchambers. 'But I wish you luck with your prisoner. As long as he's standing by the time they arrive, I'll be a happy man indeed. There may even be a new arm-ring in it for you both.'

Thorgils had more arm-rings than most on Oss and Eirik didn't think that he'd care for another, but even in his drunken state, Thorgils sat up a little taller, keen to take on the responsibility. He peered at the bodies slumped around him, hoping to locate Torstan, who he'd last seen slobbering over a comely serving girl.

He was going to need all the help he could get.

***

They were both silent with thoughts of Ren and what would come tomorrow as they lay in their narrow bed, bodies touching, trying to keep warm.

Aleksander had brought the fire back to life before they'd crawled into bed, and the bright flames helped them to see. After days apart, and about to face an indefinite separation, they were desperate to see each other.

Aleksander looked even thinner and more drawn than usual. His eyes were red-rimmed and sunken, his lips scabbed, his fingernails bloody.

Wherever he'd been, and whatever he'd been doing, it hadn't been enjoyable.

'Tell me,' Jael breathed, wanting to keep their conversation just between them. 'Where have you been?'

Aleksander was wary at first, his eyes searching hers for some sign as to her mood. He hesitated, then sighed. 'I went to find the Widow.'

'The Widow?' Jael was confused. 'What? What for? How did you find her? Surely, she's dead?'

Aleksander shook his head. 'No, she was very much alive.'

'But she must be over a hundred years old.' Jael frowned. 'And you found where she's been hiding all these years? How?'

'It took a while, but yes, I found her. She wouldn't see me, though,' he murmured, choosing his words carefully. 'Not at first. She refused. I waited outside her cottage for days, in the snow, trying to get her to speak to me. I think she had enough of me bothering her in the end because she finally let me in.'

'But how did you know where to find her?' Jael asked again.

Aleksander sighed. 'When I was a child, my mother would tell stories about her. She told me where to find her. I don't know why. I don't suppose she thought I would remember. But after my mother died, I didn't want to let go of her, so I memorised her stories, just the way she would tell them. Imagining her voice, remembering her words,' he whispered sadly. 'I just didn't want to think that you'd leave and I'd do nothing but let you go. I couldn't ask Edela to help me, and you wouldn't tell me what she saw for us. Not all of it. I had to know what would happen myself.'

'And what did she tell you?'

Aleksander looked away, shuddering with the memory of it. 'She wouldn't say anything. Nothing. After all I went through to get there. After finding her cottage and convincing her to let me in, she made it plain that she wasn't about to help me. She gave me a meal, then threw me out. But I stayed there, waiting, and eventually, she came out to me again, handed me a tincture and sent me to the very tip of God's Point, to Vidar's Tree. I had to drink the tincture and stay there for three nights, and on the last night I would be shown the visions the gods wanted me to see.'

Jael's eyes were wide. 'And what happened?'

'Well, I did as she said. I was barely able to stand in the wind up there. The tip of God's Point is no safe place to be, hanging there above the cliffs. I tied myself to the tree as best I could. I'm not sure if it was her tincture, or that I went mad from hunger and thirst, but the visions came so powerfully, as though I was in them. They were like dreams, nightmares, but I think I was awake the whole time. I don't remember sleeping at all.' He paused, the memory of it unsettling him again. 'I saw Edela tell you about Eadmund Skalleson. I heard what she said about how you were meant to be together. I saw all of that between you and her, and then, I saw more. All the things Edela didn't say.'

Jael gripped his hand tightly. 'What things?'

'That you would come back to me, with your child. Your daughter. That we would be together again.' Aleksander knew that he should feel happy because of that, but he didn't. His wild, painful dreams had been scarred by dark images; warnings of horrors to come. He didn't understand most of them, but he knew that he had to keep them from Jael.

'A daughter? With him?' Jael closed her eyes. The thought of that made her want to scream, but then there was better news: they would be together again.

That was something to hold onto.

But why hadn't Edela mentioned it?

'Yes, a little girl,' Aleksander said sadly. 'Just like you. I saw you holding her hand. Introducing her to me.'

Aleksander's story was so strange; almost more than Jael could take in. She had been preparing to say goodbye to him forever. And now there was this unexpected twist. So, it was only goodbye for a short while, or at least until she came back again with this child. Jael felt more and more removed from all that was coming. She closed her eyes, imagining herself standing in the mucky gore of a battlefield, swinging her sword in a wild, blood-making fury.

Alone. Free.

In the silence, Aleksander could sense Jael's discomfort. He knew that his story had been riddled with so many holes that soon she would start questioning him. He kissed her quickly, hoping to distract her so there would be no time for questions, only goodbyes. He tried not to see his dreams again, not wanting them to ruin the illusion that she was his and always would be.

Whatever Aleksander had told her, he knew that when Jael met Eadmund Skalleson, it would never be the same between them again.

And still kissing her, Aleksander ran his hand firmly down Jael's face, over her sharp jaw, down between her frozen breasts, nestling it firmly between her thighs.

In whatever was left of this night, she would still be his.

CHAPTER SIX

If only the snow had settled.

If only the Freeze had come.

Jael stood on the pier wrapped in her cloak, shivering in the bitter morning air. Small, ever-decreasing puddles of slush lingered on the ground, but the dark harbour water was clear of ice, the ships were almost loaded, and soon they would be leaving.

They were taking two ships, partly because they were taking two horses and neither horse would make good company, especially for the other. Tig had sailed a few times, but he hated the rocking sensation of being at sea, and he always refused to settle. They were also taking a white mare named Leada, who was younger and much more agreeable than Tig. She was to be Jael's gift to her new husband. It had been Lothar's idea, and although Jael could have cared less, she was pleased to know that Tig would have some Brekkan company on the island.

The thought of horses reminded her of Ren, and the sadness of his sudden loss pulled at her heart. It would be so hard for Aleksander to lose both him and her within days of each other.

'Warm enough?' Lothar chortled as he crept up behind his shivering niece, rubbing his hands together. 'You're not going to enjoy our journey if you think *this* is cold!'

Jael didn't reply. She was in no mood to even attempt conversation today.

Lothar didn't care. As soon as winter had done its worst, they would be at the piers again, knee-deep in ships and weapons, preparing to invade Hest with Eirik Skalleson and his mangy Islanders.

He couldn't have been happier.

'I've organised for Tiras to stay with you on Oss,' he murmured into Jael's ear, standing far too close for her liking. His breath stunk of ripe cheese and onions, and Jael wanted to turn away. 'To ensure that you stay loyal. That you represent this family well. That my part of the alliance holds true. He will be watching you.'

Jael didn't even blink. 'As you wish, Uncle.' She knew that she still had to please Lothar to keep everyone safe, as she had done these past few years, but there was just so little left inside her to care today. She wanted to be gone, to be on their way, to have said her goodbyes.

If only Lothar would shut his stinking mouth and just fuck off.

Lothar grinned, unperturbed by his sullen niece. 'There is one last thing, though. My sword.'

Jael's hand instinctively moved towards the hilt of the Furyck sword, tucked into its scabbard, hidden beneath her cloak.

'You may keep that old scabbard,' Lothar said dismissively as Jael began to fiddle with her swordbelt. 'I have my father's. It is just the sword I require.' He stepped around in front of her, and Jael was forced to look at his sneering face. Lothar looked nothing like her father, although, admittedly they both had dark hair. But whereas Ranuf had appeared carved out of stone, Lothar looked ready to melt like a sheep-fat candle. He was a man filled with so little substance that Jael was convinced that he would slither away to nothing at the merest hint of a flame.

Glaring at her uncle, she unsheathed the sword and handed it to him. Ranuf may have chosen to pass his crown to Axl, but he had left his sword to her. And now here she was, placing it into the sweaty hands of Lothar the Usurper; a man so foolishly ambitious that he was on course to destroy two thousand years of

Furyck rule in Brekka before the end of his reign.

Whatever was about to happen, whatever path the gods had laid out for her, Jael promised herself that she would return to Brekka one day and remove Lothar's head, wiping his name from their history.

Lothar wrapped his hands around the sword's iron grip, making a great pretence of inspecting every part of it. Eventually, he slipped the sharp blade into the ancient Furyck scabbard he had only just managed to tie around his rotund frame. 'We shall be away within the hour, so best say your goodbyes quickly.' Lothar's smile was smug as he waddled down the pier, his new boots squeaking through the slush.

Jael couldn't move.

She stared straight ahead, watching as the sun struggled higher into the bleak morning sky, fingering her empty scabbard.

***

'You've lost him? Already?' Thorgils was dumbfounded. He towered over the guilty-looking Torstan, who had been charged with keeping Eadmund on a leash while Thorgils helped move benches and tables around the hall. 'How is that possible? He was unconscious! Snoring! Dribbling, even!'

'Well, he's gone now,' Torstan mumbled into his blonde beard, rubbing his head in a typically bemused fashion.

Thorgils sighed. Perhaps his slightly confused friend hadn't been the best choice to help him watch Eadmund. 'Well, go and find him then!' he urged crossly, bending down to Torstan's ear, not wanting to be overheard. He glanced around the hall, but nobody was looking their way. Everyone was far too busy getting ready for their guests. 'I'll come and help shortly. Try the drying sheds, try Evaine's, try anywhere he might be likely to find a drink. And do it without Eirik noticing. If he sees you looking around, calling out, he's going to kill Eadmund and then us!'

A loud crash sounded from the back of the hall.

'Thorgils!'

'I have to go,' Thorgils muttered impatiently. 'Just go, and I'll find you soon.'

Torstan nodded, heading for the doors at his typically slow pace.

'And quickly!' Thorgils grumbled after him.

***

They were in their cottage.

It felt like the right place to do it, hidden away from everyone. The silence was awkward, though, and neither wanted to make the first move because a beginning would require an ending, and that was the thing they were dreading the most.

'Don't come down to the piers. Stay here,' Jael insisted agitatedly. She couldn't look at Aleksander. She didn't want to do the actual goodbye part, but it was here, and now she couldn't run away from it any longer.

Aleksander grabbed her shoulders, forcing her to look at him. 'I won't. I don't want to.'

Jael reached up, touching his face. 'You'll be all alone here. Not even Ren for company. Not till Axl gets back.'

'Ahhh, because Axl is such great company,' Aleksander grinned, trying to lighten the mood.

Jael's mood wasn't lightened at all.

She leaned forward, letting him hold her, hiding inside that warm, safe place he kept just for her. She clung onto him, remembering the night before; how glad she had been to see him, to be with him that one last time. She didn't want to let go. They'd been inseparable through arguments, through battles, through everything that had mattered. Aleksander had never let her go, no matter how many times she'd given him reason to.

Jael felt so annoyed with herself.

She should have fought harder to stay.

She should have fought at all, but she'd just given in, accepted the destiny of it, as though everyone else had the right to decide their future.

Perhaps they did. For now.

Jael sighed, realising that she had been so passive since her father had died. Creeping into the background. Hiding from things she should have faced. Accepting things she shouldn't have.

And now this.

She held on tighter, feeling Aleksander's tears as they ran down his face onto hers. Her fault, she told herself, it was all her fault. If only she had...

'You're coming back to me, remember that,' Aleksander mouthed into Jael's hair. He eased back her head and bent to kiss her one last time.

Gently. Slowly. Remembering her, and then letting her go.

Jael burst into tears, feeling a loss of control for the first time since her father had died. The pain was overwhelming. 'I'm coming back,' she whispered, more to herself than Aleksander. 'I'm coming back. If I have to kill the lot of them, I'm coming back to you.'

Aleksander held her tightly, wanting to believe her words, but his visions laughed at them as they stood there, wrapped around each other, not knowing how to let go.

***

They were on board and waiting.

Gisila, Lothar, and his youngest daughter, Amma, were on *Lightning*, the largest and newest of two ships charged with taking the wedding party across the treacherous Nebbar Straights to Oss. Gant was there too, with a handful of Lothar's most loyal men. Osbert was pacing around on *Storm Chaser* with Axl, Edela, and Biddy hovering nearby, all eyes on the harbour gates, watching for any sign of Jael. The horses were jittery, especially Tig, who knew that Jael wasn't there and was unsettled because of it.

The wind was getting up, the sky grimmer than ever and more snow was threatening. They had to leave now.

Gisila felt ill.

Surely Jael wouldn't just escape? Leave them all to Lothar's mercy?

'Jael will be here any moment, I'm sure. She needed to say goodbye to Aleksander. That would have been hard.'

Lothar grunted. 'A king does not like to be kept waiting, as I'm sure you know, Gisila. Not the King of Brekka, nor the King of Oss, so she'd better hurry up.' He said this through gritted, grinding teeth but his rank breath still managed to escape, wafting over Gisila, who quickly turned away.

Jael emerged from the gates then, walking towards the piers. She was not hurrying, but nor was she dawdling, so there was little for Lothar to grumble about.

'Finally! Let us be away!' he barked, glaring at both helmsmen, who nodded at the two boys standing by the mooring posts, ready to loosen the ropes.

Jael stepped down into *Storm Chaser* as its rope fell away, ignoring the good wishes from the Andalans who had formed a line down each side of the pier. It was not a moment to celebrate, and they understood that, but still, those who had known Jael throughout her life wanted her to know that she would not be forgotten.

Jael didn't care what they thought, though, not now.

Her tears had dried, her goodbyes were done, and she was

ready to sail away from all that she had been.

Raising her hood, she made her way down the deck, past the busy oarsmen, bumping into Osbert. He stared at her, caught between enjoying Jael's misery and feeling some of his own. It was strange to think that she was leaving Andala, never to return.

The ship's roll was instant as the men slotted their oars in and started to pull them slowly away from the pier, and Osbert turned his attention away from Jael as he stumbled towards the gunwale eager to find somewhere to stand.

Tig whinnied, shuffling about trying to find his balance as Jael swayed down to the mast where he was tethered, grabbing hold of his bridle. She put her face to his, blowing gently on his dark cheek, murmuring in his ear, as much for her comfort as his. He stilled, his muscles relaxing slightly, his head touching hers. Jael closed her eyes and held on, not wanting to look back, knowing that Aleksander wouldn't be there.

Hoping he wouldn't be there.

She cleared her mind of everything but the sea and sky ahead, wondering if she would ever see Andala again.

***

Aleksander stood near one of the ship sheds bordering the entrance to the piers. He waited, concealed in the shadows, watching as the ships shrank from view.

His heart felt heavy, a sudden loss of hope rendering him numb.

He knew that he would see Jael again, but what would happen between now and then would change them both forever.

PART TWO

Adrift

CHAPTER SEVEN

'I don't want her anywhere near him. Do you understand me, Morac?' Eirik grumbled. 'Nowhere! Put her away somewhere. Lock her up! Just keep her out of my sight!'

Eirik stood near the doors, surveying the hall. On edge. Nothing was happening fast enough for his liking. Dusk was already falling. Their guests would be here soon, and flower garlands were still being strung around the walls. Lamps and candles were still being carried in. Not enough, not nearly enough to convey the illusion of luxury and wealth. For, although Eirik had dreamed of turning the Slave Islands into a prosperous, free kingdom, fishing and whaling were nowhere near as profitable as slaving had been for his tyrannical father. They needed more markets and opportunities for trade if they were to truly thrive. A few extra candles and lamps would do little to mask the stark reality that Eirik's was a kingdom in decline.

'Of course. I'll make sure she stays away,' Morac said, biting down on his irritation. 'She has no wish to cause trouble, I promise.'

'No? Well, good,' Eirik muttered.

'The hall looks impressive, my friend,' Morac smiled tightly, clapping Eirik on the shoulder. 'You've no need to fear. It looks perfect. Royal.'

'Ha! If only that were true. But hopefully, it looks enough. That's all I ask. I don't wish to embarrass my son, or myself.'

'I hardly think you'll embarrass yourself, but as for Eadmund...'

'Eadmund,' Eirik snapped, 'is being looked after by Thorgils and Torstan. He'll surprise us all tonight, I'm sure.'

Morac pointed towards the back of the hall, to the green curtain that led to the bedchambers. 'You mean Torstan and Thorgils over there, who appear to be looking for someone?'

Eirik spun around, jaw clenched as he pushed his way through the busy hall towards the curtain. 'What have you done with him?' he demanded, surprising the two men who had been sneaking around, checking the bedchambers. 'When did you last see him?'

Thorgils swallowed and Torstan, who had always been terrified of Eirik, flushed bright red, staring at anything but his king's apoplectic face.

'Ahhh, it was, ummm,' Thorgils stalled. 'It was this morning. Early this morning sometime.'

'*What?*' Eirik barked, so loudly that the gentle, murmuring hubbub of the hall ceased immediately, all heads turning in his direction. '*What?* Where is he? Where did you lose him? *How* did you lose him?' He looked directly at the squirming Torstan whose face burned an even darker shade of red.

'We only turned our backs for a moment, and he slipped away,' Thorgils insisted, coming to his friend's defense. 'He was gone before we could do anything, and we haven't been able to pick up his scent since. There's no sign of him anywhere.'

Eirik felt ill. His eyes darted around the busy hall in panic.

'Father, I can take you to him!' It was Eydis. She had emerged from behind the curtain and was reaching out, trying to find her distracted father's hand. 'I know where he'll be.'

Eirik looked down at his daughter in confusion.

Eydis was already dressed in her grey fur cloak, hood up, gloves on. She tugged impatiently on his hand, turning to lead him out of the hall. 'Come on, Father! We must hurry!'

***

It had been an awful day, and now they had reached what was sure to be the worst part yet.

Storm Chaser had bounced nauseously about, buffeted by extreme winds, moody seas, and frequent snowfalls. Under sail since leaving Andala's harbour, she had raced across the black depths of the Nebbar Straights: the treacherous stretch of water between Andala and Oss, the largest of the islands in Eirik Skalleson's kingdom.

Tig had joined Jael in hating every moment of it. Osbert had complained loudly, barking at her to keep her damn horse quiet. She was sure that most on board would have happily tipped Osbert over the side and left him to be picked over by Ran, Goddess of the Sea, so she'd ignored him for the most part. But he was a perverse little bastard, and Jael didn't want him doing something reckless; so she'd spent the entire journey by Tig's side, keeping him as calm as possible, safe from Osbert, his unstable temper, and the threatening glint of his sword.

Edela hated sailing even more than Tig, and she had clung to Axl in the stern, her face as leaden as the sky that hung over them, her mouth clamped tight against the wind. Jael wondered what Edela saw in her dreams that made her so fearful of the sea. She thought about revealing Aleksander's visit to the Widow but changed her mind, deciding that it was best to keep that information to herself; hoping that his visions would prove more accurate than her grandmother's.

The ships had cautiously navigated two of the smaller islands and were now weaving and rolling their way towards the jagged black stones that rose out of the white-capped sea, guarding the entry to Oss' harbour.

Jael forced herself to look up at the island that was to be her new home. It appeared to be little more than a craggy rock discarded by the gods and dropped into the sea. No wonder it had never been settled by the Tuurans, she thought, squinting at its high, sheer-faced cliffs. It looked a wild and unforgiving sort of place.

Not like Brekka at all.

The sky was darkening rapidly as the oars dug in, and, under orders, they started to negotiate the narrow margin that existed between safe passage and torn hull. The four stone spires that towered threateningly over them made Oss a difficult place to enter. It was no surprise that Eirik Skalleson had reigned for so long.

Who would want to come here?

Jael turned around to see that *Lightning* was still following dutifully in *Storm Chaser's* wake. She had hoped that they might strike something and sink to the bottom of the sea, but then she remembered her mother and felt a slight pang of remorse.

It was only slight, though.

She was in a bitter mood, dreading what was about to happen.

***

They hurried out of the fort, into the storm, the wind screaming towards them, bringing increasingly heavy snow with it.

Eydis was sure that she knew where Eadmund was, but as to what state he would be in when they found him, she had no idea. It was a hidden place, a secret place, but she knew of it. Eadmund had taken her there once when she was much younger, and he was feeling wistful and lonely. He'd told her about it. How it had been his place with Melaena. How they had hidden away there to watch the ships come in as the sun sunk into the sea, sleeping under the stars.

'Ships!' Came the urgent call from a man up on the ramparts.

'*Already?*' Eirik felt sick as he grabbed Eydis' hand, almost dragging her off her small feet. 'Quickly, Eydis! Show me where he is!'

Eydis tried to get her bearings, to imagine where she was, though the force of the wind had her swaying all over the place. She took a deep breath and pointed to the edge of the cliff to the right of the harbour and Eirik ran, Thorgils and Torstan following closely behind. 'Stay there!' he called back to his daughter. 'Do not move, Eydis!'

The cliff fell away to reveal a gentle, sloping path leading down to an almost-hidden, grassy ledge, wide enough to fit a tiny cottage, but for now, it just contained one prone figure lying in the almost-dark. Eirik hesitated for a moment before running down to his son.

He wasn't moving.

Eirik bent down, holding his breath, laying his head on Eadmund's chest.

He was snoring. Snoring and stinking of ale.

Eirik stood up, disgusted, his cloak flapping around him, threatening to come loose.

Thorgils and Torstan were there quickly, pulling Eadmund upright. It wasn't easy as he was thoroughly unconscious, but finally, panting, arms burning, they got him to his feet. Eadmund swayed in the strengthening wind, a snow-covered dead weight hanging limply between his two friends. Thorgils and Torstan dragged him up the rise, back to the top of the cliff, both men breathing heavily from the effort. Eirik hurried behind them, cursing himself for not bringing a water bag.

He needed something to sober Eadmund up quickly.

Eydis stood there waiting for them, rooted to the spot despite the wind's best efforts to blow her over. She could sense that Eadmund was in a bad way and that her father was in a panic. 'Bring him to me! Quickly!' she called, removing her gloves. She buried one arm inside her brother's wet cloak, digging around urgently, burrowing under his tunic. Feeling his hairy armpit, she reached up and with her sharp little fingernails, pinched the delicate skin under Eadmund's arm as hard as she could. He yelped, jerking himself upright and awake, curling away from his sister, crossly shaking her off. His eyes didn't stay open, though, and he slumped straight back into a limp state. Thorgils and Torstan readjusted their hold as Eydis reached up inside Eadmund's tunic and did it again, this time even harder. Eadmund's eyes popped open, his mouth flapping like a fish desperate for water. Eirik stepped in and slapped him, and he was awake, almost alert, and momentarily able to stand on his own.

***

The two ships, finally free of the stone spires, eased into the calmer shallows of Oss' harbour. There were no piers, just a wide stone beach where a handful of ships were slumped over, wedged into the stones. Not many, though. Hardly a fleet. There had to be another harbour or a cove housing the remainder of Eirik's ships; likely keeping them safe over winter, Jael thought, trying to distract herself.

Storm Chaser's helmsman barked at his men who lifted their oars out of the water, leaving the ships to surge towards the shore. Jael held onto Tig's reins, soothing him through this last part. She wondered what she'd been thinking, bringing him to this inhospitable looking place but she couldn't have imagined leaving him behind.

As the keel grated onto the sandy foreshore, a handful of men in the bow jumped out into the cold, dark water, dragging the ship onto the snow-covered beach. With Axl's help, Jael coaxed Tig up and over the gunwale. He was unconvinced by the idea of jumping out of one unpleasant situation into another at first, but one look at the carrots in her hand swayed him quickly enough.

As the night settled in, the sea-worn travellers made their

way towards the spluttering torches that marked their path up to the fort. Lothar helped both Gisila and Amma over the snow-covered stones, leaving Osbert and Axl to bring up the rear with Jael and Edela. Gant stayed by the ships with Biddy and his men to organise the unloading of sea chests and gifts for their hosts.

Jael dragged a whinnying Tig behind her, feeling her chest tighten with every step. He hated the wind and was making her do most of the work. They swayed and slipped together, both desperate to turn and run back to the ships.

Back to Aleksander.

Jael blinked, forcing that thought away for the hundredth time, and gritting her teeth, she yanked harder on Tig's reins, tugging him forward.

The beach merged gradually into grassy plains littered with large, ramshackle buildings that stunk of fish. From there was a steep climb up a hill to Eirik Skalleson's stone fortress, which was quickly disappearing into the stormy night. The wind was coming towards them at such a pace and angle that walking was almost impossible.

Jael glanced up to where their welcoming party stood, just in time to see one man stumble, almost falling to the ground. It was hard to see much, but it appeared that he couldn't stand on his own. The men on either side of him seemed to be struggling to hold him up.

Osbert let out a roaring laugh. 'Did you see that? That has to be your Eadmund, doesn't it, Jael? What a prize you've won there!'

'Shut up, Osbert!' Lothar hissed, slapping his son on the back of the head. 'We are not here to insult our hosts, nor make enemies of them before this marriage is settled. Keep your mouth closed if you want to leave this island with a tongue!'

***

Evaine watched as the Brekkans struggled up the long hill. It was too dark to see much from this distance, but as she peered over the edge of the rampart wall, she was sure she knew which one was Jael Furyck.

She frowned, furious that she had to hide away when all she wanted to do was make herself known to her rival. To stake her claim. To show the bitch that Eadmund would never be hers.

That woman would be warming his bed every night.

Perhaps she would carry his child.

Evaine's ears hummed loudly as she fought the urge to run down the stairs and out of the fort. But this was not a contest to win in public view. She would have to sink into the shadows if she was going to keep Eadmund all to herself.

**

Eadmund swallowed, desperately searching for some saliva inside his dry mouth. His arms ached where Torstan and Thorgils were gripping him, where Eydis had pinched him so painfully moments ago. He didn't complain, though. Standing on his own appeared to be impossible, and he couldn't even remember what had happened or how he had ended up here, swaying in the darkness. The glow of torches flickered off the serious faces of those around him. His father would not even look at him. His eyes were hard, his face bitter with disappointment.

'Will you keep him upright!' Eirik growled through gritted teeth. 'And try to make it look as though you aren't. Move in closer together.' He stared straight ahead as the Brekkan party struggled towards them. Even in this wind-battered chill, he felt himself sweating.

'We're trying,' Thorgils grunted, regripping the arm he was holding, causing Eadmund to moan woefully. Thorgils moved his body as close to Eadmund's as possible, without it looking too unnatural. It was almost entirely dark now, and he hoped it would be good enough until they could take Eadmund away to sober him up.

'My Lord King!' Lothar reached Eirik first and bowed his head in greeting. 'It is good to see you again!' He smiled broadly, clapping Eirik on the shoulders in an enthusiastic show of friendship, his cloak flapping wildly around him as the snow blew into his face.

'Lothar,' Eirik smiled. 'It is good to see you too. Welcome to Oss!'

'My niece, Jael Furyck,' Lothar announced, pushing Jael forward. 'As you will see, she is not dressed for ceremony yet, but I do assure you that she has brought a dress with her!'

Jael cringed, not knowing where to look. Obviously, she should look at Eirik Skalleson, but she doubted she could do so without scowling, so instead, she stared awkwardly around herself, glancing at his face only in passing. Eirik took one of her hands in his, raising it to his mouth, and Jael froze, forcing herself not to yank it out of his icy grip.

She glared at him, then, teeth clamped together.

He was older than Lothar, older than her father would have been. His long, gold and white hair whipped across a leathery face. His beard, though, braided and weighted with silver nuggets, almost stayed in place. He had small, wary blue eyes and a tight mouth, but there was humour lurking around it. Humour that travelled up to his eyes when he looked at her.

It was not a bad face, she surmised... for an enemy.

'Jael,' Eirik said with an eager smile. 'Welcome to your new home. We are so pleased that you have come.' He nodded at Thorgils and Torstan, who somehow managed to shunt Eadmund forward without tipping him over. 'My son, Eadmund, the future King of Oss.'

Jael took a deep breath and forced her head to turn in Eadmund's direction. Her eyes lingered briefly on his bloated face before the overwhelming stench of him hit her. He smelled as though he'd vomited and pissed into a barrel of ale, then bathed in it. The stink was truly awful, and every gust of wind blew a fresh wave of him towards her.

Jael screwed up her face in total disgust.

Eadmund looked twice as wide as she remembered from when she'd fought him all those years ago. She hadn't seen his face then, and perhaps he had been handsome once, but from what she could make out now, he looked ill. A bloated, ghostly-white face covered in sweat, damp hair stuck to his forehead, round cheeks puffing in and out as he tried to catch his breath. His limbs hung lifelessly about him as he swayed, suspended on the bridge the two men on either side of him were making.

'Hello,' Jael said shortly. Then, as a small flicker of hope ignited somewhere deep inside her, she smiled.

Eadmund Skalleson looked like a man about to die.

Eadmund could barely see straight, let alone focus on the woman standing in front of him, twisting her face with such apparent distaste. She was tall but not taller than him. She dressed like a man but looked enough like a woman that humping her wouldn't be too challenging. He noticed the scar under her eye and was both intrigued and slightly intimidated. She was confident, he thought, and as Eadmund stood there, swaying, he felt anything but. He tried to feel the strength in his own feet, tried to stand a little taller, a little more proudly, but his body sagged with the effort, and he remained limply defeated. Eadmund closed his eyes, saw his father's disappointed face again and opened them, smiling as widely as he could manage. 'I'm pleased to meet you, Jael,' he said in a voice that didn't sound like his at all. He couldn't reach out a hand to hold hers and perhaps she could sense that as she didn't offer one either.

'Let's get out of this weather!' Eirik called over the keening wind as the two groups stood shivering, silently and awkwardly in front of each other. 'I have hot fires, good food, and plenty of wine to warm your cold souls!' He exhaled heavily, relieved that they were underway and as Lothar fell in beside him, Eirik looked over to see that Thorgils and Torstan were doing an impressive job of manoeuvring Eadmund through the gates. He raised an eyebrow at Thorgils, who nodded back, and, motioning to Torstan, they let everyone get ahead of them before slipping Eadmund away into the guard tower.

CHAPTER EIGHT

They sat next to each other, all nine of them, squeezed along the high table, elbows and knees almost touching. It was not a long table, nor was it a large hall, Jael noted as she glanced around, though Eirik Skalleson had certainly tried to beautify its dingy corners. Garlands hung from beams, crossing over their heads. Finely-worked tapestries rippled warmly in the mellow glow of candles and lamps. A trio of musicians plucked on their lyres in one corner of the hall, while girls with mead buckets rushed around topping up empty cups. It was good enough, Jael thought, but it was not Brekka, and the man on her right was not Aleksander Lehr, and the man on her left was not her father.

And she had no sword in her scabbard.

Clamping her lips together, Jael stared straight ahead as the conversations bubbled over and around her like a cold river.

Eadmund blinked, glancing to his left.

Had he just fallen asleep?

His face flushed with embarrassment. He felt foolish sitting at the high table in front of all of Oss. In front of these strangers. Exposed and ashamed. He wanted to be alone. To hide away. How had he become this... fool? He searched the packed hall, trying to find Evaine. He saw Morac and Runa, but Evaine was nowhere to be seen. No doubt his father had locked her out of sight.

Perhaps he could slip away to find her soon?

Eydis gripped her brother's arm – gently this time – and

smiled, reaching up to whisper in his ear. 'Don't worry. It doesn't matter. You'll be alright, Eadmund. I promise.' She kissed his hairy cheek and sat back down again, folding her tiny hands into her lap, smiling confidently to herself.

Eadmund could have cried then. He felt lower than he remembered feeling in years. He reached out his cup as the mead girl passed, smiling while she filled it. And when she was done, he put the cold liquid to his lips, feeling its soothing touch as it flowed down his throat.

He supped deeply and contentedly, eyes closed. Oblivious. Alone.

Eirik frowned, watching as Eadmund quickly drained his cup. He sucked in his lips so sharply that they disappeared beneath his beard. He wanted to reach over and slap Eadmund across the face with that cup.

How had it ended up there? Who had placed it in front of him?

No doubt the same fool who'd let him go wandering off alone all day: Torstan Berg!

Eirik puffed out an angry breath. He had to let it go. He had to focus on his guests, on Jael, who was sitting next to him, stone-like, tense and uncomfortable. She was everything now; the answer to all that he sought for Oss and Eadmund. 'I'm sure your hall in Andala is much more impressive than this,' Eirik smiled, waving his hand around the hall, trying to engage Jael. Hoping to relax her.

Jael sighed, barely turning her head in his direction. 'Well, I suppose our hall is larger, but size doesn't really matter, does it? It's more about how you use what you have.' She paused. 'You've made it look very... festive.' She stared at Eirik properly then. He seemed nervous, anxious, almost as uncomfortable as she was. He was trying to impress them all, she realised. And he was worried about how that impression was being received.

'You are kind to say so,' Eirik nodded, forgetting Eadmund momentarily. 'I can't lie, we've been working solidly since this was all decided. And I think, given the short time frame, we've not done too bad a job.'

'So far, at least.'

'Wait until you try the food,' Eirik laughed. 'You might change your mind. Or not. I'm told we have some fair cooks on our island.'

Despite an achingly empty stomach, the thought of food tugged down the corners of Jael's mouth. 'Well, after another few rounds of the mead bucket, nobody will be judging you too harshly, whatever the outcome.' She clamped her lips together, hoping Eirik would turn his attention towards Lothar on his other side.

He didn't.

'Yes, that's my hope. To have everyone as drunk as possible, so the only memories they retain, if any, are the good ones. Well, perhaps not everyone,' he said, almost sadly then. 'Some people could certainly do with more food than drink.'

Eirik was needed by one of his servants then, and Jael was relieved. Glancing to her left, she accidentally caught Lothar's eye. He inclined his head towards Eadmund, widening his eyes. Jael frowned, clenching her hands under the table, trying to ignore him. But Lothar kept staring at her as Gisila chatted away beside him, knowing that she couldn't deny him.

Jael bit down on her urge to simply refuse, and slowly turned towards Eadmund. He was talking to his little sister. She didn't want to interrupt, and if she did, what did she say?

Lothar glared at her, eyes flaring now.

For all the gods, what did she say?

'Do you expect a harsh winter?' Jael cringed, feeling ridiculous. Thankfully, Eadmund didn't respond, and Lothar had turned away to speak to her mother. She reached for her cup, deciding that mead might be the answer to everything.

'What did you say?' Eadmund mumbled. 'Did you ask about the... weather?'

'I did. Yes. My uncle insisted I speak to you. It was all I could think of.'

Eadmund laughed, quickly draining his second cup of sweet, honeyed mead. 'Well, yes, winter is always harsh here, much like summer, and spring. Autumn too. I hope you brought a warm cloak.'

Jael took a big gulp of mead, unable to think of anything else to say. The silence lengthened, and when she looked around, there was Lothar, peering at her again. In fact, as Jael scanned the hall, she saw more than a few faces turned in their direction, curious about this first interaction between the bride and groom-to-be. Jael started to wriggle. She hated being observed, and on a scale such as this, it was even harder to bear. She had no choice, though, but to keep the conversation going. 'And... how does your food supply last?' she asked dully, her lips barely moving.

'Food?' Eadmund closed his eyes, tipping the last of the mead into his mouth. It slopped over his lips, dribbling into his sparse coppery beard. He didn't appear to notice. 'We eat reasonably well over the winter months, if you like dried fish. It's the ale supply we worry most about, though. More Osslanders die from lack of ale than lack of food.'

Jael couldn't tell if he was serious. Was he foolish, drunk, or just attempting to sound amusing? She frowned. Her body rolled as though she were still at sea, and the smell of Eadmund was turning her stomach. His breath stunk less obviously now as it flowed into the general odour of the hall, but Jael wished she could go and sit near someone else.

Eadmund caught her intense green eyes inspecting his face, and he leaned in wanting to stop her. 'How old are you?'

'How *old* am I?' Jael was surprised by the question, and by the sudden sharpness of Eadmund's bloodshot eyes. 'Not as old as you, I'm sure. But older than your sister there.' She nodded at Eydis, who was talking to Amma Furyck.

'And there were no men in Brekka willing to take you on? Only an Osslander would do?' Eadmund's words rang like bells in his ears, his bravado slowly sinking into the swirling pit of nausea that was building in his stomach.

Jael narrowed her gaze. 'Take me on? Is that what you're planning to do? Take me on?'

Eadmund felt no match for Jael and her sharp eyes now. He was struggling to piece together his thoughts, afraid that they were all about to come tumbling out of his mouth backwards. The mead bucket passed by again and the girl, smiling at Eadmund, lifted up the ladle, just as he reached out his cup. He drank quickly. 'No, I'm not.' His eyes met Jael's, and they were defeated and sad.

Jael blinked, unsure how to respond, but Eirik banged his fist on the table, and everyone turned their attention to the king. She looked away from Eadmund as Eirik rose, cup in hand, watching as the hall stilled before him, the revellers reaching to grab their own cups in anticipation of the toast he was about to make.

Eirik cleared his throat, surveying the hall with a satisfied grin. 'This night, which is bitter with wind and cold, and all that winter on Oss promises. This night, we gather in our hall to welcome our guests from Brekka! To share our feast as we prepare to unite our two kingdoms and our families in a marriage and an alliance that will bring us success, wealth, and a future of prosperity unrivalled in any of our lifetimes! So tonight, my friends and neighbours, I thank you,' he nodded towards Lothar, 'for the honour you have shown my family and me. For the gift you have given us, of Jael, daughter of Ranuf. I hope to make her feel welcome here. As part of our family. As the future Queen of Oss!' He raised his silver cup and watched as Osslanders and Brekkans alike mirrored him. 'To the Furycks and Skallesons! To Brekka and Oss! And to the riches of Hest that will soon belong to us all!'

The roar around the room was enthusiastic and thunderous, cups banging on tables in a hearty show of approval.

Jael felt numb as she stared at all the cheering strangers before her. The threads of her life were being fingered apart by so many forces now.

She wondered if she would ever feel like herself again.

***

'I can't imagine how tomorrow will go,' Gisila hissed from her cot in the corner of the bedchamber the women had all been squeezed into. 'They will have to carry Eadmund out of the hall tonight. He's lucky he has such strong friends!'

Lothar's sixteen-year-old daughter, Amma, sniggered. She lay tucked up happily in the cot next to Gisila, with Jael and Edela sharing the only full-sized bed in the tiny chamber.

Jael could have done without Amma's company. She was not an overly annoying sort of girl – she was far too dull for that – but it would have been easier if her last night of freedom had felt truly free. The three women had to watch their words around the open-eared girl, so little was said of any real value by any of them.

The night in the hall had been long. The speeches had rambled on, and after an unpleasant day of sailing, they were weary and ready for sleep. Well, all but Amma, it seemed, who started whispering away to Gisila, big brown eyes not looking sleepy at all.

A faint glow seeped in from under the door, and the low drone of voices filtered in through none-too-thick walls. Jael wondered if Eadmund was still in the hall, or whether his friends had managed to drag him out. Last she saw, he was protesting sleepily, eyes closed, clinging to his cup as his friends tried to pull him to his feet. He was a mess, and he was about to become her problem. She sighed wearily at the thought and rolled over to face Edela. 'He is worse than I imagined,' she whispered, hoping that Amma was too busy gossiping with Gisila to hear.

'Yes, he is,' Edela agreed. 'Much worse. But now he has you, and you can help him.'

Jael snorted. 'And why would I want to do that?'

'Because he will be yours, come tomorrow. Your futures will be entwined. You will need him to be much stronger than this. You will need to save him from himself so that he can become king.'

There was so much Jael wanted to say, but Amma was there, so she bit her tongue and changed the subject. 'Why do you hate sailing so much?'

'Oh, it's not the sailing I hate, it's the water. I hate the water,' Edela shuddered. 'I know that water. The cold embrace of it as it squeezes all life from your bones. I felt it once before, as a child, and I cannot bear the thought of being in it again.' She shivered, the grip of old memories tight around her shoulders.

Jael was surprised. 'Is that how you see yourself dying? In the sea?'

'No, it is not a fear of the future that frightens me, but a terror from the past.'

'Why? What happened?'

Edela hesitated, inhaling deeply. She never spoke of it. She wasn't sure if she even wanted to, not after all these years. But then, sighing, she began. 'I was a child. Perhaps seven. My brother was sent off with my father's morning meal. He was working in the forest, chopping trees. They were preparing logs to build new houses, I remember. I made my brother take me with him, even though he didn't want to. He thought I was too annoying. He thought he was nearly a man at thirteen, and he didn't want to look after a child like me. We fought as we walked, as brothers and sisters do, and he ordered me home.' Edela stopped, feeling the ache of regret, even now. 'He made us go around the ice lake, you see, whereas I wanted to go across it. I was reckless, excitable, looking for adventure. He told me that our father had heard cracking. That it wasn't safe.' She sucked in a deep breath, the memories still vivid after all these years. 'So, when he sent me home, I ran across the ice, just to spite him. And, of course, it shattered, and I fell in. I could only scream once before the freezing water dragged me down. My heart slowed, and my limbs hung and my eyes closed and I sank. I have never experienced cold like that water.'

'And did you think you would die, or had you seen that you would survive?'

'No, I had not come into my dreams then. They started soon after. My mother thought that because I was so close to death, I must have met with the gods, maybe even seen Daala, and that she had given me my gift. I had shown no signs of it before, you see. Perhaps she was right, but I had no memory of it.'

'And how did you get out?' Jael wondered.

'My brother dived in and pulled me from the water. He called out for help and men came running, my father came, but it was too late. My brother had dragged me out and thrown me onto the ice, but the cold took his limbs, and he drowned before they could reach him.'

Jael was shocked. She hadn't known any of this.

'I never speak of it,' Edela sighed, reading her thoughts. 'Not even to your mother. We never spoke of it as a family. It was too painful. And no one wanted to blame me, even though it was my fault. It was all my fault,' Edela whispered haltingly. 'So yes, it is a watery grave that tortures me, but it is my brother's, not my own.'

Jael reached out, searching for Edela's hand. It was trembling and cold, and she enclosed it gently inside both of hers. 'I'm so sorry.'

Edela sniffed, resettling herself in the bed. The wool-stuffed mattress was almost comfortable enough to soothe her clicking bones. 'It was a long time ago now, but regrets leave scars that never truly heal, that I know. When I was young, I was willful. I didn't listen. I always thought I knew the right of it, and one day, for me, it was too late. And I couldn't go back and change anything.' Edela gripped Jael's hand now. 'You are at the start here. There is a chance to make good choices with Eadmund. I know it doesn't seem it, but he can be more than you imagine right now. Don't give up on him before you've even begun.'

A loud crash sounded from the hall; voices raised in argument.

Jael rolled onto her back, trying to make out if any of them belonged to Eadmund. Unlikely, she decided. He was probably lying somewhere, face down in a pile of vomit. She closed her eyes and tried not to think of him, nor of Aleksander.

Especially not Aleksander.

***

Eadmund was kissing Evaine's throat so slowly that she began to wonder if he was falling asleep. But no, he was awake, just desperate to take his time; to taste every place on her, one lingering, last time before he was married. To her. That angular, peery-eyed, stony-faced woman.

His nightmare come true. Tomorrow.

Evaine moaned, writhing beneath him but Eadmund's drink-saturated mind was now chewing over just what he had thought of Jael Furyck. And why he felt so annoyed by her. Or was it his performance in front of her that was the more annoying? He stopped kissing and sat back on a pillow, scratching his beard, his face troubled, his head pounding.

'What is it?' Evaine frowned, coming to sit beside him. 'Are you unwell?'

Eadmund blinked. 'No, no, it's just the wedding. I want it to leave my mind, so we can... so I can... but it's just... there, whenever I close my eyes. I can't escape it, no matter how much I drink, or how naked you get. It never leaves!' Eadmund smiled and the tension that had been furrowing Evaine's brow finally relaxed.

He was still here, with her. Hers.

'It's just a wedding,' Evaine soothed, wrapping one arm around his neck, trying to bring his face back down to hers. 'And when it's done, the only thing that will be different is that you'll have a wife you don't want. But nothing needs to change for you or us. Not really. Just as you said.' She kissed his jaw, her hands fingering the coarse bristles of his beard. 'You and I will still be together. You barely have to notice her. As long as your father thinks you're doing what you must to be a good husband, then your life can run as you wish. As it does now.' She kissed his lips, easing her body against his.

Eadmund wanted to be lulled into the world as Evaine saw it, but he knew that it was so different than the picture his father had in mind. But Evaine was so persuasive, and her tongue, as it expertly wrapped itself around his, teased away all contrary thoughts. He let himself believe, for a moment, that it could all be that simple. And then there was nothing to think about except the arousing sensation of Evaine's hands as they ran up and down his chest, exploring lower and lower.

Eadmund smiled, closing his eyes, but in the darkness he saw two green eyes staring sharply back at him. His stomach lurched, and he blinked, trying to catch his breath.

Evaine, sliding down his body, tempting him with her tongue, was far too busy to notice that she had completely lost his attention.

CHAPTER NINE

'I have to go.'

'I know you do, but this won't take long,' Edela promised, carefully unwrapping the large package she had brought in her sea chest.

Jael had grown increasingly irritable during the morning's drawn-out preparations. After being steamed, bathed, brushed, scented, and having her hair braided, she had been stuffed into the dreaded dress, which was now all but hidden beneath a new black cloak, a delicate silver wedding crown circling her head, her face a thunderous storm. She was not at all ready for this, but as much as she wanted to delay the ceremony, Jael was just as desperate for it to all be over.

Edela wrinkled her nose as she pulled away the old linen enclosing her surprise, which she knew had not seen the light of day in many years. Unwrapping a final layer of sheepskin, Edela lifted out a sword. It was exquisite; a piece of craftsmanship so fine that Jael gasped. It shone as if new, its long, sleek, double-edged blade swimming with liquid patterns.

Jael bent forward, trying to read the inscription. 'What does it say?'

Edela smiled. 'It is a name. Eroth. He was one of the finest swordmakers in Tuura.'

Jael was confused. 'Where did you get it? Why did you have it?'

Edela was still holding the sword. 'Don't ask me another question until you take it. Take it. It's yours!'

Jael didn't argue, quickly grabbing the weapon with both hands. Its grip was made of ridged white bone, cold to the touch. The crossguard and pommel were silver, inscribed with scenes of angry wolves devouring snakes; with symbols she didn't recognise – possibly Tuuran – and with symbols she did: Furia's axes. A large opaque moonstone glowed out of the rounded pommel.

It was perfect.

It was a sword of the night. A sword for a leader.

So why was it hers?

'Where did you get it?' Jael asked again, holding the sword out in front of her, feeling its well-balanced weight, admiring its perfect length; turning it, running her fingers over the inscriptions. It was thoroughly unique. She couldn't stop smiling.

'From my grandfather.'

'*Your* grandfather? Really?' Jael was even more confused. 'It looks unused. There's not a scratch on it.'

'It was not his sword,' Edela said, trying to remember the last time Jael had looked this happy. 'He made it for you.'

'What?' Jael's mouth hung open. '*Your* grandfather? Made it for *me*? But why? How? It looks brand new. How is that possible?'

'In truth, I don't know.' Edela sat down on the bed, folding her hands in her lap. 'He came to me on my wedding day with the sword, wrapped up, just as it was now. I never saw it until today. He told me that he'd made it for the granddaughter I would have. He made me promise to keep it safe and give it to you on your wedding day.'

Jael was stunned. The how and why of it all was too much to take in. The idea that Eroth had known he would have a great-great-granddaughter in need of a sword on her wedding day? It was wonderfully unsettling, and Jael embraced the wildness of it. 'It's just beautiful. And really mine alone?'

'Yours alone. He made it for you. I don't believe that anyone else saw it until today. He was very secretive about it.'

'Was he like you? Was he a dreamer?'

'No. No, he wasn't, but my grandmother was, so perhaps she told him about you? Maybe she saw you? Who you would become? I'm not sure.'

'Jael! Mother! Everyone is waiting!' Gisila rushed into the bedchamber, her face strained with tension. 'I'm not sure how long Eadmund will be able to stand, so you'd better hurry up.' She took one look at the sword and shook her head. 'You cannot wear that. Not at your wedding!'

Jael grinned at Edela, who smiled back.

Gisila closed her eyes, sighing dramatically. 'Well, whatever you do, just hurry up about it!'

***

Eirik had planned to hold the ceremony outside so that his guests might take in the breathtaking views of Oss' harbour, with its stone spires, and the wild Nebbar Straits foaming beyond. It evoked better luck for the gods to see the ceremony; to witness the joining of husband and wife from their lofty realm above. And Eirik knew that he would need all the luck he could gather if this marriage was to succeed. But it had snowed heavily throughout the night, and the morning that greeted them was murky and moist. Nothing could be seen but a few misty shapes, straining to escape the clouds, and snow was sweeping in again.

So it was into the hall for the festivities.

The decorations had been plumped up and repaired, more candles and lamps had been brought in, and the mead-soaked tables had been moved against the walls to make way for the wedding archway: a woven wattle structure threaded with cascading white flowers and green ribbons.

As he stood there, waiting for Jael to arrive, Eirik felt satisfied with the look of the hall. The look of his son was far more disconcerting. He glanced at Eadmund, who was swaying dangerously close to the archway. Even though he'd spent the morning being splashed and scrubbed with cold water to keep him alert, he looked worse than ever. Eirik raised a sharp eyebrow at Thorgils, who grabbed Eadmund's arm just in time to stop him toppling over.

Sighing with relief, Eirik turned away, glancing towards the green curtain as Gisila Furyck walked through it, holding it open. Despite his tension and the state of his son, he felt a charge; a growing excitement; a sense that change was coming towards them all like a white-capped wave building out at sea.

Jael strode into the hall on Edela's arm, trying to ignore how uncomfortable she felt in the evil dress, or how ridiculous she was certain she looked. She scowled as she walked, her long braids glowing like dark, fiery coals as she made her way towards them.

Eirik almost laughed out loud. She was wearing black!

That told him much more about Jael than he'd learned from their brief conversation the night before. And with a sword at her waist too! He stole a glance at Lothar's face, pinched with displeasure as it was. She was a proud woman, it seemed, and a warrior. And as much as he wanted her to mother his grandsons, he could see so much more in her now. He smiled as she approached, but Jael's eyes dismissed him as she stopped, with a sigh, next to his unsteady son.

Eirik wasn't deterred. He could feel it.

Jael Furyck had the strength to save his son.

Jael turned reluctantly towards Eadmund, but his morose face didn't register her presence at all. She looked away, scanning the hall, barely noticing anyone or anything, trying desperately to stop herself from screaming. She held her body stiffly, reaching down to touch the unfamiliar hilt of her new sword which fit perfectly inside her old scabbard.

That was a good feeling.

The ceremony was something she simply had to endure, and if she could shut out the words, the faces, and the implications of what was occurring, there was a chance of surviving. And getting home to Aleksander. Eadmund would not last long. She peered at his half-closed eyes, noticing the sweat beading across his forehead.

He would not last long.

Eadmund swallowed. He was almost entirely sober. His father had not let a drop of anything stronger than water pass his lips during the morning's preparations. He was thirsty and tired. His feet itched in wet boots, and as dry as his mouth felt, he wanted to spit. He couldn't bring himself to look in Jael's direction. He couldn't bear another glimpse of himself through those harsh eyes. Maybe he should have given in and let his father bring Ivaar back? Eadmund's body tensed immediately at the thought of that, though he was pleased to see that there was still some fight left in him; some small flicker of hope that he could return to claim the man he once was.

That man must still be inside him, somewhere.

***

Thankfully, it was a short ceremony, and when she thought about it later, Jael remembered little, just the stench of her husband and the sniffling of her mother, who was no doubt crying more for herself than her daughter.

Mumbled words of no meaning had been spoken over them by a tattooed man with an odd-looking bush of orange hair, his beard strewn with bones and silver nuggets. She had no idea who he was, but he sounded Tuuran, which would explain why she could barely understand anything he said. Contrary to his ragged appearance, his lips were clean, pink, and wet with saliva, and he spat as he spoke. As it was a choice between facing him or Eadmund, Jael chose to be spat upon.

Simple gold coiled rings were exchanged.

Neither fit.

Their hands were joined and wrapped together in cold, white ribbon to unite them as bride and groom, though they didn't even look at each other as they muttered their vows. Both Lothar and Eirik took the opportunity to speak once it was all done, congratulating themselves and each other on a job well done, and Jael watched it all as though she were watching someone else experience it. Her mind was far away, imagining her father's face and what he would do to his grinning brother if he were still alive.

She tried not to think about Aleksander at all.

Jael was so distracted, so lost in her thoughts, that she didn't hear the old man's rasping announcement that they were now husband and wife. The guests standing around them applauded loudly, and Jael blinked, suddenly wide awake.

It appeared that she now belonged to Eadmund Skalleson.

His wife.

Everyone suffocated them then, offering empty words and meaningless wishes. Jael listened, detached, as they surrounded her like a swarm of angry bees. She nodded a lot, smiling as little as possible, desperate to remove her dress, constantly squirming to loosen its hold on her.

'That's a fine sword you have there... Daughter,' Eirik grinned, coming to stand beside Jael. He saw the look of horror on her face, and he smiled. It was not going to be easy to win her over.

'Yes, it is.'

'A gift?'

'Yes, it was.'

Eirik inclined his head towards hers. 'Lothar did mention that he'd reclaimed your father's sword. I'm happy to see you found a replacement.'

Jael peered at her father-in-law, resting her hand on the hilt of her sword.

'I won't be taking it off you if that's your fear,' he said plainly. 'I'm glad to have a warrior of your reputation on Oss.'

Jael snorted loudly.

A few heads turned in their direction, so Eirik laughed to cover any hint of discomfort between them. 'It's true,' he insisted. 'I'm no fool, and nor are you, Jael. I didn't bring you here to win me wars or defend my island, but nor do I wish to make you into something you're not. Be a kind wife to my son, give me grandsons, and you may do whatever you wish otherwise. And I expect you beside me when we attack Hest in the spring. If... if you are not carrying a child, then you shall be there.' He saw the mistrust that lingered in her eyes. 'You have every reason but no need to doubt me, for we are now family, and I am no longer your enemy.'

Eirik smiled at her, then walked off to be congratulated by a small group of similarly aged men; his friends, Jael assumed. One, a tall, awkward-looking man, turned his silvery head, staring boldly at her. His face and that stare sent an unexpected shiver down her spine. He turned away to embrace Eirik, but the memory of his look lingered.

The servants rushed around, removing the archway and reinstating the tables, and as soon as they were in place, Eadmund escaped the well-wishers and headed for his seat. He felt weak, nauseous, and thirsty, all at the same time, watching desperately as the servants walked past, ignoring him. There was no cup waiting for him this time. He noticed the cups in front of every seat at the high table, on the tables in front of him, and around the sides of the hall, but nothing had been left for him. So, picking up Eirik's silver cup, Eadmund held it out to a mead girl as she bustled past. The girl glanced nervously at his hopeful face and his empty cup, her eyes darting around the hall in search of the king. Eadmund winked at her, and she sighed, hurrying to fill up his cup before rushing away, blushing as she went.

Drinking quickly, Eadmund felt his shoulders relax, before tensing again at the sight of his wife talking to Thorgils. His wife.

The words scratched at him like an angry cat. He drained the cup, putting it back in his father's place, wiping the mead out of his beard.

His new wife. Nothing like his first wife.

Melaena had been small, delicate, lovely; the complete opposite of the tall, lean, sharp-eyed killer he was bound to now.

Eadmund smiled wistfully, trying to reclaim the memory of Melaena's long-seen face. It was almost impossible now. She had faded in his mind, or maybe it was his mind that had faded from too much drink? His smile slipped then. Melaena was gone and in her place was this... thing. Not really a woman, even in that black dress of hers, and not really a man, but something awkward that fell in between. His wife. He rolled his eyes, puffed out a long breath and sat there, weighed down by the thought of what was to come tonight.

He would need more mead. Much more mead.

Jael envied Eadmund sitting at the high table all alone. No one seemed to have spotted his escape. She was stuck amongst the crowd, trapped in a tedious conversation with his large red-headed friend who was earnestly listing all the reasons why Eadmund would prove to be a good husband... in the end. Jael was desperate for a drink herself. A wedding night awaited, and she would not be able to face it sober.

'...although, it may not seem like it right now,' Thorgils sighed, coming to the end of his long-winded speech.

Jael looked at him blankly, realising that she hadn't listened to most of it. 'I'm sorry?'

Thorgils shook his head apologetically. 'You have enough to think about today. I shouldn't be boring you with my thoughts. I'm sure you'll see for yourself who Eadmund is, over time. I was just worried that your first impression would be your last. He is my oldest friend. He deserves to find some happiness.'

Jael wasn't sure what to say. It appeared that this man genuinely cared for Eadmund and she didn't want to be cruel, but at the same time, she wished he would go away. Whether

Eadmund was a lost soul who desperately needed her help, or two drinks away from his funeral pyre, it meant little to her. The only thing on Jael's mind was how quickly she could escape from Oss. 'If you were so concerned about his happiness, perhaps you should have asked his father to find him a different wife? If Eadmund's looking for happiness, he won't find it in me. Now, if you'll excuse me, I'm going to join my husband in his drinking, and hopefully, before long he'll do us all a favour and fall asleep!'

Thorgils stared after her, open-mouthed. True to her word, Jael strode up to the high table, and, adjusting her sword, she plonked herself down beside her slumped husband. Thorgils started to smile. She was like a spitting fire, and perhaps that was just what Eadmund needed to finally wake himself up.

'You'd better try looking awake, or your father will be up here soon, watching your every move,' Jael warned, poking Eadmund's arm, her eyes fixed straight ahead.

Eadmund blinked, trying to focus on Jael, who smelled of lavender, he thought sleepily, which was not unpleasant. He noticed how dark her eyebrows were as they narrowed in on him. How they drew attention to her eyes.

The mead girl passed again, and Eadmund watched as Jael nodded for her to fill two cups. And when she was done, Jael picked up one, raising it to her husband. 'Drink up!' she grinned. And with that she threw back her cup, reaching out, before he could blink, for another.

CHAPTER TEN

Osbert was drunk, or at least the hall was moving around him in an unnatural way. He peered into the tangle of topsy-turvy bodies, wondering who, in fact, wasn't drunk? Grease-soaked plates were being cleared away by man-handled serving girls. Cups held unsteadily in drunken hands were dribbling precious liquids onto the floor. Music flowed rhythmically, pulsing through his body as he swayed in time.

The wedding guests had been treated to surprisingly good food, and so much mead and wine that his head was spinning and his stomach felt ready to burst.

Osbert was reluctant to admit that the feast had surpassed his expectations, but the evidence appeared irrefutable based on the happy, overstuffed bodies falling around him.

Eirik and Lothar were inseparable as they sat at the high table, celebrating their dreamed of successes to come, though both were too stupid to realise that they were after the same prize, and Osbert doubted that either of them truly had a mind to share. Fools, he thought to himself. Old fools. Their time was nearly done, and, with their deaths, a new era would be ushered in. By him. And then everything would change.

He had plans for that.

***

'Eadmund! Eadmund!' Thorgils shoved his friend again, but his eyes didn't open.

'You'll have no luck with your little princess there. She is surely gone tonight,' came the growl of an unwelcome observer.

Tarak Soren.

Jael looked on curiously. She was almost drunk herself. It was the most relaxed she had felt in a long time, and although she was in total agreement with this mountainous beast, she didn't like the look of him.

Thorgils sighed. 'Tarak. Have you had the pleasure of meeting Eadmund's new wife?' Thorgils gestured to Jael, hoping to send Tarak on his way but he didn't budge.

Tarak Soren was so enormous that Jael had to crane her neck back to catch a glimpse of his face. It wasn't worth the effort. He was no stranger to battle, that much was obvious. Scars chased each other over thick lumpy skin that stretched across his square face. He glared at her with menacing eyes that showed no sign of humour. The bitter scowl curling from one side of his mouth prickled the hairs on Jael's arms.

Unwisely or not, she stood up.

Jael was more unsteady on her feet than she'd anticipated, but she felt consumed by the sudden urge to make herself known to this man.

Eadmund snored, blissfully unaware beside her.

'I am pleased to meet you,' Jael smiled.

Thorgils watched on anxiously.

Tarak hated Eadmund. Tarak hated women.

Tarak would despise Jael.

Tarak noticed Jael's sword as she resettled her scabbard in front of her dress. 'I don't think you'll have much use for that *toothpick* here, my lady,' he snorted. 'Not with little Eadmunds to care for. Best you leave the fighting to your sleeping princess there. He'll protect you when we all go off to war.'

Jael bit her teeth together, narrowing her eyes. She was looking for a fight and had been since Lothar had stolen her freedom, and now, here was the best invitation she could have imagined. She fingered the pommel of her sword, feeling the icy moonstone chill her itching fingers.

'Toothpick,' she mused. 'I've spent all night trying to think of a name for my sword as it happens. Toothpick... hmmm, it could work. But then again, perhaps something more descriptive would be better as this sword is so... fine... so... sharp. You wouldn't really want your teeth picked with it, would you? Not unless you'd like them removed from your mouth first?' It sounded like a threat, Jael meant it as a threat, and Tarak was not as stupid as he looked, for he took it as a threat and stepped forward.

Thorgils had enough wits about himself to lurch out of his seat, but he was slower than Gant, who stepped in from the shadows at that very moment and grabbed Jael's hand. 'A word with you please, my lady,' he said, loud enough for Tarak to hear.

Jael didn't move. Her eyes remained fixed on Tarak. She knew that Gant was there. She could feel Thorgils ready to pounce from her other side. But she remained trapped in the needy grip of her bloodlust.

It would feel so good to hurt this condescending bastard.

Gant squeezed her hand tightly now, demanding her attention, and his increasing pressure started to calm her own. Jael sighed, turning her eyes away, at last, glaring at Gant. 'Yes, of course,' she muttered, allowing herself to be led away.

Tarak, as he stood there smiling after her, looked like a man who had just found a new toy. Thorgils didn't notice; he was too busy feeling relieved that Jael had left. There was no doubt in his mind that she'd been about to take Tarak on, but Thorgils had been bested by him on more than one occasion, and he knew what the outcome would have been.

It was unfortunate that the giant turd was so useful to Oss, but that was the simple truth of it. Tarak fought bare-chested, like an angry hammer, crushing every enemy placed in front of him. He was Eirik's and Oss' champion, but as a man, he was overly confrontational, easily angered, and just plain strange. Most who called themselves his friend were simply too scared to do otherwise, and any man foolish enough to make an enemy of him didn't live long enough to regret it.

Gant hurried Jael over to a quiet corner of the hall, away from the fires and flickering lamps, wanting to ensure that their conversation remained as private as possible. 'That was a fight you were never going to win.' He turned to Jael, his eyes sharp.

'I've faced bigger men than that and won,' Jael countered boldly, unsteadily. Gant looked so unconvinced by that statement that Jael shrunk backwards, sobering herself up with every slow blink of his grey eyes.

'What did your father always tell you?' Gant whispered quickly. He didn't know how long they had. He hadn't seen Tiras for some time, which was a worry as that worm was likely to appear just where you wanted him least.

'Tell me?' Jael's head was foggy as she struggled to grasp his meaning.

'About drinking?'

Realisation came like a wave, crashing over her dulled senses.

'If you'd taken that man on, what use would you have been in a fight? Against him? When you needed every bit of this to overcome him?' He tapped the side of his head. 'And when you're full of drink, what use are you? You must think, Jael. To survive here, you must stay in control.'

They were near the musicians, still plucking away earnestly on their lyres, and she was struggling to hear him.

Gant leaned in closer. 'Jael, you're no fool. Your father didn't think so and nor do I. You *can* reclaim Brekka but only if you're smart enough to play the game and that means watching, with a clear head, all of those around you.' Gant glanced behind himself. 'There are men who want thrones, glory, and riches. Men who want you dead to achieve it. Some who just want revenge. But whoever it is, know that you must protect yourself. Your father is gone. Aleksander cannot help you, and nor can I. You must get out of here by yourself.'

Jael closed her eyes to gather her thoughts, but when she opened them, Gant had gone. She sighed, disappointed. Her head felt thick, her legs unsteady but she had received the message, at least, and as Jael made her way back through the swaying bodies, pressed together in this far-too-small hall, she started to wake up. Gant was right. She had come here on her grandmother's word, and that alone, but destiny, Jael decided, was still hers to choose. The Drunkard was not her future, whatever Edela thought she saw. There was no hope to be found in him, that much was obvious. She needed to get herself back to Brekka and Aleksander, and somehow defeat both Eirik and Lothar in the process.

Jael could almost feel the smile of her father's approval in that.

***

'We should leave. Now.' Thorgils had finally managed to wake Eadmund. He glanced at Jael, lowering his voice. 'If we can get through the ceremony of seeing you to your house while Eadmund looks awake, no one will wonder about what might not happen tonight. But if all we're depositing is an unconscious lump on your floor while everyone cheers and jeers, it will be more than bad luck, it will be a total embarrassment for Eirik.' He lowered his voice so much that Jael could barely hear him. 'A marriage not consummated on the wedding night has no chance for success. Surely you know that?' Beside him, Eadmund's head started to droop, and Thorgils jabbed him in the ribs.

Jael nodded. It was hard not to like this Thorgils. There was something decent about him, and despite her urgent desire to swim straight back to Andala, across the freezing Nebbar Straights, she found herself agreeing with his logic. He was right; get the damn thing over with and let them assume that everything happened as it was expected to.

So they did.

***

Just the four of them remained in what was a sizable, comfortable-looking house. Jael's eyes roamed keenly over its thick walls. This was no gap-riddled, wattle-and-daub house. It had been solidly built with wooden logs, the walls stuffed and plastered over and hung with thick woven tapestries. Even the wind, which had tormented them since their arrival on this freezing rock, was barely discernible from inside. The floor was made of wooden planks, covered in an abundance of skins and furs, so the main room felt dry and cosy. After two years of being squeezed into that leaking, breezy box with Aleksander and Biddy, Jael allowed herself a small smile of pleasure. It quickly turned bittersweet, though, knowing that she would have to share the house with Eadmund.

'I've put him on the floor.'

Jael turned around to see that Thorgils had appeared in the doorway leading to the bedchamber. 'Shouldn't you put him on the bed?'

'No,' he laughed. 'He's used to the ground, and I'm sure you don't want to wake up swimming in piss or worse!'

'Mmmm, you have a point there,' Jael conceded, following him to the door.

The raucous crowd who had followed them from the hall to witness the bride and groom's journey to their marital home had quickly dispersed, drunken voices fading into the night as they returned to their cups and benches. And opening the door, Jael felt an overwhelming sense of relief. An unconscious groom, a warm house, and just Biddy for company was more than she could have hoped for. 'Thank you,' she sighed. 'I'm not sure why you're such a good friend to that drunken lump, but I'm grateful for your help tonight.'

Thorgils grinned. 'You'll find out why that lump is worth the effort, eventually. I have no doubt!' And turning into the stormy darkness, he trudged off.

Jael closed the door quickly and firmly, turning the key that sat invitingly in the lock. She was alone, apart from Biddy, who was very experienced at pretending to be invisible, and Eadmund, who wasn't threatening an appearance any time soon. The rattling drone of his snores echoed from the bedchamber. There was a bedchamber. She was in a house with rooms! It was silly to think that such small things could give pleasure, but amongst all of this that was new and uncomfortable, they did.

Biddy was fussing over the large square fire pit that sat in the middle of the main room. A row of fur-covered beds lined both walls – more than enough space for Biddy and five others – and towards the back was a generous kitchen area, filled with well-stocked shelves. To her left was the bedchamber, and straight ahead a door, which Jael assumed led to the storage rooms. She wasn't bothered for now, though, there was already far too much straining her mead-addled mind.

It was almost warm in the house, so removing her cloak, Jael came to sit by the fire. Reaching her hands towards the flames, she thought about Tig and Leada. She hadn't liked the smell of the stables she'd left them in, but there had been little time to do much about it so far. She would have to check on them in the morning.

'Hot milk?' Biddy smiled, handing her a large bowl. 'There are no cups that I can see. I shall try to find some in the morning. I found some honey, though.'

'Hot milk?' Jael could barely contain herself at the thought of one of her favourite childhood treats. She greedily wrapped her numb fingers around the bowl, amazed by how well the day had turned out in the end.

Biddy poured herself a bowl of milk from the small cauldron she'd hung over the fire, and came to sit by Jael, sighing as she stared into the flames that crackled pleasantly in front of them. 'Not the wedding night I was expecting you to have,' Biddy murmured, inclining her head towards the thunderous snoring. 'I'd organised myself a few rags to stuff in my ears. Looks like I'll still be needing them, though!'

Jael laughed. 'Much better than I could've hoped for. If we can keep him that drunk, every night could be like this.'

Biddy smiled, but it faded quickly. 'It's a very nice house, but it's not Andala, is it?'

'No,' Jael admitted sadly. 'No. But I can't change that. Not quickly at least.' She lowered her voice. Even now, in this private setting, she feared the eager ears of Lothar's worm who was no doubt lurking outside, trying to find the best places to spy on her. Hopefully, it was snowing. 'All we can do is find a way to survive here until I can get us back home.'

'Even if Edela thinks that this is your destiny?'

Jael frowned. 'Edela sees many things, but I don't believe she sees everything. Not this time.' She felt tempted to share Aleksander's visit to the Widow, but she held herself back again. The Widow was not someone to discuss lightly, especially with Tiras on the island. 'Anything can happen, Biddy, if you want it enough. Anything is possible.'

They sat there in silence for a while, finishing their milk, until Jael was suddenly unable to stop yawning. So, leaving Biddy to bank the fire, she took her bowl to the kitchen and headed for the bedchamber.

One lamp burned low on a table by an enormous wooden-framed bed, each of its four posts curling like the dragon prow of a ship. Jael almost laughed. The angry creatures were hardly the last image you wanted to see before you closed your eyes. The bed was piled invitingly high with thick furs and pillows, though, so Jael took no further interest in anything but freeing herself from her oppressive dress. Throwing it as far away from herself as possible, she crawled eagerly under the furs, gasping in shock as her body shook and shivered onto the mattress. It was so soft! There was no rustle beneath her as she rolled over, seeking just the right spot; no bits of straw poking her skin. The mattress was wool-stuffed and covered in a crisp linen sheet, and as she sunk down, it almost hugged her body, quietly, supportively. Jael couldn't believe that something so perfect could exist. It felt as though she was lying on soft fluffy clouds. Rubbing her numb feet together, she thought about the warm body that would have made this bed perfect.

If only he were here.

She lay her head on the pillows, which felt just as agreeable. The dense warmth of the furs started to penetrate her cold limbs, and her tension eased. It had been the worst day she could remember in years, but, at last, it was finally at an end.

Outside the wind screamed around the walls and inside, on the floor beside the bed, Eadmund snored noisily. Jael closed her eyes, trying to ignore him. She tried to think instead of Aleksander and Andala, and all that she had left behind.

CHAPTER ELEVEN

The banging was incessant.

Jael held her hands over her ears, willing it to stop, desperate to return to her dream of Aleksander. It had been so real. She could almost taste the winter air in Andala, feel his skin touching hers.

But the banging continued.

Where was Biddy? Why wasn't she making it stop?

'Jael?' The door creaked, opening cautiously.

Jael sat upright, squinting, wondering where she was.

'I'm sorry to wake you,' Thorgils said sheepishly, tugging on his beard. 'But it's late, and they're expecting you and Eadmund in the hall.'

Jael tried to open her eyes wider, but that just made her head hurt. 'What for?' she croaked. 'Who's expecting me?' She glanced around, looking for something to drink, swallowing repeatedly, a burning sensation in her throat.

'Eirik, Lothar, everyone. There's a morning feast to celebrate the wedding. To celebrate the wedding night. They're wondering where you and Eadmund are.' He glanced at the floor.

Jael shook herself awake, blinking, trying to clear her thick head. The bed had kept her prisoner all night, and she didn't want to leave its warm embrace, but she could tell that Thorgils wasn't going anywhere without her. 'I've no idea where my clothes are,' she frowned, peering around the bedchamber. It was comfortable looking and spacious, but with only tiny windows running along the tops of the walls, there was little light, and Thorgils was blocking the rest of it with his imposing frame. Jael couldn't see anything to wear apart from that cursed dress, lying on the floor. 'Could you hand me that thing?' she sighed.

Thorgils looked awkward but did as she asked, ducking out of the room to give her some privacy. 'Have you any idea where Eadmund is?' he called from the main room.

For the first time, Jael became aware of the total absence of snoring. She looked over the side of the bed, but only a rumpled pile of furs lay on the floorboards. 'No, I don't. I didn't hear a thing all night.' She hopped out of bed, shuddering as the cold attacked her limbs, and hastily squeezed herself back into her wedding dress.

It was freezing.

'He left in the early hours,' Biddy grumbled, popping her round-cheeked face in through the doorway, a basket of berries in her arms. 'Loudly! I'm surprised you didn't hear him. Sounded like a wild boar was trying to escape. He didn't even close the door behind himself!' She looked tired and annoyed, her greying brown curls frizzing wildly around her face.

Jael was amazed that she'd slept through that. Amazed and cross with herself; she was usually a light sleeper.

Perhaps the perfect bed was a ploy by Eirik to soften her up?

She shivered into the main room, searching for her cloak and boots. Thankfully, Biddy had them warming by the fire, and Jael sat down on a stool to put them on.

Thorgils looked troubled. 'I'll see if I can find him.' He made to leave, then turned back. 'Will you wait here for me? It wouldn't look good for you to arrive separately.'

Jael nodded, rubbing her hands together over the flames. 'I'm in no hurry to see anyone in that hall again,' she said, sneezing. 'I'll wait.'

Thorgils nodded, ushering in an icy blast as he opened the door. He shut it quickly, though, thick-headed himself but eager to find his troublesome friend.

Biddy handed Jael a cup of water. 'You'll be needing this,' she said. 'Not sure who snored louder last night, you or Eadmund!'

'What?' Jael scoffed. 'I don't snore!'

Biddy looked unimpressed as Jael quickly drained the cup. 'You certainly do when you've got drink in you. It was like sleeping with a herd of goats. I'd rather have put up with some humping!'

'You do realise that you're my servant, Biddy,' Jael said, glaring at her. 'That means I can get rid of you at any time.'

'And what would you do then?' Biddy countered grumpily. 'Think for yourself? Find your own clothes?' She turned, pointing to where Jael's sea chest sat, just outside the bedchamber filled with most of her possessions, and all of her clothes. 'You may try, but you'd be lost without me, Jael *Skalleson*, as you well know!' And Biddy bustled off to the kitchen, muttering loudly to herself as she prepared her morning meal.

Jael's head throbbed, keeping time with her churning stomach, and she felt weighed down by a deep reluctance to begin the day. The night before had been an unexpected relief, in the end, but now the cold reality of her new life was waiting just outside the door, and she was not at all ready to open it.

***

'You sodding turd!' Thorgils growled as he came upon Eadmund sitting casually outside his old cottage, taking in the lightly falling snow, drink in hand.

'What?' Eadmund was bemused by the fierce expression on his usually cheerful friend's face.

'What?' Thorgils spat. '*What*? I've been roaming this fucking fort looking for you, and here you are, sitting around as though nothing was amiss. All I seem to do these days is run around after you! How or why I became your servant, I don't know!'

Eadmund's head was foggier than his face betrayed, and he had no idea why Thorgils was so livid. 'Why have you been looking for me? What's happened?'

Thorgils rolled his eyes, grabbed Eadmund's cup, sniffed it and threw it on the ground. Seizing his friend roughly by the arm, he lifted him up. 'You're supposed to be in the hall with your wife, eating with your families, not sitting out here alone, making people wonder what might *not* have happened last night.'

Eadmund could see what his friend was about now, but he was in no mood to be accommodating. 'What do you care whether I'm here or there, or what happened or didn't happen last night?'

Thorgils sighed, throwing up his hands in exasperation. Moving closer to Eadmund and wishing he could hit him, rather than reason with him, he dropped his voice. 'Do you think Eirik's patience is unending? That his threats about Ivaar are empty?' Eadmund just shrugged, looking as unbothered as anyone possibly could, at least to Thorgils, and that only served to annoy him further. 'You're on your last chance with him, Eadmund! He warned you, and now, if he finds out that nothing happened last night, he'll have Ivaar here before the Freeze. And that will be the end of Oss and the end of you.'

'He won't bring Ivaar back. Do you know how many times he's threatened that? He hasn't done it yet, and why would he?' Eadmund looked more confident than he felt. 'He doesn't want Ivaar here any more than I do. No one does!'

'Have you seen yourself lately?' Thorgils asked crossly. 'What choice does he have?'

Eadmund was in no mood for this. He was married. He had a wife.

Surely that was enough for now?

And with one last look in Thorgils' direction, he stalked off towards the hall, hoping to get it all over with quickly so he could go and find Evaine.

***

Edela sat next to Gisila at the high table, her meal steadily congealing before her eyes. She was sure that the poached fish would have been entirely edible, but Lothar had decided that they would be sailing back to Andala after breakfast, and that had put a firm hold on her appetite. Edela was not looking forward to another journey across those treacherous straights; this time with a sea that was, according to recent accounts, freezing fast.

And if that wasn't bad enough, she'd had another dream about the Darkness. Her lack of understanding about these dreams was deeply unsettling. She felt the warning in them, woke up cold-sweating from them, but was left clinging to invisible strands that connected to nothing, and, ultimately, led to nowhere. And it was all to do with Jael, somehow. She sensed that strongly. The dreams gnawed away at her constantly, and Edela cursed herself for getting so old. Perhaps it was her fading memory? Her inability to retain the dreams long enough to interpret them fully?

She sighed, feeling a sudden tightness in her back.

Glancing around, Edela was surprised to see the young girl, Eydis, standing shyly next to her, one hand reaching out to rest on her arm.

'You needn't worry about Jael,' Eydis murmured shyly. 'She will like it here. I've seen it in my dreams.'

Edela stared into those big milky eyes that could not focus on her own. 'You have?' she asked gently.

'Yes. I've dreamed about Jael many times. Of her and Eadmund together. I knew she was the one who would change Eadmund's life. I saw it. He needs her, I think, to save him.' She bowed her head sadly.

Edela took Eydis' warm hand in her own. 'I think you are right. I've seen that in my own dreams. We are similar, you and I, so I'm glad to think that Jael will have your wisdom here, just as she is losing mine. Not that she ever took much notice of me!' Edela laughed, remembering all the times Jael had told her off, scoffed at her dreams, ignored her advice, and then turned around, albeit reluctantly, and did everything Edela had suggested.

Even this. Especially this.

'And you will return, of course, when the baby comes?'

Edela's eyes lit up momentarily, before a vision of the Nebbar Straights appeared, lurching before her, eliminating any joy she may have felt. 'Perhaps. If I can be carried over by the birds!'

***

They walked in an awkward silence that only Thorgils appeared aware of. Neither Jael nor Eadmund seemed to notice his presence as they made their way to the hall. They had nothing to say to him, or to each other.

Nobody would look at anybody.

Thorgils had just finished telling himself that he was done running around after Eadmund – done being his unpaid servant too – when they stumbled upon Evaine. Or perhaps, he thought later, it was Evaine who stumbled upon them?

She was coming out of her house, her white fur cloak flapping around her, its over-sized hood almost swamping her pretty face. She had a basket over one arm and looked purposeful, although, given the rapidly disintegrating weather, that seemed ill-advised. 'Eadmund! Thorgils!' she smiled, eyes full of surprise.

Both men stopped suddenly as though struck.

Mouths open, heads empty.

'I thought everyone was in the hall,' Evaine murmured. Staring at Jael, she dropped her eyes, almost shyly, her cheeks flushing pink against her white hood.

Jael's forehead creased as she watched the girl, and the men's dumbfoundedness around her. Neither Eadmund nor Thorgils knew where to look. 'Are you on your way there?' Jael asked. 'You can walk with us.'

'Oh no, no, no, Evaine's not going to the hall, are you?' Thorgils hastily intervened, finding his voice as he hurried to extract them all from the quickening mire.

'I...' Evaine looked momentarily confused, biting her lip, wondering just which move she should make; enjoying the power she felt throbbing inside her chest at that moment.

Eadmund tried to catch Evaine's eye, wondering what she was doing; hoping to stop her from saying something they would both regret.

'No, Thorgils is right,' Evaine said, at last. 'I was just on my way to pick some herbs to settle my mother's stomach. She is unwell today, so I am tending to her, but I do hope you enjoy your celebrations... my lady. I wish you much luck in your marriage.' The last words tasted bitter on her tongue, but Evaine smiled sweetly enough, lowering her head to cover the depth of hatred lurking near her eyes.

Jael's instincts were sharply honed, like the well-worked blade of her new sword, so she sensed that there was something false about this girl; all except for her intentions, of course, which, from her not-so-subtle glances towards Eadmund, appeared very real indeed. 'Thank you. I hope your mother feels better soon.' And, eager to get to the hall, Jael strode off, leaving Eadmund and Thorgils squirming with discomfort, hurrying to catch up with her.

***

Eirik had quickly tired of Lothar's self-important, incessant babble and his inability to listen to anything but the sound of his own voice. He sat on the edge of Lothar's conversation with

Osbert and their man, whose name he couldn't remember, barely listening to their plans for attacking Hest. Eirik had been thrilled by the sharp decline in the weather overnight. The plunging temperature and foreboding skies had convinced the Brekkans to take their ships to sea immediately, or risk being stranded till spring. If only Lothar hadn't insisted upon leaving behind his little spy to keep them all watching their step. Still, winter would bring endless snow and rain and the slippery cliffs of Oss could be dangerous for strangers.

Lothar laughed loudly. It echoed around the hall like a slapping fish, and Eirik clamped his lips together, grimacing at the unpleasant sound. No wonder Jael had come so willingly into this marriage. Anything would have been preferable to staying in Andala and being forced to listen to that man's irritating laugh.

'Ahhh, there they are!' Eirik was on his feet, relieved to see Thorgils usher the married couple into the hall, both bride and groom frowning miserably beneath a thick dusting of snow.

Cheering and bellows of innuendo greeted Jael and Eadmund, who each managed to supply an unconvincing smile or two in acknowledgement. It was a start, Eirik thought to himself. Eadmund hadn't drunk himself to death and Jael hadn't killed him in the night, so he would take that for now.

Jael should have headed for her father-in-law or her uncle, but instead, she quickly sought out her brother. Thorgils had informed her that the Furycks were leaving imminently and she realised that she hadn't managed a moment alone with him. So leaving Eadmund to deal with the well-wishers, she escaped to the corner where Axl and Gisila were deep in conversation.

'You look well-rested,' Gisila murmured, eyeing her daughter suspiciously.

'It was a very comfortable bed.'

Gisila lifted an eyebrow. 'Was it now?'

'Yes,' Jael replied curtly. She had no intention of either lying or telling the truth, but she did like to keep her mother guessing. Gisila was so self-involved that it was easy fun. 'When are you leaving?'

'Now,' Axl grumbled. 'We should be leaving now! The clouds are down in the harbour, almost touching the water, and the snow is only getting heavier. You need to hurry Lothar along, Mother. We don't have time for eating.'

One look at Lothar told Gisila that he was in no mood to be hurried along. He was enjoying his own company far too much. But she dreaded to think what would happen if they were actually frozen in. She couldn't face spending the winter on this windblown rock. 'I think you're right. I'll see what I can do.'

Gisila left, and Jael grabbed Axl's elbow, guiding him further away from prying eyes. Tiras was in her sights across the hall, near Lothar. He glanced up at her, his hood hanging low, dark eyes boring into hers. 'I thought we'd have more of a chance to talk before you left, but this will have to be it,' she said, unable to stop shivering. 'I know you want to get that throne back from Lothar, but this is where you must practice the most important part of being a ruler. You have to look after your people. Keep them safe. You're responsible for our family now, Axl. Mother, Grandmother, Aleksander. You have to take care of them all and keep them alive.' Jael tried to keep her face free of the anxiety she could hear in her voice. 'You must listen to Aleksander. Gisila will try to tell you what to do. Edela will share her dreams, of course, but Aleksander is the one to go to for advice. He knows war, battles, kings. He knows how to be patient, to play the game. Osbert and Lothar will be watching you now, more than before. Looking for any reason to end you, to end all of us, and you can't give them one.'

Axl gnawed irritably on his lower lip. Jael had always shown little regard for his worth. He thought he knew the reason, and he didn't blame her, but he was no longer a boy. He was the rightful heir to the Brekkan throne, and he wouldn't be dismissed so easily. Not by his uncle or his sister. Talk of patience, of hiding in the shadows, did nothing to quell his desire for vengeance and victory against Lothar. He admired, even loved his sister, but she was no longer part of Brekka's future so he would not be dictated to by her or Aleksander.

'Jael!' Eirik had found her, and their brief conversation was over as Jael was led off to where Lothar was lecturing Eadmund.

Axl was relieved. He would show his sister that he was not the disappointment she believed him to be. She'd always thought that it was her job to protect him, but she was wrong.

He would return as the King of Brekka to save her.

Edela snuck up behind him, slipping her arm through his. 'Come along, my Axl.' She smiled up at her grandson's determined face, looking more serene than she felt. 'Let's help your mother drag that big oaf out of here before the sea is frozen solid!'

***

Blustery snow menaced the guests as they left the warm shelter of the hall and headed down the hill towards their ships. Axl was right: the snow clouds were indeed sinking into the sea.

It did not bode well for a safe journey.

Lothar was optimistic about their chances, though. 'I've sailed in worse!' he called out bullishly to Eirik. 'You shall see how mighty the Brekkan ships are! And come spring, so will Haaron and his inbred sons down in Hest!'

Jael couldn't wait to be rid of him, but at the same time, she was not prepared for her connection to Brekka to be severed so abruptly. She had imagined a more gentle easing apart than this.

Teeth gritted against the bone-chilling cold, Jael watched as the ships were readied. The snow was settling over her boots at a quickening pace. She wondered at the logic of sailing now, but wiser heads than hers seemed to think that there was still a chance to get through. The weather blew out of Oss, onto Andala so they would be able to get ahead of it if they left now, or so they all said. The one thing the Osslanders did know about was the Freeze, which every anxious face told her, was coming fast.

Gisila held on tightly as she hugged Jael goodbye. She looked genuinely upset, but Jael wondered whether it was the sadness of losing her daughter or the shame of her having married an Islander.

'I hope it's not too terrible,' she whispered in Jael's ear. 'If you just let him drink and have other women, you'll be able to do as you wish. And Biddy will take care of you, so you won't be completely alone.' She took one last look at her daughter, before turning away, going to join Amma who had already said her goodbyes.

Lothar was next, and Jael hoped that he'd hurry. She was so cold now that her legs were trembling.

Lothar did his very best to look regal as he placed his hands firmly on Jael's shoulders. 'I wish you both a profitable marriage,' he smiled, nodding towards Eadmund who looked just as impatient as his wife. 'Rich with grandchildren for your father! And, of course, I will see you both in the spring, unless you are too big and fat to join us in our war on Hest!' He leaned in and murmured near Jael's ear. 'Keep him happy, keep Eirik happy, and I will keep your family alive. But cross me....' And narrowing his eyes, Lothar pulled away to wink at her, shaking Eadmund quickly by the hand. He inclined his head for Osbert to join him, and they walked down to the ships with Eirik.

Leaving Edela and Axl.

Jael didn't want this part.

It had been hard enough to leave Aleksander, and the memory of that goodbye was still an open wound. She didn't want to expose her heart on the stormy beach; to weaken herself in front of all these strangers. 'Goodbye, Grandmother,' Jael said with a brief smile as she bent down to hug Edela tightly.

'Is that it?' Edela snorted. 'I'd hoped for a better goodbye than that after twenty-seven years of putting up with you!' Her face was a pale mask of fear, but she still managed to flash a mischievous grin. 'You'll miss me more than that measly show of affection, I'm sure.'

'I think I might. Just a bit.' Jael hugged her again, grasping her bony frame with numb hands. She held on more firmly this time, only letting go when she saw Osbert beckoning for them to hurry up. Everyone else had boarded now. 'Be safe. Take care of yourself!' There was so much more she wanted to say, but there was no privacy and no time.

Jael rushed to hug Axl goodbye. She hoped that he'd listen to her advice and try to keep everyone safe. He looked like such a boy, though, as he stood there awkwardly in front of her in a cloak that he'd outgrown, his floppy, snow-covered hair blowing into his eyes. She brushed it away. 'Be safe.' It was delivered firmly, eye to eye; more of a warning and a threat, than a gentle wish.

Axl met her eyes boldly. 'You too.' He glanced at his sister's swaying husband, not sure whether to feel sorrier for her or him. 'Good luck,' he wished them both before slipping Edela's arm through his, helping her across the slick stones to the ships.

As they reached *Storm Chaser*, which was already rocking in the undulating water, Edela turned around to wave a final goodbye and was surprised to see a girl appear on the hill behind Jael and Eadmund. She was wrapped in a white cloak, which flapped angrily about her like the wings of a gull. Her face broke into a knowing smile as she locked eyes with Edela.

A smile that froze Edela's heart to its core.

Edela shivered, swallowing hard, closing her eyes to remove the disturbing vision. But when she opened them, the girl was still there, still smiling, still staring, and this time her face was scorched, like the toasted remains of a pyre. Eyes that had moments earlier appeared so innocent, suddenly glared menacingly out of that dark face. Edela made to change direction and rush back towards Jael, wanting to warn her, but it was too late. Osbert reached down, and, with Axl's help, they pulled her onto the ship, fighting against her protesting arms and feet, ignoring her calls to stop.

She needed to go back to Jael. She needed to speak to Jael!

But Osbert ignored her, insisting that there simply was no time.

From the bottom of the hill, Jael watched the struggle to get her grandmother into the ship. She looked ill and frightened, desperately turning back to shore in the hope that she could remain. Jael closed her eyes, calling on Eseld, Goddess of Travellers, to keep them all safe. She knew how much Edela feared the sea now, and she hoped the journey wouldn't be too traumatic for her.

The oars dropped into the snow-laced water, and the helmsmen were immediately alert. Navigating their way out of the harbour and into the straights in this weather would require every ounce of skill they possessed.

'Rather them than me,' Eirik murmured to Morac, who stood next to him, shivering. 'Those straights can be an evil bitch on the fairest of days, let alone an all-out shitter like this.'

'Mmmm, I'm sure there'll be more than a few regretting their breakfasts soon.'

Eirik laughed, turning around to locate Eadmund; hoping he hadn't disappeared again. But no, there he was, swaying next to his miserable-looking bride. 'What is *she* doing here?' he hissed crossly, spying Evaine standing on the hill. 'I told you to keep her away!'

Morac turned around, furious to see his daughter staring down at the ships, a dreamy smile on her face. 'I'm not sure. I did tell her, Eirik, but she's young. She probably got bored being stuck inside with Runa these past few days.' He tried to laugh it off as nothing but an innocent, childish mistake, but deep down Morac was fuming. They needed to keep Eirik happy, and Evaine did not seem to understand the importance of her role in that.

The older she got, the harder she was to control.

'Make sure you tell her again,' Eirik warned. 'Our alliance depends upon this marriage, so ensure that your daughter has no part in it or she'll be gone. Understood?'

Morac didn't enjoy Eirik asserting his authority so overtly, but there it was, his friend was the King of Oss, and he was not. 'Understood. I'll make sure it doesn't happen again.' He turned away, heading for his escapee daughter, feeling Eirik's eyes on his back as he hurried up the hill.

Jael didn't want to watch anymore.

It was done.

Her family had left, and their fate lay in the hands of the gods now. She closed her eyes, trying to find some resolve to start her new life, but all she managed to see was Edela's petrified face calling out to her. Not wanting the reminder, Jael opened her eyes and turned to see Eadmund stumbling up the hill, following the masses hurrying back to the dry warmth of the hall. Just ahead of them, she spied that girl again, the one who was supposedly tending to her sick mother. Jael noticed the way her eyes followed Eadmund and her sharp annoyance as the pointy-faced man grabbed her and pulled her away.

She didn't think on it for too long, though, realising that if she didn't get back to the hall and a fire soon, she was surely going to break a tooth.

CHAPTER TWELVE

The stables were damp and stunk of rotting things.

Jael wrinkled her nose. There was a difference between the smell of animals and the stench of neglect. Leaving Tig and Leada in a ramshackle shed as the snow turned into a blizzard didn't sit well with her, nor them it seemed, as both horses barely acknowledged her, heads drooping low.

Tig was it for her now, and Biddy; her only links to Brekka and her family, if you didn't count Tiras, and she chose not to. So she couldn't have anything happen to him, whether it was hoof rot or freezing to death in the coming cold. Jael scratched his muzzle, tugging on his forelock, trying to cheer him up, but he shook his head away from her hand, walking to the back of his stall.

'I wondered where you'd disappeared to.'

Eirik.

Jael's shoulders dropped. She had hoped to escape anyone's attention, for a while at least. Turning around, she offered a small nod. 'My lord.'

'You don't have to be formal with me,' Eirik smiled, glancing around, checking for that strange man Lothar had left behind, who seemed to drift around like a shadow. 'Now that your uncle has left, we can be ourselves. Eirik is fine. I don't imagine you'll want to call me Father?'

Jael considered him with a frown. Her father had lost a lot of men beating back Eirik's ambitious invasions of Brekka over the years.

She didn't trust him one bit.

Eirik laughed at her expression. 'Or, we could just get to know one another first?' Jael ignored him, so he glanced at her horse. 'Is something wrong with him?' He nodded to where Tig stood, hiding in the shadows.

'He's not happy. Neither of them are. These stables...' Jael looked around at the dank rotting floor, at the hole-riddled walls, the roof that was leaking snow. 'They're a mess. He needs to be dry, warm, they all do. The straw stinks. It hasn't been changed for some time. And everything's damp.'

'He *is* a horse...'

Jael's frown intensified. She felt no warmth towards people who didn't care for their animals. 'Yes, he is a horse. *My* horse. And I'm responsible for his wellbeing. Just as I'm responsible for the horse I brought for your son.' She glanced over at the neighbouring stall where Leada stood. Neglected. She looked just as miserable as Tig. 'Valuable Brekkan war horses. Trained to fight. My horse is trained to fight with me. He needs to be dry and healthy. I need that for him. For both of them.'

'Fine. I'll have new stables built, next to your house. There's plenty of room there. Dry and weather-tight, with sweet-smelling bedding,' he said cheerfully. 'Although perhaps I can't guarantee the smell, but I can ensure a roof, walls, a door, and a stable hand to keep the straw fresh.'

Jael was surprised by his eagerness to please, especially with Lothar gone.

He was her enemy, yet now he was her father-in-law.

It was unsettling.

Tig returned to Jael, and she ran her hand down his cold cheek. 'Thank you. That would be good for *my* horses, but the rest here will suffer if these stables aren't repaired. The roof has more holes than thatch! Someone needs to fix it. Someone needs to ensure they're all looked after, not left to rot in this pile of shit over winter. If you're not going to care for them properly, you may as well eat them!'

'Well, we are more about fish here than horses,' Eirik admitted. 'But I agree, it stinks in here, and no one does well in rot.' He peered around the dingy, rundown building, memories of his childhood flickering faintly at the back of his mind. 'I'll see to it, along with new stables for your horses, but for now, you must come along with me, for Eydis has demanded your presence.'

***

Jael didn't know what to say. The right words would have been, thank you, of course, but they stuck stubbornly in her throat, refusing to come out.

'You like horses, but you don't like dogs?' Eirik wondered wryly as he watched his daughter's disappointment grow.

They were in the hall.

Eydis sat perched on a small wooden chair next to Eirik, who sprawled comfortably on his large throne, both of them sitting on a raised, fur-covered dais. The hall was crowded but quiet, filled with the low murmur of easy conversation as everyone lazed about in a slumberous state after two days of overindulgence. The fires burned high, keeping the chill at bay as snow kept piling up outside.

Jael's eyes followed Eirik's down to Eydis. It was hard not to notice how deflated the young girl appeared: her eyes were large and moist, her bottom lip trembling. Having been so excited to give Jael her wedding present – two tiny, Osterland Hound puppies that were currently biting each other's fluffy tails – she'd been met with this unexpected wall of silence.

'I...' It was Jael's turn to be haunted by memories. 'I'm sorry, I don't mean to be rude. They are a... nice gift.' But her words did little to change Eydis' expression.

Jael tried again, coming to sit on the dais beside the small chair. 'I do like dogs. And these puppies look... it's more that I, I had a dog once... when I was younger, maybe even your age. A very special dog, and she was killed.'

Eydis reached out then, searching for Jael's hand. 'I'm so sorry.'

Jael let Eydis grasp her hand, feeling uncomfortable to be revealing her private memories in this public place. She lowered her voice. 'Well, it was very sad for me. She was my best friend,' Jael said softly. 'We were inseparable. And the boy who killed her did it because he knew how much I loved her. I kept beating him in training, embarrassing him in front of his father and his friends. So he took his revenge on me by killing my dog. Making me watch.'

'That was cruel of him.'

'It was. He was a cruel boy. But he achieved what he wanted. He hurt me as I had hurt him, so he won. For a while.'

'What happened to him?'

'I killed him,' Jael said coldly, trying not to think about Ronal Killi. Or his father, Gudrum. Especially not Gudrum.

She didn't want to say anymore.

Eydis wasn't shocked by Jael's revelation at all. 'You don't have to take the puppies, I understand. One was supposed to be for you, and one was for Eadmund, but I doubt he'd be much good at caring for them anyway.'

'No, I don't suppose he would,' Jael murmured, desperately trying to keep hold of that old pain as she watched the puppies rolling about, nibbling on one another, tangled up like a black and grey ball of wool. But the thought of their company in this lonely, new existence proved impossible to ignore. 'I'll take them.' She said it quickly, before she could change her mind. 'But you'll have to help me name them.'

***

'Ido and Vella.'

'Which one's which?' Biddy asked, unimpressed, watching the puppies sniff their way around their new home, chewing inquiringly on everything they came across.

'Ido's the black one, the boy. Vella's a girl,' Jael said grumpily. She felt annoyed that she'd ended up a dog owner again, convinced that it would end in more heartache.

She had a way of making enemies.

Biddy took her broom and shooed the puppies away from her kitchen. 'I thought you were done with dogs? After what happened to poor Asta?'

'Oh, I was,' Jael groaned, sitting down to warm her cold hands by the fire. The puppies raced over, begging to be picked up. She pushed them down. 'But how do you refuse a wedding gift from the king's daughter? And a blind one at that?'

Biddy smiled, grabbing a wooden spoon to stir the cauldron of fish stew hanging over the meal-fire. 'So marriage has turned the great Jael Furyck soft already, has it? Cooing over puppies and little girls?' She lumped a generous helping of stew into a bowl and handed it to Jael.

'Marriage?' Jael's laugh was hollow. She blew on the stew to cool it down. 'If this is marriage, I'll take it. Being in this big house, with that bed?' She glanced longingly towards the bedchamber. 'And no husband in sight? Perfect. If only Aleksander were here.' He hadn't been far from her thoughts all day, as much as she was trying not to think about him.

Biddy sat down with her own bowl, pushing away Vella's eager wet nose; she seemed to be the braver of the two little balls of fluff. But then, realising that the puppies must be hungry, Biddy put down her bowl and went hunting for some scraps to feed them. 'It's strange that he hasn't returned, don't you think? Eadmund?' Biddy called from the kitchen. 'Not that I wish to listen to that snoring again! I don't think I've heard anything like it.'

'Hopefully, he'll stay away, drinking himself onto a pyre,' Jael mumbled, blowing on a spoonful of stew. 'Imagine being able to go back to Brekka soon?' She frowned. 'I wonder if they've made it back yet? Thorgils said it's not completely frozen over, and it's surely colder here than in Andala, so they must have made it through.'

'I hope so. I wouldn't want to be out on that sea in the dark. Poor Edela.'

'Mmmm, I can't imagine she'd ever want to sail again. She looked petrified getting into the ship. I've never seen her so scared.'

The puppies attacked the plate Biddy put down for them, scattering food all over the floor, eating as though they hadn't had a meal in days.

'Fleas,' Biddy huffed, sitting down. 'We're going to be sharing this place with fleas.'

'I imagine so. And plenty of vomit and piss too,' Jael smiled. 'And that will just be Eadmund!'

Biddy looked unimpressed. 'I imagine he'll turn up soon.'

Jael choked on a mouthful of fish. 'Don't say that! I was looking forward to going to bed alone.'

'You can't avoid him much longer,' Biddy frowned. 'You can't avoid what marriage means.'

'And how do *you* know what marriage means?'

'Well, I know what the *king* is hoping it will mean. Perhaps he needs to go and have a word with his son? Remind him of how things are supposed to go.' She pushed Ido away this time. He kept putting his little black paws on her leg, sniffing her stew, his dinner plate already licked clean.

'Why are you so keen to have that drunken mess here?' Jael wondered, placing her bowl on the floor for the hungry puppies to finish off.

'I'm not, but I can imagine what the king would do if he knew

Eadmund had slept on the floor last night.'

Jael rounded on Biddy, her lips set in a thin line. 'Well then, nobody had better tell him, had they? Especially not you. Leave Eirik thinking that everything is as it should be. Leave Eadmund out there doing whatever he likes. And we can stay here, undisturbed by any of them, for as long as possible!'

***

Edela had never felt worse.

She had crouched, numb from cold and fear, in the stern, imagining Saga, Goddess of Souls, coming to claim her; tortured by the thought of dying before she could help Jael.

The wind had harried them mercilessly on their journey, tossing the ship about with an anger that kept everyone half-frozen and on edge. Despite Edela's surety in her own path, which she believed was not destined to end at the bottom of the Nebbar Straights, she had remained in a state of terror, her childhood nightmares holding her firmly in their grip. But more than that, more than the threat they faced as the dark water thickened and froze around them, was the memory of the girl on the hill.

The girl.

Was it a girl?

Edela spoke to no one. Keeping all thoughts to herself, she sheltered next to Axl, who did all he could to shield her from the treacherous conditions. Edela barely noticed. Those black eyes were seared into her memory, consuming her every thought. She couldn't shake the chill they rose on her skin.

Jael was in danger. Of that she had no doubt.

When they finally, thankfully, arrived in Andala's harbour that evening, Edela had only one thing to say as her grandson helped her out of the ship. 'I must find Aleksander!'

***

Aleksander hadn't known what to do with himself after Jael left.

He felt lost, emptied of everything that resembled love and hope. The pain of losing his horse was achingly raw and having Jael wrenched away from him at the same time was more grief than he could handle. He hadn't been able to find a way to cope. Drink was the obvious answer; dulling the agony, easing the transition. He tried that, at first, but it just made everything more emotional, so he gave up and just sat in their cold, lonely cottage, trying not to think about any of it.

There wasn't even Biddy anymore, who had cooked and cleaned and cared for him since he was a boy, just as much as she had cared for Jael. She had fussed too much, coddled and nagged him as though he was her own, but in her way, she was part of his patched-together family too.

As he sat in the dark cottage, Aleksander tried to recall everything the Widow had revealed to him in his dreams. Or had she? Had she really had anything to do with them? She had given him the tincture to drink but had it created his visions, or, as she told him, had he seen only what the gods wanted him to see?

Jael was coming back.

Aleksander pushed away all other thoughts and held on to that one hope.

But after she had loved another man and had his child.

Loved another man.

That bit stuck. Hard.

Wrapping his arms around himself, Aleksander was suddenly aware of the frigid air smoking around the cottage. He knew that he needed to get up and grab a fur, but he couldn't move.

She would come back, so he would wait for her.

But how long would it take? How long would he be without her?

Aleksander closed his eyes, shivering now, trying to go back to the dream he'd had at God's Point; trying to remember how old Jael's daughter had looked when he'd seen her returning.

How many years would he have to endure alone?

The knock on the door was so faint that in his sleep and food-deprived state, he failed to notice it. But as the door creaked open, Aleksander jumped off the bed with a start, hand on his sword. Even half-conscious, his reflexes were sharp. When he saw who it was, though, his shoulders slumped in relief. 'Edela? What are you doing here? I didn't think you were due back for days?' Coming towards the old woman, he embraced her stooped frame.

Edela sunk into his arms. 'We must help Jael!'

Aleksander was instantly alert, his skin chilling further. 'What do you mean? What's happened? Why *are* you back so early?'

Edela shuddered, glancing around the dark cottage. 'We need a fire, Aleksander. There is much to discuss, and I'm not sure I've ever been this cold in my l-l-life!' Her teeth chattered as she stood shivering before him.

Aleksander hurried to find his tinderbox and some kindling, and he set about making a fire quickly. The flames burst into life, but they did little to warm Edela. Wrapped in layers of fur, sitting as close to the fire as she dared, she couldn't stop shivering, but she couldn't wait any longer. So, taking a deep breath, she told him about the girl on the hill and the nightmares she had been having, and her confusion about it all.

Aleksander's forehead worked itself into a deep frown. 'Do you think you were seeing this girl as she really is? Or were you having a vision about her? A dream?' he wondered. 'Was she a creature or a person?'

'Creature? No, I don't believe so,' Edela murmured, shaking her head. 'Although, I've never seen anything like it, so I don't know. She was a girl, looked like a girl but... I had a bad feeling that there was something on Oss, on the islands that was a threat to Jael. I couldn't see what it was. I feel as though I'm dreaming blind these days!' Edela despaired. 'I can usually make sense of what I see, but I was too late, and now Jael is trapped there, with that girl. Till spring.'

'It's not too late. I can take a ship!'

'You can't! The sea was freezing around us. By morning it will be frozen solid. There's no way through.'

Aleksander stood up. 'But if I leave tonight...'

Edela placed a shaking hand on his. 'You cannot. No one will take you, not in this weather. And if you go, you won't come back. The sea will claim you.'

Aleksander felt confused, angry, and helpless all at once.

Sighing, he sat down. 'Did you tell anyone what you'd seen?'

'No.'

'Good. You shouldn't. We should figure this out together.'

They sat in silence. The sounds outside the cottage were dying down as the night drew a veil over Andala. The fuss over the returning travellers was over, and most Andalans were securing their homes and livestock, preparing for another onslaught of snow.

'Can you contact her another way?' Aleksander wondered suddenly. 'Through her dreams? Is that possible?'

Edela stared at him, the creases on her weary face accentuated by the soft flames of the fire. She looked deeply unsettled. 'There is a way,' she said, at last. 'I've never attempted it myself, but I know of people who have. It was not accepted in Tuura. The idea of entering another person's dreams was forbidden.' She looked around. 'But Jael needs us, and we're not in Tuura, are we?'

CHAPTER THIRTEEN

Eadmund tugged on his worn leather boots, desperate to escape. Evaine had warned him that the drifts looked more than knee-deep, hoping to convince him to stay but he'd made up his mind.

'Do you *have* to leave already?' Evaine purred, her breath making smoky swirls in front of her face. She sat on Eadmund's bed, wrapped in two furs, leaving only her head exposed to the cold interior of his old cottage.

'I think it's best that I do,' he smiled, ignoring the pounding at his temples. 'No doubt Eirik will be prowling around looking for me. Wondering why I'm not getting to know my new bride.'

'Oh, don't say that!' Evaine wrinkled her pink-tipped nose. 'The thought of her being your wife makes me ill. She looks more like Thorgils than a woman! Did you see that scar on her face? Imagine what the rest of her looks like?' She paused. 'No, don't, I don't want to think about that!'

'Well, hopefully, I'll only have to look at her in the dark,' Eadmund laughed, struggling to his feet. He frowned, then, overcome with the need to sit back down.

That incensed Evaine further. She knew it was inevitable that they would be together soon, but she couldn't bear the thought of it. In a desperate attempt to change his mind, Evaine dropped the furs, revealing chilled pink nipples and a body trying its very best to undo his resolve. 'Are you *sure* you have to go?' she purred, easing her knees apart.

Eadmund didn't know what to say.

It was easy for her body to tempt his, but although Evaine had been warm company, he felt himself slowly suffocating from her attentiveness. He was desperate for some air. He needed time to think, to find a way to shake off the hopelessness that was weighing him down. 'You make it very hard for me,' he grinned, leaning forward to wrap her up again. 'Now don't get cold or you'll fall ill, and then we can't have any more fun, can we?' He was placating her with a patient, forced smile. Talking to her like a child. Hoping it would work.

'Fine,' Evaine grumbled. 'But will I see you tonight?'

'I think so. Now go and get dressed!'

Eadmund hurried to open the door before she could change his mind. A small avalanche of snow slid into the room. Frowning in annoyance, he rushed to kick it back outside again. It wasn't an effective approach, and he should have stayed and cleared an actual pathway to his door, but Eadmund was in a hurry to escape. 'And don't let anyone see you leave!' he called, turning back to Evaine who was pouting moodily.

She poked out her tongue, then pouted some more.

Eadmund shut the door with a sigh, relieved to finally be alone. He took a deep breath, surveying the blanket of bright white snow that had settled overnight, sighing as it seeped into his boots; suddenly remembering that he'd been meaning to replace them for weeks. Striding off in search of peace and solitude, he managed to walk straight into his father.

'You do like to disappear, don't you, my son?' Eirik smiled cheerfully. 'Your wife didn't know where you'd gone this morning.'

Eadmund stumbled at that, wondering exactly what Jael had revealed. He masked his guilt with a yawn, walking off, hoping to lead his father away from his cottage and far away from Evaine.

Thankfully, Eirik followed him.

'Why were you looking for me?' Eadmund wondered.

'Oh, just to see if you were still alive, I suppose.' Eirik's eyes twinkled in the morning sun; he was in a particularly good mood today. 'Do you remember the year we found you buried in the snow after a heavy night in the hall? It took a while for anybody to notice you'd not been seen for almost a day!'

'I don't remember that,' Eadmund mumbled, barely listening as he ploughed on quickly, deciding to take his father to the hall. Hopefully, he could leave him there and be on his way again.

'I'm not surprised! You were barely breathing after a day under the snow. I'm amazed you lived through that one,' Eirik laughed, nodding at a red-cheeked woman who was shovelling a path to her cottage door. 'But now that you've got a wife, I don't need to spend all my time running around after you, making sure you haven't fallen off a cliff somewhere. I'm sure Thorgils will be pleased. Torstan too.'

'I'm not that bad!'

'Not all the time,' Eirik smiled. 'And not today it seems. Why are you in such a hurry?'

'Because it's fucking cold out here, old man!' Eadmund grouched, grabbing his father by the elbow and moving him along. 'And I want to get to your fire before my bones start knocking together!'

They made it to the hall quickly enough, their trousers wet through; the snow being higher than knee-deep in some places. The hall was relatively empty, apart from some of Eirik's most valued warriors and advisors, who were huddled around the fires, defrosting their cold bodies.

'It's certainly frozen in the straights now,' Morac noted as he walked up to Eirik. 'Beorn returned a while ago. All of the ships in Tatti's Bay are locked in the sheds.'

'Good,' Eirik nodded, not bothering to join his men at the fire. He strode up to his chair and sat down awkwardly, instructing his servant to bring him a cup of something warm. He didn't mind the cold but his scarred back suffered in the winter. When the temperature dropped, the wounds his father had inflicted upon him as a child would ache, deep within his flesh. His face, though, as he sat listening to his men, betrayed nothing. 'We'll need to be ready to go at the first drip of thaw,' Eirik urged. 'You must ensure the fleet is ready, but not just ready, we must be building throughout the winter. I want that schedule from Beorn. I need to see how he plans to get the new ships built in time. What teams he has organised.'

'He's working on it,' Morac promised, coming to stand closer to Eirik. 'I don't believe it will be a problem. His men have always worked fast, whatever the weather.' He paused. 'It's not the ships that concern me, though, it's the men. We'll need to find ways to keep them ready for battle, otherwise, they'll just spend the winter drinking and humping and be little use come spring.' Morac's eyes drifted towards Eadmund.

Eirik frowned, noticing. 'Well, I've come up with an idea for that.'

The handful of men gathered around the nearest fire turned to look at their king, eager to hear his plan. All apart from Eadmund, that is, who was trying to ease his way out of the hall unseen.

'Eadmund!' His father spied him edging towards the doors. 'You must bring your wife to eat with us tonight. I have an announcement to make that's sure to interest her. Promise me, now!'

'I will, Father!' Eadmund called out as he pushed on the heavy door, shrinking from the glare of the morning sun as it reflected off the snow. 'We'll be there.' And with that, he turned to make his escape.

'Eadmund!'

Shit.

He adored his little sister, but she had bad timing. Clenching his teeth and sighing deeply, he let go of the door and turned around. 'Hello, Little Thing.' Eydis was feeling her way along the wall towards him, and he kicked himself for being such a selfish brother.

'Eadmund,' she smiled. 'I could smell you from my chamber!'

'Thank you, as always,' he bowed, before realising that the

gesture was lost on her.

'I wanted to know about the puppies,' she smiled keenly up at him. 'How are they?'

Eadmund looked blankly at his sister, happy that she couldn't see his confusion. He frowned, digging about in his useless, hole-riddled memory for a clue as to what she was talking about. She was so excited. It must be something important.

Eydis looked suspicious. 'Or have you not even noticed them?'

'The puppies? Yes, the puppies. Of course, I've noticed them! How could I not?' Eadmund swallowed a few times. 'They are well, and... and... full of energy, you know... as puppies are.'

His sister fixed him with an unsettling stare. Her milky eyes lingered somewhere near where she imagined his to be; close, but not close enough to make him feel comfortable. 'Are they?'

'Yes, they are.'

'And what are their names? Do you remember?'

'Ahhh, well, I've never been too good at remembering anything, let alone puppy names. I'm sure you know that.'

'Of course,' Eydis smiled patiently. 'And do you remember their colours at least?'

Eadmund's mouth slackened, his brain now stretched beyond its weary limits. 'I... not especially. I'm not really one for dogs, Eydis. They all look the same to me.'

Eydis looked cross as she leaned forward, searching for his arm. 'Eadmund!' she hissed, gripping hold of his cloak. 'Father will kill you. Truly, this time he will!'

'What are you talking about?'

'You haven't even seen Jael, have you? You don't even know about the puppies I gave you both! Where have you been? You're supposed to be in your new home, with your new wife, as Father thinks you are.' Her voice was quiet but loaded with warning.

'Eydis –'

'No! Don't tell me that I'm a child. That I wouldn't understand,' she interrupted. 'I understand what will happen if you ruin this.

Don't forget that I can see the future, Eadmund. All you have to do is go and see her. Spend some time with her. Do the things you're supposed to do. That will keep Father happy. That will make you happy, believe it or not.'

'Eydis...'

'Eadmund, please.' She grabbed him harder. 'Please don't ruin this. I have seen what will come for us if you do.'

***

The hammering had started early, and Jael was utterly fed up with it now. The men were obviously industrious, eager to finish the stables their king had commanded them to build, and she was just as keen for that to happen, but the noise was ruining any chance of her focusing on being truly miserable.

'How is it possible that you're *still* in bed?' Biddy wondered for the fourth time, walking into the bedchamber and prodding the submerged, fur-covered figure. 'With that noise going on outside and those puppies yapping and wailing? How is it that you're lying here, warm as bread, still asleep?'

Jael pushed the furs away from her head and glared at Biddy. The light was unusually bright in the house this morning, and Jael blinked to adjust her eyes. 'What's the point in getting up?' she scowled. 'What's the point in coming out from under here? Why should I bother?'

'Well, you could take *your* puppies outside for a shit every once in a while, so they stop doing their business all over *my* floor!' Biddy huffed as she bent down to pick up the puppies in question, throwing them onto the bed and stalking out.

They bounced over to Jael's head, greeting her with wet tongues and wiggling tails. As much as she was determined to feel sorry for herself, to stay in a dark, isolated place, Ido and Vella had other ideas. She felt their fluffy warmth as they burrowed under the furs, down towards her feet, and it roused a lighter spirit, deep inside her wallowing. Jael heard her father's voice then, urging her to get up and make a plan. To choose a way forward. She imagined Tig's furious whinnying, annoyed at her neglect of him, desperate to be ridden, to be set free.

And she felt the same.

Emerging from her warm cave, at last, she reluctantly left behind all thoughts of Aleksander and hurried to get dressed before the chill found her bones.

The puppies rushed to escape the furs, desperate to follow her.

***

'Ahhh, my annoying friend! And how are you this fine morning?' Thorgils grinned as he fell in beside Eadmund, just outside the main block of stables. The fetid stench from within wafted gently towards them.

Eadmund frowned, irritated to have come across yet another obstacle in his quest for solitude. 'Annoying?'

'More than annoying but I'm a well-mannered man and today is a good day, so I won't go any further,' Thorgils smiled through his bushy red beard.

'That's very kind of you. If only I were as well-mannered, but I can't be arsed talking to you this morning, so I'll leave you to your business.' And with barely a glance, Eadmund headed off, walking with purpose in the direction of the gates.

Thorgils stared after his friend, bemused. For Eadmund to be in such a hurry, there had to be a drink waiting for him somewhere. He shrugged, determined not to be worried for a change.

Turning around, he spied Jael, wrapped in a thin cloak, her head bent low, striding towards the stables. Well, if one-half of the new couple wasn't interested in his company, perhaps the other would be more amenable?

***

Jael was livid as she surveyed the deteriorating conditions inside the stables. The snow was thick on the ground now, and the stench was unbearable. She was determined to remove both horses to stay with the livestock at the back of her house until the stables were complete. The speed those annoying builders were going it could be as soon as later today, depending on how long the sun held power over the moon, of course. She would have to talk to Eirik about the rest of the horses, though; they couldn't stay here another night. These stables needed to be used as firewood. That was all they were good for.

Jael saw the red beast that was Thorgils trudging towards her, wrapped in a huge, white fur cloak. She sighed.

'Good morning,' he nodded cheerfully, then gagged. 'What a stink! The poor horses.'

'You don't have a horse stabled here?' Jael wondered as she fitted Tig's bridle over his twitching head. There were at least another fifteen horses shivering in the muck along with Tig and Leada; not many, so there were obviously other stables in the fort.

'Here? Not likely. Not if you want your horse to keep all four of its legs,' Thorgils grinned, running his hand down the white muzzle of Eadmund's neglected gift. 'She's a beauty.'

Jael smiled, pleased to find someone who liked horses. 'She is. Strong too.'

'Good. No point riding a timid horse into battle.' He took a carrot from his pocket and let her nibble it slowly from his hand.

'What's her name?'

A man who kept carrots in his pocket? Jael was impressed.

'Leada. She's Eadmund's gift from my family. Not that he would know that, of course.'

'No,' Thorgils sighed, 'I don't imagine he would. He hasn't ridden for years. Once his horse died, he didn't bother with a replacement.' Sadness filled his eyes as he dug into his pocket for another carrot. 'But she can't wait on Eadmund to notice her. If you want some company, I'll come along and give her a run.'

He was already reaching for a bridle, and although Jael had no real desire for company, she couldn't see a reason to turn down his offer. Besides, in this unfamiliar world of snow-covered cliffs and sheer drops, she would be grateful for a guide.

***

Outside the gates, they paused. Jael could feel her whole body sink into Tig's sheepskin-covered saddle; a comfortable familiarity that relaxed her instantly. It was freezing but freeing. She nodded at Thorgils, gesturing for him to lead the way. The snow was deeper than she'd realised, but Tig barely noticed as he strained against her hold. There was no ice, so it was perfectly safe, as long as you knew where you were going and Jael didn't, so she followed Thorgils and Leada, keeping the reins tight against her cloak.

The view from up here, on the highest peak of the island, with the sun almost directly overhead, was breathtaking. The dark sea was now ice-covered, and it looked as though it was consuming the entire island; gathering it into an ominous, wintry embrace. Jael shivered as she looked down to the beach, remembering Edela's terrified face. That face would not leave her alone.

She hoped they had all made it back to Andala safely.

'Come on!' Thorgils called, the cloudy waves of his cold

breath streaming out behind him like a veil. He was already well ahead, but Jael only had to give Tig light encouragement before he was trotting to catch up.

They rode relatively carefully, in total silence. Jael was alert and consumed with interest by everything she came across. Up here, as they were on the ridge, there was sparse foliage and not much that wasn't snow covered. It was rocky and uneven beneath the snow; she could feel that in the way Tig skidded, at times unbalanced, his hooves unsteady. It was hard to keep her mind on that, though, when there was just so much to take in. She looked hard, with a great dose of wishful thinking, to see if she could spot a glimpse of Brekka in the vast expanse of sea ice but only the outer islands were visible.

'Not such a bad view?' Thorgils suggested with a grin.

'No, not so bad,' Jael admitted. 'Do all of the smaller islands belong to Oss?'

'Yes, all seven of them,' Thorgils nodded, leaning over to give Leada a reassuring pat; she was also struggling with her footing. 'They're all Eirik's. He has a lord on each, but he's the only king.'

'And they give him no trouble?' Jael leaned back in the saddle as they started the slow descent towards the lowlands. Tig's feet came in and out of the snow deliberately as Jael swayed from side to side. She could tell that he was enjoying himself; his ears were pointing forward, and his head was high as he followed Leada down the hill.

'Not normally. He's softened in his old age, but Eirik's still a beast. He'll cut you down if you cross him.'

Jael raised an eyebrow as she pulled on Tig's reins, trying to contain his eagerness. The cold was biting into her legs now, a dull ache forming behind each knee. She wondered how long it would be before her lips were too frozen to speak. 'So, he thinks he can cut Haaron down, then? Conquer Hest, when everyone else has failed?'

'Eirik? No, that's not his game. He had to agree to join Lothar's invasion in order to get you.'

'*Get* me? You make me sound like a prize!' Jael snorted, relieved to be down on flat terrain again. Tig shook his rump and hurried to catch up with Leada.

'Well, to Eirik you are,' Thorgils said, eyeing Jael earnestly. 'He'd almost given up on Eadmund before Eydis dreamed about you. He doesn't care about Hest. He stopped trying to build an empire years ago. He just wants to secure what he has for the future. And he needs Eadmund to do that for him. And if he can't, then Eirik has to turn to Ivaar.'

Jael glanced at Thorgils. 'Ivaar? Eadmund's brother?'

Thorgils stared at her darkly. 'Yes, Ivaar. But no one wants him to resort to that.'

'And where is this Ivaar?' Jael wondered as they came to a small lake, frozen solid, its pale surface glinting menacingly under the sun.

'Ivaar's the Lord of Kalfa, one of the islands to the south of Oss,' Thorgils grunted, tugging on Leada's reins, and she turned to the right, skirting the lake. 'But of course, being the eldest son, his ambitions extend beyond that pebble. He wants the throne, you can be sure of that.'

'But if he's the eldest, why is Eadmund Eirik's heir?'

'Ahhh... well that's a long story, and my lips are probably going to freeze before I can tell it,' Thorgils grinned. 'But the short story would be that Ivaar's a cunt, and no one wants him here.'

'Ha!' Jael couldn't help but laugh. 'That was perhaps a little too short,' she shivered. 'Surely there's more to say than that? What did he do to make everyone hate him? To make his father choose Eadmund over him?'

'You truly don't know the story?'

'No, why would I? In Brekka, we only ever bothered about Oss when you were sailing over to attack us. Why should we have cared about your family squabbles?'

Thorgils shrugged. 'Fair point.' He bent down to pat the accommodating Leada, who had not complained once about her very cumbersome load. 'There's a gap between the mountains up ahead. We can let the horses run awhile.'

'Good, they need it, as do I,' Jael said desperately. 'Now, tell me this story about Ivaar.'

'Ahhh, well... Ivaar hated Eadmund before Eadmund was even born. Eirik was married to Odila, Ivaar's mother, when he fell in love with Eskild. He divorced Odila and married Eskild, and they had Eadmund. Odila was so humiliated that she killed herself. So, there you go, a very good reason for Ivaar to grow up hating Eadmund.'

'Indeed, who could blame him?'

'Well, no one I suppose, apart from the fact that he was a strange shit of a child anyway. He had a perverse sense of humour. He was jealous of Eadmund and hated Eskild too. He once even killed a dog she had given Eadmund.'

Jael frowned, immediately disliking Ivaar.

'So, that's how things went along until they all went completely wrong.' Thorgils paused as he navigated Leada around a cluster of smooth stones covered in ankle-breaking ice. 'Eirik was trying to make a trade alliance with a lord from Alekka, and his daughter came to Oss with him. Melaena.' He rolled his big blue eyes. 'That was that, both brothers fell hard in love. She was pretty, for sure, but she knew it, and she played them both like a sweet tune. They thought she was the sun and the moon and the stars in one. And she couldn't decide between them.'

'Poor girl.'

'But then one day, her father made her choose, and she chose Eadmund.'

'And?'

'And they were married,' Thorgils said sadly. 'And Melaena died that very same night.'

'How?' Jael was shocked.

'Poisoned wine.'

'So, everyone assumed that Ivaar had done it?'

They were at the pass now. Jael smiled – it certainly was an inviting flat stretch of land – and as both riders pulled up on their reins, they could feel the horses' excitement rippling through their eager muscles.

'Of course,' Thorgils said blankly. 'Who else? Eadmund demanded Ivaar's head, but there was no proof. There was nothing to tie him to Melaena's murder except reputation and motive. It wasn't enough, though, not if the law was to be upheld, so Eirik sent him away instead.' He looked into the distance, his eyes further away than the white landscape before him. 'Eirik found him a wife, gave him lordship over Kalfa, and Ivaar was never to be heard from again. Unless, of course, Eadmund ruins this one last chance with Eirik. Then he'll return. And I don't imagine that Ivaar will be feeling very charitable towards his brother, or his brother's wife.' He peered at Jael. 'Especially as Ivaar always insisted he was innocent.'

The horses were getting cold and impatient as they stood there waiting and snorting, but there was suddenly so much that Jael wanted to know. 'So, Eadmund has one last chance? To do what? Prove he's worthy of being the king?'

'Exactly,' Thorgils said, shaking as the cold started to claim his limbs. 'But will he? Can he? Perhaps that's up to you, Jael?' He stared intently at her, then kicking Leada's rump with a loud 'ha!', he took off; white horse and white rider disappearing quickly into the white distance. The only marker of their presence was Thorgils' flaming-red hair flapping ferociously behind him.

Tig skittered excitedly, flicking his tail, desperate to follow. Jael nudged him gently and let him fly. He was fast, even in the heavy, unfamiliar conditions. It only took him a few strides to remember how to gallop in the snow. Jael bent low over his neck, clinging on with a smile that grew in the bitter wind that raked her face.

She left all thoughts of Eadmund, Aleksander, Brekka, and Oss behind as she raced to catch up with Thorgils, almost happy for the first time in weeks.

CHAPTER FOURTEEN

Aleksander walked across the square, his head bent against a mean wind, trying to ignore the whispers and concerned looks. He had a purpose now, and it felt better, he felt better, but still, he had no need for anyone's pity.

Edela had sent him to collect as many items as possible for her attempt at dream walking. Dream walking? It sounded a fanciful wish, more than a possibility, but they were both desperate to try anything to contact Jael. Edela had dug into a locked iron box she kept buried under the floor of her cottage. It contained a book, passed down from her grandmother, filled with magical spells and rituals that the Tuuran Council had outlawed centuries ago. It was a book Edela had never even opened, her grandmother insisting that she only call on its secrets in her direst moment.

So far, his mission had been challenging. Many of the items Aleksander needed were herbs: fresh, not frozen. Most hadn't taken well to being buried in the snow, but he had managed to rescue a few hardy leaves last night and throughout the morning. Now he was on his way back to his cottage, looking for anything Jael might have worn and left behind. Something that might have her hair on it.

'Aleksander?'

It was Amma Furyck. He wanted to pretend that he hadn't heard her, but she was the king's daughter, and it wouldn't do him any good to fall into trouble today. He reluctantly walked over to where Amma was waiting by the side of an abandoned shed, wondering what she could possibly want with him.

'How are you?' Amma asked, her brown eyes full of concern. 'Without Jael?'

Aleksander sighed; this was what he'd been working so hard to avoid. 'I'm fine, thank you.' He wanted to leave, but she remained, staring at him with an earnest look.

'I know Jael was worried about leaving you behind, about how you would cope without her,' Amma went on. 'But I assured her that all your friends and family here would not abandon you. We'll make sure that you don't feel alone.'

Aleksander was too distracted to make much sense of Amma's words until she reached out and placed her mittened hand on his arm.

And left it there.

'If there is anything you need, you only have to ask me. I have my father's ear, you know,' she whispered to him. 'He wants to see me happy, whatever that means. And so... if I can help you with anything, it would make me very happy indeed.'

Aleksander froze, trying to decide what to do. He wanted to shake her hand away before anyone came along and saw it, but at the same time, he didn't want to insult the girl. So, he found a smile from somewhere deep within and placed his hand on top of hers. 'It's very kind of you,' he said quickly. 'I think I just need some time to adjust to things. But I won't forget your offer, I promise.' He nodded, slowly stepping backwards, still smiling, hoping to have carried off his escape with as little insult as possible.

Amma held her breath as she watched him walk away. He looked so terribly sad and thin. There had to be something she could do to help him.

***

Thorgils' face was flushed as he brought Leada alongside Jael and Tig. 'So you can ride a bit, then?' They'd let the horses chase each other through the pass, enjoying their first burst of freedom in days.

Jael smiled, her face just as red as Thorgils'. She couldn't feel a thing, but she had the sense that her nose was running, and she wiped it on the back of her glove. Patting Tig's neck, she noticed a thin trail of smoke snaking its way out of a row of trees in the distance. 'Does someone live out here?' she wondered, nodding towards the smoke. The trees formed a windbreak in front of a path that led down to an outlying neck of land.

'Live?' Thorgils mused. 'I suppose you could call it that.'

They followed the steep path down to a clearing. The smoke was in their nostrils now, the smell of food stirring their cold, empty bellies; the sound of grunting and banging in their ears.

Jael saw a boy hitting what looked like a wooden man with a wooden sword in an area that had been cleared since the snowfall. He appeared to have no ability with the sword at all. He hit his target with little direction or skill, or any understanding of what he was doing at all.

Jael frowned at Thorgils.

'Fyn,' he smiled in answer to her puzzled face. 'Morac's son.'

'Morac?'

'Eirik's man,' he tried, but Jael looked at him blankly. 'Thin, long, pointy face, looks like he's sucking on a mouthful of piss.'

Jael laughed and nodded, recognising the man from the hall who she'd taken an instant dislike to. But why would the son of the king's man be living out here all alone?

Fyn saw them then and dropped his sword in surprise.

Jael tried not to laugh. Had no one ever taught the boy how to handle a weapon? He was lucky it was made of wood, or he might just have lost a toe.

'Fyn!' Thorgils raised his arm, grinning as they dismounted.

The boy relaxed, rushing eagerly towards his visitors then.

'Thorgils! I didn't recognise you. I thought you were raiders!'

He peered inquisitively at Jael through long reddish-brown hair which flopped over his eyes. He nervously brushed it away. His face was freckled, kind, with a boyish innocence that reminded her of Axl.

'Nothing that bad, I promise,' Thorgils smiled, clapping Fyn on the shoulder. 'Although, I think we would like to relieve you of something hot to eat!' Jael pulled back the hood of her cloak, then, and Thorgils watched in amusement as Fyn's eyes bulged. 'This is Jael. Eadmund's new wife.'

Fyn's eyes widened further. 'Oh.' He bowed awkwardly. 'My lady.'

'Hello,' Jael shivered. 'This is a rather remote place to live all alone. Do you not like your family?'

Thorgils laughed, heading off towards Fyn's hut.

Fyn's face darkened, taking on an older, sadder look. 'I... I don't choose to be so far away, my lady.' He paused, staring at his feet. 'The king, he... banished me. From Oss.'

'Banished you? But you're still here?' Jael found it hard to hide her growing curiosity. It seemed a strange situation. And why hadn't he been taught how to use a sword? He was nearly a man.

She was full of questions.

Thorgils disappeared inside the tiny hut. It was almost invisible, built into the side of the hill. If you weren't looking for it, you wouldn't see it at all; only its smoke hole had given it away today. There were no windows, only a small wooden door that looked more like part of a tree trunk than an entrance to a home.

'I, I stay to protect my mother,' Fyn stuttered in the face of Jael's interrogation. 'Well, not to protect her, but to be here for her... if she needs me. I couldn't just leave her. But my father, he doesn't know.' He blinked rapidly, his large blue eyes filled with fear.

'But your mother does? She comes to visit you?' Jael wondered.

'There's hot food!' Thorgils smiled, poking his head outside, his frame filling the minuscule doorway. He watched Fyn's face fall. 'If you would be so kind as to spare just a morsel or two, my young friend?'

'Of course, of course. You must be so cold,' Fyn said. He wanted to be an accommodating host, and his mother would send her servant soon with another bundle of food, he reminded himself.

Jael secured the horses, and, bending her head, she followed Fyn inside. The hut was almost warm, which was a welcome respite from the bone-aching bitterness outside. Warm, but so dim; it was almost like stepping into the night. And smelly. Like a rat-infested cave. Damp too.

Not a nice place for anyone to call home.

Fyn had a stew cooking in a small, misshapen cauldron that hung over a very modest fire.

Thorgils licked his frozen lips, desperate for a taste. 'Do you have any more bowls?' he asked, scouring Fyn's mostly empty shelf, his stomach growling impatiently.

'We can't eat Fyn's food, Thorgils. I'm sure he needs to make it last longer than just this meal,' Jael warned, glancing at Fyn's anxious face. Though he was wrapped in a warm-looking cloak, Jael could see that he looked a little starved.

'No, no, of course we won't. But just a mouthful or two will warm us up enough to get us back to the fort.' Thorgils smiled reassuringly, giving Fyn no choice in the matter.

Fyn hunted around in a corner of the hut, where he'd stacked a pile of broken rubbish he intended to get rid of one day. He retrieved two small bowls, both cracked. They would have to do.

They sat huddled around the fire on barely-worked tree stumps, knee to knee, numb hands thawing dangerously close to the flames. Thorgils took the bowls and started ladling in the steaming stew.

'How old are you, Fyn?' Jael wondered, adjusting her position on the stool, trying to avoid the sharp splinter threatening her behind.

'Eighteen,' Fyn replied distractedly, his eyes on Thorgils' generous portioning. 'Nineteen soon.'

Jael frowned. 'And you've never been shown what to do with a sword? Your father didn't train you?'

Fyn's face fell. 'No, he didn't think there was much point. He said I was too clumsy, that there was no chance of me becoming a warrior so he wouldn't bother.' He blushed as he took the bowl Thorgils handed him, passing it to Jael. 'You saw me out there. I'm sure you know he was right.'

Jael frowned as she took the bowl. 'Well, if you're trying to learn on your own, with only a wooden man for help, what else could you expect?' Jael caught Thorgils' eye, glaring at him sternly, so he spooned a small amount of stew back into the cauldron. 'You need to be trained by a warrior. Someone who can actually help you. Someone who knows how to use a sword better than your wooden friend!' She smiled at Fyn, who bent his freckled face away from her gaze.

Jael spooned a big helping of stew into her mouth, eager to fill her body with its promised warmth. She almost gagged. Her frozen nose had led her astray because up close, the stew smelled rancid and tasted even worse. She knew she had to swallow what was in her mouth so as not to offend their host, but not one part of her wanted to. Fyn was staring at her now, greedily tucking into his own bowl as though it contained the most delicious meal he'd ever eaten. Jael closed her eyes and swallowed everything inside her mouth in one big, unappetising lump. 'Do you have anything to drink?' she croaked, her eyes watering as she tried to ignore the vile flavours flooding her mouth.

'I have some small ale,' Fyn answered, leaping up to grab a jug from the stool by his narrow bed.

Jael glanced quickly at Thorgils, who was staring apprehensively at his own stew.

'That would be good,' Thorgils coughed. 'Pour me a cup too, Fyn.'

Fyn once again had to hunt around in his rubbish pile. 'I'm

not used to many guests,' he apologised nervously. 'It's only my mother's servant who I see these days.' He managed to find two broken cups, and he poured a small measure of watery ale into each.

Jael and Thorgils drank quickly, desperate to wash down the putrid taste of Fyn's stew.

'Perhaps Jael can come and train you?' Thorgils suggested cheekily, hoping to keep Fyn from noticing that they had both stopped eating. 'She's a warrior of great repute, you know.'

Fyn looked horrified by the proposition. 'Oh no, no, I couldn't imagine that would be a good idea.'

Jael raised an eyebrow, though she wasn't sure who she intended it for.

'No, I suppose you're right. Jael really must focus on taking care of Eadmund and preparing for motherhood.' Thorgils was enjoying the twisting, turning expressions on Jael's face as he talked. 'Although...' he turned to her, 'you do have that shiny, new sword and it would be a shame to keep it in its scabbard.'

Jael couldn't help but smile as she reached down and fingered the unfamiliar hilt, running her hand over the chilled moonstone. It was reassuring to have a sword again and one that was, for the first time, truly hers. As amusing as Thorgils was attempting to be, he was actually right, the sword needed to be used. It was better to get to know its secrets now before she had to call on it.

Although, not necessarily against a boy who couldn't fight back.

'I think it's probably best if Fyn is trained by someone who can show him more basic techniques. Someone with a simple approach. Someone, maybe like you, Thorgils, who is at that sort of level.' She winked teasingly at the big man. 'Someone with my experience and skill might only end up hurting Fyn, especially with a sword as well-made and sharp as this.'

Fyn's mouth hung open, his eyes flicking back and forth, following the banter.

He wasn't sure he liked the sound of either suggestion.

Thorgils was busy forming a retort when Jael suddenly spun around. 'Did you hear that?'

'What?' Fyn and Thorgils asked in unison, eyes darting towards the door.

'The horses! I'm sure I heard someone outside!'

Fyn was out the door in an instant, and Thorgils made to follow him, still holding his bowl, before Jael hissed at him. She quickly grabbed the bowl out of his hand, dumping its contents back into the cauldron, along with her own. Thorgils hung his head at his dimness, then raced out after Fyn, remembering to duck his head just in time.

Having determined that no raiders were trying to steal the horses, Jael and Thorgils decided to leave before Fyn could offer them anything else to eat. Fyn looked disappointed that they were heading off so quickly, so they promised to come and visit him again.

Jael turned to wave to him as Tig carried her up the snowy hill, relieved to have escaped without another mention of the stew. 'That was truly the worst thing I've ever tasted,' she muttered, shuddering at the memory, and leaning over, she spat on the snow.

'The boy is turning feral if he thinks that bowl of anus-smelling, bollocks-flavoured shit tasted good!' Thorgils cursed. 'Did you see him gulping it down as though it were food from the gods?'

'I had fur in my mouth.'

'Is that all?' Thorgils gagged. 'I swallowed a claw!'

***

Eadmund had slept a lot.

That hadn't been his intention when he'd finally found some

solitude in his favourite drying shed, but the rest had cleared much of the fog out of his muddled head. Suddenly he could see himself in sharper relief, and what he saw was brutal.

The drying shed was open on two sides, lined with row after row of hanging fish carcasses. It was a stinking place. A cold place. Eadmund usually didn't notice. He was often barely conscious when he came here, desperate to escape Evaine or his father, needing to be alone in his own mess, without witnesses. But today, for the first time, there was a witness: himself.

And it was all because of her.

Jael.

He needed to think, to find a way out of the hole he had sunk into, to change who he had become, but his mind kept wandering down the path that led to her. Why? He couldn't understand it. She was prickly and stern and looked at him as he really was: a soft lump of waste. No one on Oss did that. Of course, sometimes there was a look of pity or disappointment, but most still held onto the image of who he had once been and the hope that he would return someday. He was still their friend; they could still drink with him, share stories and jokes with him. Even his father, for all his fire, still treated Eadmund as though there was still some hope there.

But not Jael. She saw nothing but the truth.

Eadmund sat on the hard dirt floor, his back against the shed wall, watching as the carcasses swayed gently back and forth above him. He'd been quite happy to let the past consume him. Secretly hoping that one day it would devour him whole.

But now he saw Jael's face, and he wasn't so sure.

***

Tarak was busy pounding someone's face into the muddy slush

when Thorgils and Jael rode through the gates, red-nosed, numb-limbed, but happy.

The snow had been cleared from a fenced training ring known, Thorgils informed Jael, as the Pit. And making the most of the fine day, Tarak was putting on a show for a large crowd of cheering Osslanders. Swords had been abandoned, and it now appeared to be an all-out wrestling match, which was rather one-sided judging by the bloody pulp that used to be Tarak's opponent's face.

'Could've been you,' Thorgils winked at Jael.

She looked unimpressed, by both the sloppy wrestling and her new-found friend's insinuation. 'Why? Because he's a giant and I'm a girl?' she sneered. 'That doesn't make him a skilled fighter. He's squashing that fool with his big fat gut. There's no skill in being able to lie on somebody to win a fight.'

'That may be so, but Tarak's skilled in winning, no matter how he achieves it. He's only been beaten once in all the time he's been here.' Thorgils looked over as a cheer rang up from Tarak's group of supporters. 'And that shocked him so much that he's never let it happen again.'

'So, you're going to tell me that it was you who beat him?'

'Me? I wish I could say so. No one would like to knock that bastard out more than me, but no... it was Eadmund.'

Jael was stunned. She pulled on Tig's reins, bringing him to a complete stop. '*Eadmund*? Eadmund can fight well enough to defeat that? When did that happen?' Her eyebrows arched in surprise.

Thorgils shrugged. 'I'm not sure, maybe eight years ago, maybe more. I can't honestly remember. It's been a long time since Tarak was beaten and a long time since Eadmund even held a sword, that much I do know. A shame on both counts.' He dismounted then. 'Do you think your stables are finished? I'm sure your servant will have something better to offer us than young Fyn did. I'm starving.' Thorgils whispered this to Jael; not many people knew that Fyn still lived on the island, and he certainly didn't want Morac to catch wind of it from him.

Jael slid off Tig with a grimace. Her legs felt stiff and sore from the biting cold. 'That's the best thing you've suggested all day.' She yawned, following Thorgils, tugging on Tig's reins. It was barely mid-afternoon, but she was already thinking about her bed.

They led the horses across the sloppy brown slush of the square that only hours earlier had been untouched snow. And amid all the muck, Jael once again spotted the girl in the white cloak, talking angrily to the pointy-faced man.

'So, do you know why Fyn was banished?' Jael wondered, unable to stop staring. She couldn't make out their words, but it was clear that they were arguing, and she was itching to know what was going on.

Thorgils followed the turn of Jael's head, swallowing hard. It was in everyone's best interests to keep Jael far away from Evaine. 'No, I've never found out the reason. We weren't told. Eirik and Morac kept that one close to their chests. I can't imagine what Fyn could have done, though. He's a bit simple.'

'Simple? No, he's not! He's nice. And shy,' Jael insisted. 'I don't imagine you can be banished for that?'

'I don't imagine so, but come on now, I need to get something hot and clawless inside me before my heart stops beating!'

Jael reluctantly turned away. 'So, Morac is Fyn's father...'

'He is.'

'And the girl... is she Fyn's sister?'

Thorgils was silent. He kept walking.

Jael laughed loudly behind him. 'You, my friend, say more with your silence than you do with your words!'

Tiras stood to one side of the hall, watching Jael walk away. Without her husband. Again. He still hadn't seen her with him.

Not once.

Turning away into the shadows of the alley, he smiled.

CHAPTER FIFTEEN

Eirik banged his fist on the table again to silence the hall. He frowned. He was having a hard time getting anyone's attention. It was no doubt the snow's fault, keeping everyone indoors for much of the day, so that they were only just now using up all of their energy. Finally, though, voices hushed and expectant faces turned towards their impatient king.

'It seems that we are now in the grip of the Freeze. We are officially frozen in!'

There were cheers at that. It was a happy tradition on Oss, and despite the hardships that accompanied the frozen sea, most seemed to embrace the challenge of having to sustain themselves till spring. Their stores were healthy enough this year, and there was a good deal of optimism in the hall knowing that they would invade Hest and refill their coffers come the Thaw.

'But we can't turn into hermits while we wait for spring, though. We can't spend all our time face-deep in women and ale!' There were a few hearty boos then. Eirik smiled, rolling his eyes. 'We must keep our minds and bodies sharp, ready for battle. So, you're all going to train in the snow, every day, no matter the weather, for I am going to hold a contest before the Thaw is upon us!'

Eirik looked pointedly at Jael, who'd barely been listening, and even now, she stared at him blankly, not sure what he was talking about.

'It has been many years, too many years, since we held one of our famous contests and now, with the arrival of my new daughter,' he smiled, and Jael cringed, 'it feels like the perfect time to return the tradition to our beloved Pit!' The hall thundered with raucous applause and table thumping, and Eirik soaked it all up. As king, all decisions were his, and not many were greeted with much enthusiasm, so this was something to savour. 'For those of you who don't know how this works,' he looked towards Jael again, 'there will be four groups of men, who will fight each other until we have one champion from each group. And we'll narrow it down from there until there is only one standing. And that bloodied and broken man, or woman, will be named the Champion of Oss!'

Jael was listening now, and she didn't like the look on Eirik's face. He kept glancing at her as though she was the prize he was holding up in front of his audience of spitting, grinning, frothing men. She couldn't deny the charge she felt in her body, the desire to exercise her sword arm again, but she was rusty, and, with a new sword, unsure of herself.

She didn't want to be anyone's prize.

The hum of excitement intensified, and Eirik sat down, content with the outcome. He nodded to Morac, sitting at the far end of the table, who looked similarly pleased, then turned to Jael, who looked anything but. 'That should be something to make you smile,' he said confidently.

Jael frowned. 'Smile?'

'It's a chance to fight. I thought you'd like that. A chance to use your new sword.'

'So you organised this for *me*?' She looked doubtfully at Eirik, taking a small sip of ale.

'Well, no,' he conceded. 'But I'm sure you won't complain about having to fight this lot, will you?'

'No, I don't suppose I will,' Jael admitted, taking in the wild bunch before her. She didn't fear them, but she knew that she'd have to start training immediately and that was a strange feeling.

She'd only ever trained with Aleksander.

'Is it a fight to the death, then?'

'No, it's a fight until I declare a winner. I can't afford to lose most of my warriors before we invade Hest!' Eirik laughed. 'Is that how you do it in Brekka?'

'Yes, of course. What's the point in fighting someone if you know you can't kill them?'

Eirik peered at Jael, looking for signs that she was joking, but he couldn't find any.

Eadmund sat anxiously to Jael's left. He had barely exchanged more than a nod with his wife over their meal. In truth, they had barely exchanged more than a nod since their wedding.

Eadmund had felt an unfamiliar sense of clarity since returning to the fort, a building desire to reclaim the man he had once been. He wanted to show his father that he would make a good king. He couldn't avoid or escape his life anymore. He couldn't run and hide inside a cup of ale. So he had walked into the hall that evening with his head a little higher than usual, his eyes more alert, his back straighter. And then he'd smelled the ale, and watched his friends drinking, and he'd started to sweat. And throughout the meal, Eadmund had stared at his cup, his teasing, tempting cup, filled with perfectly-scented ale as it called sweetly to him. He'd ignored his itching palms and jammed his teeth together, and tried to do anything but take up its seductive offer. He wanted to stay this way, this clear-headed, determined way, or did he?

Perhaps it was nothing to do with ale?

Would one drink make any difference? Certainly not after the amount he'd been drinking these past few years. No, he was sure that one drink would barely affect him at all.

But perhaps he would wait.

At least until the end of the meal.

Thorgils chatted incessantly next to him on his left, and to his right, his wife was mostly silent. Eadmund listened as his father tried to engage her in conversation, but she didn't respond with much enthusiasm. He couldn't imagine that she wanted to be here any more than he did.

He didn't know what to say to her. Jael Furyck was a wall of intimidating ice and every idea just dissolved before it ever reached his lips. Once in a while, she would turn to look his way, but there was nothing in her eyes inviting his company, or his conversation. His mood was sinking fast, and his cup's call grew louder.

'So, what do you think? Are you going to enter the contest?' Thorgils laughed, thumping his friend on the back.

Eadmund glanced at him, wiping moisture from his brow. He couldn't stop sweating. 'Very funny.' He licked his lips, fiddling with his fingers.

'Are you alright?' Thorgils wondered, noticing for the first time how disturbed Eadmund appeared.

'What? Yes, I'm fine.'

'You're not drinking?'

'I'm... taking it a bit slower,' Eadmund muttered. His head was screaming at him now, demanding that he pick up the cup. 'I'm getting too old to be sleeping on the floor every night.' He tried a casual smile in an attempt to bat away Thorgils' interest.

'Well, that's good news.' Thorgils' face broke into a crooked grin. 'Very good news! Perhaps we'll get a sword back in your hand soon?'

Eadmund panicked, feeling his body shake. 'Hold on, hold on! I hardly said I'm going to turn into you!'

'Well, no, that would be impossible, my friend, for I am sure to be crowned the next Champion of Oss!' Thorgils leaned in closely, lowering his voice. 'And I'm going to beat that arsehole, Tarak, once and for all. I'm going to push his fucked-up face into the muck and claim my long-overdue prize.'

Eadmund couldn't wait any longer. He grabbed his cup and drank from it, his desperation finally proving greater than his half-formed resolve. Thorgils frowned slightly, more in pity than disappointment, but Eadmund chose not to notice. He pretended not to care as he felt his body loosen its tense hold on him at last. His breathing slowed, relief flooding his tight chest.

Jael turned around and saw the blissful smile on Eadmund's face as he drained his cup and reached out to a passing servant for another. She saw the disapproving look on Thorgils' face, and while she knew that it was not in Eadmund's, or perhaps her own best interests for him to be drinking, she couldn't help but feel relieved.

A drunken Eadmund would surely not find his way to her bed tonight.

'Will you be fighting in the contest?' Eadmund wondered, turning towards his wife, his confidence partly restored.

Jael saw Thorgils watching with interest. 'I suppose I have no choice.'

'Well, you may be with child then,' Thorgils suggested with a cheeky grin. 'You couldn't fight if that were so.'

'Yes, yes, that is true,' Eirik interrupted. 'Hopefully, that is the case!' He stared pointedly at Eadmund, whose head was down, ignoring his father.

Jael looked just as disturbed by the thought. 'When is this contest taking place? Soon?'

'Oh, no!' Eirik scoffed. 'It's something we take seriously. It's not just a few scrappy fights. I still have to choose a day, but we will give the men two or three months to train. It should keep us from turning to fat while we wait for the Thaw. It will help prepare us for Hest.'

It was Jael's turn to scoff. 'You think that one contest is all you'll need to be ready for Hest? To have a few lean men who can fight in the snow?' She surveyed the hall, doubt flaring. 'No one has conquered Hest. Ever. Why do you and Lothar think you can change that?'

Eirik glanced at Tiras, who was slouched over at a table in the farthest corner of the hall. He had ordered the little turd to sit as far away from him as possible. As usual, though, Tiras' beady eyes were staring Eirik's way. He was beginning to despise the constant presence of Lothar's pet. He lowered his voice. 'Why? Because this will be a dual attack, of course. Haaron won't be expecting that. He won't have prepared for both of us.'

'You don't think he has spies everywhere? You don't think word has gotten back to him of your new friendship with Lothar? Of this marriage?' Jael gestured to Eadmund, who was actually listening, which surprised her. 'Haaron Dragos hasn't ruled for so many years because he's a fool. I don't imagine he thinks you and Lothar have been making friends just to share a few cups of ale and tell a few tales. He'll know what's coming and he *will* be preparing for it. And even if he's entered his dotage now, those four sons of his will be prowling around, waiting to pounce on any pretenders to the throne they have waited so long for themselves.'

Her words were iron-heavy, and Eirik baulked under the weight of them. 'And you're an expert on the Dragos family and Hest, are you?'

Jael could see that Eirik was annoyed, but it didn't deter her. She tended to get spurred on by a confrontation, especially when she was feeling miserable. Thoughts of Aleksander had been dragging her down into a dark, lonely place all afternoon, and she was in an ornery mood. 'I'm no expert on anything, but I've fought Haaron and his sons many times. He was always one step ahead of us. He always knew what was coming,' she sighed, remembering the frustration of constantly having to rebuff his attacks. 'When my father ruled, we worked hard to put defenses in place to protect ourselves against their incursions. But Haaron always seemed to know our weakest points. He knew where to strike, and when. If our army had been smaller, if my father had been weaker, we would have been overrun by them every time. But he was always ready. He knew the Dragos' would keep coming. He worked us hard to prepare for that. And with Lothar, when he attacked Hest, they defended to meet his plans of attack exactly. Lothar was never going to win. There was certainly a spy. There were eyes on Brekka, from Saala to Andala. Haaron was watching, somehow. Or more likely, he just has his own dreamer.' She looked at Eydis, who had sat quietly by her father's side throughout the evening, sharing barely a word or a smile with anyone. Jael wondered if she was even listening.

Eirik's earlier annoyance softened slightly. It surprised him to realise that Jael's experience of the Hestians was far greater than his. He had never launched a campaign against Haaron and his wild men behind their southern mountains. He had tried, once, to take Skorro, Hest's perfectly positioned little island that sat beyond the Widow's Peak. Haaron had a garrison placed there to protect his trade routes with the Fire Lands across the Adrano Sea. Eirik had wanted to free up those routes, to bring more traders to Oss, and vice versa, but it had proved a disastrous mission that had failed in a great, bloody, ship-sinking mess. As Jael had said, Haaron appeared to know his every move before he made it. He had lost many ships and too many men and not tried again, until now, to even think about claiming any part of Hest. He would not risk his men for something he did not believe could work this time, and with Lothar, he had thought it possible. Their combined armies, their two-pronged attack, it made sense, and he truly believed they had a chance for success. He didn't need or want to be thinking differently, but Eirik knew that he couldn't dismiss Jael's words lightly.

He turned to look at Eydis, realising that he had been so focused on her advice for Eadmund, that he hadn't asked her about the invasion.

He would have to find time to sit down with her soon.

The mood at the table had been flattened by Jael's words. Even Thorgils looked downcast and grim. The men and women sitting on the benches in front of them were loud, though, excited by the thought of a contest. There were a handful of eager boasters, sizing each other up, confident of their chances, predicting their success. Jael watched them dispassionately, annoyed by their happiness. Her eyes drifted towards Tarak. His little army of followers was looking up at him, gilding his ego with excessive praise and encouragement. He puffed out his thick, square chest, rolled back his meaty shoulders, and stared straight at her, smiling through the flames of the fire that separated their tables.

Jael stared at him, clenching a fist, suddenly cheered by the thought of the contest. Perhaps it wouldn't be so meaningless after all?

***

Jael was tired, or perhaps it wasn't tiredness, but more the overwhelming desire to be alone that motivated her to stand up. She yawned, thinking of her bed. The hall was still full, but she had grown bored of the drinking, and the loud, endless talk of battles and contests.

Some of the day had been good, and her spirits had lifted for a while, but now her body was heavy with sadness. She missed Aleksander intensely; nothing felt right without him. And the thought of how long it would be until she could see or speak to him again made her want to scream. Or at least escape to the house and try to find a dream.

'You're ready for your bed, it seems,' Eirik smiled, looking tired himself as he pushed back his bench and stood. He was stiff, she noticed, but he didn't complain.

'Past ready,' Jael said quickly, hoping to escape before there was any mention of Eadmund coming with her.

'So it's a good bed, is it?' Eirik wondered coyly.

'I suppose so, yes, it's a fine bed,' Jael said, confused by the question.

Eirik frowned. That wasn't the response he had tried so hard for. 'A fine bed?'

Jael glanced at him, puzzled. 'Why do you ask?'

'Oh no, no reason,' Eirik mumbled, shaking his head. 'Now, don't forget to collect Eadmund on the way out.' He winked at her, nodding towards the doors where Eadmund and Thorgils were in the midst of a rowdy conversation with their friends.

'I think he's having too much fun, so he can just come along later,' Jael said firmly. 'I'm sure he knows the way. Goodnight.'

'Goodnight,' Eirik smiled, a bit deflated. *Fine?* How could she not be salivating over that bed? He had tried it out himself, and he'd been convinced that it was going to astound her.

He sat back down again with a frown.

Jael weaved her way through the hall. Men and women were packed in around the walls, in small groups, sharing their stories and insults, clanking their cups, clapping each other's backs. She was almost at the door when she heard Thorgils' booming voice.

'Jael!'

She froze, wondering what to do.

He did it again. So, sighing in annoyance, Jael slapped a smile on her face and turned around, walking over to the swaying huddle of bleary-eyed men.

'I think you're forgetting someone, aren't you?' Thorgils slurred, his words rushing out through his damp red beard as he peered down at Jael with a foolish grin.

'Am I?' Jael wondered impatiently as Thorgils struggled to get his thoughts in order.

'Eadmund! Eadmund! You can't leave without your husband!' He grabbed Eadmund by the shoulder and pushed him forward. Eadmund stumbled, almost falling onto Jael.

'I think my *husband* is having far too much fun with you, Thorgils,' she said patiently, trying to avoid looking at Eadmund's bloated face. 'I wouldn't want to take him away from you all too soon.' She was just about to slip away, when she saw Tiras seated nearby, watching her intently. Biting her tongue in frustration, Jael sighed, turning back to Eadmund. 'Although, perhaps Thorgils is right and you should come with me now?' She tried to subtly motion with her eyes towards the watching spy, but neither man took her hint. Both were far too dumbstruck by her change of heart.

'I, I...' was all Eadmund could get out.

Thorgils grabbed Eadmund's cup and pushed him towards his impatient wife. 'I'd leave right now before she changes her mind,' he smiled, draining Eadmund's ale before tossing the empty cup onto a nearby table. 'I imagine it's not an offer that will be repeated!'

Eadmund looked caught between going along with everyone else and wanting to run back to retrieve his empty cup and refill it. Jael didn't have enough patience to wait for him to move his legs on his own, though, so she slipped her arm through his and pulled him towards the doors.

'Have fun!' Thorgils bellowed behind them. He made such a noise that a few cheers and whistles followed them to the door, but neither Jael nor Eadmund turned to acknowledge them.

Outside the hall, a searing wind attacked them, and Jael realised that she would need to get a new cloak made of thick fur if she wanted to survive in this frigid place. Tugging on Eadmund's arm, she almost dragged him along. He didn't say a word as he stumbled behind her. He was too busy trying to keep to his feet in the icy conditions.

They tiptoed quickly across the square, Jael occasionally looking over her shoulder, but there was no sign of anyone following them. She turned down a narrow alley, barely lit by a sliver of moon, then abruptly dropped Eadmund's arm, leaning into his chest. Eadmund stumbled backwards, hitting the wall of a shadowed building.

'Couldn't you see that Lothar's man was watching us?' Jael hissed, glancing around, listening for footsteps. 'He won't hesitate to talk to your father if he sees anything amiss between us.'

Eadmund shook himself awake. He was groggy and nauseous, cursing his weakness. He was cold too. In the rush to leave, he'd left his cloak in the hall. 'I didn't know Lothar had a man here,' he shivered, puzzled. 'Why?'

'To watch us. To make sure he knows everything that's happening here. To sniff out any threat to his alliance with your father.' Jael's green eyes glowed through her thick breath smoke. 'Tiras will report everything back to Lothar and believe me, he'll work very hard to find something.'

Eadmund stared into her eyes, blinking hard. She was so intense with her words, with that sharp stare. He felt trapped. And cold. He wanted her to stop talking so they could get to the house. He needed a fire.

'I assume you have somewhere you go every night?' Jael asked quickly. 'Somewhere you can stay hidden away till morning? Not going back to the hall so Tiras can spot you again?'

Eadmund was surprised. 'Ummm, yes, I can go to my cottage.'

'Good. Without being seen?'

'Yes, it's just down this alley and beyond, no need to go anywhere near the hall.' Eadmund was waking up now, his thoughts forming more clearly, his words tumbling out of his mouth.

The cold had a way of doing that to a person.

'Good, then go,' Jael ordered, turning to leave. 'I'll show you what Tiras looks like tomorrow. That way we can both stay ahead of him. Although, perhaps it would help if you drank a bit less? It's not easy to make good decisions if your head is always drowning in ale.' Noticeably shuddering, she hurried away, her black cloak and dark hair quickly merging into the night.

Eadmund stood for a moment before he started shaking uncontrollably. He turned in the opposite direction, heading quickly for home. His home. He stumbled, slipping on a patch of ice, despondent, disappointed, but at the same time thoroughly annoyed to have been taken away from his drinking so soon. But as much as he wished to sneak back to the hall, the memory of Jael's eyes warned him otherwise.

CHAPTER SIXTEEN

They sat huddled around the fire, thoughtful in the silence. Edela noticed how gaunt Aleksander looked through the flames. He had always been lean – lean but strong, he would insist with a grin – but now he just looked broken. And starved.

They were waiting on the night, neither imagining that what they were hoping for would actually work. But hoping, nonetheless.

To dream walk, Edela needed Jael to be asleep, but who knew when that would be. So they would wait, a good, long while, to ensure that Edela would find her dreaming.

Aleksander broke the silence. 'What will you say? If you contact her?'

Edela started. 'I, I will just warn her. Tell her what I saw. I've seen nothing more since that day on the beach. I know as little as I did then, unfortunately. I can only warn her and hope that it will be enough to keep her safe until I know more.' She thought for a moment, her forehead creasing. 'There are ways to help protect her. Tuuran symbols to ward off evil. I should have thought about that before she left. Hopefully, there is someone on Oss who can tattoo her in the Tuuran way.'

Aleksander looked sceptical. 'But that depends on who she can trust, doesn't it? We can't assume that this girl is the only one like that on the island, whatever she is.'

'Perhaps I'll send Jael to speak to Eadmund's sister? She is someone Jael can trust, I'm sure.'

Aleksander stared at her doubtfully.

Edela thought she heard his stomach rumbling. 'I have some bread left from supper. Would you like some?'

'No,' he muttered, shaking his head. 'No, I'm not hungry.'

'Aleksander, you cannot stop living. If you die of starvation, how will you help Jael?'

He glared at her, suddenly irritated. 'You wanted her to be with him, didn't you? You thought he'd make her happier than I ever could. That she would love him more.'

Edela sighed. 'I can't help what I see. What I saw,' she said softly, her face pale and sad. 'Yes, I did see that Jael was meant to be with Eadmund and not you. Not to hurt you. Never that. Even though, of course, it does.'

'Hurt me?' Aleksander stood quickly, built-up sadness, frustration, and fury finally overflowing. 'It isn't *hurting* me, Edela, it's killing me! To love someone so much... to have them taken away like that... not dead but given to another man who she doesn't love. Not now, at least. Hopefully not ever, despite what you see! And all I can do is stay here, alone, and know that everyone thinks this is how it must be. That I should just leave it all alone! Let it happen. Stay away. Not get involved. Let the woman I love, who loves me, be with another man. Be his wife! Have his child!' He stared at Edela in despair. 'It's not hurting me! I feel as though I'm slowly dying without her! And whether you think that sounds pathetic or not, I don't care. I can't be without her. I just can't!'

Aleksander sat down again, deflated, crying, broken.

Edela got up to comfort him, kneeling beside his shuddering body, holding his hand, stroking his hair, heavy with the guilt of her part in his pain.

***

The puppies were pleased to see Jael.

They wiggled themselves into a wailing frenzy of excitement, happy that she was finally home. Jael was being far too soft with them, she knew, but their affection was welcome at the moment, so she barely told them off as they lunged and jumped, begging for attention as she sat down by the fire. She couldn't feel her hands as she thawed them near the flames.

'So you've managed to shake him off again?' Biddy wondered with a wry smile, handing Jael a cup of milk.

Jael wrapped her fingers around the warm cup. 'I have, thankfully.' She took a quick sip, but the milk was too hot and burned her tongue. 'He spent most of the evening just staring at his ale. I thought he might have turned some corner, but it didn't last long, and he ended up a blathering mess again.'

'Poor man,' Biddy said thoughtfully. 'Must be that he can't control himself when it comes to drink. My father was a bit like that. Well, a lot like that.'

'Was he?' Jael was surprised. Biddy no longer had any family living, and her childhood was something she'd always kept to herself.

Or, was it that Jael had never asked?

'I remember my mother saying that he couldn't help himself. That he was always trying his hardest not to drink, but that he'd been born without any self-control, so it wasn't really his fault.'

'And what happened to him?'

Biddy stared down at her chapped hands. 'He ruined us all. He drank and gambled all our coins away, so my mother ended up miserable, alone, and in debt. She tried to help him, to change him, and sometimes he wanted her help, I remember that. But there was nothing to be done for him. No matter how hard she tried, he never changed. He just got worse, and eventually, he was killed in a fight.'

'Oh, I'm sorry,' Jael said quietly.

'It was too long ago to matter much now,' Biddy murmured, picking up a whimpering Ido. 'But it does make me feel sorry for

Eadmund. You might laugh and not want him here, and I can't blame you for that, but perhaps he needs your understanding more than your scorn?'

'Perhaps,' Jael considered. 'But I'm not looking for a friend. I'm not even looking for a husband. He has family and friends, many friends. Let them take care of him. They seem to have been managing that without me. I just need to survive him, survive this place, and find a way back to Aleksander. I can't waste my time trying to help someone who can't even help himself. Someone who has no future as a king or a man.'

Biddy frowned at Jael, disappointed but not surprised by her harsh words.

Jael stood, wanting to escape the conversation. 'I'm going to bed.'

Vella raced to follow her as she quickly finished the milk and took her cup to the kitchen. 'I know I could be kinder, Biddy, but if I stop to think about Eadmund, I won't be able to focus on getting us home.' She walked towards the bedchamber. 'I don't want a part of his future. If he's going to drink himself dead, it's not something I choose to worry about. Goodnight.' And shrugging off all thoughts of Eadmund, Jael headed for bed and her dreams of Aleksander.

***

Evaine was surprised to see Eadmund so early in the evening but thrilled that he had indeed come, as promised.

Eadmund had given up having a servant years ago. None could abide his ways – the mess he left, the mess he was – and so caring for him and his home was something that Evaine had eagerly taken on, without Eadmund ever really being aware of it. He was not in the cottage a lot, but when he was, she tried to make sure that it was clean, warm, well-lit, and well-stocked for him.

As he rushed to sit by the fire, shivering uncontrollably, Evaine snatched a fur off the bed, wrapping it around his shoulders. 'Eadmund! Where's your cloak?' She was horrified. 'How could you go out in the cold with just your tunic on?'

It was her turn to talk to him like a child now, it seemed. The irony was lost on Eadmund, though. He sat shuddering and silent, staring at the flames.

Had that just happened?

Had he let himself be dragged away from his friends, his drink, his fun? Thrown against a wall in a dark alley and ordered about by her? His wife. Gone along with it all like a docile dog? Ordered away from their marriage bed too? Not that he wanted to be in that bed with her, but still...

Eadmund's head continued to ring with the sound of Jael's voice. His forehead creased, his shoulders slumped in disappointment. At himself. Again.

Evaine was worried by Eadmund's continued silence. 'Are you alright? Eadmund?' She came to sit beside him, resting her hand on his leg. She'd been lying in bed, almost asleep, hoping that he would come and now she felt cold sitting around in just her nightdress. She opened up Eadmund's fur and nestled under it, inhaling the rich infusion of smoke, ale, and meat that was so familiar to her. Everyone else might want to change Eadmund, but to Evaine, he was exactly how she wanted him to be.

He was hers.

'Is there any ale left in the jug?' Eadmund wondered, looking urgently towards the kitchen.

'Ale?' Evaine got up immediately. 'Of course, I'll get you some.'

'No!' He reached out, placing a hand on her arm, shaking his head. 'No, don't. I don't want any.'

She sat back down again, under the fur, leaning into him, but he didn't say a word as he continued to stare into the flames.

***

Jael thought about Eadmund and didn't want to. She kept seeing his sad eyes, and they threatened her sleep. He was hopeless, she told herself. There was no point in trying to help him; he couldn't even help himself. She remembered what Thorgils had told her about Ivaar. About what would happen if Eadmund ruined his last chance. She wondered what Ivaar would do if he came?

Would she still be here then?

Jael kicked herself, annoyed that she was wasting her time on Eadmund, instead of dreaming about Aleksander. But it avoided having to acknowledge how alone she was in the enormous bed; how cold her feet were without his legs to warm them on. She sighed, closing her eyes, at last, remembering Aleksander's hands on her face and the kindness in his eyes when he smiled at her. She scratched her hand in frustration, annoyed that she couldn't be with him. That she wasn't free anymore. Or, at least, free enough to choose her own bed companion.

Jael tried to picture every part of their horrible old cottage: the smell, the fire, the warmth of their furs, the feel of his long straight hair as she stroked it slowly...

***

Edela checked inside the basket once more, hoping she had everything she needed. She ran her eyes over the book that sat on the floor to her left.

It was open on the right page. Waiting.

'It must be late enough now, Edela?' Aleksander asked impatiently. 'We should get started.'

Edela nodded. He was right, she thought. She had been

delaying on many more grounds than the possibility that Jael wasn't asleep yet. She felt nervous, never having attempted to use her gifts in this way. After all, it was forbidden, and that gave her cause for concern. But knowing that this was the only way they could think of to warn Jael kept her walking down that uncomfortable path. 'Blow out the lamps,' she instructed, her voice husky and low. 'I need to focus on the fire alone.'

Aleksander was relieved. He got up to blow out all three lamps, then came back to join her on the floor, next to the fire. Edela had insisted on sitting on the floorboards, but she looked very uncomfortable with her legs crossed awkwardly in front of her, peering at the book in earnest.

'What should I do?' Aleksander wondered.

'Well, you need to start tapping on that drum when I close my eyes. Keep a steady rhythm going, and don't stop. It will help take me into the trance and hopefully, keep me there.'

Aleksander picked up the wooden drum that Edela had borrowed from one of Andala's musicians. He hit the skin firmly with his hand a few times. 'Like this?'

'Yes, keep going,' she said, distracted now, removing herself from him and the darkened room. The only light now was the warm, orange glow of the fire; its flames highlighting the sharp lines of concentration on her face.

Edela reached into the basket and emptied its contents onto the floorboards in front of her. There were bunches of herbs, most of them painstakingly collected by Aleksander, but also five smooth river stones that Edela had painted symbols onto; Tuuran symbols that made no sense to Aleksander. Bending down to select each stone carefully, Edela started to place the stones at various points around herself, now and then pausing to close her eyes and breathe deeply.

After one last, quick glance at the book, she picked up a small bronze bowl that she had placed nearby, swirling its contents with her fingers. Edela started painting, thick red lines from stone to stone, creating a circle, enclosing herself within the sacred space.

She had sacrificed a young goat for its blood and felt a sharp pang of guilt as she painted. Thankfully, Jael had not taken everything with her, and they had been able to find a few strands of hair on her pillow to mix into the blood.

Aleksander kept drumming, a slow, steady rhythm as Edela picked up the bundles of herbs and threw them onto the flames. The fire spat and crackled angrily, loudly, the room quickly filling with a heady fug that made Aleksander's eyes water. He couldn't stop coughing. He peered at Edela, worried that he was disturbing her, but her head was back, her eyes closed as she swayed calmly to his rhythm, inhaling deeply, untroubled. The smoke sent Aleksander's head spinning, and he had to fight a desperate urge to rush outside and take a deep breath of fresh air. They had built the fire up so high that even on this freezing night, he could feel sweat trickling down his back.

Edela started chanting, repeating the same unfamiliar phrases, over and over. Her voice sounded deep, not like her at all. The hairs on Aleksander's arms rose in fear and uncertainty, but he drummed on.

Edela rocked back and forth now, her voice growing louder. Aleksander found himself swaying along to the rhythm, his head lost in the smoke, his mind twisting with peculiar visions.

Edela stopped suddenly and remained still, her eyes closed. The room was silent, apart from the occasional pop from the fire, and Aleksander's drumming. He tried to clear his mind, to focus on that steady rhythm she needed from him. She had gone, he realised, gone to try and reach Jael.

He closed his eyes, praying to Eseld that she'd make it there and back safely.

***

In Jael's dream, she was watching Eadmund fight Tarak. She was standing so close that she could see every bead of sweat, every drop of blood fly from Eadmund's face as Tarak hit him, again and again with his giant-sized, bloody fist.

Eadmund had his feet planted on the ground as he swayed, taking every fierce blow without flinching, smiling through bloodied teeth, daring Tarak on, goading him into hurting him, over and over.

Jael didn't understand.

Why was he doing it? Why didn't he fight back? She could see how to beat Tarak. She could help Eadmund, show him how to escape alive.

But she didn't move. She didn't speak.

Jael looked to her right. Eirik and Thorgils were watching, and Eydis, Morac, Evaine; all the people she knew on Oss. And not one of them moved. Their faces were impassive, watching Tarak destroy this man they all professed to care about. No one moved. Why? Why wouldn't anyone help him? She turned back to Eadmund. He was going to die soon. Jael was certain of it. As the fight carried on, Tarak's smile grew wider, his confidence surging, his pleasure in his opponent's humiliation palpable.

Jael turned back to the crowd, demanding that someone do something; calling out now, but no one heard her. Then she saw Edela, and her breathing slowed. Edela didn't look like the rest of them, all dressed in pale colours as they were. She was wearing her familiar dark-red cloak, her face tight with tension as she hurried towards her granddaughter.

'Jael!'

'Grandmother!' Jael called. 'You have to do something! You have to stop the fight before he's killed!'

Edela looked around, puzzled. 'What fight?'

Jael turned to show her, but it had all gone. They were nowhere now, and she felt confused. What had happened to Eadmund? Had he survived?

'Jael, I must speak with you urgently,' Edela breathed. 'I've seen a dark threat, here on Oss. Come and sit, there is much I have to tell you, and I'm not sure how long I'll be able to hold on.'

Edela motioned Jael over to a long wooden bench that she hadn't noticed before. The ground was covered in snow, but Jael didn't feel cold. She didn't even have a cloak on. In fact, as she looked down, she saw that she was wearing her wedding dress. She reached out a hand and saw her ring, too big for her finger, its small twists of gold, glinting under the harsh sun. Everything was white and bright, Jael noticed as she looked around. They were all alone. There was nothing to see, as far as her eye wandered. Nothing but this wooden bench, sitting amongst the snow.

'Are you dead?' Jael wondered suddenly. 'Did you die on the way back to Andala?'

Edela didn't have time for much of an explanation. 'No, I am safe at home with Aleksander. He is with me, helping me. I have travelled into your dreams to warn you.'

'About what?'

'A girl with a white cloak and a scorched face.'

'A scorched face?' Jael stared at Edela, puzzled. 'There is a girl with a white cloak that I know of, but a scorched face? I don't understand.'

'She was down on the beach when we left, standing not far behind you and Eadmund. She was young, I thought. Perhaps a bit older than Amma. She smiled at me so knowingly, and when I blinked and tried to clear my vision, I saw her face as a scorched mask of darkness. It was a warning. An omen. And I wanted to run back to you then, to tell you, but they pulled me onto the ship, and there was nothing I could do.'

Jael looked troubled. 'You don't think it was just a vision? A waking sort of dream?'

'I cannot tell you what it was,' Edela sighed, shaking her head. 'But I do know that you're in danger. The smile on her face? That was a threat. It was as though she had you now. That you were trapped with her.'

'Do you think it's part of your dream about the Darkness?'

'Yes,' Edela said. 'There was menace in her eyes. Her intentions are evil, I know it.'

'What should I do?' Jael wondered. 'Keep watching her? Kill her?'

Edela shook her head. 'I'm not sure what you can do about her, not yet, but no, you can't kill her without reason. You can keep yourself protected and safe from the threat she poses, though.'

'Well, I have my sword, but I don't imagine that's what you mean.'

'No, it's not. I want you to have these Tuuran symbols tattooed on your arms.' Edela turned her palms over to reveal two small grey stones, painted with dark-red symbols. 'Find someone on Oss to tattoo these onto your arms. One on the left, one on the right.'

Jael took the stones from Edela; they felt hot in her hands.

'Here,' Edela instructed, reaching up to touch the tops of Jael's arms, just below her shoulders. 'Make sure they're done up here. In woad. There will be a ritual needed with the ink. Tuuran words must be spoken. Talk to Eydis, ask her advice. Hopefully, she'll know how to ensure the ink is given the blessing of protection. I'm sure she will help.'

Jael's head was overflowing with things to remember, but more urgently, with the desire to know what had happened to Eadmund. Had Tarak killed him? Was he dead?

'Jael!' Edela hissed urgently, sensing her granddaughter's daze. 'Do you understand? You must remember these symbols. I'm not sure what that girl is, what evil she might possess. I will dream more, find any information I can, but you must keep yourself safe from her. We cannot reach you until spring, and I don't think I'll have the strength to walk into your dreams again.'

'I will, I promise,' Jael insisted, placing the stones on the bench and reaching for Edela's hands. 'Stay awhile, Grandmother. Don't go. Please. Tell me about Aleksander.'

'Jael...' Edela looked pained. 'He... he is well. He will be fine, but it will take some time. I must go. I can't stay. Be safe. Please be safe. And talk to Eydis. About the tattoos. Ask her to help you. Perhaps she might know of something like this. She is wiser and more powerful than she realises.'

Jael could feel Edela's bony hands slipping from her grasp. 'Don't go yet. Please, Grandmother. Don't leave...'

But it was too late. Jael watched as Edela's red cloak slipped away, and soon she was holding nothing but air.

***

Edela's eyes burst open. Her head jerked forward onto her chest. She started gagging, trying to find a breath. Aleksander jumped up to grab her before she tipped into the fire.

Edela's face was ghostlike, covered in a pale sheen of sweat, her breathing laboured. Aleksander helped her crumpled body onto the bed and hurried to open the door, ushering in a burst of fresh air. Inhaling quickly and deeply, he felt his head start to clear. Taking a piece of kindling, he lit a lamp beside Edela's bed and came to kneel at her side. 'Edela?'

'Water,' she croaked, her voice barely there. 'Water. Please.'

Aleksander rushed to the kitchen and brought back a full cup of water. He helped her to sit up, but she was so weak that she had to lean against him as she steadily drank it down.

'More. Please.' Her voice was coming back now.

Pouring her another cup, Aleksander bit down on all the questions that were fighting to escape his mouth. He was desperate to know whether she'd made contact with Jael, but Edela looked ready for sleep.

'Yes, I did,' she smiled weakly, reading his thoughts. 'I did. I did.' And feeling relieved, she let her head drop back onto the pillow.

The room was suddenly cold, and Aleksander covered Edela

up with furs before going to shut the door. He could still taste the residue from the smoke on his tongue, but the night air had cleared most of it out of the cottage, and his head felt almost back to normal. He came to sit on Edela's bed, smoothing her hair out of her closed eyes, hoping that she was going to be alright.

'Don't go,' Edela pleaded quietly, her eyes still closed. 'Please stay.'

Aleksander was surprised by that, but of course, he thought, she shouldn't be alone. 'I will,' he promised, but she was already asleep, her jaw slack, her breathing hoarse and slow.

Aleksander looked around the cottage. There was a chair, a few pillows, and a spare blanket that he could use. So, carefully stacking a large log onto the dying flames, he blew out the lamp and settled into the thick fur of Edela's chair.

There was no sleep in him, though, just an urgent impatience to find out what had happened. Though, that, he knew, would have to wait until the morning.

CHAPTER SEVENTEEN

Jael woke from her dream, shaking, her body vibrating like an anvil being hammered. She couldn't catch her breath. Her heart was racing. It was a feeling she remembered so vividly. Two years ago she'd woken from a dream in which she'd seen her father about to die. It had felt so real that she hadn't hesitated to act. She'd raced to mount Tig, dragging Aleksander and Ren along. They'd ridden to find Ranuf, who was in Ollsvik, visiting the King of Iskavall. It had taken days to get there, and Ranuf was already sick and dying when they arrived.

He died the very next day, and Jael was still haunted by the memories of that dream. Wishing it had come sooner. Wishing she had been faster.

There was Tuuran in her, of course, but she had never acknowledged the possibility that she shared any of Edela's gifts, no matter how much her grandmother had insisted she did.

It was still dark in the bedchamber, but the puppies were awake now, alert to Jael's distress. Vella left her spot on the corner of the bed to come and nuzzle her cheek and Ido wrapped himself into a ball on the pillow, right next to her ear. Their presence distracted Jael from the panic rising in her chest, and her breathing gradually slowed.

She lifted one hand out of the thick mound of furs and realised that it was clasped tightly as if holding something. Jael opened her fingers, but there was nothing there. No stone. Sighing in frustration, she closed her eyes, sinking back into the dream, trying to remember the symbols on the stones; the symbols that Edela had insisted were so vital to her safety. She could almost see them, but they were quite different from each other, and she couldn't remember exactly how either one looked.

She checked her other hand; nothing there either.

It was so dark and quiet that Jael knew she had hours to wait until dawn. She searched back through the dream once more, closing her eyes, wondering if she could sleep again and slip back into it. But she was simply too alert, too awake for sleep to come now. She saw Evaine's face as her grandmother had painted it, wondering what it meant. If, in fact, Evaine was in love with Eadmund, which, from Jael's observations seemed likely, then Evaine saw her as a threat. And possibly a threat she wanted to remove. But how would she do it?

Obviously not with a sword, but what was she? What could she do?

Jael opened her eyes, annoyed that she had to wait so long for the sun to shed some light on her questions. She picked up Vella, tucking her under the furs, wrapping her arms around the sleepy little body, letting the puppy's warmth soothe her impatient mind.

***

'That smells good,' Edela croaked, swinging her legs over the side of the bed. She coughed, trying to clear her throat which felt drier than she could remember. She tried to ignore the aches in her legs, her knees, her back; the list was endless. She smiled instead at Aleksander, who was cooking bread over the fire.

He straightened up, hurrying to the bed. 'Edela! Are you alright?' Reaching out, he helped her to stand, slowly guiding her towards her fur-covered chair. He grabbed another fur, draping it over Edela's shoulders.

'Oh, to be so doted on every day,' she smiled wearily at him, her eyes puffy and strained.

'Well, I think you deserve it after what you went through last night.' Aleksander turned back to the fire, hoping to save his flatbreads from burning. The little rounds needed to be removed from the skillet but they appeared to have stuck to it instead. He had watched and helped Biddy cook many times as a child, but those memories were dust-covered now, and it was obvious that he'd gone awry somewhere in the process.

'Ahhh, yes, last night,' Edela sighed, letting her head drop back onto the soft fur of the chair. 'I can't believe it worked. Well, at least I hope it did.'

Aleksander managed to scrape the three little flatbreads off the skillet without leaving too much behind. He left them on a plate to cool. 'What happened? Did you really see Jael? Speak to her?'

'I did, yes,' Edela smiled. 'Perhaps you could pour me some water, and I'll tell you all about it.'

Aleksander quickly filled a cup and brought it to her, sitting on the little stool expectantly. Edela felt sad, remembering Jael sitting there, not so many weeks ago. It felt strange knowing that she was so far away. And would be for some time yet.

'Well, I certainly entered her dream and spoke to her. I warned her.' Edela stopped to consider things. 'It felt very real to me. And Jael listened, so I can only hope she remembers what I told her about the girl and the symbols. About how she can protect herself.'

'I can't believe it worked. I was worried about you. That you wouldn't come back.'

'Oh, yes. I felt the same, for sure. I knew I'd left you behind and I could only hope that I'd be able to return. I wouldn't want to leave you even more alone.' She leaned forward, patting Aleksander on the knee. 'Thank you for staying last night. I wasn't sure what state I'd end up in, but I appear to have a beating heart and a working tongue, still!'

And a way of contacting Jael, Aleksander thought to himself. He could only hope that Jael had heard the message and was able to do something to protect herself. To keep herself safe.

He hoped that it would be enough.

***

Jael ended up lost, twice, but finally, she found her way to Fyn's hut in the hill. She'd struggled to recognise much that was familiar from her ride with Thorgils. Visibility had been poor for much of her journey. The clouds were thick and dirty with the threat of more snow, or possibly even a storm, if the ferocity of the wind was any indication.

'Jael?' Fyn was outside, practising with his wooden man again.

She smiled as she dismounted, slipping Tig a piece of bread. He seemed to have enjoyed the ride, in spite of the wind, showing more confidence with his footing this time.

'I didn't expect to see you again so quickly,' Fyn said nervously, wandering over to greet her. His face froze. 'I hope you haven't come to train me? I didn't think you'd take Thorgils seriously.'

Jael saw an opportunity. 'Well, yes, I thought I'd come to help, not train you if you don't want me to, but I could give you some advice if you'd like?'

Fyn glanced at his boots. 'I... I'm no good. I'm sure you saw that yesterday. It's not worth your time to try and help me. Although, it's very kind of you, especially as I'm sure you have so many other things you need to do.' He hid his face beneath his hair, not knowing where to look.

Jael walked Tig over to a small covered shelter where Fyn kept his woodpile and tied him up. 'What sort of things do you imagine me having to do?' she asked over her shoulder.

Fyn scurried after her. 'Ummm, well I'm not sure. You are a... princess. But I'm not quite sure what they do.'

'Princess? Yes, I suppose I am,' Jael laughed, heading for the slushy ground where Fyn had placed his wooden friend. 'But I think most princesses spend all day fussing over their hair and dresses, don't they?' She took off her cloak and sword-belt, placing them on a log, noting the sizable pile of wooden swords stacked nearby, many of them broken. Fingering through them, she pulled out one that appeared in good condition. 'But I'm not bothered about what I wear, and, as for my hair... as long as it's not flapping around my face while I'm trying to remove someone's head, I'm happy.' She spun around, pointing the sword at Fyn, her eyes sharp. 'Let's begin.'

Fyn gulped, reluctantly stepping towards her, every part of his body clenched in fear. His shoulders were up around his ears, his sword held awkwardly in front of his waist.

'Well, there's your first problem,' Jael said evenly. 'You need to face your opponent more from the side. Don't give him so much to aim at. Here, like this.' She dropped her sword back into the pile and came over to grab hold of Fyn's shoulders, turning him slightly side-on, spreading his legs into a more stable position. Fyn flinched from her touch. 'You need to be balanced at all times, especially when wielding an actual sword and shield. They can be heavy, so it's much easier to be knocked off balance, and if you have no balance you'll likely end up on your arse, and that's a hard place to defend from.'

Jael picked up her sword again. It was smooth and well made. 'You obviously have a lot of time on your hands out here. How many of these swords have you carved?'

'Many,' Fyn said sadly. 'Too many.'

Jael felt sorry for him, and as much as she was desperate to talk to him about his sister, she knew that she needed to convince him to trust her first. Fyn's eyes told her that he didn't trust anyone much. She would have to take it slowly. 'Well, perhaps you could work on some shields next?' she smiled, coming forward. 'But in the meantime, I can teach you how to defend yourself with whatever you have to hand. There'll be times when all you have is your eating knife, or maybe not even that.'

Fyn held his sword loosely, watching Jael's every move as she strutted around in front of him.

'So, here you are, someone wants to kill you, and they have a sword, you have a sword, nothing else. The ground is mucky. The sky is murky. You have no shield. There are many things against you right now, but many things in your favour also. First, you're in your own surroundings so you can use that knowledge to help you. Think of what you may have lurking around that you could use as a weapon if your sword were to break or be lost. Think.' Jael tapped her head with her free hand as she circled in front of Fyn, her two side braids flapping angrily in the wind. 'That's how you start a fight, with an alert mind. A thought-filled mind. Always thinking. Think about your opponent, too. Look into his eyes. Is he tired? Weary? Injured? Many warriors are carrying old wounds that haven't quite healed. That makes them weaker. Find those places. Look for clues. Does he favour one leg or the other? Wince when you aim for a particular spot? Keep watching, keep looking. Does he smell?'

Fyn looked surprised. 'Smell?'

'Yes,' Jael grinned. 'Sick, rotting wounds smell. They have a stink you'll become familiar with. Blood, the smell of blood, is iron-strong. It lingers on a person. Use every sense you have to keep thinking, forming ideas. You may be fighting with a sword, or your hands, or an axe, but mostly I think, you're fighting with your mind. That's what my father taught me.'

Jael lunged forward, knocking Fyn's sword out of his hand, her wooden blade coming to rest in the middle of his chest.

Fyn gasped, stumbling away.

'Always keep thinking, Fyn,' she said, bending down to pick

up his sword. 'What's my opponent doing? Why are they doing it? To confuse you, relax you, make you more comfortable than you should be? And most importantly, hold onto your sword!' She laughed, and Fyn's face relaxed.

He took the sword from her, holding it firmly.

'You need to think of it as part of your arm,' Jael insisted. 'You wouldn't want to lose the bottom half of your arm, would you? Not without a fight, I'm sure. You'd grip that arm so tightly that no one could take it. You have to feel the same about your sword. You lose your sword, you're half dead.' She watched as his hand squeezed around the grip. 'Tighter. Even tighter. Get your fingers used to it, to how much pressure you need to exert for it to feel natural but secure.'

Satisfied with Fyn's hold, at last, Jael went back to her starting position. 'Alright, so remember to stand more to the side. To think, all the time, about everything. And to hold onto your sword like losing it will mean death.'

Fyn nodded eagerly, and Jael smiled. He was standing taller now, his fingers wrapped firmly around his sword's grip. His body was positioned side-on, his legs wide enough to balance him, and his eyes were alert. He was a fast learner. And he was showing signs that he was beginning to trust her.

That was a start.

***

Eadmund vomited onto a mound of snow. He spat twice to try and clear the taste of sour ale from his throat, wiping a hand over his short beard.

'Ahhh, I can see why the ladies like you so much,' Thorgils laughed. 'Who wouldn't want to kiss that tasty mouth?'

'Shut up,' Eadmund grumbled irritably, swallowing again.

He felt worse than he could remember. Nausea, the headache, and the aches and pains were all familiar feelings, but they weren't what was troubling him. It was the realisation, finally dawning, that he was no longer a man. He'd seen it last night in Jael's eyes, more clearly than he'd ever seen it before. And it wouldn't leave. It clawed its way inside his head and would not leave.

The picture of who he had become was so sharp now.

He was desperate to escape its mocking vision.

Torstan snorted, breathing white fumes, holding his sword, waiting for Thorgils. The temptation of glory in the contest had roused more than a few Osslanders out of their cold beds earlier than usual. None more so than Thorgils. But why Eadmund was up so early was a question on both his friends' lips.

'You're not used to this hour, it seems,' Thorgils smiled as he touched swords with Torstan before stepping back into position. He was eager to get their practice underway before the weather put an end to it. The sky was dull with the promise of another heavy dump of snow that day, and small flurries were already drifting across the Pit. 'Perhaps you need to crawl back between Evaine's warm thighs a while longer?'

Eadmund frowned as his friends giggled. 'Thank you, but no, I've come to watch you two idiots try to figure out how you're going to defeat Tarak.'

Serious looks replaced grins then, as both men hardened their expressions.

'Well, there's no hope for Torstan here, of course,' Thorgils said confidently, 'for he's never even beaten me, and besides, he only comes up to Tarak's knee!'

Torstan raised his sword at that, swinging sharply at his much-larger friend. Thorgils brought his wooden blade down, expertly turning it over to crash onto Torstan's sword.

Torstan shuddered from the force of the blow, stepping back to regain his balance. 'Tarak's knee?' he wondered crossly. 'At least down at his knee I don't have to sniff his ballsack like you do!' He shot forward, extending his sword in an attempt to hit

Thorgils low but Thorgils was feeling sharp-eyed, and once again he parried Torstan's strike.

Torstan backed off, frustrated, his mind whirring.

'You could always come and show us how *you* managed to defeat Tarak,' Thorgils suggested, his eyes fixed firmly on his prowling opponent. 'If you can still remember?'

Eadmund smiled wistfully, leaning over the railings that ringed the Pit. That was an old memory, but yes, he remembered some of it still. 'I'd like to say there was a reason behind it, but likely it was just luck from the gods. I'm not sure he's beatable by anyone here on Oss. Not anymore.'

'Not even your wife?' Thorgils asked as he feinted left, leaving Torstan stumbling as he struck him across the stomach.

Torstan grumbled, annoyed with himself for taking Thorgils' bait.

'That would be one point to me,' Thorgils nodded cheerfully.

'Jael?' Eadmund scoffed. 'You think *she* could beat Tarak?'

'Me? No, I don't think she can. Perhaps with her tongue, but no, her size would count against her, for sure, just like Torstan here. Tarak would break her.'

'I'm not that much bigger than Jael and certainly not as big as you,' Eadmund pointed out. 'But I defeated him. So perhaps there's a chance for you after all, Torstan?'

Thorgils, puzzling on that, allowed himself to be distracted long enough for Torstan to make a sharp attack on his left, weaker side, hitting him on the hip.

'I believe that's one point each,' Torstan smiled smugly.

Thorgils frowned, turning to Eadmund. 'Go and find yourself a drink and stop distracting me. I have to focus both my mind and body on defeating this little turd here.'

Thorgils meant it jokingly, of course, but Eadmund's face fell. He'd woken up early, seeking a new purpose, and had come to find his friends with the half-formed idea of picking up a sword; maybe taking the first steps towards learning how to use it again. But it had been so long, and Thorgils and Torstan had forgotten who he used to be just as much as he had.

He shrugged, defeated, and turned to leave.

'Or you could get into the Pit and pick up a sword?' Thorgils called after him. 'Show us how it's done?'

Eadmund stopped. The suggestion of a drink was far more appealing than the idea of making a fool of himself. But he heard Jael's condescending voice, and some long-dormant pool of anger started to bubble up inside him, overtaking all other fears and desires. He turned around, walking back to the railings. 'Alright,' he smiled, more confidently than he felt, his knees shaking from more than the cold. 'I can do that.'

***

'So, that's what I need you to dream on,' Eirik murmured, guiding Eydis around a puddle of slush. He didn't want everyone knowing his business, nor how reliant he was on a thirteen-year-old girl's advice. He didn't want to put Eydis in that position. There was a suspicion, of course, amongst most Osslanders that Eydis had inherited her late mother's gifts, but Eirik kept her abilities close to his chest. Eadmund was only one of a handful who knew that his daughter was a dreamer.

'I'll try, Father,' Eydis promised. 'But it doesn't always work like that. Not for me. Not without any training.'

'I understand that, of course,' Eirik said distractedly, waving to Morac who was walking to the hall ahead of them. 'But if there is any sign I should pay attention to, I would gratefully receive it. I'm committing many lives to this invasion. I don't want to waste a single one of them. Not after last time.'

Eydis could hear the tension in her father's voice. She could feel the weight on his shoulders, but she didn't feel confident that she would be able to help him. She felt no mastery over her dreams.

Eirik suddenly gripped Eydis' hand so tightly that she cried out. 'Father! What is it?' She was immediately on edge, desperate to know what was happening, but Eirik remained silent.

Silent, because he had just been rendered speechless.

'Father?' Eydis turned towards him.

'It's your brother,' Eirik said, shaking his head in disbelief. 'He's in the Pit. With a sword. He has a sword in his hand!' He was amazed, almost tearful. He had almost given up hope of witnessing such a thing again.

'Eadmund?' Eydis was just as overcome. 'Truly?' There were tears in her eyes, her face shining with happiness and relief in equal measure.

'Truly.'

Eirik watched as Eadmund stumbled around the muddy Pit. He looked awkward and unsure, there was no doubting that, but he was there, sword in hand, face flushed with effort, and that was the best gift Eirik could have imagined.

There was hope.

***

'Hit me.'

'No! I can't do that,' Fyn insisted, shocked that Jael would suggest such a thing.

'True,' Jael acknowledged. '*Try* to hit me.'

Fyn had shown some improvement with his sword, but swords had been abandoned now, and Jael was teaching him how to defend himself using only his body. Despite his growing confidence, though, Fyn was reluctant to try and hurt her.

'I think, perhaps we should stop. The snow is getting heavier... we should head inside to the fire...' He started edging back to his hut.

'Fyn!' Jael glared at him. 'You want to be a warrior? Well, you can be. There's nothing wrong with you. Nothing is stopping you, except a lack of knowledge and some confidence.' She stood in front of him, her nose dripping, and despite the tension she felt about her dream, she was enjoying herself. 'It took me years to learn how to protect myself. How to kill when I had to, to keep my people safe. My father trained me so hard that I spent most of my childhood in tears, covered in cuts and bruises. But he didn't care what I thought, or how hard I believed it was, or how much I complained. He needed to know that I'd be safe. He wanted me to learn everything, to master every way I could possibly keep myself alive. So he never gave up trying. He never gave up forcing me to try.'

Fyn could see the passion in her eyes when she talked about her father. He wished he could feel the same way about his own.

'So now, because of all that work we both put in, nothing scares me,' Jael insisted. 'I have fear. I get nervous before a battle or a fight, but I never feel scared because I know I can find a way to stay alive. I've got confidence in what I can do. If you have that, then you can welcome the shakes or the shits, and you can just move forward and kill to survive.'

Fyn stared at Jael, trying to locate that pit of confidence that lived so far down inside himself, he often wondered if it existed at all. Her words resonated with him, though, so he dug deep and pushed back his shoulders, lifting his head. 'Alright,' he decided at last. 'I'll try.'

Jael smiled. She felt genuinely pleased as she stepped back and put her hands up in tight fists. 'Good. I'll defend myself a little, and you try to hit me.' She moved from side to side. 'But do try, Fyn, because my tits are freezing out here!'

Fyn looked so shocked that Jael burst out laughing.

He gulped in a deep, icy breath and came forward, circling in front of her, his fists close to his chest, white trails of winter-cold puffing from his nose and mouth. He smiled in an attempt to distract her, and then rushed one fist towards her face, but he was slow and predictable, and Jael effortlessly knocked it away.

'Go for where my hands *aren't*, Fyn,' she suggested. 'As far away from them as possible. There are no rules in a fight for your life. You want to kill your attacker as quickly as possible. So you can dance around in front of me all you like, but I'm just thinking about getting you on the ground. That's your goal. Get me on the ground.'

Fyn looked daunted but undeterred, and he started circling again, assessing his options. Jael was alert and fast in her movements, but he took her advice and tried to surprise her with a swift jab at her stomach. He used his left hand, which did surprise her, but as he wasn't naturally strong with it, the hand came at her too slowly, allowing her to anticipate its fall. Jael twisted backwards, grounded her weight on her left foot, and swung her right leg around, snapping her boot quickly into the side of Fyn's head.

He flew into the snow.

'Are you alright?' Jael asked, trying not to laugh at the look on Fyn's face as he sat up and stared at her, horrified.

'You kicked me in the head!'

'Yes. And now you're on the ground, and I can finish you off,' she grinned, holding out a hand. 'But I won't because you've promised me a hot fire, for now, my tits are truly frozen!'

Fyn took her hand. 'You kicked me in the head,' he repeated, staggering to his feet.

'Does it hurt?'

'A little, but not as much as my pride,' he smiled bashfully. 'That hurts quite a lot. I'm glad Thorgils wasn't here.'

Jael laughed, walking over to give Tig a couple of small carrots that had frozen in her pocket. Happily, his little shelter was mostly snow-tight and almost large enough to keep him comfortable. The sky was darkening, though, and she was conscious of the need to have her conversation with Fyn before conditions made their return journey treacherous.

'Did your father teach you that? Kicking people in the head?' Fyn wondered as he waited for her to follow him into the hut.

'Not him, no. He never did that,' Jael frowned, imagining her very stern, traditional father doing such a thing. 'But he found someone who did.' She followed Fyn inside, rubbing her frozen hands together. 'He brought people to Brekka from all over the world to train me. As I said, he was driven by a desire to keep me safe. So he tried to find every way possible.'

The fire barely had any life in it, so Fyn grabbed his poker and added a handful of kindling.

'You must get so lonely living here,' Jael suggested, looking around his miserable hut. 'With no one to talk to every day.'

Fyn looked up at her, trying to mask his sadness. 'Well, I've never been good at talking to people, so I don't mind it too much.' He grabbed his cauldron and hung it over the struggling fire, filling it with water.

Jael sat down, close to the flames, desperate to feel some heat. 'What about your family?' she wondered, trying to subtly edge towards the subject of Evaine. 'Don't you miss them? I think you said your mother visits you? But what about your sister?'

Subtlety wasn't Jael's strongest skill.

Fyn shuddered.

'Evaine, isn't it?' she continued. 'I met her the other day. A very pretty girl.'

'I suppose,' he said tightly. 'But not especially kind.'

'No? That's a shame for you. A mean father and a mean sister. That's some bad luck.'

Fyn saw that she looked genuinely sorry for him. He sprinkled some dried leaves into two cups. 'Do you like lemon balm?'

'Yes, perfect,' Jael smiled wistfully, remembering her grandmother's favourite tonic for any ailment.

'It is bad luck, I suppose, but I have a kind mother. A good mother,' he considered as he placed the cups on a stool, grabbing a small jar nearby and scooping out a tiny dollop of honey into each. 'It's not easy on her, that I'm here and she is alone with...

them.'

'Your sister is difficult, then?'

Fyn raised an eyebrow. 'Difficult? More than difficult. She isn't evil, she just... she considers no one but herself. Ever. She's used to getting what she wants, and she has this ability to remove anyone or anything that stands in her way.'

'How?'

'How?' Fyn peered into the cauldron, watching for bubbles. 'I'm not sure. Perhaps it's the way she looks or...' He paused. 'I don't know. Except that, of course, she didn't get her way where Eadmund was concerned.'

Jael's ears pricked up. 'Eadmund?'

Fyn realised that his tongue had wandered far away from his head. 'Oh, I...'

'It's alright,' Jael rushed to reassure him. 'I can tell that she has feelings for Eadmund. I don't care. I have none myself.'

'Feelings?' Fyn looked doubtful. 'It's not feelings that she has. It's an obsession.' He spoke freely now, encouraged by Jael's casual interest and calm words. 'She's been obsessed with Eadmund since she was a child. Which is strange, don't you think?'

'Perhaps it's true love? Perhaps they are fated?'

'It's something, that's for sure. It's all she spoke about for years. All she ever wanted to talk about.'

'And now there's me,' Jael pondered. 'Her biggest obstacle yet. So, what do you think she is going to do about me?' She watched Fyn's face, looking for any clues as to what he truly thought but might be too timid to reveal.

But she had underestimated him.

'I couldn't say,' Fyn said. 'But I'd be very careful around her. There's something about Evaine that is... dangerous. I can't explain it, but I believe she'd do anything to get Eadmund back. Absolutely anything.'

Jael ran a cold hand over her lips, frowning. It was nothing she didn't suspect already, but having her fears confirmed was a good start. She needed more, though. 'There is no Tuuran blood in her, is there?' she asked softly, keeping her voice light. 'She doesn't possess any gifts I should be worried about?'

'Gifts?' Fyn frowned, shaking his head. 'Not that I'm aware of. Perhaps that would explain some things, but no, our parents were both born as slaves, here on Oss. There's nothing special about her that I know of.'

Jael was disappointed. Fyn didn't know anything that could help her. There was no explanation for the face Edela had seen, except that perhaps it was a warning, painted so darkly that it was impossible to ignore. A warning for her to stay alert around this obsessed girl who meant her genuine harm.

Or was it more?

Jael's mind wandered back to her dream, and she was reminded of the symbols and Edela's insistence that she get tattooed to protect herself. Jael blinked watching Fyn rubbing the side of his head. 'Is your head alright?'

He grinned. 'It still works, I think.'

'That's good,' Jael smiled, standing up.

Fyn stumbled to his feet. 'You don't have to leave just yet, do you? You haven't had your tea, and I can heat us up some stew I saved from yesterday.'

'No, no, that's generous of you, but I think the snow will make it much harder to find our way back if we don't leave now,' Jael insisted very firmly, not wanting to revisit the taste of that stew ever again. 'Besides, more stew for you to enjoy. You'll need a good meal after all that training.'

Fyn looked disappointed to be losing her company.

'If you don't mind getting kicked some more, I'll come again,' Jael suggested, heading out into the snow.

'Yes, that would be good. Perhaps next time, I'll see you coming!' Fyn laughed, walking her to the shelter where Tig was starting to get impatient.

'I don't think so, but I like your confidence,' Jael grinned, untying his reins.

Fyn glanced at Jael. 'Be careful around Evaine,' he said, wiping the snow out of his eyes. 'I can't say she'd be foolish enough to try and hurt you, but I know how much she cares about Eadmund. She won't rest until he belongs to her.'

'Well, she's welcome to him. He's no use to me!' Jael said dismissively, swinging herself up into the damp saddle. 'I shall be back, hopefully, tomorrow if the weather improves, so practice, practice, practice! And start working on those shields. We could use a few of those.'

Jael tapped Tig, and he dug his hooves into the deep snow, slowly gaining traction as he carried her up the hill. She turned around to wave to the lonely figure, isolated in a landscape of almost pure white, wondering just what she was going to do about Fyn's problem sister.

CHAPTER EIGHTEEN

Aleksander failed to look up in time.

He had been meandering slowly towards the square, knee-deep in the memories of his night with Edela, still bothered by the stink of those herbs, when he saw Osbert, Lothar, and Amma blocking his path. Stopping immediately, he realised that they were all looking at him, talking amongst themselves, but watching him. Fighting the urge to turn and run in the opposite direction, Aleksander reluctantly ploughed on.

'My lord.' He acknowledged Lothar with a brief nod of his head. 'Osbert, Amma.'

'Aleksander!' Lothar smiled broadly, one of those fake smiles he used so regularly. 'I wasn't sure we'd ever see you again! Where have you been?'

'Well, I –'

'Father, that is very insensitive of you,' Amma interrupted. 'It must be a hard time for Aleksander, losing Jael as he has.'

Lothar eyed his daughter crossly, not appreciating her public rebuke.

Osbert eyed his sister curiously, noting the pink flush on her cheeks when she looked at Aleksander.

Aleksander didn't know where to look. 'I... yes, it's not the best time, but there's spring to look forward to, and a battle with Hest is always a reason to keep heart.' It sounded trite, but it was the sort of thing Lothar loved to hear, and his face lit up, just as

Aleksander had intended.

'Exactly! Those Dragos' had better sleep well this winter as I'm certain it will be their last.' He puffed out his bulging chest. 'Gisila!' Lothar drew his attention away from Aleksander and gave it to Gisila and Axl, neither of whom looked welcome of it.

'Lothar,' Gisila nodded, her eyes barely acknowledging him before turning to Aleksander. 'How are you?'

Lothar looked peevish. All the attention was on Aleksander today, it seemed.

'I'm fine,' Aleksander mumbled, dismissing her concern. 'I was just going to buy some supplies for Edela. She's feeling unwell today.'

'Is she?' Axl looked worried. 'I'll come with you. I haven't seen her for days.'

Aleksander wasn't keen on acquiring any company, but he nodded. 'She'd like that, I'm sure. I just have to head to the markets first. If you'll excuse me.' And smiling quickly at Gisila, and purposefully ignoring Amma, he slipped through the crowd, Axl loping after him.

'He looks very thin,' Amma said to Gisila. 'Don't you think?'

Gisila wished she hadn't been left behind with Lothar and his children. 'Yes, he does. I'd better go and help him. I don't expect he will make the best choices.'

'No, no, Gisila!' Lothar grabbed her arm with his heavily ringed hand. 'I was hoping you would walk with me instead. There are some matters I wish to discuss with you.'

Gisila looked ill at the thought of being alone with him. 'I, I...'

'Come along now. It won't take long. Just a little chat between old friends.' And he slipped her arm through his, leading her to the hall... the long way.

'Poor Gisila,' Amma giggled, watching them go. 'Father has her trapped.'

'But why would he want to?' Osbert sneered. 'She's no beauty anymore. She has no status, no fortune. She's worth nothing to him.'

'Love isn't about fortune or status,' Amma scolded her older brother.

'Love?' Osbert was horrified. 'You think he *loves* Gisila?' He laughed scornfully.

'You might laugh, Brother, but I'm sure you've spent many nights wishing you had someone to love your miserable soul.'

Osbert's eyebrows pinched together, and he leaned forward, his mouth uncomfortably close to Amma's. She cringed backwards. 'Well, love seems to be on everyone's minds and faces today, doesn't it, Sister?' he smirked. 'Does Father know about your little crush on Aleksander Lehr? Does he? Would he like to know, do you think?'

Amma knew her brother well enough to believe that he'd do as he threatened, but she wasn't about to be cornered by him. He was pathetic, and a bully, and although she knew that he had their father's ear, she was comforted by the fact that she'd always been Lothar's favourite. 'Go ahead. Do as you wish, Osbert. I may just tell Father myself if you don't.' And she turned away, leaving Osbert to simmer in his lonely pile of bitterness.

***

Aleksander frowned at the paltry selection of vegetables on offer at the markets. Admittedly, the weather had affected the availability of fresh produce, but still, the limp fare would hardly be what Edela was hoping he'd bring back for her.

He selected a bunch of tired carrots, a couple of soft turnips, and a withered cabbage. It was something, but not much. He would try and bring her neglected garden back to life once the snow had done its worst. It was better than wasting any coins at the markets.

Handing over two tarnished silver coins as payment, he

shoved the vegetables into his basket, glancing around, hoping the Furycks had gone. They had, from what he could see, but Axl was still waiting for him. He'd quickly grown bored of vegetables and left to talk with a group of friends. Aleksander sighed. They were empty-headed idiots, for the most part, the sort of boys who thought they knew everything. And they were the wrong sort of friends to have whispering in your ear if you wanted to stay alive.

'Axl!' Aleksander called, raising an arm, ushering him over.

Axl came willingly enough, leaving his friends behind.

'Do you still want to come and see Edela?' Aleksander wondered, walking quickly through the busy crowd, mud and snow-wet to his ankles.

'Sure,' Axl smiled, falling in alongside, raising a hand to his friends as they passed.

'What do you think your sister would say if she saw you talking to those fools?' Aleksander asked, trying to keep his voice light.

'They're not fools,' Axl grumbled. 'They're my friends, and what would it be to her anyway if she were here to care?'

'Well, keeping you safe is something she would care about, and those boys are more about making trouble, don't you think?'

'Why do you say that?'

'Because I know boys like that.' Aleksander lowered his voice as they slipped between two rows of houses set right on the street front. 'Boys that want fame and think they can get it the easy way, by riding along on someone else's cloak. Your cloak. Thinking that if you become king, they'll become rich.'

'They're not like that,' Axl insisted. 'They want me to have what I'm owed. What was given to me by my father. That's all. Why shouldn't I have friends who think that? Better than ones who think I'll just be this nothing my whole life.'

The streets merged into broad paths now, thick with uncleared snow as they turned towards Edela's. There were fewer houses, and fewer homeowners willing to shovel the walkways this far away from the square. It was quieter too as they hurried along, the crunch of their boots in the snow suddenly very loud.

Aleksander stopped, grabbing Axl's arm. 'I don't blame you for feeling that way. You've had something taken from you. I've had some experience of that recently,' he smiled wryly, but Axl's face was unmoved. 'They're not going to help you get it back, though. They're just going to get you killed.'

Axl sniffed loudly at that, wiping his nose on the back of his glove. 'So you say, but why shouldn't I give them a chance? Listen to their ideas? Who else is going to help me? Jael? She had her chance. For two years she had her chance to help me change things after Father died, but she did nothing. Both of you did nothing. And now she's gone, so it's up to me to change things. No matter what you say, Aleksander, I'm going to do something... with, or without your help.'

Axl strode off, his head in the air, his body awkwardly trying to catch up with it. He had a purpose, Aleksander thought, but little direction. And that lack of direction, coupled with his bad taste in friends was likely to make things difficult for all of them.

***

It was just Eadmund and Thorgils now. The snow had gotten too much for Torstan, and he'd abandoned them for a hot fire and a plump woman he'd had his eye on lately.

Eadmund was nearly done, though. Every part of his body, every single part, was throbbing in shock at what he'd put it through. He'd not moved this purposefully in years. Thorgils had shown him no mercy at all, relishing the opportunity to beat the shit out of Eadmund for the first time in memory; sending him into the slush, time after time.

'You must be ready to wave your little white banner now, Eadmund Skalleson?' Thorgils mocked merrily, his red beard white with snow. 'If not, I think I'll wave mine. My snow banner! For it's snowing too much to see you! Let's get to the hall and watch Torstan make a fool of himself while we melt by the fire.'

Eadmund couldn't deny that it sounded a much better plan than freezing to death, face down in the slop. He was sure that if Thorgils had knocked him down one more time, he wouldn't have been able to get up. 'Alright, let's wave the banner and be gone! I've had enough of watching you enjoy yourself at my expense. I'd forgotten what a smug bastard you were in a fight. No wonder I stopped fighting you!' he smiled, then grimaced; even his cheeks hurt.

They stored their swords inside the small shed where the training weapons were kept and headed for the hall.

'You never said,' Thorgils started, then stopped to sneeze loudly. 'How were things with your wife last night?'

Eadmund looked puzzled. 'Things?'

'You left the hall together, you idiot, don't you remember?' Thorgils laughed. 'I assumed that things occurred... of a marital nature.' He gave Eadmund a hearty dig in his aching ribs.

'Ha!' Eadmund scoffed, grimacing as he paused outside the doors of the hall. He dropped his voice, peering around. 'The only marital things that occurred were a nagging wife and a bored husband who went their separate ways very quickly. No need to nudge me about that.' He pulled on one of the hall's enormous doors and disappeared inside, desperate for a drink.

'Oh,' Thorgils sighed, catching the door just before it closed. He'd hoped that Eadmund's sudden turnaround was because things with Jael had entered a very necessary phase.

'Do you need some help there, old man?' Jael wondered, walking up to Thorgils as he dawdled in front of the open door, Ido and Vella impatiently jumping up his legs.

Smiling in surprise, Thorgils ushered Jael and the puppies inside. 'You abandoned me for our ride today,' he said, attempting to look hurt as he followed her through the hall, brushing the snow from his beard. 'Poor Leada. Poor me! I was left having to train with those useless fools all morning.' He nodded towards Eadmund and Torstan who were standing in front of a well-stoked fire, laughing with a few other men.

'Who?' Jael wondered, only half listening, distracted by thoughts of finding Eydis. 'You don't mean Eadmund?'

'I do, actually,' Thorgils murmured. 'He picked up a sword. First time in, I think, maybe five years. Maybe longer.'

'He did?' Jael stared at Eadmund in surprise. He certainly did look brighter, somehow; his face appeared flushed with something other than ale. She wasn't sure how she felt about that; annoyed probably. Most of her was still hoping that he'd die and set her free quickly, but there was a small part of her that felt sorry for him, and that very small part smiled.

'He did!' Thorgils laughed, squatting down to give some attention to the wiggling puppies. 'Never thought I'd see that again.'

'Well, maybe he's been inspired to enter the contest,' Jael grinned. 'That might ruin your plans for defeating certain people.' She glanced around, but there was no sign of Tarak. 'Ido, Vella, come, come!' Jael clicked her tongue, and the puppies ignored her completely.

There were a few chortles from the fireside group.

Jael shot them a stern, silencing look.

Thorgils, though, wasn't so shy. 'How long has it been since you had a dog?' he wondered.

'Why?'

'Well, you have to command their respect. Show them that *you're* the leader of their pack, not one of their pack.' He stood up, wincing at the aches in his well-worked muscles. 'So far, I think, they like you, but they're not following you, so you need to show them that you're in charge.'

Jael didn't want to stand about discussing the best way to train puppies; she wanted to find Eydis. 'Well, how about you come and help me do that tomorrow? Show me all your dog skills before we go for a ride. Not too early, though. Mid-morning will be fine.' And with that, she stalked off. The puppies took one last look at Thorgils before deciding to follow her.

Thorgils laughed as he watched her go. She was like a bolt of lightning, that one, he thought to himself. It was very hard not to admire her spirit.

Jael wandered to the end of the hall, peering around, wondering if Eydis was lurking in the dark shadows somewhere. She was just about to head through to the bedchambers when Morac Gallas stepped in front of her.

'Are you looking for someone?' he asked coolly, his voice sliding down her spine like a sliver of ice.

Vella sat back on her heels, growling low and menacingly. Jael was surprised by that. Pleased too. She didn't stop her. 'I was looking for Eydis. I've brought the puppies to visit her.'

Morac eyed Vella crossly. He didn't like dogs. 'Eydis is in her bedchamber, I believe. Do you know the way?'

'I do, thank you,' Jael smiled, hoping to unsettle the uptight man. She slipped past him, behind the green curtain.

Eydis was sitting on her bed, playing with a collection of wooden dolls, when Jael knocked. She could hear and smell the puppies. 'Come in, Jael!' she called happily.

Ido and Vella raced in, pouncing on their old friend, Eydis, whose smell they knew well. They were just as pleased to see her as she was them.

'I'm so glad you've come!' Eydis' eyes sparkled merrily. 'I was hoping you'd bring the puppies for a visit. I've missed them terribly.'

Jael grabbed a small stool from a corner of the room and came to sit in front of the bed. 'I'm happy to bring them whenever you like,' she said. 'You can even look after them for me when they're getting under my feet too much, or, I should say, under Biddy's feet.'

'Who's Biddy?' Eydis wondered, lifting each puppy onto the bed in turn.

'My servant,' Jael said. 'She came with me from Brekka. I

suppose she is my friend too. She's been taking care of me since I was born.'

'And you only *suppose* she's your friend?' Eydis laughed.

'I'm not one for friends,' Jael said slowly. 'I've only ever really had one friend.'

'Well, that's not so bad, as long as she is a good friend, then your life is richer, for sure. I don't think I have any real friends, apart from Eadmund. Not many children want to play with a blind girl, even if she is the king's daughter.'

Jael watched Eydis' eyes fill with sadness. 'Well, they sound like idiots if that's the case,' she reassured her. 'And no one needs an idiot for a friend.'

'True,' Eydis laughed as Ido nuzzled her cheek. 'I'm glad you brought me such wonderful company, but I think there's more on your mind than pleasing me.'

'You do?' Jael squirmed, still trying to decide how to approach a young girl with such a serious problem.

'I may be blind, but I see many things, and I hear a lot too. Is it Eadmund?'

Jael couldn't help but laugh. 'No, no, that's another conversation entirely. No, this is something you may be able to help me with. I hope you can help me with it.' She leaned forward, conscious of keeping her voice low as she told Eydis all about Edela's warning, Evaine's face, and the symbols.

Everything she could remember from her dream.

Eydis' eyes were wide as she listened, her body still, her hands tense in her lap. 'Oh,' was all she could say when Jael had finished. 'Oh.'

Jael frowned, worried that she'd upset her. 'Are you alright, Eydis?'

'Yes, yes, I'm fine,' she insisted, shaking her head. 'I'm just cross that I hadn't seen those things myself. Eadmund has been following Evaine around for the last year or so, I know that. I always thought something about her was so troubling. Now I know I was right, but why didn't I see the truth of it?' She was deeply puzzled.

'You're only young,' Jael insisted. 'I expect your gift will grow as your body does. I'm no expert, but it may be that you're only shown those things you can do something about. And if what Edela saw is true, there was nothing you could do, not on your own. Not without someone here to help you.'

'Perhaps,' Eydis murmured. 'But I could have spoken to my father. Had Evaine removed from Oss.'

Jael looked doubtful. 'You may have had a hard job convincing him of that, with her father being his friend. And at least this way we can get rid of her together, if that's what we need to do.'

'It sounds as though that's definitely what we need to do,' Eydis said firmly, her body shaking with determination. 'I'm going to put my mind to it tonight. I'm going to tell myself to dream on it. It may work.'

'Well, good, you should certainly do that, but we must try to find those symbols Edela wanted me tattooed with. Perhaps you should have them as well, if your father would allow it?'

'There's no need for that,' Eydis smiled, pulling back a sleeve of her yellow woollen dress. It was loose and rolled easily, all the way up to her shoulder, revealing a small blue tattoo.

Jael recognised it immediately, her eyes gleaming. 'That's it! One of the symbols from my dream!' She was incredulous. 'And do you have the other?'

'Yes, I do!' And a triumphant Eydis rolled up her other sleeve.

It was, without question, the other symbol from the painted stones.

'Why do you have them? Who put them on you?' Jael wondered, distractedly picking up Vella, who was trying to jump off the bed.

Eydis looked sad. 'My mother was from Tuura. She saw her death coming. She knew that she would leave me, so she made my father promise her two things. That when I was ten-years-old, he would have the symbols tattooed on me. She gave him two stones, with the symbols painted on them, just like in your dream. And on my tenth birthday, my father did as he promised. He wanted to keep me safe. He didn't want to lose me as he had lost her, so he went along with it.'

'And what was the other thing?' Jael wondered.

'He was to send me to Tuura two years later, to start my training so that I could learn more about my dreams. So that I could learn how to be a dreamer like your grandmother. Father promised he would, but then he changed his mind. The loss of my mother was too much for him, I suppose,' she sighed. 'Every woman he's loved has died, taken from him too soon. Even his own mother. So he won't lose me. He doesn't trust the Tuurans. He won't let me go there.'

Jael shuddered. Memories of her last visit to Tuura flittered briefly past her eyes. She blinked them away. 'Well then, we need to find someone to tattoo me,' she said, plonking Vella down on the furs and standing up.

'Entorp can do it,' Eydis suggested, but Jael looked at her blankly. 'Entorp! He married you and Eadmund, don't you remember? He's from Tuura. He left to come here with my mother. He was her friend,' she smiled. 'He did mine. I'll take you!' Eydis hopped off the bed, feeling her way to the door, grabbing her cloak.

'The snow is quite heavy out there now,' Jael warned.

'I've lived on Oss my whole life, Jael. It's usually snowing quite heavily!' And smiling sweetly, Eydis slipped her fur neckwarmer over her cloak, pulled on her gloves and stood ready to go.

Jael could see the determination shining out of that sweet little face, and she realised that there was not much she could do to dissuade her. She had invited Eydis into her confidence, and now it was her job to ensure that she remained safe.

***

Runa sat by the fire, a pale-blue dress draped over her knees, thread and needle in hand. She was alone, apart from their house servant, embroidering delicate white flowers onto the dress. It was for Evaine, who'd insisted the flowers were added. Not that she needed another dress, Runa thought irritably. Morac liked to indulge his daughter, though, and he'd regularly buy bolts of luxurious cloth from the merchants who travelled around the islands, to be made into equally luxurious garments. Not for Runa. There never seemed to be enough cloth left over for her. She frowned, a rare show of resentment clouding her sad face.

There were many reasons to despise the girl.

'It's so heavy out there!' Evaine exclaimed, rushing into the house, covered in melting snow. 'There will certainly be a storm tonight. The wind is getting so loud!'

Runa looked up briefly, trying to wish away the dark feeling that crept up behind her every time her daughter was near. If only Morac saw the wisdom in marrying Evaine off. Now that Eadmund was finally married himself, it was something she would have to raise again.

'Mother?' Evaine looked annoyed by the lack of attention. Her mother had quickly returned to her embroidery, barely acknowledging her arrival. 'Didn't you hear me?'

'I heard you,' Runa sighed. 'And I agree. I've been listening to the wind picking up for a while now. I'll ask Alfar to check on the house. He'll make sure everything is secure before nightfall.'

Evaine looked resolved to suffer her mother's lack of interest as she removed her wet cloak and furs, handing them to the servant.

'Where's Father?' she asked coldly, coming to sit by the fire.

Runa didn't look up. 'Still at the hall as far as I'm aware.'

'Is he now...' Evaine mused, staring at her mother's greying head. 'Perhaps I should go and get him? Make sure he's back before the storm strikes? He should look over the house, too. We can't trust Alfar to do it alone. He's so old now. I'd be surprised if he can even see out there.'

Runa looked up, suspicion creasing the corners of her gentle blue eyes. 'Why should you need to get your father?' she wondered, peering at Evaine's scheming face. 'I'm sure he'll come when he's ready. Perhaps he'll stay the night in the hall? You know how Eirik likes his company.'

'And leave us to the storm?' Evaine stood up. 'No, I think I should go and fetch him home.'

'Evaine,' Runa said firmly, and placing her needle on top of the dress and moving it to one side, she stood. 'If you go to the hall you will put your father in a very awkward position. Do you wish to be banished as Fyn was?' She looked ready to cry at just the sound of her poor boy's name.

'Fyn?' Evaine snorted. 'How is me going to the hall anything like Fyn?'

'Because Eirik has threatened your father. He knows of your friendship with Eadmund, and he has promised to get rid of you if he even sees you near him. That would shame Morac greatly. To have both his children banished by the king? I'm not sure how he could continue here. He'd be humiliated.' Runa glared at her daughter, hoping that some sense would enter her Eadmund-addled mind. 'And I, for one, believe him. After all, look at what he did to Fyn.'

Evaine screwed up her nose, pushing her hands tightly into the sides of her green dress. Her body twitched distractedly, her eyes darkening with a brewing storm. 'Fine.' She sat down, squeezing her fingers together, staring at the floor, thoughts racing around her head. Being banished wouldn't help her get rid of Jael Furyck. Being taken away from Eadmund would only open the door for him to fall in love with his wife. And no matter what her aunt had warned her, she was never going to let that happen.

***

It turned out that the ritual of Tuuran tattooing was as much about the ink and the moon as it was about the symbols themselves. Entorp had enlightened Jael on that point after she'd told him about her dream. He had not looked well, though, plagued as he was with a bone-rattling cough. Jael hoped that he'd still be alive in fourteen days time, when apparently all factors would come together to create the most auspicious moment.

It really was a bad cough, and a long time to wait.

She would have to remain alert.

The storm that had been threatening all day had finally descended upon Oss, and after taking Eydis back to the hall, Jael was keen to get home before it blew her away. She had a puppy tucked under each arm to avoid losing them in the blizzard, and neither of them were enjoying the containment. Her cloak was streaming so far behind her in the wind that she worried it would detach itself entirely. She couldn't see anything at all, just a white wall that was blowing itself horizontally into her face.

Her first clue that someone was approaching was the rumbling of Vella's furry belly. Jael stopped and waited, watching a shadow emerge from the whiteness. Her sword hung at her waist, and she wanted to allow herself enough time to drop the puppies safely and unsheath it before the threat was upon her. She waited, and the shadow took shape as it came forward. Vella's growl moved from her belly to her throat now, and Ido joined in.

It was Tiras.

'Are you lost, my lady?' he asked in that hissing voice she found so repellent. He held his hood open just enough for her to see his snow-dusted, beady eyes. Locating the source of the growling noise, he stepped back, disconcerted.

Jael was pleased to see that he didn't like dogs. Naturally. And they didn't appear to like him either. 'Lost? Hopefully not. Why? Are you offering me your assistance?'

'I assumed that you'd be looking for your husband, and I know for certain that he's not in that direction,' Tiras sneered.

Jael couldn't see his smile, the snow was too thick, but she knew that it would be there. Tiras had a full set of brown-stained teeth that he liked to show off. 'No, you're right, he's in the hall with his friends. Perhaps you should go and join them? It must be so lonely for you here without anyone to conspire with?'

'Oh, I'm keeping busy,' Tiras assured her. 'Very busy indeed.' And with a curt bow, he dropped his hood back over his face and slid away into the storm.

Jael stared after him with a frown.

He was going to cause trouble.

Tiras was definitely going to cause trouble.

CHAPTER NINETEEN

Eadmund couldn't feel his fingers. His hands were swollen from days of continuously holding a sword. He'd almost convinced himself to give up after every fight, but somehow he kept going. Thorgils had reminded him that his fingers would harden soon, that the hilt would feel part of his hand again. But they were only using wooden swords, and he was struggling with their gentle contours, let alone the grip of an iron-heavy weapon with no such sympathy.

He sighed, feeling his resolve to get up drifting away like the dull rays of light filtering down the smoke hole. Perhaps today he would rest? His body wasn't used to this much physical punishment. Thorgils and Torstan had been making a fool of him for days. He'd been ignoring Evaine every night, and not paying much attention to his ale either. Perhaps today he would stay indoors, avoid a humiliating beating, and wrap himself up in Evaine's warm body for a while?

That would make her happy.

The urge for a drink started pulsing in his veins and Eadmund realised that he was going to have to move if he was to reach the jug of ale on his kitchen shelf.

He would have to remember to leave it by the bed.

Groaning loudly, he crawled out from under the furs, creaking his way across the cottage. The fire was lifeless, and his breath smoke was thick. Not bothering to find a cup, he held the jug up to his mouth, devastated to discover that it was empty. Not even a drip would fall onto his parched tongue.

Eadmund banged the jug onto the table, glancing around for his cloak. He'd need some supplies if he was going to spend the day in this icebox.

'Eadmund!'

Eadmund froze, his shoulders sagging at the sound of that voice.

'Are you dead in there, or just dead drunk?' Thorgils yelled through the door. 'Come on, come on! My balls are shrivelling up out here! We need to get training quickly, or I'll never be able to father a child!'

Eadmund said nothing, still thinking that he had a choice to make, but it was Thorgils, so there really was no choice. He reached for his cloak, cracking his neck from side to side, grimacing morbidly.

***

It was a clear enough morning, and for a change, the wind was merely a stiff breeze. Jael leaned over the railings of the Pit watching Torstan and Eadmund tiptoe around each other in the cleared enclosure. Thorgils stood next to her, barracking them with loud insults.

'They're taking it rather easy,' Jael observed.

Thorgils eyed her. 'Oh says you, who isn't training for the contest at all.'

'I'm training,' Jael said slyly.

'With who? Where?' Thorgils wondered.

'With Fyn, actually,' Jael whispered. 'I've been training with him every morning for a week or so.'

'What?' Thorgils boomed in surprise, his voice so loud that

both Torstan and Eadmund stopped, their swords in mid-air. Thorgils waved them on. 'You have? Why?'

'Because he should know how to fight. Because he's all alone out there. Because I have nothing better to do. It helps keep me busy.'

'Nothing better to do? Except train for a big fight or a lot of them, depending on how well you do,' Thorgils said. 'That's the whole point of the contest, for everyone to practice, to get as strong and sharp as possible. Any who aren't will just make fools of themselves, at best. At worst, they'll ruin their reputations, especially if they end up in the muck, with Tarak on their back.' He laughed as Eadmund tripped over, tumbling into the snow. 'Ha! Like that one there!' Thorgils gestured for Eadmund to come out. 'I think your turn is over, my friend,' he chortled, picking up his sword and shield before glancing at Jael. 'Perhaps it's that you just feel more comfortable playing swords with a simple boy who can't fight back?' He slipped between the rails and into the Pit, beating his sword on his shield. Pointing it in Jael's direction, he issued her a challenge with his bushy red eyebrows.

Jael glared at him. And suddenly her desire to keep everything so tightly controlled was undone by a much stronger urge to wipe that stupid smile off Thorgils' face. If he wanted a fight so badly, perhaps it was time she gave him one?

Hanging her cloak and swordbelt over the rail, Jael climbed into the Pit. Eadmund looked surprised as he passed her on his way out, but she reached for his sword and shield without even looking at him.

Her eyes remained firmly fixed on Thorgils.

'Good luck,' he croaked, handing them over, almost too tired to speak. 'He won't take it easy on you.'

Jael smiled, liking the sound of that.

***

Gisila said nothing as she stared at her mother, but her worried expression told many tales.

'I'm sorry that it is not what you wish to hear,' Edela soothed. 'But often my dreams reveal an unappealing truth. Just ask Jael.'

Gisila couldn't even offer a hint of a smile at that. 'What do you suggest I say to Lothar, then?'

'Well, what can you say but yes?' Edela said. 'He will not be satisfied with any other answer, will he? He wants you as his next wife, so unless he drops dead, it will certainly happen. You cannot turn down a king. And you won't. Not if my dreams are any indication.' Edela felt sorry for Gisila, whose face paled, her swollen eyes blinking back tears. And who could blame her? Lothar was a vile lump of slime that she wouldn't wish on an enemy, let alone her eldest daughter.

Gisila sighed despairingly. 'Well then, let's not talk about it again, and certainly don't mention it to Axl or Aleksander. Axl will be wild at me for even considering such a thing.'

'Of course he will, he's wild about everything these days,' Edela said thoughtfully, sipping a warming cup of rosehip tea. 'He wants what he thinks was his, and he's going to wrap himself up in a lot of trouble trying to get it.'

'Will he?'

'Of course. You don't need to be a dreamer to see that in his future,' Edela said smartly. 'Besides, Aleksander told me about the boys Axl is friendly with. What sort of ideas they are putting into his head. Without Jael here to keep him in line, he's going to find himself in real danger soon.'

'So, me marrying Lothar could actually help Axl?' Gisila suggested, mostly to convince herself. 'If he were to get into trouble, I would have much more influence over Lothar.' She mulled that over, wringing her hands.

It was early in the afternoon, and the light was bright inside Edela's cottage. Jael wouldn't have recognised it, Edela thought to herself. Aleksander had sorted through her shelves, moved her furniture, cleaned every surface, thrown out all the old floor reeds, and replaced them with freshly scented ones. He'd even taken out all her furs and given them a good beating. Edela was certainly grateful for it. She was feeling older by the day, and the number of tasks she was able to complete on her own was diminishing.

Aleksander had insisted upon moving in to take care of her while she recovered her strength. Edela was considerably weaker after the dream walk, and although she didn't truly need that much help, his presence had become a real comfort. And she could see the direction and friendship that it was giving him in return. He'd even started to eat regularly, which had been an easy habit to rediscover once he began cooking for Edela.

'Mother?'

Edela blinked. She hadn't been listening at all.

'Have you had any dreams about Jael? Any clues as to how things are on Oss with that feral husband of hers?'

'I've had one or two,' Edela said carefully. 'But nothing of any significance that I can share.'

Gisila raised an eyebrow but knew better than to prod any further; her mother only ever revealed what she wanted to. 'No doubt she's just hidden away from them all, waiting for Eadmund to drink himself to death,' Gisila shuddered. 'I think that's what I'd do.'

'I don't think Jael's ever been the type of person to hide from anything or anyone,' Edela suggested with a smile. 'Do you?'

***

Eirik couldn't help but laugh as Eydis giggled uncontrollably beside him. She'd whispered a joke in his ear, worried that someone would overhear. It had been passed on to her by Eadmund, and was ridiculous and barely funny, but her delight in it made Eirik's cheeks hurt with happiness.

Eydis stilled suddenly, hearing a commotion at the doors.

Eirik followed her gaze. One of his men, Eadon, had rushed into the hall, straight up to the dais.

'What is it?' Eirik stood up at once, concerned.

'My lord, it's Jael!' Eadon announced loudly, slightly out of breath. 'She's in the Pit, fighting Thorgils!'

Eirik turned to Eydis, eyes twinkling, and grabbed her arm. 'I'll get your cloak, Eydis. We must see this!' And he snatched his own cloak off the back of his throne.

They were quickly joined by the rest of the hall, as everyone rushed to catch a glimpse of the fight.

***

'Before we begin, Jael,' Thorgils bellowed, more to the gathering crowd than to her. 'Are there any places on your womanly self that you'd prefer me not to hit?'

There were jeers and whistles at that, mostly from the men. Thorgils strutted about, smiling at his appreciative audience, basking in their attention. The railings around the Pit were lined with curious Osslanders now. All the other groups had cleared out, and it was only Jael and Thorgils inside the whole enclosure now.

Jael's face was impassive, stern even, as she considered his question. 'Well yes, thank you for asking,' she said, just as loudly, walking up to Thorgils, her sword extended out in front of her. 'I would very much appreciate it if you did not hit me here.' She touched her wooden blade to Thorgils' left nipple. 'And here.' She moved the sword to his right nipple.

There was much hollering then; the Pit ringing with raucous laughter at the look on Thorgils' face. 'And whatever you do, please don't ever hit me here.' And Jael gritted her teeth, swung back her leg and kicked him as hard as she could in the balls.

Thorgils uttered a pitiful, high-pitched sound and plummeted headfirst into the muddy slush. The crowd sucked in its breath, teeth bared, as they shared in Thorgils' discomfort. Then, as he started to groan and move gingerly around on the ground, the cheers started again, and laughter followed.

Jael walked off to one corner of the Pit, waiting for Thorgils to compose himself. She remembered all the times she had trained with Aleksander; thousands of times. He knew her so well that it was almost impossible to surprise him, but Thorgils knew nothing about her or her fighting style. She was keen to sit back and learn about him, to see if she could draw him out.

'That's your game, is it?' he coughed, finding his voice again, trying to shake off the aching in his balls, and the sick feeling in his stomach. She had a kick on her that he'd have to watch. 'Kick a man in the balls, and the fight is done? Well, I'm afraid you haven't met balls like these before, Jael *Skalleson*!' he called. 'They're iron-tough and super-smooth. Just ask any of these lovely ladies who've had the pleasure of sucking on them!'

Jael didn't even blink as the crowd roared with laughter and Eirik covered Eydis' ears. She stayed where she was, fixing Thorgils with a blank stare.

He paced around in front of her, still playing up to the crowd.

'Ahhh, so now that you've realised how strong my balls are, you're going to stand back and let me run around you like a pecking chicken?' And he made to walk like a chicken, the crowd laughing along with him.

Jael said nothing. Her mouth was set in a straight line that betrayed no emotion. He's right, she thought, I am going to make him run around me. He just doesn't know it yet. She saw her father's smile in that idea. It had been one of the first things he'd taught her.

So she waited. And watched.

Thorgils could sense the crowd's patience slowly wavering. They wanted to see some action now, not just listen to his witty barbs. Apart from his hammering in the balls, there'd been nothing to watch, and Jael looked uninterested in even starting to fight. Was she worried that he was going to humiliate her? Hurt her? Thorgils' mind started whispering so loudly that he found himself unsettled, uncertain how to move forward. He shook his head, walking from side to side, talking some hard sense to himself.

Looking across the Pit to the railings, he saw Eirik with Eydis, and he realised what a difficult position his big mouth had put him in. If he were to hurt or humiliate Jael, Eirik would not be forgiving. But if he were to do nothing and have her humiliate him – he couldn't help but glance at Tarak, who was watching on curiously – then it would be *his* reputation tarnished.

And still, Jael did nothing.

The air was bitter, but Thorgils was sweating now. The crowd were no longer tolerant. They were calling out for him to do something, to make her fight. His shoulder blades tightened, his groin jiggling moistly in his trousers. He felt itchy all over as he continued to walk around, crossing in front of Jael from one side to the other and back again. His face twisted anxiously. His palms felt sweaty, and he loosened his grip on his shield.

And that was when Jael came.

She flew at Thorgils with such pace that he managed to get his shield up on instinct alone. He staggered backwards, almost slipping over on a small patch of snow. Jael slashed quickly, taking him in the torso, on his right arm, down at his left hip. He chased her sword with his shield as swiftly as he could, always a step behind, feeling the sharp jab of her wooden blade biting at his muscles. She lashed out with her shield, knocking the rim of his into his chin. Again, Thorgils almost lost his footing.

It was all Jael. Her eyes were cold, hard, and fixed on him, her dark hair flying wildly behind her. Thorgils backed away as quickly as he could to recover.

And she let him.

There was silence around the Pit. A few mouths hung open.

No one seemed to know what to say. Jael accidentally caught Eadmund's eye, and he looked just as stunned as the rest of them. She could feel her ribs hurting, but she didn't cringe or smile at her first victory. She walked left, then right, trying to let her breathing calm naturally. She was not in good shape, she realised.

Aleksander would have had her on the ground by now.

Thorgils spat a mouthful of blood onto the ground, rubbing his chin. There were a few cheers then. He frowned, not sure whether they were for or against him. His confidence was flapping in the wind, a tattered mess, but at least he had an idea of how things would go if he didn't get his head right. He lifted his shield up to the crowd, banging it with his sword in a bold show of intent. 'I thought it only fair to let Jael have a turn. What sort of man would I be to deny a woman what she so desperately craves?' He snuck a quick glance at Eirik and was happy to see him smiling. 'Now, my lord, Eadmund, I'm sorry to say, but it's time for me to show your wife what a true spanking looks like!'

Thorgils smiled with such confidence that everyone forgot what they'd just witnessed and started cheering for him again. There were notable exceptions, of course, like Tarak, who hated Thorgils, and Eirik, who was supporting Jael.

Eadmund remained quiet, unsure who he wanted to win.

'You talk a lot,' Jael observed as she glanced at the condition of the ground in front of her. She turned her back on Thorgils and walked away.

The crowd stilled, wondering what was coming now. Thorgils did too. This time he kept a firm grip on his shield, holding it high, just below his bruised chin, which was exactly what Jael had been hoping he'd do.

When she'd walked far enough, she turned, and, taking a deep breath of freezing air into her lungs, she started running at him. There were gasps of surprise as Jael kept up her pace. Thorgils lifted his shield to protect himself, leaning slightly back; he had no idea what she was planning now.

Just before she reached him, Jael jumped up onto his shield, lunging at him with her sword, catching him on the side of the neck, knocking him down to the ground. As shocked as he was, Thorgils recovered quickly, rolling away from any attempt Jael might have made to finish the fight then. He scrambled for his sword and shield, which he'd dropped in the fall, and hurried to his feet.

Jael followed.

They came together quickly, and there were no smiles anymore as they exchanged countless fast blows, blade to blade, parrying every challenge issued, shields banging and deflecting with ease and speed.

Thorgils jabbed Jael in the waist, and she jerked away as the force of that bit at her. He didn't pause to enjoy the victory of it, though. Jael could see that he'd focused now, desperate to beat her, ignoring, for the moment, the worry that he wouldn't.

It was Jael's turn to step back as Thorgils came at her with increasing force, giving her no respite, his stamina greater than hers. Jael's feet were damp in her boots, her footing less secure now as she moved about, seeking firm ground. She was on the defense as Thorgils attacked her repeatedly, his powerful strokes flowing with ease. And she let him come, ducking underneath his blows, sweeping her sword around, catching the backs of his legs.

Thorgils was much bigger than her and Jael knew that she could turn that to her advantage. She started stepping back, letting him come at her, again and again, until she was only defending, saving her energy, protecting herself. He slashed at her repeatedly, but now that she was pulling back each time, he kept missing, his face pulsing with red-bearded fury.

Thorgils finally made contact with Jael's shield, and it broke. She quickly threw away the shattered pieces, slipping her hand out of the grip. Thorgils looked unsure what to do now that she had no shield. He was thinking too much again, worrying over the fact that she was a woman; Eirik's prize; Eadmund's wife.

Jael could read Thorgils' darting eyes.

He might still have a shield, but she could sense that his mind was vulnerable.

She decided to end it quickly. She was hungry and cold, ready for a fire. So, heaving in another deep breath, she spun around, unsettling Thorgils once more. He didn't know which way to expect her to come at him. Jael used that to her advantage, aiming at his left, but, as he threw his sword and shield to counteract her move, she shifted her weight to the right and hit him across his exposed stomach. He grunted and stumbled, and she rushed at him. Thorgils' shield went up, but she'd hurt him, and his sword arm didn't respond as quickly as he needed. Jael jabbed him in the thigh.

There were gasps from the crowd as she continued her assault, coming at him again and again, her sword making contact with nearly every strike. Thorgils stumbled against the railings, and as she lunged forward, Jael saw Eadmund's worried face. She tried to shut it out, but for a moment, her focus blurred. She saw the fear in Thorgils' eyes. Not the fear of being hurt, but the fear of humiliation. She had taken the advantage, she could finish it, and he could sense that. So could the crowd. Their cheering was whisper-thin.

Jael wasn't one of theirs. They weren't supporting her victory.

It was her turn to stumble as she lost her footing in a puddle. She tipped slightly sideways, off-balance. Thorgils was at her quickly, using the advantage of his shield to butt her harshly to the ground. There was nothing Jael could do but fall, and although she still had her sword, Thorgils brought his hefty foot down on her arm in one quick move, his blade at her throat.

Fight over.

Cheers rang out and Thorgils, breathing more heavily than he could remember, rolled his eyes in relief. He looked down at Jael, lying on her back on the frozen dirt and felt the pleasure of his victory settle sweetly into his chest. Reaching down, he pulled her up. She frowned at him, uninjured, he was pleased to see.

'Well done,' was all Jael could say before Thorgils' friends invaded the Pit and started the back-clapping celebrations.

Jael stepped away from the crowd, trying to catch her breath. 'That was very *kind* of you.'

Tarak had crept up behind her.

Jael froze, surprised. 'Kind?'

Tarak leaned in closely, his sour breath warm in her ear. She flinched. 'Letting him win like that,' he rasped.

Jael spun around. 'Letting him?' she hissed. 'I fell, he won. There was no letting.'

Tarak just smiled, not taking his eyes off her as he walked away.

***

It hadn't been so awful to fight Thorgils, Jael decided, watching him celebrate with his friends. He kept looking over at her as she sat quietly at the high table with Eirik, Eydis, and Morac, raising his cup to her, motioning for her to join him.

Jael shook her head each time.

She wasn't a bad loser, but she didn't feel like celebrating.

'Do you think he has a chance of beating Tarak?' Eirik wondered, following Jael's gaze.

'Thorgils?' She grimaced as she turned towards Eirik, her side aching from one of Thorgils' shots. 'None at all.'

'That's not very generous of you,' Eirik snorted.

'I wouldn't put any coins on him beating Tarak,' Jael muttered. 'If that's what you want to know, but perhaps I'll help him, and then he may have more of a chance.'

Eirik couldn't help but laugh. 'But he beat you!'

'Yes, that's true,' she smiled. 'He did.'

Thorgils had staggered up to their table now, tired of her shaking head. 'Come on, Jael, come and have a drink with me. After *that* fight? That was some fight we had, you and I!' he slurred into her face. 'Come, come on!'

Jael smiled reluctantly at his red-faced happiness. 'Alright, just one. Just for a moment. I can only stand listening to you tell the story of your victory one more time!' And she stood, wincing at the ache in her legs.

Eadmund was draining his cup with vigour as Jael stepped into the tight little circle of friends. He looked surprised and uncomfortable to see her, his easy smile quickly replaced by a tense frown. He stood up straighter, wiping his hand over his beard.

'Do you know everyone here?' Thorgils wondered, handing Jael a cup of ale. 'Well, Torstan, of course. Eadmund? Perhaps not...' He laughed at his own joke, but neither Jael nor Eadmund joined in. 'Then we have Erland, Klaufi, and Orvar, three pieces of shit we've known since we were hairless boys. And all still standing!' All five men raised their cups to Thorgils with a smile.

Jael nodded briefly at the three new faces, trying to avoid Eadmund's eyes. He wasn't as drunk as usual, and her awareness of that made her slightly irritable. She didn't want to do anything to encourage him to her bed. Not tonight. Not ever. It was unavoidable, of course, she knew that, but she was happy to keep living this deluded existence a while longer.

Thorgils smiled, leaning down to her ear. 'I beat you, then.'

Jael laughed at the pure, drunken pleasure on his beaming face. 'Yes, you did.'

'So now, I think, you must agree that I have a good chance against...' he looked around, still retaining enough wits to keep his volume measured, '...Tarak.'

'Well...' Jael looked unconvinced. 'I'd say no. No chance.'

Thorgils almost fell over backwards. 'What?' he roared with laughter. 'I didn't pick you for a bad loser, Jael Furyck, nor a foolish one!'

'I think you might have a chance if I were to help you. I could train with you, teach you some ways to improve.'

'*You*? Who was just beaten by *me*? Help me?' Thorgils' eyes rolled wildly at her as he chewed on that, confused. He fixed her with a wobbly stare, then leaned in, throwing waves of ale towards her face, his expression lightening suddenly. 'Yes, you know, I think that is a *very* good plan actually. I've no idea how you did some of those things out there, and as for what you did to this,' he tapped the side of his head, 'that's something I do need to know. Let's do that, then. Let's be a team. The team,' he whispered, placing one arm around her shoulder, breathing into her ear, 'who'll destroy Tarak Soren.'

Jael smiled, catching Eadmund's eye. He didn't look away, and for some reason, neither did she, and she felt her stomach flip. The sensation was so unexpected that Jael almost bit her tongue. She swallowed, finally dragging her eyes away, staring into her cup before taking a quick sip, thinking that it was time she left. But Thorgils had slipped away to talk with the men whose names she'd already forgotten and Eadmund moved in to speak with her.

Eadmund wasn't drunk. He'd had a few cups of ale, but his feet were steady, and his head felt clear as he stepped towards Jael. He didn't know why he felt compelled to talk to her. Perhaps it was that his father was watching him? Perhaps it was the look he'd seen on her face during the fight when she'd slipped? It hadn't been a look of surprise. He'd been sober enough to notice that; clear-headed enough to see what she'd done. Something in that moment had given him a feeling that wasn't dislike, or fear, or even disgust. He'd finally witnessed a person behind those scowling eyes.

The person he was married to.

'Are you going to train with us, then?' Eadmund asked quietly.

'With you?' Jael was surprised. 'Are you training? I didn't realise.' She narrowed her eyes, looking him over, and most of Eadmund's loosely-put-together confidence dissolved.

'What did you think I was doing in the Pit every day?'

'I wasn't sure,' she smiled. 'Finding a new place to sleep?

Every time I saw you, you were lying face down in the mud.'

Eadmund saw humour lurking at the corners of her eyes, and he relaxed. 'Well, it has been a long time. So yes, mostly I've been lying in the mud. But it's a start.'

Jael had no choice but to look at him now. He was quite close to her, having been bumped forward by Thorgils, who was gesticulating madly behind him. 'It's a good thing, to make a start. Now you just have to keep going. Less drinking. More fighting.'

'Maybe,' Eadmund muttered, suddenly anxious. 'Maybe on both counts. I'm not sure I'm ready for either of those suggestions. All I know is that if I can get up and get into that Pit each morning, there's a chance.'

His face looked so much better, she thought. Less bloated. He was still fat, of course – a week of being chased around by Thorgils and Torstan wasn't going to shed much of that – but overall he seemed more alive. His eyes were focused on her, almost alert, and she suddenly felt awkward.

Swallowing, Jael quickly excused herself.

'I'll see you in the Pit tomorrow!' Thorgils called after her as she slipped through the hall, and up to the table to retrieve her cloak.

'You're leaving?' Eydis wondered. 'I don't blame you. They'll be drinking for hours yet!' She rolled her eyes in the way a young girl does when she thinks about something revolting; usually boys.

'I know,' Jael yawned, wrapping her cloak around her shoulders. 'But I'll come and visit you tomorrow, Eydis, and we can go walking together. Goodnight.'

Eydis looked pleased.

Eirik looked surprised. She was an unusual creature, he thought to himself. And, hopefully, a fertile one. He watched as she moved through the crowd. There were a few cheers after her, a few goodbyes, a small show of affection that had not been there before. And who could blame them? Jael had put on some show in the Pit. What a fighter, he smiled. He wondered why Lothar had been foolish enough to let her go? Well, perhaps there was the answer: Lothar was a fool.

As Jael hurried to escape the hall, Eirik looked for Eadmund who was still there, talking to his friends, but his head had turned in the direction of the door, staring after his wife.

***

The bed was freezing.

Jael had thrown both puppies under the furs with her in a desperate attempt to warm herself up, but they'd wriggled out as soon as she'd let them go, preferring to lie on top, and, in Vella's case, as far away from her as possible.

Jael thought of Aleksander and Edela. She worried about Axl. She wanted to sink into another dream where she could speak to her grandmother again. She sighed, trying to convince her mind to wander back home. She tried to remember the faces, rooms, and touches that had felt so familiar. But her mind wouldn't let her twist away from Eadmund for long. He kept coming up.

She saw his face at every turn.

Jael opened her eyes and frowned. She tried to think about the fight instead. Her body ached, and from experience, she knew that the aches and pains would only intensify tomorrow. She thought of Thorgils, and of the slip that had gifted him victory. Hopefully, it was only Tarak who had seen that she had done it on purpose. Jael didn't regret it. She'd had her fun, and beating Thorgils would have meant nothing to her; no one would have cheered for her. Well, maybe Eirik, or Eydis, maybe Fyn, when she told him the tale, but no one else. She was a stranger to them, and an awkward one at that, she knew. Thorgils' win held much more value to him. To all of them. Perhaps one day they would cheer her on, and if that day came, maybe she'd care enough to win?

Jael shook her head irritably. What was she thinking? Thinking about Oss and its people as though she wanted them to like her, as though she wanted to belong? She squeezed her eyes shut, trying desperately to remember Andala. But Andala without Ranuf had felt like living with strangers. Strangers who had betrayed her family. It was proving harder to remember that place with any warmth now, as much as she wanted to. Except for Aleksander. Her eyes relaxed as she saw his face, the tension in her body easing. He knew her better than all of them. She yawned, her body unwinding further.

Eadmund's face suddenly jumped into her mind again, and groaning loudly, Jael rolled over and put the pillow over her head.

CHAPTER TWENTY

Eydis looked out of sorts, Jael thought, as they walked briskly along the snow-covered street. Snow had been falling steadily all afternoon, and no one had been out to clear it yet. Jael didn't blame them. It was mean-spirited weather; weather only the truly hardy could enjoy.

And she was not one of them.

She gripped Eydis' hand tightly as they walked past a huddle of fur-wrapped warriors. The men nodded at Jael as she passed, their smiles visible beneath low-drawn hoods. It was time for her tattooing and Jael was not looking forward to it. She dropped her head, distracted by thoughts of tattoos and Evaine, failing to notice that Evaine was actually heading straight for them.

'Jael!' Eydis squeezed her hand urgently, and Jael's eyes came up just in time to avoid a crash.

'Oh, I'm sorry!' Evaine straightened up, pulling back her white hood to reveal red cheeks and innocent eyes. 'I was so busy trying to hide from the snow that I didn't see you coming!'

Jael was unsure how to respond to this girl, who she was on her way to protect herself from. Despite Evaine's childlike appearance, her right hand was itching to slip inside her cloak and touch *Toothpick*.

'Nobody's fault but the weather's,' Jael said shortly.

But that didn't send Evaine on her way.

'And how are you, dear Eydis? I haven't spoken to you in so

long!' Evaine smiled at Eydis, who gripped Jael's hand tightly.

Eydis frowned and didn't say a word.

Jael was pleased to see that it unsettled Evaine. 'Eydis is unwell today,' she explained. 'I thought some fresh air might help, but the snow is so bad, we may as well give up.'

'Well, there is always plenty of cold air on Oss, isn't there, Eydis? Cold air and darkness. Especially at this time of year. Nothing but darkness it seems, surrounding us all.'

'But the darkness won't last,' Jael said firmly, narrowing her eyes. 'Spring will be here before long. Now, I must get Eydis walking before she freezes to the street. Goodbye.'

They left quickly, both of them unsettled by Evaine, eager to get out of the snow.

When they reached Entorp's door, Jael turned to Eydis. 'Are you alright? You haven't said a word since we left the hall.'

Eydis dropped her head, keeping her mouth closed.

It was snowing heavily now, but Jael didn't want to go into Entorp's if Eydis had something important on her mind. There was a lean-to on the opposite side of the street that appeared unoccupied, so Jael grabbed Eydis' hand, dragging her towards it.

'Where are we going?' Eydis protested. 'Entorp is expecting us!'

'That may be true, but I think you should tell me what's wrong first,' Jael insisted. 'Something is wrong. I can feel it, and it was there before we ever bumped into Evaine.' She wandered to the back of the shelter, checking for anyone lurking in the shadows. Thankfully, there was no one to be seen. The snow had sent most people to work on indoor chores for the afternoon, it seemed.

Eydis looked uncomfortable but resigned. She felt her way to a hay bale, and sat down, slipping her gloved hands under her legs. 'I've been trying to dream a lot these past few weeks, for my father, and for you. It hasn't been easy. I've had some very dark dreams,' she said faintly, so faintly that Jael had to sit down next to Eydis to hear her.

'What about?'

'About Ivaar. He is coming. I see it so clearly. He'll be here soon. Before the Thaw.'

Jael was shocked. 'But how? The sea is frozen. That would be impossible, surely?'

'Well, there is one place to the south of the island where the winds blow warmer. The seas do not freeze so much there, and that is how you can get to Oss from Kalfa, where Ivaar is. He could make it. He *will* make it. I've seen it. He'll bring his whole family. He will come.'

Jael rubbed her gloves together, her dark eyebrows pinched into sharp lines. She wasn't sure how she felt about that. Thorgils believed that Ivaar would kill Eadmund, and who else? She glanced at Eydis, who still looked troubled. 'What is it? What else have you dreamed?' she wondered, watching Eydis squirm.

'I, I...' Eydis stuttered awkwardly. 'I saw Evaine... carrying Eadmund's child.'

A dull blow struck Jael somewhere deep inside. She swallowed, moving around on the hay bale. 'Oh.'

'And that isn't good for Eadmund or my father. Or Oss. None of it is,' Eydis sighed, shaking her head.

'No, I can see that.'

'Ivaar will destroy everything. He can't come, Jael. He can't!'

Jael frowned. 'But can we do anything? Stop it from happening? Perhaps she's already pregnant?'

'I don't know,' Eydis said quietly. 'Maybe it's just a warning? Of what will happen if Eadmund doesn't stay away from Evaine? He needs to keep getting stronger, to show Father that he doesn't need Ivaar here. But I don't know if we can change anything I've seen. It may be that it's already decided.'

Jael stood up. 'Hmmm, I've a feeling you're right.' She grabbed Eydis' hand. 'But at least I can get the symbols tattooed on me so I can stay safe from whatever's coming. Whether it's your brother or any threat that girl poses. That's a start. We can figure out the rest as we go along.'

Eydis tried to smile, but her face was clouded with fear and confusion.

'I won't let anything happen to you, Eydis,' Jael insisted, helping her up. 'I promise. You have nothing to fear from Ivaar. Don't worry.'

***

Evaine sat by the fire, fingering her long blonde hair. The wind terrorised Oss, and her beautiful hair was always in tangles. If only she were as sensible as her friends, her mother would always say, the ones who wore their hair in braids. Evaine frowned, thinking of Runa who seemed to be doing everything she could to keep her away from Eadmund. Although, Eadmund seemed just as keen to stay away from her himself lately. She had barely seen him in weeks, and when he had invited her company, like tonight, he was so distracted, he hardly noticed she was there.

'What did you say?' Eadmund sat beside her, sipping a cup of mead.

Evaine had brought him a full jug of mead in the hopes of earning his affection, and while he'd seemed pleased to see her, his reaction to the mead had been mixed. He was trying to stop drinking so much, it seemed, and that thought unsettled her. 'I was just wondering how the mead was?' she said, smiling sweetly. 'It was from my father's private store. He was saving it, but I don't imagine he'll miss one jug.'

'You shouldn't have done that, Evaine,' Eadmund said harshly. 'I'm not interested in taking another man's drink, especially if he's been saving it. I'll stopper it up, and you can take it back when you leave.' He put his cup on the floor and got up to seal the jug.

Evaine looked as though she'd been slapped.

Anxiety burst in the pit of her stomach as she stared after Eadmund. They'd eaten without any conversation, then sat silently around the fire together, and now, he had scolded her. He hadn't even looked like touching her or wanting her for days. She didn't know what to do.

He was slipping through her fingers faster than she'd anticipated.

Eadmund saw how upset Evaine was when he came back to sit beside her. He had invited her to his cottage, but he wasn't being very good company, he knew. He was just so distracted by other thoughts: ale, sword fights, the contest, and things he didn't want to name, even to himself. 'I'm sorry,' he smiled, lifting her chin with one finger. 'I know you were only trying to make me happy. It's just that I don't need to be drinking mead, especially not your father's. It's not easy to say that, and it's even harder to do.'

'But why?' Evaine asked desperately, moving closer to Eadmund, thrilled that he was talking at last. 'What's wrong with drinking mead all of a sudden?'

'It's not the mead,' Eadmund explained patiently, putting an arm around her shoulder. 'It's drinking. All things.' He stared into the flames, realising that this was the first time he was putting words to his thoughts. 'I seem to have decided that I'd rather be able to stand, sleep in a bed, hold a sword, become a king than have too much to drink.'

'Oh.'

It sat there between them: a shift in their relationship. Eadmund had shifted it. He was changing himself, and therefore, what they had and how they had been with one another would inevitably change. Evaine felt a rush of fear flood her veins. Her body started shaking, and she stilled one hand by placing the other on top of it.

She was losing him.

Eadmund saw the tension in her face, and he sought to reassure her. 'It doesn't mean that I don't want to see you,' he said, trying to convince her. And himself. 'But if I don't make these changes, my father will bring Ivaar back. And if Ivaar comes, then he'll be king, and no one wants that, especially not me.'

'Nor me.'

'So I have to show Eirik that I can make the changes he needs to see,' Eadmund sighed. 'It's taken me far too long to realise it, but now that I've started, I can't go back. I don't want to.'

Eadmund could feel the vibrations in Evaine's body as it leaned against his.

'You'll have less time for me.'

'Evaine!' Eadmund laughed at her down-turned mouth. 'You've probably spent most of our time together watching me sleep! This, I hope, will be better for you as well.'

'Of course. I'm sure it will be just as you say.'

'It will,' Eadmund promised, bringing his hands up to her face, leaning in to kiss her.

She flinched from his touch.

It was different, she knew, despite the fact that he was kissing her, eagerly it seemed. Eadmund was different.

And something had to change before he slipped from her grasp entirely.

***

It hurt, much more than she'd imagined it would. Jael didn't let it show, though, as she clamped her jaw shut, looking away from the constant tapping on her arm. There was a lot of blood. She could smell it and was happy that Eydis couldn't see it.

Entorp was a fast worker, though, and despite his bone-jangling cough, he'd managed to keep a steady hand. He had talked throughout the process, about the symbols and their history, and although Jael thought it was no doubt worth listening to, her mind kept wandering. She couldn't stop thinking about what Eydis had revealed about Evaine. A pregnant enemy was going to be trickier to defeat. Or remove. Would Eirik get rid of her if he found out, or keep her around, happy for a grandchild from any source?

She groaned as Entorp tapped into a particularly sensitive spot.

'Are you alright, Jael?' Eydis wondered. She was sitting on the bed in one corner of the small house, playing with Entorp's trio of snow-white cats.

She appeared to have relaxed since they had spoken.

'I am,' Jael grimaced. 'We're nearly done, I think, and then I can walk you back home before your father wonders what's happened to you.'

'Almost there,' Entorp croaked, concentrating hard on her right arm. 'I'll apply bandages to stop the blood, but you'll need to keep the tattoos moist until they've completely healed.' He sat back and cocked his head to one side, admiring his work with a blue-eyed squint. 'I have a salve for you to apply. It reeks, but don't let that stop you from using it.'

'And is that all I'll need? Tattoos? Salve? And I'll be protected from all the evil that's coming for me?' Jael smiled cynically, grinding her teeth together as he tapped a few finishing touches on her arm.

'If only it were so,' Entorp murmured, brushing his wild mop of orange hair out of his eyes. 'No, there is plenty of evil these tattoos will offer you absolutely no protection from. These symbols are old magic from the Tuuran gods. They will keep you safe from all those who mean to do you harm through maleficent ways, such as alchemy or bewitchment, trickery or enchantment. No one will be able to command you. These symbols are the gateposts to your soul and your mind. They will protect them both.' He coughed, a deep hacking cough, right next to Jael's ear. 'But as for your mouth, if they wish to poison you, or your flesh, if they try to cut you, only you can save yourself there. And from what I've heard, you have a good chance of doing just that.'

Jael's face lightened; she was suddenly less bothered by the discomfort. Entorp was right. She knew how to protect her body, but now she had the confidence of knowing that she could enter the fight with her mind and soul safe.

She closed her eyes, thinking of Edela.

Her grandmother may just have saved her life.

***

Aleksander squirmed on his stool. Amma was sitting right there, next to him, chatting to Edela, and he didn't know what to do with himself. He'd only sat down to be polite, and now he didn't feel as though he could leave without appearing rude.

Why was Amma here?

She'd brought a large basket of food for Edela, that part was obvious at least. It was gratefully received, no doubt stolen from Lothar's stores, and Edela seemed very pleased about that. But why else? He knew the answer, of course he did, but he couldn't admit it to himself. It was not something he even wanted to consider.

'We'll be an even closer family soon,' Amma smiled at Edela. 'With my mother dying and Getta being married off, our family has been shrinking, but soon I'll have you and Gisila. You'll be like a grandmother! I certainly don't remember either of mine. They died before I was born.'

Edela nodded, distracted by the tension in front of her. 'Well, I'll be very lonely without Jael to annoy, so I shall expect many visits from you, then.'

'Of course!' Amma said. 'And there is the wedding to look forward to. I'm just so glad that Gisila and Father are waiting until spring so I can wear a pretty dress, rather than a big old cloak. I thought I'd freeze to death at Jael's wedding!'

Aleksander felt the blow of that reminder, and his polite mask slipped.

Amma carried on, blissfully unaware. 'Perhaps Jael will come to the wedding?' she suggested. 'I'm sure Gisila would want her there.'

Edela lifted her eyebrows, trying to stop Amma before she tangled herself up into a complete mess. 'Oh, I don't know if that will happen, my dear.'

'Yes, you're right, I suppose Jael could be with child by then, so she might not want to make the journey.' Amma finally noticed Edela's pleading eyes and the morbid look on Aleksander's face. Flustered with embarrassment, she rushed to get up. 'I should be going,' she mumbled. 'I didn't want to take up your day. I just know how hard it is to come by fresh food at the moment, so hopefully, you'll be able to enjoy what I found.'

'We are most grateful for it,' Edela said warmly as she stood. 'I shall put Aleksander to work right away. He's turning into an excellent cook, and I'm sure he'll be glad to have something more than a limp old cabbage to serve up tonight.'

'Yes, it was very kind of you,' Aleksander admitted, showing Amma to the door. 'But make sure you don't get yourself in trouble with your father on our behalf. We'll be fine to make it through the winter on whatever I can scrape together.' He was firm, hoping to dissuade her from coming back. Amma Furyck was a well-meaning girl, but he didn't want to be around her; she had a way of making him feel uncomfortable.

'I understand,' Amma said, ducking her head as she pinned her cloak to her shoulder. 'I hope you enjoy the food. Goodbye.'

'Goodbye,' Aleksander said quickly, closing the door before she'd even left the doorstep.

'Are you sure you didn't just shut poor Amma's finger in the door? You couldn't have closed it any quicker if you'd tried!' Edela laughed as she returned to her chair, grabbing a fur off the bed to wrap around her shoulders; the cold was in her bones today, and not even the fire would warm her through.

Aleksander frowned as he started to unpack Amma's basket. For all his discomfort and annoyance with her attention, he couldn't deny that she'd provided an impressive hoard of produce; much better than anything he'd been able to find.

'There's nothing wrong with Amma, you know,' Edela called to him over the spitting fire. 'She's not like her father or her weaselly brother. She'll make good company when she grows a little older, I think.'

'She's a girl, a little girl with the wrong ideas,' Aleksander said coldly, turning towards Edela. 'And she's wrong about me. I've no plans to forget Jael and find someone new. It may take some time, but you should know that I'm waiting for Jael to come back. And she will. I've seen it.'

He stared at Edela with such fierce determination that she shuddered at both his expression and his words.

Seen it? How?

What had he done?

CHAPTER TWENTY ONE

Fyn was thrilled to see Jael. It had been days. Days of nothing but howling whiteness. He was frozen, lonely, and sick of his own company.

Jael dismounted with a strained gasp and half a smile.

Fyn grabbed Tig's reins, leading him away to the little shed. He came back, handing her a practice sword. 'Are you alright?'

'Fine,' she sighed, feeling the ache in her upper arms. The tattoos had been annoying her for days now, and although the pain had lessened, she was finding it hard to sleep without lying on them.

'Are you sure?'

'Yes,' Jael said irritably, pushing away the sword. 'At least let me take off my things before we begin!'

While Jael removed her cloak and swordbelt, Fyn trotted around the cleared practice area, slashing the air with his sword. She couldn't help but smile; his confidence had grown so quickly. 'I brought you some food,' she remembered. 'It's in my saddlebag. Remind me to get it when we're done.'

'Really? That's very kind of you,' he smiled. 'I was wondering what I was going to eat today!'

He did look thinner, Jael thought as she picked up her sword and trudged towards the energetic figure. 'So, you have no food?'

'Not really,' Fyn admitted with a cheerful shrug. 'I should ration it more carefully. Respa can't make it out here with supplies from my mother when the weather is bad.'

'Yes, you should,' Jael grumbled, raising her sword to touch his. 'And you should get on with those shields. You'll need to learn how to hold onto one of those too!'

Fyn laughed. 'They're a lot tougher than a sword, but I am trying!' He lashed out at Jael, surprising her, hitting her shoulder.

She yelped, stumbling backwards. 'Had we begun?'

'I, I, I thought we had!' Fyn dropped his sword arm, coming to see if she was alright.

Jael pounced, knocking the sword out of his hand.

It fell into the snow.

'Oh,' Fyn sighed, bending down to pick it up.

'Yes. Oh,' Jael growled. 'Never let go of your sword. Never loosen your grip. Never allow yourself to become so distracted that someone can surprise you. Hold onto your sword!'

'I was worried about you!'

'I don't need you to worry about me, Fyn, I need you to hold onto your sword!' she said, happy to see him firm up his grip.

Jael went easy on him then, and they trained for a while in a slow, methodical way, working on the idea of predicting shots, getting behind them, blocking, protecting your body, staying alert.

The ache in Jael's arms from the tattoos and the cold eventually got too much. 'Let's take a break!' she called, and without waiting for an answer, she dropped her sword, hurrying to the little shed to retrieve the packet of food she'd brought with her.

Fyn's eyes widened at the shape of the well-stuffed packet as he followed Jael into the hut; he really was starving.

Jael took a stool in front of the fire, which, Fyn noted, was starting to burn low. He hurried to build it up, knowing how much Jael hated the cold. He would need to bring in some more wood soon. 'Is something wrong?' he wondered, tearing off a piece of the bread Jael offered him. It had been warm when she left the fort, but it was almost frozen now.

'Wrong?' she mumbled, trying to swallow a hard lump of

bread. 'Well, if you'd paid attention, you would have realised that I had wounds on my arms. You could have been aiming for them, instead of pissing about trying to hit my stomach for the past hour!'

'Your arms? What happened?'

'I've been tattooed.'

'Tattooed? Why?'

'They're Tuuran tattoos. Symbols of protection,' Jael said distractedly, looking around.

'Protection from what?'

'Your sister, mainly,' Jael smiled. 'Do you have anything to drink in here?'

Fyn was too shocked to respond, so Jael got up, and, finding a jug beside Fyn's bed, she poured herself a cup of very watery ale.

'Evaine? You think you need tattoos to protect yourself from her? Can they? Protect you, I mean?'

Jael sat back down. 'I hope so. But if not, I shall look very pretty,' she grinned.

Fyn was silent. He had so many questions, but he didn't know where to begin. So Jael told him about her dream, about what Edela had seen on the beach, and how she had come to warn her.

'I don't understand what it all means,' was all Fyn could say when she'd finished. 'The scorched face? I've never seen it, or anything like it. Evaine is the worst person I've ever known, well, not the worst, but I've never seen her like that. Ever.'

'We don't know what it means. None of us do,' Jael admitted, taking a sip of ale. 'But hopefully, I can keep myself safe, and Eydis too. And perhaps it's time you got away from here? Made a new life in Alekka, or on one of the other islands?'

Fyn sighed. 'I can't do that, Jael. I can't leave my mother.'

'But you don't even see her,' Jael said. 'You're out here, starving, all alone, with no family, no one to talk to, not even a horse for company!'

'I know...'

'And how long do you think you can live this way?'

'I...' Fyn looked defeated.

'You should have friends, and fights, and fall in love, have adventures, have a family, or at least someone to talk to,' Jael implored. 'You have to leave here, Fyn. Surely your mother wouldn't want you to exist like this? She'd want you to have a life of your own.'

'But who would protect her if I go?'

'Protect her from what? Your sister, or your father?' Jael wondered.

'Both of them, I suppose,' Fyn said quietly. 'I know I can't do much all the way out here, but I didn't want to leave my mother. She's not like them. I wanted her to come with me, and I know she thought about it, but I think some part of her still loves my father. She told me about this hut, said she'd send food for me. So I stayed here... for her.'

Jael was troubled. She liked Fyn. It was like having a little brother again, but easier; she didn't resent him. She wanted to help him have a life again, somehow. 'I could talk to Eirik,' she suggested. 'He seems to like me well enough. I'm sure I could convince him to bring you back. You could go home again.'

'No!' The look on Fyn's face was pure terror. 'No, please, Jael. Please don't do that!' He reached out, grabbing her hand. 'Promise me you won't say anything to the king, or to my mother or father. Please!'

His eyes were desperate and something else. Scared.

'Alright, alright,' Jael soothed. 'I won't say anything, I promise. On one condition, though. Tell me why you were banished.'

Fyn's blinking eyes told her that he wanted to run and hide, but he kept staring at her, until finally, he dropped his head, sighing.

'Alright, I will.'

***

'And where is your wife this morning? Trying to seek revenge on Thorgils?' Eirik grinned, prodding the fire.

Eadmund leaned into the flames. 'No, not this morning. Thorgils is busy wrestling Torstan and Klaufi in the Pit. I haven't seen Jael. She probably went riding.'

The hall was relatively empty, just the servants tidying up, and Morac and Beorn talking about ships over the map table. Eirik felt a sense of relief, enjoying the peace and quiet. He glanced at Eadmund, who seemed reasonably sober, and alert. More like the son he remembered from years ago.

They were sitting around the fire in the middle of a snowy day. Just the two of them. Eirik hadn't felt so content in some time. 'She's always riding, that one, or fighting it seems. Not the sort of wife I imagined you'd end up with! I wonder how she'll be when my grandsons start arriving?'

Eadmund squirmed. It had been playing on his mind these past few weeks that he had to change things with Jael. He needed to find a way to break down the wall between them before his father grew suspicious about his lack of grandsons. He just hadn't found the opportunity to do so. 'I imagine she'll be much the same. I can't see her sitting around the fire with a circle of women, embroidering a tapestry,' he grinned.

'No, nor should she,' Eirik smiled. 'That would be like putting a wolf in a room of children and asking it to play nicely. It would end up a big, bloody mess!'

Eadmund laughed, remembering the look on Jael's face when she'd fought Thorgils. She certainly was wolf-like with those eyes of hers. They followed him everywhere; he saw them constantly, even when he was with Evaine.

'Will you be placing a few coins on your wife in the contest, then?' Eirik wondered. 'Or perhaps Thorgils?'

'Or Tarak?' Eadmund suggested, nodding to Erland and

Orvar who'd wandered into the hall, shaking snow from their cloaks.

'I think most people's coins will be on Tarak,' Eirik muttered, shuffling his stool closer to the fire. 'Although, I'm a bit bored with him winning every damn contest we have. I'd rather bet on Jael or Thorgils instead.'

'I can't see Jael beating Tarak,' Eadmund mused. 'He's a giant. She wouldn't be strong enough against him.'

'Thorgils isn't that much smaller, and she coped well enough with him. Although, Tarak is the better fighter, for sure.'

'Don't tell Thorgils that,' Eadmund smiled. 'He thinks he has a chance this time.'

'And maybe he does, with Jael helping him.'

'Maybe, but I'd still choose Tarak. He's made of stone. It's like hitting a wall. Nothing moves him. He's unbreakable.'

'But you defeated him,' Eirik reminded his son. 'Don't you remember?'

'Not really,' Eadmund said dismissively. 'It was so long ago. I was probably drunk at the time! I almost didn't, I think. I had a lot of luck that day.'

'I've never been in a fight that didn't involve some luck,' Eirik noted. 'The gods are always watching. They choose to help the one they think worthiest.'

Eadmund looked scornful. 'Well, what does that say about them if they keep picking Tarak as their champion?'

'Ahhh, well, they like a man who knows how to win. Say what you like about him, but he never gives in, no matter how the fight is going. He always finds a way to come back and win. Except against you, of course,' Eirik smiled. 'Perhaps you need to step up your training now, see if you can be the one to defeat Tarak? I know it would make a lot of people happy to see him lose.'

Eadmund laughed. 'Me? Ha! I don't think so, not this year at least. But it would be nice to see someone give him what he's had coming these past few years. Whoever it is.'

***

Fyn had stalled, insisting upon going outside to the woodpile to bring in another armload of logs. The hut was too cold, he insisted, and Jael hadn't complained because, well, he was right.

Now the fire was spitting happily, and the room had warmed up so quickly that Jael was almost considering removing her cloak. Fyn sat quietly next to her, vibrating with nerves.

'Tell me what happened,' Jael urged. 'It can't be that bad, can it?'

Fyn swallowed, gulping a few times, his eyes wandering from the flames to the bed, avoiding Jael's face. 'It *was* bad,' he whispered quietly. 'For me, it was very bad.'

Jael waited. She didn't want to rush him.

'My father, he... didn't like me. I don't know why, but he never liked me, so when he... when he found me, as he did, he knew he'd found a way to get rid of me. He wasn't going to listen to anything I said because his own ideas were already planted in his head. So, he told the king everything he'd seen and gave him no choice. He had to banish me.' Fyn saw the confused look on Jael's face and tried to unmuddle his thoughts. 'He found me,' he mumbled, coughing nervously, 'being raped.'

Jael gasped. She couldn't help it. Her eyes widened in sympathy as she stared at him.

'I was face down on a table being raped,' Fyn shuddered, the memories painting torturous pictures in his scarred mind. 'And my father didn't stop him. He didn't stay and try to stop him. He just left. Left me being raped. The look on his face... disgust, that's all he felt. He didn't try to save me. He, he thought I was doing it, part of it, finding pleasure in it. I don't know. But he didn't do anything to stop it.' Fyn's eyes were full of tears as he stared into the fire, wanting to disappear. 'He told the king, though. He couldn't wait to do that.'

'I don't understand how you could be punished for being

raped?' Jael frowned, her heart throbbing loudly in her ears. 'How is that possible?'

'There are rules, laws on the islands. About men laying with other men,' Fyn said awkwardly. 'It's acceptable to be the man doing it, but to be the one... receiving it... that is to be like a woman. Not a man. No one like that is acceptable on the islands. They are banished.'

Jael was horrified. 'What? But you were *raped*, Fyn! Didn't you tell your father that, or Eirik?'

Fyn was silent, lost in his memories.

Jael reached out, touching his arm.

He jumped.

'No, I didn't tell my father. I didn't speak to the king. I just left when my father told me to. He warned me to never come back.'

'But why? And what about the man who did this to you? He should have been punished. *He* should have been the one banished!'

Fyn laughed bitterly. 'Not him. They would never banish him. There was no point in me ever saying anything, not against him.' He looked angry now. 'He didn't just rape me that night, Jael. He had done it to me since I was a boy.'

Jael's body clenched. Her breathing stilled.

'He would find me, no matter where I went, or where I hid,' Fyn went on, numbly. 'He would come and get me, and hurt me, and make me do things that made me want to vomit. And he would scare me so much that I never said anything to anyone. He told me that he'd hurt my mother if I did. So I never said a word. Not once, till now.' Fyn dropped his head to his hands, sobbing, his shoulders heaving with the force of his pain.

Jael put her arm around his back, holding onto him while he wept.

She felt sick. Sad for Fyn. And angry, so angry that this man had tortured him and ruined his life, while he was still living in the fort, free and unpunished. 'Who was it, Fyn? she asked, her voice as hard as stone. 'Who did this to you?'

He sat up, sniffing, considering things, not wanting to speak that name again. Then looking at Jael's determined face, he suddenly felt reassured. Not alone.

She was his friend.

'It was... Tarak.'

***

Thorgils was waving his arms around, retelling his battle victory to two attentive women, when Jael strode past, climbing through the railings, into the Pit. She shrugged off her cloak but kept her swordbelt on.

'Let's try with real swords today,' she snapped, glaring at him intently as she unsheathed her new sword.

Thorgils' attention was immediately drawn away from the attractive faces, towards the fearsome creature who stood there, waiting for him. She had a look in her eye today that creased his forehead. 'Real swords?' He smiled politely at the women, excusing himself with a bow. 'You think you can handle that? Have you even used that sword of yours before?' Thorgils removed his cloak and clambered into the Pit. He wasn't sure that this was the wisest game to play, but he was too intrigued to stop and think about it for long.

'No,' Jael said quickly. 'But I need to know how to, so you can help me. Unless you're scared of my little *Toothpick*? He has a very sharp blade, you know. I wouldn't want to hurt you.'

Thorgils flinched. 'Hurt me?' he asked, his smile wavering. 'Go ahead, if it will make you feel better.'

They had trained together, many times since the fight, but without much intensity. Jael had tried to give Thorgils some advice, which he'd almost listened to; shown him ways that he could play with Tarak's mind to help him win. But after her conversation with Fyn, she wanted the pleasure of beating Tarak herself. And she needed to get stronger and sharper in every way possible if there was a chance of that happening.

'Better?' Jael scoffed. 'This won't make me feel better, but it will help me on the way.' She squatted slightly, shifting her legs apart to balance herself, scuffing the ground until she could feel the certainty of earth beneath her boots. 'Come at me as hard as you can, with everything you have. Let's see where we're at. How ready we both are for this contest of yours.' Jael was so angry. She felt so enraged by what Fyn had told her. She didn't know what she could do to help him, but right now, she needed to release all the furious tension that was threatening to drown her.

'I can do that,' Thorgils smiled confidently, noticing that the two women had remained behind to watch. 'If you think you're ready for it?'

'Oh, I'm ready.'

And gripping *Toothpick* tightly, Jael went for him.

CHAPTER TWENTY TWO

'It's stopped bleeding, I think,' Biddy murmured, stepping back to admire her needlework. 'You'll live.'

Thorgils groaned, unconvinced.

'It's not that bad,' Jael insisted with a grin. 'Hardly worth a stitch really.'

Biddy and Thorgils glared at Jael, neither of them impressed by her lack of empathy.

'You nearly took my balls off!' Thorgils grumbled, wincing at the sight of the small wound on his upper thigh.

'How big *are* these balls of yours, Thorgils? I scratched your leg!'

'That's not a scratch,' he snorted. 'That sword of yours is deadly!'

'Good!' Jael laughed, sitting on the bed next to him. 'There wouldn't be much point to it otherwise.'

'But perhaps it wasn't the best idea to practice with it, not unless you're actually trying to hurt someone?' Biddy suggested, bringing Thorgils a cup of ale to settle him down. 'Surely that's what the wooden swords are for?'

'They use real swords in the contest,' Jael told her, leaning back against the wall, enjoying a sip of cool ale. 'And I need to learn how to use mine, and quickly if I'm to make an impression.'

Thorgils looked surprised. 'You want to make an impression now, do you? Why the change?'

Jael glanced at her cup, the memory of her talk with Fyn still fresh in her mind. 'Well, I suppose, revenge for one thing,' she said, looking up. 'I can't have everyone thinking I can be beaten so easily, especially by a big girl like you. And maybe... maybe I want a chance at Tarak too. Why not? Somebody needs to put him on his giant arse.'

Thorgils laughed at the determination on her face. He didn't doubt that she had more than a chance, especially after today. She'd been in the red mist when she'd fought him. If he hadn't started bleeding so quickly, she would have shown him no mercy, he was certain of it.

Something was troubling Jael, that much was obvious.

'Well then, here's to destroying Tarak!' Thorgils raised his cup, knocking it into hers. 'As long as the contest ends with him in a crying heap of his own shit, we'll both be happy.'

'Agreed. If only it were a fight to the death...'

And looking into Jael's eyes, Thorgils saw that she meant it.

***

Jael lay in bed that night consumed with sadness for Fyn, and anger about Tarak. She wanted to kill him. She'd wanted to kill people before, of course, and she had, but not for a long time. Nothing had made her feel this desperate for justice. But how? Where was justice to be found? Not in the laws of Oss, it seemed.

She'd promised Fyn that she wouldn't say anything to Eirik, or Morac, or even Tarak. But how could she help Fyn, and how could she ensure that Tarak was punished if she didn't do anything? Nobody deserved a painful death more than that vile, child-abusing bastard.

Jael was full of angry steam as she lay there, unable to sleep, incapable of relaxing. And lonely. She would have talked to

Aleksander about Fyn. He would have been annoyingly practical, and she would have dismissed his advice completely, but still, it was always nice to hear it; to know that he cared enough about her to try and help.

The loss of him was hard to accept.

She felt as though she was missing a part of herself; that only half of her was here, lying alone in her large, empty bed.

Jael wondered if he was waiting for her, or if he'd decided to find someone to warm his own bed until she came back? In his vision, she had returned to Andala with a child, so that was some way off as she'd not even touched Eadmund yet. Jael shuddered. He was improving, and there were signs of hope, but she couldn't imagine sharing her bed with him. Eadmund wasn't Aleksander. And Jael loved Aleksander. But if she wanted to get back to Aleksander, she needed a child.

And for that, she needed Eadmund.

***

Runa felt sick.

She grasped hold of Evaine's hair as her daughter bent over, retching into the bucket again. It was the third time this morning; it was the third time this week.

The sick feeling in her stomach had grown every day, fuelled by the look of her daughter, who was both pale and glowing at the same time, whose appetite had changed, who complained about feeling uncomfortable, whose body seemed rounder somehow. There was simply no denying it, but Runa was still determined to do so.

'Water,' Evaine coughed. 'Forget my hair, Mother! Just get me some water!' She flapped a hand at Runa and straightened up, holding her aching back.

Runa returned with a cup of water and Evaine sipped cautiously from it. Everything was making her ill, but as miserable as her body felt, she couldn't have been happier. 'When do you think I should tell Eadmund?' she asked coyly, coming to sit by the fire, smoothing her rumpled dress over her growing bump.

Runa swallowed, conscious that their servant, Respa, was sweeping the kitchen floor.

'Tell me about what?' Morac asked irritably, pushing open the door, shaking off a layer of snow.

Runa and Evaine stared at each other, mouths open, neither wanting to be the first to speak. Evaine's confidence dissolved; her father was not going to be pleased with her at all.

'Evaine?' Morac demanded. He was feeling old, and cold, and his day with Eirik had frustrated him. They'd talked incessantly about ships and Hest, and Eirik had ignored most of his advice. He was in no mood for childish games.

'Yes, Father?' Evaine smiled sweetly, moving to sit beside him.

'What do you need to tell Eadmund?' Morac wondered impatiently, tugging off his boots.

'Oh, that. It was nothing, just talk between women,' Evaine giggled. 'Perhaps you need a drink to warm you up? It looks as though you've had a hard day.' And getting up, she rushed away to the kitchen to speak to Respa.

'What is she up to?' Morac asked Runa, who came to help him with his boots, which, being wet, were not coming off easily.

Runa tried her best not to look guilty, then giving up, she simply turned her face towards Morac's boots. 'Nothing, as she said. She's just being silly, thinking of Eadmund all the time. As she always does. She's having a hard time getting his attention lately, I think.'

'Well, as long as it's only thinking she's doing,' Morac grumbled as Evaine returned to the fire. 'You stay away from him like I told you and we'll all be better for it. I'm sure that once this marriage stops being new, and Eirik has the grandson he wants so desperately, he'll be more relaxed about everything. But until then, you must keep your distance. Don't let Eirik catch a glimpse of you!'

Evaine didn't enjoy being reprimanded.

She bit her bottom lip and sat sullenly next to her father, simmering.

When she was the Queen of Oss, no one would be able to tell her what to do.

Ever.

***

There was only darkness.

Edela strained her eyes, but there was nothing to see, just pure darkness. It wrapped around her, inside her, and she was struggling to breathe, to clear her throat and mind. She felt herself getting sucked into it, as though she was becoming part of it, as though her life-force was slipping away from her, into it. She tried to scream, to call for help, but her screams echoed back to her.

All around her.

She was trapped in a cave, all alone. In the dark.

Then she heard screaming: women's voices, wailing in agony.

Edela spun around, finally spying a light, a hint of flames in all the blackness. She could hear her breath rasping as she hurried forward.

The fire grew bigger, brighter, then disappeared entirely to reveal a town.

Tuura.

There was nothing she recognised, nothing to tell her where she was, but she knew, in her knotted stomach, she knew this place.

The screaming died down, replaced by low, keening moans.

A crowd stood around in the night air; a huddle of raven-haired Tuurans in winter cloaks, snowflakes drifting all around them. Some were holding onto each other in grief and despair, while others, it seemed, looked less upset, more relieved. As the crowd parted, Edela stepped forward, peering past the people, who didn't appear to notice her at all.

Two men in boiled-leather aprons were cleaning up a mess. A mess of blood and bodies. Two bodies. Two heads. Each man picked up a head, and with an emotionless face, jammed it onto a long pointed spear. Edela glimpsed the gruesome death masks, inhaling sharply. They were young women, no more than girls. Long, dark, blood-soaked hair hung down from their crudely chopped off heads.

Edela wanted to vomit, but she couldn't even retch. She tried to turn and run from those ruined faces, but her feet wouldn't respond. Her body wouldn't move at all, and as the men shoved the spears firmly into the hard earth, leaving the heads to drain of all their blood, Edela was forced to stare into those glazed eyes. Not even her head could turn itself away, nor her eyes close against the horror.

'We have to find the other one,' she heard from somewhere behind her. 'She must have taken the book.'

Edela woke, gagging, coughing, spluttering.

Aleksander was at her side immediately. 'Edela!' He had been awake for some time, watching her dreaming, her body twisting relentlessly in her bed; uncertain whether he should wake her. 'Edela, are you alright? What's happened? Is it Jael?'

Aleksander handed Edela a cup of water, which she quickly pushed away. She wasn't thirsty, she needed air. The room was suffocating her. She felt as though part of her was still trapped in that cloying darkness. She needed to breathe. 'Open the door,' she croaked urgently. 'Please!'

Aleksander hurried to the door, pulling it open. The dull morning light fell gently into the cottage as Edela scrambled out of bed, and, with Aleksander's help, headed to the door. Her body sunk into his supportive arm as she felt the frigid air on her face. She breathed deeply, closing her eyes, letting it fill her lungs and cool her panic. 'That's enough,' she shivered eventually. 'I'll get frostbite if I stand out here any longer!'

Aleksander sighed, relieved that Edela had recovered. Desperate to know what had happened. 'Come and sit down,' he urged, guiding her to her chair. He put another log on the fire, poking the embers before coming to sit on the stool before her. 'What happened? What did you see?'

Edela didn't know what to say. She gazed into his worried eyes, trying to make sense of it all. 'I'm not sure. It wasn't about Jael. Not really,' she mumbled, noting his relief. 'I think it was about the Darkness. And perhaps it was another clue.'

She told him all about her dream then, about the beheaded girls, and the missing one. The one with the book.

'Do you think the book could be the Book of Darkness?' Aleksander wondered eagerly. 'Perhaps your theory is right? That it all comes back to that book? That it's real?'

'Yes, possibly,' Edela frowned, uncertainly. 'But it's all so very muddled. I have no real answers, and no one to talk to about any of it. I think you and I might need to go to Tuura. The vision I had in my dream, it was Tuura, I'm sure of it. It seemed a different time, though. Something that had happened long ago. I'm sure we can find someone in Tuura who might know of it. Someone who can help us help Jael.'

Aleksander squirmed, feeling himself panic. 'But Tuura...'

'I know,' Edela murmured, standing up, desperate for that water now. 'We don't want to go back there, none of us do after what happened, especially you. I know it will be hard, but we need to find out more. We won't be able to help Jael until we do, and I certainly can't help her without you.'

Edela eyed Aleksander with a determination that reminded him of Jael.

He shuddered, never imagining that he would consider returning to Tuura.

Not after what had happened.

***

Eadmund felt dreadful as he trudged towards the Pit. The snow was up to his ankles, and his balance was unsteady. He'd drunk too much for the first time in weeks, and his body was punishing him mercilessly. His limbs felt heavy, and his head banged with every step. He wasn't looking forward to Thorgils' rollicking either. The day was dull and grim, but Eadmund could tell that the morning was nearly over. His friend wouldn't be impressed by his late arrival.

'Ahhh, you're awake at last, sleeping princess,' Torstan grinned, eyeing the dishevelled figure before him. 'You really did have too much last night, didn't you?'

'Maybe one or two more than I should've,' Eadmund admitted. 'But I'm here. I might vomit at any moment, but I'm here.' He looked around, rubbing his eyes; he might have been here, but no one else was. 'Where is everyone?'

'They've gone to eat, most of them,' Torstan said, throwing his cloak around his shoulders. 'Ketil knows how to drum up business, that's for sure. He started cooking in the middle of training, and no one could think with their sword arms after that, just with their bellies. Come on, you can buy me something to eat!'

'Where's Thorgils?' Eadmund wondered, following his friend towards Ketil's. 'And Jael?'

'Oh, they just left. Thorgils went riding with her. On your horse. Again.' Torstan blew on his hands, most of which were exposed in well-worn blue gloves. 'Anyone would think she was his wife instead of yours, the amount of time they spend together!'

Eadmund was irritated by the observation, though he wasn't

sure why. His head was thick with regret, and he was struggling to form any clear thoughts at all. He was relieved to know that Jael had left the fort, though. He could spend the afternoon trying to wake himself up, ready to face her again. She was always so sharp and fast, and he felt like a blundering fool in front of her. An addled head was hardly going to help him improve upon that.

'Thorgils is welcome to her!' Eadmund grinned, attempting to appear more cheerful than he felt. 'I'm sure Eirik won't suspect a thing. As long as his grandsons don't come out with bright red hair!'

***

They rode along silently, into the dark grey morning. It was an awkward silence, and Thorgils felt as though he'd missed something. There was definitely a tension he wasn't a part of. Not an unfriendly one, but he sensed that something had occurred. He dismissed it for now, though, determined to enjoy the ride, despite the moodiness of his companions and the gloom of the day.

It had been Thorgils' idea to take his horse, Vili, with them so that Fyn could join them for a ride. And he had something in mind that would put a smile on both their miserable faces. 'You'll be speechless, I promise,' Thorgils winked at Jael. 'Oss has some secrets that will amaze you. Secrets that most people on the island don't even know about. It may be that this will surprise you too, Fyn!'

Fyn looked unconvinced, but Jael smiled. Thorgils had quickly forgiven her for nearly severing his enormous balls, and he seemed as cheerful as ever, unlike Fyn, who had barely spoken to her for weeks now. She had tried to broach the subject of what to do about Tarak, but he had backed into his shell so quickly, that she'd left it alone. Trawling up memories from such a dark pit hadn't been easy for him, and Jael knew that it would take some time for him to release them back into the abyss again.

Despite the sinking clouds, there was much to take in. Oss was a wild, windblown place, and Jael found it unexpectedly appealing. Whereas Brekka was lush, rolling, and serene, Oss was a jagged, angry mess of dark mountains, frozen lakes, sharp cliffs, and wide valleys. The scenery was a constant surprise, even hiding beneath a good blanket of snow as it had been since she'd arrived.

They rode at a leisurely pace through a winding valley, mountains rising up around them on both sides. Jael hadn't been this way before; in fact, she hadn't explored much without Thorgils, so she had no idea where they were going at all.

'You won't say where you're taking us, then?' she wondered.

'Not a chance! I want to see your faces when we get there. I think you'll like it. I know you will!' Thorgils was enjoying leading them along, his chest puffing out bullishly in his new, brown fur cloak. 'We turn here,' he said, tugging Leada to the left, towards the mountains.

Jael and Fyn shot each other puzzled looks behind Thorgils' back.

Where was he leading them?

***

It was perfect. Tender, smoky, and the ideal remedy for his grumbling belly and muddled mind. Eadmund chewed happily on his meat stick as he sat opposite Torstan amongst the crowd of Ketil's satisfied customers, enjoying the noise of the square as it buzzed around them.

He started to relax.

'I meant to tell you,' Torstan mumbled. 'Your father came by, looking for you this morning.'

Eadmund's face dropped, his shoulders tensed, and he stopped eating. 'And what did you tell him?'

'I didn't tell him anything, but Thorgils did. He said you were unwell,' Torstan snorted, wiping a greasy hand over his short blonde beard. 'Not that Eirik thought much of that! He rolled his eyes and left.'

Eadmund's improved spirits quickly sank. It had been a nice change to feel his father's approval these past few weeks. He had been embarrassing Eirik for so many years, and his father had endured it better than most would have. Eadmund felt that he owed him something for keeping faith in him for so long.

'Speaking of which, here he comes again!'

Eadmund quickly abandoned the rest of his meat, and, clapping Torstan on the back, he hurried to meet his father, who had stopped to talk with Ketil.

'You're awake, then?' Eirik smiled, although his good cheer did not extend much past his lips.

'Almost,' Eadmund grinned, keeping his tone light. 'Though, perhaps I had one or two more than I should have last night.'

Eirik raised a woolly eyebrow. 'One or two? Or maybe ten or twenty?'

'It wasn't *that* many!'

'If you say so,' Eirik smiled wryly. 'I've just had Morac this morning, telling me that our ale stores are running low, which is not the thing I want to hear when we're not even at Vesta yet. He didn't mention your name, but I've a feeling he was trying to suggest it might have something to do with you.'

'Well, it sounds as though Morac needs to plan a little more carefully if you're running out of ale this quickly. Perhaps I should make some suggestions about how much he should allow for in future?' Eadmund's tired eyes sparkled with a little humour. He was making an effort to smooth over any cracks his lapse had caused. It was working, he sensed, as his father's face started to lose its sharp edges.

'I'm not sure anyone should take advice from you. Not when it comes to ale, my son.'

'Eadmund!' Eydis smiled, coming towards her brother, using a long stick Eirik had carved for her. It enabled her to be independent around the fort while keeping her safe, although Eirik still hated to let her out of his sight. She was growing up, he knew, but he couldn't stop worrying about her. He was terrified of losing her, as he had her mother.

Eadmund grabbed his sister, spinning her around. 'How are you, Little Thing?' he asked, genuinely pleased to see her.

'Hungry! And you smell like what I want to eat,' she said cheekily.

'You want to eat dirt? Ear wax? Snot? Stale ale?'

'No, but you can buy me one of Ketil's meat sticks please.' She dug inside the little purse hanging from her belt.

Eadmund put a hand out to stop her. 'Eydis, no. It's my turn to treat you,' he insisted. 'You wait here.' And he went off to stand in line for her.

'He seems happy,' Eydis said, feeling her father wrap his arm around her shoulder. 'Maybe last night was just a hiccup?'

Eirik watched Eadmund, who certainly did look alert and cheerful as he chatted with his friends. 'I hope so. I don't want to lose him all over again.'

'Well, maybe you could let the ale run out completely?' Eydis suggested. 'Then you'd always have him like this.'

'Ha! I would, but the rest of the men would plot to kill me, for sure!' Eirik laughed, squeezing Eydis, enjoying her smile. Eadmund did seem alright, he thought. If only he would stay this way, always; no hiccups. Then he could sleep through the night for the first time in years.

Next to him, Eydis tugged on his cloak. He turned to see Runa approaching. Eirik had always liked Runa, but the years had not been kind to her. She walked in a shadow these days, her heavily lined face mostly turned towards the ground. He wondered if that was the loss of her son, or perhaps the trial of her daughter, or was it Morac who had worn her down? His old friend had become increasingly ornery of late. 'Runa!' he smiled warmly. They'd been friends since childhood, perhaps even bed companions in their youth; although, he'd spent much of that time as drunk as Eadmund, and couldn't say if that was a true recollection.

'Eirik, Eydis,' Runa nodded, returning his smile, though her eyes flitted around anxiously.

'Are you looking for Morac?' Eirik wondered.

'Yes, he wasn't in the hall, and since everyone seems to be at Ketil's today, I thought he might be here.'

'I haven't seen him, but I'll tell him that you're looking for him if I do.'

'I would be grateful, thank you.'

Evaine snuck up behind her mother then, and Eirik watched Runa's expression freeze in horror as she saw her daughter. He imagined that his face didn't look much different.

'Hello, Mother, my lord,' Evaine beamed, her pale cheeks showing spots of pink. 'Eydis, I didn't see you there! I hope you're feeling well again?'

No one said a word.

Eydis reached for the assurance of her father's hand to steady them both.

Runa looked as though she wanted to run away.

Eadmund returned, not noticing Evaine until it was too late.

'Hello, Eadmund,' Evaine smiled coyly, looking down at her clasped hands which sat just below her belly. She could hardly contain her happiness; it had been days since she'd last seen him.

Eadmund handed Eydis her meat stick, nodding in Evaine's direction, making no attempt to look directly at her.

No one said a word.

'Have you been training for the contest, Eadmund?' Evaine asked sweetly, trying to ease the tension that was building. 'I'm very much looking forward to it. Of course, Tarak will be the favourite, but I imagine there'll be a few new challengers. Perhaps even your wife?'

Eadmund didn't reply. He was confused, wondering what Evaine was playing at with her pointless chatter. Getting herself into trouble with everyone, it seemed. His father's face was turning red.

That was a bad sign.

'We must be getting along to find your father, Evaine,' Runa hissed at her daughter, her composure withering under Eirik's furious stare. 'I wish you luck in the contest, Eadmund.' She nodded quickly to Eirik, grabbed Evaine firmly by the arm, and pulled her away.

The three Skallesons stood in silence. Evaine had somehow managed to make each one of them feel uncomfortable.

Eirik spoke first. 'I should get rid of that girl.' He looked ready to spit.

Eadmund suddenly felt sorry for Evaine. It was his fault for leading her on. He'd encouraged her for purely selfish reasons, and if she were to be punished, or worse, banished, it would surely be his fault. 'You can't do that, Father,' Eadmund pleaded, turning towards him. 'She's done nothing wrong. Nothing to be banished for at least. You may as well banish me. It's my fault!'

'Well, don't think that I won't,' Eirik grumbled. 'You need to be spending time with your wife, not some childish girl who wants to play games with you, and me, it seems'. He looked around, frowning. 'Where is Jael, by the way? It feels as though I haven't seen her for days.'

'She's gone riding with Thorgils.'

'Again?' Eirik's eyebrows knitted together in displeasure. 'It's time you remembered how to ride a horse. She's horse mad, that one, so you'd better get back in the saddle if you want to spend some time with her,' he huffed. 'Eydis, you stay with your brother and finish your meal, I'm going back to the hall to get warm.' And mumbling crossly to himself, he stormed off.

'Well, he's easily annoyed today,' Eadmund laughed,

watching his father scurry away.

Eydis didn't say anything as she stood there holding onto her meat stick, her appetite suddenly gone. For she had just seen the strongest image of Evaine.

She was glowing; surrounded by light.

Pregnant.

CHAPTER TWENTY THREE

The cliff they stood beneath reached up so high that Jael had to strain her neck to catch a glimpse of its peak. It stood there, staring back down at her, streaming with cold moisture, its sheer exterior, dark and imposing amongst the low-lying mist.

'We go in here,' Thorgils smiled, his eyes twinkling as he pointed at the cliff-face.

Jael and Fyn looked around, confused at first, but a slight turn to the left revealed a light emerging from the rocks, and a natural opening wide enough for Thorgils to slip through. They followed him; Fyn as curious as Jael now.

He certainly hadn't been here before.

The smell when they entered the cave was intense, like rotten eggs, Jael thought, wrinkling her nose. The air was much warmer than outside, though; warm, and glowing blue! Looking up in amazement, she saw that the high, curved ceiling of the cave was covered in thousands of tiny blue lights. Glow worms. She remembered seeing something similar in one of Andala's sacred caves, but nothing that matched this.

This place felt like magic.

They followed Thorgils down a ragged path towards a huddle of large rocks. 'Careful, it's slippery,' he cautioned. 'I'd suggest you close your eyes before you get to the surprise, but that would likely kill you both!' He stopped, waiting for Jael and Fyn to come beside him, smiling at their puzzled expressions as he gestured over the rocks.

To a little pool.

A shimmering, steaming pool, rippling under the sky of lights. Fyn's eyes widened. 'It's a hot pool, isn't it?'

Jael's numb lips parted. 'Hot? It's hot? Hot water?'

Thorgils looked triumphant. 'It is! A hot pool, just for you, the coldest woman on Oss!' He laughed at the look of sheer joy on her face. 'I've seen you shivering since you arrived. Moaning and miserable in that thin cloak of yours, so I thought you needed something to warm you up. And I remembered this place,' he smiled. 'Eirik found it and named it Eskild's Cave after Eadmund's mother. Only those people Eirik trusts know about it, and luckily for you, one of those people is me!'

Jael was touched that he would think to bring her here, but impatient too; her frozen body was demanding that she throw herself into the steaming hot water immediately. 'I can't think of anything to say, except, thank you, and get out so I can get in!' She smiled ecstatically at the men as she rushed to remove her gloves and cloak.

'Alright, alright, give us a chance to leave!' Thorgils panicked, hurrying back to the entrance with Fyn. 'I don't want to see you naked before your husband does!'

Fyn stared curiously at Thorgils as they made their way outside.

'Don't ask!' Thorgils laughed.

Jael didn't even look up to see if they had gone. She was undressed in a heartbeat, folding her sword up into her damp clothes, happy to escape their miserable embrace for now. She caught a glimpse of her tattoos as she approached the water. They had almost completely healed; she hoped they wouldn't mind the heat.

Her body went limp as she slid one toe into the dark pool. The water felt hot enough to melt her icy bones. She slipped into it quickly, feeling the heat devour her shivering flesh.

The water was deep enough for Jael to stand and still be mostly submerged, but the heat quickly made her limbs heavy, so she found a little hole in the side of the pool, just big enough for her backside, and she sunk into it. Laying her head back against a smooth rock, she stared up at the sparkling ceiling, marvelling at the lights. Jael's body sagged contentedly, and she closed her eyes. She saw Eadmund's face immediately and frowned. What had happened to him this morning? Perhaps the changes in him had just been fleeting? A false hope for everyone to cling to? Maybe it just was, as Biddy had said, the way some people were born? Perhaps Eadmund would end up as miserable as Biddy's father had?

She hoped not.

Jael opened her eyes. She suddenly felt low and didn't want to feel that way in this perfect, perfect place. Shaking her head in frustration, she tried to stop Eadmund from entering her thoughts. She cleared her mind and closed her eyes again. Her body was utterly limp now, and it was impossible to resist the sense of unravelling she felt as the water softened every part of her. Her mind kept wandering back to Eadmund, though, and eventually, she didn't resist.

She wondered if should she try to help him? He was her husband, after all, for now at least. Perhaps there was something she could do? He would likely need all the help he could get if Eydis was right about Ivaar coming back to Oss.

But what *could* she do?

If Evaine fell pregnant, nothing was going to stop Eirik bringing Ivaar back.

***

Kalfa was a small island, not even a quarter the size of Oss, and Ivaar hated it.

Though not as much as he hated Oss.

The people of Oss had never liked him. His father had never liked him. His brother had hated him, and the feeling had been entirely mutual on every count. But Ivaar had spent every day of the past seven years imagining a way to get back there and reclaim the life he'd once had as the king's son.

As the true heir to the Slave Islands.

He was a lord here, on Kalfa. *The* lord. It was his island as much as it was his father's. His father never came here, and Ivaar never went to Oss, so Kalfa had become his whole world, and him its prisoner. A tiny, unimpressive, rocky stone of a go-nowhere world. He was lord of nothing much and going slowly insane because of it.

Ivaar was ambitious; desperately so. And not prepared to wait any longer. He'd had word that there had been a wedding on Oss; that his pathetic brother had married, and married well. A Furyck. His father had pulled a surprise there. Jael Furyck was a real prize, the woman he would certainly have chosen for his own wife if he'd been given any choice in the matter. Furia's daughter, they called her, and a battle-hardened warrior too. That was a woman to have beside him, not like his permanently miserable wife, Isaura, who was as exciting as a bowl of cold porridge.

Forced upon him at the last moment before he'd been thrown from Oss to Kalfa, she had provided him with four living children – one of them a son – so she had done her job, but nothing about her excited him, just as nothing about Kalfa excited him.

And Ivaar was desperate for excitement.

Desperate to turn everything upside down in his boringly predictable life.

He sat impatiently on his large wooden chair inside his ugly little hall on his small pathetic island, stroking his finely groomed beard.

There had to be a way back to Oss. If only the gods would help him.

Perhaps he needed to talk to his dreamer about making a sacrifice?

There might be hope in that.

***

'Did Jael give you that bruise?' Thorgils wondered, pointing to a large, greenish mark on the side of Fyn's face.

Fyn blushed, ducking his head. 'Ummm, yes, she did. One of many.'

They were standing by the horses, jiggling and shivering in the freezing air, both wishing that Jael would hurry up so they could take their turn in the hot pool.

'Ha!' Thorgils laughed, stroking Leada's cold face with one hand, feeding her a carrot with the other. 'That doesn't surprise me. She doesn't go easy on you, that's for sure.'

'No,' Fyn agreed. 'But if she'd treated me softly, I'd probably still be tripping over my feet, dropping my sword every time she looked at me. Now I just need to learn how to avoid being kicked in the head!'

Thorgils looked shocked. 'She kicks you in the head? How does she do that?'

Fyn laughed, relaxing for the first time in a while. 'Easily, it seems, as she's done it countless times, and I've not seen it coming yet!'

'That's what the bruise is from, then? Her boot?'

'Mmmm,' Fyn mumbled, gnawing on a piece of salt fish he'd found in his pouch.

'But how does she kick that high?' Thorgils was still stunned by the thought of it, reaching his arm out to measure the height of Fyn's bruise from the ground. 'I'd like to see that.'

'I'm sure she'd happily show you,' Fyn laughed. 'But you'd probably end up in the snow!'

'Show you what?' Jael wondered, emerging from the hole in

the mountain, folding her hood around her wet hair, her red face glowing.

'Nothing,' Thorgils muttered, quickly slipping past her. 'Nothing for you to worry about. You just keep those horses happy, and we'll be back soon.'

Jael looked at Fyn, but he just shrugged, following Thorgils into the cave.

She smiled, pleased to see a flicker of life in his eyes again.

***

Eydis knocked on the door, but there was no answer. There was no one around at all, she thought, listening intently. Not even a horse and certainly not any puppies. She couldn't hear a soul.

Her shoulders dropped in disappointment. She'd been hoping to see Jael, to talk to her about Evaine. To try and decide what they could possibly do, as futile as it all seemed now.

Biddy smiled down at the little girl standing outside the door. 'Hello, there. You must be Eydis.'

The puppies rushed joyously at Eydis, jumping up her legs. She bent down with a smile, happy to be showered in their sloppy affection again. 'And you must be Biddy,' she said shyly.

'I am,' Biddy said, unlocking the door. 'Now, why don't you come inside and warm yourself up, young miss. I'm sure Jael won't be long.

***

'You need to go there often, I think,' Thorgils grinned. 'You look like a different person with that silly smile all over your face. I think in this mood, you'd even give Eadmund a kiss or two!' He laughed loudly at the sudden grimace on Jael's cheerful face. 'Oh, he's not so bad that you can't even imagine kissing him, is he?'

'Well, he's not my choice,' Jael tried to explain, suddenly awkward. 'He's not who I would choose to kiss, or choose to be married to.' Her eyes drifted away gloomily then. 'If I'd ever chosen to be married at all.'

'So you had someone in Andala, then?' Thorgils suggested delicately.

Jael eyed him as they ambled up the hill towards the fort, the horses blowing hard after a fast ride from Fyn's. 'I might have.'

Thorgils looked at her with deep sympathy. 'Well, that's a hard thing, Jael, and I'm sorry for you. But you can't go back, can you? What's done is done. You're married now. And I tell you, in Eadmund you have a good man, and if you give him a chance, you might find a reason or two to kiss him, at least once. And who knows where that might lead...'

'You should stop worrying about me and Eadmund, and focus on your own chances for getting kisses, my friend,' Jael grumbled, giving Tig an encouraging nudge with her boot. She was starving and desperate to get back to see what Biddy had cooking. 'Why aren't you married, then?'

Thorgils' face fell so heavily that Jael immediately regretted her words. She'd never seen him look so serious or sad, but within moments he'd masked his eyes, and shaken it off with a light-hearted grin. 'Oh well, I'm the picky type, you see,' he insisted, trying to keep his voice casual. 'I like to sample the goods rather than go through with the purchase.' It didn't sound like him at all, and he knew it, and he knew that Jael knew it, but both of them left it alone. 'Besides,' he continued. 'I watched my mother nag my father till he died, so I was never keen on the idea of living under the thumb of a woman, no matter how comfortable her tits might be to snuggle into at night!'

Jael rolled her eyes. 'Oh, with talk like that, I can imagine the line to receive your favours stretches long and deep.'

'Yes, just like my cock!' Thorgils couldn't help the laugh that roared out of his chest as he firmly shut the door on the painful memories Jael had uncovered. They were so dusty now that it was an easy door to keep closed.

Most of the time.

Jael shook her head, nudging Tig again, who, getting annoyed now, dug his hooves into the thick snow and started to climb faster, leaving Leada with her much heavier weight, and the extra burden of towing Thorgils' horse, in his wake. Jael turned around in the saddle, laughing at the frustrated face staring back at her. 'You'd better hurry up, old man, or there'll be no stew left for you!'

***

There wasn't even any stew for her, it turned out. Eirik had sent word that he expected Jael at the hall for the evening meal, so Biddy hadn't prepared anything, which was just as well, as Eydis was desperate to talk. Thorgils left them to it and headed to the hall, his stomach rumbling loudly.

'What's happened?' Jael wondered, pulling off her wet boots, worried by the troubled look on Eydis' face.

Eydis hesitated, unsure where Biddy was.

'Oh, you needn't worry about Biddy,' Jael insisted, gripping Eydis' hand. 'Biddy wouldn't dare reveal anything we talk about. She knows what I can do with a sword!'

Eydis smiled nervously, almost reassured. She felt strange putting words to her thoughts; strange talking about such adult things.

'Tell me what happened, Eydis.'

'It's Evaine,' she spluttered. 'She's pregnant. I know she is.'

They both heard Biddy's gasp from the kitchen, but Jael was too stunned to say anything.

'She was in the square today, with her mother,' Eydis went on. 'She sounded so happy, and I could see a light around her. I could see a child inside her. I'm certain of it, Jael. I saw it this way in my dreams.' Eydis turned her head towards the floor, worry shrouding her pale little face. 'She is pregnant. Now.'

'Well, alright,' Jael muttered, almost to herself, scratching her nose distractedly. 'There's not much we can do about that, is there?'

'Isn't there? Anything?' Eydis pleaded hopefully. 'She can't have Eadmund's baby. You're supposed to do that!'

Jael didn't know what to say. She felt uncomfortable. All this talk about Eadmund was getting under her skin. If only Eirik had married him to Evaine, they could all have saved themselves a lot of trouble. 'Well, all we can do is try to keep your father calm when he finds out,' Jael suggested, trying to imagine Eirik's reaction. 'He's seen the changes in Eadmund, so he may not be as quick to call for Ivaar as everyone thinks.' She glanced at Biddy, who had come to join them by the fire.

Biddy's face reflected the doubt on her own. 'Perhaps you just need to get yourself pregnant before he finds out?' she suggested helpfully.

Jael didn't welcome that piece of advice. 'I think I'd rather have Ivaar here than suffer that!' she snorted.

'No, no, don't say that, Jael!' Eydis cried, her eyes full of fear. 'You don't know what he's capable of. You don't know what he'll do!'

Jael sighed. She felt as though she was rushing towards everything she had spent her whole life avoiding.

But rushing towards it, she was.

**

Axl sat, simmering furiously, watching his uncle pawing his mother. Their marriage plans were gathering pace, and Lothar assumed that his upcoming nuptials gave him the right to touch Gisila where and when he wanted, and he chose the King's Hall, in front of anyone who mattered in Andala.

Axl was sure that he'd never felt so helpless and angry at the same time. Lothar sat there in the seat that had been Ranuf's, touching the wife who had been Ranuf's, wearing the sword that had been Ranuf's. Axl could barely contain himself. He chewed on his lip, clenched his jaw, rolled his fingers over and over, his mouth set in a firm line of displeasure.

'You should learn how to craft a better smile than that,' Gant whispered hoarsely in his ear. 'It might save your life.'

Axl didn't turn around to acknowledge him. Gant was Lothar's man now, why should he care what he said? He'd abandoned them all when they'd needed him most and chosen to follow his bloated, ridiculous uncle, so Axl had no need for Gant's advice now. He picked at the food on his plate with his knife and remained silent and sullen.

Gant tried again, keeping his voice low. 'Your sister's not here, and your mother won't be able to save you if you keep to this path, Axl. Don't think they're not watching you.'

Axl looked up, catching Osbert's eyes boring into him.

Without acknowledging Gant, and completely ignoring his mother and Lothar, he stood up from the table, leaving to join his friends at the front of the hall.

He was too angry to speak.

'Axl doesn't seem very happy these days,' Osbert noted pointedly to Gisila. 'Does he not approve of you marrying my father?'

'Well, no, he is not too pleased,' Gisila admitted nervously, worried by Axl's mood and Osbert's interest in it. She tried to keep her face calm and her tone light. 'He misses Ranuf greatly. It's hard to lose your father when you're still a boy. He's missed out on so much guidance these past few years. And now, with

Jael gone, it's even harder for him.'

'He's hardly a boy, Gisila,' Lothar scoffed, turning his bulging belly towards her. 'And, of course, we all miss Ranuf, but Axl must accept that you deserve to find some happiness.' He picked up a carrot from her untouched plate, chomping into it, mouth wide open. 'He must see how it benefits him to be the king's stepson? Surely he can be happy for you and put a smile on his surly face for once?'

Gisila wanted to push Lothar off her. His body kept rolling towards her, touching her, and the look in his eyes made her want to recoil. She smiled blankly, knowing that there was nothing she could do. 'I will try and talk to him. Perhaps I'll ask Aleksander to speak to him before he leaves?' Gisila tried to look happy as she reached out a hand, reluctantly placing it on Lothar's sleeve. He beamed from her touch, slipping a hand under the table to rest on her thigh.

Gisila swallowed sharply, trying not to flinch. With Lothar on one side and Osbert on the other, she felt like a trapped animal, ready to be pounced on if she made one false move.

Watching from his table, Gant saw terror flare in Gisila's eyes. He watched the way Osbert was staring at Axl. And he saw Lothar, oblivious to anything that did not directly involve him, trying to stick his hand up Gisila's dress. There was no Jael, and no Aleksander, who was packing to leave on his trip with Edela.

He saw Ranuf's face and felt the rebuke in it.

They had been closer than brothers. Ranuf's family had felt like his own for so many years. Guilt weighed more heavily on his conscience with every passing day. He should have done more to help them when Ranuf died.

Perhaps it wasn't too late?

CHAPTER TWENTY FOUR

Jael couldn't get their faces out of her mind. First, there was Fyn's troubled one, then Thorgils' broken-hearted one, and now Eydis' terrified one. Her three friends on Oss, and each one of them traumatised by something she could do nothing about.

And then, of course, there was Evaine...

Ido and Vella rolled about in the snow at her feet, but Jael was too distracted to notice how happy they were to be let outside at last. It had snowed relentlessly for days, so heavily that most Osslanders had simply hibernated in their homes to wait it out. But this day had begun without a hint of bad weather, and everyone was finally emerging outside again.

'You'll lose them if you're not careful,' Eadmund grinned, coming to stand beside Jael at the railings of the Pit. He looked happy and relaxed, warm too, in a thick fur cloak.

No one was training today. It would take a long time to clear the ground. The snowfall had been the biggest dump so far, and no one seemed inclined to tackle the task of clearing such a large area this early in the day.

Jael stared at Eadmund, uneasy in his presence. He'd never approached her like this before. Not in daylight. Not when he was near-sober. She fiddled with her cloak, wanting to leave.

'You really should have a warmer cloak,' Eadmund tried, watching her squirm. 'Something more suited to Oss' weather. That thing will never keep you warm here, not even in summer.'

'I know. I've been thinking about wearing one of the furs from my bed instead,' Jael said awkwardly.

'*Your* bed?' Eadmund raised an eyebrow, leaning casually over the rail, watching the puppies disappear into the deep snow.

'Yes, *my* bed,' Jael replied, lowering her voice. 'I'm the only one who's slept in it, so yes, it's my bed.' She glanced at him, noting the glint of amusement in his eyes.

'For now, maybe,' Eadmund murmured, looking straight ahead.

That surprised Jael.

He'd been quite different lately. She hadn't seen him drunk in some time. Perhaps he knew about Evaine's baby? But if that was the case, why wasn't he with her?

The puppies decided that Eadmund should be their new friend, so they raced towards him, pawing his legs, demanding his attention. He laughed, bending down to give them just that. 'What are your names, then?' he grinned, stroking their snow-covered, wriggling bodies, trying to avoid their frantic tongues.

'Vella's the grey, Ido's black, although right now they both appear to be white,' Jael smiled as the puppies fought for Eadmund's affection.

'It's been years since I had a dog,' he sighed wistfully.

He likes dogs, Jael noted, annoyed. 'Well, perhaps it's time you found yourself one, then?'

'Found myself one? I thought these were *our* dogs?' Eadmund frowned. He stood up, closer to her than he'd anticipated, but he didn't move away.

'*Our* dogs?' Jael snorted, trying to mask her discomfort. He smelled almost pleasant, she noticed with surprise. 'No. *My* bed. *My* dogs.'

'Is that right? Your horses too?'

'Well, one certainly is. As for the other... you'd have to talk to Thorgils about that. He's the one who rides her. You don't even know her name.'

'True. But perhaps it's time I did? Thorgils has his own horse.

He doesn't need mine.'

Jael was just about to offer a clever retort when she noticed Eadmund's smile fade and his attention drift. She followed his gaze, watching it fall on Evaine, who was standing at the entrance to an alley across the square, trying to catch his eye. Eadmund was immediately distracted.

'It seems that you have to go,' Jael said briskly, consumed by a sharp burst of irritation. 'Ido! Vella!' She clicked her tongue for the puppies to follow her and thankfully, they did.

Striding off quickly, Jael didn't look back.

Eadmund frowned after her, disappointed by the abrupt end to their promising conversation. He reluctantly turned his attention back to Evaine. He'd been doing his best to avoid her for days, even sleeping at Torstan's. He knew that he had to face her and put an end to things, but he had no appetite for it. It would devastate Evaine and the coward in him didn't want to be responsible for breaking her heart.

Taking a deep breath, Eadmund waded through the knee-deep snow towards her, realising that if he didn't tell her the truth, she would never leave him alone.

He turned around, hoping to catch a last glimpse of Jael but she'd already gone, and that made him even more irritable. 'Are you trying to get yourself banished?' he grumbled, grabbing Evaine's hand and pulling her down the alley, away from public view.

Evaine looked crestfallen. She'd watched Eadmund smiling with his wife, enjoying her company, but now he was utterly furious. At her. She felt tears falling down her cold cheeks as she hurried along behind him. 'Eadmund, wait!' she sobbed loudly. '*Please!*'

Eadmund stopped, turning to her, still holding her hand, but Evaine quickly shook him loose, running to a pile of dirty snow, and bending over, she started vomiting.

Eadmund looked worried, and then disturbed as he came up behind her.

There was no one around. They were in a back alley, barely used, and he was grateful for the privacy. 'Are you alright?' he asked dully as Evaine straightened up, wiping her mouth. She was a dishevelled, tear-stained mess and his anger started to cool as his panic rose.

'I'm pregnant, Eadmund, so no, I'm not alright. I'm carrying your child!'

She hadn't lowered her voice, and he rushed a hand to cover her mouth. 'Sssshhh,' he implored. 'Anyone could hear!'

Evaine pushed his hand away. 'There's no one around,' she whispered crossly.

And she was right, Eadmund saw, as he glanced down the street and back again, but he still felt uneasy. Grabbing Evaine's hand again, he hurried her along, hoping to get back to his cottage before she said or did another thing, his head spinning with the consequences of what this might mean for them both.

***

'I wish you didn't have to leave,' Gisila sighed, gripping her mother's hands, her face pinched with anxiety.

'You will be fine,' Edela assured her with a squeeze. 'And we'll be back by spring. We won't stay away any longer than we need to.'

'But couldn't you wait *until* spring to go?' Axl frowned, looking almost as anxious as his mother. 'It would make travelling much safer, especially for you, Grandmother.'

'Well, no, not really,' Aleksander said, boosting Edela up onto her horse. 'When spring comes, we'll be leaving for Hest, won't we? I need to be here then. Lothar has been very clear about that. Besides, if your aunt is unwell, we don't have time to wait.'

They had three horses, six saddlebags, and at least six days supply of food. It would take four days to get to Tuura, but Aleksander was not sure how slowly they would have to travel to accommodate Edela's age and lack of experience. She hadn't ridden much these past few years, and he worried at the toll the constant riding would take on her old body. The snow wouldn't help much either. It was a fair day, but the winter cold would make a difficult travelling companion.

'Perhaps we should come with you, then?' Gisila suggested, her eyes brightening at the thought. 'If Branwyn is very ill, I could help. I should be there for her.'

'Mother, you don't really want to go back there, do you?' Axl asked, shuddering. 'I certainly don't.'

'No, of course not,' Gisila murmured, dropping her eyes. Her memories of Tuura, though seventeen-years-faded now, were still raw enough to give her nightmares. 'But Branwyn's my sister. I just hope that she'll be alright.'

'So do I, which is why I'm going now,' Edela smiled down at her daughter. 'And I promise you, my dear, you'll still be here when we return. I've seen your wedding, and I am there!'

Gisila's shoulders slumped at the thought of it.

'How about me? Will I still be here?' Axl wondered, with a hint of his old smile.

Edela frowned. 'You? You must watch yourself, my Axl. Ahhh yes, I know,' she said as he scowled at her, anticipating another lecture. 'But you aren't living by yourself on some rock out at sea. Everyone is watching you, especially the people who matter. So take care of your mother and stay away from those boys!'

Axl grumbled; all three faces were staring at him with the same stern expression, and he didn't like it one bit.

Amma came rushing towards them, her breath swirling around her in great white clouds as she stopped by Edela's horse. 'Oh, I'm so glad you're still here! I wanted to say goodbye. Wish you safe travels.' She reached up and took Edela's hand. 'I hope your daughter will be alright, and that the weather will be kind on your journey.'

'You are a sweet girl, Amma,' Edela smiled, squeezing her hand affectionately. 'Perhaps you can help look after my other daughter there, while I'm gone. Make sure she doesn't feel too lonely without her old mother to keep her company.' Edela glanced at Gisila's miserable face and felt a pang of guilt. She hated to leave when things were so hard, but she knew that going to Tuura was necessary for all their futures.

Both Aleksander and Edela had agreed to leave as quickly as possible. It had been Edela's idea to suggest that she'd had a dream about her youngest daughter, Branwyn, being ill. Nobody had questioned her story nor her urgency to depart.

'Of course, yes, I will,' Amma replied eagerly, slipping her arm through Gisila's. 'We can work on the wedding together!'

Everyone's faces fell at that and Amma squirmed uncomfortably to see it. Her father's unpopularity didn't surprise her – she was more than aware of his flaws – but he was still her father, and since her mother's death, and her sister's marriage, he was all she had; not counting Osbert, of course, which she never did. It upset her to see the strength of feeling against him, especially amongst her own family.

'We should go before the morning runs away,' Aleksander insisted into the awkward silence, sensing, but trying not to catch Amma's eyes as they sought his own.

'Yes, I'm already feeling ready for a rest!' Edela laughed.

'We haven't ridden anywhere yet!' Aleksander said with a frown as he mounted his new horse. She was a young, gentle mare with a red-and-white dappled coat. A beautiful horse. But he couldn't bring himself to name her yet.

'It was only a joke,' Edela chuckled, tapping her heels against the flanks of her dirty, white horse, Deya, who looked almost as old as she was. 'Now, come along before the morning runs away!'

Aleksander tapped his own horse's flanks, hurrying to get in front of her, their pack horse trailing behind him. He turned to wave goodbye and accidentally met Amma's eyes. She smiled keenly at him, happy to have caught his attention at last but Aleksander looked away so abruptly that he didn't notice her disappointment.

Axl did, though. 'Come on, Cousin,' he smiled kindly, putting one arm around her shoulder. 'How about we go for a walk, and you can tell me all the reasons why Aleksander Lehr is the greatest man you've ever known, and how you're going to convince your father to let you marry him as soon as possible.'

The sheer embarrassment on Amma's burning face quickly had him roaring with laughter.

***

Eadmund's mind was clear of ale but thick with panic. How was he going to get out of this mess? How was Evaine? She was certainly going to be banished now, as was he. And it was all his fault.

He sat on the end of the bed, his head in his hands.

'I wasn't trying to get pregnant,' Evaine sniffed next to him.

'I know that,' he mumbled.

'It just happened.'

'I know. It's my fault, of course it is.' Eadmund sat up, sighing heavily. 'There's no ale is there?'

'No,' she said sadly, holding his hand.

Eadmund wanted to rip it out of her grasp. He wanted to be reasonable and calm, but the more he gnawed on the situation, the more annoyed he felt.

'What are we going to do?' Evaine wondered quietly. Eadmund's reaction had been nothing like she'd imagined when she'd rehearsed this moment as she lay in her bed, dreaming of him. In those fantasies, he'd been so excited and happy at her news, convincing his father to grant him a divorce so that they could marry and raise their child together.

Looking at Eadmund's angry, distant face, she couldn't see that happening now.

'Do?' he asked crossly. 'Well, nothing for now. You mustn't tell anyone, Evaine. The moment my father hears of this is the moment he banishes you, and in all likelihood, I won't be far behind. He'll not take this well. Not at all.'

Evaine had never seen Eadmund so angry before. She didn't know what to say to make things any better. There wasn't a single drop of affection in his eyes; nothing that wasn't cold and hateful. 'But Eirik wanted an heir, he wanted you to have a son. He wanted you to show him that you could be the king, and you've been doing that,' she tried. 'The only problem is your wife. If you divorce her, then we can marry, and our son will be your heir.'

Eadmund shook his head, standing up. He'd just noticed how cold the cottage was, and he made to start a fire. 'You don't know my father or what he wants,' he said morosely, grabbing his tinderbox. 'Eirik doesn't want you, even if you gave me ten healthy sons! He wants Jael to be the mother of my children. He wants the Furyck line, the Furyck name. He'll not want your baby, for him or me. He'll not let you stay here to have it. It would shame him.' Evaine shook, with fear or cold, Eadmund couldn't tell, but as the fire sparked to life, he came back to sit with her, his ire cooling, his head clearing. 'Perhaps you need to get married? To someone else?'

'What?' Evaine looked horrified.

Eadmund turned towards her, his eyes alert now. Reaching out, he grabbed her hands. 'If we find someone to marry you quickly, then you could pass this child off as his. My father would never know. No one would, except you and I. That way you and the baby could stay on Oss.' He paused, looking at her sharply. 'You haven't told anyone else, have you?'

'Just my mother.'

'Good, then keep this secret, and we can think of someone for you to marry. You're the most beautiful girl on Oss, Evaine.

There'll be many contenders.'

'But Eadmund –'

'I know, it's not what you want, but it will keep you here,' he smiled, hoping to convince her of the plan, which had suddenly given him hope. 'If my father finds out, he'll send you away, and I'll never see you or the baby again.'

Evaine didn't look pleased. Tears were threatening her eyes again, and her bottom lip was quivering. She placed her hands on her belly, which Eadmund realised, did have a slight curve he hadn't noticed before.

'I'll think on it,' she said quietly.

'Good!' Eadmund said desperately, feeling the small flicker of hope in that. He clung on, determined not to let go, and wrapping an arm around Evaine's shaking body, he pulled her close. 'Just take your time, and make sure that in the meantime, you don't tell anyone. It's the only chance we have. If my father finds out about this child, he'll not hesitate to send us away and bring Ivaar back.'

CHAPTER TWENTY FIVE

The crackle and spit of the fire echoed amongst the tall fir trees, and nearby, their three horses nuzzled through the snow, looking for something more to eat.

Aleksander sipped his cup of icy-cold ale and sighed. It was a relief to finally stop. It had been a steady days ride, and they'd made reasonable progress. Edela was hardier than he'd imagined possible for a woman of her age. He'd watched her nodding head and weary eyes, but he hadn't heard any groans or complaints as she'd trailed behind him throughout the day.

Camping in the snow was not going to be easy, though. Aleksander had hoped to find a cave before nightfall, but they hadn't travelled far enough to make it there before the sun started sinking. So, instead, he'd made a camp for them in a sheltered grove of trees, a little way off the main road. It wasn't ideal, but it would have to do.

After digging out an area of snow to form a pit to lie their bundles of furs into, Aleksander had unpacked their tent. With Edela's help, they'd joined the wooden poles together, secured them into the ground, and to each other, and finally slipped a thick linen tent over the frame. It would be enough to keep out the worst of the night, and hopefully, give Edela a restorative sleep.

'Do you think you'll be able to do the same again tomorrow?' Aleksander wondered anxiously as they leaned into the first flames of the fire, desperate for warmth after a day that had left them both numb.

'Of course!' Edela insisted. 'I'm old, but not weak. I can sit on a horse for many more hours if I have to, and I'll do so again tomorrow. As long as there's a hot fire and a warm bed at the end of each day, that will be enough to keep me going,' she smiled with tired eyes. 'This is too important to worry about a few aches and pains. I'm an old woman... I'll have them anyway!'

Aleksander felt relieved. She sounded determined, although he did still wonder if they should've taken a cart. But the strain on the horses, the lack of a clear road to follow in the snow, and the worry about getting stuck had all played a part in his decision to simply go on horses and hope for the best. 'Well, get as much sleep as you can. You'll need more strength for tomorrow.'

'I don't think sleep will be a problem,' Edela chuckled, her smile still bright, despite the trials of the day. 'I'm sure I'll sleep deeper than I have in my whole life!'

'Good. Maybe you'll have another dream to help us too?'

Edela's face paled, despite the warm glow of the fire. She stood, trying not to give in to the intense pains shooting through her aching limbs. 'We do need to know more,' she sighed, grimacing. 'But my dreams have been so terrifying lately. I'd rather stay awake than fall into that dark pit again.'

'It must be hard to see those things and feel as though you're in it. Living through it.'

'It is, of course, but still, I'm being shown them for a reason. The gods think that I can help Jael.' She looked worried, wondering how Jael was faring on Oss. She missed her fiery granddaughter's company more than she ever let on. 'I have a feeling there is so much more hiding in the shadows, but I'm just not sure I want to peek inside.'

Aleksander got up to help her to bed. He snatched at her fur to stop it falling into the fire. 'Well, you're not alone out here, at least. I can't come into your dreams and save you, but I'll be waiting here if you need me.' He squeezed her shoulder reassuringly, easing her down onto her furry bed.

'You're a good man, Aleksander,' Edela said with a yawn. 'And tomorrow perhaps you'll finally tell me why you think Jael is coming back to you?'

Aleksander blinked at her, regretting his big mouth. He wasn't looking forward to having to explain that.

***

Eadmund hadn't made eye contact with Jael once. He hadn't even turned her way. It felt strange after their conversation at the Pit, which had been their friendliest so far. Strange also, because they were sitting next to each other, eating supper in the hall, their bodies almost touching.

Jael had been talking to Eydis instead, but she had just left for bed.

Thorgils saw the empty space and took it. 'Eirik's going to announce the groups for the contest tonight.'

'So he said.'

Thorgils looked unimpressed by her lack of enthusiasm. 'It's important to get into the right group, to see which one of us has a chance. You know,' he whispered, moving closer to her, 'with Tarak.'

They both looked over at Tarak, who must have sensed their attention, for he stared straight back at them.

They quickly looked away.

'We're not ready,' Jael said bluntly. 'Neither of us are.'

'Well, speak for yourself!' Thorgils scoffed. 'My sword arm's never been in such fine shape. And thanks to you, I've gotten more in control of this.' He tapped his head. 'Stronger with my technique too. Surely you're being hard on yourself there? I'm not saying you could defeat Tarak, or even me, but you don't look that bad. I doubt many could beat you.'

Jael barely acknowledged Thorgils' words. She felt agitated being in the same room with Tarak. He made her skin crawl. She'd tried to avoid him ever since her talk with Fyn, but it was impossible; he was loud, large, and always showing off somewhere nearby. Whenever she heard or saw him, Jael thought of Fyn – Fyn crying, Fyn as a little boy, Fyn being raped – and that made her so wild that she had to bite down hard on her tongue to stop herself from doing something rash.

So far, she'd managed it, but only just.

'If I were training with my old partner,' Jael said, her voice softening as she saw a glimpse of Aleksander's face for the first time in days, 'he would have won every fight against me. Easily. That's how I know I'm not ready for Tarak. I'm nowhere near sharp enough.'

'He was good, then, this partner of yours?'

'Not as good as me, but close,' Jael smiled sadly. 'We'd trained together since we were children, so we learned the same techniques over and over again. My father brought in warriors to teach us. We learned everything together, practised it together. Constantly. It's strange to fight without him.'

The look on Jael's face told Thorgils more than her words. 'And yet, you were beaten by a nothing sort of Osslander named Thorgils!' he laughed, trying to cheer her up. 'So either I'm better than I thought, or you were having a bad day!'

Torstan grabbed Thorgils' attention, then, and Jael was once again reminded of her silent husband. Was it Evaine? Had she told him about the baby? It would certainly explain his silence. He wouldn't know what to do if that were the case. In truth, *she* didn't know what to do.

And more importantly, what would Eirik do?

Jael reached out, touching Eadmund's arm, retracting her hand quickly, immediately regretting her sudden show of affection.

Eadmund looked around, surprised; he'd almost forgotten she was there. He stared down at his arm, wondering if he'd imagined her touch.

Jael tried to smile, but it was awkward and only half-formed, so it came across as more of a grimace. 'You're very quiet tonight,' she mumbled as he looked away again.

Eadmund drank from his cup, not looking back at her. 'I have some things on my mind.'

'Ahhh, woman troubles, is it?' Jael smiled, trying to be friendly, wondering at the same time why she felt such an urge to be friendly.

Eadmund's tongue tangled in his mouth, and he ended up gaping at her. 'I...'

'Or, were you thinking that you must come around and look at that horse of yours before Thorgils takes her home to live with him and his mother? He does love that horse, and she loves him, so no doubt you were planning to bring her a carrot to try and lure her away. It won't be easy, their bond is a strong one, but she does like a good carrot.' The words kept tumbling out of her mouth, as much as Jael wanted to stuff them back inside. 'Perhaps you were thinking that you should act fast, so tomorrow would be the best time?'

Eadmund's mouth hung open some more, but the look in Jael's eyes was warm and inviting; in fact, everything about her was inviting, now that he considered it. She was sitting close to him, her body turned in his direction, her head inclined his way, her eyes staring into his.

Eadmund slowly put his cup on the table, not taking his eyes off her. He suddenly forgot about Evaine and the problem of the baby and his father that he had been eye-deep in all evening long. He forgot about everything except those eyes, which were deep-green and not at all harsh and judgemental right now. They were almost concerned, certainly friendly, and definitely open to him. He didn't look away. 'I... yes, I... that's just what I was thinking. About the horse, and tomorrow. It would be good to come. Over. To see the horse.' He felt flustered, clumsy with his words.

'Good. I'll make sure I'm back by mid-morning,' Jael said,

enjoying flummoxing him, but then realising that she felt just as flummoxed herself. She looked away, grabbing her cup, hiding her heated face in it.

'Back? Are you going somewhere?' Eadmund broke his trance to take a deep breath and a long drink.

'I like to ride, every morning,' Jael mumbled between sips of ale. 'Tig's a moody horse. It's best to keep him well exercised and happy. He's more likely to do as he's told then.'

Eadmund smiled. He didn't know what to say, or what had just happened.

He felt better, though, less alone.

Eirik stood up to quiet the hall, which had been low-humming with anticipation all evening. They hushed easily for him tonight as most were waiting to hear which group they would be in for the contest. Eirik was in a particularly good mood as he surveyed his warriors. The plan to keep everyone eye-bright and focused had, for the most part, worked, and he'd been pleased to see how full the Pit had been in the best and worst conditions that winter had thrown at Oss so far.

The first part of the Freeze had gone better than he could have imagined. Eadmund had pulled himself out of his ale-soaked ditch. He had a Furyck wife now, and soon their sons would run around their old grandfather's legs, if there was time.

He hoped he had time; he would like to see that.

Eirik looked wistfully at Eadmund, remembering the scrawny little boy whose golden hair was always being braided by his beautiful mother who had loved it too much to ever cut it off. Eirik felt a sudden yearning for Eskild, his second wife, who he had loved so passionately.

He was wandering too far away from the hall, he knew, so, inhaling a deep, ale-rich breath, he brought himself back to the present. There was no point in looking behind him. He still had much to do before his time was at an end, and Vidar came to take him to his hall.

'Right, I have the list!' Eirik bellowed, holding a piece of vellum high for everyone to see. 'Morac and I have placed you into four groups. Your opponent will be drawn before you fight. After four rounds of fighting, we'll drop down to two groups, who will fight until we are left with just two men standing!' Eirik didn't mean to, but he stared at Tarak, whose scarred face rippled with confidence. 'And, of course, those two will fight for the champion's honour!'

Thorgils clapped Jael on the back, whistling loudly, joining in the chorus of cheering Osslanders. Jael wasn't sure how he was going to contain his excitement over the next few weeks; it was already boiling over.

As Eirik started to read out the names, Jael noticed that Eadmund was looking around the hall, staring at each warrior in turn. 'Assessing your competition?' she wondered quietly.

Eadmund blinked. 'No, no, not me. I'm not in the contest. Not this time.'

'Makes sense. Best to wait until you're ready. No point getting squashed by Tarak for no good reason.'

'Mmmm, I have a memory of him trying that the last time we fought. I suppose it makes up for his lack of skill with a sword.'

Jael heard her name mentioned but wasn't especially interested.

Thorgils was, though. 'You're with Torstan! Ha! Look at his face!'

He was right, Jael saw, as she caught Torstan's eye. His friends were slapping his back, pointing at Jael, laughing. Torstan had trained with Jael twice, and both times she had defeated him harshly, to the amusement of many in the Pit.

He didn't look pleased at all.

'At least we're not in the same group,' Thorgils sighed with relief. 'I wouldn't want to humiliate you any further.'

Eadmund laughed loudly at the look on Jael's face. She smiled at him, feeling relaxed, almost enjoying herself as she looked around the hall. The men were genuinely happy, she saw. Eirik too. He stood up there, proudly reading out the names of his warriors, basking in the glow of their victory dreams as they sat around the fires, enjoying the respite from the bitter winter hiding just outside the hall doors.

Jael took another sip from her cup, feeling her shoulders loosen their tense hold on her. Eadmund had turned her way and was toasting Thorgils, who appeared to have landed in an easy enough group, or so he said. Eadmund's leg was resting against hers under the table. Jael felt a twist in her stomach as her body responded to his, but she didn't flinch, and she didn't move away.

She saw Aleksander's face and swallowed.

'You'll have it hard, Jael. Your group has a couple of good men in it,' Thorgils said, attempting a sympathetic smile, his eyes alive with thoughts of facing Tarak. 'But we have a few weeks to get ready, and even though I haven't trained with anyone who wasn't a piece of shit, no offence, Eadmund, I'm sure I can give you just as good a beating as your old partner!'

Eadmund saw Jael's smile slip. She recovered it quickly, but this time it didn't reach her eyes.

'Perhaps we should go our separate ways now?' she suggested. 'We might meet each other in the final, and we wouldn't want to give away all our secrets, would we?'

Thorgils scratched his beard; she had a fair point. He considered it, then bent his head towards her ear. 'The only thing that truly matters is that one of us beats that giant turd. And if I can't stop him, then it will be up to you. We both need to enter that Pit with the best we have, so let's help each other. Let's spend the next few weeks out of sight from everyone else. We can go and train at Fyn's. Perhaps together we can cook up a few surprises for whoever we're drawn against?'

He sat back, one bushy red eyebrow raised in her direction and Jael nodded, reflecting the fierce determination she saw in his eyes. 'Agreed,' she whispered. 'But, if that's what you truly want, then I'll have to stop being so easy on you!'

Thorgils' snorted happily, and Jael couldn't help laughing.

For all that she missed Aleksander, for all that she needed

him to make her better, what she did have now was Thorgils and Fyn, and somehow, they would have to be enough.

She turned around to speak to Eadmund, but he had gone.

***

'Aleksander! Aleksander! Wake up!'

Edela shook the sleeping lump with both arms, trying to rouse him out of his nightmare. He had been wailing and tossing about loudly enough to wake her. She tried again, shaking herself as much as him. It was bone-numbingly cold inside the tent, and Edela was desperate to crawl back under her frozen pile of furs.

'What?' Aleksander yelled suddenly, sitting up in surprise, reaching instinctively for his knife which he always kept under his pillow.

'Sssshhh, it's me, Edela. You've had a nightmare.' Tired of bending over inside their little tent, she sunk down by his legs, listening to the gentle cracking of frost on his furs. The moon was full enough for her to make out his face. It shone with sweat, ghostly pale. He was shaking.

'I'm sorry I woke you,' Aleksander shivered. 'Get back to your bed before you freeze.'

He made a move to get up and help her, but Edela put her arm out to stop him. 'You keep warm, I'm alright, it's not that far,' she chortled, heaving herself up and over to her own bed, wondering at the wisdom of taking a trip in the depths of winter. Edela lay down, feeling aches in many new places as she tried to get comfortable. Her body was telling her off loudly. 'What was your nightmare about?' she wondered, jiggling her arms and legs, trying to warm herself up.

Aleksander crept out of his bed, prodding the fire to see if there was any life in it; there was, just. So, wrapping a fur around his shoulders, he grabbed a handful of dry twigs and leaves that he'd collected earlier and made a little nest around the glowing embers. They didn't catch. 'It was about my parents,' he murmured, feeling around for his tinderbox. 'Watching them get killed again.'

'Of course,' Edela mumbled from under her furs. 'I imagined that going back to Tuura would stir those terrible memories. I'm so sorry for you, truly sorry for what happened to them.'

Aleksander struck his firesteel on the flint, still lost in his dream. He could hear the screams of his mother as she lay over his father's dead body before she too was slaughtered before his ten-year-old eyes. His memories before that night were forever coloured by their traumatic loss. He only felt sadness when he looked back now. They had been good parents, he thought, good to each other, and he knew that he'd been loved, but when they died, all of that had been replaced by a sense of loss, and emptiness and nothing else.

Aleksander blew on the burning touchwood and carried it carefully to the little nest he'd made, his hands shaking with cold. It smoked, then burst into flame. 'I'll never understand why it happened. What reason there was for any of it.' His voice sounded lost and far away. 'Why did those men attack us? Why did they kill my parents? Why didn't you see it coming?' he sighed sadly, blowing on the struggling flames.

'I wish I had answers for you,' Edela sighed. 'But even after all these years, I still have none. No one in Tuura saw it coming. There was no warning from anyone. But you must always remember that your father died trying to protect Jael. Without him, I'm not sure she would have lived.'

Aleksander considered that. It was a consolation, of course. His parent's deaths had brought him into Jael's family, and that was something that had changed his life, for the better, ultimately. But still, he'd always lived with the nagging question of why they had to die. 'Come and sit by the fire,' he urged, shaking away the last remnants of the dream, roused to life by the welcome heat.

'Warm yourself up a while.'

'Not likely!' Edela snorted, her head under her furs now. 'I plan to leave my bones here till morning, so if you're planning on having any more nightmares, you shall have to save yourself!'

***

Evaine rested her head on Eadmund's shoulder. She was completely still, watching his chest rise and fall, listening to his breathing as he thought on what to do.

It hadn't unfolded as she'd planned. She had taken too long to fall pregnant, and he had drifted away from her; she could see that now. She kept remembering the way he'd been with Jael at the Pit, the way he'd placed his body so close to hers, the ease of his smile. All of it told her that Eadmund wanted his wife, perhaps even loved her. He'd made all those changes to himself, but they were for Jael. He wanted to be different... for her.

She felt morose and nauseous, but there was still a flicker of hope inside her. And placing her hands on her belly, she closed her eyes, inhaling deeply. She knew that there were other ways to keep Eadmund, to bring his attention back to her, to make him forget his wife entirely.

She needed to find a way to visit her aunt.

Morana would know how to help her.

CHAPTER TWENTY SIX

'Aarrghh!' Jael skidded on a patch of snow, just managing to keep to her feet. She touched her cheek, which Thorgils had just caught with his sword, blinking rapidly, her eyes watering.

'Are you alright, Jael?' Fyn was at her side immediately, attempting to examine her face, but Jael jabbed him with her sword.

'We're in the middle of a fight, Fyn!' she barked. 'You can't just walk in between us to check my wounds!' Her cheek stung, and her ears buzzed loudly.

'Jael's right, you little turnip! Get out so I can finish her off!' Thorgils growled, his face clear of any sympathy. 'I want to sup on the sweet taste of my revenge before we're snowed in!'

It had snowed steadily all morning. It wasn't getting heavier, but the wind was building, blowing it straight into their faces now.

They were both struggling to see.

'Alright, alright, I'm going inside. I'll heat up the stew,' Fyn sulked, stomping off towards his hut in the hill.

Jael and Thorgils exchanged nervous glances through the mess of snowflakes. Fyn had been threatening them with his stew all morning, and they were both determined to be gone before they had to face it.

'Forget the revenge, we should leave now!' Thorgils laughed loudly, walking over to Jael, eyeing her cheek. 'It's not bleeding, but I think you'll be finding your way home with one eye.'

Jael grimaced. 'I think you're right there. We should go before the snow gets worse, or we'll be stuck eating furry claws again!'

The wind screamed around them, so loudly that Thorgils barely heard her as he headed towards the hut. Jael glanced over at Tig and Leada who were sharing a shelter made for one. Neither looked terribly impressed by the conditions. The sound of the wind was making them jittery.

It was going to be a difficult ride home.

'Your eye is closing up,' Fyn noted as Thorgils and Jael shook themselves by his fire.

The stew didn't smell bad... yet, but both Jael and Thorgils looked away from it with fear on their faces.

'It is, so we'll head back to the fort,' Thorgils said firmly, plonking his boots near the modest little fire. 'But first, I just need to feel my feet again!'

Jael placed her boots next to Thorgils'. Her face ached, but she didn't think on it for long; her mind was occupied with thoughts of Eadmund. He would be at the house soon, and that agitated her. Why had she thought to invite him? Why had she reached out to him at all? She told herself that it was mere curiosity, to see what Evaine might have revealed, but she knew that things other than that were stirring her body and rattling her nerves.

'Hello?' Thorgils stared at Jael, slightly concerned. 'Has that bump knocked your thinking parts about in there?'

Jael shook Eadmund out of her head and drew her eyes and feet away from the fire. 'No, no, I just have things on my mind.' She jiggled her hot toes around inside her steaming boots.

'Eadmund things, is it?' Thorgils wondered cheekily. 'I saw you two speaking to each other last night. Things are moving along at a rapid pace now. Before long, you might even decide to get married!'

Jael frowned. '*You're* the one who wanted me to speak to him.'

'True, and I'm pleased you did. But he didn't look so happy.

Something's nagging at him, and I don't think it's you.'

Jael opened her mouth to share her suspicions, then closed it.

The look on her face was one of guilt, though, and Thorgils cocked his head to one side. 'What is it? What's wrong with Eadmund?' He leaned towards her.

Fyn sat down next to Jael, his face echoing a similar curiosity.

Jael stared at both men, listening to the thick sucking of the stew, the spitting of the fire, and the wind screeching past the door, loudest of all. They were her friends, she was certain of that. And she would need their help if everything fell to pieces, which it seemed, was about to happen. 'It's Evaine,' she began.

Fyn swallowed, squirming on his stool.

'I think she may have told Eadmund that she's pregnant,' Jael said quietly, sensing two pairs of eyes bulge from either side of her.

'Wh-wh-what?' Thorgils stammered. 'What makes you think that?'

'Eydis saw it in her dreams. I have a feeling Evaine told Eadmund yesterday. It would explain his odd behaviour last night.'

There was silence as each man digested Jael's revelation.

'It would be something Evaine would do,' Fyn said at last. 'If she were to have his child, it would tie her to Eadmund forever.'

'Well, she didn't do it alone,' Jael noted, wryly. 'I think Eadmund may be partly responsible.'

Thorgils pulled on his beard, his eyebrows knitting together. 'This is terrible. If Eirik finds out, he'll be in a wild fury, for sure.'

Jael looked into his troubled eyes. 'Eydis has seen Ivaar coming.'

Thorgils' face fell.

Fyn drew in a sharp breath.

'When?' Thorgils could barely speak; his mind was whirring.

'Before the Thaw is over, she said. Soon.'

'We need to leave. Now!' Thorgils glared sternly at Jael as he hurried to his feet. 'We have to talk to Eadmund. We have to stop Eirik finding out. It might be too late already, but we have to try.'

'Eadmund is coming to the house when I get back, to meet Leada. I can talk to him then.'

'What do you mean, *meet* Leada?' Thorgils frowned, pulling his hood over his bushy hair. 'He's decided he wants a horse now, has he?' And ducking out of the door, he muttered crossly to himself.

Fyn stood up. 'But what about the stew? Wouldn't you like something hot to eat before you go?'

Jael shook her head, pulling her own hood up. 'Thorgils is right. We need to find out what's happening and see what we can do. If Ivaar is as dangerous as everyone says, we have to find a way to stop Eydis' dream coming true.'

The weather had disintegrated further, and the horses were in no mood to leave their shelter.

Thorgils was in no mood to care what they thought, however. 'We may or may not be back tomorrow!' he called to Fyn, throwing himself up into Leada's saddle. It was covered by an old sheepskin that helped make winter riding bearable, but the wind had blown so much snow into the shelter that it was now wet through and half-frozen; he barely noticed, though, as he tugged on the reins. 'It depends on what we find when we get back. If we can even find our way back in this shit!' He kicked his heels sharply into Leada's flanks, and took off, not waiting for Jael.

'Well thanks, Thorgils!' she called after him, her voice lost in the blizzard.

Tig wouldn't stand still long enough for her to mount him – he was too spooked by the screeching wind – so Fyn grabbed his bridle, gently stroking his face, whispering soothing words into his ear as Jael clambered quickly up onto him. 'Don't be too hard on Thorgils!' he called up to her. 'He has more reasons than most not to want Ivaar back!'

Jael wanted to ask what those reasons might be when she heard Thorgils bellowing at her from up on the ridge. 'Tomorrow! You can tell me tomorrow!' Jael yelled, racing to catch up with Thorgils.

***

'I want you to prepare the children's things,' Ivaar whispered hoarsely, bending his thin face towards his wife. 'We're going back to Oss.'

Isaura didn't know where to look. When Ivaar was on top of her, she tried to keep her face over his shoulder so he didn't notice the look of empty disinterest she found hard to disguise. She endured his touch because she had no choice; it wasn't even the worst part of their marriage. It happened less now that they had a living son, but still, he came to their bed regularly, using her to scratch whatever itch he might have at any time of the day or night.

At least tonight she got to lie on her back.

Isaura turned her sad face towards her husband in surprise. 'Oss? Why?'

Oss was a long-ago memory that she'd shut behind an iron-strong door.

She didn't want to open it again. Not ever.

'I spoke with Ayla today. She sees word coming soon. From Eirik. We'll be going back there, at long last.' Ivaar continued to thrust into Isaura with an increasingly steady rhythm, though his face expressed no pleasure in what he was doing or saying.

Isaura tried not to let anything that might have stirred in her heart just then, show on her face; if she still had a heart left after all these years. Of course she did, she chided herself. She had four children and a son who had died before he'd even taken his first breath. They filled her heart with hope. There was room for nothing else. No one else lived there anymore, she'd made sure of that.

'What? You've got nothing to say? You're not happy to be going home again?' Ivaar narrowed his cold blue eyes, peering down his nose at her. 'I'm sure there's at least one person you'll be happy to see, isn't there? If he's still alive.'

Isaura stared blankly at her husband, keeping calm despite the threat of his cold glare and taunting words. She despised him, but she had never allowed herself to be completely destroyed by him. She had always been determined to survive for her children, doing whatever it took and becoming whatever Ivaar needed in order to keep going for them. 'I don't know how I feel about going back to Oss. It was all such a long time ago now. I'm not sure anyone would welcome us back, would they?'

Ivaar looked annoyed by her question. His rhythm broke, and he stopped, staring fiercely into her pale, brown eyes. 'Seven years,' he hissed at her. 'That's how long we've been exiled here. Do you think we should *care* who wants us back?'

Isaura shook her head, trying not to blink. 'I suppose not.'

Ivaar closed his eyes, arching his back as he pressed himself into her again. 'No, my father made a big mistake sending me here. And he'll be making an equally big mistake bringing me back. He just won't realise it until it's too late.'

Ivaar bent over, his head towards the pillow, and Isaura allowed her face to sink back into misery. Returning to Oss was everything she'd once wished for, but Ivaar was right, seven years was a long time. Too long, she feared, convinced that everything would have changed.

Certain that nothing would be as she'd left it.

***

'What's that smell?' Jael gagged, screwing up her face as she guided Leada and Tig towards the stables. She'd convinced Thorgils to let her speak with Eadmund alone. He'd not lost any of his furious anger during their ride back to the fort, and she didn't think his mood would help things at all. Thankfully, Thorgils was not blind to his own madness, and he'd seen the wisdom in that, although he had urged her to find out the truth of it quickly.

Biddy looked up irritably, messy curls blowing about her face. She was squatting in the snow under the shelter that linked the stables to the house, trying to control both puppies who she'd trapped in a wooden tub. The sight of Jael was too much for them to bear, though, and they wriggled out of her grasp, splashing out of the tub, happy to leave the cold water behind.

'The smell, you're about to find out, is them!' Biddy grumbled, wet hands flailing as she tried to catch her escaping prisoners. They weren't keen to go back into the tub, however, and quickly slipped away from her.

'Down! No, no, get down!' Jael snapped as the puppies jumped up her legs, spooking the horses who skittered about wildly.

'I caught them in the stables, rolling in all the horse shit before Askel had a chance to muck it out,' Biddy sniffed, wiping her nose on a soggy cloth she'd tucked up her sleeve. 'For some reason, they love the stinking stuff, but nothing has ever smelled worse, and I'm not letting them back into the house until they're clean, no matter how cold the water is!'

Jael ushered the horses inside the stables and shut the door. She scooped Ido up in one arm, and Biddy captured Vella. 'I'll help you. Then I'll sort out the horses. Eadmund will be here soon.'

'What?' Biddy almost dropped Vella into the tub. 'What do you mean *here*? Why is he coming here? What for?' She was suddenly on edge. Anxious about the state of the house: the fire which had probably burned down to nothing, the lack of food, the mess she'd been in the middle of clearing up. She ran it all over in her mind, and it set her nerves jangling.

'He's coming to visit Leada. I think he might start riding her soon.'

'Oh,' Biddy sighed, relieved. 'Well, perhaps he won't go inside the house then, just the stables?'

'What?' Jael dumped Ido into the cold water and started

scrubbing his shivering body with a lump of soap. The smell was unbearable, and she had to turn her head away. 'You think he should stay out in the stables? In *this* weather?' She cringed as Ido shook all over her. 'I think he'll want to go into the house. He must be curious about it. I'm not sure he's even seen inside it before?'

Biddy wrestled Vella into the tub. 'Well, let's hurry up then as everything's upside down in there. I was cleaning before these two monsters put a stop to it. It's a complete mess!' She snorted, trying to clear the shit smell out of her nostrils.

'Ha!' Jael laughed, lifting Ido out of the tub, promptly getting showered with icy water as he shook all over her again. 'Perhaps you haven't seen Eadmund before? *He's* a mess! He'll feel very comfortable if everything's all over the floor, I'm sure.' Jael smiled to cover her own anxiety.

She felt oddly nervous about him coming too.

Wrapping the shivering Ido in a blanket, Jael took him inside to the fire, happy to be out of the blizzard at last. After rubbing him briskly, she set him free.

'See what I mean?' Biddy muttered, gesturing around the main room. 'It looks like a herd of goats lives here!' She handed Vella to Jael. 'Here, you dry her, and I'll get started.' And rushing to hang her cloak on the back of the door, she grabbed her apron, tying it around herself.

Jael glanced at Biddy's wet clothes as she rubbed Vella's wriggling body. 'Hadn't you better put something dry on first? You're a little wet.'

Biddy looked down at her sodden dress, but she didn't have time to worry now. She ignored Jael completely as she sat down to take off her wet boots, her eyes racing around the room, deciding where to begin.

Jael let Vella go, laughing as she chased Ido around Biddy's legs, much to her annoyance. She headed outside to tend to the horses, wondering exactly how she was going to ply Eadmund for information about Evaine.

***

He wasn't coming.

Jael and Biddy sat around the fire in silence, the puppies fast asleep, warm, fluffy, and snoring gently on a pile of rugs by their feet. Jael sipped her lemon balm tea and sighed.

'Should I make us something to eat?' Biddy wondered quietly.

'I'm not hungry.'

It was well past mid-afternoon now. The day had grown increasingly grim, the storm taking a determined hold on Oss. It was almost completely dark outside.

There was a sharp knock on the door.

Ido and Vella woke with a start, barking, slightly confused and excited.

Both women stumbled to their feet. Jael straightened her favourite blue tunic as she walked to the door, glancing around at Biddy, who was standing awkwardly behind her, smoothing down her apron.

Swallowing, Jael opened the door.

To Eirik.

PART THREE

Into the Storm

CHAPTER TWENTY SEVEN

Thorgils couldn't settle. He'd tried sitting at the table in his mother's house, listening to her mutter and moan, but he'd wriggled about and been so irritating that she'd kicked him out. Into the blizzard. And now, here he was in the hall, unable to sit still, his eyes darting around, wondering what Jael and Eadmund were talking about.

There weren't many in the hall, which didn't surprise him. Blizzards tended to gather everyone into their cottages. Families grouped together, keeping each other and their livestock safe. Most of the men camped in the hall were single and alone with no one to care for. Thorgils felt guilty. Perhaps he should go back to his mother's house to make sure she was alright? The wind was a high-pitched wail now and who knew how deep the snow would get.

'There's something funny going on,' Torstan whispered, flopping down onto the bench beside Thorgils.

The hairs on the back of Thorgils' neck stood on end. 'What do you mean, funny?' he whispered back, just as cautiously. There was no one within hearing distance but still...

'I don't know, just things. Things that make me think something has happened,' Torstan murmured. He wasn't usually the most perceptive man, but the peculiar look on his face told Thorgils that something was wrong. 'Eydis is in her bedchamber. I heard her crying.'

'What about Eirik?'

'I haven't seen him or Morac all day, not in here anyway. Nor Eadmund.'

Thorgils glanced around. Everyone appeared relaxed. There were no odd looks or whispered conversations. The men sitting around the fires were talking and laughing openly. But something was wrong, and Thorgils could feel it. 'You wait here,' he ordered. 'I'll go and speak to Eydis.' He left a worried Torstan by the fire and strode off towards the green curtain, looking for answers.

Afraid of what he might find.

***

Eirik looked tense as Jael ushered him inside, out of the snowy gale. His usual spark of good humour was gone, replaced with a sullen glare.

'This is a surprise,' Jael smiled cautiously. 'We were expecting Eadmund.'

The puppies sniffed Eirik's legs, satisfied that he wasn't an enemy.

Jael wondered if they were right.

'Were you? What for?' Eirik made no move to step any further into the house; his back remained to the door.

'Would you like to come and sit by the fire?'

Eirik said nothing as he followed her to a stool.

'Something to drink?'

'I had an interesting visit from your little Brekkan friend this morning,' Eirik started, ignoring her offer as he sat down. 'It was early. He couldn't wait, I suppose, after all his hard work. He couldn't wait to lay it all at my feet. To enjoy his gloating at my expense. I'm sure he can't wait to tell Lothar about it either.'

Jael's heart was racing now. Eirik spoke as though she wasn't there.

She could feel everything slowly starting to fall down around her.

'Seems that little bitch got herself pregnant,' Eirik spat.

Jael heard Biddy's stifled gasp from the kitchen.

'You don't look surprised,' Eirik noted, glancing towards Jael for the first time. 'Did you know?'

Jael took a deep breath and sighed. 'No, not really but I guessed. I was hoping to talk to Eadmund about it. To find out the truth.'

'Were you now?' Eirik looked to the fire, his tone flat and defeated. 'So you are *talking* to him now? Not lying with him, not sleeping in the same bed, but *talking* to him?'

It was Jael's turn to ignore him. 'It doesn't matter that she's pregnant, does it?'

Eirik eyed her sharply. 'Doesn't it? Not to you? You don't care that your husband will have a child with another woman? You feel relieved, do you?'

'It's nothing to do with me,' Jael said coldly. She felt anger spark inside her, rising up from where it had been simmering for so long. 'I didn't ask to come here, to be in this place with your son. What he does with other women... what control do I have over that? What has it got to do with me?'

'You're his *wife*!' Eirik growled, standing up, his fury overwhelming him. His face reddened as his voice rose. 'I brought you here to be his *wife*! To have his sons, to bring your name to my heirs! To be a *wife*! Not to ride around with other men, to fight with your sword, to do everything and anything you wanted to avoid being his *wife*!' His small eyes bulged angrily at her.

Jael stood and stepped towards him, her own fury on the edge of consuming her reason. She saw Biddy's worried face out of the corner of her eye, and that checked her a little but not enough to stop her. 'You're angry at the wrong person, Eirik!' she began loudly. 'Your son spent the first part of our marriage drunk! Nowhere to be seen! I never even knew where he was, let alone had the chance to speak to him. How was I going to be a wife to a man I couldn't find? What did you expect me to do? Hunt him down? Drag him out of her bed and into mine?'

'Why not?' Eirik countered. 'You certainly could have if you'd wanted to!'

'Of course, but why *would* I want to?' Jael was wild now. 'I didn't even want to come here! I never wanted to be married to anyone! Ever! That was the choice I made, but you and Lothar decided that I didn't deserve a choice! You took it from me! Forced me to come here! You took me from my family and my home! You made me come here and be a wife to this hopeless drunk, who could barely even stand! And what was I supposed to do? *Fix* him? Turn him into the son you wished he was? How was I supposed to do that when none of you could?' She shook with anger. 'I'm no goddess. I have no powers to do anything like that. What you asked of me was too much. It's Eadmund who needed to save himself, not me!'

Jael sat down, not wanting to go on. Weeks and weeks of pain was tumbling out of her, and she needed to stop. Yelling at Eirik wouldn't change anything, no matter how good it felt.

Eirik sat down beside her, his face stripped of all anger now. He just looked sad. 'You're right, of course,' he said quietly, his voice trembling. 'It was always Eadmund who needed to change himself.'

'And he has!' Jael implored, turning to her father-in-law. 'Haven't you seen how hard he's tried lately? How different he looks? He's been drinking less. He's started training with a sword, and today he was even coming here to look at his horse. It was a start. It could have been a beginning.'

Eirik looked bereft. 'It's not enough.'

'What do you mean?'

'Tiras, that vile bastard. He had a lot to say,' Eirik sighed, looking away. 'About your wedding night.'

Jael frowned. 'What about our wedding night?'

'That nothing happened between you and Eadmund that

night. That your marriage was not consummated. That it has never been consummated. That Eadmund hasn't even set foot in this house since your wedding. That he slept through that night on the floor!' Eirik stared at her intently, challenging her to deny Tiras' accusations.

Jael thought that over. How would Tiras know all of that? Did he sit outside the house all night with his ear to the wall, listening to Eadmund snore? She clenched her jaw, hating that spying little maggot more than ever. 'It's all true,' was all she could say.

That set Eirik off again.

He lurched to his feet, pacing around the fire, scratching his hands fretfully through his long white hair. 'But that's the worst kind of luck there is! Not to consummate a marriage on the wedding night? The gods will curse such a misformed union! Nothing good can come from your marriage now. Nothing at all!'

'You're wrong,' Jael insisted, standing up. 'You're wrong! There's hope in Eadmund. In both of us.' She instantly regretted her words, no matter how true they might have been.

'It's too late!' Eirik glared at her, his mouth set in a decisive line. 'It's too late, Jael. That was Eadmund's last chance with me. I warned him. He knew it. He only had that one chance, and now it's gone.'

'Why? What have you done?'

'I've had Morac take the girl away,' Eirik said coldly. 'And I've sent for Ivaar.' Eirik removed all feeling from his face as he turned to leave. 'I wish you luck with your marriage, Jael. Both you and Eadmund. You're going to need it!' And, yanking open the door, he disappeared into the blizzard without another word.

The door banged loudly in his wake, snow blowing inside, but Jael made no move to go and shut it.

She remained frozen to the spot.

***

'Have you told Jael? About Isaura?' Eydis wondered shyly.

Thorgils sat in front of her on a chair that was far too small for him, his bushy head cradled in his hands, his mind flooding with painful memories he'd never imagined having to face again. 'No.' His voice was dull, muffled.

Eydis sniffed. She'd spent most of the day sobbing after her father had raged at her about Evaine. She'd never felt so much anger in him, mixed with so much disappointment. He felt betrayed, she knew, but he was reacting harshly and too quickly. Eydis had pleaded with him to change his mind, but he wouldn't listen to anything she had to say. He felt that she was a conspirator, that she'd kept things from him, important things he needed to know.

It was too late, he'd warned her. Too late for Eadmund.

'I thought you'd be happy to see her at least?' Eydis suggested hopefully.

Thorgils lifted his head. 'Oh, Eydis,' he smiled ruefully. 'But you know nothing about love, do you? Who knows, maybe you will, one day soon?' He sighed, reaching out to grasp her little hand. 'You see, love can feel as though your heart will burst with happiness. And love can feel as though your heart will break with pain. With true love, there's no easy middle ground. Just happiness or pain. And with Isaura, we had happiness. More than I ever thought to deserve. We were so happy that I foolishly thought we'd always be that way.' He looked wistfully at Eydis, trying to picture Isaura's face. He frowned because he couldn't. 'When your father took her from me and gave her to Ivaar, I thought I'd die from the pain. Just like Eadmund, when he lost Melaena. He had the pain of knowing that she'd never return to him, and me... I've had the pain of knowing that Isaura was only a ship's ride away, married to your bastard brother. And there was nothing either of us could do to stop it. There still isn't.'

'Isaura didn't want to go, did she? She had no choice. She would never love Ivaar.'

Thorgils smiled uncertainly. 'No, I don't suppose she'd ever love Ivaar. Only Ivaar could truly love Ivaar.'

'So that means she still loves you,' Eydis said encouragingly. 'And if there's still love, then there's still hope that you can find happiness together again, isn't there? Unless, of course, you've given up?'

Her words were a challenge, and Thorgils thought on it.

He *had* given up, he realised. On Isaura. On hope.

'But now she's coming back. And even though no one wants Ivaar to come, at least it gives you another chance with Isaura. Somehow, maybe? If you don't give up,' Eydis smiled. She could feel Thorgils' pain so intensely. She wanted to help him. Guide him in the right direction.

But in her mind, she saw Ivaar coming, and her heart turned cold.

***

Eirik had thrown him out of the hall, insisting he never step foot in there again. Tiras didn't care; he felt a charge inside himself, thrilled to have finally unravelled Jael and Eadmund's sham. He hadn't been sure how he was going to use his knowledge about their wedding night to his advantage, but when he'd overheard Eadmund and Evaine arguing in the alley, it had all come together perfectly. All those cold nights huddled outside houses, lurking in the shadows, hoping for some sweet morsel to take to Eirik, had finally paid off.

Tiras smiled gleefully as he built up his fire in his sparse little shack. He'd been treated worse than a slave since he'd been here, so he couldn't have been happier knowing that his revenge had played out against them all. Unfortunately, despite his revelations, he was stuck here, having to endure their company for the rest of the winter, and what a bitch of a winter it was already proving to be.

Tiras shrugged his hunched shoulders, knowing that nobody was as good at appearing invisible as him. He would just hide away, keeping his ears and eyes open until spring. There were a few on the island who were keen to bring him information for a reward. He didn't need to show his face to continue his work for Lothar. He was confident there would be more to find. More ways to undermine Eirik and Jael. Oh, how he'd have loved to have seen her face when Eirik told her everything.

The door flew open, slamming against the wall, shaking the cottage.

Tiras shook too because standing in the doorway, ready to kill him, was Jael.

She saw him crouching by the fire and didn't hesitate.

In two strides, she had him in her hands, one around his neck, the other on his shoulder. She rushed him backwards, pushing him down to the floor, pinning him there with her weight, one knee in his ribs. Tiras was certain that he was heavier than her, but he could do nothing to push her away. The full weight of Jael was upon him, her fingers pinching his throat.

He couldn't breathe.

Tiras flapped his hands against the hard dirt floor, trying to gain some purchase, wanting to bat her away, but he couldn't even reach her.

'If you take a fish out of water, how long do you think it can breathe before it runs out of air?' Jael asked slowly, coldly, her eyes as hard as iron, her face betraying no effort as she held him down. 'I've often wondered that. How reliant we are on a simple thing like air. What happens when it's taken away from us? Just like that.' She leaned down harder, pressing her knee further into his ribs, squeezing her fingers around his throat, and now Tiras' ears were buzzing and ringing. He started to get dizzy, seeing black patches dancing before his eyes, his head thick with confusion.

Jael had come here wanting to frighten him, threaten him, punish him. But now that she had his mean little life in her hands, now that she knew how easy it would be to keep going like this until he stopped breathing, she found herself not wanting to let go. Tiras was a shit-stained piece of nothing who'd worked hard to destroy Lothar's enemies.

Jael felt her breathing slow, everything around her fading away. All she could see were Tiras' eyes jumping out of his rodent-like face. She watched the panic in them, the fear that she was truly about to kill him. His arms and legs flailed underneath her, but she knew she'd weakened him enough now that it would make no difference.

She could finish him. Take her revenge quickly.

Jael bent her head towards his face, slipping a knife out of its scabbard with her free arm. Tiras' eyes darted to the left. There was still enough life in him to fear that sound.

He knew what was coming now.

Jael readjusted her weight, bringing the knife past his eyes, forcing him to watch its blade shimmer in the fire's light, its finely honed tip coming to rest on his pulsing throat. She smelled Tiras' bladder open then, flooding the floor with the bitter stench of his terror.

And staring into his eyes, she smiled.

***

The mood of the hall grumbled around Eirik as he sat, picking over the remains of his supper. Everyone avoided looking his way, gossiping quietly amongst themselves, rolling his words around their heads, chewing things over with one another.

Eirik felt more isolated than he could remember as he sat at the high table, alone. There was no Morac or Runa. There was no Eadmund or Jael. Eydis wouldn't come out of her room – she wouldn't even speak to him – and there was no Thorgils either.

Eirik had other friends, other advisors, but they were rarely invited to sit near him, so he had faced the hall on his own, too furious to care how many people he'd upset with his announcement that Ivaar was coming back.

Jael and Eadmund had deceived him. Eydis and Thorgils too. They'd all known things they should have told him. And Morac and Runa should have kept that girl locked away.

Eirik's mind raced.

No one wanted Ivaar back, that much was obvious. Eadmund was beloved amongst the people of Oss, as his mother had been, but he wouldn't make a good king. Eirik was sure of that now. Yes, he'd picked up a sword again, but what did that really show? A few training matches in the Pit was hardly a commitment. True commitment would have been paying attention to his marriage. Actually being in it. Sleeping in the same bed as his wife, especially on his wedding night when all the gods were watching, waiting to give their blessing!

Eirik felt embarrassed, imagining Lothar's smug face. Lothar would blame him, of course, and he'd be right to do so. Eirik couldn't honestly see how Jael was to blame for any of it. There was certainly no reason for her to want to be with Eadmund. It had been up to him to take the lead with his wife, as her husband. He had that responsibility as a man. But Eadmund had failed. At every opportunity, he had failed, and no matter how hard he might be trying now, it was too late.

Ivaar was his choice now, and all of Oss would have to get used to it.

Eirik simmered angrily as he drained his cup of mead, the taste of it oddly bitter on his tongue. He was confident that Ivaar could show them that he was everything Eadmund had turned out not to be. He pictured Eydis' tear-stained face, pleading with him as he left to send a note to Kalfa, warning him that Ivaar would destroy Oss. That he would destroy all of them.

Eirik hadn't listened. It was too late.

He had simply had enough.

***

Isaura's hopes sunk as she watched the ship being pulled up onto the beach, her one-year-old son, Mads, grizzling on her hip. Her three daughters ran down to the shore, filled with excitement; they didn't often get visitors to Kalfa, especially during the Freeze. Ivaar's face glowed with satisfaction as he waited expectantly beside her. She could feel the vibrations in his body as his shoulder brushed against hers.

Isaura shivered, knowing that the opportunity for his long-awaited revenge was about to be delivered to him by the very man he had always dreamed of destroying.

CHAPTER TWENTY EIGHT

'Are you alright?' Aleksander asked for the third time, glancing behind himself. He hadn't yet decided if it was better to ride in front of, or behind Edela. He'd tried both, switching regularly, and each position had kept him in a constant state of anxiety, wondering whether she was falling behind, or stumbling off the path. He carried the responsibility for her safety like a heavy pack on his back.

'Yes, yes, of course!' Edela croaked crossly. 'It's just a bit of bread caught in my throat. I'm still breathing back here!' She tapped Deya lightly, and they moved up alongside Aleksander. 'You must stop worrying so much. I've not seen my end on this journey, I promise!'

The look on her face relaxed his, a little. He sighed, feeling the pain in his shoulders. The tension that had kept him prisoner since Jael left still offered him no respite. Aleksander wondered how life was for her now. If she thought of him anymore? If she was carrying her child yet? He shuddered at the image of her and Eadmund together, but at the same time, if his visions were to be believed, it would mean that she was one step closer to coming home.

'So, tell me, then,' Edela smiled craftily. 'Why you think Jael is coming back to you?'

Aleksander started, unsettled by the timing of her question. He'd been expecting it, but he still wasn't sure how much to reveal. 'Well, I just believe that she is.' He stared into the distance, watching light-grey clouds rush towards them. He couldn't see any snow on the horizon yet, which was a good thing; there was plenty enough snow already. 'I've had my own dream about it.'

Edela made a noise somewhere between a cough and a groan. 'I see. Different from mine, was it?'

'I'm not sure,' he wondered, honestly. 'Did you ever see Jael coming back to Andala? To me?'

Edela rolled words around her tongue, considering which ones to pick. In the end, she couldn't see any other path to take; he needed to know. 'I did see her returning to Andala, yes, but Eadmund was with her.'

Aleksander said nothing but she could see that she had shocked him. His mouth hung open, his eyes flooded with despair.

'You were so certain that she was returning to be with you?'

'I had a dream, a vision,' he said faintly. 'I only saw Jael and her child. Not him. In the dream, we were together again. I'm sure that's how it was.' He frowned, digging back into his memories, hoping to find any clue he may have missed. Wanting to prove Edela wrong.

'But it was just a dream,' she said kindly, ducking under a drooping branch, heavy with snow. 'And you've had dreams and nightmares your whole life. Why did you believe this one so much?'

Aleksander watched the lean of the trees in front of them. The wind was picking up again, he thought absently. The further north they climbed, the more challenging the weather would become.

'Aleksander?'

'I saw the Widow.' He couldn't even look at her.

Edela said nothing but her body froze in horror.

That was a name she hadn't heard whispered for many years.

Aleksander felt her shock, and he rushed to fill the frosty silence, his words tumbling out now. 'She gave me a tincture, told me to drink it, said that the gods would send me the dreams

I needed to have. That's when I saw it, Jael and her daughter coming back to Andala. But I never saw him. He wasn't in my dream. I'm certain of that. He wasn't there.'

'The Widow,' Edela began, then shivering, she stopped, inhaling a deep breath. 'The Widow is no one you should ever seek guidance from. She would not have helped you for any reason other than to cause pain, to you, or someone else. That is her reputation. She doesn't help or heal, she hurts. Everyone she meets. You should not have sought her out.'

Aleksander saw the fear and anger in Edela's eyes, but he wasn't prepared to let go so easily. He had clung to the hope of that dream. It was all he had.

He wasn't going to let it go, no matter what Edela thought.

**

The new snow made for slow walking. It was well over her knees, and Jael had barely stepped away from the house before she considered going back to change her trousers. She decided against it, though, and kept walking, listening to the plaintive wails of Ido and Vella, who were not going to be let out for a while yet.

Jael wondered how Tiras was faring in his piss-stained trousers.

Had she truly intended to kill him?

Possibly not, but it had taken an enormous amount of willpower to keep her blade from tearing open his throat. She'd felt nothing watching his distress. Nothing but pleasure in the terror she saw in his eyes. But, in the end, it would have cost her more to kill him than to let him go. He was Lothar's favourite pet, and his death would have caused trouble for them all.

Jael sighed, lifting her legs higher, trying to step over the snow instead of wading through it. There were too many shit-filled people walking about, she decided, on Oss, and in Brekka. Too many people who didn't deserve the breath that filled their lungs.

Surely it was time one of them met their end?

Jael trudged on towards the hall, wanting to see how Eydis was faring. She imagined that her father's news would have been a hard thing to hear, no matter how much she'd seen it coming.

As she walked past a block of stables, Thorgils staggered into her path. He faltered when he saw her, squinting at the blanket of snow spread before him.

'Slept with the horses, did we?' Jael smiled, then grimaced. Her cheek ached, and her eye was no better. She could barely see out of it.

Thorgils blinked groggily at her, trying to make his mouth work, but it was too dry, so he tried to clear his throat instead, which hurt his head and made his eyes water. 'I'm either going to fall into the snow and drink it, or you can drag me to the hall so I can get something to wet my tongue,' he croaked, staring at her pitifully; a slouched wreck of a man.

Jael grinned, slipping her arm through his, hoping he wasn't about to lean his substantial bulk on her. Thorgils stunk, almost as much as Eadmund had when they'd first met, and she turned her head away as she helped him limp towards the hall.

The cold air started to revive Thorgils, and before long he was almost upright. 'Have you seen Eadmund? Did you speak to him?' he wondered, noticing the stares they were getting as they staggered through the deep snow. There were not many people about this early, but those who were seemed intent on whispering and staring.

'No, he never came, but Eirik did.'

'Oh... well, you know everything, then,' Thorgils muttered, hanging his head, the misery of yesterday's events snuffing out any hope of a better day.

'Yes, and by the look of it, so do you.'

'I do, indeed.' He shook his head, then remembered how sore it was and stopped. 'We should be at Fyn's, but I don't even know if I can lift a sword today.'

'Well, that's good news for me and my one eye, then,' Jael grinned as she helped him up the snow-covered steps to the hall. He stumbled. 'Careful! You'll have us both on our faces if you don't open your eyes wider!'

Thorgils tried blinking to clear his vision, but everything was just a white blur. He sighed morosely as Jael opened the door, pausing, unsure how he felt about seeing Eirik this morning. 'I think... maybe we should get a drink elsewhere?'

'Why?' Jael stopped and let the door close.

'I'm just not sure I can face it yet. Why don't we ride to Fyn's? I can cling onto Leada, let the breeze blow some sense into my thick head.' He stared down at Jael sadly. 'We can talk about some things.'

'We can do that, although, with all this snow, I'm not sure the horses will be too happy.'

'True,' he nodded. 'But I think they'd be unhappier stuck in the stables all day. Besides, at least one of us needs to practice and even more now,' he muttered, lowering his voice. 'With Ivaar coming, who knows what's going to happen on Oss. I don't imagine either of us will be safe much longer.'

***

Eydis knew all of Eadmund's hiding places; he'd had so many over the years. He'd not been intentionally hiding most of the time, but somehow he'd just ended up falling asleep in the same places, over and over again.

They'd checked four of them now, without any luck, but Eydis had a strong feeling that Eadmund would be in the fifth place. He had to be. She had run out of ideas.

'Are you warm enough, my lady?' Biddy wondered anxiously for the third time.

Eydis had come early, seeking Jael's help to track down Eadmund but she'd wound up with Biddy instead, who had no intention of letting her go exploring on her own. Not in this much snow.

'You must call me Eydis, Biddy. My lady sounds like I'm my mother,' she smiled sadly.

'Well... Eydis,' Biddy said severely, pulling the shivering girl towards her to avoid an oncoming group of snow shovellers. 'You're shaking, and I think we should go back now. We've found no sign of that brother of yours, and you need to change your clothes. All of them!' She looked down at Eydis' wet cloak and boots. Her own clothes were clinging to her legs, and she couldn't stop thinking about how nice it would be to go back to the house and sit by the fire.

'Just one more,' Eydis pleaded, arms out in front of her now, feeling around. 'I think we're here. Is it a small cottage, all by itself? With antlers over the door? No windows?'

'Well, I suppose so. They all look much the same around here. But it could be the place. There is one antler. The other appears to have broken off.'

'Good, then I'll go in and see. You can wait for me here,' Eydis smiled confidently, pushing on the slightly crooked door.

Biddy looked distressed as she called after her. 'Well, I'm not sure I should just let you go in there! It doesn't look the cleanest place for a young lady to go...' But her words fell onto the snow and stayed there, ignored, as Eydis disappeared through the door.

The air inside the cottage was frigid, and Eydis couldn't hear or feel a fire. She shuddered, noticing for the first time just how wet her clothes actually were. She heard nothing but the hollow sound of her boots on the floorboards as she walked forward, arms constantly moving, trying not to fall over anything or anyone.

'Eadmund? Are you in here?' Eydis sensed someone nearby,

certain she could hear breathing. The cottage stunk of stale ale and other things she didn't want to imagine, and following the faint, snuffling noises, Eydis eventually found a bed, and, feeling around, she found a leg and a space, and she sat down. 'Eadmund!' Eydis squeezed the leg as hard as she could.

Eadmund jerked upright, blinking in shock as the cold grabbed hold of his body. He gasped, surprised to see the shadowy little figure of his sister sitting nearby. 'Eydis! What are you doing here?' He squinted at her with one eye. 'You shouldn't be here, it's freezing!' His head was full of fog, but he had enough sense to scramble up and wrap his bed furs around her. 'How did you get here? You're wet through!' he croaked, shaking his head, trying to wake himself up.

'Biddy brought me. She's outside, so perhaps you could put your head out and tell her that she can go home now. I don't want her standing around in the snow getting cold.'

'Biddy?' Eadmund mumbled, stumbling towards the door, his head pounding with every step. 'Who's Biddy?'

Eydis rolled her eyes and sighed. 'That's how we got into this mess in the first place!'

Eadmund opened the door to see a middle-aged woman, dressed in a plain, brown cloak, with a fierce look on her face. She appeared ready to break into the cottage. Seeing him, however, she took a step back, and her face relaxed.

'I take it you're Eadmund?' Biddy said, wrinkling her nose at the foul odours escaping through the door.

'Yes, and you're Biddy?' Eadmund shivered, wondering where he'd left his cloak. Again. 'Eydis is sending you home. I'll bring her back to the hall when she's done telling me off.'

Biddy couldn't help but smile at his swollen-eyed, miserable face. Despite the look and the stink of him, there was something about Eadmund that she quickly warmed to. 'Well, you're both more than welcome to come back to *your* house instead, if you like. I shall have something hot waiting, and I know two puppies who would like the company.'

Memories started shifting around in Eadmund's head, and he put them all together with a crooked smile. '*My* house?' he said slowly, then frowned. 'What about Jael?'

'You needn't worry about her. She's gone riding with Thorgils. I don't imagine they'll be back for hours.'

Eadmund scratched his head. 'Perhaps we will. That does sound more appealing than seeing my father.'

'Good. I'd better hurry back and start cooking then,' Biddy said, nodding quickly, remembering all the chores she'd been in the middle of when Eydis had whisked her away. She would have to move fast.

Eadmund closed the door and came back into the room. 'Ahhh, Biddy...' he sighed, joining his sister on the bed. 'My wife's servant.'

'Your servant too, if you ever went to your own house!'

'Well, it's too late for that, isn't it? It hardly matters now.' Eadmund hung his head, remembering his conversation with his father. Eirik had been wild with rage. But sad too. Eadmund had seen that in the brief moments Eirik had stopped to catch his breath. He'd never seen him look so disappointed.

Eydis reached for her brother's hand. 'It's not too late.'

'I can't get Evaine unpregnant, or make Jael pregnant in one day, Eydis. It's too late,' he told her firmly. 'Everything's too late.'

'Eadmund, listen to me,' she pleaded. 'I saw Ivaar coming. I saw Evaine with your child. I have seen many things, some of them far into the future, but I don't believe we can't change them. Why else would the gods show me what's coming? It's a warning, isn't it? They're giving us a chance to do something. To stop the bad things from happening.'

Eadmund felt ashamed of his own weakness as he glanced at his little sister's face. She was desperately clinging to hope, whereas he was ready to fall down and give up. Every part of his body was trying to convince his mind that going back to sleep was the best way to deal with the situation.

Or ale.

If he could just find more ale.

***

'Well, that makes sense of all this,' Jael said, flapping a hand at Thorgils' miserable face as they rode carefully down the slope towards Fyn's hut. 'I don't blame you at all. But surely seeing Isaura again is something you can look forward to?'

'With him? Seeing her with him? What if she loves him? What if she's stopped loving me?' He sighed deeply. 'What if she hasn't?'

Tig's hooves slipped, and Jael had to catch herself from tipping forward. 'Whoa, Tig.' She gave him a reassuring pat, resettling her weight backwards. 'You can't worry about any of those things, can you? Not now, at least. When you see her, you'll know the answer to all of your questions. But until then, don't think about it, it won't help you. You have to keep your mind and your body on the contest. That's the only thing you have any control over. Any more mornings like this and you won't even get a chance to meet Tarak, let alone have any hope of defeating him.'

Fyn waved his sword at them, an eager smile on his freckled face. He must have been out clearing the practice area since dawn as he'd moved enough snow for them to begin right away. Although, Jael thought, feeling her swollen eye, and glancing at Thorgils yawning and clutching his belly, he might have done it all for nothing.

***

Morac frowned, remembering the look on Eirik's fuming face when he'd ordered him to remove Evaine from Oss.

Ordered him.

Like he was a servant.

Is that what Eirik truly thought of him after all these years? As no more than a servant? Morac supposed it was true. He'd put himself in that position. Eirik was so used to him bending to his every whim now that he took more and more advantage as the years wore on.

It had all been so different when they were boys. Eirik had been like a little brother to him then. Morac had looked out for him, taken care of him. All those nights when Eirik's father used to beat him, it was Morac and his sister, Morana, who had tended to his wounds. Who had given him comfort and friendship. Who had ultimately helped him escape and take revenge upon his father.

But that was so long ago now, and they'd both forgotten so much, it seemed. Morac had been the leader then. He had saved Eirik's life.

They had both forgotten.

But Morana hadn't.

She looked as withered as an ancient tree, Morac thought, staring at his younger sister. Her black-and-white hair hung about her like curtains, wild and matted together. Her skin was wrinkled like weathered bark. But her dark eyes were still sharp, and they sought his in the dim light of the cottage. 'Without us, he would've turned to ash before he'd even begun!' she spat. 'Does he not remember? Is he so old that his memory box has broken?'

Evaine sat on a small bed, leaning against the wall, barely listening. She stared at her hands, her eyes hurting, her breasts aching, her heart breaking.

'Time will do that to memories,' Morac said wryly. 'It twists and shapes them into whatever we want them to be. Whatever comforts us and allows us to sleep at night. Eirik is not alone in that.'

'No, I suppose he is not,' Morana conceded reluctantly, sipping a foul-smelling brew. 'But he owes you more than he's ever acknowledged. He's the King of Oss *because* of you. And now, instead of giving you his thanks, he's ripping your family apart, piece by piece. Soon it will just be you left, and then... no one.'

She was being dramatic, Morac thought. But Eirik had banished three members of his family now. How was he to hold his head up on Oss ever again?

'Eirik Skalleson is old. His death is coming. And soon.'

Morac looked up sharply. 'You've seen this?'

'I have, and he has too!' she snorted. 'Why do you think he's made all this fuss about having an heir? His time is rushing away from him, and when he's gone, you will have your chance. We all will!' She grinned at Evaine, showing off two crooked rows of rotting teeth.

***

Jael felt weary as she pushed open the door. She'd barely been able to see, and Thorgils had barely been able to stand, but somehow they'd managed to use most of the daylight to fight one another, much to Fyn's amusement. He'd enjoyed his improved chances against both of them, taking a few gleeful helpings of revenge for the punishment they'd served up to him recently.

The house was warm and quiet, apart from the crackle of the fire, and an odd rumbling sound that reminded Jael of... snoring? She glanced around the main room then bent down to pat the very sleepy Ido and Vella who had come to greet her. She saw Eydis sitting by the fire and Biddy tidying her kitchen corner, but where was that noise coming from?

Biddy put a finger to her lips. 'That would be your husband,' she whispered, pointing towards the bedchamber.

Jael's eyes rounded in surprise. She shivered, glancing back at the door, wondering if she should go and check on the horses.

'Sit by the fire,' Biddy insisted, taking Jael's wet cloak. 'You're shaking.'

Jael felt awkward as she sat down next to Eydis in a... chair. 'Hello, Eydis,' she smiled. 'Where did this come from?' It was a very nice chair: smooth oak, with a high back, and ample armrests. Jael sunk back into it, comfortable but confused.

'I had it brought around for Eadmund,' Biddy whispered, coming to perch on a stool. 'I thought he needed something more comfortable.'

Jael raised an eyebrow. 'I see. But the stools are alright for me?'

'Well, your rump fits perfectly on them, so I haven't been worried about you, no.'

'But you've been worried about Eadmund?'

'Of course! I want him to feel at home here.' Biddy lifted Ido onto Eydis' knee. 'Here you go, Eydis. He's looking for a cuddle.'

'He's getting so big,' Eydis laughed, stroking Ido's fluffy coat. 'I don't think he'll fit on my knee for long.'

'Good,' Jael said. 'That way I'll be able to take them walking without worrying they're going to drown in the snow!' She watched Eydis' expression change, and turned to see that Eadmund was standing in the doorway.

'I do believe that's *my* chair you're sitting in.'

He looked terrible, Jael thought, with his crumpled face and wild hair. She couldn't help but smile. 'Feel free to move me out of it, if you like.'

'I wouldn't think of it,' Eadmund croaked, heading for the fire. 'You look like you've had a rough day.' He pointed to his eye.

Jael reached up, touching her own. 'Oh, that? That was Thorgils.'

Eadmund looked surprised as he pulled a stool close to the

flames, sitting down with a groan.

Biddy was right, Jael realised, he was far too big for it.

'You were training together? I haven't seen either of you in the Pit lately. Where have you been going?'

'We... ahhh, we've been fighting elsewhere.' Jael tried to construct a story that didn't involve Fyn. 'Just somewhere Thorgils likes to go for privacy. I've no idea what it's called. He's worried about Tarak knowing his secrets. He's taking the contest very seriously.'

'I can't blame him,' Eadmund said. 'Tarak's humiliated Thorgils every time they've fought. Not just beaten him, but worked hard to make him look like a fool in front of everyone.' He scratched his beard. 'I don't know what makes someone want to be that way. To get pleasure from hurting others.'

'Well, there are a few like that around here, wouldn't you say?' Jael noted wryly. 'And it seems that your father is about to welcome one more.'

Eadmund grimaced, sighing. 'Yes. That.' He didn't know where to look or what to say, but suddenly the room felt too hot, his tunic too close to his skin, the lamp too bright near the corner of his eye. 'It... is unfortunate, but I suppose I shouldn't be surprised. Eirik made it clear enough what would happen if I were to... let him down. It's my own fault.' Eadmund could feel Biddy's eyes and Eydis' ears taking everything in, and he felt embarrassed. 'I should get you home, Eydis, or at least walk you to the hall steps. Father will no doubt be wondering where you've been all day, though I hardly think he'd like to see me.' He stood, his head hanging low, his spirits even lower.

Eydis lifted the sleeping Ido onto the floor and let Biddy wrap her up in her cloak. She'd had such an enjoyable afternoon, sitting and talking with her by the fire, cuddling the puppies, listening to Eadmund snore, eating far too many bowls of nettle soup. She was reluctant to leave, but she could hear the distress in Eadmund's voice. He needed to go.

Jael got up and followed them to the door. 'Do you have a

cloak?' she wondered. Eadmund was only wearing a tunic and already looked cold.

Biddy had already found it, though, and she handed it to him with a sympathetic smile. He really did look like the saddest man she'd ever seen. 'Here you are.'

'Thank you,' Eadmund nodded. 'Thank you for the meal and the company, and the bed, of course. That bed is a hard thing to leave. I've never slept in something like that.' He shook his head. 'My father worked so hard on that for you.'

'He did?' Jael was surprised.

Eadmund laughed. 'He wanted to impress you so much. I think sometimes he doesn't feel like a real king, not compared to your family, at least. I suppose it's hard letting go of who we used to be, no matter how far away we end up from where we began.'

Jael could see the sadness behind his smile as he bent down to pat the puppies, but she didn't know what to say, or how she felt about any of it. 'You should come again,' she tried. 'We can talk about *my* horses and *my* chair and *my* puppies.' She started to smile, but her eye hurt, and she cringed instead.

Eadmund laughed, pleased to have caught a glimpse of kindness in her eyes; that meant something. 'Perhaps I will.' He turned to his sister. 'Come on, Eydis. We need to go.'

Jael squeezed Eydis' hand. 'You must come and keep Biddy company again. She's getting lonely without me these days, and old people always like to be around the young, don't they Biddy?' She winked at Biddy, whose face twisted into a scowl.

'Yes, you should come again, Eydis. It will make a nice change to be around a real lady.' And bending down, she picked up Vella, who'd been pawing her leg.

'Goodbye, Eadmund.'

'Goodbye, Jael.'

He smiled briefly, his lost eyes lingering for just a moment before he opened the door, ushering Eydis outside, quickly shutting it behind them.

***

'You're in the best place possible now,' Morac promised, clambering into the small ship. He felt reluctant to leave his daughter. Angry that Eirik was forcing him to.

Evaine didn't look convinced.

Her pale face was drawn, her body shaking. She didn't want to be left on this miserable island with her aunt, without Eadmund. 'Will you come back? Will you come and take me home?'

Morac stumbled, unsteady in the rocking vessel. He blinked away his uncertainty. 'Of course, of course, I'll come back. And so will you. Ask Morana. She sees everything, which she will no doubt tell you over and over again!' He smiled, hoping it would relax her, but Evaine appeared ready to cry.

'Perhaps Eadmund will come and visit me?'

Morac looked away, not sure he could face disappointing her further. The oars were in now, and the helmsman was demanding they leave. The sky didn't look threatening, but the wind would make it a difficult journey back to Oss. The narrow slip of sea that remained unfrozen was notoriously tricky to navigate, even on a calm day.

'Go back to the cottage, Evaine!' Morac called to her as the ship backed into the waves. 'Get yourself warm. You must take care of that child. And yourself!' His words blew away on the wind, and he held up his hand instead, waving to her, watching her disappear, hoping she would be alright.

Evaine sighed, trying not to vomit. And gathering in her flapping cloak, she turned to climb the hill back to her aunt's stinking little cottage.

CHAPTER TWENTY NINE

Thorgils kept swallowing as he stood there, waiting. He could feel the tension growing at the base of his neck, the straining of his nerves as he watched Isaura slowly coming towards him. He wanted to look away, desperately afraid of what he would see in her eyes, but not wanting her first look of him to be a disappointment. He tried to keep his shoulders high, his face impassive but strong as he waited.

The small party from Kalfa had spent nearly two days making their way from the very south of Oss, overland to the fort. The trip had, for the most part, been uneventful, but with four children and a large group of servants, most of whom were women, it had been a tediously slow journey. Ivaar was thoroughly sick of them all by the time they approached the rise of the hill where the fort stood, exactly as he'd left it, seven years before. He felt his left eye twitch in a burst of anger as he caught his first glimpse of the figures waiting for him and his outcast family. Oss had been his home, and he'd been thrown out of it in the most humiliating way. He clenched his jaw, knowing that he had to bite down on all of his resentment if he was going to achieve everything he had dreamed of for so long.

Eirik could feel his beard starting to freeze.

He wished they'd hurry up.

As much as he was looking forward to meeting his grandchildren and seeing Ivaar again, he was beginning to wonder what he'd done. A few days without Eadmund had cleared his mind, allowing him to wander far enough back into the past to remember why he'd removed Ivaar in the first place. But still, he told himself, he had to make a choice. There was no time not to. His responsibility as king was to leave his people in the hands of someone who could keep them safe and prosperous.

He hoped that Ivaar would give him reason to think that it could be him.

'Father!' Ivaar beamed, dismounting his horse. He stepped forward, embracing Eirik in an awkward hug. His father looked smaller than he remembered, but those blue eyes were still sharp as they peered up at him.

'Ivaar,' Eirik smiled. 'It's been a long time.' He stepped back, pleased with what he saw. Ivaar looked well indeed. His handsome face had barely aged since he'd last seen it. He had cut his blonde hair short, which made him look more severe than he remembered; though his pale blue eyes still had the same hungry look. After watching Eadmund's decline, Eirik was relieved to find that his eldest son was mostly unchanged.

He glanced towards Ivaar's wife, who was helping the children out of an overloaded wagon. 'Isaura! My dear girl, and look at all these grandchildren of mine!'

Isaura spun around, smiling nervously at Eirik. She had left as a nobody seven years ago and returned as the daughter-in-law of the king. She didn't know how to behave at all. Her weary eyes remained at chest level, staring straight ahead. She didn't want Ivaar to catch her looking for Thorgils, but she knew that he was there. She could sense him watching her. 'My lord,' she smiled politely, bowing her head.

'Oh no, you must not be that formal with me,' Eirik grinned, tickling each child's chin in turn, paying particular attention to the little boy, who promptly started grizzling. 'Eirik is fine. But now, who are these fine young Skallesons before me?'

'This is Selene... Annet... Leya... and the baby is Mads,' Isaura mumbled, pointing to each blonde-headed child in turn. They all looked ready to cry, she thought anxiously. The journey had been tiring, and much of it had been spent in tears.

Eirik looked genuinely delighted, Jael thought, as she shivered nearby, holding Eydis' hand. She hoped that he would send them to the hall quickly, though, before she froze to the ground.

'Eydis!' Ivaar came over to greet his little sister. 'You've grown so big!' He lifted her up, kissing her cheek. He chose not to notice the look of horror on her face or the rigid way she held her body, as though she was trying to escape his clutches. 'And *you*, you must be Jael,' he murmured, returning Eydis to the ground, giving her no further thought.

Jael nodded, studying Ivaar closely. He did look like Eadmund, she supposed, but a narrower, leaner version. His smile was not warm, though, and his eyes did not sparkle. 'I am, yes.'

'I'm pleased to meet you, at long last,' he said, letting his eyes roam the length of her. 'I've heard much about you over the years. All the stories of your victories with your father. What little news filtered through to me on Kalfa, at least, which was not much.' He drew his eyes towards Thorgils then. 'And Thorgils! It *has* been a long time, but you're still as big as ever!'

Thorgils bit his teeth together, clamping down on all the words that were threatening to rush out of his mouth. 'Ivaar,' he nodded shortly. 'Welcome back.'

'Thank you.' Ivaar returned the nod, then leaned in closer. 'Perhaps it won't be so easy between us, not as it once was, but I'm sure we'll smooth things over quickly enough.'

Thorgils wanted to rip those slimy words out of his throat and shove them up his arse. He swallowed, trying not to speak until he had control of himself; unsure if that would ever be possible. Thankfully, Eirik gestured for everyone to head to the hall, and Ivaar turned away, giving Thorgils a chance to take a few quick breaths.

Ivaar caught up with his father, leaving Isaura to usher the children along behind him. As she turned around to gather them all into the same general direction, she looked back, letting her eyes wander just far enough to find Thorgils. It was as though no time had passed between them at all. He suddenly felt hot, the unfamiliar burn of tears stinging his eyes.

Isaura looked away, grabbing her youngest daughter's hand, hurrying to catch up with her husband.

Thorgils didn't move.

He wanted to stay there, remembering those eyes, reading everything they had said to him in two tiny heartbeats.

'Come on,' Jael smiled kindly, stopping beside him. 'Let's get inside and have a drink.'

***

Eadmund knew that they would all be in the hall by now. He knew that he should be there with them. If he was going to turn his father back towards him, he had to show more fight than this.

He sat on the bed in his lonely, dark cottage, dressed in his cloak and boots, ready to join them, but he couldn't move. He remembered the warmth and company of Jael's house. His house. No, he shook his head, it didn't feel like his house. He didn't feel that he'd earned the right to be there, sitting in his chair by the fire. He smiled sadly. Not yet.

Eadmund thought of Evaine, and wondered how she would fare on Rikka, with Morana. He felt the guilt in that. She would have his child in the spring, but would he even know when it happened?

He imagined his father's face, staring at the doors of the hall, wondering if he was ever going to step through them. What would Jael think? Would she care that he wasn't there beside her?

Eadmund drank deeply from the jug. He'd drunk more than he'd planned, and now he didn't know if he was right enough in the head to be in the hall, with Ivaar and his sharp eyes, and Jael and her harsh tongue.

But what about Thorgils, he thought guiltily? How would he be coping, having to face Isaura again, knowing that she was married to Ivaar, who would no doubt be making it as torturous as possible. At least Thorgils had Jael and Torstan, he convinced himself. They would help him, he was sure.

Eadmund hung his head as it swum with memories and fears, but no direction. He couldn't see a way forward, not even with Jael, as pleasant as that had felt lately. He wanted to be all those things everyone assumed he could be; the person his father had hoped for, or Eydis believed in. But his father only saw the faded hope of his mother in him, and Eydis saw nothing at all but dreams.

None of it was real.

He took another swig from the jug, his head lolling from side to side, knowing that it was too late for him. He couldn't go to the hall now, it would only embarrass everyone he cared for.

Let them talk to Ivaar.

Let them welcome him back to the island with open arms.

He would rather stay in his cottage, where there was no one to judge him but himself.

***

Aleksander sighed with relief as Tuura finally came into view. Or was it discomfort? He almost couldn't tell. He'd felt so irritable and been so quiet since his talk with Edela about the Widow, that he'd barely noticed anything but his own thoughts. But now, here they were. Tuura was staring him in the face, and he suddenly felt ten-years-old again. Aleksander reined in his horse-without-a-name and waited for Edela to come alongside.

'We made it,' she sighed heavily, leaning forward to pat her faithful horse. 'I wasn't sure I'd ever feel happy to see this place again, but after four days of sitting like this, I'm delirious!' Edela glanced at Aleksander, who still looked morose. She felt responsible for that, knowing that every time she opened her mouth, she was dashing every hope he had for his future with Jael.

'Well, at least you'll be able to sleep tonight knowing you don't have to sit on a horse tomorrow,' Aleksander said. He tried to smile, but his frozen lips barely moved.

He nudged his horse forward.

'Aleksander, wait!' Edela called, reaching out to stop him. 'We mustn't forget why we are here. What we are hoping to find out. I know you're mad at me, but we must stay true to our purpose. We cannot reveal any of our suspicions, not unless we're with someone I trust. You cannot talk about my dreams, especially not the book, and definitely not the Widow.'

Aleksander held the reins tightly in one hand and turned to stare at her. 'Why *definitely* not the Widow?'

Edela looked down at the imposing stone fort, watching smoke plumes rise into the darkening sky, and sighed. 'The Widow was banished from here a long, long time ago. We don't need anyone discovering that you sought her out. That she helped you. It would not reflect well upon us at all. And I'm sure there are more than a few elders who would like to know the whereabouts of that... woman.'

Aleksander mulled that over as their horses snorted impatiently beneath them. They could smell civilisation and were eager to get to it. 'What did she do to get banished, then?'

'I'm not actually sure,' Edela admitted, shaking her head. 'My grandmother used to tell me tales of her, tales to frighten me into using my gifts for only good things. Whatever she was banished for has always been a well-guarded secret, though. Only the elders would know something like that.'

'Well, don't worry, I want to find out what's going on as

much as you do,' Aleksander insisted. 'No matter what you see in my future, I'll always try to help Jael. Whatever is out there for us, nothing will stop me trying to help her.' He bent his head, not wanting Edela to see how hard those words were for him to say. Tapping his boots lightly against his very agreeable horse, he moved off ahead of her again, riding down towards the very place that had ripped his life apart, and put it all back together again in the darkness of a blood-splattered night.

***

'There's no chance, Daughter!' Lothar bellowed, his eyes mocking her. 'Not while I'm alive. No chance that such a marriage will ever take place! Why would you think I would ever agree to such a thing?'

Amma shook from embarrassment, from humiliation, and from something else: anger. She stood in front of her father in the King's Hall, but they were not alone. Some of his men were gaping at her in amusement, a handful of servants were preparing tables for the evening meal, and Osbert sat behind Lothar, smirking in his chair. Why had her father chosen to make this such a public rebuke, she wondered? What had she done to deserve this low treatment? 'I never suggested such a thing, Father,' she tried, but her voice was so quiet that he rolled over her again.

'But you thought it, didn't you? Wanted it to be so?' He strutted back and forth in front of Amma, his ample girth jiggling, his rich, blue cloak swishing angrily across the floor. 'I'm sure it was only a matter of time before you brought it up yourself. Tried to win my favour for the match.' He stopped and glared at her, dark eyes bulging. 'But it was never going to happen. It *will* never happen!' And harrumphing loudly, he stepped back to sit on his throne, which shuddered beneath his weight. 'The only wedding we shall be celebrating is mine, my girl, and you will do well to remember that!'

Amma could feel her bottom lip quivering. Tears were dampening her eyes. Perhaps she should let her father see her cry? Maybe it would soften him? Remind him that he loved her. That he cared about her happiness.

'And you can stop those tears! If you think that's going to make a difference, it won't!' Lothar turned and whispered to Osbert.

Amma ducked her head, wondering if she could leave without him yelling at her any further. She was desperate to escape.

'Amma,' Lothar's voice softened as he motioned for her to come to him. 'Come, come here.' She reluctantly walked to stand in front of the throne, and he leaned forward, peering at her. 'Aleksander Lehr is no one. And you are the daughter of a king. Not just any king, either, but the King of Brekka. A Furyck king! I will not allow my daughter to marry a no one.' He grimaced, lifted one buttock, and farted loudly. 'I only want the best for you, just like I did for Getta. She is now the Queen of Iskavall. A Queen! And she's not much older than you. Can Aleksander offer you that? No! He can offer you a tiny cottage, a few rags, and not much else. But you will have more than that, I promise you. So much more!'

Amma feared what he meant by that. She saw Osbert out of the corner of her eye, enjoying her discomfort, a knowing smile on his nasty little face. She thought about Aleksander and felt embarrassed; relieved that he wasn't there to witness her humiliation.

She felt foolish. Foolish, and so very alone.

***

Jael wondered where Eadmund was. She wasn't the only one. There were a few faces turned towards the hall's closed doors, waiting to see if anyone else was going to open them. She glanced at Ivaar with his keen eyes and decided that it was better if Eadmund stayed away. He would need a clear mind and a quick tongue to face his brother, and she didn't imagine he'd find either of those in a cup of ale.

'They make a good couple, don't you think?' Thorgils mocked, motioning with his head towards Ivaar who was clapping Tarak on the back; the two of them apparently old friends.

'It's hardly a surprise. Rats will gather together,' Jael said softly.

'He certainly is that. I don't blame Eadmund for staying away,' Torstan mumbled.

Ivaar turned to stare at their little group, and such was the look on his face that Torstan froze.

Jael laughed. 'It's alright, Torstan, I'll keep you safe.'

That managed to raise half a smile on Thorgils' face. He distractedly sipped a cup of mead, doing everything he could to avoid looking for Isaura. He had a sense that she was talking with Eydis, but he didn't want to be caught searching for her, especially not by Ivaar, whose eyes were patrolling the hall.

'She looks so sad,' Jael whispered quietly to him as Torstan slipped away to top up his cup.

'Ahhh, best we don't talk about it,' Thorgils muttered, dropping his head, wanting to hide the unhappiness he could barely keep off his face. 'There's nothing I can do about it.'

'Not yet, anyway,' Jael said, staring at Tarak and Ivaar. 'But don't lose hope. There'll be something we can do.'

'Hello again,' Ivaar smiled as he approached. Thorgils nodded and raised his empty cup, quickly leaving to fill it.

He was handsome, Jael thought as she considered Ivaar closely by the high flames of the fire, with his well-groomed beard and his carefully cropped hair. He looked as though he spent a lot of time on his appearance; that what people thought of him mattered. He appeared confident, his eyes continually roaming her body. She had to fight the urge to slap him to make him stop.

'Are you pleased to be back, then?' Jael asked.

'I am. Very pleased.' Ivaar didn't blink. 'It's been a long time, an unfortunate time for us all. I'm just relieved that my father decided he was ready to bury the past and make a new future. One that we can all benefit from.'

Ivaar was standing too close to her. The hall was noisy, but not so loud that he needed to stand this close. Jael couldn't risk stepping back, though. He was testing her, seeing if he could make her uncomfortable. She kept her eyes up, her body rigid. 'Yes, your father seems very intent on creating new futures for everyone, it seems.'

Ivaar laughed. 'Mmmm, I was surprised when I heard Eadmund had married you. It was an interesting choice, and one I don't imagine you made for yourself.'

'No?'

'Eadmund? No.' Ivaar shook his head dismissively, his lips turned up in a smirk. 'Even when he was at his finest, when they called him Eadmund the Bold, even then I couldn't imagine he would have been your choice. That a Furyck would wish to marry an Islander? One step removed from a slave?' He laughed, and it sounded bitter. 'But I suppose we're all tokens in our father's games, until we become the kings and queens ourselves and then the games are all ours to play.' He angled his head towards her.

Jael continued to smile at him, but thoughts were chasing each other around her head. Ivaar was supposedly her enemy, but he didn't know that for certain, did he? Here he was, talking to her, looking to find out which side she wanted to be on. He would have seen her with Thorgils and assumed a lot from that, but perhaps she could confuse him now? Make him wonder where her true loyalty might lie... if she even knew herself.

'Yes, that's true,' Jael said, her smile friendly and open. 'I didn't come here willingly. Yet, here I am. The threads of our lives are often pulled in different directions, far away from what we may have imagined was being woven for us.'

'I had thought your father would make you the Queen of Brekka.'

Talk of her father always made Jael uncomfortable. He was not long enough dead, not yet. Her eyes faltered, and she was happy to let Ivaar see it. 'Yes, well, there you have it. The kings do make all the decisions, don't they? Although, it seems you have a good chance of becoming one yourself now, which I imagine you'd all but given up on.'

She was blunt, Ivaar noticed, and he liked that. Attractive too, despite her bruised face, and that scar that sat dangerously close to those very green eyes. He saw a fire in her that heated him quickly. After so many years of enduring his insipid wife and a handful of thick-headed servant girls, here was a real woman. Blade-sharp and strong. He would love to see what she could do with a sword. More than that; he would love to see what she could do to him in bed. 'Well, perhaps. I had thought I would just wither and die on that shit heap of an island, but here I am, rising from the ashes. Back where I belong, and happy for it. It does feel good to be home.'

Ivaar stared at Jael with such blue-eyed intensity that she had to work hard not to flinch. She remained still, her smile hardening, her eyes narrowing, holding his gaze. There was a chance here, she saw, a chance to be part of the game, and for all their sakes, she was going to take it.

CHAPTER THIRTY

Tuura was an ancient stronghold; a tiny, remaining speck on the land that had once belonged solely to its people. Before the Furyck settlers had arrived, escaping the burning ruins of Osterhaaven, they had roamed their land with freedom. Now, eight-hundred years later, they were feasting on mere scraps, their grip at the northern tip of Osterland becoming increasingly precarious. There were regular incursions from the Alekkans across the sea now. Even raiders from Iskavall, to the south, tried to break through their defenses, stealing what food and treasure they could find. And so, Tuura had been forced to build its walls even higher, hoping to keep its ever-encroaching neighbours at bay.

It was not how she remembered it, Edela thought sadly as she stared at the stone walls through the sinking gloom of the afternoon. Tuura had once felt like a free place. There had been some walls, of course, but they had felt much less oppressive than what she was looking up at now. Now, Tuura resembled a prison; its thick walls, topped with new ramparts, reached as high as a small mountain.

Aleksander glanced at Edela, sensing her unease. They halted the horses just before the wooden gates, waiting patiently behind a line of farmers and traders. He had been to Tuura only once, and it was not a place he had planned to revisit. His eyes tried not to seek out much, not wanting to find ghosts lurking in the places that tormented his dreams. Aleksander just wanted to stable the horses and find something hot to eat, preferably indoors. The sun was trapped behind a thick hedge of clouds, and the air was cooling down quickly. He shuddered, wrapping his cloak tightly around himself

He didn't want to be here again.

The line moved quickly enough, and despite a brief interrogation and inspection of their horses and saddlebags, they were ushered inside the gates with ease.

It was darker in here now, Edela noticed as her eyes flitted eagerly around her long-forgotten home. The high walls imposed themselves upon the town, leaving much of it in shadow. She had left here with Gisila over thirty years ago, on their way to a new life in Brekka with Ranuf Furyck. Tuura had remained close to her heart, though, and she'd returned many times to visit her mother and Branwyn, until that night when everything had changed. She had never felt the same way about it again and had barely visited since.

They rode on, down the main thoroughfare, which was broad and thick with well-trodden slush. Edela looked around in distress, noting the buildings in need of repair, the paths whose boards had worn through and not been replaced. Even the children who ran alongside her and Aleksander looked ragged and dirty. Despite the illusion of wealth and power the new fortifications created, Tuura felt like a crumbling ruin.

'Mother?'

Edela turned to see her daughter, Branwyn, rushing towards her, bustling her way through the curious onlookers standing around in the snow, peering at the visitors. Her face creased into a smile. It had been so long since she'd seen her youngest daughter. She felt a pang of guilt, but blinked it away as Branwyn grabbed her hand.

'Mother! This is a surprise! What are you doing here?' Branwyn's gentle brown eyes were wide with happiness. She had similar features to Gisila, but whereas Gisila was lean and refined, Branwyn was buxom and soft, her round face rippling with the gentle wrinkles of a happy life. 'Did you ride all the way on that?' She pointed to her mother's horse, blinking in surprise.

Aleksander reached up to grab Edela around the waist, gently lowering her to the ground. She couldn't help the groan that escaped her frozen lips when her boots touched the snow, nor the series of loud creaks as her joints readjusted themselves. 'Yes,' she smiled, sighing heavily, 'I did. I had a dream that I must come and visit you. That it had been far too long. So I forced dear Aleksander here, to accompany me on an old lady's whim.' She gingerly stretched out her back. 'Although, I'm not sure I'll ever be the same again!'

Branwyn laughed, hugging her mother. 'You look so well! Truly. It is so good to see you.' She smiled at Aleksander, who was trying not to make eye contact with anyone. 'Come, come along, and we'll take the horses to the stables. I'm sure they've plenty of room. Then we can find something warm to fill your bellies. You look frozen!'

Aleksander considered Branwyn's smiling face. There was a woman to admire, he decided. Horses first, then food; Jael would have approved. He grinned, and picking up the reins of their two leading horses, he fell in behind Edela and Branwyn, who were already thick in conversation, their heads bent towards each other in an easy familiarity.

***

'I can't believe how grown-up you are,' Isaura smiled at Eydis. 'I remember when I used to braid your hair. You hated it so much that you'd run away crying whenever you heard me coming. Do you remember?'

Eydis smiled shyly. 'I do. You would tighten the braids so much that my head would ache. I begged my mother to keep you away from me!'

Isaura looked horrified. 'Oh no, did you? That's terrible. I must have gotten better at it, though, as my daughters are not scared of me yet, and I've been braiding their hair since they were very young!' She patted Eydis' arm. 'It is so good to see you again, dear Eydis. To see this hall again. Your father has improved it greatly.'

'So he tells me,' Eydis sighed. 'My dreams are filled with pictures of how it must be in here. I'm sure I imagine it as the grandest hall there ever was.'

'Which is a good thing to do. Sometimes, all we have are dreams to hold onto, so it's best to make them grand.'

Isaura sounded so forlorn that Eydis felt uncomfortable. She didn't know where Ivaar was – there was too much noise in the hall for that – but she couldn't feel him nearby. Still, she didn't want to say anything out of turn that would cause problems for Isaura.

'How's Eadmund?' Isaura asked, scouring the hall again, but there was still no sign of him. 'I don't imagine he was happy about us returning?'

Eydis hung her head. 'No,' she whispered. 'Is Ivaar nearby?'

'No, no, he's talking far away. You can speak freely. I'll tap your arm if he comes close.'

Eydis nodded, relieved, but she whispered anyway. 'Eadmund is not himself. He has not recovered since Melaena died. I thought Jael would be able to help him, and she did for a while, but in the end, it was all too late. Evaine fell pregnant, and Father sent her away.'

'Evaine Gallas?' Isaura was shocked. 'Oh, dear. I imagine your father wasn't happy about that. I do remember Evaine,' she murmured, frowning. 'She was such an annoying little girl, always following him about. He could never get rid of her.'

'Well, she never stopped, not even when he got married to Jael.'

'What did your father do with her?' Isaura wondered, her

eyes wide, her voice hushed.

'He banished her to Rikka, to live with her aunt.'

'Oh well, they'll make good company for one another, won't they? That old crone Morana was always a strange one.' Isaura watched as Ivaar walked over to speak to Jael, for the second time, she noted. He was already busy playing his games it seemed. 'And what about Eadmund's new wife? How is she?'

Eydis' troubled face broke into a smile. 'Jael? She's perfect for Eadmund. She's everything he needs. He had gotten so much better before this happened. It was certainly because of her. I'm not sure what will happen now, though. I don't know how Eadmund will cope with Ivaar being here. I imagine he'll go back to being drunk all the time,' she sighed.

'Oh.'

'What is it?' Eydis could hear the strain in Isaura's voice, and a sudden hush murmuring around the hall. 'Isaura, what it is?'

'It's Eadmund. He's just stumbled inside. He doesn't look good at all, Eydis. What has happened to him?'

***

The house was thickly insulated, and after three nights of sleeping outdoors, Aleksander was grateful for it. Tuura was a bitterly cold place, but with the door shut and a change of clothes, he found that he had no complaints at all. There was even a fur-lined chair for him, placed right next to a blazing fire.

Branwyn's servant had fed them well, and as he sat with his legs stretched out near the flames, Aleksander could almost feel his toes again. He sighed contentedly, sinking back into the chair, his shoulders easing down, his muscles relaxing for the first time in days.

Branwyn's two sons, Aedan and Aron, had run in and out.

Her husband, Kormac, had also stopped by to welcome their visitors before returning to work at the smithy. But now the house was almost still. The women were nattering softly to each other on one of the beds that lined the walls of the main room, and Aleksander allowed his eyes to close and his thoughts to wander far away, back to Jael.

Always back to her.

He remembered how she had been that night when his parents were killed. She'd come to him in Gant's arms, covered in blood, her small body shaking, too numb to speak. She'd just stared blankly at him with those big green eyes. He must have looked much the same, he thought.

Gant had put Jael down beside him, firmly instructing Aleksander to look after her. He'd shaken him by the shoulders, making his tear-filled eyes focus, forcing him to understand the importance of keeping her safe. Gant had handed Aleksander his long knife and then left, his sword drawn, ready to find the men who had done this to them. And Aleksander remembered that feeling of being so incredibly lost and distraught at that moment, but forgetting it all when he'd looked into Jael's eyes and seen how broken she was. He knew he had to help her then, to watch over her, because Gant had told him to, but also because he had seen something in her that he truly wanted to care for.

He wanted to keep her safe.

And now, he didn't know how it was for her – whether she loved her husband or not – but he knew that he would do anything he could to help her, for as long as he had breath in his lungs.

***

This was not good.

Jael caught Thorgils' eye, and he nodded, grabbing Torstan and heading swiftly towards Eadmund's swaying figure. Every head had turned in Eadmund's direction, watching as he barged towards Ivaar and Jael.

'My brother!' Ivaar called, his lips forming a tight smile. He opened his arms in a show of friendship, determined to appear conciliatory before his father and the people of Oss.

Eadmund saw nothing except the fact that his brother was standing next to Jael. Next to his wife. He'd seen their faces as they stood talking. As mixed up as his mind was, it had only taken a heartbeat to conclude what was happening from her silly grin, and his brother's intense stare. Eadmund brushed away Ivaar's outstretched arms and stopped in front of Jael instead.

'My wife,' he slurred into her pinched face. He turned to glare at Ivaar. 'How long did that take you, Brother? Ha! You do seem to like my wives. But you're wasting your time here, for your interest in *her* will do nothing to hurt me. You're welcome to this one!' he spat, grabbing a cup of mead from the tray of a passing servant, draining it quickly. 'Just ask our father. We have no real marriage at all.' Eadmund glared at Jael, trying to focus. 'I'm not even sure why she's still here!'

Jael felt the shock as Eadmund's words echoed around the hall. Thorgils and Torstan came up behind him, their arms out, ready to pull him away but she shook her head slightly, warning them to keep back. Something had to be rescued from this mess. Eadmund was not about to go quietly, and if she didn't do something, the only winner would be Ivaar, gloating as his brother was forcibly removed from the hall, humiliated before everyone. Out of the corner of her eye, she saw Tarak striding towards their little huddle. Was he merely keen for a closer look, or about to add to the trouble? He moved to stand just behind Ivaar, raising a challenging eyebrow in her direction.

'Ahhh well, it's no secret that Eadmund prefers his women younger and blonder,' Jael smiled sarcastically, turning to Ivaar. 'Which, of course, is why you're here.'

Thorgils' face froze in surprise. He stared at Jael, demanding her attention, but she wouldn't look at him.

What was she playing at?

Eadmund's face froze in shock. Jael was glaring at him so fiercely that his reply tripped over the tip of his tongue, and didn't come out his mouth.

What was she playing at?

'But as to why *I'm* still here?' Jael looked at Ivaar as she spoke, pointedly ignoring Eadmund. 'I can assure you, it has nothing to do with my *husband*.' She shot Eadmund a look that was thick with scorn. 'It is for the weather that I stay. For the cold, and the snow, and the wind, of course!' she smiled, sensing some of the curious faces around her relax. There were a few chuckles, a handful of grins. Even Eirik looked slightly more at ease. 'And though I am no great beauty myself...' She bowed her head slightly. 'Nor am I delicate and blonde.' She aimed another sharp look at Eadmund. 'I hope that the people of Oss will, in time, be glad of my presence, even if my husband is not. Although... after the contest, I'm sure there will be many of you wishing I'd left for Brekka before the Freeze!' She played up to the crowded hall, grinning cheerfully, rewarded with a smattering of cheers.

Jael rested her eyes on Tarak for as long as she could stomach it, then walked away, barely noticing the amused faces turned in her direction. She headed straight for the high table and sat down next to Isaura, who looked too shocked to move. The Osslanders' eyes followed Jael, watching as she drank from her cup, and their attention wandered back to Eadmund and Ivaar, wondering what would happen next.

***

'Go away,' Gisila murmured, not even wanting to look up.

'Pretend you didn't find me.'

'You know Lothar's looking for you, then?' Gant wondered gently as he stepped into the cottage. He found her huddled by the barely-there fire, staring into the feeble flames, a blanket draped over her shoulders.

'He always is,' Gisila sighed. 'I thought I could avoid him until the wedding, but he won't leave me alone.'

'So I've noticed.' Gant glanced around the small room. 'Where's Axl? Gunni?'

'Gunni's gone somewhere, visiting her sister or something. Axl, I don't know about. Perhaps he's with a girl? He's never here anymore.'

Gant rolled his eyes, but Gisila didn't notice. He doubted that Axl was staying away for a girl. 'You can't refuse him, you know.' He crouched down, taking her hand. 'Gisila, look at me. You can't say no to Lothar. It will only mean bad things for all of you.'

She looked up then, and he saw that her beautiful eyes were swollen, tired, and bereft of any hope. 'I've been sitting here, remembering so many things today. When there's no noise, no one talking to you, your mind can truly get lost.' She stared into the flames again. 'I was the queen here, for thirty years. That's no small amount of time, is it? For more than half of my life, I was the queen here. And now look at me, Gant. Look at my family. It's broken into unhappy pieces, and I don't know what to do. Without Ranuf and Jael, and now my mother and Aleksander...' She looked up at him. 'What am I supposed to do?'

'You're about to become the queen again,' Gant said quietly as he grabbed a stool and came to sit beside her. 'Don't forget that. I'm sure you never thought that would happen. That your fortunes would turn again.'

'Not in this way, I didn't,' Gisila spat. 'Not like this. I never wanted this.'

'That may be so, but it will help all of you get out of here,' he insisted, motioning around the dingy cottage. 'And who knows what else it will be useful for?'

'Of course,' she sighed, staring into his concerned grey eyes. 'Of course, it all makes sense as you say. And I shall have fine dresses and eat well again. And once I thought that truly mattered. But now... now I'd rather have this hovel and these rags, and be free of that disgusting man and his irritating son.'

Gant knew that it was his job to convince her to come with him, but at the same time, the last thing he wanted to do was take Gisila to that slug so he could drool all over her again. She deserved so much better than that, especially after what she had been through. 'Perhaps we can wait here a little while before we have to go?' He looked at her kindly. 'Lothar doesn't need to know.'

***

Eadmund wasn't sure what would happen next. He was so confused about what Jael had just said and done that his head felt as though it was swimming backwards, searching for a way to turn around and move forward again.

He wasn't sure what to do.

He was surrounded, about to be pounced upon, but who was to be his captor? Tarak was glowering at him from behind Ivaar, and his father was quietly simmering on his right. He knew Thorgils and Torstan were behind him, and, of course, Ivaar was right in front of him, looking just as surprised as he felt. And as for Jael... she was sitting next to Isaura, drinking as calmly as anything, after all of that.

What was that?

Isaura. Eadmund's face lightened suddenly as his eyes met hers. She looked at him with such gentle pity that he faltered, feeling the years since they had last seen each other tumble away. Seven years since they had cried on each other's shoulders. He had just lost Melaena, and she was about to lose Thorgils; they were both bereft. She had been a true friend throughout his childhood; cared for him like a brother. He didn't want her to see him this way, in this pathetic state. He tried to blink some sense into himself, to salvage something from the mess that he'd made.

'Where are all your children then, Ivaar? Where are my nieces and nephews?' Eadmund asked through gritted teeth. He was still unsteady, in both mind and body, but he wanted the hall to relax away from him so he could find another drink, and a chance to speak to Isaura. All eyes were still turned on their conversation, waiting for the fight Eadmund had suddenly lost his appetite for.

Ivaar frowned, disappointed by the sudden change in his brother's mood. 'My children?' He looked around the hall distractedly. 'They're resting with their servants, I suppose. It was a long day for them. They're very young.'

'Well, perhaps I'll meet them tomorrow, but in the meantime, I shall go and welcome back their mother.' Eadmund stared at Ivaar but made no further threat, brushing past him as he walked towards the high table.

Eirik caught Thorgils' eye, suggesting he follow Eadmund, but that was the last thing Thorgils wanted, for Eadmund was heading for Isaura.

'It's alright,' Torstan whispered, 'I'll go.' And he followed Eadmund towards the other end of the hall.

'I suppose it could have been worse,' Ivaar laughed as his father approached. 'I had thought he might have come in with his sword drawn!'

Eirik didn't feel as light-hearted as Ivaar was attempting to be. He was uncomfortable, for more reasons than he could count. Eadmund was rotten drunk again, Jael seemed to hate both him and Eadmund, Eydis still wasn't talking to him, and Ivaar was acting as though the kingdom had already been promised to him. Eirik supposed he had given him that impression when he'd sent his note, asking him to come back, but still, Ivaar's confidence rankled.

Eirik watched sadly as Eadmund hugged Isaura. It had all been going so well. How had they ended up back here again?

'You look surprised,' Eadmund mumbled, barely meeting Isaura's eyes as he released her from his arms. 'Is it because I didn't kill Ivaar? Or because I'm as fat as a pig ready for slaughter?'

Isaura laughed. 'Both!' she smiled, relaxing at the reappearance of the twinkle in his eye that she remembered so well. It was still there. He was still in there, somewhere. 'But yes, you are very fat, Eadmund. What have you been doing to yourself?'

'Thank you very much, my dear Isaura. How I've missed your honesty!' he laughed, looking around for something to drink. He was getting far too sober now. His wife had a way of doing that to him, it seemed. She sat there, so close to him, but she didn't even look his way. All of her attention was now on Eydis. Eadmund lost himself, watching her, remembering her words, puzzled by them.

He blinked, suddenly, remembering that he needed a drink.

'Do you really think more ale will help?' Isaura wondered, reading his mind.

'Help?' Eadmund shook his head. 'No, but I will feel better for a while, and that's enough for right now.' He stopped a passing mead girl and grabbed a freshly poured cup from her.

'But a while will not last long, and then you'll feel nothing but regret. Regret, and a pounding head,' Isaura scolded lightly.

'Are you speaking from experience?' Eadmund asked with a crooked grin. 'Is that how you survive my brother? Ale or mead? I don't know what they drink on Kalfa. Fermented sheep's milk?'

Isaura laughed, distracted. 'No, not for me. I have my children to help me survive, that's all I need.' She smiled tightly, watching Ivaar, who was still talking to Eirik, not looking at her at all. She felt momentarily free, but still, she kept her voice hushed as she leaned in closer. 'How is Thorgils? Is he married?'

Eadmund saw the despair and longing in her eyes. He knew how she felt, how tortured and lonely she would have been without Thorgils all these years. He looked around, checking for Ivaar but saw only Torstan, who seemed to have been sent to watch him. He frowned in his friend's direction, then turned back to Isaura. 'No, he's never married. His heart never mended. He wasn't looking forward to you coming back.'

Isaura looked devastated. 'Oh.'

'No, no, I didn't mean it like that!' Eadmund said, scrambling about inside his muddled head, trying to find the right words. 'I mean that he didn't know how he'd be able to see you, with Ivaar. I imagine he thinks you may have forgotten him, or even fallen in love with your husband.'

Isaura snorted so loudly that even Ivaar turned in her direction. She looked embarrassed and said nothing for a moment, waiting for him to resume his conversation. 'No.' She shook her head. 'Never. Never that, not with him. Never.'

Isaura looked terrified, Eadmund thought, and that sobered him up quickly. The years had been hard on her, he realised. Her cheeks, which he remembered plump with dimples, were dull and pale. They matched her eyes, which looked empty. She had always been the happiest person he knew, but she didn't look as though she'd smiled much in years.

Isaura grabbed his arm to let him know that Ivaar and Eirik were walking towards them. 'Tell Thorgils that I've not forgotten him,' she whispered, trying to keep the tears out of her eyes.

'I will,' Eadmund promised, moving quickly to avoid having to sit next to either arrival. The only seat left was next to Jael. He coughed, stumbling down onto the bench, trying to avoid touching her. It felt odd. He desperately wanted to catch her eye, to know what she was thinking, but at the same time he was afraid of what he would find, so he kept his eyes down, focused on the plate full of food he had no appetite for.

Jael made a point of not looking at Eadmund. She could feel him there, his shoulder almost touching hers. She wanted to move, just enough to brush against him, to let him know in some small way that they were still friends.

She shook her head.

Is that what they were... friends?

She tried to ignore her confused feelings which were busy tangling themselves into a knot, keeping her face towards Eydis. But as she glanced up, she caught Ivaar staring at her. He smiled, his eyes locking with hers. She smiled back, deciding that it was the best path to take.

Surely it would be useful for all of them if she made friends with Ivaar?

Thorgils walked past at that very moment, catching the friendly exchange between Ivaar and Jael. He stormed past, quickly taking his seat, his face a thunderous storm.

He was going to have to have a very serious conversation with Jael tomorrow.

***

Jael stroked Vella's soft, thick fur. After the tension and noise of the hall, it was soothing to sit in the silence, with only the occasional crack from the fire as she ran her hands over that shaggy mane. Vella seemed to like it too as she lay there, flopped contentedly over Jael's knee.

'I hope Eadmund will be alright,' Biddy said with a frown. 'At least you managed to calm him down in time.'

'I suppose I did,' Jael muttered distractedly. 'But I'm not sure what he'll think about any of it. He was a complete mess, though, so he probably won't remember it tomorrow.'

'Well, that's a shame for him,' Biddy sighed. 'He seemed to have made a change, didn't he? For a while there.' She sipped her milk, enjoying the quiet of the evening as it settled around them.

'But as you said, perhaps some people are just born that way? Maybe Eadmund will never be able to escape it, like your father? Maybe it will kill him too? It certainly could have tonight, the way he came into the hall ready to murder Ivaar.'

'But if Eadmund keeps drinking, if he gets worse, then this Ivaar will certainly become the king, won't he? And Eydis sees bad things for that. So, we have to help Eadmund stop drinking.' Biddy put down her cup and stood up, disappearing into the kitchen.

'I'm not sure that's possible,' Jael sighed. 'There's always going to be ale, or mead, or wine about, wherever Eadmund goes. What chance has he got of controlling himself with all that temptation?'

'Well, there may be one way,' Biddy smiled triumphantly, returning to her stool. 'With this.' She held a little brown bottle out towards Jael. 'Edela gave me this tincture to help Eadmund, when you thought it was time.'

'Did she?' Jael leaned forward, taking the bottle. 'What does it do?'

'It's supposed to stop him drinking. To stop the urge for it,' Biddy said, somewhat doubtfully. 'Edela said that you must keep him restrained, keep him away from any drink while the tincture does its work. And watch him. Don't let him out of your sight.' She stared at Jael. 'It may take days, of course, for him to work through it, but Edela said that if he were to finish the bottle without anything else touching his lips, then he would have a chance to be free of it for good.'

Jael stared down at the tiny bottle. 'And you believe that? Do you think it could have helped your father if you'd have known?'

'My father was a bastard, so I wouldn't have wasted it on him in the first place,' Biddy spat, her face twisting harshly before the fire. 'My mother and I were better off without him.'

'So drinking too much is not always a bad thing, then?' Jael suggested, surprised by the venom in Biddy's eyes. 'I suppose it just depends on the person caught in its trap.'

Biddy shook herself away from that dark place. 'Yes, it does, and Eadmund is one who I think we must save. Don't you?'

Jael frowned at her, thinking it over, but she didn't say a word.

CHAPTER THIRTY ONE

'It's a bad idea, Jael!' Thorgils grumbled. 'You don't play with Ivaar. He plays with you!'

He was barracking her from his wooden stump as she circled Fyn, trying to ignore his disgruntled mumblings. 'Are you ever going to come at me, Fyn? I may as well fight the snow for all the use you are today!' Jael was irritable. She hadn't slept much. Her dreams had been terrifying and vivid: thoughts of Edela and Evaine, threats of darkness and dead bodies, storms and blood, Ivaar and Eadmund. She'd woken up frowning and weary, and had stayed there, trapped in that scratchy place.

Thorgils had barely spoken to her on their ride; his mood as fractured as her own.

Fyn felt stuck in the middle of two rapidly approaching storms. He didn't know what to say or do. Perhaps it was better to let the two of them fight it out? 'I'm going for a drink,' he decided, and throwing down his sword, he headed off to his hut.

Thorgils blinked after him in surprise.

Jael picked up Fyn's sword, handing it to Thorgils. 'Well, come on then, I'm going to freeze solid if I don't start moving soon,' she sighed, stretching her neck. 'We both need the practice.'

Thorgils stood up, still annoyed with her, but he took the weapon, happy not to be fighting with real swords today. The mood they were both in, it would likely end up a bloody mess, and it was better to save that for the contest. 'I wish you'd hear me, Jael. You're making a mistake playing games with Ivaar.' He raised his sword and took three quick steps towards her, slashing his blade down in a hail of fast, aggressive strokes.

Jael rushed her sword up to defend herself, then ducked and lunged quickly, hitting him in the ribs. It did little to improve Thorgils' mood. He flinched, taking a step back.

'If Eirik dies and leaves Ivaar as his heir, what will happen to all of us?' Jael wondered, too distracted to fight now. She lowered her sword. 'What will happen to Eadmund?'

Thorgils glared at her. 'You think you can protect him by becoming Ivaar's lover? How will that help anyone?'

Jael laughed loudly. 'Ivaar's lover?' She shook her head. 'I wasn't thinking of being *that* friendly!'

'You didn't notice the way he was looking at you?'

'Of course I did, but I'm not interested in playing the game that seriously,' Jael insisted. 'I just want to confuse him, distract him while we try and sort Eadmund out. If we can do that, then Eirik will have a reason to change his mind. He doesn't really want Ivaar, he's just angry, but that will pass, especially if Eadmund can stop drinking and start training again.'

Thorgils looked unconvinced. 'Maybe, but playing with Ivaar is only going to end badly, for all of us. Ivaar's a fucking arse, but he's no fool. He won't believe you, no matter how convincing you were last night.'

'Do you have another plan?' Jael muttered crossly. 'It makes sense. I'm going to distract him. We're going to fix Eadmund and make Eirik change his mind. That's our plan. If you have something better, then tell me, otherwise, *that's* our plan!'

Thorgils mulled it over, his bushy eyebrows working hard as he stared at her. He didn't like the sound of it, but he didn't have anything else to offer. Besides, if Jael was so determined to keep Ivaar busy, it might give him a chance to speak to Isaura alone. Eadmund had passed on her message, and his hopes had lifted considerably. He raised his sword, tapping it against hers. 'Alright, it's our plan. For now. It's a bad plan, and I want you to remember I said that when it all comes shitting down on our heads. But be careful. Remember what happened to Eadmund's last wife!'

Jael rolled her eyes and casually turned back towards the shelter where Tig and Leada were huddled together. 'I am *nothing* like Eadmund's last wife,' she promised darkly as she stilled, taking a long, deep breath. 'But I'll remember the warning.' And she swung around quickly, raising her leg as high as she could, snapping her boot into Thorgils' jaw.

'Aarrghh!'

Fyn came rushing out of his hut in time to see Thorgils staggering out of the snow, gripping his face, eyes bulging in shock. He couldn't help but laugh. 'She got you, then? That'll be a nice bruise tomorrow.' And smiling, he picked up a sword and headed towards Jael, reminding himself to watch out for that leg of hers.

***

Morana was a slow walker, much to Evaine's irritation. She wanted to stop and explain the use of every plant she picked, but Evaine had stopped listening some time ago. She yawned, rubbing her tired eyes. She'd not slept for more than a few hours since she'd arrived, traumatised by the thought of never seeing Eadmund again.

Surely that couldn't happen?

Not when she was carrying his son.

Morana poked Evaine with her nobbly staff. 'You're not listening, child!' she grumbled, and not for the first time. 'There doesn't appear to be much between those pretty ears of yours. Certainly no patience at least!'

Evaine eyed Morana. They had walked in circles for hours,

it seemed, and for what? A few plants and an aching back, to go with a swirling stomach, and a throbbing head. She was truly miserable, and her bottom lip remained firmly turned towards the snow they waded through.

'Do you not care to know the magic of these plants? How they can help you achieve all that you desire?'

Evaine lifted her head, her eyes suddenly full of interest. 'What do you mean, all that I desire?'

'Is it so long since you last visited me that you've forgotten what I can do?' Morana crept towards Evaine, her torn and dirty black cloak slithering across the snow behind her. 'What I have helped you do in the past?'

They were standing in a small cluster of trees, hidden from any sun that might have escaped the thick, morning clouds. It was bone-achingly cold in the shadows. The tall, gnarled ash trees looked as though they were closing around Morana as she stepped forward, pointing her staff at Evaine.

'No, no, of course not,' Evaine muttered quietly. 'It's just that I don't see what I can do from here. What use is your magic when there's no one to use it on? How can I achieve anything when I'm so far away from Eadmund?'

Morana smiled. 'There is always something we can do. Besides, that child won't stay in you forever, and you won't stay here forever either. Just long enough for us to make our plans. We have much to talk about, you and I.'

***

Edela was thrilled that there was nowhere to ride to this morning. Her body felt weak, as though it was held together by a few loose stitches. She was convinced that if she moved too quickly, she would crumble apart, so she sat by the fire, nibbling warm bread and hard cheese, chatting to Kormac and Branwyn.

'It's so different here these days,' Kormac said thoughtfully, shaking his mop of curly brown hair at the wedge of cheese Branwyn was offering. 'You can see that, of course. Raiders were coming so frequently. We were easy prey, but now the army is everywhere. The elders keep building the walls higher, making the army bigger and stronger, which, I suppose is good for us blacksmiths,' he admitted with a wry smile. 'But the elders have shut themselves further and further away from the people. They barely come out of the temple, except to announce decisions by the council, and they no longer let anyone in, besides the dreamers, of course.'

'Really?' Edela coughed in surprise. 'Why is that?'

'We're not sure,' Branwyn admitted, handing her mother a cup of skullcap tea. 'They won't say. Since Marcus Volsen became the elderman, it has all changed. The elders have become almost invisible.'

That was not good news for Edela's plans. She would have to tell Aleksander when he returned from checking on the horses.

Branwyn could see the worry in Edela's eyes. 'What is it, Mother?'

'Oh, nothing, I suppose,' Edela smiled lightly, uncertain how much she wanted to reveal. 'I was just hoping to speak to someone... I have some questions about... Tuuran history. I had thought I would simply go to the temple and find an elder, but it seems it will not be that simple now.'

'What sort of questions, Edela?' Kormac wondered as he tended to the fire. 'Perhaps we can help? The elders aren't the only ones who know Tuura's secrets. We have our own ways of finding things out.'

Edela frowned. It had been many nights since her last dream, but every detail of it was carved into her memory with a sharp blade. She wasn't sure who she could trust besides Aleksander, but she rested her eyes on Kormac and let her body relax, clearing her mind. He'd always seemed a very decent man, and he had made Branwyn happy, she saw. Kormac turned his kind brown eyes towards her with such genuine concern, then, that Edela felt a certain push towards him. She leaned forward, aware of the creaking pains in her back, and told them both, in hushed tones, about the girl with the scorched face, the nightmares, the book, and the danger she had seen for Jael.

Kormac and Branwyn listened with wide eyes and furrowed brows. Neither said a word until she was done. Edela sipped her tea, resting her feet close to the fire. She glanced at their faces, hoping they would be open to helping her, but doubting there was much they would know. Kormac was a blacksmith and Branwyn had not inherited her mother's gifts, and neither of them were particularly close to any dreamer or elder that she knew of.

'That is very troubling, Mother, but I'm not sure what you'll be able to find out here,' Branwyn frowned. 'There are people who know more than most about Tuura's history, but those people are in the temple, hidden away with all the secrets they keep. I can't imagine they'll be eager to reveal anything to you.' She shook her head, glancing at Kormac.

'Branwyn's right, they guard their secrets well,' Kormac said. 'But, of course, you know that. It has not changed these many hundreds of years. The dreamers tell the elders what they see of the future. The elders have their scribes write everything down, and they keep it all safely hidden away. All those prophecies... hidden from the ones they concern the most. They never share them with us, do they? Not in all these years. We've watched as they turned this village into a town, and now a fortress, and we wait, knowing that something is coming. Something must be coming, but they won't tell us.' He lowered his voice, staring into the flames. 'But there are others here who have secrets. Others who have knowledge that has been passed down through the centuries. Not all Tuuran secrets are housed in the temple.'

That surprised Branwyn, who eyed her husband curiously. 'What do you mean?' she whispered, suddenly conscious of how loud their voices sounded echoing around the large house. Her eyes darted to the door.

'Well,' Kormac whispered hesitantly. 'I know about the sword.'

***

'You're back, then?'

Morac could barely bring himself to raise his head as he walked towards Eirik's chair. 'I am, yes.'

'That didn't take long.' Eirik was out of sorts and not at all pleased to see his friend again. His presence was a bitter reminder of all that had happened. Of the betrayal he felt by the people closest to him.

'I only stayed as long as I needed to.'

'Well, who could blame you? Morana is hardly the best company,' Eirik muttered crossly as he leaned back, resting his head against his wooden throne. He was feeling weary today, disturbed and unsettled by the events of the past few days, and in no mood to be generous with his words.

Morac eyed him just as crossly. 'She's still my sister, Eirik, no matter how ill your feelings towards her may be.'

Eirik sat up, feeling the full weight of that rebuke. He bit his tongue, not wanting to say something more to regret; there had been far too much of that lately. 'You're right. Let's not talk about her, or that girl. I'm in no mood to grumble at each other like old women.'

'That may be so,' Morac said, trying hard to control his rising anger. 'But you have insulted my sister, and now you dismiss Evaine as though she is nothing.' He ran a hand through his lank grey hair, trying to calm himself down. 'She may be just *that girl* to you, but she is my daughter, and you have sent her away from me!' He was shaking now, vibrating angrily with decades of resentment and fury towards this man who he'd always thought of as his closest friend.

Eirik rose out of his chair, eyes bulging with irritation as he stepped down towards Morac. '*I* took her away?' Eirik smiled coldly. '*Me*?' He laughed, and it sounded hollow in the almost empty hall. He leaned forward, his breath white in front of Morac's face. 'I warned you. How many times did I warn you?' he growled, shaking his head. 'I should never have let that girl come here in the first place, but I did, for you. She was only here because of you, but now look at what that weak decision all those years ago has cost me!'

'And you blame Evaine for that? She's just a girl! It's Eadmund who used her. He did this to her!'

Eirik laughed. 'Just a girl? Ha! I didn't take you for such a fool, my friend. You really think this had anything to do with Eadmund?'

Morac was momentarily thrown. 'What are you saying?'

'I'm saying that your little bitch of a daughter has had her claws in my son and one eye on my throne since she could walk. You're blind if you can't see that! The way she followed him around? Everyone could see it. Everyone but you!' Eirik was becoming furious; he could feel his tongue loosening and his chest throbbing. Morac was blinded by his loyalty to that girl, and there was nothing he could do to make him see the truth.

'You should choose your words more carefully, Eirik,' Morac warned, his eyes narrowing, his voice threateningly quiet. 'That bitch, as you call her, will be mother to our grandson. You would do well to remember that.'

'Ha! *Our* grandson? You seem a long way from the truth of anything today.' Eirik shook his head, returning to his throne. 'That child is nothing to me. It will be born a bastard, and you may do with it as you wish, but you'll not bring it here, and you will never mention it to me again. Or her. Never again. Do you understand?'

Morac shuddered. In all their years of friendship – over fifty years of it now – they had never fought like this. His heart was pounding loudly inside his chest, his hands shaking by his sides. He knew that something had just broken between them. There would be consequences to pay for it, of that Morac was sure. 'I understand. Perfectly.' He spoke with barely any volume, and, nodding his head, he turned and strode out of the hall.

***

A fresh afternoon breeze had managed to blow away most of Thorgils' cobwebs; that, and a stop at Eskild's Cave on their way back to the fort. Jael had suggested that a soak in the hot pool would make him feel better, and she'd been right, annoyingly. Thorgils glanced at her bright red face as they dismounted. She was still determined to go ahead with her ridiculous plan, and he was still convinced that it would end badly.

'Seems you're very popular after your little speech last night,' Thorgils noted as they passed a group of warriors smiling amiably in her direction.

'Ha!' Jael scoffed. 'I can't imagine that's why they're looking at me. They're probably just staring at my tits.'

'You have tits?' Thorgils raised an eyebrow in surprise. 'I didn't notice that about you. Where are you hiding them, then?'

His humour had returned, despite his swollen jaw, bruised ego, and turmoil over Isaura, and Jael was happy for it. 'Nowhere you'll ever find them!' she laughed, glancing up at the sky as the first gentle flurries of the day started to drift down. 'Looks as though we made it home just in time.' She caught sight of Tarak then, and her face froze. He was walking towards them with Ivaar, the two of them sharing a joke, indulging in much back-slapping.

Jael scowled.

'Ahhh, our two favourite people,' Thorgils mumbled. 'Let's

turn here so we can avoid them.'

But he was too late for Ivaar's keen eyes. Spotting Jael, he smiled, striding towards them, Tarak trailing in his wake like a giant dog. 'A beautiful beast you have here, Jael,' he smiled, stroking Tig's muzzle. 'Eirik told me how much you like to ride, you and Thorgils here.' He acknowledged Thorgils with a brief nod, noticing his swollen jaw. 'What happened to your face?'

'Oh... I, ahhh...' Thorgils looked awkwardly at Jael, his mouth empty of words, his cheeks starting to burn.

'He fell off his horse,' Jael said quickly. 'We came across a lot of icy patches today, didn't we? It must have rained last night.'

'Mmmm,' Thorgils nodded, happy to let her do the talking.

'Well, perhaps we need to ask Vidar to send us more rain? That will make the contest more interesting,' Tarak growled. 'There's more than one person I'd like to watch sliding about on their arse.' He glared at both of them, one corner of his mouth curling down in disdain.

Jael felt something snap inside her. 'I heard you had a thing for arses, Tarak,' she said sharply, digging her toes into her boots, trying to control her boiling anger. She felt Thorgils stiffen beside her, but her eyes were fixed on Tarak.

The look of horror on his hideous face was a start.

He recovered well, though. 'What man doesn't?' he laughed boorishly. 'And, just like your husband, I prefer mine small and blonde.' His smile appeared confident as he shared it with Ivaar, but his eyes were anxious.

'Oh? Really? That's not what I heard,' Jael said, cocking her head to one side. 'I'd heard it was tall, red-haired. Young, with freckles...'

Tarak stumbled then.

It was only a small movement, but it was obvious to everyone that Jael had her finger on something that Tarak didn't want her to have her finger on. His mouth gaped open, his discomfort palpable.

Jael took a quick breath, deciding to leave it there. And with one last pointed look at Tarak, she dismissed him entirely, turning to Ivaar. 'Will you be fighting in the contest, then?'

Ivaar blinked. 'No, no, I haven't trained properly in a long time,' he laughed dismissively. 'I'd be slaughtered in the first round, for sure. Besides, this way, I can sit back and watch you fight. I'm looking forward to that.'

Jael was barely listening. She was trying hard to cool her fury, but with that bastard staring at her, breathing on her, it was nearly impossible. She felt her right hand clenching instinctively, eager to reach for her sword. Jael heard her father barking at her then, remembering the look on his face whenever she'd given in to her temper, and she relaxed her hand, regaining a small measure of control at last.

Thorgils grabbed her arm, deciding that it was the only way he was going to get her out of the hole she had determinedly dug her toes into. 'We should get the horses back to the stables, don't you think? Rub them down?'

Jael shook her head, waking herself up. 'Yes, you're right, we should. No doubt we'll see you in the hall tonight, Ivaar?' She smiled at him, softening her face deliberately, reminding herself of the plan.

'I hope so,' he smiled back, stepping aside to let them pass. 'I look forward to it.'

Behind him, Tarak stared after Thorgils and Jael. His body remained still, but inside he was shaking.

What did she know?

And if she did know anything, what was she going to do about it?

CHAPTER THIRTY TWO

The four of them sat huddled around the fire.

Edela had insisted they wait for Aleksander before Kormac revealed what he knew about the sword. Thankfully, he'd been on his way back to the house, and they were able to begin without much delay.

'Did you lock the door?' Branwyn wondered nervously, glancing back into the darkness. It was a dull day, and despite a healthy fire, there was barely enough light to see by.

'I did,' Kormac said calmly. He felt relaxed enough, but still, he didn't want to be overheard.

Aleksander edged forward, eager to find out what this was all about. He had no idea what he'd been dragged into, but by the looks on everyone's faces, it appeared to be serious.

'So, you said you knew about the sword?' Edela prompted, feeling a sense of excitement surge through her body. She had wondered about the meaning of that mysterious weapon for much of her life.

'I do,' Kormac said hoarsely. He took a long breath and blew out a puff of cold, white smoke. 'You see, the elders are not the only ones who keep secrets in Tuura. The guilds do as well, at least the Blacksmith's Guild does.' He stroked his bushy brown beard, smiling. 'I don't suppose many of our secrets are of great importance, though, to everyday folk. Most of them are just about tasks we are set by the elders. They always need someone to do something for them, to make something, go somewhere, even deliver a message. They don't do much for themselves.'

'That's very true,' Branwyn muttered, looking at Aleksander. 'They sit in that temple, with all those prophecies. No one sees them, and no one knows what they mean for any of our futures. What the point of it all is, I don't know.'

Kormac looked patiently at his wife, waiting for her to finish. She nodded bashfully towards him, realising that her tongue had run away with itself.

He continued, lowering his voice even further. 'But some of the secrets are a little more interesting.' That had their attention, he saw, as Aleksander's eyes widened expectantly, and Edela leaned further forward, not wanting to miss a word. 'Some three or four hundred years ago, I forget which, the elders asked the Master Blacksmith, Wulfsig, to make them a sword. He was not told what the sword was for, or who it was for, just that they needed it made urgently. They insisted that its very presence was to be shrouded in the utmost secrecy. That no one could ever know about. So Wulfsig forged the sword to their precise instructions, gave it to the elders, and never saw it again. Obviously, he told another member of the guild, for the story has passed down from blacksmith to blacksmith throughout the years.'

Edela's forehead creased. That made no sense to her, and she wondered if Kormac was telling the story of a different sword.

'But then,' Kormac continued, noting Edela's puzzlement. 'Some fifty years ago or more, the elders brought the sword to your grandfather, Edela. They gave it to him and told him to give you the sword, to put his mark on it, as though he had been the one who'd forged it. That it was for your granddaughter, to be kept safe until it was ready for her.'

'What?' Aleksander's mouth hung open. He stared at Kormac, then Edela, who looked just as surprised as him. 'You had this sword? For Jael?'

'Well, yes,' Edela admitted. 'I knew it was important. My grandfather insisted I keep it a secret, so I hid it from everyone.

Not even my husband knew about it. No one saw the sword until I gave it to Jael on her wedding day.'

'But how did they know?' Branwyn asked, then chided herself. 'Well, of course, the dreamers told them. But what does it mean? What is Jael supposed to use the sword for? And why her?'

Kormac shook his head. 'I don't know.'

'What was it made of? What makes it so special?' Aleksander wondered.

'That remains a secret, taken to the pyre, I'm afraid,' Kormac said. 'Wulfsig only revealed the fact that he'd been asked to make the sword, not what it was made of. Not long after he gave the sword to the elders, he died.'

Three faces froze.

'How?' Branwyn whispered.

'I have no idea, my love, but it is suspicious, of course.'

'And now Jael has it,' Aleksander frowned, running a hand through his dark beard. 'Does anyone else know about it, do you think?'

Kormac thought on that. 'Outside of the guild? Probably. I often wonder if that's why we were attacked that night all those years ago. Did those men come looking for the sword?'

Aleksander looked from Kormac to Edela. '*Were* they looking for something?'

'I don't know,' Edela admitted, climbing back into her memory of that night. 'It didn't feel as though they were looking for something in particular. Did it?' she asked Kormac.

'I'm not sure,' he said, shaking his head. 'They were raiders, as far as I'm aware. They're naturally going to be looking for something to take. They wanted the treasures of the temple, they wanted the elders, but they left with nothing, that I know of at least.'

'Perhaps we're trying to squeeze too many pieces into this puzzle?' Branwyn suggested, her face troubled by the unwanted reminder of that terrible night. 'Perhaps the sword is nothing to do with any of these things?'

'Well, it certainly has something to do with Jael,' Aleksander said anxiously. 'If anyone knows Jael has it, they'll go after her, won't they? It must be a weapon worth having.'

Edela looked just as worried. 'But it's Jael. We can be grateful for that,' she said, trying to reassure them both. 'If anyone can look after herself, it's that granddaughter of mine.'

***

'What was that about?' Thorgils wondered, eyeing her suspiciously.

'What?' Jael looked up innocently. She was crouched on the ground, drying Tig's legs. Thorgils stood next to her, rubbing a towel across Leada's back. Both horses were cold and damp from the ride.

'That, with Tarak. Whatever that was.' Thorgils nodded towards the stable door, closed against the blustery snow. 'It was something, and don't say it wasn't.'

Jael straightened up. 'I'm just trying to prepare Tarak for the contest. We need his nerves jangling,' she said lightly. 'It doesn't hurt to mess up his head a little, does it?'

'What does that mean?' Thorgils grumped, hanging his damp towel on a peg and fishing a carrot out of his pocket. 'What do you know that would make that pig's arse nervous?'

Jael thought on it. More than anything, she wanted to tell Thorgils what Fyn had revealed, but at the same time, she knew that it was Fyn's secret to share. Besides, it would unhinge Thorgils when he was already unsettled by Isaura's return, and he'd need to have his head together if he were to defeat Tarak. 'Perhaps one day I'll reveal my secrets,' she smiled. 'But until then, you'll have to keep guessing and trust me.'

Thorgils just looked cross, mumbling irritably as he opened

the door. 'Well, if you're going to be like that, I'll go in search of friendlier company for the afternoon. Perhaps Eadmund might have woken up by now?'

Their eyes met, and they exchanged worried looks.

'He's getting worse,' Jael said quietly as she hung up her towel.

'He is, yes,' Thorgils admitted. 'But it's his own fault of course. If he'd stayed away from that scheming girl, none of this would have happened.'

'True, he's an idiot, but,' Jael looked around, lowering her voice, 'if we're going to change Eirik's mind, we're going to have to stop Eadmund drinking. Quickly.'

Thorgils sighed, coming back into the stables and shutting the door. 'Well, how in the name of Vidar do we do that then? I doubt we'll even be able to find him today. He was such a mess last night. He's probably wandered off a cliff. Ivaar coming back has wrecked him.'

'Well, we have to try,' Jael insisted. 'I have something that may help him. Something my grandmother gave Biddy.'

Thorgils looked interested. 'What sort of something?'

'A tincture to help him stop drinking.'

'So your grandmother saw the trouble you were going to be in with your husband, did she?' he smiled. 'Did she see a good ending? Or do we lurch from this shit to more shit, and then all die in our own shit?'

'Ha! I don't know,' Jael admitted. 'Perhaps we don't even survive the contest? Tarak looks ready to kill me.'

'True, but I'm sure he's not the only one,' Thorgils grinned, his mood lightening. 'Alright, I'll go and find Eadmund, and we'll see what we can do with this potion of yours.' He bent his mouth close to her ear, just in case Tiras was on the prowl again. 'I'm willing to do anything if it means getting rid of Ivaar.'

Jael looked at him and nodded. 'Then find Eadmund and let's get started.'

***

Aleksander had been desperate to escape Branwyn and Kormac's house. Aron and Aedan had arrived with Aedan's pregnant wife, Kayla, to feast with their guests, and the noise and revelry had quickly worn on him. Edela, sensing his discomfort, had suggested they take a walk to check on the horses and he'd leaped at the chance.

As they headed out into the frozen darkness, Aleksander tucked her arm through the crook of his, worried by the ice he saw sparkling under the moon.

'I did just spend four days upon a horse, you know,' Edela snorted as he refused to release her arm. 'I'm not so feeble that you must hold me up like a doll!'

'Alright then, I'll let you go, and you can skate across the street!'

Edela caught sight of the ice herself then, and she gripped hold of Aleksander. 'Well, since you insist, you may as well help me until we reach the stables. If it will make you feel better?'

Aleksander laughed, helping her along the darkened streets, his eyes firmly turned towards the ground, avoiding both the icy patches and any reminders of that night he didn't wish to find.

There was no one about when they entered the large stable block. Helpfully, a torch was burning by the doors. Aleksander removed it from its sconce and guided Edela through the ramshackle building, looking for their three horses. They had been stabled together, and all three jostled about, nickering softly, pleased they hadn't been forgotten.

'You must name your horse, you know,' Edela said gently, patting each animal in turn. 'She deserves that, I think.'

Aleksander sighed, placing the torch in a nearby holder. He stroked his horse's cold muzzle, and she butted his head, seeking his affection. 'I suppose I must.' He tried not to look into her big brown eyes.

It was always the eyes that got him.

'She's yours now. Maybe yours for many years,' Edela smiled. 'She needs a name.'

Aleksander brushed his horse's red mane out of her eyes. 'She does, of course, but naming an animal means they're something to you,' he said sadly. 'I'm not sure I can stand the pain of any more loss. If anything were to happen to her...'

'I know, but if you risk nothing, you'll have nothing,' Edela said gently as she walked towards Deya who eagerly sucked up the tiny apple she offered. 'If you only focus on the pain at the end, you'll have an empty life, filled with fear and loneliness. Death will claim us all, eventually, you can't stop that. But you can choose how you live before it does. Give her a name. She's yours.'

Aleksander couldn't quite raise a smile, but he nodded, glancing around the stables. He knew they were alone but still, he bent towards Edela, his voice a whisper. 'I've been thinking about the sword.'

'Mmmm, I'm not surprised. So have I.'

'The elders wouldn't have had that sword made without a reason. Without a prophecy from one of the dreamers. And if they record all the prophecies, they'd surely have recorded this one. A sword like that? There must be a reason for it being made in such a secretive way. Saved for someone who wasn't going to be born for hundreds of years? There has to be a way to find out why.'

'I agree. There will be a prophecy in the temple, and we need to see it. But we have no chance of getting in there. None that I can see, at least.'

'Really? None? There's no one you know of who could help you?' Aleksander paused as a thought popped into his head, his eyes widening. 'But Edela, *you're* a dreamer! Dreamers are allowed into the temple, aren't they? So why wouldn't you be let in?'

Edela frowned, ready to argue before realising that he was right. 'I will go tomorrow then, or at least try to,' she muttered quietly, suddenly nervous. 'I'll have to go alone, of course. Hopefully, they'll let me in.'

'I'm sure they will,' Aleksander said reassuringly. 'But I don't imagine they'll show you the prophecy, and I don't think you should ask about it either. Not yet. That part might take a little more figuring.'

Edela nodded distractedly, remembering her dream of the beheaded girls. Something had happened in Tuura long ago, and she was certain the elders did not want anyone finding out about it.

***

Thorgils hadn't been able to find Eadmund.

There had been no sign of him anywhere. No one knew where he was, and the worry of that ate away at him as he stood drinking with Torstan, Klaufi, and Erland in the hall that evening. He'd convinced them all to help in the search, but each one had returned with empty hands. Thorgils watched Jael chatting with Ivaar out of the corner of his eye and frowned. It was all well and good trying to keep Ivaar busy, but if something had happened to Eadmund, what point was there to any of it?

His eyes drifted across to the high table where Isaura sat. He was desperate beyond words to speak to her, or even look at her without fear of being caught. To touch that soft skin of hers; run his fingers over the dimples which he hadn't even seen a hint of yet. She looked so melancholy, so unlike the woman he remembered... when she had been his. He kept having to remind himself that he no longer had the right to walk up to her and tilt her head, kiss her lips, coax her smile back when she was feeling sad.

'Thorgils,' Torstan whispered hoarsely, elbowing him in the

ribs. 'You need to stop looking at her.'

Thorgils shook himself awake, realising that his friend was right. He quickly turned away, sighing. 'I think I'll go and have another look for Eadmund. Better than standing about here all night, gaping at Isaura like a speared fish.' He nodded to his friends and eased his way through the crowded hall towards the doors.

Jael watched Thorgils leave, noticing the slumped curve of his shoulders.

Ivaar followed her gaze. 'You and Thorgils are good friends?'

Jael looked away, blinking any feeling out of her eyes. 'We've been training together for the contest, but no, he's Eadmund's friend, not mine.'

Ivaar nodded, pleased to hear it. 'He's a good warrior. Not as good as Eadmund was but not bad.'

'Was Eadmund better than you?' Jael wondered, trying to turn the conversation around to him and far away from Thorgils.

'Me? I suppose so,' Ivaar said casually. 'Although now? By the look of Eadmund last night, I'd say even Eydis could beat him!' He watched her expression as he laughed, testing her.

Jael laughed along with him. 'Having seen Eadmund train, I agree with you. And easily too. Most of the time he defeats himself, just by tripping over his feet!' It felt oddly disloyal to talk about Eadmund that way, but it was just what Ivaar wanted to hear. His smile grew wider, almost reaching his eyes, so she kept going. 'So don't mark him down as the head of your army when you take the throne!'

Ivaar stilled. 'Is that what you think will happen? That I'll be king here?'

'Isn't that why Eirik called you back?'

'I suppose it is,' Ivaar said, his eyes darting about uncertainly. 'It's just so long since it was taken from me now. It feels strange to talk about it after all this time. And, of course, looking at my father, he could rule for another decade at least, don't you think?'

Jael glanced at Eirik, who was trying to talk to Eydis. 'Well, no one knows what plans the gods are making, do they? It would be no fun for them if everything went as we expected.'

Eirik frowned, watching Jael and Ivaar smiling at one another. 'Jael appears to be making more of an effort with Ivaar than that husband of hers,' he muttered to his daughter.

'You can't expect Eadmund to want to talk to Ivaar,' Eydis whispered crossly. 'Not after what he did to Melaena.'

Eirik dragged a piece of bread around his plate, mopping up the leftover juices of his meal. 'No, I don't suppose I can.' He stopped and sighed, feeling his eyebrows release the giant crease they had been working into the middle of his forehead. He had been irate, on edge, and ornery for days now and nothing seemed to be shifting his foul mood. Eirik knew that he had to do something, though, before he ended up completely isolating everyone he cared about.

'You must give Eadmund some time, Father,' Eydis warned. 'This will have set him back again.'

'Mmmm, well let's hope he doesn't take seven years to recover this time as I certainly won't live to see it!' He peered at his daughter, wishing she could see him. Wishing she could see the fear that lived behind his rheumy eyes; the threat of his impending death, which haunted him daily.

But then, he remembered, she was only thirteen-years-old.

Why should he terrorise her with his nightmares?

As much as she worried about her father, Eydis was still cross, and she didn't feel like talking to him at all. She was anxious to know what had happened to Eadmund, what Jael was doing befriending Ivaar, and whether Thorgils had spoken to Isaura. She felt frustrated as she sat on the outside, waiting for someone to tell her what was going on. There was too much noise: spitting fires, the low hum of constant chatter, servants clearing plates, warriors jeering, sometimes singing. Eydis had struggled to pick up anything that would tell her exactly what was going on. And if she didn't know what was going on, how could she help anyone?

'I think I'll go to my bed now, Father,' Eydis decided, standing up. 'Goodnight.'

'Already?' Eirik frowned. 'Are you unwell?'

'No. I'd just rather be by myself now,' she said firmly. 'It's too noisy in here for me. Goodnight.'

Eirik watched his daughter leave, resisting the urge to get up and help her, knowing that it would only irritate her further.

'Sleep well,' Isaura murmured, looking up as Eydis felt her way to the wall.

'Goodnight, Eydis,' Jael called as she took her seat next to Isaura, thankful to have escaped Ivaar at last. She smiled briefly at the small, golden-haired woman who quickly returned her gaze to the plate she'd been picking at. Jael wasn't usually concerned with being friendly, but she felt compelled to attempt conversation. Isaura might be Ivaar's wife, but she was Thorgils' woman. And Thorgils was her friend. 'I hear you were all very close growing up, you, Thorgils, and Eadmund,' Jael said lightly, sipping her ale.

'We were,' Isaura sighed. 'It was a long time ago now, though. We're all much changed.'

'Even Thorgils?'

'Well, no,' Isaura smiled. 'He looks much as I left him.'

'On the outside, perhaps,' Jael suggested carefully. 'He has a thick hide, that one.'

'I'm glad of it,' Isaura whispered. 'It hasn't been easy, all these years away.'

'But now you're back.'

'And that's even worse,' Isaura grimaced, forcing a smile on her face as Ivaar glanced her way. 'Worse because now we can't even look at one another, and yet we are finally close again.' She shook her head, annoyed with herself. 'I shouldn't speak so. There's no point to any of it.'

'Perhaps you should talk to Eydis? She might have a dream for you.'

Isaura looked puzzled. 'Eydis is having dreams? She's a dreamer now?'

'You didn't know?' Jael was surprised. She leaned in, lowering her voice. 'She saw you and Ivaar coming. Saw Evaine getting pregnant. What else she's seen I'm not sure, but I don't think much of it is good.'

'No, I'm not surprised to hear that. I don't think any good is going to come from our return at all.'

Jael didn't know what to say. Isaura obviously didn't like her husband, and from the few looks she'd seen Ivaar give his wife, the feeling appeared to be mutual. So, if she was hoping to construct a friendship with Ivaar, Jael realised that she could hardly start one with Isaura, which suited her just fine. She'd never had a female friend apart from Biddy, who was simply Biddy, and neither man, nor woman in Jael's eyes, or Eydis, who was a child and didn't count. 'I'm sorry to hear that,' Jael said shortly, turning towards the doors, wondering if Eadmund was going to burst through them tonight. It felt odd without him sitting next to her.

She hoped Thorgils would be able to find him.

***

'You won't find what you're looking for here, Edela.'

It was just a voice. In the darkness. She couldn't see anyone, but the voice rumbled around inside the black, foul-smelling mist that hung everywhere. It rolled and echoed, and she felt the warning in it.

Edela could hear her breath, ragged in her ears as she stood, listening in the nothingness.

'Go back to Andala. Keep out of those things which do not concern you, Edela. This is not something you want a part of. This will end in death, and there is nothing you can do about that, I promise,' the voice cackled. 'Everyone you love will die, and there is nothing you can do to stop it!'

And then laughter.

Wild, hysterical, female laughter.

Edela could feel a shiver race over her skin as the darkness came to claim her.

CHAPTER THIRTY THREE

Osbert was bored, wishing that winter would hurry up and be done. He was ready for something to happen. The invasion of Hest, planned by two, old, addle-brained kings was sure to end in disaster, but he couldn't wait for it to begin. He was desperate for any form of excitement, even if it ended in a bloody death for them all. Anything would be better than this endless, white, bone-chilling boredom that he'd plodded through since Jael's departure.

How strange, he thought to himself, as he turned towards the hall, that he should miss his cousin. Well, not if he were honest, he supposed. She was an exciting woman, despite her obvious flaws. When he was around her, he felt alive. He missed her scowls and insults; missed the opportunity to tease and torment her. And now there wasn't even the heartbroken Aleksander to entertain himself with. He truly was bored. And no matter how many women writhed beneath him every night, his days had become a shadowy existence of predictable nothingness.

Osbert shook his head, kicking out at the snow in front of him. Cross. Bothered. Aimless. Then he heard a voice and looked up, a smile curling one corner of his thin lips.

Amma.

By the droop of her head and the slowness of her walk, he could tell that she was unhappy; still stewing over her public humiliation, no doubt.

He smiled. 'Amma!' he called, watching as she froze.

His sister didn't look around, but her two companions did. They glanced anxiously behind themselves, and, seeing Osbert, they squeezed Amma's arm and hurried away, leaving her to his mercy.

***

Jael had wandered far away from Oss in the night and she'd woken up lost and unsettled. Her dreams had been filled with childhood memories: memories of her father, of training with Aleksander.

Vella crept over to Jael, curling up against her chest. She sighed, reaching out to stroke her, wondering if Aleksander was waiting for her?

Did she still want him to?

She saw Eadmund's sad face and felt confused, and then annoyed with herself for daring to feel confused.

How could she think of Eadmund, when she loved Aleksander?

Jael pulled the furs around her neck, sinking further down into them, wanting to feel warm again, to fall back into her dreams. She smiled sadly, remembering how Ranuf would bark instructions at them as they trained, his face always a dark mix of disappointment and fury. She spent most days crying in the beginning, wanting to be so much better than she was; desperate to please her father and earn his elusive approval. Ranuf would roll his eyes and huff and puff his way over to Gant, who would soothe his nerves and send him back over, calmer and ready to give both children a second chance.

It felt like a lifetime ago.

And now her father was dead, and Aleksander was gone,

and Jael felt very alone.

***

'Where have you been?' Thorgils sighed in exasperation. 'I've spent a whole day and night looking for you. And not for the first time!'

Eadmund hung his head. He didn't know what to say.

And not for the first time.

'We thought something had happened to you! Are you alright?'

'We?' Eadmund lifted his head.

'Everyone! Torstan, Erland, Klaufi... we've all been looking for you.'

'Oh.' Eadmund hung his head again, staring at the floor. He didn't know what to say. He'd wanted to be alone, desperately so, but it was embarrassing to think that his friends had wasted their time searching for him.

They were standing just inside the doorway of Eadmund's cold cottage.

There was no hint of a fire.

'You haven't been here all night, have you?' Thorgils grumbled, peering past his friend into the darkness. 'I came here at least three times, but there was no sign of you.'

'No, I was down on the beach, in the drying sheds, for some of the night at least. I wandered around a lot. I wasn't trying to be found, I suppose,' Eadmund mumbled as he ushered Thorgils inside, albeit reluctantly. He was in no state to make sense of his thoughts and turn them into words, and he certainly wasn't looking for company.

'We have to talk, you and I,' Thorgils said firmly. 'You can't allow Ivaar to send you back down into that dark place. You were just climbing out of it. You can't let him have that power over you again!'

'It's not as easy as that,' Eadmund sighed, sinking onto the bed.

'I know, believe me, if anyone knows, it's me,' Thorgils said sympathetically, dragging a stool in front of Eadmund, and plonking himself down.

'What was Jael doing with him like that?' Eadmund frowned, his mind wandering. 'That's what I don't understand. The way she was smiling at him... I don't understand.'

Eadmund looked so genuinely hurt that Thorgils didn't know what to say. He thought about revealing Jael's foolish plan. It would have eased Eadmund's mind, yet there was a part of him that almost believed Jael was doing the right thing. And he knew that Eadmund was not to be trusted. Not until he was sober and able to keep his mouth shut around Ivaar.

He couldn't know about their plan. Not yet.

'I wouldn't worry about it. Women can be fickle, even Jael, it seems,' Thorgils said dismissively as he got up and started examining the contents of the cottage. 'I have to go before Jael leaves without me, but you've enough to get a fire started in here, so get one going before your balls drop off!' He headed for the door, then turned around, worried. 'And stay here, please, just stay here today, and we'll talk more when I get back. I know something that will help you, I promise. There may be a way that all of this will start to get better.' Thorgils opened the door with a frown. 'Just stay here, Eadmund. Don't go wandering off again!'

***

'Do you feel like some company?' Ivaar wondered, leaning over Jael.

She was crouching down, inspecting Tig's hooves, checking for any rot. Thankfully there was none, but there was the sudden problem of Ivaar. She stood up, trying not to show her annoyance. 'Company?'

'On your ride? Unless you'd rather be alone?' He looked at her keenly, trying to read her expression. It was early morning; he thought she looked tired.

Jael tried to smooth away her frustration. 'No, I'll take some company,' she smiled tightly, wondering what she was doing. Thorgils was not going to be pleased with her. 'You can saddle up my other horse, Leada. She's in the stables. I'll be back in a moment.'

Jael headed into the house.

'Biddy,' she hissed urgently, closing the door, pushing Ido and Vella away as they jumped up, begging to go with her. 'Biddy!'

Biddy emerged from the bedchamber, frowning. 'What is it?'

'Find Thorgils, and tell him that Ivaar invited me for a ride, so we can't train this morning.'

Biddy raised an eyebrow, sticking her hands firmly into her hips.

'It's the best thing!' Jael insisted. 'Tell him I'll be gone with Ivaar for a good while, so he can go and speak to Isaura. That should keep him happy.'

Biddy followed her to the door. 'I hope you know what you're doing,' she whispered sternly.

'So do I,' Jael said uncertainly. 'For all our sakes.'

***

'What do you want, Osbert?' Amma snapped as she spun around, her long brown hair flapping angrily behind her. She was still smarting from her father's words, and she knew that the whole scene had only played out because of her brother's petty trouble making.

'My sister! My last, unmarried sister,' Osbert purred, smiling his way towards her. 'It is so brave of you to show your plain little face again after your very public humiliation.'

Amma frowned, stepping forward. She was slightly taller than her brother, and she peered down at him, her face full of disdain. 'Well then, I suppose I *am* brave, which is a compliment, don't you know? So much better than people calling you small, or petty, or mean.'

Osbert squirmed. He hated the way she was leaning over him. Dropping his shoulders, he sucked in his stomach, rising on his toes. 'Well, let's see how brave you are when Father introduces you to your *new* husband.'

Amma's face paled, and she shrunk backwards.

Osbert smiled, his chest puffing out with renewed confidence. 'Oh, that's right,' he said slowly, with wide, innocent eyes. 'You don't know about that, do you?' He shook his head in mock horror. 'Oh, I shouldn't have said anything, should I? Father is going to be so cross with me.' And smiling, he stepped around his sister and started to walk off. He assumed that she'd say something, call him back, but Amma just stood there, frozen to the spot. Osbert paused, realising that the game would end if he didn't do something, so he turned around, walking back to her, placing his mouth near her ear. 'I wouldn't worry, though. I hear the weather in Hest is so warm in winter that you don't even need a cloak!'

Osbert heard Amma's sharp intake of breath.

He smiled, happy with the outcome.

He'd be able to sit back and watch her crumble over the coming days, too afraid to even talk to their father about it. He turned and walked off, feeling as though the day, barely started, was already a success.

Amma shuddered as he left, realising that her life was about to unravel. She could see how Jael must have felt, and that was Jael who was capable of killing any man in Osterland. And if her cousin had been unable to stop her marriage to that drunken fool, what hope did she possibly have?

***

The sun was out for the first time in days, and despite the frigid air, Jael was relieved to be freed from the confines of the house and her suffocating thoughts. She tried to forget her unease about Ivaar's company and her anxiety about Thorgils, letting everything blow away into the wind; lost and forgotten, just as she wished to be today. It proved impossible, though, and eventually, Jael gave up, everything tumbling back into her head.

Ivaar looked at her with concern as he came alongside. 'Are you alright?'

'Yes, fine. I didn't sleep much last night.'

'I'm sorry to hear that,' he said sympathetically, walking Leada slowly next to Tig. 'We don't have to stay out long.'

'No, no I love it out here,' Jael insisted. 'Riding away from the fort is my favourite part about living here!'

Ivaar laughed. 'Well, I can't blame you there.'

They carefully navigated a narrow path that led them down into a small valley. 'I've missed this place,' he sighed, his eyes travelling up and down the dark, chiselled cliffs that bordered their route. 'Kalfa is a nothing sort of place compared to Oss. Oss is full of bold shapes and hidden surprises. There's so much I'd forgotten.'

Jael stole a quick glance at his face. He appeared genuinely happy. 'It must have been hard being away for so long?'

Ivaar turned to look at her. 'Hard?' He considered that. 'Yes, it was. I suppose you can understand how it felt. You didn't want to leave Brekka, did you?'

'No.'

'Neither did I, but I had no choice.'

'Well, after what you did...' Jael couldn't help herself.

Ivaar didn't even flinch. 'You've heard all the stories about me, then?'

'And they're just stories, are they?'

'I didn't kill Melaena, if that's what you mean,' Ivaar said sharply, and clicking his tongue, he nudged Leada ahead of Tig. They slipped down another narrow path, leaving Jael staring after him with an open mouth.

She caught up quickly, edging Tig up to Leada as soon as the path widened. 'You didn't?'

'Of course I didn't,' he insisted. 'Why would I? I loved her. Desperately. Why would I kill someone I loved?'

'Because you couldn't have her for yourself? Because she chose your brother? Love and hate are similar passions. It's easy for one to overwhelm the other,' Jael suggested.

'Of course. But she didn't choose Eadmund,' Ivaar said quietly. 'She chose me.'

'That's not the story I heard.'

'Well, I can imagine how the story went if Eadmund or Thorgils were doing the telling.'

Jael pulled on Tig's reins, determined to look at Ivaar as he spoke. She needed to know the truth, and she couldn't discover that without looking into his eyes. 'What *is* your story, then?' she asked, peering at him.

Ivaar reined Leada in, his face dark with old memories. 'Melaena...' he sighed heavily. 'She was incredibly beautiful, and she tormented us both. That's how it was for a long while. She came with her father, who was keen to make an alliance with Eirik. They stayed some time, enough time for her to tie the both of us up in knots.' He looked away, searching for the right words. 'She would say that she couldn't decide who it was she wanted more. Eventually, when I told her that I wouldn't share her with

Eadmund, that I couldn't go on like that, she told me that she loved me. She chose me.' He stopped, seeing the strongest vision of Melaena's face for the first time in years. It faded quickly, though, and he frowned. 'But her father had a different plan. He wanted her married to the future King of Oss. Not some spare.'

'But why was that?' Jael interrupted, soothing a restless Tig with her hand. 'Why had Eirik made Eadmund his heir? What had you done?'

'Done?' Ivaar's laugh was hollow. 'You've so many bad ideas about me, Jael! Done? I was just born to the wrong woman. Eirik had married my mother for her riches, for an alliance, but he despised her, in the end, so he divorced her to marry Eskild. When he fell in love with Eskild, nothing else mattered. No one did.' His eyes were those of a little boy for a moment, but he blinked his memories away quickly.

Tig skittered about under Jael, and she tugged sternly on his reins. He might have been ready to move on, but she was eager to hear the rest of Ivaar's story.

'When Eadmund was born, Eirik simply made him his heir. He loved Eskild, and he wanted her son to be the king. It was too much for my mother,' he said quietly, dropping his head. 'She couldn't live with the shame of it all. She killed herself.'

'I'm sorry,' Jael said sympathetically. The pain on his face looked very real. Perhaps he was playing a game, but if so, he was playing it expertly.

She felt completely fooled.

'Shall we keep riding?' Ivaar wondered with a hint of a smile. 'Before your horse runs away with you?'

'I think we should. He's not very happy with me today it seems.'

Jael wondered if Tig was mad at her out of loyalty to Thorgils. She didn't blame him, but what Ivaar was revealing was worth the price of both his and Thorgils' anger, she was sure.

CHAPTER THIRTY FOUR

'Gone? With Ivaar?' Thorgils shook his head as he stood on the doorstep, dressed in his thickest cloak, his pockets full of carrots. 'But we're supposed to be training!' He stared at Biddy in confusion. 'Why would she do that?'

'I don't know,' Biddy shrugged. 'But she did suggest that you could go and see Isaura. She was sure they'd be gone a long time.'

Thorgils stilled at the suggestion. Jael was clever to twist the story that way, he smiled to himself. He would certainly have stern words with her when she returned, but until then... 'Well, perhaps I could do that,' he said uncertainly. 'Although, it has been a long time. She may not wish to speak to me,' he mumbled into his beard.

Biddy grabbed his arm, forcing him to look at her; glaring up at him in a way that reminded him of his mother. 'There's only one way to find out. And if you stand here on my porch jiggling in your britches any longer, you'll never know because Ivaar will be back!'

Thorgils blinked rapidly, realising that she was right. He readjusted his cloak and ran a hand through his beard. 'Right, I shall go, then.' He looked down at Biddy but didn't move.

'Thorgils! Go!' And she shooed him away with her broom.

***

Edela drifted away, lost in old memories as she stared up at the massive doors of the ancient Temple of Tuura. They were just as imposing as she remembered; large wooden panels, latticed with strips of dark wood, secured at every corner by huge iron rivets. Tall carved steeples raged out of its roof, calling to the Tuuran gods, welcoming them to this sacred place.

This was no place for ordinary people.

The elders had made sure of that.

The temple had stood for over a thousand years, little changed in all that time. As the lands and the people of Tuura had slowly vanished beneath its dark glare, the temple had remained, impenetrable and remote. It offered no sanctuary, though, no welcoming embrace for its vulnerable, frightened people. It kept all of their hopes for the future locked away behind those doors.

A tomb of secrets hidden from all but the powerful elders.

Edela shuddered, remembering her dream. She had not known that voice, a woman's voice, but it had been a voice to fear. There was danger coming, a darkness that threatened to consume them, of that Edela was certain now. But she had no idea what she was supposed to do to keep everyone safe.

'Edela?'

As she turned around, her face broke into a smile, blue eyes blinking with surprise. 'Alaric! My old friend!'

'Old, is it now?' Alaric Fraed smiled shyly, embracing her.

'Yes, that is what we have both become, it seems,' Edela chortled as she stepped back, considering his long-seen face. 'Older, but wiser, I hope.'

He was a small man; only as tall as her, if that. Smaller than he used to be, she thought, noticing his rounded shoulders which he was working hard to straighten. They had been childhood friends, although Alaric had once wanted more; once, she reminded herself, when they were young enough to care for such things.

'Wiser or more foolish, I am yet to decide,' Alaric said, his watery eyes darting about nervously as he reached up a hand, trying to tame the few strands of white hair left on his head.

'I feel much the same, I must admit,' Edela frowned, staring at the temple doors again.

'Are you going in?'

'Me?' It was her turn to look nervous. 'I'm not sure. Branwyn tells me that many things have changed since my last visit. I hear that all are not welcome through those doors anymore.'

Alaric nodded. 'Things have changed, that is true. But you're a dreamer, Edela. You will always be welcome there. It is only the rest of us who aren't.'

His words were weighted with sorrow and something else, Edela noticed: fear. She smiled kindly. 'It has been so long, my dear Alaric, since we were last together. You must tell me how your life has unfolded since I was last here.' And slipping her hand through the crook of his arm, she turned him away from the temple steps. 'I'm eager to hear all about it.'

Alaric relaxed, his shoulders sinking in relief as she led him away; happy to talk to her about anything other than that temple and the secrets he wanted no part of anymore.

***

They rode silently for a while, but Ivaar's words kept themselves busy in Jael's head. She felt confused and unsettled by them. Was he just twisting the truth into a palatable story to win her over? Probably, she decided, but nothing about him appeared false. There was real pain there, she saw, when he spoke of Melaena and his mother. But could it be possible, truly possible, that Eadmund had spent all these years heartbroken over a woman who hadn't even loved him?

Jael slowed Tig down again, waiting for Ivaar. She needed more.

'If you loved her and she loved you, as you say, why is she dead? And why does everyone assume that you did it? Obviously more than assume. You were banished for it,' Jael said bluntly.

Ivaar scratched his beard and frowned. 'They assumed it because Eadmund told them I did it. Convinced them all of it. But he didn't know Melaena loved me. He didn't know that we never stopped being together, even after she was betrothed to him. We couldn't be apart, couldn't stay away from one another,' he breathed, staring into Jael's eyes. 'I had no reason to kill her.'

'So you're without blame in the whole mess?'

'I'm certainly not without blame. I was in the middle of it, so of course, some of the blame is mine. I could have, should have backed away, left her alone, left her to my brother,' he sighed, feeling his body vibrating with the memories now. 'She was intoxicating. I loved her desperately. So yes, I am to blame for that. But killing her? No.'

Jael narrowed her eyes, trying to find the lies in his. But she couldn't see any, and that worried her. If Ivaar hadn't killed Melaena, who had?

And if Ivaar hadn't killed Melaena, was he really their enemy at all?

***

Thorgils had almost convinced himself to give up, certain that Isaura wouldn't want to talk to him, when he suddenly saw her. She was down on the snow-covered beach, standing by the drying sheds, feeding seabirds with her children. Her three daughters were racing about in the snow, throwing crumbs into the air as the birds screeched and swooped down towards them. The little boy sat grizzling on her hip, a fat fist in his mouth.

Isaura didn't look happy to see him.

'You can't be here,' she hissed as he walked up to her. 'Ivaar will find out. He has a dreamer. She will know.'

Thorgils looked down at the fair-haired little boy, who stopped his grizzling, staring in shock at the big, red-headed man peering down at him. Thorgils smiled sadly as he held out his thumb for him to grab hold of. 'I'll go then,' he mumbled.

Isaura looked at him, not wanting him to go at all. Tears quickly filled her eyes, and she tried to wish them away, inhaling his scent as it blew towards her on a stiff breeze. It was so achingly familiar, as was that face, albeit with a few new lines and scars. She sighed. It wouldn't help him or her if she lost control now. 'There are too many things we could say,' she quietly. 'And none of them will make any of this better. None of them will take away the past seven years. We are both damaged by it, but we can't change what has been. I have my children, and they have a father, and Ivaar is not someone to cross. You know that.' She wiped her eyes and looked across the frozen sea, towards the sharp, mist-covered stone spires as the seabirds wailed and called around them.

Thorgils looked down, seeing that Isaura's son had a firm hold of his thumb. He sighed, wishing that everything was different; that it was their children they stood watching on the beach; that they could go back to their house and sit around a warm fire and eat a meal together. They had talked about it when they were growing up, longingly planning the time when they could escape his mother and her father.

When they would be free to be together, alone.

'Ivaar's gone riding with Jael,' Thorgils murmured.

Isaura looked anxious. 'You need to warn her about what he's doing. It will end badly. I've seen the way he looks at her. I remember that look.'

'I know, so do I. She won't listen, though. There's never been a more stubborn creature than Jael Furyck.'

Isaura's eyes were fierce as they sought his. 'Then you must make her.'

Thorgils nodded, easing his thumb out of the little boy's wet hand. 'Just tell me one thing, and then I'll go. Tell me you would still choose me if there was no Ivaar. If you had a choice.'

Isaura looked away, watching as her daughters started running towards them. 'Go now, before the girls come, please.' Her face was pained as she stared imploringly at him. 'Thorgils, you never need ask me such a question. What we were, what we had, that will never change in my heart. Now go!' And she turned away from him and started walking towards the girls, hoping to cut them off before they had a chance to investigate her visitor.

Thorgils hesitated for one, thick, white breath, watching her go before turning and walking slowly away.

***

Alaric's cottage was a tiny, dark hole, thick with dust. Sparsely furnished. Just a simple bed with a threadbare fur, a poorly made table and stool, a few vessels for cooking stacked around his firepit, and not much else.

Edela felt sorry for her friend and the poverty of his existence. She sighed, feeling the ache in her weary shoulders. How quickly their youth had rushed away from them. 'You never married, then?' she wondered quietly as Alaric pulled the solitary stool out for her to sit on.

He shook his head, bending over the firepit, poking the charred logs, looking for flames. 'No, in the end, it all just passed me by, I suppose.' He glanced at her, sadly. Wistfully. 'Some things just aren't meant to be. You know that, of course.'

'Yes, better than most,' she shivered. It was almost colder in here than outside. 'But what about your work, as a scribe? Why is it that you're not allowed into the temple anymore? I thought the scribes were just as important as the dreamers to the elders?'

Alaric screwed up the wrinkled folds of his face, his eyes almost disappearing beneath them. He looked hesitant. 'Well...'

'You don't have to tell me, of course,' Edela reassured him. 'I don't wish to make you uncomfortable. If it's something you'd rather not say...'

Alaric looked back to his dead fire, hanging his head. There was no life in it, nor in him anymore, it seemed. But here was Edela, a bright-eyed reminder of a time when there had been hope in his heart. He stood up, his hips clicking in protest, and came to sit on the edge of the firepit in front of her. 'There are many secrets here, of course. Always secrets,' he said softly. 'The elders grow more and more worried about them escaping the temple. They don't trust anyone now. The dreamers are different, the elders need them, but the scribes?' He leaned in closer now, resting his arms on his knees, lowering his voice. 'Someone stole a prophecy, many years ago. They decided that one of us was responsible. Marcus interrogated us all. He's the elderman now,' Alaric shuddered. 'It was very important, this prophecy. I don't know of it. It was not written in my time at least. But they wanted it back, desperately. In the end, they decided it was Arbyn Nore who did it. That he had told someone about it or stolen it himself. Arbyn insisted he was innocent. Nothing would compel him to confess, but, in the end, they found him guilty and beheaded him.'

'Oh!' Edela's eyes widened in shock. He had been one of their childhood friends. 'I didn't know that. Poor Arbyn. Do you think he did it? That he told someone about the prophecy or took it himself?'

Alaric shook his head. 'You wouldn't choose to steal a scroll, would you? That is hardly a treasure, not unless you have knowledge of what it contained. Someone knew that it was valuable, which is why it disappeared. But no, I don't believe Arbyn did it. He was devoted to his work,' Alaric insisted, shivering. 'But someone revealed its presence and let a thief into the temple, or took it themselves. After the prophecy was stolen, the elders shut everyone out and turned their attention towards strengthening the army, building the walls higher. It does not fill us with any confidence to see what they are doing. I often think about what that prophecy might have contained. What its loss could mean for us all.'

Edela felt confused. There were so many threads dangling hopelessly inside her head, all loose and unattached. If she was to help Jael, she had to start weaving them together in a way that made sense.

Before it was too late.

***

Thorgils hadn't come back, and Eadmund wasn't going to sit and wait any longer. He didn't need anyone to look after him. He was perfectly able, just slightly pathetic, but his legs and arms were all working fine. So, forgetting Thorgils entirely, he threw his cloak around his shoulders and headed out in search of food. And maybe some ale.

He left the door to bang behind him, grimacing as the cold attacked his face and his boots sunk into the deep, wet snow.

'I wondered what had happened to you. I'm glad to see you're still breathing!'

Eadmund froze, closing his eyes. He reluctantly turned around, his mood suddenly as murky as the clouds sinking above him. 'No doubt you were hoping I'd dropped off the cliffs somewhere.'

Eirik frowned, then sighed. 'One day you will know the feeling of having a child, and for the most part, never wishing they'd drop off a cliff.'

'Not even if they murder someone?' Eadmund spat crossly, his stomach growling loudly to match his angry mood.

Eirik chose to ignore that. He peered at his dishevelled-looking son. 'Ketil has just opened for the day. I'll walk over with you. I could do with something to eat, and by the look and smell of you, you're going to need someone to prop you up soon.'

'And you think you've got enough strength in that sack of bones to hold me up?' Eadmund grumbled, unable to bring himself to say anything nice.

'Ha! I didn't make myself king by sitting around scratching my arse all day,' Eirik smiled as they started walking towards the square. 'I think even these old bones would make it further in the contest than you.'

Eadmund frowned at this father, feeling the familiar itching in his throat. He really did want that ale now. 'Well, I can't deny that. You probably could.'

Eirik looked at his son, feeling a twinge of sorrow. Finally, something other than anger was stirring inside him. He wished he could reach into Eadmund and fix everything that was wrong, but he couldn't.

That, he decided was the curse of being a parent.

'And what about Jael, then? She seems to be disappearing to train with Thorgils often enough. She must be taking it seriously?' Eirik suggested.

'Jael?' Eadmund looked even lower then. 'I'm not sure. You'd have to ask her. We haven't spoken in a while.'

Eirik stopped, grabbing Eadmund's arm. 'She's your *wife* now,' he said firmly. 'I've had three wives and loved two. Truly loved. And I recommend it very highly indeed. A bloody death awaits us all, my son, if we're lucky, so we have to hold onto those few things that give us happiness. Otherwise, what's the point of any of it? To just be miserable and alone until we die?' He sighed, sensing that Eadmund wasn't even listening. 'They're both gone now, but I don't regret that I loved them. After your mother died, I didn't imagine ever finding happiness again. But then I saw Rada. It would've been easy for me to stay sad and alone, to wallow in that place without Eskild, but the gods offered me another chance. I didn't want to take it at first. I remembered how it was when your mother died,' he said quietly. 'But I did, in the end. I took the risk, and I found another six years of happiness I hadn't expected. So, now I'm here, all alone, without Eskild or Rada, but with you and Eydis and a head full of memories. And I don't regret any of it. If I'd let those chances slip away, I'd be like you now. Still broken. In pieces. Trying to drink enough ale so that I didn't feel any of it.' Eadmund looked away, uncomfortable, and Eirik grabbed his arm harder. 'But Jael is *here*. Your chance for happiness is *here*. Now.' Eirik shook his head. 'This isn't about heirs or legacies, or being the king. You're my son, Eadmund! Find a way out of this. Be happy. You have a chance to be happy.... take it.'

Eirik blinked the tears out of his eyes. He could feel more coming, so he ducked his head, not wanting to say anymore. The despair of all these years of watching his son drift away from him was just too much. His own helplessness and Eadmund's hopelessness overwhelmed him, and he walked away, not looking back.

Eadmund felt tears stinging his own eyes. It was a hard thing to see his father like that. He felt shame and embarrassment burn his cheeks. He wanted to sink to his knees, into the freezing snow, and just scream away all the memories, all the pain that he couldn't escape, no matter how much he wanted to be free of it. No matter how tired of it he was. His father was right, of course he was. He had a wife, and he had felt things; seen in her eyes that she had felt things, but now he wasn't sure about any of it. He would never know the truth, though, if he didn't try to find out what could be.

Sharp pains attacked the base of his neck, and Eadmund's stomach growled impatiently again. He really did want some food, he thought, glancing around. He was just across the street from Jael's house, he noticed with a wry smile. There was smoke twisting its way out of the hole in the roof. He imagined Biddy stirring a stew in her cauldron, his chair by the fire, the puppies lying at his feet. Jael and Thorgils would probably still be training, so he had time.

He took a deep breath and made the decision to try.

Eadmund stopped himself before he'd even begun, watching as Jael and Ivaar walked towards the house with the horses. *His* house. *His* horse. Ivaar was patting the white horse, smiling at Jael. Eadmund slunk back, hiding amongst the shadows, not wanting to be seen but still, wanting to see.

Jael's face was flushed from riding, he could tell. Her cheeks and nose were bright red, and her teeth were showing as she laughed with Ivaar. She seemed comfortable with him, he noted. Very comfortable. And Ivaar couldn't stop looking at her. Eadmund clenched his jaw, ignoring the urgent call of his stomach.

He wanted to see what was about to happen.

What he feared was happening all over again.

CHAPTER THIRTY FIVE

Amma sat sobbing on one side of Axl. His mother sniffed morosely on the other. Axl didn't know who to try and comfort first. He wished that Edela were here. She always seemed to know what to say. 'It's no easy thing being a woman,' he tried awkwardly.

'Well, it was a lot easier when your father was here,' Gisila muttered crossly. 'He'd never have married Jael off. Not to an Islander. And if he were here, then I wouldn't be marrying Lothar.' She glanced quickly at Amma.

'It's alright, Gisila,' Amma mumbled, wiping her running nose on a cloth Axl had found for her. 'Say what you like about my father. I've seen the truth of who he really is with my own eyes, and it's an ugly truth. I had thought that Osbert was simply a freak, my mother being so gentle-natured, but I see now where Osbert's character truly comes from.'

'Amma,' Axl said quietly, leaning towards her. 'You'll only make things worse for yourself if someone hears you talking like that. As angry as you feel, you must find a way to keep control of your thoughts. Keep them off your face.'

'Well, isn't that what everyone has been saying to *you*?' Gisila scolded him. 'And have you listened?'

Axl sighed; it was true, of course. Perhaps it was just easier to see a way to help someone else? He hadn't cared about the danger his behaviour could have brought to his own door, but he should have thought more about what it could mean for his family.

He felt the vulnerability in Amma and his mother and with it a responsibility to care for them. He'd been treading a dangerous path listening to his friends, and as desperate as he was to reclaim the throne meant for him, it would feel a hollow victory if he lost everyone he cared about in the process.

'There must be something we can do, Axl?' Amma wondered desperately. 'Some way to stop all of this happening? To stop my father and Osbert?'

Axl felt his mother's eyes turn towards him. He was frozen, wondering what his father would do. What Jael would do. But he was not like either of them, so why had his father thought to make him his heir? How could he look after a kingdom of people when he was struggling to think of a way to protect just two women?

'We can stay safe,' Gisila said calmly, sensing Axl's panic. 'And wait. Pray to the gods and don't do anything foolish. Something will turn in our favour. It has to.'

**

Jael was starving, wishing that Ivaar would hurry up and leave so she could go inside and eat. It would have been polite to invite him in, she supposed, but he had a wife and children, and besides, she was not overly interested in being polite anyway. She wanted to stick her toes by the flames, drink a cup of ale, eat a large bowl of something tasty, and talk to Biddy about everything Ivaar had revealed on their ride.

But first, she had to get rid of him.

Jael handed Tig's reins to Askel, her stable hand, who was waiting to rub the horses down and turned to Ivaar, ready to send him on his way.

'Perhaps we could go riding again?' Ivaar murmured, sensing that she was ready to go but not wanting their conversation to end just yet.

'Yes, of course, although I'll be training with Thorgils tomorrow.'

'Oh, perhaps another day?' He looked disappointed, then smiled. 'I'm looking forward to seeing what you can do with a sword. I've heard all about your fight with Thorgils.'

'Ha! That. Well, who knows. I might fall on my arse in the first round and spend the rest of the day watching everyone else.'

'I doubt that, but you never know, it might rain.'

'Well, if Tarak is praying to the gods it will,' Jael snorted.

'You really don't like him, do you?'

'No, I really don't.'

'You're a brave woman to play with a man like that,' Ivaar frowned in warning. 'Eirik won't protect you against him. Tarak's too valuable to Oss, and he knows it. He isn't someone to make an enemy of.'

'Ahhh, so that's your plan? Make friends with the big, scary ones?' Jael smiled.

'Of course! Better than having them slit your throat in the night, don't you think?'

'Perhaps, but I have excellent hearing,' Jael said smartly, 'so, I'll take my chances with Tarak.'

Ivaar looked doubtful. 'Well, I've warned you at least. I'm sure you can take care of yourself, as you say. I'd better go and find my father. He wants to talk to me about Oss, Eadmund, everything it seems.'

'I look forward to hearing all about that, if I live long enough,' Jael grinned. 'Who knows, Tarak might sneak up on me tonight?'

'I hope not, Jael,' Ivaar smiled as he walked away. 'Who would I go riding with?'

Jael kept her smile fixed on her face until he'd walked across the street, then spinning around, she quickly let it fall as she hurried into the house, desperate for some warmth, thinking about that chair by the fire.

Eadmund's chair.

She smiled sadly as she opened the door, hoping that Thorgils had found him.

'You're back, then,' Thorgils growled, pushing himself out of Eadmund's chair. 'Sounds as though you and Ivaar had a lovely time together.'

***

Eadmund lost his footing and clattered against the side of a cottage. The noise turned Ivaar's head in his direction, and he came stalking towards his brother.

'Are you alright, Eadmund?' Ivaar wondered. He checked behind himself to make sure that Jael had gone inside. 'You look as though you need a hand back to bed.'

'I don't think so,' Eadmund muttered, straightening up, sinking further into the snow. 'My legs work just fine.' He moved to step past his brother, but Ivaar blocked his path.

'Were you spying on us from over here? Eavesdropping?' He looked at Eadmund with one eyebrow raised, a condescending smile on his unsympathetic face.

Eadmund frowned. 'Spying on what? I was on my way to Ketil's.' His stomach rumbled to support his argument. He tried to step around his brother, but again Ivaar moved to stop him.

'You can't blame her, you know.'

Eadmund's shoulders sagged. He wanted to get away from Ivaar; he didn't want to play the game. It was an old game he remembered well from their childhood. Ivaar would dangle a tasty morsel to torment him. Eadmund would eventually rise to take the bait, and Ivaar would have him trapped, torturing him mercilessly. 'You're welcome to talk to anyone, Ivaar. I don't care. As I said in the hall, do what you want with Jael. She means nothing to me. I didn't choose her, and I don't want her. I believe you'll discover the feeling is mutual.'

Ivaar studied his brother, his swaying, stinking, bloated brother. He looked truly pathetic. There was nothing about him that resembled the man he remembered. But he felt no pity or sympathy, just a growing sense of pleasure to think that his brother had suffered so badly since Melaena's death.

There was some justice, after all.

'Hmmm, there are many things I'd forgotten after all these years. So many things. We were apart for such a long time, but I've just remembered what a bad liar you are,' Ivaar laughed. 'Perhaps you're even lying to yourself, and you don't know it? In this state, I doubt you know anything at all,' he sneered. 'But I will tell you one thing, Little Brother, you love your wife. It's in your eyes. It's all over you. You forget that I've seen you in love before. I know the look. I recognise the signs. You have it all again. And there's nothing you can do to stop it.'

Eadmund blinked rapidly, clenching his fists by his sides. He wanted to kill his brother more than he'd wanted anything in a long time. Ivaar was shorter than him, just, but he stood on a higher piece of ground, towering threateningly over him. Eadmund felt like a small nothing standing in the shadow of Ivaar's scorn. He'd wasted his strength over the years, and now his body had no fight left in it. As angry as he was, though, he knew that the only outcome he could expect if he fought Ivaar, was humiliation and pain. The pain he wouldn't have minded, but he couldn't stand any more of his brother's gloating. There was only one way out of this if he was to cling to any self-respect and it had to be with his head held high. 'Well then, I wish you luck,' Eadmund said quietly, his lips tight, his body pulsing with barely contained fury. 'My wife is a strong woman. You'll need all the luck you can get if you're going to play with her.' And he stepped past Ivaar as quickly as he could.

Ivaar let him go, disappointed that Eadmund had not taken his bait.

But there would be plenty of time to hook him. He was sure

of that.

***

'Lovely time?' Jael asked irritably as she sniffed around Biddy's cauldron. Hot, good smelling things were bubbling away inside, and she was desperate for a taste. 'Well, lovelier than you, by the look on your face.' She handed Biddy her cloak and sat on a stool to remove her wet boots.

Thorgils stayed standing and frowning. 'I thought we were training today. We were supposed to train today!'

'It's only one day. We won't miss it. Don't forget, we have a plan. I could hardly say no when he asked to come along with me. Besides, it was well worth it. Ivaar did a lot of talking.' Jael placed her wet boots next to the fire to dry, and her feet by them. She was frozen solid, desperate for the heat from the flames.

'About what?' Thorgils wondered crossly.

Jael patted the stool next to her. 'Well, I'm not going to yell it up to you. If you want to hear the story, sit your hairy arse down here.'

Thorgils harrumphed and reluctantly plonked himself down. 'Go ahead, then. My arse is ready.'

Jael shot him a sideways look. 'I thought you'd be happy, me leading Ivaar away like that. I thought you'd be able to talk to Isaura alone.'

Thorgils looked away from her, towards the flames. 'She didn't want to talk to me.'

'Oh.'

'She was worried it would cause problems for me. The truth is that it would cause problems for her, so I left.'

'That's a shame. I'm sorry.'

Thorgils shook away all thoughts of Isaura for now. He was

too cross with Jael to think about anyone else. He hated the idea of her befriending his worst enemy. 'So, what did Ivaar say that was so interesting?'

'Well... he explained how it was, with Melaena.' Jael moved her feet away from the flames, which, having rapidly thawed them, were now scorching her socks. 'He said that she'd loved him, not Eadmund. That she'd wanted him, but her father made her choose Eadmund because he was Eirik's heir.'

'Ha! Of course he thinks that's how it was. Are you surprised?'

'He didn't appear to be lying.'

'And you can tell a liar from an honest man, can you?' Thorgils raised an eyebrow, peering at her. 'You've probably never heard Ivaar tell the truth, which is why you can't see the lies in his eyes, nor hear them from his lips. But believe me, everything he says is *his* version of events. He's so in love with himself that he never sees his own fault in anything.'

Jael frowned. She had believed Ivaar. Nothing he'd said or done had led her to think that he was lying. 'He told me that he didn't kill Melaena.'

Thorgils laughed loudly, startling Biddy, who was standing next to him, ladling stew into a bowl. 'And let me guess, you believed him about that too?' He got up, his irritability overwhelming him. 'What has happened to you, Jael? I thought we were on the same side? But now you seem to be flying Ivaar's banner. What about Eadmund? What we were trying to do to help him?'

Jael stood up, looking just as cross now. 'Lower your voice,' she hissed. 'Tiras is probably sliding around out there.' She shook her head as Biddy offered her a bowl. Her need to make Thorgils listen was suddenly stronger than her hunger pains.

'He did kill her, and you need to realise that, Jael,' Thorgils growled deeply. 'And Melaena did love Eadmund. She chose Eadmund. Whatever Ivaar is telling you, believe the opposite, otherwise, you'll find yourself in a real tangle. It's his game, what he's doing to you, what he's always done. Isaura told me to warn you that Ivaar had started to play with you. He does that. He watches and sees what Eadmund loves and then he goes and takes it for his own. He's always done that. He wants to hurt Eadmund. It's how he feels good about himself.'

Jael shook her head, suddenly feeling very odd. 'What? Eadmund doesn't love me. Why would Ivaar think that?' She could feel a burst of warmth on her cheeks, and it wasn't coming from the fire.

Thorgils glared at her. 'Listen to me. Hear my words, please, Jael. We can't keep going with this plan of yours if you forget what the plan is... if you get lost with Ivaar.' He ran a hand through his wild hair. 'He's a handsome man...'

'What?' Jael looked insulted. 'What does *that* mean?'

Thorgils sighed uncomfortably. 'I'm just saying that perhaps you're getting distracted. You've been on this island a while now. You must be lonely, and you have a husband who spends much of his time in a... bad way.'

Jael was tired, hungry, and mad. She couldn't believe that Thorgils was so full of doubt over her intentions and her character. She glared at him. 'Yes, you're right, I have been on this fucking cold island for a long time now, and if I'm lonely for anything, it's for a real friend. Someone who knows I'm not a dim-witted idiot about to be fooled by a man because of the way he looks, or how careful he is at crafting a lie!' She huffed irritably, shooing away Vella who had started chewing her sock. 'A real friend. Someone who knows me, who knows they could trust me to find the truth without getting lost along the way!' She turned around to Biddy, who was still standing there, holding a bowl of stew, watching the bickering friends with troubled eyes.

'Right then, well I'll leave you to your meal,' Thorgils snapped. He was hurt and angry, and both emotions fused together into a bright red face and a burst of fire inside his belly. 'I wish you luck in the contest, Jael. Not that you'll need it, of course.' He adjusted his cloak, nodded to Biddy, and headed out the door in a rush.

Jael sat down, staring at her hands. Biddy tried to offer her the bowl of stew, but she was no longer hungry.

Her appetite had left with Thorgils.

***

'Where have you been?' Eirik called impatiently as Ivaar opened the door and stepped into the dimly lit chamber. 'I was beginning to wonder which one of my sons I'd asked to see. It's usually Eadmund I end up waiting for!'

Ivaar ignored his father's grumbles, laughing as he sat down opposite him. 'What's the hurry? Have you nothing else to keep you busy?'

Eirik sat back in his chair, trying to decide whether Ivaar's attitude was meant to annoy or relax him. It was an even choice. 'No, I've nothing else to do today, except wait on you, it seems. What were you doing?'

They were sitting in one of Eirik's chambers, a place he reserved for his more private conversations, of which there were not many, but he had seen the eyes following Ivaar since he'd arrived on Oss. It was better to talk away from them and their accompanying ears.

'I went for a ride with Jael,' Ivaar said casually, warming his hands over the inviting flames. His father's chamber was plush and well heated, its floor covered in layers of hides and furs. It was the chamber of a king; one day his, if this conversation went as he expected.

'Jael?' Eirik didn't look impressed. 'That's no way to endear yourself to your brother, nor anyone else here.'

'Why? Eadmund doesn't seem to like her. Why would he be bothered?'

Ivaar was fishing for information and Eirik could see it in his eyes. He said nothing more on the subject. 'What do you think of the place after all these years, then? Better than Kalfa?' he wondered evenly.

'The stables are better than Kalfa,' Ivaar sneered. 'Yes, of course. It's not been easy, being away. We're all relieved to be back.'

'I'm not sure your wife looks relieved. I haven't seen her smile yet.'

Ivaar blinked. 'Well, no, I suppose it is harder for her. Her father is dead now. She had no one to come back to. She doesn't have fond memories of how she left either.'

'No, well that would be my fault, I suppose, but I did owe her father a favour,' Eirik admitted. 'Still, she's given you fine children so far. Another son or two will be necessary if you become my heir, though.'

'If?' Ivaar narrowed his eyes. He didn't want to appear too keen, but he was desperate to hear the words he had been dreaming of for most of his life. 'I didn't think I was here for just a visit.'

'Didn't you now?' Eirik snorted. 'Well, I don't suppose you've ever had a problem with confidence, have you, Ivaar?'

'I'll make a good king, Father, and Eadmund is obviously in a bad way. Do you have any other choice?'

Eirik leaned forward, irritated, ready to defend Eadmund but then his shoulders sagged, and his irritation eased when he realised that he couldn't. Ivaar was right: Eadmund had given him no choice. 'When I am ashes, drinking in Vidar's Hall, and you are here, sleeping in my bed, sitting in my chair, what sort of king will you be?' Eirik wondered, studying his son carefully. Ivaar was thirty-four-years-old now. Any youth had vanished, leaving his face sharp-edged. His clear blue eyes held no emotion that Eirik could see, just cold, hard ambition.

He didn't need an answer.

He could tell what sort of king Ivaar would be, and that worried him, but what else could he do?

CHAPTER THIRTY SIX

Aleksander turned to Edela. 'Are you sure about this?'

'I am most certainly not sure about this,' Edela murmured uneasily as she stared up at the never-ending doors. Her conversation with Alaric had kept her awake for much of the night, and Edela knew that she'd never get any closer to the answers she sought unless she entered the temple.

But now that she was here, she felt hesitant.

'I would come with you if I thought they'd let me in,' Aleksander smiled, sensing her anxiety. He squeezed her arm reassuringly. 'Just don't forget that you're welcome in there. You're a dreamer. They like dreamers!'

Edela glanced up at him, relaxing her face slightly. 'So I hear. But not all, I'm sure.' It was snowing, and she didn't want him freezing out here while she dithered about like a foolish old woman. She shook her head, waking herself up. 'You go, go on back to Branwyn. I'll walk there when I'm done.' She tried to look brave, but her bottom lip quivered.

'I'll come back. I'll keep coming back to see if you're here,' Aleksander insisted. 'The snow is only going to get worse, so I'll just spend some time in the stables... thinking of a name for my horse.'

Edela laughed, forgetting her tension as she stepped forward. 'I'm glad to hear it. Now, come on, help me up these steps and then go. I'll be fine.'

Aleksander guided her up the snow-covered steps to the temple, then hesitated, watching as she stood there, knocking on the door. Edela turned and shooed him away. Aleksander backed down the steps as one of the large doors slowly opened, the light of the temple falling out into the dark afternoon.

And with one final, anxious look at him, Edela disappeared inside.

***

Fyn was getting good at this, Jael thought to herself, watching him strut into the centre of their circle, his sword pointing confidently at her, his grip firm.

It was an unpleasant day for fighting, the coldest one yet, and blowing such a snow-gale about her face that Jael could barely see. She couldn't imagine anything she'd rather be doing, though. If only Thorgils were here. She shoved that thought away quickly; she was still too angry at him.

'Are you sure you have the strength to go again?' Fyn asked cockily.

Jael raised one eyebrow, tightening her numb fingers around the wooden grip of her sword. 'Really? You think my panting is because I'm tired, you little weed?' She shook her head, walking towards him until their swords were almost touching, her smoky breath lost in a haze of sweeping snow. 'No, that's just me trying to calm my fury before I unleash it upon you!' She smiled, and Fyn laughed.

That was a mistake.

Jael lunged forward, jabbed her sword into the side of his ribs, stood on his foot so he couldn't move, and smacked her elbow into his jaw. She jumped back quickly, leaving Fyn to stumble, grumble, and feel his face before he recovered, blinking the snow out of his eyes, raising his sword and thrusting it towards her.

Again, it was a mistake.

Jael skipped to the side, avoiding his sword, smacking hers across the backs of his legs. Hard. He stumbled again but didn't go down. 'Lucky for you, my sword is made of wood, little boy!' she warned, turning to hit him again. She went for Fyn's face, but he managed to get his sword up just in time. She changed angles, hitting the inside of his wrist. He flinched but didn't drop his sword. Jael was impressed, but she didn't let it show. She didn't have time to because he was coming at her again.

Fyn lowered his sword, aiming for her belly but his jab was laboured, and Jael moved aside easily, quickly, bringing her sword up to his left side, cracking his ribs. He grimaced but didn't stumble.

Jael frowned. Surely it was time for him to go down?

'I'm watching your legs, Jael,' Fyn smiled, teasing her. 'I know what you're thinking, but you won't get me this time.'

Jael turned her back on him, walking away. It was so cold. It felt as though her sweat was freezing on her face. She wanted to get inside to the fire and heat herself through. But first, she had to find a way to end Fyn's fun.

Cocking her head to one side, Jael smiled.

Fyn shivered uncontrollably in his frozen boots, steadying himself as he waited for her. He knew that she wouldn't take his goading well, and she'd surely come at him with speed. He pushed his right leg back into the ground, feeling it slip slightly on fresh snow, and waited, gripping his sword with determination.

Jael turned, and her face was utterly blank. It unsettled Fyn. It felt as though she was staring right through him. She didn't move. The wind flapped Fyn's hair into his face, and he tried to shake it away without taking his eyes off her. He should have braided it, he thought irritably.

Jael rushed forward, and Fyn braced himself.

She moved that leg of hers, and he felt a half-smile form on his face, knowing what was coming, surprised she'd be that predictable. He moved his sword up to the left, preparing to protect his head but before he could blink, Jael dropped to the ground, sweeping her leg in a fast circle, knocking his legs out from under him. He fell onto the snow with a thud, feeling a small rock lodge in his side, grimacing at the pain of it, cringing at the shame of it, and staring up into the thick, white storm as it blew around him.

And then Jael's face as she leaned over, smiling.

'I hope your fire's still going!' she grinned, holding out a hand.

***

It was vast, bigger than she remembered and much quieter, Edela thought as she shuffled down the length of the temple, her eyes adjusting to the soft glow of light that coloured the high stone walls. Fires were burning down the middle of the large, vaulted room, and their loud crackling was the only sound she could hear; that, and the soft squelching of her wet boots as she trailed after the woman who had let her in. Edela didn't know who she was, or where she was leading her to, but she had no time to ask as she hurried across the flagstones, desperate to keep up.

Towards the back of the temple was a corridor; a narrow, dark passage leading to a handful of private chambers. Memories suddenly flooded back, like old friends. This was where the dreamers would come and talk to the elders, to share their visions and learn how to interpret them as more than just pictures or words. Edela had been so young in these rooms once; young and intimidated but excited by her new gifts, eager to learn, wanting to see more, always wanting a new dream. But now? Now she was terrified when she closed her eyes every night. She was tired and needed answers more than she needed dreams.

The woman led her to a door at the very end of the corridor and knocked on it, leaving Edela without even a nod. It was much colder in the narrow passage without the warmth of the fires, and Edela was suddenly conscious of how wet her cloak was as it clung to her shaking legs.

'Come in!'

Edela thought she recognised the voice. She frowned, trying to picture the face it belonged to as she turned the handle and eased open the door. A burst of heat welcomed her, and she was relieved to see a large fire and lamps burning. It was bright in here, bright enough to recognise the woman who stood before her. 'Neva,' Edela breathed in surprise. 'I didn't know you had become an elder here.'

Neva Elgard had been Branwyn and Gisila's childhood friend many years ago. A very pleasant girl, Edela remembered, but now? She didn't know what to think of this middle-aged woman who stood there so calm and still, her face completely unreadable in the firelight. Her hair was gathered back in red and grey streaked braids that hung to her waist. Her figure had wasted away somewhat, Edela thought, and despite the attractiveness of her pale blue dress, she looked thin and frail.

Neva smiled as she came forward. 'It has been many years since I came to the temple. Many more since I raced around with your girls.'

'Yes, I think you're all a bit too old for that now, aren't you?' Edela said wistfully.

'Come, please, sit down.' Neva helped Edela to a simple wooden chair by the fire and took the one opposite. 'I have been waiting for you.'

Edela stilled at that, her senses heightened. She didn't know where to look.

'You have many questions, I know,' Neva said softly. 'More than I am able to answer, I warn you. But let us begin and see where we end up.'

***

Jael's hands were dangerously close to the flames, but her body was still shivering. 'I've never been this cold,' she chattered.

Fyn sipped his hot nettle tea next to her. 'That's not good. I've known it to get much colder than this,' he warned. 'It's been a mild winter so far.'

'What? Don't say that!' Jael looked horrified. 'Well, perhaps next time I need to bring Leada, and we can ride to the cave and warm ourselves up?'

Fyn frowned. 'What about Thorgils? You still haven't told me why he hasn't been coming with you lately.'

Jael frowned back at him. 'Thorgils is being an idiot. It's as simple as that. When he stops being an idiot, I'm sure he'll be back.' She looked more confident than she felt. She hadn't seen him in days.

'Oh,' Fyn shivered as the wind raced under the door. 'Well, I hope so because I'm not sure I can offer you much in the way of a challenge. You need more help to get ready for the contest than me and my little wooden sword.'

'Don't think like that,' Jael smiled. 'You're getting better. Better than I thought possible when I first saw you dropping your sword all over the place. Your father was an idiot to think that you wouldn't make a warrior. Truly.'

Fyn ducked his head, uncomfortable with both her praise and talk of his father. 'I don't think I'm ever going to become a real warrior, though. Fighting with an army.'

'Not if you hide out here, you won't,' Jael said crossly. 'We need to do something, get you back to the fort before you die out here, especially if it's going to get colder than this! You can't hope to have a life out here, Fyn. On your own, in this hole.'

'No, Jael, no!' Fyn glanced anxiously at her, his eyes darting around in fear. 'You promised you wouldn't say anything! Please, don't. I'm fine here. I don't mind the cold at all. I like my own company, I really do.'

Jael sighed. He was terrified, and she didn't know how to change that. 'Alright then, I won't mention it again. At least not for a day or two,' she said as an idea formed. 'But promise me this, if Thorgils or I manage to defeat Tarak in the contest, let me talk to Eirik about you coming back.'

Fyn shifted about on his stool, looking away from her. He didn't imagine that Jael could defeat Tarak, as good as she was. No one could. Tarak was simply too big and too used to winning. He sighed heavily. 'Alright, I promise.'

'Good!' Jael was happily surprised. 'That's extra motivation for both of us, then. Yet another reason to destroy that bastard. As if we needed any more.'

Fyn shuddered; just hearing that name made him feel sick.

He tried to shake away the memories, but it was impossible. They haunted him, asleep or awake.

He couldn't escape them.

***

'It took a while to find you,' Tarak rumbled at the hunched figure lurking in the shadows. 'No one knew where you'd crawled away to. I thought that Brekkan bitch might have thrown you off a cliff.'

Tiras scowled. He didn't like the look of the giant beast glowering down at him, but he could see the opportunity he provided, especially when he glanced at the man standing next to him.

Ivaar Skalleson.

If there were two sides on this island now, then this was the only side Tiras would pick. The side that had a chance of defeating Eadmund, and with him, that cunt of a woman. 'She wouldn't dare,' he hissed. 'Despite all her threats, she's afraid, that one. She let Lothar take the throne for himself and did nothing to stop him. She could have killed me, but she didn't.'

'Maybe that's not afraid,' Ivaar said coolly, dismissing Tiras as a nothing kind of fool. 'Maybe it's clever. She'd only create problems for herself by killing you, and she didn't have the support to defeat Lothar, from what I hear.'

Tiras and Tarak stared at Ivaar, his defense of Jael surprising them both.

'Why have you sought me out?' Tiras wondered, trying not to appear nervous under Ivaar's steely-eyed glare and Tarak's towering frame.

Ivaar narrowed his eyes. 'Well, you're the reason I was brought back, from what Tarak tells me, so I came to thank you.'

'Thank me?' Tiras' beady eyes popped open.

'Yes, thank you,' Ivaar said coldly. 'And make you an offer of my protection.' He leaned towards Tiras, who flinched back into the shadows.

They were standing, hunched over inside the tiny hut that Tiras had found for himself in the farthest corner of the fort. It was barely big enough for a dog, Ivaar thought dismissively, and, looking at the filthy animal-like creature before him, he thought it a fitting hole.

Tiras raised an eyebrow. 'And in return?'

'In return, you'll place your very useful ears back to the ground, and to the doors, and the windows of every place in this fort, and you'll bring me anything and everything I need to know, especially anything to do with Jael or my brother. I want to know every word they speak to one another. Every person they meet. Bring it to me, and in return, Tarak here will keep you safe from Jael, and from my father, and most of all, from me. Do you understand?'

Tiras stared into those cold, humourless eyes and nodded.

Caught in a trap.

***

Edela fumbled nervously beneath Neva's calm stare, not knowing where to begin, nor what to reveal. She had no idea who she could trust or what danger she was in.

Neva reached out and gently patted Edela's hand. 'I didn't mean to intimidate you,' she smiled reassuringly, her pale grey eyes softening. 'This is about your granddaughter, isn't it? Jael?'

'It is, yes.' Edela felt her heart racing as she looked into Neva's encouraging eyes. 'I... I've had many dreams these past few months, about her, about what threatens her. And now the sword...' She peered at Neva, but she didn't even blink. 'I've always known there was something special about Jael. Something she was meant for. Why else was I given that sword to hold for her?'

'She has the sword now?' Neva asked.

'Yes, I gave it to her on her wedding day, as my grandfather told me to.'

'Good,' Neva nodded, smiling briefly. 'It is good that she has the sword... and Eadmund.'

Edela frowned. 'Eadmund?'

'You always saw that, didn't you?' Neva wondered. 'That she was meant to be with him?'

'Yes, I did.'

'You will need to go back to Oss,' Neva said. 'Jael will need you to keep her safe, to save her life. You are right, Edela, she is in danger. She will be in danger soon.'

Edela swallowed, shivering, despite the warmth of the small room. 'What sort of danger?'

'Danger that the sword cannot protect her from, I'm afraid, no matter how well she learns to use it. But *you* can save her. You will find a way when the time comes. Do not fear Edela, we all have confidence in you.'

'But what is the sword for if it cannot protect her from the danger that seeks her?' Edela puzzled. 'Why was it made?'

Neva sat quietly, her face betraying none of the anxiety of Edela's. 'The sword has a very particular purpose, but what that is, I cannot say. Our prophecies, as you know, are sacred messages from the gods to the elders. We are trusted to keep them safe. We must never reveal their contents, not when what they promise is yet to be realised. It would put many in danger, especially the people the prophecy concerns.'

Edela felt frustrated, but one look at Neva's face told her that she would not be moved, so she tried another approach. 'I've seen a girl with a face of darkness. I've had dreams of dark things coming. Is that the danger? These dark forces?'

Neva stilled. Her voice, when she spoke, was smooth and light. 'As you know, Edela, there are many ways to interpret your dreams. You must work to understand what the darkness could represent. Darkness may be the way you are being shown danger. This girl you speak of?' Neva leaned forward, her face suddenly sharper. 'She *is* dangerous. She is the greatest threat that Jael faces right now. Her name is Evaine Gallas, and she is desperately in love with Eadmund. She has always believed that she is meant to be with him. That he will be hers and hers alone. It is something that has been promised by her mother. And now they will plot together, against Jael.'

Edela moved towards the edge of her seat, her body rigid with fear. 'She wants to take Eadmund away from Jael?'

'Oh yes, she does, and urgently, for she is carrying Eadmund's child.'

'Oh.'

'As soon as the Thaw comes, you must cross the Nebbar Straights, back to Oss and keep Jael safe.'

'I will, of course,' Edela insisted, her eyes wide. 'But will she be safe in the meantime?'

'Do not worry too much, Edela,' Neva said, relaxing her face. 'Evaine is not on Oss now. She has been removed by the king, but she will return. You just need to make sure that you are back in time.'

'And this girl's mother? Who is she?'

'Her name is Morana. She is very skilled in the use of dark magic. Everything that Evaine thinks or feels or does comes from Morana. And Morana wants to destroy Jael.'

Edela was gripped by uncertainty. She didn't feel equipped to battle against dark magic, and if she failed, what would happen to Jael?

'We will talk again before you return to Andala,' Neva assured her as she stood up. 'I will show you ways that you can protect both you and Jael against what is coming. There is time, do not fear.'

CHAPTER THIRTY SEVEN

Ido and Vella chased each other around Eydis as she sat on the floor of the hall, laughing as she tried to catch their slippery bodies.

'Your dogs are growing,' Eirik noted awkwardly, coming to sit beside Jael on the long bench she had dragged next to the fire.

Jael was surprised, but not unhappy that he'd sought her out. They had barely spoken since that night at the house, and she was ready to make things right between them. 'They are. I'll have to start training them properly, I suppose.'

'You haven't already?'

'Not as well as I should have. Perhaps they're just a stubborn breed,' she frowned. 'I've never had any problems with dogs before. They're obedient to most commands, but they simply refuse to come when I call.'

'Sounds like good practice for having children to me!' Eirik laughed. 'If my children had done as they were told, I would've had more sleep and less of these!' He pinched the sagging folds of his wrinkled cheeks.

He was smiling, but his eyes were sad, Jael thought as she turned to face him. 'It's not too late for Eadmund, you know.'

Eirik frowned, a sigh escaping his down-turned mouth. 'Yes, it is, it's far too late. I've made up my mind, spoken to Ivaar. It's done.' A hint of uncertainty flickered in his eyes, though. 'Ivaar is my heir now.'

Jael glanced around, lowering her voice. 'But what if Eadmund changes? I can help him. I can help him stop drinking and start fighting again.'

'Why would you want to do that?' Eirik asked, his eyes reflecting little belief in her words. 'After what you said about him? How your marriage has been? Not even a marriage.' He shook his head sadly, the disappointment of how everything had turned out still raw. 'Why do you suddenly want to help him now?'

Jael wasn't sure she had an answer to that. 'I think he's a... good man,' she stumbled, feeling uncomfortable, aware that Eydis was listening. 'He'll make a good king here, and you know that too. He will care about your people and keep them safe. Look at Lothar and my father. My father did everything he could for the Brekkan people, but Lothar is only interested in himself, and Brekka is suffering because of his greed. I don't know Ivaar, other than by reputation, but I'm sure you know who your people would choose for their next king.'

Eydis coughed loudly, and both Jael and Eirik turned to see Ivaar and Isaura walking towards them with their children.

Jael stood, hurrying to the puppies who were jumping all over the littlest girl, Leya, as she leaked great big tears. 'Vella, get down!' Jael called crossly, and for once, Vella listened, racing back to her. Ido loped after his sister, leaving poor Leya to fall into her mother's arms.

'You've trained your dogs well,' Ivaar grinned, ignoring his sobbing daughter as he stopped just a little too close to Jael.

Jael frowned, glancing at Isaura who was only two paces behind him. 'Well, you would think so. It's a start.'

'You like dogs?'

Jael looked at Eydis, who was now being hugged by her nieces. 'They were a wedding gift from your sister,' she whispered, rolling her eyes. 'I couldn't refuse.'

'Oh, well I suppose they could get lost on a walk one day?' he winked.

'That would not be good preparation for motherhood,' Jael smiled. 'I'm sure any child I have will be far more annoying than a couple of puppies.'

Ivaar laughed. 'You're right there. I could say that children are better left to the women, but I don't imagine that's what you want to hear.'

'Good morning, Jael,' Isaura smiled politely as she joined them, Mads wriggling on her hip, drooling, red-faced and ready to burst into tears at any moment. 'Hello, Eirik.'

Eirik rose to greet her. 'Isaura. And how is my grandson this morning? I heard a lot of noise in the night.' He smiled at the little boy, who looked back at him sternly.

'Oh, yes, Mads is a troublesome sleeper,' Isaura blushed. 'I'm sorry about that.'

Ivaar raised an eyebrow in her direction. 'Yes, troublesome is certainly the word I'd use with that boy.' He turned to Jael. 'I'm not sure we've had any sleep since he was born.'

Jael looked horrified.

'He's not that bad, Jael, I promise,' Isaura insisted. 'He has teeth coming through, that's all.'

Jael cringed. Everyone saw her having this future child, but the thought of it made her toes curl. She enjoyed sleeping far too much.

Isaura smiled at her. 'Don't worry, when they're your own, you will love them through all the sleepless nights, all the teething, all the bad behaviour. Just ask Eirik.'

'It's true,' Eirik admitted. 'It's the only thing that keeps you from flinging them out into the snow every night!'

'There's always a servant,' Ivaar suggested helpfully. 'Or you could build another house next door?'

'Oh, please stop!' Jael pleaded, only half-joking. 'It's not something I want to think about. Not now or ever,' she sighed. 'I'm going for a ride, so if you'll excuse me.' She patted her leg for the puppies to come.

'Would you like some company?' Ivaar asked quickly. 'I

enjoyed our ride the other day.'

Jael saw Isaura's face pale slightly. She noticed the tension around Eirik's mouth. She could feel Eydis' stern glare, but what could she say? 'Yes, alright. Leada needs someone to ride her. She's not getting much exercise these days.'

'Why? What's happened to Thorgils?' Eirik wondered, ruffling his grandson's blonde hair. Mads' lips turned down and started wobbling.

'Oh, he's decided to train on his own for a while,' Jael said lightly. 'He couldn't cope with being beaten by a woman every day.'

Eirik and Ivaar laughed, but Isaura looked upset. Jael felt sorry for her, standing there with Ivaar, and Ivaar's children.

It was not the life she had dreamed of for herself.

Jael knew exactly how she felt.

***

'What happened to you?'

'What happened to you?'

'You look like shit.'

'Thank you. So do you.'

Thorgils sat down opposite Eadmund, irritably picking at a hanging fingernail.

'I thought you'd be out training with Jael?'

Thorgils snorted loudly.

Eadmund raised an eyebrow. It hurt. 'What's happened?'

Thorgils leaned over, sighing. 'I suppose we're fighting.'

'Fighting?' Eadmund almost laughed. 'About what?'

'Her bad judgement, mainly,' Thorgils said, looking up. 'She's stubborn. Won't listen. Just like you.'

Eadmund smiled. 'Poor you, having such difficult friends.'

'Yes, you're right, you're both idiots.' Thorgils scratched his head. 'But you, I can forgive. Jael... that may take longer.'

'Is it Ivaar? The way she is with Ivaar?' Eadmund asked, glancing around. They were sitting outside Ketil's, surrounded by many ears and eyes. He didn't want to be overheard. Who knew how many people Ivaar had already managed to slip into his pocket.

Thorgils avoided Eadmund's keen eyes as they sought his. Despite his fury at Jael, he still didn't want to involve Eadmund in her scheme. By the stink of him and the bloat of his face, he was struggling more than ever. Now was not the time to bring him into his confidence. 'Well, that doesn't help things. She seems to find him very interesting, doesn't she?'

'Who could blame her, with that hair of his? It brings out the colour in his eyes, don't you think?' Eadmund's lips curled into a smile, but his eyes were heavy with sadness. He hadn't spoken to Jael in a long time. There was a wide valley between them now, and she was standing on the other side of it with his gloating brother.

Thorgils laughed loudly, slapping the table, his frown easing for the first time in days. 'You're so right! That hair! Ha!' He bent over suddenly, lowering his voice, realising how loud he had become. 'At least it won't get in his eyes when he's swinging his pretty sword around.'

Eadmund's smile faded as he thought back to his brother's sneering face. 'If only he were swinging it at me as he was going down beneath *my* sword.'

'Well, why not?' Thorgils said hoarsely. 'It wasn't so long ago that you picked up a sword. If things hadn't gone so wrong, imagine where you'd be now? We can start again. I can help you now that I'm not training with Jael.'

Eadmund was surprised. 'It's that bad between you?'

'It is. For now. No doubt I'll forgive her when she sees sense, but until then, she can fight herself for all I care.'

'Ido! Vella!'

Both men turned to see the puppies racing through the snow towards them. They had grown so big that the snow barely troubled them now. Having sniffed out Thorgils, they jumped up to say hello, pawing his knees, licking his hands. There was food about, and they were eager to see if he had any to spare.

Jael trudged after them, cursing herself for their lack of obedience. She may as well be the wind for all that they listened to her.

'Hello, hello,' Thorgils smiled, patting the puppies' snow-dusted heads. 'Looks as though you'd better run along now before your mother tells you off.' He didn't look at Jael, but he could feel her cold glare aimed in his direction.

A few days without each other had not softened either of them, it seemed.

Eadmund watched the frosty exchange and was so distracted by it that he forgot his own awkwardness. His eyes met Jael's, and she blinked, then frowned at him. He looked away as the puppies, having abandoned Thorgils, raced around to try their luck with him.

'Ahhh, so fickle. Just like their mother,' Thorgils noted wryly.

Jael ignored him. 'Well, I'd love to stand around and share stories with you ladies, but I must get back to the house. Ivaar and I are going riding. Leada's in need of exercise, and since both of you have abandoned her now, Ivaar is helping me out.' She watched the pinched expression on Thorgils' face with some satisfaction. 'Come on, Ido! Vella! Let's go, come on!' And walking off without acknowledging either man, she clicked her tongue and patted her leg. The puppies, realising that she wasn't coming back, dashed after her.

Thorgils turned to Eadmund, his face bursting with irritation. 'Well, there you go. I say we go to the Pit and get you a sword.' He stood up and walked around to Eadmund, leaning towards his ear. 'You're never going to get rid of your bastard brother if you're pissing your pants, asleep under a table every night.' And with that, he strode off in the opposite direction to Jael, towards the Pit, not waiting to see if Eadmund would follow him.

Eadmund considered things.

The idea of cutting Ivaar to pieces was one of the better thoughts he'd had lately. The lure of ale remained ever-present, though, despite the ache in his head and the bile swimming around his throat.

Perhaps he would keep Thorgils company for a while?

Then he could find a drink.

***

Jael slammed the door behind her. Biddy jumped, and so did the puppies as she stormed past them into the bedchamber and slammed that door too.

She threw herself onto the bed and screamed into a pillow, so loudly that she felt her throat burn with the strain of it. She was furious with Thorgils, annoyed with Eadmund, ready to kill Tarak, and completely fed up with Fyn.

Pushing her face into the pillow, Jael screamed again.

Her body went limp then, and she rolled over, staring up at the rafters, wishing she was under the blue lights of Eskild's Cave, deep in that hot water. Wrapping herself up in a fur, Jael lay still, trying to calm down. Ivaar would be coming soon, and contrary to her appearance around Thorgils and Eadmund, she was dreading it. He was not unpleasant company, she supposed, but he was not her friend, and she couldn't relax around him. She was permanently on edge, trying to maintain a facade, lest he see her real intentions; just as she supposed he was being falsely interested in her. It was all a game, and she had never been very good at games.

Her temper and tongue always seemed to get in the way.

Jael closed her eyes, thinking about Aleksander. There was

another reason to scream. Being apart from him was torturous. She hated the fact that she couldn't just talk to him or look at him. She missed everything about him.

Sighing, she buried herself deeper into the furs, knowing that before long she would have to get up and face Ivaar.

There was a knock on the door.

'When you've finished having your little tantrum, I've filled up the tub with hot water for you, so you can come and have a bath,' Biddy called through the door.

Jael rolled out of the furs, her tension unravelling itself at speed. She may not have Aleksander, but at least she had Biddy.

And Biddy was a gift from the gods.

Jael opened the door and was instantly pounced upon by two hairy bodies, who were relieved to find that she was alright again.

'Well, come on, then, come and soak away all that rage,' Biddy grumbled, pointing her towards the back room.

Biddy had shifted the goats and chickens into the new stables once they'd been built, so the back room had been left empty, apart from their food stores and the large barrels of ale she'd brought in for Eadmund. She had recently acquired a wooden tub, and this was the first time she'd filled it up.

'Are you sure you're not a dreamer?' Jael wondered, stepping into the softly glowing room where a row of lamps burned generously in front of the tub. It felt almost warm in here; almost, but her skin still shivered as she undressed, desperate to feel her toes again.

'Ahhh, if I were a dreamer...' Biddy smiled wistfully. 'I wouldn't still be here, bathing you after all these years!'

Jael laughed, and wriggling out of her clothes, she threw them at Biddy.

There was a loud knock on the door.

'Who is that?' Biddy wondered irritably, covered in clothes.

Jael paused, one foot dangling just above the water, her face pained in despair. 'Ivaar,' she groaned. 'I forgot about Ivaar. We're going for a ride.'

'*Again?*'

Jael stood back on the stool, reaching for her clothes, her expression sour. 'Yes, again. Into that fucking cold. Again.'

'Well, at least you can come back to a hot bath,' Biddy promised her. 'I'll keep it warm for you somehow. But don't do anything silly out there. Don't forget about Eadmund, now.'

Jael frowned at her as she hurried to put her clothes back on. 'You're starting to sound like Thorgils! I haven't, and I won't. I won't forget about him, don't worry.'

'He needs our help,' Biddy reminded her.

'I know he does,' Jael sighed crossly. 'I know what we're trying to do. It was my idea in the first place! Why does everyone think I'm going to fall under Ivaar's spell?' She grabbed her cloak out of Biddy's hands and wrapped it around herself, pinning it to one shoulder. 'Can you go and open the door now? And please, stop fretting.'

Biddy gave her one last fretting look and disappeared back into the house. Jael shook her head. How was it that her friends thought her so easily manipulated? Did they truly think she was so weak?

There was nothing that Ivaar Skalleson could say or do to lure her over to his side. Not one thing.

***

'Don't you think it's time for a drink,' Eadmund panted, his body heaving as he bent over, trying not to vomit.

'You look like a drink is the last thing you need right now,' Thorgils suggested. 'Let's sit down for a bit. Then we can go again.'

Eadmund straightened up, wincing. There wasn't one part of him that didn't hurt. He was right back at the beginning again, doubting the wisdom of even trying. What was the point anyway? He wouldn't be able to keep it going.

Thorgils strode over to him, smiling encouragingly. 'Come on, don't give up. Let's just sit for a while. I'll go easier on you, I promise.'

'You're wasting your time!' Eadmund snapped, throwing his sword away in frustration. '*I'm* wasting your time! There's no point to any of this,' he sighed, rubbing his neck. 'All I'm thinking about is where I can get a drink from. I need some ale! I know I should care about swords and fighting and Ivaar, but I just don't, not right now. Not while I don't have a cup in my hand. It's all I can think about, Thorgils.' He looked up at his friend. 'There's no point in doing any of this because,' he hung his head, 'I'm always going to ruin it. I can't see any way out of this feeling. It never leaves. I can't stop!' Eadmund gritted his teeth, his eyes wild with despair.

Thorgils noticed that some of the training sessions had paused and more than a few faces were watching them with interest. 'Come on, let's get you that drink,' he said kindly. 'We don't have to do any more of this today.' He picked up Eadmund's sword, taking it to the training shed with his own. 'But don't ever think that you're wasting my time. You're my friend. We swore a blood oath to each other, don't you remember? How old were we when we made that? Eight? Nine?' he smiled wistfully. 'Sometimes I could punch you in the head, but most of the time, I just want to help you be alright again. It's been such a long time, but I don't think it's as far away as you do. Truly, I don't. You have everything you need now. It's just about getting your head right.'

As they walked off towards the hall, Thorgils realised that he was going to have to go and have words with Jael. Peace-making words. He had to get help for Eadmund, and if that meant swallowing his pride and apologising, he could try that.

Surely it wouldn't be too hard?

***

They dismounted by a frozen waterfall. It was the first one Jael had seen on Oss, and it was breathtaking: a mountainous burst of glimmering, icy shards, hanging from the cliff, waiting to be released again.

'This is one of my favourite places,' Ivaar smiled, walking towards the edge of the cliff. 'There's something so powerful about these falls. Dangerous. Free. Exhilarating. But even they are no match for Oss' winter!' He turned to look at Jael, and his eyes were full of more than just waterfalls.

Jael had been distracted on their ride, her thoughts bouncing between Eadmund and Aleksander. She'd barely noticed Ivaar at all, but now, here he was, moving too close to her again. She heard Thorgils' voice warning her that she would end up in a tangle, but she had no intention of letting him be right.

Turning quickly away from Ivaar, Jael stroked Tig's cheek, slipping him a carrot.

Ivaar stepped even closer to her then. 'Have you thought about what will happen when Eirik dies, and I become king?'

Jael was never one for stepping back, but she also didn't like physical closeness with anyone she didn't have plans to be physically close with. So far that had been everyone she'd ever met, apart from Aleksander. It seemed that Ivaar was intent on doing everything he could to change that. 'What do you mean?'

'I can break the alliance with Lothar. Grant you a divorce from Eadmund. Give you an army to help you take back the Brekkan throne, for you or your brother.'

Jael was stunned. He had spoken so casually, and quietly that she wondered if she'd heard him correctly. 'What?' She shook her head. 'Why would you do that?'

Ivaar leaned in, his lips almost touching her ear, his breath hot on her neck. 'Why wouldn't I? It's what you want, isn't it? To return to Brekka? To be rid of Lothar? I can do that for you.'

Jael moved her head back to look at him. 'And you want to make an enemy of Lothar as soon as you become the King of Oss?'

'No, I want to make a friend of *you*,' Ivaar murmured, staring into her eyes. She was uncomfortable, he could tell, and he enjoyed the feeling of power he had over her at that moment. Ivaar smiled to himself. He wanted her, desperately, to hurt Eadmund, of course, but also to satisfy his own burning need. She was beautiful, confident, strong, and everything about her excited him.

Jael's thoughts tangled themselves inside her head, just as Thorgils had predicted. She blinked, trying to regain control of herself. Ivaar had unsettled her so quickly with his closeness, and now he was promising her everything she'd wanted so desperately, and more.

But what did he want in return?

'Well, those are nice words,' she said bluntly, 'but it might take you years to become king, and by then I'll be old, and my house will be filled with Eadmund's children. What use is your offer to me, really?' Ivaar's eyes told Jael that he knew more than she did and she hated that. She had an overwhelming urge to punch him in the eye just to make him stop squinting at her in that knowing way. The thought of that made her smile, which only served to encourage Ivaar, and he stepped forward, his face bending towards hers.

It was suddenly very clear what he wanted from her in return.

'My father will not live long,' he breathed.

'Why? Are you planning on adding another victim to your collection?'

'Ha! You make me laugh. I'm not sure I've smiled this much in years. At least seven of them.' And Ivaar leaned in to kiss her.

Jael had no choice then but to back away. Abruptly. 'No! No, that is not a good idea!'

Ivaar looked puzzled, but not deterred, as he glanced around. 'Why? We're completely alone out here. Unless,' he narrowed his gaze, 'you have feelings for Eadmund. Do you?'

Jael had to think fast. 'No, not Eadmund,' she laughed. 'Someone else. Why do you think I've worked so hard to stay away from your brother? I have someone in Andala. He is waiting for me.'

'I see.' Ivaar frowned, annoyed and curious. 'What's his name?'

'His name?' Jael squirmed, wondering how far she was going to walk down this icy road. But then again, she knew Aleksander; he would be able to protect himself, no matter what trouble she unwittingly sent his way. 'His name is Aleksander Lehr.' Her eyes filled with sadness. She had not spoken his name aloud in such a long time.

'I see.' Ivaar's voice was clipped now. 'I've heard of him. The two of you used to fight together, didn't you?'

Tig shook his head impatiently, hitting Jael's shoulder, bumping her towards Ivaar. 'We did, yes. We grew up together, trained together. We were inseparable until your father brought me here.'

'You're very loyal,' Ivaar said tightly, his mind whirring. She was not to be moved, not yet it seemed. He would have to find another way to get her to succumb.

'Of course,' Jael insisted strongly, although inside she felt anything but. 'We made an oath to each other. We love each other. We should have married, but we saw no need, which was our downfall, of course, when Lothar and your father decided to make peace. I'm only here until I can figure out a way to get home, back to Aleksander.' The words felt so strange on her tongue that she wondered if she believed them anymore.

She hoped her face looked more convincing.

Ivaar considered her quietly. He backed away and threw Leada's reins onto her back, climbing into the saddle. 'My offer stands, Jael,' he decided at last. 'As I said, my father will not live long. And when he dies, I will grant you a divorce, set you free from Eadmund, and you can go back to Brekka to be with this Aleksander. Lothar Furyck is an idiot from what I hear, so I'd much rather have an alliance with you than him, or his son, who appears to be an even bigger fool.'

Jael was unsettled, not expecting that. She threw herself up into Tig's saddle, gathering the reins in her frozen hands, a sharp crease forming between her eyebrows. 'Why do you think your father will die soon?' she wondered as Tig skittered about underneath her. 'Who told you that?'

Ivaar turned Leada around, bringing her alongside Jael. 'I have a dreamer,' he said quietly. 'She saw us coming back here, and she's seen Eirik's death very clearly. He will die quite soon. He will not last another year.'

CHAPTER THIRTY EIGHT

Aleksander had waited. Patiently. But now his curiosity was itching so loudly inside his head that he couldn't give her any more time. He simply had to find out what had happened.

'Edela! Wait!' Aleksander raced to catch up with her as she hurried down the street. A storm was brewing, and he could taste it on his lips. Soon there would be rain, and perhaps thunder and lightning. He looked up, and the sky glared back down at him, its threatening clouds dropping lower and lower over Tuura's high reaching walls.

Edela turned around, sighing as Aleksander ran towards her. She had hoped for some more time alone. Her talk with Neva had unsettled her so much that she was afraid of saying anything to anyone. She had not breathed a word about it, despite all the expectant looks she had been plagued with since returning from the temple.

Edela knew that she could trust Branwyn and Kormac, and certainly Aleksander, but still, what little Neva had revealed to her would worry him. He would want to head back to Andala immediately and find a way to Oss, but there wasn't any way across that frozen sea, and she knew that, so they would have to wait. Wait and know that Jael was in danger and they could do nothing to help her.

Not yet.

Edela frowned in frustration. She felt as though she was

always reaching for more information. She never seemed to have quite enough.

'Where are you going?' Aleksander slid to a stop beside her, his trousers wet to the knee.

Edela looked uneasy. 'I thought I would visit my friend Alaric again,' she muttered. 'He seems very lonely. I thought he might like some company.'

Aleksander stared at her, wanting her to look at him, to notice he was there. Edela had seemed so far away since her visit to the temple. As though she didn't hear or see him anymore. He reached out, touching her arm. 'We need to talk, don't we? About what happened? I've been as patient as I can, but Edela... I need to know.'

Edela hesitated. She wasn't afraid of Neva or the elders. She hadn't avoided Aleksander for that reason. It was just that every step they took together seemed to take him further away from Jael, and he blamed her for all of it.

She didn't want to hurt him again.

The sky rumbled, and they both looked up anxiously.

'Let's stand over there. You can tell me quickly before the rain comes.' Aleksander grabbed Edela's elbow, guiding her across the street, wading through the snow, around a flock of sheep being quickly shepherded home. 'We can't go back to the house. It's full of people.'

'I know, why do you think I left!' Edela grumbled.

'What did you find out that you're afraid to say?' Aleksander asked as they huddled beneath the drooping porch of a small cottage. 'You have me thinking every sort of dark thing imaginable.'

'I didn't find out enough,' Edela said, frowning, cross with herself. 'But hopefully, there will be more to learn soon.'

Aleksander glanced around as lightning streaked through the darkening sky. 'Did you find out about the sword or the prophecy?'

Edela shook her head. 'They don't want me to know about

either of those things. We didn't speak of them. Not really.' She took a deep breath and braved those sad dark-brown eyes. 'The elder I spoke to knew about Eadmund. She told me that he was meant to be with Jael, just as the sword was meant to be with her. That it was important they were together.'

Aleksander froze.

How could he have expected anything else?

Everyone wanted to take Jael away from him, it seemed. There wasn't a single soul on his side, apart from the Widow, he supposed, unless she had just been playing a game with him? 'I see. Well, that's not a surprise, is it? Can he help keep her safe?'

Edela looked extremely doubtful, her mouth opening and closing while she thought on it, remembering her last glimpse of Eadmund Skalleson swaying on the beach. 'Well, that depends on whether Jael has managed to get the tincture into him. He certainly couldn't if he's in the state he was in when I was there. But I don't know if she would want to help him, and if that's the case, no, Eadmund will be of no use to her.'

The clouds opened up, and rain teemed down, suddenly and violently. More thunder followed. They were under the narrowest of ledges, and icy shards of rain found them quickly.

'We should go!' Aleksander called over the noise, grabbing Edela's hand.

'No, wait, listen to me!' she said urgently. 'Jael needs our help. That is what I learned above all things. She's in danger. The girl I saw, she is trying to kill Jael. *Will* try to kill her. Her mother knows dark magic. We have to get to Oss as soon as the Thaw comes.'

Aleksander frowned, his body tensing. 'But will that be enough time? What if something happens before then? Spring is months away!'

Edela shook her head. 'The elder, Neva, she said that the girl was not on Oss. That she would not be back for a while. We have time.'

The rain was soaking them now, and Aleksander could see

Edela's body shaking in the glare of another bolt of lightning. 'Come on, let's get back to the house. You can go and visit your friend tomorrow.'

Edela nodded, cringing beneath the fury of the storm.

Aleksander pulled her along as fast as he could, trying to ignore the tightness in his chest. The elders were confident that there was enough time for them to get to Oss and help Jael, but what if they were wrong?

***

Jael grumbled as she hurried to get undressed for the second time. She was colder than ever and more unsettled. Her limbs shook, and her head was a mess. She hadn't said a word to Biddy about any of it since she'd arrived back. She was in no mood for a lecture. Her mind had been solely focused on getting into the hot water as quickly as possible, hoping its soothing warmth would clear her mind. She wished she could talk to Edela; to have her peer into the future and forge a clear path for her.

At the moment everything was suddenly fog-heavy.

Jael hopped up on the stool, dipping one foot into the water. Biddy had managed to keep it warm! She smiled and sunk her whole foot in, hopping over the side of the tub and standing in the water, letting her body acclimatise. It was so used to being permanently frozen that the heat came as a shock to her numb limbs. She sat down, closing her eyes, leaning her head against the back of the wooden tub, enjoying the sensation of the water as it lapped around her neck.

And then a knock on the door.

Jael's eyes burst open.

Biddy popped her head into the room, eyebrows raised. 'Who could that be?'

'Well, whoever it is, *you* can talk to them! I'm not getting out!' And Jael slipped further under the water, letting its wet warmth wrap around every part of her. She kept one ear out, though, wondering who their visitor was. She hoped it wasn't Ivaar; she'd had enough of him and his hot breath for one day.

'Hello, Biddy.'

Jael sat up immediately. She knew that voice.

It was Thorgils.

***

Eydis looked forlorn as she wandered through the square, her long stick disappearing into the snow as she walked, her ears soaking up all the sounds around her. It was a quiet day in the fort, it seemed. Nothing stood out as interesting or unusual. Warriors were training in the Pit, smoky, cooking smells blew towards her from Ketil's fire, and she could hear the general hum of the Osslanders working steadily away at their daily tasks. But still, Eydis could sense an uneasiness, or perhaps that was just within her?

She hadn't spoken to Eadmund in days, and every time she was around Jael, Ivaar seemed to be there too. She could hear how intrigued he was by her and that worried Eydis. More so because of the dreams she'd been having about Ivaar and Jael recently, and what they would mean for Eadmund and Oss.

Eydis stilled suddenly, hearing footsteps close behind her, smelling an unfamiliar, feminine scent. She turned around quickly, anxiously. 'Who's there?' she called, blinking rapidly.

'My name is Ayla,' the woman smiled, edging towards her. 'I thought I would seek you out, Eydis. Your brother Ivaar told me about you. I'm a dreamer, like you. His dreamer. There are not many of us that I know of, on any of the islands,' she said sadly.

'It would be nice to speak to you, I think. Perhaps for both of us?'

Eydis stilled, her face clouded with uncertainty. Ayla's voice did not disturb her greatly, and she heard no threat in it, but she was Ivaar's dreamer, and that was enough to put Eydis on edge. Still, she had not met many dreamers in her life, and her desire for more knowledge piqued her curiosity. 'Yes, alright,' Eydis said cautiously. It was so hard when she couldn't look people in the eye and assess their true intentions. She could tell much by a voice and by the sounds a body made when it spoke, but she was always filled with longing to stare into someone's eyes. To see right into their soul.

'Perhaps we could walk?' Ayla suggested gently. 'I could take your hand?' Eydis nodded, and Ayla reached out for the little gloved hand, leading her through the square. 'Ivaar tells me that your mother was a dreamer. Have you been to Tuura yourself?'

'Tuura? No, I haven't.' Eydis couldn't keep the disappointment out of her voice.

'So, no one has taught you about your dreams?'

'No, my mother died when I was small, before I had any.' Eydis ducked her head. 'I haven't been having dreams for that long. They do not come all the time.'

'No, you are too young for that,' Ayla smiled. 'But soon, as you grow older, they will become more and more urgent. Soon you will dream constantly. The gods have chosen us to help people, to advise them, warn them, comfort them... so many things.'

They walked for a while, Ayla's words hanging in the air between them. Eydis tried to paint a picture of her. She imagined her to be her mother's age; her voice was certainly young enough to be so. She was of medium build, Eydis decided, as her footsteps had weight to them, but not too much. Her voice was not too far away from her, so she wasn't that tall, and she appeared to walk easily enough. 'But how did you end up with Ivaar?' Eydis wondered suddenly. 'On Kalfa? So far away from Tuura?'

Ayla stumbled, her boots slipping on a patch of ice. 'Well, I... I fell in love with a merchant. I left Tuura with him, and we were married. I sailed everywhere with him. And on one voyage he took me to Kalfa and we... never left.'

Ayla gripped Eydis' hand tightly as she led her down a back alley, away from any prying eyes or ears.

Eydis suddenly noticed the lack of noise. 'Where are we going?' She felt the air cool around her. There were boards under her feet now.

'I just thought, perhaps we could talk more easily if we were alone.'

Eydis stopped, dropping Ayla's hand, her eyes darting about uselessly. 'Why? What is it that you really want from me?'

Ayla glanced awkwardly around herself. They were standing close together, between two narrow rows of houses. It was not as private as she'd hoped, so she lowered her voice. 'I want nothing from you, Eydis.' She ran a hand through her loose dark curls which fell well past her shoulders towards her waist. 'I had a dream. I wanted to share it with you, in case it was something you hadn't seen for yourself.'

'What dream? What have you seen?' Eydis asked quietly, swallowing hard.

'About your father. I have seen his death. He does not have long.' Ayla looked down at the girl who stood shaking in front of her. 'I don't mean to scare you, but I didn't want anyone to overhear. I thought that you should know.'

Eydis didn't know how to feel. She too had dreamed that her father would die soon, but part of her had always hoped to be proven wrong; that further dreams would come eventually to contradict her first. But now, this was a confirmation of all her fears. She felt her heart breaking with the knowledge that soon, she would become an orphan. 'I understand,' Eydis sighed. 'I have seen it too. My father knows all about it. I have warned him.'

'I'm glad,' Ayla said with relief. 'Glad that he knows and can prepare things for Oss, and the islands. And you.'

Eydis was confused by this woman. She was with Ivaar, which made her an enemy, despite her clumsy attempt at friendship. But perhaps she had more information? Perhaps she had seen more than Eydis herself had? 'How will he die? That I don't know.'

'I've not seen his death,' Ayla said thoughtfully. 'I have only seen his funeral pyre and the ceremony with it. I have seen Ivaar as king, here on Oss. How it all unfolds or is connected, I don't know. But it will not be long. I have seen you there, and you are not much older than this.'

Eydis shuddered. It was well into the afternoon now, and the air felt ice-tipped. Darkness would fall soon, and Eydis felt an overwhelming need to be back at the hall. She wanted to be alone, to think, to try and understand what Ayla's presence meant. To decide whether she could trust her.

'Shall I help you back to the hall?' Ayla wondered softly. 'I've upset you, and you look very cold.'

'Thank you, yes,' Eydis nodded quickly. 'I'd like to go back to my father.'

Grasping her hand, Ayla turned Eydis around, leading her back down the street and out into the brighter light of the square, her mind jumbled with nerves. Ivaar had ordered her to befriend his little sister, to earn Eydis' trust so that she could ply her for any information that would serve his needs.

But Ayla saw more than Ivaar realised. More than she had told Eydis, and now she found herself caught between needing to obey her master, and a strong desire to help a fellow dreamer.

***

Thorgils' voice was low as he spoke with Biddy. Too low. Jael tried to make out what they were muttering about, but it was impossible. As eager as she was to find out, though, she was in no hurry to get out of her long-awaited bath. 'You may as well come in here if you've got something to say!' she called out crossly from her tub.

Thorgils blinked, glancing at Biddy, who had been in the middle of trying to convince him to come back later. She shrugged, pointing to the doorway at the back of the house. Thorgils looked uncertain, but he wandered towards it anyway, poking his head into the dimly lit room.

Jael sat there in a high-walled wooden tub, only her head visible. She turned to look at him with a frown. 'What do you want, then?' Her voice was sharp and not at all forgiving, which was unfortunate since forgiveness is what Thorgils had come seeking.

He looked around for a stool, not wanting to stand there, peering over the edge of the tub, no matter how dark the room was or how submerged Jael appeared. He felt awkward enough already.

There was nothing suitable to take his great weight, so he disappeared into the house and came back with a stool, which he promptly plonked near the tub. 'I want to talk about Eadmund.'

Jael lifted an eyebrow. 'Why? What's happened?'

'To Eadmund?' Thorgils sighed. 'Well, before all of this between us,' he waved his hands about, 'we were going to help him. With your tincture. Remember? But then...' He couldn't look at her. He was no good at apologies, and he didn't really believe he should apologise anyway, it being all her fault. 'Eadmund's in a bad way. He needs our help. Now.'

Jael frowned. That was hardly an apology, and he owed her an apology.

As for Eadmund... after her ride with Ivaar, she didn't know how she felt or what she wanted to do about Eadmund.

Thorgils sensed her hesitation. 'Have you changed your mind about helping him?' He narrowed his eyes, glaring at her. 'Has Ivaar changed your mind for you?'

Jael's eyes flared angrily.

There they were, back in that place again!

She ignored the fact that he had a point and turned around to attack him, all the frustrations she'd been stowing away, spitting out of her mouth. 'Ivaar? Ivaar! Why do you think I'm such a willing victim to Ivaar? I don't understand it. How can you and I be friends when you think so little of me? *Still!*'

'You didn't rush to help Eadmund then, did you? I saw it on your face, the hesitation. It wasn't there a few days ago, but it is now. And that's Ivaar. That's what he does. I've seen it!' Thorgils' face was a mass of frothing anger. 'He's like a blood-sucking tick, crawling under your skin, taking what he wants. He does it to everyone. He gets his way, every time.' Thorgils shook his head in frustration. 'You're my friend, Jael, and I don't think you're a willing victim at all, but there are ways Ivaar can play with you. Things he can use against you, and he has, I can see it in your eyes. You've changed! Something's changed!' Thorgils stood and paced the room, suddenly not caring what he saw in the tub.

Jael simmered, wishing he'd go away. She'd missed his company more than she'd admit but not his judgement. He could go and take that with him. She turned away from him, staring straight ahead.

She had nothing more to say.

Thorgils ran both hands through his hair, pressing his fingers against his forehead. This was not going well. He needed a white banner. They had to make a truce.

Eadmund needed them to.

'I'm sorry,' he muttered, reluctantly pushing the words out of his mouth.

'What?'

'I'm sorry. I don't want to fight with you, not because of Ivaar anyway. There are better things to fight about than that nothing.' He grabbed the stool and brought it closer to the tub, sitting down again. 'Eadmund needs that tincture. If you don't want to help him, then give it to me, and I'll do it on my own.' Again he saw her reluctance, and it worried him. Ivaar had her. He had something over her. Thorgils could smell the stink of it.

Jael turned to him. 'Biddy has it. You can get it from her on your way out.'

Her voice was bitter, and Thorgils shuddered from the chill in it. There was no forgiveness to be found here, he realised. Not today. 'Thank you.' He got up and left the room, wishing he could say something more, but knowing that there was no point. Not now. Jael had gone far away from him, and Eadmund.

Jael watched Thorgils leave and did nothing.

Inside she was screaming at him to stop and come back, wanting to help Eadmund with him, but she couldn't. Because Ivaar was offering her Aleksander.

And Jael loved Aleksander.

CHAPTER THIRTY NINE

The storm that had blown through in the night lingered the next morning, so there was no riding to Fyn's, and thankfully, no riding with Ivaar. Jael couldn't face him again, not until she had her head in order, and currently it was a scattered mess.

She'd spent the night revisiting her conversations with Thorgils, Ivaar, Aleksander, and Eadmund, and even now, as she sat by the fire with Biddy, listening to the wind battle the rain outside the house, she had no idea what she thought. She wondered if Thorgils was with Eadmund, and felt guilty because she wasn't.

Biddy handed her a hotcake, fresh off the skillet. 'Careful,' she warned. 'You'll burn your tongue.'

Jael blinked, bringing herself back into the room. She looked down at her fingernails, which she'd gnawed to nothing since yesterday, then up at Biddy who was staring at her with concern in her eyes. She closed her own eyes and sighed.

'Well, I could pretend not to notice that something's wrong,' Biddy said matter-of-factly. 'But I've never been very good at pretending. Much like you.' She looked at Jael's lost face. 'Tell me what happened. On the ride with Ivaar. It might help.'

Jael couldn't meet Biddy's eyes, and she didn't want to say anything. Not yet. 'I think I'll go and see Eydis,' she decided suddenly.

'In *this* weather?'

'Mmmm, I think Eydis would probably like to escape that hall for a while and visit the puppies, don't you think?' She didn't wait for an answer, though, grabbing her boots, pulling them on. 'I haven't spoken to her in days. It will be nice to see her.' Jael wrapped her cloak around her shoulders, not bothering to pin it, and pulled up her hood. 'Perhaps you could heat up some milk? Eydis would like that,' she mumbled distractedly as she headed to the door, slipping out before the puppies had a chance to escape with her.

***

It was hard trying to help someone you couldn't find, Thorgils grumbled to himself as he trudged through the storm. He'd had the tincture in his pocket since yesterday, but there had been no sign of Eadmund. He wasn't sure that Eadmund was even avoiding him, he just tended to wander about whenever he was drunk, and at the moment, that was constantly.

Thorgils was crossing the square, heading back towards Eadmund's cottage when he saw Jael walking up the steps to the hall. She didn't notice him as she pulled on a door and disappeared inside. Perhaps she was going to see Ivaar? He frowned, anger pulsing at his temples. She was a strong woman, and he had no doubt that she could defeat Ivaar in a sword fight, but Ivaar had other weapons at his disposal. He knew how to manipulate people's thoughts, twist them, turn them, use their weaknesses against them.

Thorgils sighed, trying to imagine what Ivaar was doing with Jael.

To Jael.

Why had she been so different yesterday? He'd never seen her look so cold.

Thorgils shook his head, trying to get the freezing rain out of his eyes as he turned his face away from the dark doors of the hall. He hoped that whatever temptations Ivaar was laying out for Jael, she would find a way to see the lies in them and come back to him. And Eadmund.

They needed her.

***

'I didn't expect to see anyone today!' Ivaar smiled at Jael, who had stopped to shake herself by a fire. He glanced back to where Isaura and Eydis sat, playing with the children. 'But I'm glad for the company,' he sighed. 'Even my father has taken himself away from the constant prattling and whining of that lot.'

'Well, perhaps you should do the same, for I'm not staying. I just came to get Eydis.'

Eydis lifted her head towards Jael, her eyes suddenly bright.

'Eydis?' Ivaar looked both surprised and annoyed.

'Yes,' Jael said loudly. 'I promised her a visit with the puppies today.'

'In *this* weather?' Ivaar scoffed.

'Well, we don't plan to play outside!' Jael laughed as she walked over to Eydis. 'I'll go and get your cloak and then we can go. Biddy has some milk and hotcakes waiting for you.' She headed for Eydis' bedchamber without waiting for a reply.

Ivaar stared after her, puzzled. Isaura dropped her head, trying to stop the smirk that was threatening her face. It made a pleasant change to watch Ivaar twist and turn.

Jael was back quickly, in no mood for conversation as she wrapped Eydis up in her cloak, helping her on with her gloves. 'I'll bring her back this afternoon before it gets dark,' Jael said firmly, slipping her arm through Eydis'. 'In case Eirik wonders where she's gone.'

'Have a nice time!' Isaura called out cheerfully from the floor as her children clambered all over her.

Ivaar scowled at his wife's happy face, before turning to watch Jael and Eydis hurry towards the doors. He frowned. Yesterday he'd felt confident that he had hooked Jael with his tasty bait, but now? She'd barely even looked at him, and as for taking Eydis to her house... what was that for?

Ivaar glanced at his father's throne, which sat empty, tempting him with the promise of what was to come. But it was all too far away for his liking. Still too up in the air. He shook his head, trying to release the frustration that was building like a storm. He had no fear of Eadmund, or Thorgils, or any of their idiot friends.

But Jael?

If he didn't get her onside, she was going to cause him problems, he could feel it. He would have to speak to Ayla. She needed to find a way into Eydis' confidence and quickly. He had to find out what was going on with Jael.

***

Eydis sipped her warm milk, relieved to be away from the hall. She loved spending time with Isaura and the children, but the feeling of Ivaar prowling around in the background left her in a constant state of anxiety.

'Are you sure you're warm enough?' Biddy fussed. 'I can throw another log on to heat the fire up a bit more?'

'No, I'm fine, I promise,' Eydis smiled. She reached out with her empty cup, not knowing where to place it. Biddy grabbed it from her quickly and took it to the kitchen.

Jael lifted Vella onto Eydis' knee. 'Here, she's just small enough to fit on there, maybe for the last time.'

'Oh,' Eydis laughed as her knees sunk with the weight of the fluffy lump. 'She is getting bigger, isn't she?'

Eydis looked sad, Jael thought, despite the sweet smile on her face. 'How has it been in the hall with so many children?'

'Oh, it's been very noisy!' Eydis laughed. 'But they are good company when they're not crying and moaning. Isaura is too. But Ivaar...'

Biddy came back to sit by the fire, giving Jael a pointed look. Jael frowned it away, turning her face towards Eydis, listening.

'He has a dreamer, you know,' Eydis said, her eyes suddenly filled with fear. 'I didn't know that before yesterday, but she came and found me while I was out walking. She took me down an alley, told me things about my father that only I knew. I'm not sure why she did that, really. I don't know what to think of her. She's Ivaar's dreamer, so I don't think I should trust her.'

Jael's eyes met Biddy's as she leaned forward, concerned. 'What things about your father?'

Eydis sighed, her eyes quickly brimming with tears. 'That he will die soon.'

'Oh.' Jael didn't know what to say. Ivaar had implied as much, but still, she felt unexpectedly sad. 'How soon?'

'Before I am much older. I don't know when exactly, but it does not feel far away at all now,' she said miserably, tears running down her face. 'And then, what will happen to me? I won't have a mother or a father anymore. I'll be completely alone!' Her bottom lip wobbled anxiously.

Jael put her arm around the sobbing girl, pulling her close. 'Eydis, Eydis, you won't be alone. You'll have Eadmund. He will take care of you, and you'll have me, and Thorgils. Biddy too.'

Eydis pulled back, sniffing. 'But I won't, I won't, don't you see what is coming? Can't you see what he'll do?'

'You mean Ivaar?'

'Yes, Ivaar! I think you're friends with him now and maybe that will save you, I'm not sure, but Ivaar will kill Eadmund as soon as he can. As soon as my father is burning on his pyre, he will kill Eadmund and Thorgils, all their friends, anyone loyal to Eadmund. He will take their heads. All of them! And then, what will happen to me? What will he do with me when he has his own dreamer? When he has no need for me? No need for a useless blind girl?' She cried so loudly that Vella jumped off her knee in fright.

Jael didn't know what to say.

Everything Eydis said made sense. Ivaar would certainly want revenge for all the years he'd been banished, and before, when Eirik had chosen Eadmund over him. He couldn't rule as king when most of the people didn't want him. Not until he'd removed Eadmund's loyal followers, and then, Eadmund himself.

And what would he do with Eydis when there was no one left to protect her?

Eydis sniffed, wishing she could see Jael, wanting to know how she felt about all of it. Jael wasn't speaking, though, and that worried her.

Biddy handed Eydis a cloth, shooting Jael a look that said nothing Jael wanted to hear.

'Have you dreamed all of this?' Jael wondered, listening to the fire spitting and hissing under the steady stream of rain dripping down the smoke hole.

'Yes,' Eydis sighed, blowing her nose. 'But it's so muddled now. I can't see what it all means. It's a handful of pieces, and I'm not sure how to put them all together. In my dreams, my father is dead, and Ivaar is the king, and he kills Eadmund and Thorgils.'

Jael frowned. 'And what about me? Do you see me in your dreams?'

'No. Not anymore,' she said sadly. 'I used to, but not anymore.'

Jael felt a sick feeling building inside her stomach. She glanced towards the fire, imagining her father's face in the flames, but it was unreadable. She couldn't hear his voice as she always did when she didn't know what to do. He would want her to take Ivaar's offer, though, wouldn't he? To go back to Brekka, put Axl on the throne? He would urge her to do what was right for Brekka above all things; demand it of her, she was certain. It would be a way for her to repay the mistake she'd made when she didn't challenge Lothar for the crown after his death.

Brekka was important. She was a Furyck.

It was her responsibility to care for their people.

She sighed, looking at Eydis, who seemed so very helpless and lost.

And then, of course, there was Aleksander...

Jael put her fingers up to her mouth to chew on a nail but realised that there was nothing left.

***

'What a day!' Alaric laughed to himself as he bustled around, preparing cups of small ale. It was all he could afford to give his guests; the ale part of it being much smaller than most would expect. 'I've not seen weather this fierce in many a year.'

Aleksander barely smiled as he glanced at Edela. She had brought them here in search of more information, but looking around this sparse little hut and at this frail little man, he wondered about their chances.

'It certainly reminds me of how troublesome the winters can be up here,' Edela smiled. 'And how cold. I've had too many years living a soft life in Brekka, it seems because I haven't stopped shaking since we arrived!'

Alaric smiled nervously as he handed out the cups. He had no food to offer his guests, and he felt embarrassed by the lack of it. The few stores he had left had to see him through winter, yet what he was still living for, he did wonder at times. Every year brought with it more aches and ailments, and an ever decreasing amount of joy, especially since he'd left the temple.

At least he had a fire today, Edela thought as she took her cup. She felt sorry for Alaric and wondered how things had gone so terribly wrong for him. As a scribe, surely he would have earned enough coins to be living a richer life than this?

'I went to the temple yesterday,' Edela murmured to her old friend as he came to sit beside her on his bed.

Alaric's face paled. 'Did you now?' he mumbled nervously, his breath coming in short, white bursts.

'I saw Neva Elgard, which was a surprise. I didn't know she had become an elder.'

'Neva...' Alaric's face relaxed some. 'She is a good woman. I'm glad it was her you spoke to and not Marcus.'

'Who's Marcus?' Aleksander asked with a frown. He'd heard that name mentioned a few times now and no one seemed to like the man.

'He's the elderman, remember?' Edela said patiently. 'He has a reputation for being...'

'Firm?' Alaric suggested.

'Yes, firm is a good word,' Edela smiled. 'Although, perhaps it is a little soft to describe his true nature, from what I hear.'

'But you saw Neva, so perhaps there is no need to see him?' Aleksander suggested, worried for Edela.

'Yes, yes, Marcus is not someone you will see unless you end up causing problems,' Alaric warned. 'Then you will wish you had never come here at all.'

Edela could sense Aleksander's unease, but they needed to know more, whatever the consequences. 'Do you remember what happened to my family when they came here all those years ago?' she asked, turning to Alaric.

He looked puzzled for a moment, then disturbed by her question as the memories of that night revealed themselves. 'Yes, I do. That was a terrible, tragic night, wasn't it?' He shifted about uneasily, sensing that Edela was only just starting to divulge the real reason for their visit.

'Aleksander lost his mother and father that night.'

'Oh.' Alaric's eyes bulged with surprise. 'I'm very sorry for you,' he murmured uncomfortably, glancing towards the solemn-looking man.

'Thank you,' was all Aleksander could manage. He knew they needed information, but he had no desire to talk about that night.

'Yes, his father was killed trying to protect Gisila and the children. It has been hard for him to come back here, to the place that orphaned him.'

'I see. Of course,' Alaric muttered.

'But we had to come for my granddaughter, Jael, because of the danger she is in now.'

One wild, snowy eyebrow shot up at the mention of that name.

Alaric didn't look surprised, Edela thought. She studied his face. They had been so very close once, and if her memory held true, he knew more than he was prepared to reveal. But she had no plans to leave until he did. 'Why did those raiders come that night? Do you know?' she asked him directly. 'Were they looking for something?'

Alaric took a quick sip of small ale, his face puckering at the insipid taste. 'Edela...' He shook his head. 'There are things the elders... they don't take well to having their secrets discussed. You know that.'

'Alaric, please. Jael is in grave danger. Neva confirmed it to me, and we are trying to help her,' she sighed. 'Neva didn't reveal much, but if you know anything that could help, you must share it with me, please, Alaric. Please.'

'About that night?' Alaric saw the determination in Edela's eyes, and he felt defeated. It had always been impossible to refuse her. 'Yes. They were looking for something, yes, well... someone.'

Edela and Aleksander leaned forward. They hadn't been expecting that.

Alaric hesitated, then sighed. 'They were looking for your granddaughter. But they got the wrong one.'

Edela gasped loudly, her mouth hanging open in shock. She could feel the tears coming then, remembering how it been that night when those men had burst into their cottage. There had been three of them. She remembered it so clearly. They were so large and fast. They'd knocked down the door and ripped her granddaughter out of her mother's arms. But it wasn't Jael. It was Evva, Branwyn's daughter by her first husband. She was Jael's age, and they took her quickly, their swords flying around the cottage, threatening anyone who tried to stop them, but it was a house filled with women and children, and no one could do anything. Gant and his men had rushed in, but they were too late. One of the hooded warriors had held Evva up by her hair. Gant had lunged for him, but the hooded man had slit Evva's little throat as Branwyn and Edela begged and screamed, and the swords clashed all around them.

Edela blinked, tears running down her face, trying to drive the blood-splattered memory from her mind. They thought they'd killed Jael, she realised, and everything else that had happened was a way to cover it all up.

But they hadn't.

When had they realised that?

Aleksander felt lost. 'Do you mean your other granddaughter? They thought she was Jael? That's why she died?'

Alaric nodded solemnly, patting Edela's arm.

'How did the elders know that the men were looking for Jael?' Edela's voice was barely a whisper.

'How do they know anything?' Alaric sighed. 'A dreamer told them. I don't know who it was. I did overhear a conversation in the temple the next day, but it was all so muffled. They spoke about being relieved that Jael was safe. That the raiders had made a mistake. But they were worried. They didn't know how someone had found out about her. About how important she was. They said that someone would have to tell Ranuf Furyck. That it was time he knew so he could try to protect her. They said that she would never be safe again.'

***

Eydis had calmed down now, and she was curled up in Eadmund's chair, stroking a snoring Ido, her eyes swollen and red-rimmed.

'I'll go and talk to this dreamer of Ivaar's. Tell her to stay away from you,' Jael said firmly, chewing things over. The storm had retreated, along with Eydis' tears, and the house felt much quieter now.

'Thank you, Jael,' Eydis smiled gratefully. 'You'll be able to see what you think of her. She sounded kind, I thought, but when she led me away like that, the things she said...' Eydis shuddered. 'I wasn't sure what to think after that.'

'But she knew about your father, so Ivaar knows he's going to die,' Biddy murmured.

'Yes, which is why he sounds so happy. He knows that no matter what happens, he'll be the king here soon.'

'What do you mean, no matter what happens?' Jael wondered.

'Well, even if my father changed his mind and made Eadmund his heir again, Ivaar knows that he could come back and defeat Eadmund easily. That he'll rule here either way,' she sighed. 'There is little hope in Eadmund being strong enough to defeat him, is there?'

Jael thought on that. 'Does Ivaar have a large enough army to do that?'

'On Kalfa?' Eydis frowned. 'No. It is a small island, but he will likely get support from the other islands once my father dies. Eadmund has done nothing to win any of their respect, not for years. But Ivaar has Tarak and Tarak has a lot of loyal followers here.'

Jael reached down, picking up Vella. She wanted to go to bed and find Edela waiting for her in a dream with a calm face and a steady stream of advice. Her head was a swirling storm of dark clouds, and she couldn't make sense of any of it. 'How is your father going to die?' Jael asked gently.

'I've been trying to dream on that, but I don't see anything at all,' Eydis sighed. 'He keeps asking me to see if the invasion of Hest is a good idea. But I can't. I can't see anything about it.' She paused. 'Maybe it's because he dies before it happens? Maybe it never happens at all? Or maybe he dies in it? I don't know. I don't want to think about it at all.' Tears threatened her eyes again. 'It makes me feel so helpless. So sad. I don't want him to die. I don't want to be alone.'

Jael's eyes were full of sympathy as she glanced at Biddy.

Biddy's eyes were full of questions as she looked at Jael.

But despite what Eydis had said, she still had no answers. Not yet.

***

Eadmund had waited out the storm in a ramshackle hut on the outskirts of the fort. It was an abandoned heap of sticks, ready to fall down, but Eadmund often took his chances there, just for a night or two. He knew that Thorgils would have been looking for him and his shoulders were heavy with the guilt of that. His friend deserved better than a life spent chasing after him.

The rain had stopped, and the wind had retreated to just a whimper, but the ground was slippery with ice, hard for a mostly drunk man to navigate, especially in the near-dark. He tiptoed cautiously through the square on the way to his cottage, convinced that he'd stored a few jugs of ale there. There was barely a hint of moon, though, and it was slow going; every few steps resulting in another heart-stopping slip.

Eadmund looked up as a hall door creaked open. One of the doors had always had a loud and distinctive squeal that nobody had been able to silence in all the years since Eirik had replaced them, no matter how much fish oil or sheep fat he'd ordered rubbed onto its hinges. Eadmund smiled to himself. The sound was so familiar that he didn't even notice it, except now when everything else around him was shrouded in a bone-chilling silence.

He turned to see who was leaving the hall and froze.

Despite the darkness, he could tell that it was Jael. He couldn't help but watch her, his white breath swirling around him as he stood there in the silence. Her head was down, and he was far enough away so that she wouldn't see him, he was certain. He stayed still and watched, a wistful smile on his face as she walked... straight into Tarak.

CHAPTER FORTY

'Ahhh, my favourite Brekkan whore!' Tarak boomed, loud enough for anyone to hear, if there had been anyone around. 'Been plying your trade inside? Looking to tempt Ivaar again with your sagging tits and your dried-up cunt?'

Jael frowned. She was in no mood to be clever with Tarak. She was far too confused to think clearly at all. 'From what I know about you, Tarak,' she spat coldly, 'you'd be far more interested in tempting Ivaar than I'd ever be.'

Tarak glared down at her, anger spiking in his pitch-black eyes.

Jael didn't back away, nor did she try to move around him.

'What do you think you know about me?' he growled, leaning into her, his voice much quieter now.

'About you?' she asked with wide-eyed innocence. 'Much more than you'd want Eirik to know, and certainly more than Ivaar would be happy to hear about, I'm sure.' Somehow, Jael managed to grab hold of her tongue, just before everything she'd promised Fyn she wouldn't say, tumbled out of her mouth.

Tarak peered at her. He needed to find out what she knew, or at least, he needed to shut her up before she said anything that would weaken his position with Ivaar, for Ivaar would soon be the King of Oss, and Tarak was first in line to become his most trusted advisor. 'You should think hard on whether you've got the balls to play this game, whore,' he hissed through bared teeth, 'because between you and I, there'll only ever be one winner.' And slamming his hands forward, he shoved her in the chest. There was no traction, nothing for her boots to grip onto, and Jael flew through the air, landing on her back, her head banging onto the hard ice with a loud crack.

Tarak laughed as he pulled open the hall door, quickly glancing around to check that no one was watching before disappearing inside.

Jael lay on the ice, feeling her cheeks burn with embarrassment. The pain in her head was overwhelming, but all she could feel at that moment was the shame of being knocked down so easily by that grinning turd. She sighed as she lay there, grimacing as everything started throbbing, staring up at the starless night sky. And then she smiled as a few flurries of snow drifted down towards her. Better to let Tarak think she was easy to defeat, Jael decided.

There was plenty of time to take her revenge.

'Do you need some help down there?'

Eadmund leaned over and stuck out a hand. He blinked uncertainly into her eyes, wondering if she was alright.

'I might,' Jael croaked, reaching up to grasp hold of him. She felt the friction in his touch as their eyes met, groaning loudly as she stood, listening to the clicking and cracking in her back and hips as they protested the shock of the fall.

Eadmund winced in sympathy. 'That doesn't sound good.'

Jael hung her head for a moment, gritting her teeth. 'At least it was dark, and there was nobody to see, apart from you that is.' She frowned. 'What are you doing here? I thought you'd be with Thorgils?'

'Thorgils?' Eadmund looked confused. 'Is he looking for me again?'

'You haven't seen him today?'

'No, I've been ummm...' Eadmund looked down at the ice, trying to locate any words that could explain his situation without making him appear as utterly hopeless as he knew he was.

There were none.

Jael touched his drooping chin, lifting it up, ignoring the clanging in her ears. 'Eadmund, why don't you come back to the house. Biddy will have something cooking, I'm sure. You can rest there, and I'll go and find Thorgils.'

Eadmund frowned, stepping away from her, his feet slipping. 'Why Thorgils? Why do I need to see him? I'm fine, just on my way home,' he slurred. 'Thought you needed some help, but you go, I'm fine. I don't need Thorgils, or you.' Eadmund saw the pity in her eyes; those eyes which were wide with something he couldn't interpret at all. His shoulders sagged, and he felt desperately ashamed. He needed to get away. To be alone. To find that ale in his cottage.

'Eadmund, wait!' Jael called as he stumbled away, sliding on the ice. 'I can help you!'

'I don't need your help, Jael!' he shouted crossly, not bothering to turn around. 'I don't need anyone's help!' And he disappeared into the darkness as the snowflakes thickened and danced through the bitter night air.

Jael stared after him, all thoughts of Tarak and revenge forgotten. All thoughts of Ivaar, and Brekka, and Aleksander were gone too as she turned and walked away.

***

'Oh, it's you,' the old woman grumbled.

She couldn't have been that old, Jael supposed, but she had so many lines on her face that it was hard to imagine that she'd ever been young at all. There was certainly nothing to admire about her now, but that was more because of her sharp glare and turned-down lips, which were mean and miserly. Her hair was wrapped in a faded yellow scarf, her hands firmly wedged into ample hips.

It was not much of a welcome, Jael decided.

'What are you doing here?' Thorgils' head appeared over the top of his mother's. Her head came up to just past his waist, only half the size of his.

'I need to speak to you,' Jael said, raising an eyebrow, hoping to convey the need for privacy as his mother looked on with an open mouth.

'Mother, this is Jael –' Thorgils began.

'You think I don't know who this is?' Odda Svanter hissed up to her son through a handful of teeth. 'My eyes work fine, same as yours.' She turned back to Jael. 'I saw you beat her. I was there when you defeated this *woman*. I know who she is.' And she glared at Jael, her baggy eyes bulging with dislike.

'I need to go, Mother,' Thorgils said, disappearing to grab his cloak. 'I'll be back later.'

'Later, when?' Odda barked.

'Later, when I return,' he smiled, kissing her scarf before ducking through the door. 'Don't worry about any food for me. I'll have something in the hall.'

They walked away from the long-reaching scowl as it followed them from the doorway, without a word, too busy concentrating on the icy ground than the need to smooth everything over right away.

'You've saved me from another evening with my mother, and for that, I'm in your debt,' Thorgils winked at Jael with a flash of his old humour. He'd seen something in her eyes when she'd come to his doorway, as though she'd returned from that dark place.

He hoped he was right.

***

'We can't tell Branwyn,' Edela insisted as they walked away from Alaric's cottage.

'No, I agree,' Aleksander said. 'That would be hard for any parent to hear. That their child was killed accidentally? Mistaken for someone else?' He shook his head, still in shock.

It was dark now and the cold bit at their legs as they walked. Despite the plummeting temperature, neither were in a hurry to return to Branwyn and Kormac's house. There was too much to discuss.

'Evva was so gentle, so innocent,' Edela said sadly, tears threatening her eyes again. 'They murdered her because they thought she was Jael. But who were they? Where did they come from?' She shuddered. 'I wish Alaric had known more, but I'm certain he told us all he could.' She gripped Aleksander firmly as they came upon a noisy crowd gathered outside a meat vendor. The smell of cooking meat called to Edela's empty stomach, and it rumbled back in return. They had been at Alaric's a long time, and he hadn't offered them anything more than that insipid small ale. Poor man, she thought sadly.

'If those men thought they'd killed Jael, how long do you think it took them to realise she was still alive? And did they try again?'

'I don't know. It would make sense for them to try again, though, wouldn't it? But I suppose getting into Andala was a lot harder than coming to Tuura that night. There were barely any fortifications back then. Not like now.'

'Do you think that's why Ranuf started training Jael as soon as we were home? That one of the elders told him about what had happened?' Aleksander wondered.

'Possibly, but what we really need to find out is who those men were. What sort of men kill a ten-year-old girl because they fear what she will become? What does the prophecy say Jael will do?'

'Well, I don't imagine your elder friend will be telling you *that* in a hurry, will she?' Aleksander smiled as they came to a stop outside the house.

'No,' Edela murmured. 'But we know a lot more than we did, and that's something. Now we just have to sleep on it, and hopefully, I can dream on it. And tomorrow, perhaps we can think up a list of possible enemies. If we can do that, it might take us even closer to the answers we need.'

Aleksander nodded and opened the door, ushering Edela inside, wondering as he did, just who had led those raiders to Tuura that night? Who had let them in? He shook his head, tired of there being so many unanswered questions swimming about in there.

***

Thorgils stopped and turned around, surprised. 'You're not coming?' The snow was heavy in his beard, and he shook it out, peering at Jael.

Jael didn't move. 'I think it's better that you do it. You go. On your own.' She'd stopped, not far from Eadmund's cottage, uncertainty flaring again.

Thorgils frowned, walking back to her. 'I don't think it's going to work without you.'

'Why do you say that? It's a tincture. Anyone could pour it into his mouth.'

'I don't think that's the point of it, do you?' Thorgils said softly. 'Your grandmother made this for you to give him. Not me, but *you*, when you were ready to do it. Do you really think it will work if *I* give it to him?'

Jael had a mouthful of words ready, reasons why she didn't need to go with him, but she kept her mouth closed, staring at Thorgils blankly, her insides turning over.

Thorgils smiled kindly at her, sensing her unease. 'You came and got me for a reason, Jael. You want to help him.' He stared into her eyes. Despite the thickness of the snow, he could see the panic as it flitted across her face. 'Don't run away now.'

***

Eadmund had quickly drained the contents of the two jugs of ale he'd found in his cottage. His head was throbbing, and he felt a little sick, but despite that, he was wondering how he was going to get some more, and quickly. He yawned as he sat on the edge of his bed, trying to convince himself of the need to stand up, but unsure if his legs still worked. His stomach rumbled, but he didn't care for food. He was thirsty, though, but ale wasn't about to come to him, so if he wanted more, and he definitely wanted more, he would have to go and find some himself. Hopefully, without being seen by his father, or Ivaar, or Jael, or Thorgils. Even Isaura, he grimaced guiltily.

It was completely dark in the cottage. The fire he'd hastily put together had not taken and was now just a pile of scorched logs. He'd not been able to find lamps or candles and had given up on the idea of light and warmth altogether.

He just wanted ale.

Eadmund's mind wandered back to the bed at Jael's house. His whole body sighed with longing, but he didn't think he'd be welcome there anymore, not when Jael had become so friendly with his brother. He remembered her face when she was with Ivaar. Ivaar's too. There was definitely something there, and he wanted no part of it. He was done with Ivaar's games.

Eadmund shook his head, driven to stand by his overwhelming desire for another drink. He would take the risk, gather his supplies, return to his cottage, and drink all thoughts of Ivaar and Jael far away. He stumbled towards the door, wrapping himself in his fur cloak, already missing the warmth of his lonely bed.

The door swung open, knocking into him. He quickly lost his already unstable footing and fell over backwards, his head hitting the floorboards with a loud crack.

'Eadmund!' Thorgils rushed over to his prone friend. 'Are you alright?'

Jael laughed awkwardly as she closed the door behind them. 'What were you doing standing behind the door?'

Eadmund groaned as Thorgils tried to help him to his feet. He was mostly dead weight, and despite his size, Thorgils could barely lift him. Jael stepped in to help and between the two of them, they managed to get Eadmund up, his head wobbling about, his eyes opening and closing as he moved in and out of consciousness. The stench of his breath had them both blinking.

'How were you even standing on your own?' Thorgils wondered.

The cottage was dark, but Jael could just make out Eadmund's bleary eyes trying to focus on her. He looked confused, a little cross, and thoroughly drunk. She sighed, wondering at their chances of success.

This tincture would surely have to be magic if they were to have any hope.

'Come on, come sit on the bed,' Thorgils said, helping Eadmund down onto his pile of furs. 'I'll go sort that fire out. We need some light in here.' He watched as Eadmund swayed unsteadily on the bed, then glanced at Jael, who was standing there, watching, obviously still doubting her decision to be there. 'Perhaps you can go and hold him up? I need to get the wood.'

Jael sighed and sat down next to her unstable husband, grabbing his arm to steady him.

He flinched.

'Why are you here?' Eadmund slurred angrily, his head bobbing towards her face. 'Is Ivaar busy?'

Jael let go of his arm, pushing him backwards. 'Perhaps it's best if you have a little sleep now?' she murmured.

Thorgils walked back into the cottage with an armful of snow-covered logs and saw Eadmund lying on the bed with his eyes closed; Jael sitting on a stool by the firepit. He raised an eyebrow. 'Your soothing voice put him to sleep, did it?'

'Something like that,' she smiled, helping with the logs, placing a few of the smaller ones into the firepit.

Thorgils added some twigs and tinder, and together they resurrected the flames. Eadmund's cottage was frigid, so they had to make it habitable, or they'd all freeze tonight.

***

Isaura lay still, her heart thudding anxiously in her chest as she listened to Ivaar's steady breathing. He'd barely wanted to touch her since their arrival on Oss which had been both a surprise and a wonderful relief. No doubt he'd found some poor servant girl to molest. Or perhaps Jael was the reason that Ivaar seemed so distracted and uninterested in her anymore? Isaura had assumed that he was merely playing with her to torture his brother, but perhaps there was more to it than that? She could certainly see the appeal of Jael to a man like Ivaar. Not so much for Eadmund, or at least the Eadmund she had known. This new Eadmund looked nothing like the man she remembered. He was trapped in the past, never escaping his heartbreak.

She knew how that felt.

Ivaar rolled towards her, flinging one arm across her chest. Isaura froze, holding her breath as she waited. He snuffled, groaned, and started snoring loudly again, his breathing resuming a steady rhythm. Isaura closed her eyes, imagining how different life would have been if she'd married Thorgils.

She thought of Ivaar and their children, and that small flicker of hope was snuffed out. Now it was even worse. Now Thorgils was close. Closer to her and closer to Ivaar.

One wrong move and Ivaar would kill him.

She had watched him train every day on Kalfa. She had seen the care he had taken of his sword, the disciplined way he'd practiced day after day. He had been driven, determined to find a way back to Oss, to take his revenge. And now here they were, at last, and she didn't know what he was about to do.

***

'Why are you here?' Eadmund was awake now. He felt confused, and although his head seemed clearer, he couldn't put his thoughts into any order that made sense.

Jael looked hesitantly at Thorgils, who was busy staring at his feet. She sighed. 'We came to help you.'

Eadmund snorted. 'And why do I need *your* help?'

Thorgils looked up, frowning. 'Why? Well, let's see... your brother already thinks he's the king and you're hiding out here, wobbling about as drunk as an ale-soaked apple, with no hope of stopping him.'

'Stopping him?' Eadmund scoffed. 'You think *I* could stop Ivaar? Ha! How am I supposed to do that?'

'Well, you could breathe on him,' Jael suggested tartly.

Thorgils glared at her, although, he had to admit that Eadmund did reek. 'You can stop him by convincing Eirik that you deserve a second chance.'

Eadmund shook his head. 'He's not about to give me that. He's made his choice. He's too proud to go back on his word now.'

'Eirik doesn't want Ivaar as king,' Jael insisted. 'He wouldn't have gone to all the trouble over our marriage if he'd been thinking of bringing Ivaar back. Ivaar has always been his second choice. You just have to remind him of why you were his first.'

Eadmund didn't want to look at Jael, or even listen to her. It was all too confusing. He closed his eyes and saw her with Ivaar, then blinked and looked away.

'Eadmund, we can help you,' Thorgils said quietly, leaning closer to his friend. 'Jael's grandmother is a dreamer. She made this tincture here to help you.'

Eadmund looked suspiciously at the tiny brown bottle that Thorgils pulled out of his pouch, watching the way the glass glinted ominously in the firelight. 'Help me do what? What did she see I needed help with?'

Thorgils squirmed, glancing hopefully at Jael.

'Well, you're a big, fat drunkard, Eadmund,' Jael said bluntly. 'The tincture is supposed to help you change all of that.'

Thorgils sighed. 'What your sweet wife over there means is that this can help you stop drinking.'

'*What?*' Eadmund staggered to his feet, swaying, his cloak flapping close to the flames. Thorgils stood up to grab him, but Eadmund ignored him and stomped away from the fire. 'I don't need help with that!'

'No?' Thorgils wondered sarcastically. 'You can just stop it on your own, can you? Because nothing will change until you do. Not for you, and certainly not for Eirik. If you keep drinking like this, Ivaar will have everything he wants. You'll be giving Ivaar the kingdom. And worse than that, you'll be giving Ivaar your life and mine, Isaura's, Eydis', Jael's. Eydis has seen your father dying soon, and whatever happens, you have to get better, or we will *all* die.'

Eadmund walked over to his bed, sitting down with a thud. He could feel the bile rushing up into his throat. He grimaced, dropping his head, wishing it all away. He needed to think, but at that moment, it seemed to be the one thing he was completely incapable of.

Jael came and sat beside him.

'Why the sudden change?' Eadmund snapped at her. 'Why do you want to help me? You and Ivaar are such good friends.

Why help me defeat him?' He couldn't bring himself to look into her eyes, afraid of what he would find.

Thorgils laughed as he sat down on Eadmund's other side, the bed creaking angrily under his additional bulk. 'Oh, that was Jael's plan, didn't you know? She was trying to distract Ivaar.'

Eadmund frowned but at the same time, his spirits lifted ever so slightly. 'Your plan?' He raised his eyes as high as he dared, just catching hers.

'It was a good plan!' Jael grumbled at Thorgils, then turned to Eadmund. 'Ivaar seemed to like me well enough, so I thought I might as well encourage that. Lead him away from any games he might be planning for you. Let him play with me instead, which he's been very keen to do.'

Both Eadmund and Thorgils raised their eyebrows at that.

'What do you mean, *play* with you?' Eadmund wondered dully, shaking his head. 'You never want to let Ivaar play with you. He's a sick bastard. He'll always find a way to get what he wants.'

'I agree,' Thorgils said, poking the fire. 'He's dangerous. You don't know him like we do.'

Jael shrugged their concerns away. 'Look, the most important thing is to get you right, Eadmund. To get you back in front of your father so he can believe in you again. So that he remembers why he stood by you for all those years while you drunk yourself into this mess. You owe him something, and the people of Oss, and Eydis, and even Thorgils here. They've all cared for you, and helped you, and wanted you to come back to them. And if you don't, if you stay like this, if Ivaar becomes the king, who knows what will happen to them? You don't want to be responsible for that, do you?'

Jael's words hit Eadmund like a hammer, and he lurched forward, stumbling off the bed, running for the door. He opened it just in time to get his head out before vomiting loudly.

Jael cringed at the violent retching sounds coming from outside, turning to Thorgils, who smiled crookedly at her.

'You have a way with words, it seems.'

CHAPTER FORTY ONE

Eydis didn't know why she was there.

Her father had asked her to sit with him as he met with Sevrin, the head of his army, and Otto, his fleet commander. She was pleased that she couldn't see their faces, but she could almost feel their eyes turning quizzically in her direction. Eydis kept her head down, still disturbed by her meeting with Ayla; uncertain how she felt about the woman. The dull droning of the men meandered around her as she sat there, preoccupied, barely listening.

'But if we fail?' Eirik couldn't help but glance at Eydis then, annoyed that she didn't appear to be paying any attention. He frowned, not wanting to even consider such an outcome, but still, as the king, he needed to ensure the safety of his people. 'If we fail and they come after us?'

Otto scoffed, which was typical of him, Eirik thought regretfully.

Otto had led their last disastrous attack on Skorro. He should have removed him from his position before now, but there was no one as experienced to take over. No one he trusted, at least. Eirik shook his head, trying to focus, but it was hard. He hadn't seen Morac since their argument, and he was beginning to realise how much he'd relied upon his old friend. After all these years, Morac knew how Oss should run without the need for endless debate. But now, without Morac's planning and foresight, Eirik was flailing about like a child. He knew there were things he needed to do to keep their plans for the invasion rolling along, and the contest, and Vesta, which was coming too. But the what, when, and how of organising it all was overwhelming him.

'If we fail,' Sevrin murmured, running a hand over his dark beard, 'we need to know that the fort is defended. If our fleet is crippled, it won't make it back in time to help. If it makes it back at all. I don't believe Haaron will let us get away with such a bold attack. He'll surely send his fleet to Oss, and if we've barely dented them, the damage they inflict could be catastrophic.'

Eirik glowered at the wooden figures on the table in front of him. He had sequestered one of the hall's tables for their battle planning, and it now stood to the right of his throne, permanently covered in wooden figures as Eirik plotted his ever-changing strategies for the invasion. Without Morac's calm reassurance, he found himself doubt-riddled and fretting, constantly fiddling with the figures.

He picked up two of the wooden ships, bringing them back to join the couple he had left on Oss. 'We won't send so many ships, then.'

'But if we don't take enough ships, we have no hope of defeating them,' Otto urged. 'The men on Skorro are some of Haaron's best. If the invasion is to be a success, we have to eliminate them and quickly. It will determine the outcome of everything. The more ships we send, the better chance we have. Besides,' he said, looking pointedly at Sevrin, 'you forget how much trouble they'll have coming through the Widow's Peak. If they try to follow us, most of them won't make it through in one piece.'

Sevrin snorted. 'You think they won't have learned how to navigate that handful of stones by now?' He glared impatiently at Eirik. 'We underestimate them and put ourselves in grave danger if we simply assume they won't be able to chase us.'

Eirik pulled on the ends of his beard, regretting that he'd allowed himself to become so dependent upon Morac's advice.

His own mind had become lazy because of it.

He glanced at Eydis as he walked back to his chair, sitting down. So far she'd had no dreams about Hest at all. None. And it worried him. He needed luck for this invasion. Perhaps her lack of dreams was already a sign that no good thing would come of it? Eirik sighed. He simply couldn't lead his men to another heavy defeat. Or, he stilled, perhaps that was how it was going to end for him? Sinking into the black depths of the Adrano Sea, watching his men drown alongside him. He shuddered, plagued by swirling doubts, desperate for some insight.

'We'll continue this tomorrow. I'll think on your suggestions overnight,' Eirik muttered distractedly, rolling his hands over the armrests of his chair. 'Go, get yourselves a drink.' He waved his hand, dismissing them with a frown. The two men nodded, turning away. Eirik barely noticed; he'd already moved his attention to Eydis. 'What do you think, then, my daughter? What chance do we have of taking Skorro?'

Eydis blinked, squirming in her seat. 'I can't say, Father. I've tried to dream on it, but nothing will come.'

'Just my death, that's what's coming, isn't it?' Eirik whispered. 'Coming faster each day, and still I'm in this muddle with Eadmund and Ivaar.' He leaned his head back, his body slumping in defeat. 'My life was not an easy one, but all of this,' he swept his hand around the hall, 'is mine. All of it. And where did I come from? I was the shit on my father's boot, kicked about like a dog from the day I could walk. I scraped around this hall, waiting for the blows that would come, watching the way he treated us, all of his slaves, as though we were nothing.' Eirik stared into the far reaches of the hall, back to a time when it had belonged to Grim Skalleson. It had been a smaller, darker place then, filled with the rotting stench of slavers and their perverse ways. 'I saw what he did to my mother, and I swore I'd destroy him. Destroy all the slavers. Take this place back. Free us all. And I did. But what was the point of any of it, if it all returns to a pile of picked-over-bones when I'm gone? How do I know that it won't?'

Eydis' eyes were wide with concern as she felt around for her father's arm. He sounded morose and very lost. 'Where is Morac? I haven't heard his voice for many days. Don't you need his advice more than mine? He can help you, can't he, Father?'

'Morac...' Eirik sighed. 'We've had a... disagreement, he and I. I'm not sure if he's still on Oss, or whether I'll see him again.'

He closed his eyes, wondering if he even wanted to.

***

Runa was tired of this endless silence. She loved silence most of the time, but this? She'd had enough of this. Something had to change.

Morac sat, staring at the fire. It felt as though he'd been sitting there for days, and Runa didn't know what to do to shift him, both out of his stupor and out from under her feet. She felt as though she couldn't breathe. He needed to get back to the hall and make amends with Eirik. Another few days of this and she would lose her mind.

'I was thinking that we should leave.'

Runa looked up from her embroidering, horrified. She was adding details to a new cloak for herself; a luxury she'd not had the pleasure of for many years. 'Leave? And go where?'

'To Rikka.' Morac's drawn face was suddenly brighter, the clouds in his head finally shifting. 'Evaine will need us. Morana can care for her and help with the birth, when the time comes, but she lives in a tiny old shack. Evaine will be suffering, of that I'm sure.'

Runa wanted to say how pleased she was to hear it, and that the two of them deserved one another, but she bit her lip and thought quickly. 'Rikka? But surely if you do that, there would be no way back to Eirik's hall. You'd be banishing us all. Forever.'

'What makes you think I want back into that hall?' Morac spat bitterly. 'What has Eirik Skalleson done for me after all these years of me doing everything for him?'

Runa put her work to one side and came to sit beside her husband. 'Well, we have this home, surely the finest on Oss?' she tried. 'Remember when we were children, and you had to dig about for scraps just so we could eat? We shivered in Grim's hall every night with not even a blanket to cover us. Look at how far we have come *because* of your friendship with Eirik. *Because* of your service to him. Without that, none of this would have been possible.'

Morac looked scornfully at his wife. 'And you think that when I'm taking my last breaths, I'll be glad I lived in a fine house? That it is my thick walls and wooden floorboards I'll be thinking of as I die? As if *that* is all my life truly meant?' He looked disgusted. 'I haven't done all of this to have a house, Runa! To go from being a slave to a servant with a nice house. That is no life! Where is the power in that? What power do I have over my own life or that of my family's? That Eirik could just send my daughter away because he's annoyed with his son?'

'Well, he is the king,' Runa tried. 'No matter who you become on Oss, Eirik is the king, and the king will always have his way.'

'Will he, though?' Morac wondered, smiling to himself. 'Will he?'

***

It had snowed throughout the night, and Jael was relieved to be wading through soft, wet powder instead of skating around on treacherous ice. She grimaced, remembering the pain of her fall and the look of satisfaction on Tarak's face as he watched her fly. Grumbling into her cloak, she took another bite of the hot loaf of bread she was bringing back to Thorgils who was in the cottage, watching Eadmund.

So far the tincture had been trouble.

Eadmund had initially decided to accept their help, but not long after his first dose, he'd become edgy, irate, desperate for a drink, and difficult to control. He'd paced anxiously around the cottage for some time, then decided to try and escape. Repeatedly. They'd restrained him, tied him to the bed, and Thorgils had brought Eadmund's chair from the house and some more rope.

It had been a long few days, listening to Eadmund growl, bark, yell, shake, and vomit.

No one had slept much.

'Hello,' Ivaar smiled, sneaking up behind Jael.

She froze, her mouth stuffed full of bread.

'I didn't realise you had such an appetite!' Ivaar grinned, peering at her bulging face and the loaf of bread she was attempting to conceal beneath her cloak.

Jael swallowed, trying to decide exactly how she felt about her Ivaar plan now that she'd made the decision to help Eadmund. 'Well, it's hot,' she mumbled. 'I like it when it's hot.' She cringed, deciding that she needed more sleep.

Ivaar laughed. 'It feels as though we've not spoken in days. Not since the waterfall. Not properly, at least.'

Jael looked around. It was mid-morning, and a fair amount of people were milling about the square. She felt awkward and exposed. 'Ahhh, that.'

'Yes, that.'

'Well, you tried to kiss me, so I suppose I'm avoiding you,' she smiled, unsure whether honesty was the best approach with a man like Ivaar, whose eyes were always shifting about.

'Ha!' he laughed again, relief on his face. He'd been worried that Jael had gone over to the other side. That he'd lost any hope of having her on his, but she seemed fine. More than fine. 'Well, I can't blame you there. Although, it's probably the only time I've ever been turned down.'

'Really?' Jael acted surprised, playing along. 'Well, you do have nice hair. I imagine it's impossible to resist a man who makes such an effort with his appearance.'

Ivaar felt a surge in his body as he looked into her eyes. He'd missed her company, more than he'd realised. She was completely unafraid of him, and he was fascinated by her. 'Let's go for another ride today,' he suggested. 'I promise not to try and kiss you this time.'

Jael narrowed her eyes. 'That may be what your mouth is saying, but your eyes are saying something else entirely,' she grinned, walking away. 'Perhaps tomorrow? You may have cooled down enough by then!'

Ivaar watched her go, frustrated but excited.

There was still hope to be found in Jael Furyck.

He was sure of it.

***

Runa came back to the house after finally escaping for a long, cold walk to find Morac in their bedchamber, packing their clothes into their sea chests. She gasped. 'What are you doing?'

Morac barely looked up. 'We can get to Rikka tomorrow. I've been out to speak to Edrun, and he's happy to take us in the morning, all being well with the weather overnight.'

Their house was well insulated and warm, but Runa couldn't stop shivering. How was she going to talk him out of this idea? Morac seemed to have made up his mind, but she couldn't go to Rikka. The thought of being with Evaine again made her ill, but having to endure Morana as well terrified her. And there was no way she could leave poor Fyn. Not that she ever got to see him, but at least she could ensure he was sent food regularly.

She wouldn't abandon him.

'But what about Eirik?' Runa tried. 'What will you tell him?'

'Why do I need to tell him anything?' Morac snorted. 'I'm not bound to him, not anymore.

'But you made an oath.'

'Bah!' Morac spat, closing the lid on his sea chest and moving over to start on hers. 'He broke that oath when he banished Evaine. Why should my loyalty remain true to a man like that? A man who doesn't respect my family? Our oaths were made when we were boys. What do they mean now? Just lies and empty promises. I don't care about any oath that lies in the dirt, trodden on, year after year.' He sighed, sitting back on the bed, his body suddenly weary. 'Runa, come here. Come, sit down.'

She did as she was bid, still shaking, her eyes darting about desperately.

She would not go to Rikka. She couldn't go to Rikka.

'You don't want to come, do you?' he asked quietly, taking her hands in his.

Runa looked down. 'I don't want to leave Oss,' she mumbled. 'It's our home. If we both leave, there'll be no way back for our family. Not ever.' She looked up and saw some hope on the horizon, then. 'But if you go on your own, I can keep our house here, for when you return with Evaine and the child. Who knows what would happen to the house if we were both to abandon it? Eirik might not take things well and have it destroyed. And you know how much Evaine loves this house.'

Morac frowned. She did have a point, he realised. It would be easy for him to slip away without any fuss, but if they were both to leave, there would certainly be loose ends and a lot of people whispering in Eirik's ear. And he didn't want to make things worse where Eirik was concerned.

Not yet, anyway.

Morac lifted Runa's hand to his lips, kissing it softly, his eyes lingering on hers for a moment. They had been together for most of their lives. It would not be an easy thing to leave her, but then he thought of Morana, and Evaine, and the promise of the future, and he smiled.

CHAPTER FORTY TWO

'You took your time,' Thorgils muttered as Jael crept into the cottage. His empty stomach was torturing him, joining in the misery of his aching back and his pounding head.

'I got waylaid by Ivaar,' she sighed, then wished she hadn't said anything. She didn't want to start another argument. But one look at the bread Jael pulled from her cloak, and Thorgils forgot all about her much-discussed and forever-maligned Ivaar plan. The packets of cheese, dried fish, and salt pork she took out of her pockets, made him even happier.

'It's still warm!' he exclaimed gleefully, grabbing the bread.

Eadmund groaned from the bed, starting to wake up. They both froze, holding their breaths. Jael frowned at Thorgils, who looked sheepish as he shrugged back at her. Eadmund was certainly easier to manage when his eyes were closed, and he wasn't trying to escape.

They hoped to keep him that way as much as possible.

Jael kept her cloak on as she sat in front of the fire. Despite the height of the flames, the room was bitterly cold. Thorgils helped himself to the only plate-like object he could find and came to sit beside her. He ripped off some of the bread, smiling again; there was nothing he loved more than warm bread. And making himself a serving of bread, fish, pork, and cheese, he shovelled most of it into his mouth; the rest crumbled into his beard for him to collect later.

'I'm not sure I brought enough,' Jael grinned as Thorgils started filling the plate again.

He paused, mid-chew, and picked up the loaf, handing it to her.

Jael tore off a corner. She was just as hungry, but she felt too tired and preoccupied to eat much. 'When do you think I need to give him another dose?' she wondered, looking over at the large sleeping lump.

'I say as soon as he wakes. If there's any chance of it helping, you need to get more of it into him and quickly,' Thorgils mumbled, studying her worried face. 'What did Ivaar say?'

'He wanted to go riding again.'

'And you said?' Thorgils leaned forward, his voice an irritated whisper.

Jael glared at him. 'I said, maybe in a day or so. We have enough to worry about right now without another Ivaar argument, don't we?'

'We do, yes,' Thorgils agreed. 'Let's forget about him for now, then. Focus on the nicer brother.'

Jael handed back the bread, which Thorgils had been eyeing. 'Shall I go back and ask Biddy to make another loaf?'

'At least.'

***

'Not long till Vesta,' Ivaar grinned at his father as he sat down by the fire.

Eirik's shoulders drooped, matching his already miserable face. 'Mmmm.'

Eydis' eyes lit up. 'Ooohh, I can't wait!' she squealed, feeling a rush of joy for the first time in weeks. 'That's something to look forward to!'

Isaura didn't look as enthused as she bent down to stop Leya poking a stick into her brother's ear. 'At least the days will start to get longer again. More chance for the children to play outside.'

'Well, there's something to look forward to,' Ivaar said pointedly, staring at his wife, who ignored him and reached down to take the stick away from her very persistent daughter, who promptly started wailing.

'You always love Vesta, Father,' Eydis said excitedly. 'Why not this year? The games, the feasts, the songs. It's the best part of winter!'

Eirik sighed. 'Well yes, apart from the fact that Morac usually organises all of that. Without him, I've no idea what to do.'

'Oh.' Eydis looked heartbroken.

'I can help if you like?' Isaura said shyly, scooping Leya into her arms to try and stop the tears. 'Help you organise everything, I mean. I used to plan our own Vesta on Kalfa, much like the ones I remember from here. Just a smaller version.'

'She did,' Ivaar agreed. 'It always went well, from memory. You should let her help you, Father.'

Eirik stood, allowing himself half a smile. 'Well, I'm sure whatever you can manage would be better than any poor show I'd come up with, Isaura.'

'Good,' Isaura said, her eyes blinking nervously, unsure what she had just walked into. 'I'll shepherd the children off with the servants, and we can talk over some ideas.'

Eirik nodded, only half-listening as he wandered over to the fire. He was wondering how to go about making peace with Morac. It had taken a while for him to realise that he'd been harsh; harsher than was fair. But how was he going to heal the gaping wound? They were both far too old to let things fester this long.

He would have to go and see him.

***

'I need a drink!' Eadmund rasped furiously, pulling against the ropes.

They had tied him to the chair when he'd woken, given him another dose of tincture and left him to fall asleep. He'd been weak and tired, and thankfully, had barely protested at all.

Thorgils had gone for some air, and Jael was lying on Eadmund's uncomfortable little bed, trying to find some sleep. Her mind had jumped about, though, and she hadn't been able to keep her eyes closed for long.

She sat up, groaning, trying to stretch out her back.

'Are you alright?' Eadmund wondered, noticing the discomfort she was in.

'Fine,' Jael frowned, padding towards him, her feet numb in damp socks. 'But I do owe Tarak a good beating.'

'What did you say to make him do that to you?' Eadmund wondered, forgetting his desperation for a drink for a moment.

Jael opened her mouth, but she couldn't think of anything that would make sense to him. She searched around for the tincture, trying to remember where she'd placed it. The fire had burned down to embers, and it was already dark outside, making it hard to see. 'He just doesn't like me very much, I suppose,' she mumbled. 'But perhaps we'll meet in the contest, and I can finally have a turn at him.'

'You won't be able to push him over that easily,' Eadmund croaked. 'He's made of stone. He's a tower that won't go down unless you take out his foundations.'

Jael removed the stopper from the bottle and headed for Eadmund. 'I suppose not. Now open your mouth so we can get this over with.'

Instead, Eadmund turned his head away. 'That's *not* the sort of drink I had in mind.'

'No, but you won't save yourself or anyone else if you don't try *this* drink. Come on,' she urged, careful to stand just out of reach in case he knocked the bottle out of her hand.

'Where's Thorgils?'

'Eadmund,' Jael said firmly. 'Take the tincture. Please. I'd rather you opened your mouth on your own. I don't want to have to knock you out and pour it down your throat myself.'

He turned around, glaring at her, his fingers gripping the arms of the chair. 'I'll take your fucking tincture... if...if you get me a cup of ale. Just one cup. It doesn't even have to be big. A small cup of ale for one drink of tincture. That's a fair trade, don't you think?' His voice was high with desperation.

'No. No ale. No liquid. Nothing but the tincture.'

'How do you even know it will work? How do you know what it does?' Eadmund shook angrily against the ropes, banging his wrists up and down on the arms of the chair, growling in frustration. 'I don't feel any better or any worse, just the same!' he hissed, teeth bared.

Jael stoppered the tincture, placing it far away from him, and walked back to the bed. She grabbed the furs and pulled them over her aching back, facing the wall in silence.

Eadmund's eyes followed her, at first furious and then, when he realised that she wasn't coming back, desperate. He was so thirsty that his tongue kept sticking to the roof of his mouth. He could barely swallow. He needed some form of liquid in his throat, and if it wasn't going to be ale... 'Alright, I'll take it.'

Jael didn't move.

Eadmund bit his lip in frustration, his forehead creased, his toes tapping the floorboards beneath his feet. He'd lied to her. His whole body was vibrating with the need for ale. His head felt as though a giant tick was crawling around inside it, biting at his thoughts. He wanted to reach his hands inside his head and scratch till he bled. Not one part of him wanted to go through with this anymore. He didn't want to think about any of them. They could save themselves. He just needed ale, ale, ale, but right now he would take liquid in any form, just to feel some moisture in his throat.

'Please, Jael.'

Jael sighed and got up, wondering why she'd been stupid

enough to lie down again. Eadmund's horrible little bed was not helping the pain in her back. 'Alright, but if you've made me get up just to turn your head again, I'll have to slap you hard.'

She wandered over to the kitchen, which really was just a broken bench and one shelf, both covered in a thick mess of dust and cobwebs. Grabbing a stale-smelling cup, Jael poured some tincture into it, deciding that it was better to keep the bottle well away from Eadmund. She could hear the desperation in his voice now, no matter how much he was trying to convince her otherwise. 'Here.' Jael held the cup up to his face, urging him to tilt his head.

Eadmund scowled at her, his jaw tensing, which was not the action of a man who was about to open it. He breathed loudly through his nose, fast, quick breaths, watching as Jael stepped away. 'Alright, alright,' he snapped, tipping his head back, opening his mouth.

Jael leaned forward, dribbling the liquid inside, shaking the cup, and moving away as quickly as possible. The wind was starting to pick up outside; a breathless howl creeping its way around the walls. She grimaced, her stomach rumbling as she left Eadmund to sit by the fire.

Hopefully, Thorgils would be back soon with some food.

'Why are you doing this?' Eadmund asked faintly, trying to take his mind off the overwhelming desire to scream and rage at his wife, demanding she release him.

'Helping you, you mean?'

'Well, *you* may call it help,' he muttered, his teeth chattering suddenly. 'But it feels more like torture to m-m-meeee.'

'I think you have that wrong,' Jael said sadly, placing another log on the fire. 'What you've been doing to yourself all these years, *that* was the torture. This part is the help.'

'Grrrrrrrr!' Eadmund snapped, his eyes popping open. 'You have no idea what this feels like! If you did, you'd rip these fucking ropes off me and give me something to drink!'

'And then what?'

Eadmund blinked.

'What will you do then? Drink, and then drink some more and go wandering about, falling asleep, disappearing, while your brother slowly takes over Oss and kills everyone you love?'

Eadmund rattled his arms against the chair. 'My father is still the king, isn't he? He's in no hurry for anyone to take over.'

'But he knows he's going to die soon, doesn't he? Ivaar knows it too.'

Eadmund was almost still, then. Jael could hear his breathing, shallow and ragged. His eyes lost their fire for a moment as he lingered on the thought of losing his father. 'We have to destroy Ivaar,' he whispered finally, feeling the clarity of that singular thought; trying to grasp hold of it.

'We do, but first, we have to save you.'

***

'I need you to approach her again,' Ivaar insisted softly to the ample breasts he lay between. 'You can't enter her confidence if she doesn't get to know you. You can't give up without even trying, Ayla. This time, just do it differently. Put her at ease. Become her friend.'

Ayla tried not to sigh as she shivered beneath Ivaar's sprawling body. She was freezing, wishing she could just tell him to grab the furs, but from experience, she knew not to interrupt Ivaar when he was talking. He enjoyed the sound of his own voice far too much. 'I'll try again, perhaps tomorrow,' she said sadly. 'I don't think Eydis trusts anyone much, not when she can't see them. It must be very hard for her.'

Ivaar sat up, finally cold himself, retrieving the furs which had been tossed off the bed. 'She's always been shy, but don't you see,' he said, throwing the furs over Ayla and climbing under them, 'you're a dreamer! Eydis doesn't know any dreamers. She'll want to get to know you. She won't be able to ignore her curiosity. That will win her over, I'm sure.'

Ayla opened her mouth to speak, but one look at Ivaar's face made her close it. She smiled tightly. 'Of course, you're right. She did look keen on that idea, I think.'

'Good,' Ivaar yawned, lying one leg over hers, pushing himself firmly into her side, seeking her warmth. 'I need to know what she's seen. And dreamers don't always reveal everything they see, do they, Ayla, my love? Not unless we find ways to make them.'

Ayla froze, watching his eyes close, a sly smile lingering on his lips. Ivaar had a way of finding out anything he wanted to know, and she was terrified that he'd find a way into her dreams and discover the visions she was hiding from him.

***

They lay Eadmund down on the bed again, securing him as tightly as possible. He looked up at them furiously, hating them both, smashing his arms onto the bed, trying to loosen the ropes, but with little strength remaining, he had to stop after only a short while.

Leaving their prisoner grumbling, yawning, and frowning at them, they moved away to sit by the fire.

'What's wrong with you?' Thorgils wondered. They had not spoken much since they'd stumbled upon peace, but he'd noticed that Jael was making a lot of strange faces.

Jael looked up as snow started drifting down the smoke hole, sizzling the flames. She stretched her back. 'Tarak.'

Thorgils leaned forward, worried. 'What did he do to you?'

'He wanted to see if I could fly,' Jael smiled wryly. 'So he pushed me, as hard as he could, onto the ice. Just another reason to defeat the bastard. As if we needed more.'

'But why? What did you say to him?'

'Well...' Jael mumbled. 'I suppose I threatened him, taunted him, that sort of thing.'

'And you thought it would end well, did you?' Thorgils looked unimpressed. 'You could have broken something! Ice is an unforgiving bitch.'

'True, but it was worth it, and I don't think I did.'

'Worth it? How?'

Jael smiled. 'He doesn't see me as any sort of threat now. Just a smart-mouthed woman he can push over. So if I do come up against him in the contest, he'll be overconfident about his chances. It might even up the odds.'

Thorgils laughed, almost happy for the first time in days. He'd missed Jael's company and her crazy insistence on trying to out-think everybody. Leaning in, he lowered his voice. 'And what about Ivaar? How's that plan going?'

'Ahhh, well, it's going along at a steady pace, I suppose,' she muttered, jiggling about on her stool, avoiding Thorgils' enquiring eyes. 'He seems to like me well enough.'

'Oh, does he now? And what does that mean?'

Jael glanced over at Eadmund, but he appeared to be sleeping. 'Well, he tried to kiss me.'

'What?' Thorgils growled. 'That bastard! What a shit. What a fucking shit!' He stared at her. 'I told you this would happen.'

'Ha! I don't believe you told me *that* would happen but stop fretting. Ivaar knows I'm not interested.'

Thorgils gave her a doubt-filled look, and she gave him back a pair of determined eyebrows, and they were just about to pick up their argument again when Eadmund started shaking violently, his body jerking about as though he was having some sort of seizure. The only look Jael and Thorgils exchanged then was one of panic as they raced to the bed.

'Quick, untie the ropes!' Jael cried, fumbling with the ropes at his feet.

Thorgils froze, watching Eadmund's shuddering body.

He didn't move.

'Thorgils!' Jael yelled. 'We have to turn him onto his side! You need to untie the ropes!'

Eadmund's head was banging onto the pillow, his feet were hitting the end of the bed's frame, and now his eyes were open, rolling around. Thorgils suddenly woke from his daze, hurrying to untie the knots around Eadmund's wrists. It wasn't easy, though; they'd tied them very tight.

'Let's roll him over!' Jael urged as the ropes came undone. 'I'll lie behind him. You come here, make sure he's breathing.'

Thorgils didn't argue as he swapped places with Jael, who crawled up onto the bed, which was creaking from Eadmund's jerking body, and her extra weight. It held, though, and she managed to grab hold of Eadmund and stop his arms flapping about. She could feel her heart thudding loudly against his moving back. She closed her eyes, begging Vidar to save Eadmund.

He couldn't die. Not like this.

She wouldn't let him.

CHAPTER FORTY THREE

'Mother!' Branwyn grabbed Edela by the shoulders, trying to wake her. 'Mother! You're having a bad dream! You need to wake up! Mother?'

Edela sat up quickly, her eyes still closed, her breathing shallow. She frowned, trying not to wake fully until she had a firm hold on the threads of her dream.

Branwyn looked worried; her mother's face was very pale. 'Are you alright?'

Edela remained silent as she tried to remember the fading visions. There had been a note, and a cup, and what else? Eadmund, that's right. Something was wrong with Eadmund. She blinked her eyes open, staring at Branwyn's troubled face, shivering as the chill of the room quickly wrapped itself around her.

She looked keenly towards the fire.

'Mother?'

'Yes, yes, I'm alright, my dear,' Edela groaned, easing herself out of bed. Her hip clicked, and she felt the pain in it. The colder weather was making her familiar aches worse, but there was no time to dwell on that now. 'I'm just trying to keep my dreams afloat. They can disappear so quickly these days.'

Branwyn grabbed the fur from her mother's bed, tucking it around her shoulders. 'Here, warm yourself by the fire, and I'll bring you something hot to drink.'

Edela smiled gratefully as she settled into the comfortable, fur-covered chair, closing her eyes, disappearing back into the darkness of her dream. She'd seen the two girls again, as though she was standing barely an arm's length from their heads on the spikes; two pairs of dead, glazed eyes staring at her. A hooded figure had been crouching on the ground, catching some of the dripping blood in a bowl. It had been dark, but she remembered the flash of a knife as it tore off a clump of each girl's long hair.

Edela opened her eyes. It was an unpleasant dream to revisit, but she was glad for having retained it. She shook her head, cross with herself for forgetting those girls. What had happened to them was important, somehow. She needed to discover if anyone knew about them.

'Here you are,' Branwyn smiled, handing her mother a cup of fragrant lemon balm tea. 'Have you managed to remember your dreams, then?' She sat down beside Edela, grabbing the iron poker, shivering herself.

'Yes, I think so,' Edela croaked, still only half awake. 'Some of them at least. It felt as though I hadn't dreamed for many days, and then suddenly, there were so many at once. I'm sure most of them slipped away in the night, but I do remember dreaming about Eadmund. Something is wrong there.'

'Jael's Eadmund?'

'Mmmm,' Edela murmured as she tried a sip of tea, but it was too hot. 'His soul is far away from him, wandering lost. He must decide whether it's life or death he seeks because he can no longer have both at the same time.'

Branwyn's forehead creased, not understanding what Edela was talking about. 'What else did you see? Anything about the sword?' She'd noticed how secretive her mother and Aleksander had become. Anything they were uncovering was not being shared with her or Kormac.

'The sword? No, but I did see something that confused me,' Edela frowned, trying to make sense of everything. 'I saw a note. Someone wrote a note about us coming to Tuura all those years ago. They were alerting someone to our visit.'

Branwyn swallowed. She hated talking about that night. It had been the single worst moment of her life. She felt sick reliving it, but the thought of discovering the why of it all piqued her interest. '*You* were the reason those men came? They wanted you or something you had?' Branwyn looked upset. 'Then why did they kill Evva?'

Edela's face blanched as she realised how careless she'd been. She'd forgotten that she was talking to Branwyn and not Aleksander. She could see the faded misery in her daughter's eyes, and she felt guilty for making her relive that night again. 'Well, it was not much of a dream, I must admit,' Edela said quickly. 'I think I've woken up more muddled than when I went to sleep. Perhaps a soak in your tub would clear my head?'

'Of course.' Branwyn rushed to get up. 'I'll ask Berta to heat some water for you. That sounds exactly what you need. Maybe some of your dreams will come back to you while you soak? Perhaps things will be clearer then?'

'I do hope so,' Edela sighed. She was already wandering far away again, desperately searching her memory for more clues. The note had been written in a woman's hand; she could see that very clearly. And that hand had a very distinctive ring on it. A ring she recognised.

And if she could just remember who it belonged to...

***

'And he hasn't opened his eyes since?' Biddy peered down at Eadmund, her eyebrows pinching together.

He did not look well at all.

Thorgils and Jael stood beside her, all three faces registering deep concern.

'Not once, and one of us kept watch all night,' Jael said quietly, her eyes straining to stay open.

'But he's breathing,' Biddy said, almost to herself. 'That's the main thing.'

'He looks as pale as snow, though,' Thorgils murmured. 'And the stink...'

'Yes, perhaps I need to air things out a little in here?' Biddy suggested, resisting the urge to gag. How anyone had managed to sleep in the vile stench was a miracle. Ido and Vella ran around her feet, sniffing everything.

There was a lot to keep their noses occupied this morning.

'What do we do now?' Jael wondered. 'He still hasn't finished the tincture, but what if it's not even working? Just slowly killing him?'

'Of course it wouldn't be killing him!' Biddy scoffed with as much confidence as she could muster. 'You trust Edela, don't you? With your own life, I'm sure. She would only have prepared something that would save Eadmund, not hurt him. Never that.'

Jael sighed, scratching her head. She felt anxious about Eadmund, worried about Tig and Leada needing a ride, not to mention poor Fyn, who would be wondering what had happened to her. But most of all, right then, she was starving. Sitting down, she dove into Biddy's basket. Thorgils came to join her, along with the puppies, who'd decided that the basket filled with food was the best smell in the cottage by far.

Thorgils pushed their wet noses away and peered into the basket himself, his face troubled. 'I've never seen a thing like that,' he muttered, shaking his head. 'What happened to Eadmund last night. Whatever that was.'

Biddy glanced over her shoulder at Jael as she grabbed a broom and started sweeping.

Jael didn't say a word.

'How did you know what to do?' Thorgils continued, stuffing a boiled egg into his mouth.

Jael chewed slowly and thoughtfully, her eyes far away. 'My

eldest brother, Stellan, had seizures like that. Nobody knew what to do when it happened, except my grandmother. She would tell us to put him on his side, that it would keep him safe. And it always worked, and he would recover quickly.' She stopped chewing and looked up at Thorgils. 'One day, he didn't come back from a walk, and my father found him in the woods, lying on his back, dead. He died, I suppose because he was all alone when he had a seizure. There was no one to help him. He was only twelve-years-old.'

Biddy walked past, opening the door, letting in an icy blast of fresh air.

'I'm sorry,' Thorgils said, glancing at the bed. 'That is no easy thing, I know. But thanks to your brother, you knew how to save Eadmund.'

'This time, yes,' Jael said thoughtfully. 'But who knows what else is coming his way? Who knows what the tincture will do to him next?'

***

'That worm Tiras has been having fun, creeping around in the snow,' Tarak laughed loudly.

Ivaar glared at him, inclining his head towards Isaura, who was well within hearing distance; although with three children all talking to her at once, it was unlikely she could hear a thing, but still... 'Have some thought in your head about where you are,' Ivaar growled. 'If we have private business, we can discuss it in a private place. And anything to do with *him* is very private indeed.'

Isaura wandered off after the girls, who were chasing their crawling brother, and Tarak moved closer to Ivaar. 'He says the Brekkan bitch has been holed up in your brother's cottage these past few nights.'

Ivaar almost dropped his cup into the flames. 'What?' That was unexpected. He'd planned to seek Jael out shortly, hoping to go riding with her but now...

Tarak was triumphant, unable to contain his glee. He hated how obsessed Ivaar was with Jael, but this was surely the beginning of the end now. 'Yes, she's barely left the place, he said.'

'Is that all?'

'Well, he did mention that the big, red idiot has been there as well for some of the time.'

Ivaar frowned, feeling the burn of anger as it surged up into his throat. Had Jael been playing with him? Was that possible? 'Tell our friend to keep his ears open. I want to know what's going on inside that cottage.'

Tarak smiled, the look of rage on Ivaar's face warming his heart.

It appeared that the Brekkan bitch's downfall was about to pick up speed.

***

Edela found Aleksander in the stables brushing Sky, the horse who finally had a name. He was talking to her softly as he ran one hand over her dappled red-and-white coat. She smiled sadly. Life had been hard for him lately. If only she could promise that it was going to get any better, but it appeared that her dreams were warning her otherwise.

'Awake at last!' Aleksander grinned when he saw her. He'd left the house early to go riding, desperate for some air that felt fresh and non-Tuuran. He hated the close, cloying feel of the place and its people as they squirmed about miserably beneath its growing walls. 'I thought you'd decided to sleep the day away.'

'Oh, if only I could!' Edela chuckled. 'Imagine that? But at my age, I'd probably just end up stiff, sore, and even more crotchety. Better to be shuffling about in the freezing cold looking for you!' She wandered over to Deya, holding out a carrot.

Aleksander glanced around, happy to see that the stable boy had left. 'You've had a dream, haven't you? I can tell by that crease between your eyes. Whenever you've been dreaming, you walk about with that big line all day.'

'Do I?' Edela had never been told that before. She laughed, relaxing her crease a little. 'It's hard to keep hold of the dreams. You might not think there is much work in having them, but dreams are like clouds. They all float past you, and you have to grab hold of those things you think could be important. Go after them, follow them, go deeper. Until you learn that, it all just feels like a muddle, and you can't tell which are true visions, and which are just your fears and desires leading you astray.' She sighed, moving along to pat Sky. 'I can't hold onto them as I once did. I suppose I am old.'

'Well, yes, you are!' Aleksander laughed. 'But think of all that you *have* been able to find out so far. We're only here because of you, and now we know that we have to get to Oss to help Jael. Don't be hard on yourself. You're the only reason we have *any* idea about what's going on.'

Edela smiled, patting his hand, then froze.

She looked up into his dark eyes, and was immediately back in her dream, seeing the hand with the ring and the note. She shivered. That golden ring, with a blue sapphire set in a gold star... she could see it so clearly now.

That beautiful ring had belonged to Fianna Lehr.

And Fianna Lehr had been Aleksander's mother.

***

Jael yawned as she stepped through the snow, which seemed much deeper today. Walking felt harder than it usually was. Or perhaps it was that her aching limbs were as tired as her aching eyes? But she thought of her bed and smiled. Biddy had sent her away for some real sleep, and as worried as Jael was about Eadmund, she realised that without sleep, neither she nor Thorgils would be able to keep watch over him.

She caught sight of the stables and sighed. Tig and Leada had been so neglected while she'd been looking after Eadmund. She would have to try and take Tig riding tomorrow, but she couldn't face asking Ivaar to ride Leada, and there was no chance that Thorgils could come with her, so poor Leada would have to wait for another day.

'Ahhh, there you are!' Ivaar called, striding towards her. 'You look dressed for our ride!'

Jael tried to keep her shoulders up, and her face calm as her body sagged. She'd really led herself into a thick forest with this stupid plan of hers. She took a deep breath and tried to smile. 'I was actually thinking about coming to find you,' she said with effort, cursing herself for the stubborn creature that she was. Eadmund was not going to recover for some time, and if she could keep Ivaar busy and away from him, even for a while, then it was worth it. 'I may be ready to ride with you again. If you promise that you'll only try to kiss Leada this time.'

Ivaar came closer, wanting to see her eyes. 'I can only try,' he breathed softly. 'But it won't be easy.'

Jael shuddered, staring into those icy blue eyes.

Something was wrong.

It was the sort of shudder usually followed by an urge to grip her sword, to feel the comfort it provided when she felt under threat. And right now, for some reason, Jael felt in danger.

***

'What is it?' Aleksander grabbed Edela's hand. Her face had gone completely white, her eyes blinking at him in horror as she stumbled in the straw. 'Edela, what have you seen?'

Edela closed her eyes in an effort to calm her rising panic. Aleksander loved Jael, she knew that. Aleksander would never, ever hurt Jael.

She trusted him... didn't she?

'Oh, it's nothing, nothing,' she mumbled, suddenly overcome by the need to sit down. 'I just saw a vision from my dream again.' She glanced around, lowering her voice. 'It was about the two girls, the beheaded ones. I saw more this time. Someone collected their blood. Took some of their hair.'

Aleksander's thick eyebrows shot up. 'That sounds like magic.'

'It does, most certainly,' Edela agreed, although she was only half-listening. The other half of her was desperately trying to think of a way to find out more information about Aleksander's mother without causing him any distress. Fianna had been one of Gisila's closest friends. She had helped raise Jael. Why would she have sent those men to kill Jael, especially as they ended up killing her and her husband? It made little sense to her muddled mind.

'We have to find out who those girls were,' Aleksander said. 'There must be a reason you're being shown them again. As though you missed something the first time?'

'Dreams can be like that,' Edela agreed unsteadily. 'Sometimes, there are just too many pictures and not enough of me to make sense of them all. As I said, I'm getting far too old for this now.'

Aleksander slipped Sky a piece of bread from his pouch and wrapped his arm around Edela's shoulder. 'I'll take you back to Branwyn. It's too cold to stand around in here for long. Unless you're a horse, of course, and even then I'm sure they'd much rather be sitting by a warm fire given half a chance!'

Edela smiled distractedly, allowing herself to be led away,

her heart sinking with every wet squelch of her boots. If Fianna had conspired to have Jael killed, what did Aleksander know about it?

***

They'd ridden so fast that the bitter slap of wind on Jael's face had managed to keep her awake. As much as she needed sleep, she also needed to feel free from the confines of that horrible cottage, and the worry that lay cloaked around Eadmund.

Although, there was the nagging problem of what was wrong with Ivaar.

His mouth was tight when he smiled, his eyes evasive and yet predatory. Something had happened, but what?

Pulling on Tig's reins, she decided to find out.

'Had enough already?' Ivaar breathed, slowing Leada to a stop. His eyes lingered on her, but although they were still full of desire, there was no warmth in them anymore.

'No, not yet, but it's hard to talk when we're chasing the clouds like that,' Jael said, smiling as brightly as she could manage; it wasn't only Ivaar who could play games, she decided. 'Besides, I wanted to know what was wrong.'

Ivaar blinked, his eyes shifting about uncomfortably. 'Wrong?'

'Mmmm, you're not very good at hiding your feelings,' Jael said. 'Did you know that? You look ready to kill me rather than kiss me.'

'Kill you?' Ivaar muttered. 'Why do you say that?'

'Well, there is some dreamer in me, you know. I do have the occasional vision. I can see things more deeply than most,' Jael almost-lied, wondering how easily she could tease the truth out of him.

Ivaar opened and closed his mouth, surprised by that. 'Well, I...' He ran one hand over his cropped hair, suddenly anxious under Jael's inquisitive stare. Her bluntness had surprised him, and now he just felt confused. 'I know about you and Eadmund.' His blood ran hot just speaking his brother's name before it was whipped away from him on the wind. They had stopped the horses in a wide, flat valley, and the wind raced between them with a ferocity that matched his darkening mood.

Jael tried her best to look only puzzled, but her mind was racing, trying to quickly piece together what that actually meant. She looked at him and smiled. 'Ahhh, so you've made friends with Tiras, have you?' It was a guess, but what other explanation could there be?

Tig hated the shriek of the wind, and he skittered about restlessly under her. Jael soothed him with a pat, leaning down to murmur in his ear, giving herself a chance to think.

What would Tiras have found out?

Eadmund's walls *were* very thin...

'Well, I thought he would come in useful,' Ivaar said carefully.

'To spy on me?' She tried her best to look hurt.

'No, no, not you, in particular.' Ivaar looked down at his reins to avoid her eyes. 'But I'm going to be king in a place I no longer know, with loyalties I need to determine. There'll be a lot of people unhappy with Eirik putting Eadmund aside. I need to know of any problems I'll face before I have to face them.'

'And you see *me* as one of those problems all of a sudden?' Jael wondered, her braids whipping across her face. 'Because Tiras told you I was with Eadmund?' She was putting it all on him, making him do the work, not backing away for a moment, her eyes challenging him.

'Well, weren't you?' Ivaar demanded sharply.

Jael nudged her stubborn horse closer to Ivaar. 'You make me an offer of friendship, and then a few days pass, you hear a rumour, and suddenly you decide we're enemies? It's hard to be friends with someone like that. Someone so quick to jump to conclusions. Who has a spy follow you.'

Ivaar could see her point, and he felt cross with himself, but still... 'You told me that you loved this Aleksander. That you were waiting for him. How easy is it for *me* to be friends with someone who lies?'

'Ha! *Lies?*' Jael looked cross now, although truly she was cold, wind-whipped, and desperate to end the game of words and race home to bed. 'I was with Eadmund because Thorgils asked me to go. He begged me to help him because Eadmund is a mess. He's drunk himself into such a state that he's bedridden. So, I've been in that rancid hole, looking after someone I don't want to be married to, while he vomits and pisses all over the place, and your little spy creeps around outside! Maybe next time you should tell him to knock on the door and see what's really going on, because I promise you it's not as exciting as either of you've imagined!' And with that, she turned Tig's head, tapped her heels firmly into his flanks, and steered him for home.

Ivaar blinked after her, his mouth gaping open, the sting of her words sharp on his cheeks.

That had not gone as he'd planned.

CHAPTER FORTY FOUR

Gisila bit her tongue so hard that her mouth filled with blood. Next to her, Axl spluttered Lothar's wine all over the table, Amma choked on the tough piece of chicken she'd been gnawing on, and even Gant coughed in surprise.

The only person who carried on eating his meal without pause was Osbert.

'I hardly think it's *that* shocking!' Lothar laughed, peering at the startled faces. 'I just thought it made sense to bring the wedding forward. Come spring, we only need to be thinking of the invasion, not of feasts and guests. Surely you agree, Gisila? Our focus must be on Hest.'

Gisila's tongue ached, but the pain of Lothar's news was worse. 'Five days? That is not much time to organise a wedding.'

'Well, it's time enough for our needs. You will have plenty of dresses to choose from, I'm sure, from your time as queen... if the moths have been kind. It will be dark, so it doesn't need to be that new anyway, does it? And as for the ceremony, we can make do with whatever you can organise in time. Surely the most important thing is that we're married and can be together... *properly*.' Lothar gave Gisila a look that left everybody sitting at the high table in no doubt as to why he was rushing the wedding forward.

Lothar may have been the king, but Gisila had been determined to keep him at arm's length until they were married, so he'd decided that it was time to remove the remaining obstacle and finally claim her. He had dreamed about having Gisila since the first hairs sprouted on his face, watching with envy as Ranuf made her his bride, all those years ago. She had always been the most beautiful, desirable woman in Andala, and even now, he was tortured with the need to claim her for his own.

'But Father, what about Jael and Edela? What about Aleksander?' Amma wondered quietly. 'Gisila's family will not be here.'

'No, that is true and unfortunate,' Lothar mumbled cheerfully between large gulps of wine. 'But this is not your first marriage, and you are no longer at an age where that sort of thing matters, does it, my dear?' he smiled, leaning towards Gisila. 'Besides, I already have plans for a large feast when we get back from Hest. I'm sure that Eirik and his family will be here then, ready to celebrate our victory and our union.'

Gisila rinsed her mouth with wine, dabbing the corners of her lips with a napkin, resisting the urge to sob. 'Well, yes, you're right, of course. It would have been nice to have my mother here, and even my sister, if she were well enough, but as you say, we can make up for it in the spring.' She glanced quickly at Lothar, avoiding Axl's eyes, which she could tell, were desperately seeking her own.

Lothar belched triumphantly. 'Exactly! Which is why you and I are such a perfect match. Our two heads already think as one, don't they?' And he leaned forward, touching his lank black curls to the side of her head.

Gisila froze, blinking tears away as she caught Gant's eye. He gave her the smallest of reassuring smiles, but Gisila was too filled with panic and despair to notice. Five more days and it would be her wedding night.

She wanted to die.

***

Thorgils could barely keep his eyes open. The silence was sleep-inducing.

Biddy had gone back to the house to make something for their evening meal, and Eadmund was quieter than falling snow behind him. Thorgils sat hunched over the fire, wishing the flames were warmer and that his roughly-hewn stool was a large, soft bed, complete with Isaura and a stack of thick furs. He sighed forlornly, closing his eyes, remembering her eyes, breathing in the thick wood smoke that was being blown back down the hole by the angry wind.

The door creaked open, and he jerked himself awake.

Jael stood there, looking even worse than when she'd left.

Thorgils blinked. 'Couldn't sleep much?'

Jael rushed towards the fire, her face as weary as his. 'I didn't sleep. I went riding.' She ripped off her wet gloves, holding her red hands to the flames.

'Well, I'm not sure that was the best idea.'

'Blame Ivaar,' Jael yawned as she sat down, tugging off her wet boots, which were difficult to budge, much like her foul, Ivaar-tainted mood. 'He came along just as I was about to go into the house, as he always seems to do.'

'Oh, really?' Thorgils looked unimpressed as he stood. 'Try for another kiss, did he?'

Jael shook her head, beckoning him over.

Thorgils frowned. 'What?' he whispered, glancing around.

'Tiras has been creeping around outside apparently, telling tales to Ivaar.'

'Oh, has he now?' Thorgils murmured, his red mop of curls shaking irritably. 'Ivaar does keep good company, doesn't he? First Tarak, now Tiras. A trio of turds.'

'We'll have to be very quiet in here,' Jael warned. 'Ivaar thinks I've turned against him since I'm holed up in here with

Eadmund.'

Thorgils snorted unsympathetically, scratching his beard. 'Well, bad luck for him. I hope he cries himself to sleep tonight! Perhaps I should lay a trap behind the cottage, just underneath the snow? We'll know if someone's crawling about then!'

Jael smiled for the first time in a while. 'More likely one of us will stumble upon it, half asleep, and end up with one less foot!' She rubbed her eyes, nodding towards the bed. 'How is he?'

Thorgils sighed sadly as he wrapped his cloak around his massive frame. Its thick brown fur made him look like a red-headed bear. 'The same. Not a movement, nor a sound. Nothing at all.'

'Well, we have no choice but to wait.'

'Mmmm, we can't do anything else, I suppose. Although,' he mumbled, 'I was wondering if we should tell Eirik? What if this is it? What if Eadmund doesn't wake up?'

'Of course he'll wake up!' Jael insisted. 'He will. The tincture is going to help him. I'm sure it *is* helping him... healing him.'

'By putting him to sleep?' Thorgils asked doubtfully. 'How can that possibly help him? Eadmund needs to be awake. He needs to live again, not lie about like a corpse. This is not helping him, Jael.'

Jael nibbled her bottom lip, not wanting to think that Thorgils was right. She didn't want to believe that Edela could have been wrong about the tincture. They'd all seen that she was supposed to save Eadmund.

But how could she do that when he was just lying there asleep?

***

He watched them, again.

They wandered away towards a place he'd never been: over a hill, into a small, dark grove of trees. It was their secret place. He heard Ivaar whisper that to Melaena as he bent his face close to her ear, his lips brushing past the place on her neck that always made her purr like a cat.

Ivaar smiled then; he must have heard her soft, sweet sound.

He turned around, staring straight at Eadmund, and the smile on his face was so satisfied that Eadmund wanted to run at him, as much as he wanted to run in the opposite direction.

He was trapped here, in these dreams, but they were more like nightmares. Seven-year-old nightmares. So many of them were new, and every one of them was torture. He was desperate not to see any more. To be forced to watch the illusions he'd spent seven years holding onto crumble into dust before his eyes.

Melaena loved Ivaar. Not him. Was that real?

Or was this dream Ivaar's evilest plan so far?

Eadmund didn't think so, as desperate as he was to believe that it was all his brother's well-crafted lie. It felt too real. Melaena felt too real. He'd watched them together, as they kissed and rushed at each other's bodies with urgency; heard the way they laughed at him with such scorn and pity. Her father had forced her to choose Eadmund because he was going to be the King of Oss, she told Ivaar.

Eadmund shook his head.

If only her father had been able to see into the future.

He wanted to scream as he watched them disappear over that hill, Ivaar's arm around Melaena's waist. He closed his eyes, and, at last, there was darkness. Cold, soothing darkness. He would stay here, he decided, in this place where nothing existed. Where nothing was real or false, just this blissful emptiness. There was nothing to see here, and for a moment, he was at peace.

'Eadmund!'

His eyes flew open. His head jerked back.

She was standing there before him in her wedding dress.

Eadmund blinked.

That dress.

Her dark brown curls fell over slender shoulders, cascading over the bright green of that dress. It was perfect, and so was she, standing there in the warm glow of the fire. He couldn't help but smile, as sad as he was, as angry as he wanted to feel. Then he saw the tightness in her eyes. He'd never noticed that before. Her lips were turned upwards as though she was smiling at him, but was she really? He blinked and saw that her eyes were not soft, nor happy, not really.

'Eadmund, what is it? You're looking straight through me,' Melaena laughed, turning around to pick up her goblet. 'You're not nervous, are you?'

What did he say? She was about to die.

What did he say?

The poison was moments from her lips, and Eadmund stood frozen before her, doubting every single thing she'd ever said to him. Every look, every kiss, every moment they'd shared when she was wishing that she was with Ivaar instead. But still, he should stop her, shouldn't he? Warn her? Something! 'I'm fine,' he lied, his voice a nothing echo inside his head.

'Good,' she said. 'Now go and get your goblet because this is the wine my father saved for our wedding night. I want you to have the first taste.'

Eadmund frowned, slowly turning around. His goblet was waiting on a small table next to his side of the bed. Was that going to be his side of the bed, he wondered? If he stopped her, maybe; stopped her drinking that wine.

But he didn't, not yet.

He knew that she was waiting for him. He remembered how it went.

Thunder boomed above their heads, and Melaena jumped, giggling nervously, nearly spilling the wine, but she didn't, not yet. Not until she was falling to the ground would she spill it. All over her perfect wedding dress. All over the snow-white furs that lay beneath their feet. They would be burned, along with her stiff body, wrapped in that perfect dress.

But not yet. Not until she drank that wine.

Eadmund came back to her, stood in front of her, raised his goblet to hers and watched as Melaena smiled again, lifting her goblet to her mouth.

He gulped, his heart beating so loudly inside his ears that it was all he could hear. The goblet was touching her lips, and his mouth hung open, waiting, his breath shallow as everything slowed around him...

'Wait!'

She stopped, staring at him.

'I don't want you to die!' Eadmund rasped, his breath ragged, tears in his eyes. 'I don't want you to die!' he sobbed. 'Please, please don't drink that wine, Melaena! Please...'

Eadmund blinked and she was gone, and he was all alone in the dark, outside, ice under his boots. He felt unsteady, his breath smoking out in front of him in quick, urgent puffs. And then he saw Jael walk out of the hall.

He remembered this.

He started walking quickly towards her, desperate to stop her before she bumped into Tarak; before Tarak pushed her over.

He'd get there in time, he was certain of it.

But just before he was upon her, he watched her walk straight into... Ivaar.

Eadmund stopped.

Jael smiled at Ivaar, placing her hand on his arm, his shoulder, his neck, curling his face down towards hers, kissing him passionately. Ivaar reached around with his arm, pulling Jael to him, kissing her back, not stopping. Eadmund turned around to leave, desperate to escape, but the ice was slippery, and he fell and hit his head, so hard that it started ringing.

And in the distance, he could hear Ivaar's laughter echoing with the pain as it spun and danced, around and around, inside his head.

CHAPTER FORTY FIVE

Eirik was ready to stop being nice.

He'd listened for three interminable days to Isaura prattling on about Vesta. She had ideas – more than he could have anticipated – but at every turn, she came to seek his approval. He'd quickly grown sick of the sight of her as she tiptoed nervously towards him, grizzling toddler permanently attached to her hip. Eirik had done his best not to let his eyes roll and his throat growl, but now he'd simply run out of patience. 'Isaura!' he bellowed, standing up and stalking towards her as she mumbled at him. 'That's enough!'

Isaura looked mortified, quickly backing away. Mads burst into tears of terror, and the entire hall, which had fallen silent, echoed with his distressing wail.

Eirik took a deep breath as he approached the shrinking woman, trying to calm himself down. 'I know you want to help and you have many good ideas,' he said, trying to make himself heard over his grandson's noise. 'But I simply don't care about any of them! You organised your own Vesta for many years so please, please stop asking me to decide everything! To pick every song! Every dish! I simply do not care enough to waste my breath on it! I leave it all up to you. All of it!' And, harrumphing loudly, he stomped past her and all the wide-eyed, shocked servants, heading for the doors, desperate to escape them all.

Isaura didn't move. She knew she needed to try and soothe

Mads whose noise was only getting worse, but she was too stunned to even turn her head in his direction. She felt as though she'd just been slapped, and her cheeks burned with the shame of it.

'Isaura,' Eydis said, trying to get her attention. 'Give him this.' She held out the filthy-looking cloth Mads loved to suck on.

Isaura blinked at the cloth, which Mads quickly snatched out of Eydis' hand, promptly sticking it in his mouth. The sound of quiet sucking was welcome, but she still couldn't bring herself to move.

'Come,' Eydis said gently. 'Come and sit down, and you can tell me all about your ideas. I can help. We can make plans together.'

Isaura followed Eydis to a table by the fire, where Ayla sat. She looked crossly at the dark-haired dreamer, not wanting her company, but Eydis had already sat down, and she didn't see that she had much choice.

'Hello, Eydis, Isaura,' Ayla breathed softly.

Eydis jumped. She hadn't heard or felt Ayla come into the hall. She wouldn't have sat down if she'd known that she was there. Eydis had managed to avoid the dreamer since their first meeting, but she didn't appear to have any choice now.

'I'm sorry,' Ayla smiled. 'I didn't mean to scare you.'

Isaura had started to wake up from her shock now, and she noticed how uncomfortable Eydis was around Ayla. She didn't blame her. She could see what Ivaar found so useful and exciting about the woman, but she didn't believe it had anything to do with her dreams. 'If you don't want to scare people, it would be best not to sneak around so quietly, especially when you're approaching a blind girl,' Isaura grumbled.

Ayla looked embarrassed. 'Yes, of course, I'm sorry. I simply didn't know what to say in the middle of all that noise.'

Now it was Isaura's turn to look embarrassed. She hid her reddening face, running a hand over her son's fine blonde hair. 'Well, I imagine the king has much on his mind, but perhaps you would know more about that than me?'

'He does,' Eydis interrupted, hoping to cool Isaura's ire. 'He doesn't have Morac around to help him, and he's worried about many things,' she sighed sadly. 'But I'm sorry that he was so rude to you.'

'What's happened to Morac?' Isaura wondered, not wanting to dwell on her humiliation any longer.

'I'm not sure, but they must have had a bad disagreement, for I've not heard his voice in weeks. I can tell that Father misses him, but I think he's just too stubborn to say.'

Ayla frowned. That was a name she'd heard in her dreams lately: Morac. She closed her eyes, trying to find him lurking in the depths of her memories, but he was hiding out of sight. She held onto the name, though, and tucked it away, reminding herself to think on it later.

***

'I'm sorry to have kept you waiting, Eirik!' Runa looked mortified as she ushered him inside. 'I forgot that I'd sent Respa on an errand.'

Eirik frowned, peering around the elaborately decorated main room. It was a warm, comfortable house, he thought. Morac had certainly done well for himself over the years. 'Morac is not here, then?' he asked shortly, ignoring Runa's attempts to offer him a seat.

'Ahhh, no.' Runa looked down at the floor and then away to the door. Anywhere but at his face. 'He has gone to visit Evaine.'

Eirik's eyebrows shot up. 'Oh. Has he now?' He was instantly irritated. 'Just a visit, is it?'

'Yes.' Runa had known that she'd have to face Eirik's wrath eventually, and as awkward as it was, it was worth it to have been left behind. 'He was worried about leaving her with Morana. You know what Morana can be like.'

Eirik jerked at the mention of that name. 'I do, indeed,' he murmured, trying to keep his temper under control. 'And when do you expect him back, then?'

Runa's face froze. 'I... I'm not sure. He wasn't happy when he left. He was upset. I don't imagine he'll be away too long, but truthfully, I don't know.'

'I see.'

'Can I offer you something to drink? Some wine or ale?' Runa said lightly.

She could barely meet his eye.

Eirik shook his head briskly, annoyance flaring in his eyes. 'No, it was only Morac I wanted. I really must go and attend to matters in the hall. Vesta is only days away, and there is much to do. I had thought that Morac would be here to help, but no, it appears that he has more important matters to attend to than those of his king.' And with one sharp look at Runa's nervous face, he turned and made his way out through the door.

Runa couldn't move. She was relieved that it was over but worried to think what it all would mean in the end. Eirik was not going to welcome Morac back with open arms, if, or when, he decided to return.

***

Isaura had left to deal with a bleeding knee, and Ayla was pleased to have Eydis to herself. She knew that Isaura disliked her and that her presence would only enhance Eydis' mistrust. As much as she wanted to leave the girl alone, she knew that Ivaar would demand to know if she'd spoken to her.

'I'm sorry about the other day, Eydis,' Ayla said softly, sliding closer. There weren't many left in the hall now, and most were far away but still...

'Did Jael speak to you?' Eydis wondered. She hadn't seen Jael for days, but she was hoping that she'd done as she'd promised.

'Jael?'

Eydis' face fell. She shook her head. 'It doesn't matter.'

'You needn't worry about me, you know,' Ayla tried to reassure her. 'I don't mean you any harm. I went about our first meeting all wrong. I shouldn't have led you away like that. I frightened you when I was only trying to befriend you.'

'Why?' Eydis turned to her. 'Because Ivaar wants you to?'

Ayla couldn't blame her for that. She looked around quickly but saw no sign of Ivaar. 'He wants me to get to know as many people as I can, yes. He needs to know who will be loyal to him when he is king.'

Eydis' milky eyes were troubled. She hated to think about what was coming, knowing that Ivaar was at the centre of it all. 'I'm not sure he really cares about whether *I'm* loyal, does he? I'm just a child. Why should I matter to him? Besides, you don't need to talk to me to find out. Can't you see everything in your dreams?'

Ayla smiled. 'I'm sure you know that dreams don't always answer the questions you have. Sometimes they can just be a confusing mess of even more questions.'

Eydis picked at the well-worn grooves in the table. There was so much she wanted to know and learn, and here was someone who could finally help her; the closest she was going to get to any lessons in mastering her dreams. But still, Ayla was loyal to Ivaar, and there was no way that Eydis could trust her.

'I can help you,' Ayla said quietly, sensing Eydis' turmoil. 'I can teach you about your dreams. You are young, and they will be hard to manage without guidance,' she warned. 'When I first came into my dreams, I believed that everything I saw when I closed my eyes was a prophecy, and I couldn't stop warning everyone, revealing what I thought was the future. It took me some time to learn how to tell a true vision from just a dream. To keep quiet until I was sure.'

'There's a difference?'

'Of course!' Ayla laughed. 'That's what they teach you in the temple. How to sort through what you see. To hold onto what is important and useful. To disregard that which is not.'

Eydis' eyes were wide with possibilities, then. What if everything she'd seen about her father and Ivaar, about the terrible things that would happen... what if those weren't real dreams at all, just her own fears for the future? What if it was just her imagination, rather than a vision?

But then she sighed as the light was extinguished.

Ayla had come to her with the same dream.

'You see Ivaar becoming king, then? There is no mistake in that?' Eydis wondered sadly.

Ayla hesitated. She despised Ivaar, but she needed to give him what he wanted to keep him happy, and that kept her cautious.

Eydis could sense her hesitation in the silence, and she suddenly felt more confident. 'I see Ivaar as the king here, and in my dreams, he does terrible things to us all,' she whispered. 'He kills my brother and all those loyal to him, and in my dreams, he kills me.'

Ayla gasped. She had not seen that. 'But perhaps that is just what you fear will happen,' she said quickly, trying to soothe away Eydis' panic. 'Dreams are always filled with our own worries. You must feel very concerned about what will happen after your father's death. It is natural, I promise you, to be seeing such things.'

Ivaar walked past then, and Ayla froze. He had been in a terrible mood since yesterday, but when he saw her talking to Eydis, he raised one corner of his mouth in a half-smile. She nodded at him and looked away, trying to focus on Eydis again, but those eyes of his haunted her, as did Eydis' words.

With Ivaar, anything was possible, and the guilt of what he might be planning to do lay heavy on her heart.

***

Neither of them had much of an appetite anymore.

'Perhaps we do have to tell Eirik?' Jael sighed reluctantly, staring at the lifeless figure before them. Eadmund had shown no signs of coming around since his seizure, and that had been days ago. She glanced at Thorgils, who looked as forlorn as she felt.

'I think so,' Thorgils agreed. 'Someone's bound to come looking for him soon. Let's give him the night, and if he's still like this in the morning, then I think we have to tell him.'

'Perhaps we don't mention the tincture, though?'

'No, we definitely don't mention that,' Thorgils agreed, shaking his head. 'Eirik might think your family tried to kill Eadmund.'

Jael couldn't raise a smile, though, and neither could he.

'You go, take Tig for a ride, see Fyn. It's been so long. He's probably starved to death out there,' Thorgils said quietly. 'Try to sneak away without Ivaar cornering you again, though.'

Jael rolled her eyes, remembering her last conversation with her brother-in-law. She doubted that he was very pleased with her, but she honestly didn't care what he thought anymore. She was done with the plan. 'I do want to go and see Fyn,' Jael sighed, reaching for her cloak. 'Tell him what's been happening. But I won't be long. I don't want to be away long.'

Walking over to the bed, Jael looked down at Eadmund's ashen face. His breathing was almost silent, his body so still. She bit her lip in frustration and turned away. 'Perhaps prod him with something sharp while I'm gone,' she suggested, finding a smile at last. 'He's obviously having far too many good dreams to be bothered waking up.'

Thorgils walked her to the door. 'Well, at least one of us is,' he grumbled. 'When he's back from his dreaming, I'm going to bed until spring!'

***

Ivaar kept whispering in her ear and then she would turn towards him, and they would laugh at some shared joke that no one else was privy to. His leg was pressed against hers, Eadmund noticed, as he stood there watching. She looked different; so cold and far away. Her eyes were only for Ivaar.

Eadmund couldn't understand it at all.

'It's such a shame,' Ivaar said as he rose and started walking forward, 'that it should come to this. But what choice have you given me? What choice have you given us?' He turned around, holding his hand out for Jael to join him. 'As king, I demand loyalty, Eadmund. But what loyalty have you ever shown me? And now? You and your friends here...' He waved his hand dismissively and Eadmund turned to see Thorgils and Torstan standing near him. 'You plot to try and overthrow me, to take *my* crown, the crown our father gave to me!' Ivaar's voice was rising as his eyes narrowed into blade-sharp slits. He let go of Jael's hand and started circling Eadmund, his eyes never leaving his face. 'Jael wanted me to kill you right away. Remove the threat you posed. But I told her that I wanted to trust you, to give you a chance to prove your loyalty to me. To earn a place here on Oss.' Ivaar sighed heavily. 'But my faith in my family was misplaced, it seems.' He nodded at Tarak, who was waiting nearby, his sword glinting in the sunlight.

'Ivaar,' Eadmund croaked as Tarak came forward, dragging a screaming Eydis behind him. Eadmund's eyes bulged in terror. 'Ivaar, please!' He couldn't move. His arms were being restrained by two of Ivaar's bulky warriors. He was too weak to break free. He turned to look at Jael, but her face was an emotionless mask; her eyes wouldn't meet his. 'Jael, you must stop this! Please! Don't let him hurt her!'

Tarak shoved Eydis forward, knocking her to the ground. She was sobbing uncontrollably, her little body shaking in terror as she cowered beneath his shadow. Eadmund tried to lunge for her but he couldn't move. 'Eydis, it's alright! It will be alright, I promise! Just look at me. It's alright, it's alright!'

Eydis started wailing as she kneeled in the dirt, her head spinning desperately, trying to follow his voice.

'I'm here, Eydis. I'm right here behind you. It's going to be alright, I promise!' Eadmund called as calmly as he could. He could feel his heart racing. He could see Thorgils and Torstan trying to wriggle free from their restraints, their panic matching his. 'Ivaar, no! I'll do anything! Anything! Please let her go. I'm begging you! *Please!*'

Ivaar smiled as he looked into Eadmund's desperate eyes, then nodding at Tarak, he walked away, back to Jael, where they waited and watched, unaffected by the screaming, the tears, or the begging.

Tarak raised his sword.

Eadmund shouted, crying out in despair, jerking forward, but it was no use.

The iron-bright blade flew down, sending blood splattering everywhere.

Thorgils blinked. He'd almost fallen asleep by the fire, but as his eyes were closing, he was sure he'd seen Eadmund move. He got out of his chair and leaned over the bed, frowning. Something about Eadmund's face was different.

He looked as though he was in pain.

CHAPTER FORTY SIX

'What's happened?' Fyn demanded as Jael dismounted. 'Where have you been?'

She looked pale and tired, he thought. Something was wrong.

'Oh, that.' Jael tried to smile, but it wouldn't come, and her face remained tense. 'It's Eadmund. He's been unwell.'

'Unwell?' Fyn stared at her, confused.

'More than unwell,' she admitted, leading Tig to the little shelter, tying him to the sturdiest-looking post. 'He's not woken up for a few days.'

Fyn frowned. 'Not woken up? But he's still breathing?'

'Yes, he's still breathing.' Jael yawned as she followed Fyn towards his hut. 'But that's all he's doing. Thorgils is with him now.'

'What happened to him?' Fyn ushered Jael inside and was happy to see that he'd left a good fire burning. He motioned for her to sit down.

Jael sighed heavily and didn't argue, overcome with relief at being away from the cottage, but at the same time, afraid of what might happen while she was gone.

She told Fyn about the tincture and Eadmund's seizure.

He looked just as worried as she felt. 'If only you could talk to your grandmother. If only she were here,' he murmured. 'Surely she'd know what to do to help him since she made the tincture?'

'I'm sure she would,' Jael said wearily. 'But she's not, and I'm not her, so I don't know what to do, except wait.'

Fyn distractedly prodded the fire with his poker, moving the logs around. 'But if he dies... there'll be no one to stop Ivaar.'

Jael leaned into the flames. 'As it stands, Ivaar will get the crown either way. Eirik hasn't changed his mind about that. But yes, without Eadmund there's little hope of getting rid of Ivaar, which is not good news for anyone, except Tarak. He loves Ivaar.'

Fyn cringed, and Jael felt guilty for speaking so thoughtlessly. She tried to lighten the gloom. 'Unless, of course, I manage to accidentally kill him in the contest!'

Fyn gave her a crooked smile. 'That's a nice dream to have, Jael, but it's just a dream. If anyone's going to be accidentally killed, it won't be him.' He blinked repeatedly, trying to shake away the nightmare of that face... those hands.

'Come on, then, let's grab some swords,' Jael said, heaving herself up with some effort. 'I need more practice if I'm going to make that dream of mine come true!'

***

Ivaar leaned over the railings of the Pit watching Tarak train, although he wasn't really watching. He was staring in Tarak's general direction, but in his mind, he only saw Jael. He couldn't stop thinking about their fight – if that's what it had been – and he didn't know what to do next. She had been furious with him, and now he was utterly confused by the whole situation. The thought of taking her from Eadmund was so pleasurable that he didn't want to let her slip through his fingers. Not yet. And then there was the part of him that wanted her body. The frustration of that gnawed away at his already dark mood.

Tarak bellowed loudly as he lifted his opponent up, throwing him into the slush as if he were just an empty sack. He looked triumphantly towards Ivaar, seeking his approval, but instead, Ivaar sighed irritably and turned around, just in time to see Ayla walking towards him. She was a beautiful, shapely woman, he thought to himself, despite her perpetually sad face.

He'd been so lucky to stumble upon her.

She was going to be the key to what would happen next, he was certain of it.

Ivaar raised an eyebrow in Ayla's direction, shutting away all thoughts of Jael. There was more than one woman who could tempt him with her body. 'What did my little sister have to say for herself, then?' he murmured.

Ayla glanced around, trying to avoid Ivaar's hooded eyes. 'She didn't say much. I didn't ask her much. As you suggested, I was just trying to make friends first.'

'Oh.' Ivaar's annoyance twitched his lips.

Ayla watched the darkening clouds on his face, and she scrambled to think of something to clear them. 'But she did say that she saw you as king. She had dreamed that.'

His face lightened. 'And?'

Ayla hesitated for a moment. She felt confused, but ultimately, she knew it was Ivaar who would choose whether she lived or died. 'And... she saw you killing her and your brother.' She waited, watching his face for any signs that Eydis had been right.

The slightest of smiles played around Ivaar's lips, and his eyes, when they peered at hers, were bright like a summer sky. 'Did she now?' He scratched his chin. 'Hmmm, perhaps she's a better dreamer than you already? Maybe that's a reason to keep her alive.'

Ayla felt chilled to the bone as she stared at him. She couldn't tell if he was serious, but surely not? He wouldn't really kill his own sister, would he?

'Come,' Ivaar said, his eyes full of something else now, 'I need to see you naked.' And he walked off without looking back.

Ayla sighed with dread and turned to follow him, desperate to shut away the terrors that were lurking in her mind.

For she saw dark things coming for them all.

***

'You look better,' Thorgils said wearily as Jael sat down with a thud, her whole body numb from the ride.

'Perhaps. A little,' she admitted. 'It was good to see Fyn again and beat him about with a sword for a while.' She bent down, tugging off her boots. 'Although, he's getting so good he did a bit of beating himself.'

'Really?' Thorgils looked surprised as he hunted around for his cloak. 'It's been a long time since I saw that scrawny runt. Perhaps I'll take Leada for a ride tomorrow, stretch out my own sword arm?'

'You should,' Jael smiled, pulling off her wet socks. 'You're going to need some practice before you fight me again.' Her smile faded quickly as she looked towards Eadmund. 'No change, then?'

Thorgils wrapped his cloak around his shoulders. 'Well, actually, he looks different, I think.' He peered down at Eadmund. 'His face has changed somehow. I was falling asleep, but I thought I heard him move or speak, and when I looked at him, it was as though something had shifted. What do you think?'

Jael got up immediately and bent down to inspect Eadmund's face. It was nearly dark outside, and the light from the fire didn't illuminate much, but Jael could tell that Thorgils was right. 'He looks as though he's in pain,' she frowned. She reached down, touching the deep crease that had formed between Eadmund's eyebrows. 'Right here. As though he's having a bad dream.'

'Well then, he must be dreaming about Ivaar,' Thorgils muttered. 'That bastard brings nothing but pain.' He shook his head, eager to get Ivaar out of it. 'Biddy came by while you were gone. Said she'd bring something hot for you later, which I'm sure will be better than anything Odda has planned for me!' He rolled his eyes in terror. 'That woman does not cook well.'

Jael smiled. 'Well, why not go and eat with Biddy, then? I'm sure she's made enough, and honestly, I'm not hungry at all.'

Thorgils looked at her uncertainly.

'Really, go to the house, eat some food, and I'll see you in the morning. And so will Eadmund,' she said firmly. 'I've grown quite bored of this now. I'm going to have him awake by morning, I promise.'

Thorgils opened his mouth to argue, but the fierce look in Jael's eye made him close it. She was determined, it seemed, and he saw no reason to doubt her.

***

Edela was relieved when Aleksander left.

Branwyn's eldest son, Aedan, had come to take him to the tavern, and Aleksander had not hesitated. Edela couldn't blame him. They'd been cooped up inside Branwyn and Kormac's house all day, and she hadn't been able to think of anything to say to him. She'd dreamed of the note writer again, and this time she had seen more than the hand and the ring; she'd seen Fianna's face. But how could she discover more information when the only person she could ask was the one person she was trying not to?

'Mother?' Branwyn wondered into the silence of the room. 'Are you alright? You look very tired today, I think.' She came towards Edela with a cup of warm milk.

'Thank you,' Edela mumbled distantly as she took the cup into her chilled hands. As pleasurable as it had been to see Branwyn again, she missed the solitude of her cottage, which had always provided her with all the quiet she needed to untangle her dreams. 'I'm alright, my dear. I suppose there are just so many things on my mind. It's hard not to feel anxious and frustrated. We don't appear to be making much progress.'

Branwyn pulled a stool next to Edela's chair and sat down, frowning. 'You must have made some, though? You and Aleksander always seem to have your heads together, whispering about something.'

Edela could sense Branwyn's eagerness to find out more. There was also a little resentment there, for which she could hardly blame her. They had opened a door, let both her and Kormac into their secrets, and then promptly shut them out. 'We've not found out much at all, I promise,' Edela smiled gently. 'I will always tell you what I can, but you cannot know everything, nor can Aleksander, and even I'm not allowed to know all the secrets. There's always someone who seems to be one step ahead of us all.'

'You mean the elders?'

Edela sighed. 'Yes, them. If only they'd reveal what they know, then I'm certain we could just get on with things, but it's all a big secret, and, as you said, they like to keep their secrets locked away.'

'Yes, while the rest of us suffer,' Branwyn said crossly. 'I thought Neva would have been different. We were all so close once, but now, I suppose, she's just like the rest of them.'

Edela peered at Branwyn. 'You *were* close, weren't you? You, Gisila, Neva, and Fianna.'

'Yes, once, before we all married. Before Neva went to the temple, and Fianna left for Brekka with you and Gisila. We were all like sisters,' she smiled wistfully into the flames. 'How different it is now. And poor Fianna... what a terrible end she had. Aleksander looks just like her, doesn't he? I've been thinking about her a lot since he arrived.'

'He does, yes,' Edela said, feeling her chest fill with hope. 'He is a very kind man, and he has been very good to me, especially since Jael left. But I wonder, do you think he got that from Fianna or Harald?'

Branwyn was puzzled by the question, and by the intense look on her mother's face. 'Well, I didn't know Harald at all really. But Fianna... she was always very serious, often quiet. She would keep to herself a lot, so perhaps it is her he takes after. But why do you ask?'

'Oh, I just had an odd dream about Fianna the other night,' Edela said lightly, taking a quick sip of milk to shield her eyes from Branwyn's keen stare. 'I suppose it was only natural for her face to appear as I've been spending so much time with Aleksander. But it was just very odd. She seemed different in my dream, almost untrustworthy.' Edela shook her head, unsure of how to lead Branwyn on without opening up a gaping hole of trouble.

'Fianna?' Branwyn frowned. 'No, you'd never say that about her. She was incredibly loyal, especially to Gisila. Gisila trusted her with everything, including Jael.'

'What do you mean, including Jael?'

'Well, don't you remember, there was that incident when Jael was a toddler, and she went missing?'

Edela's eyebrows shot up; she had completely forgotten about that. 'I do, yes. She disappeared for an entire afternoon, didn't she?'

'Gisila told me about it. How everyone in Andala had been looking for her, fearing the worst, and eventually, they'd found Jael in the forest, all alone.'

'Yes, they thought a servant had tried to take her away, as she disappeared at the same time and never came back,' Edela breathed, her heart racing.

'That's right,' Branwyn nodded. 'Well, after that, Gisila trusted no one to care for Jael, apart from Biddy and Fianna. She trusted her completely. So, perhaps you're right to think that Aleksander is like her. She was a good woman.' Branwyn smiled sadly at her mother, losing herself in the events of that terrible night again.

Edela didn't know what to think. Someone had tried to take Jael as a toddler. How could she have forgotten that? And Branwyn was right; Fianna had been very close to Jael, so why would she have sent men to kill her?

It made no sense.

'I think I may head for my bed,' Edela mumbled, almost to herself as she eased her aching bones out of the chair.

Branwyn looked up, surprised. 'Already? But we haven't eaten yet. Kormac's not even home!'

But her mother wasn't waiting.

'Oh, don't worry about me. I just need to go and dream awhile.' And Edela crawled under her bed furs, wriggling into the softest spot she could find before closing her eyes.

She needed to find answers.

***

Jael yawned as she clambered onto the bed beside Eadmund. She had no idea why she'd promised Thorgils that she could wake him up by morning. She had no idea how to do it at all.

Sighing, she wedged herself in between Eadmund and the wall, listening to his barely-there breathing, occasionally interrupted by a loud pop from the fire.

As a young girl, Jael had hated being alone at night, and would often crawl into Edela's bed and listen to her soft voice as it soothed her to sleep. Edela would stroke her long hair and tell her that she would become a dreamer when she grew up, just like she was. Jael would get so cross to hear that. She didn't want to be a dreamer at all. She wanted to be a warrior, like her older brothers were training to be. She wanted to be like her father.

She wanted to rule Brekka.

Jael tried to ignore her dreams when they came. They didn't

come often because she wouldn't let them, or at least that's what she told herself. But Edela insisted that she had inherited the gift of dreams and that it would always be with her, waiting until the day she was ready to acknowledge it.

Turning to look at Eadmund's face, Jael reached out, stroking his cheek, almost shyly. It felt like ice, and she shivered, pulling the furs closer to her body, tucking them over Eadmund. He didn't move and nor did she.

Jael sighed.

If Edela couldn't be here to save Eadmund, then she would have to.

Somehow.

***

It was quiet in the hall. Uncomfortably so. Most of his men and their families were eating in silence, Eirik noticed, looking up from his plate. He took a long drink of ale and frowned. He'd walked himself to a standstill during the day, trudging through the snow, wandering far away from the fort, trying to get rid of the cloud that he'd carried over himself for weeks.

He could see now how much everything had changed.

And how far away he was from all that he'd hoped for.

Turning to his left, Eirik saw Ivaar smiling to himself as he ate, oblivious to the mood of the hall. That was a worry. A king needed to be aware of his people, to anticipate their needs, to manage their expectations. Ivaar gave him the impression that he'd be happy to ignore any needs but his own, much like Lothar Furyck. Then there was Isaura, who wouldn't meet his eye. But who could blame her?

That was it.

There was no Morac, Eadmund, Jael or Thorgils, no Eydis

even, who didn't like to eat with Ivaar, it seemed.

Eirik had thought a communal meal in the hall would help bring everyone together, but all it had done was show him how much everything had fallen apart. 'I was harsh on you, Isaura,' he admitted, running a hand through his beard as he turned towards his daughter-in-law. 'Perhaps we could try again tomorrow? I know Vesta means a lot to Eydis. I'd like to see her smile again.'

Isaura looked up tentatively. 'I understand,' she said quietly. 'Our return has not been easy for anyone.'

'No, that is the truth,' Eirik said sadly. 'But perhaps Vesta is a chance to smooth everything over? Leave all the broken things lying in the past? A time to start again. We could all benefit from that, I think.'

Isaura didn't know what to say. She nervously sipped her ale. 'Eydis has been helping me today. Perhaps we can all meet tomorrow and finalise our plans? We made a lot of decisions so there won't be much to talk about, I promise.'

Eirik laughed. 'Well, I'm sorry for barking at you like a rabid dog. I'm sure I can stand a few more questions before I do it again!'

Isaura glanced at her father-in-law. His face had relaxed, and he appeared less inclined to attack her now. 'Perhaps we should ask Jael to join us? She can tell us how they do Vesta in Brekka?'

'I imagine that one would rather stick herself in the eye with a sword than do that, but you can always try!' Eirik winked, missing his other daughter-in-law suddenly. He hadn't seen her for days, and he felt the absence of her feisty company. Everyone was avoiding him, it seemed, and who could blame them? He would have to go and find Jael and Eadmund tomorrow and see about making peace.

He had to find a way forward for all their sakes.

***

Eadmund stood in the smoke as it belched from the pyre. He tried to blow the stench out of his nostrils. It was not a memory he wanted to keep: the smell of her as she burned. Not that she was there anymore, he told himself. The flames were dying down, retreating, shrinking, revealing all that was left of Melaena.

Eadmund felt cold, but it was summer, he remembered.

He could feel himself shaking with unhappiness, with anger, with the overwhelming desire to merge into the smoke and drift away with Melaena's ashes. He coughed as the smoke found its way to the back of his throat.

'Here,' she said. 'You need a drink.'

Eadmund turned around, angry before he even saw her face. He ignored her outstretched arm and the cup she was holding for him. 'Get away from me before I kill you!'

Jael blinked, confused.

'I know all about you and Ivaar. About her and Ivaar too,' Eadmund spat, turning back to the fire. 'I've been blind to everything, but now I can see.'

'You know nothing, Eadmund,' Jael said firmly. 'Nothing that is real. You're dreaming. Nothing is real in here.'

He turned back to her, taking the cup.

He was so thirsty.

It tasted horrible, though, like that cursed tincture. Eadmund spat it out, throwing the cup away. 'You and Ivaar, that was very real. The way you were with him.'

'No, it wasn't,' Jael insisted, stepping closer. 'That was your fear. That what happened with Melaena will happen with me. That I'll be trapped by him too. But look at me... do I look like I'm going to let Ivaar trap me? Really? You think I'd choose a man like that?'

Eadmund stared at her. She was dressed in mail, her sword at her side, her hair braided. Ready for battle.

She looked exquisite.

'I've come for you, Eadmund. I've come to take you back.'

'Why?'

'Because you have to save Oss. You have to kill Ivaar. And if you stay here, he'll destroy everyone and everything you love.'

'Including you?'

'Me? No, Ivaar won't destroy me, but I won't be able to stop him destroying everything else. Not without you.'

The bitter smoke made Eadmund cough again, and he stepped away from the pyre, away from Jael, and she let him go.

'I've seen a lot of things,' he said slowly, turning back to her. 'But most of all, I've seen how stupid and weak I've been. How much I let Ivaar take from me. And I did nothing about it, nothing at all.'

'Well then, come here so I can take you back. So you can stop him.'

'And how will you do that?' Eadmund wondered, stepping slowly towards her. 'How will you get me out of these nightmares?'

'Like this,' Jael breathed, and reaching up, she gently kissed his lips.

Eadmund blinked, surprised and unsettled. He looked towards the pyre, but it had gone. And they were in the snow. And that smoky taste in his throat was seven-years-old, and he wasn't there anymore, and nor was Melaena.

But Jael was, and he took her face in his hands and kissed her back.

CHAPTER FORTY SEVEN

Gisila shivered as Arnna hobbled around the bottom of her dress, muttering away to herself. Arnna's fire was only spluttering, barely there, but she didn't appear bothered by the chill.

'Hmmm, it's a shame there was no time for a new dress,' Arnna grumbled. 'This is well-made but old now, and the moths have had their way with it somewhat.'

Gisila didn't care. She'd simply pulled out the first dress she had come across in her old chest; the chest where she kept her memories of a different life. She thought of Ranuf regularly now, wishing he was here to slit Lothar's throat from ear to ear. He would have been furious with the damage his waste of a brother had inflicted upon Brekka and his family. Gisila sighed, letting his face slip helplessly back into the past. What was the point in such fantasy, she told herself, when she was marrying Lothar in two days.

Arnna straightened up, taking Gisila's hands in hers. 'We will make the best of it, I promise. You'll look like a queen again, don't worry.'

Gisila could feel tears sliding down her cheeks, but she made no attempt to wipe them away. 'I don't care if I look like a servant when I marry that man,' she sniffed. 'So don't trouble yourself too much, Arnna. Just tighten it a bit, and that will be enough.'

Arnna frowned, peering up at Gisila's morbid face. 'Oh, my dear, you must think of how good it will feel to be the queen again!

You forget how much power there is in being a queen, especially one with a husband who desires her as much as Lothar does you.' She bustled off to her kitchen and poured Gisila a cup of wine. 'Here, drink this. Better than an old rag to stop your tears!' She bent down, continuing to assess the prospects of the dress.

'Lothar might desire me, as you say,' Gisila cringed, sipping the tart wine, 'but I can't think of anything good that will come of that. For me, at least.'

'There are many ways a woman can get what she wants,' Arnna cackled. 'And there is also much a woman can endure if she has a mind to. How many women do you know like Jael, who can take what they want with a sword? None! And even *she* couldn't get herself out of a marriage she didn't want. But that daughter of yours is tough. She'll find a way to make it right.' She straightened up again and started to creep around the middle of the dress, pinning the waist; Gisila had lost a lot of weight since she was last the Queen of Brekka. 'There are many ways to feel powerful that don't require a sword. You just need to think of them. Stop seeing yourself as weak. There is strength in you, Gisila. You must remember that. Surely Jael didn't inherit all that fire from Ranuf alone?'

Gisila took a large gulp of wine, letting Arnna's words swirl around her head. She dropped her shoulders back and held her head a little higher, remembering how it had felt when she'd walked around Andala as queen. It had not been that long ago at all. How had she forgotten so quickly? Arnna was right; there was a chance here to take back some of what she had lost. If only she could survive the disgusting things Lothar planned to do to her. She shuddered but didn't retreat.

Surely she had enough strength in her to withstand that?

***

'Thorgils! Where have you been hiding?' Eirik called, walking towards the fur-covered figure who had stopped, frozen to the spot, not far from Eadmund's cottage. 'I was just going to find that son of mine. I haven't seen either of you for days!'

Thorgils hadn't seen such a genuine smile on Eirik's face in a while, which was unfortunate as today was the day they were going to tell him about Eadmund. He didn't want to do it now, though, not until he had a chance to speak to Jael, to see what had happened in the night.

'Oh, well, things have been... difficult... lately,' Thorgils said awkwardly, ducking his head, afraid his eyes would betray him. 'I don't suppose either of us have enjoyed the changes around here very much.'

'No,' Eirik agreed, his smile fading. 'No, I suppose not, but there is no choice. Ivaar is here now.'

'For how long?' Thorgils wondered.

Eirik frowned. He hadn't thought about that. 'Well, I suppose he will return to Kalfa soon. I know he wants to stay for the contest, so perhaps he'll leave after that? He has to sort out his affairs in Kalfa, and I'll need to find a new lord for sure.'

'Maybe you could send Tarak to Kalfa?' Thorgils suggested cheekily. 'I'm sure he'd love to be a lord.'

'A good idea!' Eirik laughed. 'If only I didn't need his sword so much.'

'Ahhh well, wait till the contest is over, then you'll see if you still need Tarak,' Thorgils warned.

Eirik raised an eyebrow. 'That's confident talk after what he did to you last time.'

Thorgils blinked that memory away. 'Time has moved on. I'm better than I was.'

'I'm glad to hear it,' Eirik smiled. 'If only Eadmund could say the same.' He stepped past Thorgils, who moved to stop him.

'Thorgils?' Eirik stared at him, puzzled.

Thorgils dropped his head. 'There's something you should know,' he muttered into his beard.

Eirik tensed all over. 'What is it? What's happened?'

***

It was the cold that woke her.

Jael's teeth were chattering so much that she bit her tongue and jerked awake, her eyes bulging from the pain. The fire was long gone, and the cottage was freezing in the early morning light. Jael leaned over, peering at Eadmund's face.

She shook her head and sighed.

He hadn't moved.

Nothing had changed at all.

Jael crawled out of bed despondently, wrapping a fur around her shoulders. She shuffled over to the fire, grimacing at the now-familiar pain in her back. Thankfully, Thorgils had left everything she needed nearby, and she yawned her way through setting a new fire, trying not to send sparks into her fur instead of the tinder she had placed in front of the kindling. As the flames started to take, Jael sat back, leaning against a stool, staring at the bed. So much for thinking that she could do anything, she told herself miserably.

So much for her being the one to save Eadmund.

Everyone had been wrong there.

She'd had no dream that she could remember. Nothing had happened at all, and now they would have to tell Eirik. She was not looking forward to that.

Standing up, Jael took her fur to the bed and laid it over Eadmund, tucking it around him, brushing her hand over his cheek, making sure she could still feel his breath, warm on her skin. That was something at least. She stood there for a moment, shivering, wondering where she'd left her cloak.

The door banged open, and Jael jumped in surprise, reaching

for the sword she didn't have. It lay wrapped up in the cloak she couldn't find.

It was Eirik, and Thorgils was not far behind him.

Jael glared crossly at Thorgils as Eirik barged past her, striding towards the bed. She moved to stop him. 'Wait! Eirik, just wait a moment!'

'I want to see him!' Eirik demanded crossly, his eyes tight with concern.

'He's resting,' Jael tried again.

'Resting?' came the faint croak from behind her, and she spun around to see Eadmund, starting to move, his eyes fluttering open. He coughed, trying to sit up, but fell back, exhausted. 'Is that what you call it?'

Jael couldn't move. She stared at Eadmund in shock.

Eirik sat down on the bed, relief flooding his body. 'Thorgils said you'd been unwell, very unwell. And by the look of you, he had it right.'

Eadmund was so weak that he could barely keep his eyes open. 'Well, you can blame these two here for that,' he rasped crossly. 'They've been trying to cure me. They stopped me drinking. Tied me to a chair.'

'Really?' Eirik murmured, raising his eyebrows in Jael and Thorgils' direction. 'Sounds like a good idea to me,' he smiled. 'I wish I'd thought to do that earlier. I wouldn't have needed to call Ivaar back.'

Eadmund flinched at the sound of his brother's name but his gaze remained sharp as he rested it on Jael. 'I don't suppose everyone is disappointed that Ivaar's here, though, are they Jael?'

Thorgils and Eirik blinked at Jael, and she blinked at Eadmund. She didn't know what to say. What *had* he been dreaming about?

'Hello?'

They turned to see Biddy standing awkwardly in the doorway, struggling with a basket of food that looked far too heavy for her small frame. Thorgils rushed over to take it, ushering her inside.

'You're awake!' Biddy smiled at Eadmund, then noticed the

cross look on his face and the tension on everyone else's. She frowned, confused. 'I've brought food if anyone's hungry?'

Eadmund managed to sit up, groaning and light-headed. 'Have you anything to drink?' he asked desperately.

Everyone turned towards him, mouths open.

'I have some milk,' Biddy offered cautiously.

'Perfect,' Eadmund croaked. 'Please.'

Four sets of shoulders relaxed as Biddy went digging into her basket.

Jael could feel Eadmund's eyes boring into her. This wasn't how she imagined it would go. He looked ready to kill her.

Eadmund turned away from Jael. 'How long have I been asleep?' he asked Thorgils, who was caught between being thrilled that his best friend was awake, and confused as to why he was in such a foul mood. Although, when he thought on it, they had kept him prisoner, and after that, he probably would've felt ready for a fight too. 'A few days, I think. We've barely slept while we looked after you so I couldn't say for sure.'

'Three days,' Biddy said, handing Eadmund a cup of milk.

'Wait!' Jael called out, snatching the cup out of Biddy's hand. 'You have to finish the tincture first. There's only a drop left, but you need to have it all before you drink anything else.'

Eadmund glared at her. 'Well, go on, then, let's finish it.'

Eirik looked at Thorgils, confused. 'Tincture?'

'It's a long story,' Thorgils smiled wryly, enjoying the relief of thinking they had made it to the end. At least he hoped they'd made it to the end.

Jael brought the bottle to Eadmund, shaking the last drops of the vile liquid onto his tongue. He didn't look pleased, but he didn't protest either.

They all held their breaths as he swallowed it down, before holding a hand out to Biddy. 'Can I have that milk now?'

Biddy looked towards Jael, who nodded.

The tincture was done.

Now they had to wait and see what would happen, though

with the mood Eadmund was in, Jael wasn't sure what that would mean for any of them.

***

'What happened to your husband?'

Ayla almost dropped the bowl of apples she was carrying to the table. 'He, ahhh... he died.'

'Oh, I'm sorry,' Eydis said sympathetically. 'That must have been very hard for you.'

'Yes, it has been... difficult,' Ayla said sadly as she placed the bowl down and came to sit beside Eydis, handing her the reddest apple she could find. 'Here, take this.'

'Thank you,' Eydis smiled, biting into the sweet-smelling fruit. She was becoming more comfortable around the dreamer now. She didn't feel threatened at all; not like the first time. Eydis didn't trust Ayla, but she no longer feared her, and that was enough to keep her talking.

Isaura bustled over to the table, her forehead wrinkling in displeasure to see Ayla sitting with Eydis again. She'd suddenly become a very visible presence, and Isaura had a bad feeling about it, convinced that Ivaar had her spying on them all. She would have to find time to speak to Eydis and warn her, but first, she had to survive the next two days. Agreeing to organise Vesta had been a bigger undertaking than she'd imagined, and she felt nervous about speaking to Eirik again.

Ivaar sauntered over to the table and sat down beside Ayla, close enough for their shoulders to touch, Isaura noted sourly.

'Ladies,' he smiled to Ayla and Eydis, ignoring his wife.

Eydis' smile quickly disappeared, and she squirmed on the bench, desperate to leave.

'Good news!' Eirik announced as he entered the hall, Thorgils trailing reluctantly behind him. Eirik had insisted that Thorgils tell him everything about Eadmund and the tincture and he'd made him follow him all the way back to the hall while he listened to the tale.

Ivaar looked at his father with interest, but Isaura glanced away, not wanting her eyes to betray her. She hadn't caught a glimpse of Thorgils in days, and she was desperate to know how he was, but Ivaar didn't need to know that.

'Eadmund is awake!' Eirik smiled widely.

'Eadmund?' Ivaar laughed. 'At this time of day? That's good news indeed.'

No one joined in Ivaar's joke. In fact, Eirik ignored him entirely and spoke instead to Isaura and Eydis, much to Ivaar's annoyance.

'He's been ill. Very ill. Jael and Thorgils have been looking after him. He's finally through the worst, so we should be seeing him around here again, once he gets his strength back.'

Ivaar was surprised. Jael had been telling the truth then. He felt a brief surge of pleasure at that, which was quickly extinguished by the look of happiness on his father's face. Eadmund was well again.

So what did that mean?

What did Eirik want that to mean?

Ivaar quickly shut those thoughts away. He was going to be king. Ayla had seen it. Eydis had seen it. Eadmund wasn't about to take his birthright away from him again. 'Well, that is good to hear, Father,' Ivaar said as he stood, smiling with forced enthusiasm. He caught Thorgils peering at him. 'And just in time for Vesta too.'

Eirik turned to his son with a genuine smile. 'Yes, it is perfect timing. We shall have to make this Vesta the most memorable one yet. If you think we can manage that between us?'

Isaura swallowed nervously, not daring to look up. 'I think we can,' she said with absolutely no conviction at all.

'Good!' Eirik smiled, handing his cloak to a servant who was hovering expectantly near him. He rubbed his hands together, sitting down opposite her. 'Now, tell me your plans. I want to hear everything!'

Isaura gulped.

Thorgils, with one, quick look in her direction, turned and headed for the door, his chest tight with joy for Eadmund, and sorrow for himself.

***

Biddy had cleared everything away after they'd eaten, leaving quickly. The tension between Jael and Eadmund had only increased, and she had no desire to be there when one of them lost control.

Jael sat in front of the small fire, freezing, wondering why she hadn't followed Biddy back to the big house with the large fire and the thick walls. She nibbled a fingernail, feeling Eadmund glowering at her, as he had been doing since he'd woken up. She couldn't understand it at all. They had been trying to help him. Was he truly that mad at them? 'Perhaps you need to go back to bed?' she suggested, glancing at his pale face.

Eadmund frowned. 'I've had enough of that bed for a while.' He shifted about uncomfortably on the stool, his body aching from lying down for so long. He did feel weak and tired, but nothing was getting him back into that bed in a hurry.

'Well, perhaps I should go, then? Leave you alone?' Jael said irritably, standing up. 'You look as though you'd rather I left.' She grabbed her cloak, wrapping it around her shoulders, her face as moody as his.

Eadmund stood up, too quickly. He felt light-headed, swaying for a moment.

'Are you alright?' Jael moved towards him, concerned, but he shook his head quickly, and she backed away towards the door. 'Fine, then I'll go.'

'I saw you and Ivaar in my dreams.'

'Saw us? Doing what? What does that mean?'

'Oh, kissing, killing my sister, that sort of thing.'

'What?' Jael looked horrified. 'Killing Eydis? Me?'

'Well, you were there,' Eadmund said frostily. 'You didn't stop him. You watched while Ivaar had Tarak kill her.'

Jael frowned. 'But it was just a dream. Eydis is alive. I haven't seen Ivaar for days. I've been here looking after you! It was just a dream.'

'It didn't feel like a dream. It felt so real. The way you looked at him, kissed him, wanted him.' Eadmund came towards her, his eyes full of simmering resentment. 'Just like her.'

'Who?'

'Melaena.' Eadmund shook his head. 'I saw her with Ivaar too. Saw the truth in that. She never loved me at all. She wanted him, not me. She had no choice but to marry me.'

'They were just dreams, Eadmund,' Jael said, trying to calm him down. 'You aren't a dreamer, so they were just dreams. But you're awake now. You have to let them go. You're not there anymore. You came back.'

'Because of you.'

'Me?'

Eadmund grabbed her arm. '*You* made me come back.' He closed his eyes, remembering when she'd reached up to kiss him. 'You brought me back here. I came back for you.'

'Good. Because I was trying to bring you back. I wanted you to come back... to me.'

Eadmund stared into Jael's eyes, feeling his tension relax at last. He reached out a finger, tracing her cheekbone, touching her scar, leaning in until their lips were almost touching. He could feel tears coming as he closed his eyes and kissed her. Softly. Slowly. And Jael came into his arms, pushing herself against his body, her cold skin touching his, his tears wet on her face. Eadmund grabbed her head, holding it tightly in his hands, pulling her towards him, running his hands down her neck, feeling the throbbing of her heart against his.

Jael pulled back and looked at him, fearlessly.

She wasn't going anywhere now.

And reaching up, she kissed him, running her hands over his chest, feeling the chill of his skin through his worn tunic. She pushed him backwards, towards the bed and they fumbled their way onto the furs, quickly, awkwardly, rushing to remove their clothes despite the chill of the cottage.

'Jael,' Eadmund breathed into her hair. 'You saved me.' He looked at her again, smiling. 'You saved me.'

Jael stared at him, her eyes never leaving his. 'Stop talking,' she whispered, reaching a hand underneath his tunic, kissing him again, more urgently now. 'Before I change my mind.'

PART FOUR

Fury

CHAPTER FORTY EIGHT

Gant looked nervous as he approached Gisila. It was the day before the wedding, and he didn't imagine that she'd be in a very stable place.

'What has Lothar sent you to do now?' Gisila asked crossly, spinning around.

Gant was surprised. She had changed since he saw her last. She reminded him of the woman he used to know. Her shoulders were straight again and her face, although cold, did not look self-pitying. If he'd dared to come closer, he would have seen the fear and misery lurking in her almond-shaped eyes, but he didn't, so all Gant saw was the illusion of confidence Gisila had decided to construct to help her survive Lothar.

'He, ahhh, he wanted to know if you had everything you needed? If there was anything he could do for you? Anything you wanted?'

Gisila looked around her small cottage and thought on that. Axl had only just left. She noticed his pile of things flung on top of his bed, spilling onto the reeds.

He had always been her messiest child.

'You can tell Lothar,' she said firmly, walking towards Gant, wanting him to see her face, to see that she'd come back. 'You can tell the king that I want Axl to have his old bedchamber in the hall. I'll be able to relax and feel much more comfortable if I know that Axl is nearby. If I can keep a close eye on him.'

Gant raised one scarred eyebrow at that. 'Osbert's room?'

'Yes, Osbert's room.' Gisila didn't take her eyes off him. 'Which was Axl's room.'

'Well... I can try,' Gant said slowly, shaking his head. 'Although I'm not sure what Lothar will think about that. Or Osbert.'

But Gisila wasn't finished. 'I would also like a new crown. I have no wish to wear the hand-me-down crown his dead wife stole from me. If Lothar is taking a new queen, then his new queen wishes to have a new crown.'

Gant didn't know what to say. What had gotten into her? He didn't dislike it, though, not at all. Gisila looked fierce, and she reminded him very much of Jael in the fading light of the fire. He smiled. 'I'll let him know. Is there anything else?'

'No, but I shall send Gunni to find you if I have any other ideas,' she said coolly.

Gant bent his head. 'Good, well I'll be at the hall organising everything for tomorrow.' He was unsure of what to say to fit the moment. Despite this show of strength, he knew how much Gisila was dreading it. He could see the slightest tremble in her hands now as she clasped them in front of her dress. He took two steps forward and spoke quietly. 'I wish you luck, Gisila. I'll do whatever I can to make it easier, I promise.' And backing away quickly, he turned and opened the door, closing it quietly behind himself.

Gisila's shoulders fell into a rounded heap as all the air in her tight chest rushed out of her mouth. Her head drooped, and her eyes burned with tears.

Luck? She didn't need luck.

She needed an intervention from the gods.

***

Eadmund was sound asleep. Jael was naked and freezing under the furs next to him, filled with an urgent desire to escape. For all that she'd wanted Eadmund, she'd spent the night dreaming of Aleksander. Her head was a confused mess of guilt and desire, her body clenched tightly as she lay there shivering.

She just wanted to leave.

Jael crawled out of the uncomfortable bed as it creaked and groaned, but Eadmund didn't stir. Quickly glancing at him, she hoped he hadn't slipped back into those dreams again. More likely he was completely exhausted, she decided. They had spent the best part of the night awake. She frowned, the memories of it torturing her. It had been a beautifully strange experience. Eadmund wasn't Aleksander, though, and she'd only ever known Aleksander's touch. But, as much as she was cursing herself for her disloyalty, and her lack of self-control, part of her was just as eager to crawl back under those furs and do it all again.

Jael shook her head, furious with herself, and grabbing her frozen clothes, she hurried them on. She needed to get out of this vile cottage and feel the wind on her face. Perhaps it would whip some sense into her?

Pinning her cloak to one shoulder, she eased open the door, and, with one last, guilty look at Eadmund, she disappeared outside.

'So that went well, then?' Thorgils wondered with a lopsided grin as he stood knee-deep in the snow, staring at her. 'Did you break our prisoner?'

Jael jumped, then frowned. 'Sssshhh, he's asleep in there.'

'And you're trying to sneak away, are you?' Thorgils laughed hoarsely. 'I've done that before, many a morning.'

'Oh, really? Well, don't feel any need to tell me about it on our ride,' she grumbled quietly, stalking away from the cottage and Eadmund, and all those confusing feelings which nagged and poked inside her.

'*Our* ride, is it?' Thorgils smiled, hurrying to catch up with her. 'You're bringing me back into the fold, then?'

Jael turned to look at him sharply. 'We've much to do, you and I, if we're going to get anywhere in this contest.' And glancing around, she lowered her voice. 'For us to get anywhere, it means defeating Tarak, and neither one of us is ready for that yet, are we?'

Thorgils nodded, his face quickly matching the seriousness of hers. 'We are not at all ready.'

'Let's get going to Fyn's, then,' Jael said shortly. 'We need to spend the entire day there, training until we can't stand. We have a lot to catch up on.'

Thorgils smiled to himself as he trailed after her. 'You're a little feisty this morning, Jael, I must say. Are you sure Eadmund was still breathing when you left him?'

Jael wasn't even listening. She needed to fight, to release the panic that was building inside her. And more than that...

She needed to defeat Tarak.

***

'Are you talking to me today?' Aleksander wondered, peering at Edela's troubled face. He no longer took it personally when she went quiet and ignored him – he knew that she was trying to unravel her dreams – but the way Edela had looked at him yesterday had unsettled him greatly. It felt as though what she was working on was all about him.

'Of course, of course, I am.' Edela looked up, smiling. 'I suppose there's just too much on my mind. Sometimes, I disappear.'

Aleksander grabbed her arm, pulling her towards him as soldiers came riding at speed down the middle of the street, flinging snow and muck at everyone they passed. Aleksander wiped some out of his eye. 'Lovely! This place never fails to irritate me.'

Edela laughed, wiping her own eyes. 'Well, hopefully, we can leave soon and get back to Andala.'

'Soon?' Aleksander was surprised. 'But do we really know anything much at all? We've a lot of breadcrumbs, but none of them lead anywhere, do they?'

Edela didn't know what to say to that. It was a clear enough day, but as they walked down Tuura's main street, she felt a dark cloud hanging over her. And that cloud was Fianna Lehr. Unbeknownst to Aleksander, that was the biggest breadcrumb of all. If only she could ask him about his mother without completely isolating him. He would not take her questioning well.

How could he?

'Have you thought about going to the temple again?' Aleksander wondered.

'I'm waiting to be asked,' Edela mumbled, only half listening. 'Apparently, I'm going to be called back, but who knows when?'

Aleksander bent low to her ear. 'This place is so odd. No one speaks plainly, do they? They just bustle about, hiding the truth of everything behind their doors. They're a bunch of cowards. I mean, what could be so bad that telling everyone would make it worse, not better? Surely the more people you tell, the more everyone can help?'

Edela could see the similarities between herself and the elders, then. And that was not a comparison she felt especially proud of. She had failed to find any further clues about Fianna in her dreams. Maybe the gods were telling her that the only way to move forward was with Aleksander's help?

She grabbed his sleeve and stared into his eyes. 'I need to tell you something.'

***

Eadmund stood at the railings of the Pit, struggling to locate a smile.

Jael had been gone when he'd woken, and he wasn't sure why. He was surprised to find that he'd not thought of ale or drinking at all yet. Not in the way he once had. But he was constantly thinking of his wife as he stood there, watching everyone train. Everyone but him. He felt so weak, especially after last night. He smiled, remembering the feel of her, the fire in her. It was the most alive he'd felt in years, but now, he just felt tired and troubled.

Jael had saved him, but now that he was saved, what did he do?

He was almost as fat and useless as he'd been before; still as far away from being any sort of man that his father could believe in. Eadmund bent forward, leaning on the wobbly railings, feeling the heavy ache in his arms and back. He sighed and turned around, thinking that perhaps he would go and find Eydis.

She could always help him see the things he couldn't.

'So, it's true, then? You're alive!' Ivaar sneered, walking up to his downcast brother.

Eadmund cringed at the sound of that slippery voice. He pulled himself up, feeling the pain in his shoulders as he pushed them back, raising his head higher than was comfortable. 'Seems so,' he spat angrily. 'And I'm coming for you, so you'd better watch your back.'

'Ha! I like your spirit,' Ivaar said without blinking. 'Coming for me? I'm terrified. Truly, I think I just pissed myself. You have me shaking, Brother!'

Eadmund did nothing but stare.

They weren't just words, he realised. He knew what he had to do now. Jael had told him as much in his dream. He had to kill Ivaar. Ivaar could never be the King of Oss. He didn't need Eydis to help him see that. He stepped forward, straighter and taller than Ivaar. 'Good. Shake away, because I *will* kill you. Has your dreamer seen that? Perhaps she's too scared to tell you how you'll die because it will be the longest, slowest, bloodiest death you can imagine.' And turning around, Eadmund walked back to the Pit, heading for the shed.

He was going to find a sword.

***

'What?' Osbert choked on his porridge, which was not surprising; the thick mulch of oats was so dense, it felt as though he was swallowing dried mud. '*My* chamber?'

'Yes, your chamber,' his father mumbled, handing him a cup of ale. 'It makes sense. Axl is young. He needs to be kept in line, and Gisila and I can't do that if he's roaming around the fort all night. Better that he's under our roof, where we can keep him safe.'

Osbert took a sip of ale, swilling it around his mouth. 'And where will I go?'

'Well...' Lothar mused, spooning honey into his porridge. 'You're old enough to have a wife and a house of your own now. After Hest, we can think of a suitable marriage for you, but in the meantime, go and find somewhere you like. There are plenty of good-looking houses near the hall. Anyone would be honoured to give up their home to the son of the king.'

Osbert glared at his father, wondering if he'd gone mad.

This was Gisila's doing. Or was it Axl's?

Perhaps they were working on a way to remove him? And who could blame them? Gisila was about to be the queen again. Why wouldn't she want to raise her son up to the status he once had.

Osbert frowned.

Axl was fast becoming a problem he needed to do something about.

***

Ayla had woken late, and she was only now finishing dressing in the cottage Ivaar had found for her in the middle of the fort. It was small but private, and except for Ivaar's regular visits, she was able to enjoy the luxury of being unobserved by strangers for the first time in a year.

She had barely slept, tortured by endless dreams, but nothing she saw showed her a way out of the prison Ivaar had so carefully trapped her in, and everything else was just a mess of blood, and death, and darkness.

Ivaar burst through the door in a rush of red-faced fury. 'You and I need to talk!' he growled, glancing around.

Ayla blinked in fear, stumbling backwards. Ivaar's eyes had narrowed into dangerous slits, which either meant he wanted her clothes off, or he had plans to hurt someone, and right now she couldn't tell which one he had in mind. 'What is it?' she asked nervously, falling onto the bed, one strap of her pale-blue dress hanging down, still unpinned.

'Have you seen my death?'

'What?' Ayla looked genuinely shocked as she stared up at him. 'Why do you ask that?'

'Answer me, Ayla!' Ivaar grabbed her shoulder, his lips twisting angrily. 'Have you seen my death?'

'No,' she breathed. 'No, I haven't. I promise I haven't.'

Ivaar sat down beside her, watching her eyes dart about like fleeing beetles. She looked so surprised that he found himself believing her... just.

'What about my brother? Tell me, what will happen to him? He seems different. He suddenly wants to kill me.'

'Oh.' Ayla swallowed, beginning to understand the cause of Ivaar's outburst. 'But hasn't he always wanted to kill you? After what happened to his first wife? Doesn't he blame you for her death?'

Ivaar thought about that. Ayla was right. That wasn't new, so what was, and why did he suddenly feel threatened? Why now? 'Tell me about him,' he urged. 'What do you see for him?'

Ayla looked away, closing her eyes, hoping it would give her enough time to clear her face of anything she didn't want him to see. What Ivaar needed to know was not what she actually saw, but what would make him feel reassured. And it was her job to put him at ease. She shuddered. 'Your brother, as I've told you before, meets his end under your hand, with his wife next to you.'

Ivaar frowned. 'Yes, you have said that many times, but how do I know it's the truth? How can I trust you? They're just words, Ayla, and you can pick any you want to placate me!'

Ayla tried to look insulted. 'Why would you doubt me? I have no choice but to tell you everything I see. You'll find no secrets in my eyes, Ivaar!' she lied as boldly as she dared. 'You must remember that dreamers don't see everything that will happen. We're only shown what is important. I've seen you as king, and you will destroy your brother as you want to. I can't tell you any more.'

Ivaar stared at her so intensely that she felt her stomach lurch.

'You have, you have told me that many times, and I want to trust you. But I promise you, Ayla, if I ever find out that you've been lying to me, or not telling me everything you see in your dreams... I will cut your husband's throat myself and make you drink his dying blood.' And with that he pushed her back onto the bed and tore off the other strap of her dress, ripping it angrily away from her body, pushing his lips onto her chest, down over her breasts, as they shivered in the morning chill. 'Hear my words, Ayla,' he breathed. 'You will not get away with betraying me.'

***

Thankfully, Branwyn had gone to visit Aedan's family. His wife was heavy with child and Branwyn had started to spend much of her time there, fussing over her daughter-in-law, excited about the birth of her first grandchild.

It meant that the house was empty.

Even the servant had gone off on an errand.

'Is this why you were so quiet yesterday?' Aleksander wondered, pulling a stool towards Edela's chair.

She shivered nervously, leaning towards the fire. 'Yes. It is.' Edela was finding it hard to meet his eyes. 'I had a dream... about your mother.'

Aleksander looked puzzled. He stared at her blankly. 'What was my mother doing in your dream?' He shivered. 'Is this about that night? The night she died?'

Edela looked at him, wringing her gloved hands, trying to think of how to order her words in a way to lessen the hurt she knew would follow. 'Yes. I dreamed about her writing a note to someone. I don't know who, and that is part of the problem. It was certainly her. I saw her wedding ring. It was very distinctive. That's when I suspected, but then I also saw her face in another dream. It was certainly Fianna.'

'A note? What did it say?' Aleksander felt odd. Edela looked so serious.

This was not going to be something he wanted to hear.

'It was alerting someone to our visit,' Edela sighed, taking a deep breath. 'The note said that Jael would be going to Tuura and it said when.'

'It mentioned Jael?' Aleksander could hear his heartbeat louder than the crackle of the fire now. His breathing had slowed, but his heart was racing. 'Why?'

She was going to have to lead him there slowly, Edela realised. 'The men that came to Tuura that night were looking for Jael. They killed Evva, thinking she was Jael. But no one knew why they had come or what they wanted. But now I know who sent them there...'

'What?' Aleksander stood, blinking at Edela. 'What do you mean? My mother?' he spluttered. 'But she was killed by those men! My father was killed by those men! Are you saying she sent people to murder Jael? And then herself? No! Why would she do that? She treated Jael like a daughter. She adored Jael! I used to be jealous of how much she loved her.' He shook his head, walking around the fire, lost in the memories of that night. 'She loved my father too! She wouldn't have sent people to kill either of them. Or anyone. My mother was gentle! Don't you remember her, Edela? You must remember how she was! She was so kind and...' He came back to Edela, kneeling before her. 'No! Don't do this to me. *Please*. Don't take my mother away from me. Not the memory I have of her. Go back into your dream. See it again. See the note again. You must!' Aleksander grabbed her hands. 'You're wrong. You're so wrong about this, Edela.' He sat back on his heels, losing his breath. 'You must be...'

'Then help me,' Edela pleaded, her eyes full of tears and guilt for the pain she was causing. 'Help me understand what I've seen. Dreams are hard to interpret sometimes, but I've been doing this for so many years now. I know what I saw. I wouldn't have told you if I wasn't certain that what I'd seen was real. If I didn't think it could help Jael.'

Aleksander sighed, staring at Edela, seeing the sadness on her face.

She wanted to help Jael, not destroy him, he could see that, but his mother? He shook his head. 'I don't see how I can help you. The woman I knew didn't write a note to have a little girl killed. Jael was like her daughter.' He hung his head. 'I can't help you, Edela. I just can't.'

Edela sighed, rubbing the tears out of her eyes, cursing her dreams for only ever giving her half a story.

If Aleksander couldn't help her, who could?

***

Ido and Vella were beside themselves as they jumped up on the weary figure who stumbled in through the door.

Biddy got up to join them, helping Jael off with her cloak. 'You look ready to fall down,' she said sternly. 'What have you been doing all day? Although, perhaps I shouldn't ask?'

'I've been training with Thorgils,' Jael yawned, handing Biddy her swordbelt and sitting down to take off her boots, her eyes barely open. 'All day long.' She yawned again.

'Well, the stew will be ready shortly,' Biddy murmured, coming back to peer into her cauldron. She gave the thick, brown gluck a stir and sat back down with her mending. Jael had a habit of putting holes in her socks quickly, and she'd been working through a pile of them all afternoon.

Jael looked up with little enthusiasm. She bent down to pat the furry faces that were demanding her attention, then yawned again and straightened up. 'I just need to lie down for a moment. Just a moment,' she mumbled, almost to herself as she headed for bed.

Oh, how she had missed her bed.

The puppies followed her, jumping onto the bed before she did. Jael blinked in surprise. Surely she hadn't been gone long enough for them to grow that big? They burrowed under the furs and lay there, waiting for her, taking up a lot more of the bed than they once had. There was still plenty of room for her, though, and Jael crawled in beside their warm bodies, pulling the furs over herself, closing her eyes, her head already full of dreams of Eadmund.

And Aleksander.

***

'Torstan tells me you were training today,' Thorgils began, sitting down with a groan, every limb throbbing after his day with Jael.

'Ha!' Eadmund laughed. 'If you can call holding a sword and swinging it around a few times training, then yes, I suppose I was.'

'You have to start somewhere,' Thorgils smiled wearily, rubbing his wrist where Jael had caught him with her sword, more than once. She'd been in an unforgiving mood, and he was certain he was bruised from head to toe.

He'd needed it, though. They both had.

'True.' Eadmund leaned forward, staring into Thorgils' eyes. 'I'm going to kill Ivaar. I always thought about taking revenge on him, but today I decided I was actually going to kill him. So, yes, it was a start, but I'm a long way from being able to kill anything more than an overfed flea right now.'

'What made you decide that, then?'

Eadmund added another log to the fire. 'I had a lot of dreams while I was stuck in that bed. Confusing dreams,' he frowned. 'But one thing I'm certain of is that Ivaar has plans to kill us all, including Eydis. So I'm going to stop him.'

'And what about Jael?' Thorgils wondered, noticing the smile that crept its way into Eadmund's eyes when he said her name. 'Where was she in all of this?'

Eadmund shook his head. 'In my dreams, she was with Ivaar.'

Thorgils looked surprised.

'But then she came and got me, brought me back,' he smiled. 'So, I'm choosing not to believe that part of the dream.'

'Sounds right,' Thorgils agreed. 'But why are you still here, then? In this pile of shit? Alone? Surely you have warmer options than this now?'

Eadmund laughed, then frowned. That was a good question.

What had happened to Jael today? Was she regretting everything? He was plagued by doubts but trying hard to hold onto the belief that last night had meant something to them both. He hoped it was the start and a way forward, not a mistake. 'I'm not sure. Jael's a complicated woman.'

'She is that,' Thorgils said, rolling his eyes in agreement. 'You're in for a very interesting marriage with that one, I'm sure. Best you keep up your training. Could come in very handy!'

CHAPTER FORTY NINE

Aleksander was cross with himself.

He'd drunk more than he could remember in a while and somehow he'd ended up here. In bed. With her. He'd forgotten her name, or perhaps he'd never asked it? He closed his eyes and sighed, feeling the pounding intensify, like a hammer between his eyebrows.

She was awake, he could tell. Awake and naked next to him, just as he was naked next to her. If only his head would stop hurting so much, then he could move, find his clothes, find a way out of wherever he was, and quickly.

'You can leave,' she said then, her voice soft. 'The door is not locked.'

Aleksander opened his eyes, feeling foolish. He turned awkwardly towards her and smiled. 'I'm sorry, it's just that I...'

'You don't need to explain anything to me,' she said shortly, sliding out of bed, searching for his clothes.

The light in the sparsely furnished room was dim. It was very cold, and Aleksander could see his breath blowing out before him. There were rays of light seeping through the holes in the walls, and the sound of voices filtered in loudly as the fort roused itself to life for another day.

The woman found his cloak, weapons, and clothes on the floor, near his boots. Wrapping them all up in a pile, she brought them back to his side of the bed and left them there before rushing back under the furs, shivering in the icy air.

'Thank you,' Aleksander mumbled, unable to even look her in the eye. He felt guilty for what he'd done, but at the same time, he wondered why? Jael was married, sleeping with her husband now. Why shouldn't he be doing the same?

But it was different, he knew. He had a choice, Jael didn't.

And in his heart, he'd wanted to wait for her.

Aleksander grimaced as he sat up, trying to ignore the stabbing pains in his head, the urgent need for water. Still, the room was cold enough to make him move fast, and he dressed quickly, attaching his belt, ready to leave. He looked over at the bed, then. At her. She was not Jael. There was no dark hair or mesmerising eyes. No scars. She was softer, and her round face was plainer, plumper, but it was kind, he thought to himself. Gentle. He must have had some idea of what he was doing when he ended up with her.

Just.

'Take care of yourself, Aleksander,' she said in a whisper. 'Don't do your drinking in such a public place next time. People are watching you.'

Aleksander's eyebrows shot up, and that hurt his head. He was puzzled.

What had he said? What had he done last night?

He was here to help Jael, but how was he going to get past the fact that Edela believed his mother responsible for sending those men to Tuura? He couldn't. It was as simple as that. He'd have to go back to Andala now, leave Edela to find her own way home after she'd found out what she needed to.

He wanted no part of it anymore.

Aleksander headed for the door, then paused, wading through even more guilt. 'Thank you...' he mumbled quietly.

'Hanna' she said. 'My name is Hanna.'

Aleksander showed her the briefest of smiles, then ducked his head and slipped through the door.

Hanna looked after him for a moment, her face troubled.

He didn't realise how much danger he was in.

She wondered if she would ever see him again.

***

Jael used to like Vesta. All that eating and drinking, celebrating Vesta, Goddess of the Sun. Honouring her with gifts and sacrifices, trying to tempt her out of hiding. Inviting her to bring spring and warmth, and light to feed the land.

But now?

Now she just wanted to crawl back into bed and sleep. Her mind and body felt like a heap of twisted brambles. She felt awkward and disloyal; uncomfortable in her own skin.

Jael pulled on the door with a heavy sigh, wishing she was going to Fyn's instead of having to endure this very public feast. Her tired eyes widened as she entered the hall. It had been transformed into a magical grove, draped with hanging rows of fir branches, interlaced with white flowers and red berries. It reminded her of the King's Hall in Andala, and memories of her childhood came rushing back. Her mother would take such care over decorating it for Vesta, she remembered, just as Eirik had here. Every table was ornamented with fruit and branches, pinecones and leaves. There was so much white; beautiful, snowy white. White linen hung around the walls, with white flowers and green leaves strung across it. Candles, lamps, and torches appeared to have tripled in number. It was warm and fresh smelling.

Jael almost felt cheerful.

'There you are!' Eirik smiled in relief, grabbing her hand. 'I didn't think you were coming!'

'Jael!' Eydis came up beside her father, feeling her way to Jael's waist, wrapping her arms around her.

'Well, this is all very nice,' Jael admitted.

'It looks better than I've seen it in years,' Eirik said proudly. 'All thanks to Isaura and Eydis. They did everything. I just grumbled along beside them. It's definitely better to let a woman handle this sort of thing.'

'Where's Eadmund?' Eydis wondered. 'I thought he'd be with you.'

'Did you?' Jael looked surprised, noticing the smiles on their faces. 'No, I haven't seen him.'

'Oh.' Eirik looked disappointed. 'I thought...'

'Jael!' Ivaar slipped in beside his father, leaning forward to kiss her on the cheek. 'Happy Vesta to you.'

Jael did her best not to cringe, but she certainly didn't smile. 'Ivaar.' She met his eyes without any warmth as he stood there, right next to the little girl he had plans to kill – if there was any truth to the dreams people had been having lately.

'I hear your duties have ended now? Your patient has made a full recovery?' Ivaar smiled. It was good to see her. She looked very out of sorts, though. Her face was drawn and cross, but he'd missed looking at it, more than he'd realised.

'Well, hopefully,' Jael murmured, trying not to yawn. 'Although, I haven't seen him for a while, so who knows?' She frowned, realising that she really should have checked on Eadmund. What if he was ill or drinking again? She'd just run away without much thought at all.

Another thing to feel guilty for.

Thorgils wandered up to her with an easy grin, and her shoulders relaxed away from her ears. 'Are you alright?' she smiled at him, noticing a bruise that had formed near one eye which must have been her doing.

'I can still see, if that's what you mean?' Thorgils tried to look annoyed, but he was in a good mood, despite Ivaar's presence. 'Enough to find where our good king placed all his best wine!' He raised his cup, acknowledging Eirik, and took a big gulp, determined not to let Ivaar ruin his favourite time of year.

Thorgils froze as Eadmund walked into the hall. He looked

tired and weak, but there was no stumbling this time. He was steady on his feet as he raised a hand in acknowledgement and came walking over to the group.

Jael followed Thorgils' eyes, surprised to see Eadmund. Her body responded to him with an almighty shiver. She smiled quickly, then glanced away, noticing the intense look on Ivaar's face. She didn't want him knowing anything about her feelings for Eadmund, which she didn't even know herself.

Jael tightened her lips and furrowed her brows, attempting to look as irritable as possible, which wasn't hard.

Eadmund saw Ivaar standing next to Jael, and though he clenched his teeth, he tried not to let his desire to kill his brother overwhelm him. He picked up his little sister and gave her a squeeze. 'Happy Vesta, Little Thing,' he whispered. 'I have a gift for you, but you'll have to wait until tomorrow to open it.'

'Ooohh, really?' Eydis exclaimed excitedly. 'You've not remembered a gift for Vesta since I was little! I can't wait!'

Eirik drunk from his favourite silver cup, enjoying the sensation of the cold wine as it slipped so pleasantly down his throat; enjoying seeing Eadmund and Eydis again, and Jael was there, Thorgils, of course, and he didn't even mind Ivaar's company. He admired the festive decorations, listened to the musicians wandering around with their lyres and flutes, smelled the juices of the roasting pigs, and felt a genuine burst of happiness.

Life, he decided, was still with him, so he would stop worrying about what end the gods were planning for him, and enjoy what he had right now. 'Well then, you'll be receiving two gifts, as I have one for you too!' Eirik smiled at Eydis, enjoying the look of happiness on her face.

Eydis clasped her hands together. 'I knew you'd make this Vesta happen, Father! I knew you wouldn't let me down!'

'Come on, then,' Eirik said. 'Come and help me find where the serving girls have all gone because if the wine disappears, you'll be the only one who is happy with me!'

That left four of them.

Thorgils squirmed, ready to rush off, but quickly reconsidered when he looked at the simmering tension on Ivaar, Jael, and Eadmund's faces.

Perhaps it was wiser to remain?

'Are you going to get yourself a drink too, Brother?' Ivaar wondered coolly. 'It's so unusual to see you without a cup in your hand.'

Eadmund kept his face impassive. He didn't even blink. 'If Eirik can find the wine, I'm sure I'll find my way there.'

Jael and Thorgils exchanged a nervous glance, both trying to think of a way to dampen the fire building between the brothers.

'What sort of Vesta things do you do on Oss?' Jael wondered. 'Do you play any games?'

'Well, yes, lots of games, naturally,' Thorgils smiled. 'Usually after drinking most of Eirik's best wine, so they tend to end up very messy. A lot of stumbling about, more drinking. Some take off their clothes, slide around on the ice. A few races, tug-o-war. That sort of thing. You'll enjoy it, I'm sure. Maybe even partake yourself?'

Jael looked doubtful, but in truth, she was barely listening. She felt an overwhelming need to talk to Eadmund, or to run away from him entirely; she couldn't decide which. But one thing she knew for certain was that she wanted to get away from Ivaar. He kept moving towards her, and she could feel his eyes trying to claim her, and Eadmund's eyes sharpening because of it. 'Well, the food looks good, so I'm going to eat!' And, ignoring Thorgils' pleading eyes, she left.

Eadmund stared after her, disappointed, but his head was clearer now, and despite the weakness in his limbs, he felt more capable than he had in years. He wasn't about to let her slip away from him as quickly as she seemed to want to. 'I agree with my wife, the food does look very good,' he said shortly and disappeared after Jael.

Ivaar looked ready to scream, Thorgils thought, as he stood there awkwardly, wondering how to make his own escape. It was nice to see the twist on Ivaar's face, but Eadmund wasn't ready to play games with such a deadly snake.

Not yet.

***

Gisila had lost her confidence in the night. She'd lain there, unable to sleep, listening to Axl snoring, worrying about how she was going to keep him safe. Worrying about what Lothar was going to do to her, whether Branwyn still lived, how her mother was faring, how Jael was surviving her marriage to that drunken oaf.

She hadn't fallen asleep, not once, and now, as she stood in the hall, about to walk to Lothar, she felt ready to fall down, just when she needed all the strength she had to endure the worst day of her entire life.

Gisila had not wanted to marry Ranuf Furyck. She had felt too young and not at all ready to be his queen, but despite her reservations, she hadn't disliked him. She had never feared him. Ranuf had been handsome, strong, and powerful. Of course, when she got to know him better, he was also moody, argumentative, stubborn and sometimes cold. But he had been good to her and treated her with kindness and respect.

With Ranuf, Gisila had felt safe from the very first moment, but with Lothar...

'I'm so sorry, Mother,' Axl murmured, his eyes tense, watching Lothar, who was waiting for them on the fur-covered dais. 'I promise I'll do everything I can to protect you. I won't let him hurt you. Not ever.'

Gisila tried to shut Axl out. She didn't want to cry. If she had any hope of surviving, and even thriving, she had to show Lothar her strength, hiding away any sign of weakness that either he or Osbert could use against her.

Lothar watched with barely contained excitement, as Gisila glided towards him on Axl's arm. He had not loved Rinda, the dead mother of his three children. He had endured her miserable body, her barely-there tits and her lack of any desire, but Gisila? He sighed happily as his eyes roamed over her chest. He couldn't wait to run his fingers through her long dark hair, rip that snug fitting dress off her, feel the heat of her perfectly soft flesh beneath his hands. He blinked, trying to shake himself out of that place, realising that he still had some time to wait, and besides, he wanted to make sure that she was ready for what he had in mind.

Amma gave Gisila a sympathetic smile as she passed, but Gisila barely noticed. She had hidden herself away now, behind a wall of strength that she would need to keep high if she was going to survive. She had Axl, and her mother, Aleksander, even Gant, and, of course, Jael.

She knew that, eventually, Lothar would meet his end at one of their hands.

If she didn't manage to kill him first.

***

Eadmund followed Jael as she approached the high table. He was determined not to let her slip away from him without a word or a look. He hadn't come back for things to be the same as before.

He had come back for her.

'Hello,' Isaura smiled, grabbing Eadmund's arm as she stepped in front of him.

Eadmund tried not to appear as annoyed as he felt. He smiled but feared it looked more like an angry grimace. 'Isaura. Happy Vesta.'

'And to you,' she said quietly. 'You look well. I heard you were very ill. I didn't know if you were going to be here, but I'm so glad you are.'

Eadmund felt embarrassed. 'I was, yes, but I'm fine now. Well, almost fine.'

'You do look much better than when I last saw you. It will be good to have you around again.' She peered behind herself, lowering her voice. 'Ivaar is already acting like a king, collecting himself a loyal band of followers. After the contest, we're going back to Kalfa to sort everything out and bring our household here. To stay.'

'What?' Eadmund felt sick. 'You're coming to *live* here? Now?'

'I know. It truly is the worst thing for you. And Thorgils,' she whispered. 'Eirik is going to appoint a new Lord of Kalfa soon.'

Eadmund shook his head. He'd thought that there would be time to change his father's mind while Ivaar was back on Kalfa, but now? 'Well, perhaps we should swap places? Jael and I could go and live on Kalfa? You and Ivaar could come here,' he laughed, not meaning it.

'How is Jael?' Isaura wondered quickly. She knew she had to go and make sure everything was flowing smoothly, but she'd barely spoken to Eadmund since they'd arrived.

Eadmund frowned. He wasn't sure how to answer that. 'She is well, I think. Tired from looking after me, no doubt. Looking forward to the contest, I imagine.'

'You think? You imagine?' Isaura mused, one eyebrow raised. 'I see. So it's not going well then, your marriage? She seems quite... distant. Angry.'

Eadmund had his mouth open, ready with a defense, when Ivaar and Tarak joined them.

'Ahhh, there she is, my wife! The woman responsible for all this... festivity.' Ivaar swung his hand around, slightly drunk. 'She's going to make an excellent queen, don't you think, Brother? Our hall will always look well-dressed!' His smile was heavy with intent. 'Here, I brought you a cup of wine since you seem to be without one.'

Isaura squirmed uncomfortably, wanting to leave, but as she turned, she saw Thorgils watching her, so she turned back around. Ivaar was drunk and who knew what he would do if he saw her near Thorgils.

She certainly didn't want to find out.

'That's very kind of you, Brother,' Eadmund smiled cheerfully, taking the cup, determined not to let Ivaar win any more games. 'What a shame I can't agree with you about Isaura, though. I don't believe she'll ever make a queen, not on Oss at least. I already have *my* queen picked out, and I'd not want to take your wife from you.' He took a small amount of pleasure in the sour look on Ivaar's face.

Jael made her way into the fray.

She'd seen Ivaar hand Eadmund a cup, and that had her up from the table and hurrying towards the huddle by the fire. She wasn't in time, though. Eadmund poured the wine down his throat just as she reached him. She looked at him in horror, but he wouldn't meet her eye.

Now she was mad.

Jael could feel the stir of her temper as it vibrated hot and red in her chest. She didn't know who she wanted to yell at first: Ivaar or Eadmund? In the end, she decided to ignore both of them and direct her fury at Tarak. 'How are you, Tarak?' she smiled, her green eyes narrowing on him. 'I haven't seen you since you pushed me onto the ice that night. Although, I do see your face every time I get a pain in my back.'

Tarak froze, feeling Ivaar's furious eyes as they snapped to him. He knew how Ivaar still felt about that bitch, and Ivaar wasn't going to be pleased with him at all.

'You pushed her over? Why?' Ivaar wondered crossly, all thoughts of Eadmund momentarily forgotten.

'Oh... well...' Tarak tried to laugh, but his thick-skinned face only managed to twist itself into a terrifying grimace. 'We were just laughing with each other about the contest. A few insults were thrown, that sort of thing. It was not serious, more of an accident. I hadn't realised how light she was when I pushed her. I didn't imagine she'd fly through the air like that.' Tarak's eyes bored into Jael's, and they were triumphant.

He was certain he'd played that well.

Jael glanced at Eadmund, waiting for him to rush off and grab another cup of wine, but he stood there calmly, his eyes fixed on Tarak. 'Well, Tarak,' he grinned. 'I'd advise you to keep your hands off my wife. If you poke a wolf, you only make it more likely to attack. I'd hate to think what trouble you've made for yourself there.'

Tarak snorted. 'As you say, but if you'd seen the way she flew, like a piece of cloth, you'd hardly think she was a threat to anyone. It's hard to be scared of a wolf with no teeth.'

Jael took a deep breath, trying to calm herself, but it wasn't working. She had to leave. Her eyes darted about, and she spied Thorgils. 'Well, since Eadmund is doing such a good job of defending my honour, I'll leave him to it.' She nodded quickly and made her escape as Tarak, Eadmund, and Ivaar stared after her.

Isaura glanced at the three men, who all appeared ready to kill each other, before hurrying away, deciding that she'd be better off in the safety of the kitchen.

***

Edela stood outside the tiny cottage, shivering. The snow was falling at an increasingly heavy rate, and she didn't know how long she could wait before needing to leave and seek shelter.

At last, the door opened, ever so slowly, and Alaric's sleepy face peered at her. 'Oh, Edela!' He looked horrified at the state of her, covered head to toe in snow as she was. 'I'm so sorry! I didn't hear you. My hearing is not what it once was, I'm afraid.'

Edela bustled past him, desperate to get to his fire; hoping it had some actual flames today. 'Well, I know how you feel there. Getting old is no fun at all.' She shivered uncontrollably, shaking the snow from her cloak.

'I'm surprised to see you without your young friend,' Alaric noted as he checked the water in the cauldron that hung over his moderately bright fire. He had enough dried dandelions to make tea for two, so he shuffled towards his kitchen shelf and found another cup. 'I did see him last night, though, stumbling out of the tavern. He looked rather unhappy with his lot.'

'Did he?' Edela muttered, her eyebrows pinching together anxiously. 'Well, that's hardly surprising... I accused his mother of being evil.'

'Oh?' Alaric looked at her in surprise, placing the cups on the table. 'Please, take a seat,' he smiled nervously, trying to make up for his lack of hospitality during her last visit.

Edela moved the stool closer to the fire and sat down, pulling off her wet gloves. 'I had a dream about her. Fianna. It made me doubt the sort of woman she was, the woman I remembered,' she said sadly. 'I wondered whether you knew of any loyalties she had that might have caused her to want to hurt Jael?'

Alaric's eyebrows rose at that. 'Fianna? She always seemed a nice girl,' he murmured, shaking his head. 'It's so long ago, though. My memories of her are faint indeed, but I do remember her mother, of course... Rhea.'

Edela sat back on her stool. 'Rhea Thorsen.' It was as if the snow clouds in her head had suddenly shifted and she could see what they'd been masking. 'Rhea. Of course.'

'There was something slightly strange about her, wasn't there?'

'Mmmm, there was. She was thrown out of the temple before she'd really begun her dreamer training. We were friends for a time, as children. I'm not sure what she did, but they never allowed her back in the temple. It made her quite bitter. We were never close again after that. She removed herself from all of us.'

The snow continued to fall outside and down the smoke hole, dropping into Alaric's cauldron. He peered inside, deciding that the water looked hot enough. 'She died quite young, didn't she?' he murmured, removing the cauldron and carefully pouring the water into the cups, his arm shaking from the strain.

'Yes, Fianna was only eight or so, I think. That's why she spent so much time with my girls and Neva,' she smiled wistfully. 'I do remember now. She was a very quiet child. Sweet but shy. The pain of losing her mother was always in her eyes.'

Alaric handed Edela a cup and came to sit on the bed. 'So what is it that you think she did?' His curiosity quickly overrode his fear of talking about such secret things. 'What made Aleksander so upset?'

Edela looked down at her cup, not wanting to meet his eyes until she knew what she wanted to do. But she had to trust someone, for without Aleksander, what hope did she have of finding anything out?

***

Amma squeezed Gisila's arm, smiling at her. 'You're braver than I could ever hope to be,' she whispered, pushing her empty plate away. 'But I suppose you've had a lot of practice being a queen and a wife. Perhaps it's easier this time?'

Gisila had quickly drunk three goblets of wine after the horrible ceremony, and she was feeling both morose and giddy. She'd experienced some terrible days in her fifty-two-years; some days she wasn't sure she would ever recover from. Her two eldest sons had died as boys, she had endured a stillbirth, several miscarriages, not to mention that night in Tuura, but this, somehow this topped them all. Because throughout everything else, there had always been Ranuf. He was like the biggest tower that she could crawl behind. He would protect her while she healed, care for her while she built up her strength, and came out again, stronger. But now?

Now she was completely exposed.

Now it was all up to her.

'You're right, dearest Amma, and completely wrong too,' Gisila smiled wistfully. 'But I've decided to remember how strong I can be. As you will have to when your time comes.'

Amma looked terrified. She'd watched enough women forced into marriages they didn't want recently to know that it was something she could never face. She would rather die than be pushed into such a union, especially, as Osbert had implied, with someone from Hest.

'Although,' Gisila smiled gently, seeing the panic in Amma's eyes, 'now that I'm your stepmother, I'm sure I'll be able to exert more influence over your father than Osbert.'

Amma looked up, blinking. That sounded like hope.

Gisila watched Osbert and Lothar talking with Gant, who smiled her way.

She ignored him, turning back to Amma. 'Just because we are women, we don't need to be the victims here, do we? When Edela returns, she'll be able to help us with your father, I'm certain of it.'

CHAPTER FIFTY

Jael decided that there were better ways to spend Vesta than knee-deep in insults and worries, so she'd asked Thorgils to keep an eye on Eadmund, then slipped away to the kitchen, making herself a parcel of meat, vegetables, and bread. She even helped herself to a jug of wine before heading to the stables, where Biddy helped her pack everything securely onto the horses.

And together they rode to see Fyn.

It was the first day of Vesta and Jael had no intention of leaving Biddy to sit alone in the house all day with just the puppies for company. Biddy wasn't the surest horsewoman, but she was Brekkan, so she certainly knew her way around a horse, especially in the snow.

She'd almost been excited to come.

As they rode slowly down the slope towards Fyn's hut, gentle flurries were falling. Jael dismounted, looking up at the sky which had darkened considerably on their ride. By the look of it, they wouldn't be able to stay long.

'Jael?' Fyn was surprised as he emerged from his tiny hole; quickly nervous to see that she'd brought a companion.

'This is Biddy,' Jael smiled. 'I've told you about Biddy, haven't I?'

'You have, yes,' Fyn grinned with relief.

'Happy Vesta,' Biddy said, looking the gangly boy up and down. He reminded her of Axl, albeit skinnier, and that gave her a sharp pang. How she missed and worried about that boy.

'Happy Vesta,' Fyn smiled shyly, grateful to have company on a day which had made him feel lonelier than any other. 'There's something cooking in my cauldron that we can all share.'

Jael raised her eyebrows at Biddy who looked worried, having heard the tale of the claw stew. 'Well, that's very kind of you, Fyn, but we've brought food from Eirik's hall. You may want to try that instead?'

Fyn's stomach flipped with joy at the thought of real food; he had grown tired of his terrible cooking. Jael unpacked their saddlebags, handing him the jug of wine and the cloth-wrapped bundle of food, and sent him inside with Biddy to get everything underway while she secured the horses.

'Oh!' Biddy exclaimed as she entered the hut, horrified by Fyn's living conditions. 'Perhaps we should have brought some furs to keep you warm in here?'

Fyn ducked his head in embarrassment. He placed the wine and food on the floor, looking anxiously around for a plate and cups. 'Well, it's not the warmest of places to live, that's true. Still, I can always sit by the fire to keep warm.'

Biddy instantly wanted to take care of him. 'Here, let me do that,' she smiled as he fumbled about. 'You go and add a few logs to that fire. I'm far too old to sit around in this ice bucket!'

Jael opened the door, not surprised to see Biddy already organising everything. Fyn sat by the fire, looking quite put in his place. Jael pulled out a long package from behind her back and handed it to him. 'Here, Happy Vesta!'

Fyn was almost speechless as he stood up to take it. 'But... but, it's only the women who get gifts for Vesta.'

'Well, that's what they say, but I thought you might need this.'

Fyn looked puzzled as he unwrapped the very long, thin package. He knew what it was, of course, by its shape, but he wouldn't allow himself to truly believe it until all the cloth had been removed and the sword lay gleaming in his shaking hands.

'Jael... I...' he mumbled, tears in his eyes.

Jael could feel tears threatening her own eyes, but she blinked them away. 'You've earned it, Fyn. You deserve to have a sword that isn't made of wood! You've come such a long way from that boy who couldn't even hold onto one. And, when I get you back to the fort and Eirik sends us all to Hest, I expect you by my side. Understood?'

Fyn's face went from pure joy to utter terror in a heartbeat. 'Jael, I'm no warrior. I can't –'

'I wouldn't have had this sword made for you if you were no warrior, Fyn,' Jael insisted as she took a cup of wine from Biddy and sat down by the fire.

It was a fine sword, Fyn thought to himself, not quite believing it was real. He wrapped his fingers around the cold, leather grip, running his eyes down the well-worked blade. 'You had it *made* for me?'

'I did,' Jael said, sipping from her cup of icy wine. 'You've earned it. It's yours, and you're allowed to be happy about that! And happy about some wine and good food too. It's Vesta, and we came to spend it with you!' She smiled, raising her cup.

Biddy handed Fyn a cup of wine and went back to sorting out the catastrophe of his broken little kitchen. She shook her head, feeling sorry for the poor boy.

Fyn took a quick drink, smiled, and placed the sword carefully against the wall. 'I have a gift for you, too.' He disappeared into the corner of his hut, which only took one step, and rustled about under his bed. 'It's not much, of course, not like that perfect sword.' He came back and sat down, suddenly shy. 'Thank you, Jael. For everything you have done. All of it. I... you have helped me so much. More than I deserve.' He ducked his head nervously, handing her a tiny ball of dirty-looking cloth.

Jael frowned as she unwrapped the parcel, then smiled. It was a small, delicately-carved wooden sun on a thin leather cord. She held it up so Biddy could see. 'It's beautiful, Fyn! How did you make something so fine?' Jael slipped it over her head, smiling. The sun nestled comfortably between her breasts, sitting right alongside the bronze pendant of Furia's axes that her father had given her.

'It's the symbol of Vesta. She will protect you from the Darkness, I hope. If it comes.' He shuddered, glancing at Biddy, who handed him a plate overflowing with an abundance of meat and vegetables; so many things that he hadn't eaten in a year or more. His eyes bulged, and his stomach growled happily.

Jael laughed as she took her own plate, glancing down at her new pendant. She thought of Eadmund and hoped more than anything that he wasn't drunk again.

She would have to go and speak with him.

She couldn't ignore him forever, as much as she was trying to.

***

'You can't be afraid of her,' Thorgils murmured as they made their way to the Pit. There was still enough light, and both of them had been eager to get away from Ivaar. Despite it being Vesta, Eadmund had suggested they try a little training, and even in his slightly merry state, Thorgils thought that sounded better than more wine. For Eadmund at least.

'I'm not *afraid* of her!' Eadmund scoffed, ducking through the railings and making his way into the shed.

'Really?' It was Thorgils' turn to scoff. 'She's quite scary, that one, especially with a sword in her hand!'

'Ha! Well, hopefully, I won't have to face her like that,' Eadmund laughed as he picked up one of the less battered-looking training swords. He ached all over from his brief attempt yesterday, but he was desperate to get stronger quickly. All this tension with Ivaar would come to a head soon, and he couldn't be a bumbling fool when it did.

'No, I don't imagine it's a good idea to bring swords into a marriage,' Thorgils smiled. 'Unless you were married to Ivaar, of course, and then I would certainly advise it.'

'Poor Isaura,' Eadmund said, following Thorgils out into the snow-covered Pit. No one had cleared it as today was a feast day, and work was forbidden, for most. The games would come tomorrow, and the Pit would be swept clean as soon as the sun was up. 'Still, once I put my sword through Ivaar's neck, she'll be free to marry you.'

Thorgils looked doubtful. 'You have it all planned out, don't you? Does Ivaar know that you're about to behead him and take his promised crown again?'

'He does,' Eadmund frowned, looking up; the sky was darkening so rapidly that he doubted they'd have much time to practice. 'He knows I want to kill him.'

'But does he care?'

'Probably not,' Eadmund admitted, taking a few steps forward, his hand firm around the grip of his sword, ignoring the blisters that had formed since yesterday. 'Perhaps he's forgotten what I can do? I'm sure everyone else has, and who could blame them? But things are different now. I'm not going to sit back and watch Ivaar take another thing from me.'

Thorgils felt a surge of energy. He remembered this Eadmund.

This Eadmund *did* have a chance of defeating Ivaar.

He smiled, edging forward. 'Well then, Eadmund the Almost Bold, why don't we see how much work you need to do.' And with a quick lunge, he slashed his sword into Eadmund's side.

Eadmund bit his lip as he stumbled backwards, almost tumbling into the snow. 'I think I'll need a shield.'

***

Kormac peered at Edela with concern. She looked ready to cry, and it was no easy thing to watch an old woman cry.

'He took all his things?'

'He did, yes,' Kormac said sadly. Something had broken between Edela and Aleksander. He was not sure what but Aleksander had taken everything and gone to stay with Aedan and Aron. It had left him puzzled.

Edela sighed. It was Vesta, she remembered wistfully. In Brekka, not in Tuura. There had never been any celebration in Tuura for this time of year. Tuurans didn't believe in honouring their gods in such an overt way. It was only the elders who spoke to the gods here. Whatever midwinter ceremonies were celebrated in Tuura, they were held in the sanctity of the temple, for the elders alone.

'Come and sit by the fire, Edela,' Kormac smiled. 'I've just found a large flagon of mead I'd forgotten I had. I'm sure a cup of that is just what you need. Aleksander will be fine, and probably much happier with the boys. Gives him a chance to feel like a man again.'

'I suppose you're right.' Edela sat down in her favourite chair, not even removing her cloak, her mind still occupied with thoughts of her visit to Alaric. He'd had no knowledge about what trouble Rhea Thorsen had gotten herself into, but just the mention of that name had helped Edela.

Now she had another breadcrumb, and she knew which path she had to follow to find the next.

***

Eirik noticed that Ivaar was stalking around the hall in an increasingly irritable state. He had drunk more than usual, and his cool facade was slipping now. Eirik watched him from his place at the high table, yawning from too much wine. Eadmund had left, Jael too, long ago, and Eydis had made her way to bed, and so he was left with Ivaar for company.

Ivaar. His new heir.

Eirik shrugged away the doubts that crowded his mind. Eadmund had walked out of the hall sober, only one drink passing his lips. Eadmund sober. He shrugged that away too. It wouldn't last. Oh, how he wanted it to, but after seven years of watching his son struggle, Eirik knew that it wouldn't. Not without Jael by his side, certainly, and she seemed no closer to Eadmund than before.

Ivaar was the right choice.

Eirik shook his head.

No, Ivaar was the wrong choice, but he was the only choice.

His eyes narrowed as he watched the dark-haired woman wind her way up to the table. Ivaar's dreamer. What was her name? She was effortlessly beautiful, and Tuuran and that reminded him of Rada, Eydis' mother, and he suddenly felt morose. The dreamer looked up at him quickly as she passed, then her eyes ran away, and so did she. Eirik blinked, confused. He'd drunk far too much wine, of course, but her eyes had pleaded with him, he was certain.

She looked fearful.

Was it for him? Or herself?

He turned around quickly, but she had gone, leaving him wondering if she had even been there at all. He blinked, pushing away his cup.

It was time for him to find his bed before he became as drunk as Ivaar.

***

Jael lay under a mountain of furs, happy to feel almost warm for the first time all day. Ido and Vella snored on either side of her, adding extra insulation. She stroked Vella's fluffy mane and sighed, closing her eyes.

It was Aleksander, she realised, at last.

Jael had wanted Eadmund, but by losing control of herself, by hopping into his bed, she'd betrayed Aleksander. She shook her head, trying to remember him, but it was only Eadmund's face that would come now.

Rolling over, she sighed, listening to the wind as it picked up outside, howling painfully around the house now. It sounded like a baying wolf. She smiled, remembering how Eadmund had stood up to Tarak for her. She hoped he wasn't lying drunk somewhere, or with someone. That thought made her frown intensely. But who could blame him, after his wife had saved him, then left him before he'd even caught his breath?

Jael didn't know what to think.

If Aleksander and Eadmund were standing before her now, who would she choose? She opened her eyes, peering into the emptiness of the dark room, surprised to discover that she didn't know the answer.

**

Gisila was completely sober as she stood before Lothar. She'd drunk more than she could remember, but nothing had helped quell the ever-increasing panic that flooded her body.

Her knees started shaking.

'You look cold, Wife,' Lothar smiled, his eyes oozing with lust as they narrowed in on his prey. 'Come, come stand by the fire. I have more furs over here to warm your feet, or your back, however you feel more comfortable.' He raised an eyebrow, smiling at her. 'Come to me, Gisila, and let me warm you through.'

Gisila fought the urge to vomit.

This was not her first wedding night. She knew how it would go. Somehow she knew that this would be so much worse than her first night with Ranuf, which had not been particularly pleasant for her either.

There was something about Lothar that made her uneasy.

Gisila edged forward, towards the fire and the furs, of which there were indeed many. She tried to keep her head high as she came closer to Lothar. She could almost hear the growl that rose out of his body for her, and she fought against every instinct that told her to turn and run.

This had been her bedchamber once. Hers and Ranuf's. The memories of their bed were achingly close, sullied now by Lothar and whatever foul things he was about to do to her. She sighed and thought of Arnna and her advice. She had to make Lothar bend to her, not the other way around. Somehow, she had to exert her power over him before he consumed her.

Gisila closed her eyes for a moment, calming herself. She took a deep breath and looked into her new husband's burning, bulging eyes and reached for the strap of her nightdress, pushing it off her shoulder. Lothar gasped. She chose not to notice the hideous expression that deformed his very pink lips. Keeping her eyes fixed on his, she pushed the other strap over her shoulder, letting her silk nightdress fall to the furs beneath her feet.

It was freezing, and not one part of her wanted to give herself to him like this, but if Gisila wanted any control, and she did, then she had to use whatever she could to claim it.

Lothar lunged at her like a rabbit released from a trap, his chubby hands pawing her breasts, his lips on hers, his hands in her hair. He was beside himself, unbridled desire coursing through every vein. He had her at last! Ranuf's wife was now his. It was intoxicating. And her body, that delicious, milky body he had long dreamed about, was now his to do anything he liked with.

Oh, how he had plans for that body.

Gisila gulped, her eyes frozen in terror over Lothar's shoulder as he pushed her down onto her knees, grunting at her, demanding she place her lips on him.

Gisila shuddered, praying for Furia to avenge her as she bent forward.

***

'You think you're getting closer, Edela?' the voice crowed darkly. 'But you haven't even scratched the surface of what this all means!'

The loud echo of that voice rolled around Edela's head. A hint of flame lingered near the corner of her eye, and her breath came in short bursts. She tried to move forward, to find her way towards the light; turning, turning, but the flames moved with her, and she could never find anything but absolute darkness.

'Rhea Thorsen? You want to know what she did? Well, that is no secret. You don't need to go to the temple to find that out. But it won't help you. Finding out about Fianna Lehr? That won't help you either!' the voice laughed, crashing like waves over Edela. 'You can follow that trail, that path of tiny morsels, and bit by bit you will get somewhere, but by then, it will be too late. By then, you will be dead.'

Edela gasped. She saw it in the darkness then, the briefest glimpse of her own death. The first time she had ever seen such a thing.

There was truth in that vision, she realised.

'You didn't know, did you?' the voice hissed coldly. 'How close you were to the end? And yet you've had your whole life to solve this mystery of mine. I have been warning you since the day of your birth, Edela,' she scoffed. 'But have you ever remembered your dreams of me? Oh, Edela. Grandmother to Furia's daughter? The one they say will save you all? And you can't even remember a simple dream?'

Edela was shaking all over. She couldn't catch her breath.

She felt as though she was being swallowed by the suffocating darkness.

'But if you don't remember in time, then what will happen to your precious Jael? To your Tuurans? Or your Brekkans? Who will save them if you can't remember your dreams, Edela? Who will save them from me when you are gone?'

CHAPTER FIFTY ONE

Isaura glanced nervously at Eirik. He didn't look too upset, she thought hopefully. There was still a hint of a smile lurking near his eyes.

He turned to her, sensing her unease. 'It's alright. We have the contest to look forward to in a few days. And you can't predict what the weather gods will bring us. Not in the armpit of winter. Not on Oss.'

He was right, Isaura thought, stroking Annet's golden hair as she slept with her head on her knee, but still, after all that planning, she was disappointed to think that it had all been for nothing. The blizzard that swept through Oss on the first night of Vesta had been vicious, battering them without respite. Only a brave few had ventured into the hall on the second day, and no one had left their homes today. It was too dangerous to go outside. Isaura listened to the screaming wind rattling the doors and sighed.

'Who knows, perhaps it will die down out there, and we might get a few stragglers coming in later if we're not all in bed?' Eirik tried to coax a smile out of Isaura, but he could see that none was forthcoming. He turned, glancing around the empty hall. It looked like a perfect winter's day. Everything felt frozen by time, untouched. They would take all the decorations down tomorrow, of course, which would be a shame, but it was bad luck to leave them up when Vesta was over.

He wondered if he would live to see another?

'You'll be the queen here before you know it, Isaura,' he assured her. 'And your Vestas will last the whole three days, I'm sure.'

Isaura frowned. She never wanted to think about being the queen and what that would mean for Eadmund and Thorgils. She knew that Ivaar was obsessed with his plans for revenge and that he would not rule here without making them suffer.

If he let them live.

'What is it?' Eirik leaned forward. It was just the four of them by the fire: Isaura with Annet on her knee and Mads snoring gently on his.

Eirik was enjoying the silence of his grandchildren, who usually made more noise than he could remember from any of his own children.

Isaura squirmed uncomfortably. Eirik had certainly been friendlier these past few days, and his face glowed warmly in the firelight now, but still, he was Eirik the Bloody and Ivaar's father. She hardly felt free to speak her mind.

'Isaura, tell me,' Eirik urged, watching her eyes dart around the hall like a deer sensing danger. 'Is it Ivaar?'

Isaura froze. 'You don't need my opinion on Ivaar,' she whispered. 'I'm sure you made your choice for many reasons that have nothing to do with me.' She dropped her head, not wanting him to see the fear in her eyes.

Eirik was intrigued. It was true. Sometimes it did seem as if everyone had an opinion on Ivaar, and as much as he knew that he couldn't, and certainly wouldn't abandon his decision, the worry he had over it was keeping him awake at night. 'Tell me,' he insisted quietly but firmly. 'Tell me your reasons, Isaura. Why don't you want to be queen?'

***

The knock on the door surprised them all as they sat around the fire eating. Kormac frowned at Branwyn, and they both watched as Berta opened the door. They couldn't hear a thing, though, nor see a face.

Berta closed the door quickly and came over to her mistress. 'It was a messenger from the temple. The elderman wishes to see you, my lady,' she said, nodding at Edela.

Branwyn and Kormac's faces revealed just what they thought of that news. Edela wasn't as disturbed, though. She knew that the elders wanted her to keep Jael safe, so she didn't imagine she could be in any danger from this Marcus. She had no memory of him from her own time in Tuura, but no one said his name without a fearful look on their face.

'Mother,' Branwyn said nervously as she placed her bowl on the floor and came over to sit next to her. 'Mother, you must be careful around Marcus. You must watch your words. He knows everything that happens in Tuura and beyond. The dreamers tell him everything they see. He will catch you out in any lie, be sure of that.'

Kormac studied Edela quietly. 'I'll walk you to the temple. After that rain last night, I fear it is very icy outside.' He got up to put on his cloak and gloves.

Edela handed Branwyn her bowl and eased herself out of the chair, grimacing in discomfort. She felt a heaviness in her body that had only intensified over the last few days. The absence of Aleksander was affecting her spirit greatly. She had not seen him since their talk about his mother, and she was growing increasingly worried about him. She had not had a single dream, nor any further insight into Fianna or Rhea, but perhaps there was more to be found at the temple?

If this Marcus would tell her anything.

Branwyn held out her cloak, and Edela turned around so that she could slip it over her shoulders. She kissed her mother on the cheek. 'Be careful. Please.'

***

Aleksander knew that he had to stop or he was going to turn into everything he despised: a man who had no control over mind or body, who lurched about the streets like a mad fool, causing people to turn away from him in distaste or fear.

He'd seen men like that, and he had no intention of becoming one.

Pushing his cup away, he decided it was time to leave. He wobbled to his feet, his head ringing loudly as his eyes moved in and out of focus. Grabbing the table, he tried to steady himself.

She touched his arm. 'Come,' she whispered, 'lean on me.'

Aleksander peered at her, trying to remember her name. He was happy to see someone he knew, but at the same time, he wished she would go away. He didn't want her to see him, not like this. He didn't want a reminder of what they had done.

What he had done.

'No, no,' Aleksander grumbled, pushing her arm away. 'No!'

But she saw the state he was in and the looks from the men around the dark little tavern. Soon they would throw him out into the snow, she was sure of it. He was a stranger here, alone, and making another fuss. She tried again. 'Come, just let me help you back to your house. That's all. Come on.'

Aleksander frowned at her and let go of the table, trying to prove that he didn't need her, but the room moved away from him, and he stumbled again. She reached out, grabbing his arm, placing it over her shoulder.

He didn't argue. He didn't want to be here anymore.

She led him through the door and into the chill of the night, or was it night? The sky was dark, but surely it was barely midday? He was confused and disoriented as she led him away. He wanted to stop her, to make her turn around. He needed to go back to Aedan and Aron's. He was sure they were going the wrong way. He didn't want to go back to her cottage again, not that.

Aleksander's shoulders sagged in defeat as his feet slid around beneath him.

Hanna, he remembered as the wind rushed the sweet smell of her over him.

Her name was Hanna.

***

'Ivaar's not here,' Eirik assured her. 'We both saw him leave this morning and he hasn't been back. You can speak freely, unless you think your children here are spies for him?' He smiled encouragingly at her, but inside, his stomach was twisting into knots.

Why was he asking questions he didn't want answers to?

Isaura bowed her head and spoke quickly before she changed her mind. 'I worry for Eadmund and Thorgils. For what Ivaar has planned for them.'

Eirik's frown was sharp. 'Planned for them?'

Isaura didn't flinch. 'He is driven by revenge, for what Eadmund did to him, for what he sees as Eadmund's fault. He's always insisted that he didn't kill Melaena. He blames Eadmund for his banishment, for turning everyone against him. But, of course, it goes so much further back than that, doesn't it?' she sighed. 'He blames Eadmund for all the things that have gone wrong in his life.' She paused, nervously glancing around again but there wasn't even a servant in the hall now. 'When he is king, there'll be nothing to stop Ivaar taking his revenge. Nothing at all.'

Eirik nibbled his bottom lip. Eydis had said similar things, but in the heat of his anger at Eadmund, he hadn't wanted to hear any of it. Oss was his priority. Oss had to be protected. But what if they were all right? What if Ivaar's revenge destroyed everyone he loved? 'Tell me about Ivaar's dreamer,' he whispered. 'Is she good?'

Isaura looked puzzled. 'Good?' She shook her head, trying not to let her distaste show on her face. 'I don't know. Ivaar doesn't let anyone speak to her. He takes her advice very seriously, though. He is never without her.'

Eirik scratched his head, suddenly as anxious as Isaura. He remembered the sad eyes of the beautiful dreamer as she'd passed him the other night. When the blizzard had done its worst, he would have to seek her out. Draw her away from Ivaar.

He needed to see if she had any insight into what his son's plans were.

***

Eadmund was going mad. He sat on his bed and stared at the door, tapping his boots on the floor. The wind was still whipping snow around outside but was it slowing down? He fidgeted with his tunic, readjusted his cloak, stretched his neck, and got up.

Again.

To open the door and check outside.

Again.

The wind whipped the door out of his hands, and he had to step outside to retrieve it as it banged violently against his cottage. Part of him was hoping the storm would sweep the cottage up into its fury. He was sick of the sight of its pitiful four walls. Sick of the scream of the wind as it raced through the holes in them.

Eadmund wandered back inside and sat down by the fire. What was left of the fire. He was almost out of wood and was either going to have to face being blown away by the storm, or simply just freeze. He sighed, glancing at his bed, remembering the night Jael had been there with him. Naked. On top of him. Her hair loose and wild about her as her eyes devoured him.

He frowned.

Where had she gone? Why had she disappeared?

Eadmund looked down at the parcel that sat by his feet; a gift he hadn't been able to give because of the storm. But perhaps, when the snow and the wind eventually retreated, perhaps he could try?

His head was clear now. He was tired of waiting.

***

'Come in, please, Edela. I have a seat waiting for you by the fire.'

Edela shuddered at the sound of his voice. She didn't know why. There was nothing especially threatening in it, but it was cold, and he spoke slowly, and she feared him instantly. She quickly glanced at his face as she made her way to the seat. She didn't know him, but how was that possible? How had he risen to become the elderman without her even knowing him?

'We have not met, you and I,' Marcus Volsen breathed as he walked behind her, the soft thud of his boots barely noticeable on the stone floor. He was a large man, but he made little sound.

Edela sat down on the small wooden chair, shaking with both cold and fear. 'No, we have not,' she croaked, clearing her throat, trying to imagine herself younger, stronger, less vulnerable in front of this powerful man. 'Which is strange, I think, don't you?'

He sat opposite her, placing his hands on his legs, his amber eyes resting on her. 'I believe we may have simply passed one another. I came here from Helsabor as a young man after the death of my parents. I am Tuuran, on my mother's side.'

Edela was not at ease, and she knew that put her at a disadvantage. Every sense in her aching body was warning her that this man posed a threat that stretched far beyond his polite chatter. She could sense it in the tightness of his shoulders and the tension in his thick, black eyebrows. In the way his head barely moved when he spoke. He sat before her like a mountain that wanted to crush her with its force, and her mind was scrambling about helplessly before him.

'Well, that would explain it, I think,' she smiled freely, taking a deep breath. She saw Jael standing behind him then, and her jaw clenched, her focus sharpening. 'You are young to have risen to become the elderman,' she said. 'It is a great achievement.'

'Perhaps,' Marcus said, one eye twitching. 'But then we are all given gifts. It is how we use them that dictates where we end up, wouldn't you say?'

Edela sat forward confidently. Life was a game of shadows, she knew. And in the shadows, many things could remain hidden. 'I would, yes. But, of course, not everyone who has a gift uses it wisely, or indeed, to its full potential.'

Marcus inhaled sharply and stood, walking towards a table in the corner of the room. He poured wine into two silver cups and brought them back to the fire. 'Please, have a drink.' He didn't smile as he held out her cup.

'Thank you,' Edela said, placing the cup on her knee with absolutely no intention of drinking it.

'We must speak of your granddaughter,' Marcus began.

'I am glad to hear it,' Edela said quickly. 'There is much I wish to know.'

'*You* wish to know?' Marcus was surprised. 'Neva has already informed you of what you need to know. I have brought you here to discuss what you must do when you return to Oss.'

Edela tried not to let her annoyance show. His manner was curt, and it riled her, but he was the most powerful man in Tuura, and she needed to keep on good terms with him for now. 'I thought Neva was going to speak with me about that?' she frowned.

Marcus looked slightly unsettled. 'Neva is... unwell. I thought it best that I spoke to you instead. You will need time to study, to ready yourself for Morana.'

'Who is this Morana? How is she so dangerous and yet still alive?' Edela wondered, watching Marcus' face harden with each word she spoke. 'Why has no one tried to stop her before?'

'All things happen as the gods will it, Edela. As the gods lead us, we will always follow.' He spoke as though reading a prophecy. 'And Morana's death will come when it is time. That, however,' he shook his head, 'is not your concern. Your concern is to protect Jael from Evaine, her daughter.' He reached under his seat and brought out a black leather-bound book, holding it out to Edela with some reluctance.

'This is for you to see. You alone,' he said firmly, his fingertips still gripping the edges of the book. 'You will not show another soul. Do you understand me? Morana has magic of the darkest sort at her disposal,' he warned. 'She has her own book, many of them, I imagine, but this is ours. And you must take it and learn how to defend yourself and Jael against whatever she is planning. Everything you need to know is in here.'

Edela put down her cup and took the book. It smelled as though it had been buried in a damp, dark hole for centuries. Edela felt the weight of it sink into her knees. 'But I....' She looked up at Marcus, suddenly anxious.

'Jael must live,' he said firmly, his eyes probing hers. 'You will help her to live, Edela. You will learn what the book has to teach, and you will go to Oss, and you will save her. Do I make myself clear?'

Edela shivered and shuddered as she sat there by the intense heat of the fire, her mouth dry, and the stench of the book filling her nostrils. She must have nodded her head, for he looked at her, satisfied, then stood and walked away.

***

Jael ran the brush down Tig's neck, her hand following its silky path. He hated being shut up in the stables. She would have felt the same if it weren't for the fact that she was trying to hide from everyone.

The storm had been an unexpected Vesta gift. She had been able to hibernate in the house with Biddy and the puppies, and in the stables with the horses. They had a wealth of food and wood, and an abundant store of ale and mead, so it had been a thoroughly pleasant few days. She had pushed every thought of Eadmund out of her head as soon as it had arrived, along with every guilty pang and stirring desire. Nothing had existed for Jael except the howl of the wind and the warmth of the fire.

She kissed Tig's cheek, stroking his mane. 'Perhaps tomorrow, my friend,' she promised.

'So you prefer to kiss your horse?' Eadmund smiled, standing in the doorway, covered in a thick dusting of snow. 'I see now why you ran away. I must say, it's unexpected, but I do understand, he's a handsome creature.'

Jael frowned, unhappy at being caught off guard. She squirmed, uncomfortable that he was blocking her exit. 'Well, we have been together a long time, Tig and I. We're very close.' Her eyes did not reflect the smile in his.

'I see,' Eadmund said, stepping forward. 'But then again, I'm your husband, and that entitles me to certain rights that your horse can never have.'

Jael wanted to step back, but she couldn't move; she was already hard up against the door to Tig's stall. 'Rights?'

'Yes, don't you remember our vows that day? It was not so long ago, was it?' Eadmund stopped just in front of her, brushing the snow out of his beard, reaching a hand out to touch her face.

Jael flinched, her eyes sharp. She pushed his hand away and stared at him coldly. 'You were so drunk you couldn't stand, so how you can remember anything that was said at our wedding, I don't know.'

'Well, you forget, I've been married before,' he smiled. 'I've suffered through those vows twice now, so I do remember how you promised to love and obey me, to care for me, nourish and nurture me, to share a home with me. So...' he continued, reaching for her hand, but she shook it away again, 'I think it's time for us to do just that, don't you? You can either come back to my shit-heap of a cottage, or I can come here. But one thing I know for sure, Jael, is that you're my wife and where you are is where I'm going to be, whether you like it or not.' Eadmund's eyes softened, and there was a small flicker of uncertainty in them. 'I've wasted enough of my life. I'm not going to waste any more.'

Jael glowered at him.

She hated being told what to do. She despised it more than anything.

She had been ordered about by Lothar, and Eirik, and now Eadmund had decided to come and claim his husbandly rights.

After all this time?

She wanted to punch him in the face.

Eadmund's smile faded, his hazel eyes full of sadness. 'Don't run away from me, Jael. You didn't save me to push me away, did you?'

Tig whinnied, banging his head into Jael's, nudging her closer to Eadmund.

She stumbled, losing some of her composure.

Eadmund laughed, grabbing her, pulling her reluctant body into his snowy cloak. She stood stiffly in his arms, rigid beneath his hold.

She wouldn't even look him in the eye.

'You're not drunk, then?' she muttered.

'No? Why would I be?' Eadmund wondered over the top of her head. 'You cured me, didn't you? You and that evil bitch of a tincture.' He smiled and stepped back, lifting her chin. 'And now I'm here to get you.'

Jael's eyes darted around the stables as she tried to think of what to do. She tried to think of Aleksander, but all she saw were Eadmund's eyes and nothing else. And then all she could feel were his lips as he leaned forward to kiss her, and his hands as they gripped her head, and his body as it pressed against hers. And then there was no time for thinking as the wind screamed like an angry ghost outside, and the horses whinnied impatiently in their stalls, and the straw rustled under their feet, scratching Jael's back as Eadmund laid her down and smiled.

CHAPTER FIFTY TWO

His willpower had most certainly deserted him, or was it something about her that he found so hard to resist? Perhaps he was just desperately lonely and tired of being broken?

'Why do you drink so much?' Hanna wondered quietly as she lay her head on his chest.

Aleksander wanted to ask her to move, to lie away from him. He didn't know her. He didn't want her to be so close, as if they were something more than what had just happened.

Again.

Why had he let it happen again?

'I suppose it's something to do,' he said distantly, not wishing to reveal anything about himself. He wasn't looking for a friend. He wanted to leave.

'Well, seems to me that you should find something else to do,' she murmured. 'You're making yourself known as trouble. They don't like trouble in the temple. People who cause trouble don't stay around here long. Especially outsiders.'

Aleksander frowned, pulling the furs up over his naked chest. He was cold to the bone and too thick-headed to make much sense of Hanna's warning. 'Why do you care so much about what trouble I get into?'

She sat up and looked at him, shyly covering her breasts with one arm. 'I don't. I just thought you needed to know,' she muttered, dropping her head to avoid the scowl in his eyes. 'You looked very sad. Alone.' She lay back down.

On her side of the bed.

Aleksander was caught between wanting to throw something and needing to cry. His head hurt too much to do either, though. 'I suppose I am,' was all he could get out, his voice heavy with pain. He rubbed his head. 'I should go.'

Hanna looked up at him, worried. 'Do you *have* somewhere to go?'

'Of course.' He sat up, thinking about Edela. He was worried about her and felt disloyal for abandoning her, but he couldn't go back to Branwyn's and face her. He didn't want to know what else she had seen about his mother. He would never believe it, no matter what she said.

No matter what she saw.

Aleksander glanced at Hanna. 'I have some coins in my pouch...'

'For what?' Hanna looked insulted. 'What do you think I am?'

He cringed, caught in the awkwardness of the moment. Wishing he was anywhere else. 'I... I thought –'

'You should go.'

Aleksander reached for his trousers, which he'd dropped by the bed. 'I'm sorry. You've been very kind to me.' He slipped his tunic over his head, shrugging it on. 'I'm sorry.' He didn't look at her again as he grabbed his cloak and belt, and headed for the door without bothering to finish dressing.

***

Ayla opened the door with a heavy sigh.

'My lord,' she gasped in surprise at the shivering figure who stood knee-deep in the snow, frowning at her. 'Please, come in.' Her face burned with the memory of Ivaar's recent visit, and she struggled to meet Eirik's eyes, wondering why he had come.

'You're Ayla?' Eirik murmured, handing her his wet cloak and hurrying to the fire. 'You're Tuuran?'

'Yes, yes, I am.'

'And how did you find your way to Kalfa, then? A long way for a Tuuran dreamer to go.' She was incredibly beautiful, he thought. She reminded him so much of Rada with those gentle dark eyes.

'My husband was a merchant from Silura. I left Tuura to be with him.' She tried to smile, but her lips barely moved as she poured ale into a cup, bringing it to the king. 'We stopped at Kalfa once and decided to stay.'

'In Kalfa?' Eirik raised an eyebrow. 'Thank you,' he nodded, taking the cup.

Ayla sat down opposite him, nervously running over all the reasons why he may have come. 'My husband liked its location. He had good trading opportunities there.' She'd told that lie so many times now that the words fell off her tongue without much effort.

Eirik sipped the cold ale, glancing at the fire. 'How do you see me dying, then?'

Ayla swallowed, unsettled by his bluntness. 'I... I don't see your death at all, my lord.'

He glared at her coldly. Her curls bounced nervously over her chest. She was shaking, but was it from fear? Eirik couldn't tell. 'Was it not you who advised Ivaar that he'd be coming back to Oss? Did you not prepare him for that? Warn him? Tell him I would die soon?'

'Well...' Ayla felt trapped. 'I saw that you would send for him. I saw Ivaar as the King of Oss. I saw your pyre. I saw all of those things, but never your actual death. I'm sorry.' She hung her head, wanting respite from his piercing blue eyes. 'I cannot tell you about that.'

Eirik sighed. 'It seems that no one can tell me about that, which is a shame, as it's all I can think about. My death and what will become of Oss.' He pulled his stool towards hers. 'My children, my legacy. Tell me what you have seen about that. All of it.'

Ayla squirmed. He was much like Ivaar with those penetrating eyes which could turn so cold and demanding. They searched her face, desperately seeking answers she didn't have, and information she couldn't give.

She couldn't. Ivaar held the key to everything she wanted.

She couldn't help his enemy.

***

Where had his father gone?

Ivaar leaned back in the chair he'd moved next to the fire. Mads was wailing on the floor next to him, and he kept glancing around for Isaura or any of her countless servants to come and get him. He was trying to think, and that awful noise was not helping.

Ivaar rubbed his head, trying to gain some clarity. He was losing control of himself, losing a firm grip on his plan. Because of her. Jael. She was inside his head more than anyone else these days, and that was becoming a problem. His goal was Oss. Becoming king, destroying Eadmund. But trying to play games with Eadmund by playing with his wife had only ended up confusing him, and now he felt like the one being played with.

'Will somebody come and get this fucking child!' he yelled into the quiet of the hall.

Mads stopped grizzling, staring up at his father in shock. Ivaar looked down at his little blonde head, remembering when Eskild had come and taken his father away from him and his mother. She had given Eirik a new son, a better son, *her* son, and his father had never wanted anything to do with him again. Until now, when Eskild's son had ruined his chance, finally, and now

Ivaar had his again. He wasn't about to let it slip away from him. No matter what Eadmund did, no matter what Eirik thought or wanted, or what games Jael was playing. Nothing was going to stop him claiming what was rightfully his.

Not this time.

A servant rushed over to Mads, but Ivaar shooed her away. He bent down and picked up his son, sitting him on his knee. No one was going to stop the vision he had for Oss and the revenge he had been dreaming of for most of his life.

***

'Is Ivaar so powerful that you fear what he'll do to you if you tell me the truth?' Eirik was frustrated as he leaned towards Ayla. He could tell that she knew more, despite her insistence that she'd told him everything.

'My lord,' Ayla said nervously, her eyes shifting about. 'Ivaar knows all that I've told you, and I have told Ivaar all that I know. There is nothing more. Perhaps Eydis can see things that I can't?' she suggested, hoping to distract him.

'Well, the gods do not seem to think my death very important, do they?' Eirik grumbled as he stood, shaking his head. 'I'm sure you think you're doing the right thing, Ayla. Choosing the right side. But the choice about Ivaar is mine, entirely mine. Almost no one wants him here. Almost no one wants him for their king because they remember him, and they do not like the things they remember.' He reached for his cloak which Ayla had hung over a stool to dry. 'I've chosen Ivaar to lead my people when I'm gone, to grow my kingdom, to keep my family safe.' He stared into her eyes. 'If I had another option, I would choose a different man, but I don't. That is just the way it has to be. But if there is a chance that my decision will end up killing everyone I love, I would not make that choice. Do you understand?'

Ayla nodded slowly as she stood, her eyes hooded.

'Perhaps you can dream on that for me? Perhaps you can try and see if I'm making the right choice for my people? For Eadmund and Eydis?'

Ayla followed him to the door.

'Eydis likes you, I hear.' He turned to her, wishing he was a younger man as he looked down at her attractive face, her smooth olive skin glowing in the firelight. 'Perhaps you could help her with her dreams? Maybe the answers I need will come to her?'

Ayla blinked, an idea flickering inside the darkness of her mind.

Eydis.

***

Thorgils trudged through the deep snow, happy to finally be freed from his mother's company. What a torturous Vesta that had been. Imprisoned. Forced to listen to her grating nag and endure her tasteless cooking for two whole days.

And it had all started so well.

He sighed sadly, remembering how beautiful Isaura had looked as she sat at the high table next to Ivaar who'd barely even noticed her. But Thorgils had, if only out of the corner of his eye when he'd checked to make sure that no one was looking. He wondered how he'd ever speak to her again? Ever snatch a moment when it was just the two of them alone? As much as he hated the idea, perhaps Jael needed to take Ivaar off for another ride?

He laughed, doubting she'd be in a hurry to do that.

The blizzard had wreaked havoc for two days and nights and then vanished as if it had never been, leaving behind a fort strewn with thatch and wattle and broken things, and a sky so blue that it glinted in the sun with a blinding force.

Thorgils stopped by the Pit, blinking as he watched two figures approach. It was Jael and Eadmund, leading Tig and Leada.

Perhaps Vesta hadn't been so bad for everyone?

'Thorgils!' Eadmund smiled. 'You're alive! I thought Odda might have killed you with her cooking or whipped you to death with her tongue!'

He looked well, Thorgils thought. Better than he could remember, and that smile? 'Well, it's true, I nearly ran out into the blizzard, hoping it would sweep me away!' he laughed. 'Thankfully, my mother likes to sleep, so it was not always so bad.' He nodded towards the horses. 'Going somewhere?'

'Of course,' Jael said quickly. 'Training.'

Eadmund smiled happily. 'You should go and get Vili. Come with us.'

Jael turned to Eadmund. 'Us?' She shook her head. 'There is no us. You can stay here and find Torstan. Thorgils and I are the ones leaving.'

Thorgils laughed, helping himself to Leada's reins. 'Thank you, my friend,' he said politely. 'I appreciate it.'

Eadmund glared at Jael. 'Torstan?'

'You're no use to us,' Jael said shortly, sticking her boot into a stirrup and throwing herself onto Tig's back. 'We have to train hard. We don't have time to be teaching you how to use a sword again, so try Torstan.' She turned to see that Thorgils had mounted, and clicking her tongue, she nudged Tig forward through the dense snow. It was going to be a slow ride. 'We'll be back later.'

'Much, much later,' Thorgils grinned, his eyes sparkling with mischief. He tapped Leada gently, and they fell in behind Jael and Tig.

Eadmund glared after them but neither of them even looked back.

Frowning, Eadmund turned towards the Pit, his shoulders sinking.

Torstan?

***

Torstan had him on his knees within minutes. 'This will go much better if you keep to your feet, Eadmund,' he laughed, turning around, walking back to his spot.

Eadmund scrambled to his feet with a groan. The ground had been cleared, but slush still lingered, and Eadmund was wet through already. He didn't feel defeated, though; the memory of his wife leaving with his best friend was enough to have him crouching again, sword ready, determined to do better.

'Don't say *you're* going to enter the contest, Brother,' Ivaar laughed, approaching the Pit with Tarak. 'That would make things very interesting. At least for a heartbeat. I think that's all it would take, don't you?' He winked at Tarak, who glared at Eadmund, eyes full of scorn.

'Well, not as interesting as what I plan to do to his wife.'

'Eadmund,' Torstan warned through gritted teeth as Eadmund straightened up and stalked towards the railings.

'My wife?' Eadmund glowered. 'You have *met* my wife, haven't you, Tarak? The angry, fighting one? The one who knows how to use a sword better than most? That one?' He smiled, turning back to Torstan. 'I wish you luck with your plan, but I fear it'll end with a sword up your arse. But then again, perhaps you'd like that?'

Torstan's mouth hung open as Eadmund crouched before him again, his back to Ivaar and Tarak.

Tarak looked ready to lunge into the Pit, straight through the railings, but Ivaar put a hand out to stop him, shaking his head.

'Cool your anger,' he warned. 'They're only words. Big words from a weak man with a strong wife. Perhaps you can hide behind her when we attack Hest, Brother? If you can manage to stay on your feet by then?' Ivaar was in no mood for games. He had control of himself again. He had slept well and felt much calmer today.

Eadmund's time would come.

There was no point in rushing things. He didn't want to unsettle his father or give him any reason to see him as a problem, especially in light of Eadmund's sudden turnaround.

***

They trained without swords. Thorgils wouldn't stop grumbling as Jael wrestled him to the ground, time after time.

Fyn sat watching, laughing as somehow, every time, Jael managed to twist and turn Thorgils against himself until he was wrapped up in a tangle, lying on the ground.

'I think it's time young Fyn swapped places with you,' Thorgils growled as he staggered to his feet, shaking snow from his tunic. 'Let's see if I can wipe that arse-crack of a smile off his hairless face!'

Jael grinned, happy to take a seat. She wondered how Eadmund was faring with Torstan, grinning even more as she remembered his jaw-dropping shock as they left him behind. He might have felt as though he had come far, but it was good for him to realise how far he still had to go, she thought. He was only at the beginning. He needed her help and Thorgils' to get better but not now, not when they had the contest to prepare for. They had to do everything they could to defeat Tarak. They had no time for Eadmund.

Even Fyn was better than him at the moment.

'Keep your eyes open, Fyn!' she called. 'Watch for every

movement. Remember what I did, how I took him to the ground. It doesn't matter how much bigger he is than you if you know how to bring him down. And if you can bring him to the ground, you can control him and finish it.'

'Will you shut up!' Thorgils barked at her. 'We're trying to concentrate over here!'

Jael laughed, taking a drink from the jug of ale she'd brought Fyn. It was cold and refreshing after a long morning of grappling with Thorgils. She watched as Thorgils and Fyn circled one another, but her mind was back at the house with Eadmund. It hadn't felt as strange as the first time. Aleksander's face still flickered in and out of her mind constantly, but so did Eadmund's. And Eadmund was her husband. And that thought made her smile. She closed her eyes for a moment, picturing his face as he lay beneath her, looking deep into her eyes, his hands on her body.

'What? No! Ha! I don't believe it! Jael, I did it! I did it!'

Jael blinked herself away from Eadmund and saw that Thorgils was once again pulling himself out of the snow, and it was Fyn this time who was dancing around him like a mad hare, revelling in his victory.

'I did it! I did it!'

Jael laughed, then gasped as she watched Thorgils come up behind the celebrating hare and take his feet out from under him in one fell swoop.

Fyn plummeted into the slush, face first.

'Ha! Now *I* did it!' Thorgils snorted. 'Best you remember to watch your back, you little turd!' And he strutted over to Jael, snatching the jug away from her and taking a long drink, the look on his face one of disgruntled triumph. 'Time for swords, I think. I have a little revenge to dish out.'

***

Edela opened the book as soon as Branwyn closed the door. She had thankfully taken Berta with her who had left behind a comfortable fire and a plate of fresh hotcakes. Edela sat beside the fire, wrapped in a smoky fur, turning each page with great interest, her mind humming as she scanned the thinly-scrawled words and symbols. The smelly old book appeared full of ways to protect herself from the darkest magic. Is that what this Morana was planning to use against Jael? Hoping to kill her or enslave her? Turn her against everyone she loved? Edela frowned. She wished Aleksander were here. She felt far too old to enter a war of magic on her own, if such a terrifying thing did exist.

Edela had until spring to master these symbols and spells. To memorise all that she needed to know from the book. She doubted they would let her take it when she left. Symbols and spells to ward off evil, to keep Jael safe from Morana and her daughter. But Edela knew that there was so much more to all of this.

They needed Jael safe. Why?

Fianna had sent men to kill Jael. Why?

Edela's head was full of questions as she lay it back against the chair, sighing heavily with the burden of the last few months. There was so much more she needed to find out. What about those headless girls? What about the Book of Darkness? They had not appeared in her dreams without reason.

She shook her head in frustration, wishing that her dreams were being more helpful.

There was a faint knock at the door, and Edela lurched forward in surprise, hurrying out of the chair, slipping the book under her pillow. She smoothed down her dress and ran a hand over her hair before going to open the door.

'Alaric!' Edela was surprised by the stooped figure before her. 'How lovely to see you.' He looked worried, she thought as she ushered him inside, his eyes quickly sweeping the room.

'You're alone, then? I saw Branwyn leave.'

'Did you now? Well, come and sit down and tell me what has happened, because I can see, dear Alaric, that you have a lot on your mind.'

CHAPTER FIFTY THREE

They were in Eydis' bedchamber, well away from Ivaar's prying eyes, and hopefully, his little spy's eavesdropping ears.

'You must close your eyes and think of a word that describes what you're seeking,' Ayla explained as she sat next to Eydis on her bed. Her face was strained. She had not slept much since Eirik's visit. 'You'll see that word in your mind as you're going to sleep.'

'And that will help bring dreams to me?'

'It will help focus them, yes, but in the end, it's the gods who will choose what you see. You can only ask, as clearly as you can,' Ayla warned her quietly. She watched as Eydis closed her eyes, wondering if it made any difference to her. 'The other thing you can do is find an object. Something to represent the person or thing you're seeking answers about. For instance, if it were your father, perhaps you would take an arm-ring, or an item of his clothing, and hold it in your hand when you went to bed.'

Eydis frowned. 'And will that help me understand what is real and what is not?' She turned towards Ayla. 'Will I be able to tell the difference between my fears and my visions?'

Ayla saw the panic on Eydis' face. She patted her hand. 'When the clouds of your dreams come, you must concentrate. This is when you'll use your word again. Keep it in your mind. See it. Say it. Over and over again. This will help the clouds part, and what you'll be left with is a true vision. That's the one you must grab hold of.'

'But how do I do that?'

'Well, that is the hard part. The elders teach us to walk into a dream. By walking into a dream, you become part of it. It becomes part of you. You are there, inside the dream, so it is easier to hold onto once you wake up. But Eydis, that is the hardest part of all. It may take some time for you to learn how to do that.'

Eydis took a deep breath. Her chest fluttered with nerves, but also some hope that hadn't been there before. It had all felt so confusing and overwhelming, but now she saw a way forward. A way that she could help.

Ayla stood. 'I should go,' she said quietly. 'Ivaar will be looking for me.'

Eydis didn't need to see her face to know how she felt about that. 'Will you come again, though? Perhaps we could talk some more? I'll try to do as you say, but I'm certain it won't be as easy as it sounds.' She smiled shyly, reaching for Ayla's hand.

'I will, of course,' Ayla smiled, squeezing her hand. 'But you must not forget that dreamers go to the temple for years to learn how to master their dreams. You shouldn't expect to have control after one night.'

'No, but at least I know more than I did before you came. Thank you, Ayla. I hope I'll find some answers when I go to sleep tonight.'

Ayla looked down at Eydis as she wrapped her blue woollen cloak around her shoulders, her forehead creased into a deep frown. 'I hope you will too.'

***

'Who is that parcel for?' Jael wondered, peering at Eadmund over a bowl of soup.

They were eating around the fire, and he had barely spoken to her, much to her amusement. He had a black eye, and he'd limped back to the house with her, filthy, wet, and in a foul mood.

'Do you have any other clothes?' Biddy asked, handing Eadmund a second bowl of soup. 'I should like to wash those.'

'Thank you,' Eadmund mumbled. 'Clothes? Well, none that I've worn in a long time. I suppose they're shut away in my chest. In my cottage.'

'Good. I'll have Askel fetch your chest tomorrow, then, and we can see what's in there. I'm sure you have something else you can wear.'

'You'd think so, wouldn't you?' Eadmund muttered, devouring Biddy's fish soup. Her cooking was almost reason enough to smile.

But not quite.

He was still too annoyed with Jael for that.

'The parcel?' Jael asked again, nodding towards the large lump Eadmund had brought with him on his first night in the house. He'd left it by the door and not mentioned it since. Both Jael and Biddy had been keen to know what it was.

'That?' Eadmund didn't look up. 'That was something I bought for you. A Vesta gift. But I haven't made my mind up whether I want to give it to you yet.'

'Oh, really?' Jael looked less than impressed.

'Yes, really.' Eadmund put his empty bowl on the floor, running a hand over his beard. 'You had me lead my horse out as if we were going training together, and then you just left me there, like a small child, while you rode off with my horse and my best friend!'

Jael laughed. 'Well, what did you expect?'

'I expected to go training with *you*! Not to spend the day having my face pushed into the mud by Torstan! Torstan, who I used to beat every time we fought. Torstan, who couldn't stop smiling as he ran me around like a little dog!' Eadmund glared at Jael, but there was a hint of humour in his eyes now. He was finding it impossible to stay as angry as he had a mind to be. Not when he could see her. Not when she was this close to him, and they were sitting around the fire together in *their* house.

Jael handed her bowl to Biddy and patted Vella who'd been patiently sitting next to her. 'We have to beat Tarak,' she said seriously. 'One of us does. It's more important than you know. To me. When the contest is done, you can be our friend again, I promise,' she smiled.

'That's very kind of you,' Eadmund snorted. 'I'll look forward to that, but in the meantime...'

'In the meantime?'

'I think I should like to stay here. Or will you be sending me out to stay with Torstan and moving Thorgils in?'

Jael raised an eyebrow. 'Well, I was quite happy here with just Biddy and the puppies,' she said with a straight face. 'We've gotten used to it being just us, haven't we, Biddy?'

'Don't drag me into your game!' Biddy called from the kitchen. 'I've far too much to do for any of your nonsense!'

'How about you give me your gift and then we'll see?'

Eadmund frowned. 'No, I think I'll hold onto that a little longer. I want to make sure you're not going to run away from me again. Perhaps, if you're still here in the morning, I'll give it to you then.'

Jael stared at him, and he stared back at her, and she couldn't look away. It was surely going to be much harder to run away this time.

***

Alaric's eyes flitted nervously around the spacious house. Compared to his tiny cottage, it was truly luxurious, with thick furs scattered over the wooden floor, plastered walls that retained the heat of the room, and beds that actually looked comfortable. There was obviously some reward to be found in blacksmithing, he decided, smiling as Edela handed him a cup of ale and a plate of hotcakes and berries, smothered in honey. 'Thank you,' he murmured appreciatively.

'Has something happened?' Edela wondered, bringing a stool towards the chair she had forced Alaric into. 'You seem distressed.'

'Well,' he shuddered. 'Not so much. I just wanted to help. You.'

'I'm glad to hear it,' Edela smiled. 'Without Aleksander, I do feel very alone in all of this now.'

'I'm not sure you should be delving into these things, Edela, but if you are,' Alaric tried to smile, 'you can't do it all by yourself.'

'No, I expect not,' she admitted sadly, thinking that she must find Aleksander. She needed to try and get through to him. Shaking her head, Edela brought her attention back to Alaric. 'So what can you do to help me?'

'Well... there is a scribe called Merya. She is very, very old now. Older than even us,' he smiled. 'She was the personal scribe of Fritha, who was elderman when you were in the temple. When Rhea Thorsen was removed.'

Edela's eyes widened. 'I remember her, and, of course, I remember Fritha. She was a very fair woman, wasn't she?'

'Yes, she was,' Alaric nodded. 'Which is why I thought it worth asking about Rhea and what she had done. Fritha would never have removed someone from the temple without a serious reason.'

'And?'

'Well, Merya is no longer quite right in the head, it seems,' Alaric said awkwardly. 'So our conversation was rather meandering, to say the least. Much of what she said sounded like jumbled ravings, but when I finally got around to mentioning Rhea's name, she went completely white. Her face froze, and she hurried away into a corner of her cottage and stayed there.'

'Oh.'

'It took some time, coaxing her out, calming her down. I told her all about you and how you had returned, trying to help Jael.' His stomach rumbled impatiently, and he popped a berry into his mouth. 'She knew all about Jael, and her words suddenly became clearer. I told her about Fianna so that she would understand the importance of finding out what Rhea might have done. And eventually, she told me.'

Edela edged forward, holding her breath.

'Apparently, Rhea boasted about the Widow. About knowing her and visiting her,' Alaric whispered anxiously. 'She said she'd been taken to see her as a child, by her own mother.'

Edela was surprised by that. 'They threw her out of the temple because she knew the Widow?'

'Of course,' Alaric said. 'They could not have someone in the temple, exposed to all their prophecies and secrets, who had a connection to that witch. Although I have to say, perhaps it was just the fantasies of a young girl? Surely the Widow couldn't have been alive?' He took a long sip of ale, trying to calm his screeching nerves.

But the Widow was very much alive according to Aleksander, who had known where to find her because of his mother, who must have known because of her own mother. A terrifying shiver crept up Edela's spine. Perhaps everything was finally starting to make sense, but what that meant for Aleksander, she didn't know.

***

When Eadmund rolled over the next morning, he came face to face with Vella.

Vella licked his face affectionately, but she was not Jael.

He frowned, fumbling around for his clothes which were missing, convinced that he'd thrown them over Jael's chest when he'd gone to bed. He wrapped a fur around himself, groaning at the pain in his arms, not to mention his legs, which were aching and heavy.

There was no Jael when he walked out into the main room, either. The fire was burning high, and Biddy was sweeping madly, but there was no Jael.

'Good morning,' he mumbled, trying not to sound as irritable as he felt.

'And to you,' Biddy smiled, placing her broom against a wall and going to stir the cauldron. She'd been keeping his porridge warm while he slept.

'Where's my wife?'

'She left already,' Biddy mumbled, not wanting to meet his eyes.

'Really?'

'She went to find Thorgils. They've gone training again.'

'Of course. Have you seen my clothes?'

'I've scrubbed them clean, and I'll be getting your bath ready as soon as you've had this.' She handed him a bowl.

'So I have no clothes?' Eadmund frowned, taking the bowl of porridge to his chair.

'None. Not until your chest arrives.' Biddy grunted, lifting the cauldron off its hook and carrying it to the kitchen. 'And hopefully, that won't take long, but I expect I'll have to wash those too. You may as well get comfortable!'

'Hmmm,' Eadmund grumbled, unsure whether to be grateful for the food, which tasted better than it looked, or angry because Biddy was treating him like a child. He decided on the former. 'I need to get training too, though. I can't sit around naked all day.'

'Well then, I'd better get that bath water ready, hadn't I?'

Eadmund spooned another lump of porridge into his mouth, glancing at the parcel, still sitting by the door. It looked as though it would be sitting there a while yet.

***

'Jael, wait!' Eydis called, tapping her stick, trying to navigate her way across the square with speed, which was not easy in the snow.

'Eydis?' Jael turned around and walked towards her, holding Tig's reins, Thorgils following not far behind with Leada. 'What's wrong?' She'd been eager to leave as early as possible, hoping to avoid talking to Eadmund. She still felt odd and out of sorts most of the time and the only answers she'd found for that were riding and fighting.

Eydis was wrapped up warmly in a thick cloak, with a fur tucked around her neck, woollen arm warmers, and gloves as well, but she still looked chilled to the bone. 'I wanted to talk to you,' she whispered. 'Hello, Thorgils.'

'Miss Eydis,' he smiled. 'Shall I leave?'

'No, no, it's not a secret really. It's just that I had a dream.'

Jael glanced at Thorgils. 'Should we go somewhere less public?'

'Is Tarak around? Or Ivaar?' Eydis wondered quietly, her head turning from side to side, trying to listen for any clues.

'No, no one at all really,' Jael assured her. She looked at Thorgils. 'Why don't you come with us? You're certainly dressed for it.'

Eydis' eyes lit up.

Thorgils, though, looked less convinced. 'Well, we're going to be training for most of the day. That won't be very interesting for Eydis.' He raised his woolly eyebrows at Jael.

'But she might find someone to talk to where we're going, mightn't she?' Jael smiled, thinking that it was time Eydis made a friend and she knew the perfect person.

Eydis looked intrigued. 'I'd like to come,' she smiled eagerly. 'I haven't been riding since Eadmund used to take me, but that was many years ago.'

'Good, I'll go and tell your father and maybe grab something from his kitchen. I imagine you'll need feeding before long!'

Thorgils frowned after Jael, but he saw how happy Eydis looked, and he felt the guilt of his morning moodiness. 'Well, come on then, Eydis, let's see about getting you and Leada acquainted. How about you give her a carrot? That's always a good way to impress a lady, I find.'

***

Axl couldn't raise a smile. Suddenly he had finer clothes again; his mother had seen to that. He was sleeping in his old bedchamber, eating at the high table, but it all left a bitter taste in his mouth. He walked through the snow, kicking it absently, listening to the crack and squeak of the fresh powder beneath his boots. His mother was trying to be brave, but he knew her better than anyone, and he could see how hard it was for her. She didn't deserve this.

Somehow, he had to do something about Lothar.

'It's freezing this morning!' Amma shivered, creeping up beside him, slipping her arm through his. She was covered from head-to-toe in furry things, and Axl laughed to see it.

'How can you possibly be cold wearing that many animals?' he wondered, taken out of his misery for a moment. They had become very close lately, and Amma was the only person who could make him smile these days. Axl had finally listened to his mother and abandoned most of his friends. He supposed he'd always known the underlying motives of their friendliness, but now he could see just how much danger he'd put his family in. He needed to be smarter if he was to survive, and he needed to survive to keep Amma and his mother safe.

'Well, that may be true,' Amma laughed. 'But it is still the coldest morning I can ever remember. Although I'd rather be out here than stuck in the hall watching your poor mother suffer. My father won't let her out of his sight.' She cringed, peering around quickly, imagining herself in the same position one day soon. She saw it constantly now, and the worry was making her ill.

'Agreed,' Axl said sadly. 'It's not what she deserves at all.' He pulled Amma closer as they walked down to the piers. 'There is hope, you know. A way we can all get out of this. I'm certain of it. I will find it Amma, I promise.'

***

'Stealing from the king?' Ivaar purred, stepping in front of Jael. 'Dear, oh dear, that crime is punishable by... hmmm, I'm not sure what my father does these days, but I'm sure that whatever it is will be nothing compared to what I have planned.'

'I shall look forward to it,' Jael said coolly, holding a packet of food close to her chest. 'Luckily, though, the king himself gave me this food, so no punishment is necessary.' Her skin prickled. There was no warmth between them anymore.

No games to play.

'I see,' Ivaar murmured, circling Jael as she stood by the fire, waiting for him to finish his performance. 'But what about the punishment for lying? Will you escape from that so easily?'

Jael frowned impatiently. 'Lying? About what in particular?' She wanted to leave.

'Well, my little spy tells me that you and Eadmund are very much together now.' Ivaar leaned towards her face. 'Apparently, his return from the dead has prompted a sudden change of heart from you. You've forgotten all the things you told me, it seems. Forgotten Aleksander Lehr. Forgotten Brekka. Forgotten all that I could offer you. Your freedom, for one.'

'Your little spy?' Jael bit her lip, trying to stem the fury rushing towards her mouth. Why hadn't she killed Tiras when she had the chance? 'Well, he seems to be a spy with only one ear, as he only ever tells you half a story.' Her eyes were cold and hard, as was the line of her mouth as she spoke. 'Does he know anything about what happens inside here?' Jael asked, pointing to her head. 'Or here?' she hissed, pointing to her chest. 'Then how could he tell you everything and how could you suggest that I'm a liar if you only have half a tale? A tale from a spy who's spent years trying to destroy me? How could you possibly believe anything he says?' Jael snorted. 'He knows, what? That Eadmund is in my bed now? Well, do you love everyone you lie with, Ivaar?' She let that hang in the air, hoping to confuse him a while longer. She didn't care what he thought anymore, not really. But it was always better to keep an enemy guessing.

Jael stepped around Ivaar and his pinched, angry face, heading for the doors. 'It's a shame, you know,' she said sadly, 'the choice of friends you made. It could all have been much different between you and I. I thought so much more of you when we first met.' She sent one final, frosty look in his direction, then pulled open a door, keeping her smile hidden until it had closed behind her.

Ivaar glanced around, but he was alone, apart from Annet and Leya who were playing with their dolls on the floor by the fire. He was frozen to the spot, furious but unsure if he was angrier at Jael or himself.

He watched the door close, his eyes boring into its thick, wooden panels, his hands shaking by his sides.

Jael was with Eadmund now, and Eadmund was with Thorgils, and they were all against him. But he had Tarak, and it was time to show Jael what a terrible mistake she had made.

CHAPTER FIFTY FOUR

There was not much room in Fyn's hut with Eydis squeezed in as well, so Thorgils moved to sit on the bed, which heaved beneath his fur-wrapped bulk. Jael shot him a worried look, but he brushed it away as he made himself comfortable, happily ignoring the warning creaks.

Fyn had learned to have his fire high and his cauldron boiling in the morning so that his visitors could thaw out and warm up before training began. He sat around the fire, pouring hot water into the new cups Jael had brought with her. He was nervous around Eydis, who he knew, of course, but she was the king's daughter – the king who had banished him – and her presence had him on edge.

Eydis had been very upset to learn what had happened to Fyn. He had always been very kind to her, and she couldn't imagine why he would have been banished. Jael knew Eydis wouldn't say anything to her father, but she made her promise not to reveal Fyn's location anyway.

'Now that we're here, you can tell us about your dream,' Jael said encouragingly. 'You can trust Fyn. He's not going to be telling anyone out here!'

Eydis smiled, but she looked anxious as she began. 'Ayla, Ivaar's dreamer, has been teaching me how to control my dreams. How to focus on what I want to know.'

Jael raised an eyebrow. 'Ayla? I thought you didn't like her?'

She cringed. 'I was supposed to speak to her, wasn't I? I'm sorry, Eydis. With what happened to Eadmund, I completely forgot.'

'It's alright,' Eydis insisted. 'She's trying to help me, and I'm grateful for that.'

'You don't trust her, though, do you?' Thorgils grumbled from behind them. 'She works for Ivaar. You can't trust her.'

'No, of course, I don't,' Eydis said firmly. 'But I can take her advice without fear, I'm certain of that. And besides, it helped, it really helped, for last night I had the clearest dream I've ever had. But it was very bad for you.' She turned towards Jael, her eyes filled with panic. 'I saw Tarak about to kill you.'

***

Eadmund dragged the chest forward and lifted the lid. The stench that drifted out of the old box had them both gagging.

'I think we might need to set fire to everything, rather than wash it,' Biddy suggested, wrinkling her nose at the fusty dampness emanating from his chest.

'Mmmm,' Eadmund agreed, fingering through his mouldy memories. 'I doubt there's anything worth keeping in here at all.'

There were tunics, undertunics, a stinking old cloak, that when he held it up, was more holes than fur. He found a belt, a few odd socks, a comb, and then, as he dug deeper, Eadmund discovered his battered iron helmet, which he pulled out with a wistful smile. There were handfuls of rust-stained arm-rings his father had given him, and a mail shirt which was in a poor way, but, he thought, could be saved. He laid it down next to his helmet and rummaged through the box again, pulling out some arm guards.

'These could all do with a polish,' Biddy hummed happily. She looked them over with interest. 'Most definitely worth keeping.'

Eadmund picked up a white tunic. Well, once it had been a white tunic, now it looked like a yellowish, moth-eaten rag. He held it up, his face suddenly sad. He'd worn it when he married Melaena. 'This is not one for keeping,' he said quickly, handing it off to Biddy who was piling the rubbish beside her. 'But this...' Eadmund lifted out his long-neglected sword, his face breaking into a smile at last. 'Hello, old friend,' he murmured, holding the blade up towards the light. He twisted and turned it, but the rust had consumed its shine entirely.

'Well, I see you'll be busy today, then,' Biddy laughed as she started organising her piles. 'And I'll have to go and speak to the tailor. You can't get about in any of these rags!'

But Eadmund wasn't listening.

He had his sword in his hand again, and he couldn't stop smiling.

***

Aedan's wife, Kayla, opened the door. 'Edela! This is a surprise. Please, come in.'

Edela hesitated, happy to see that her pregnant granddaughter-in-law looked in such good health. The baby was due soon, but by the cheerful look on Kayla's face, she had a while to go yet.

'No, I won't, thank you, I just wanted to speak to Aleksander,' she said hopefully. 'I thought he might come for a walk with me. We have some matters to discuss.'

Kayla's face fell. 'I'm sorry, he's not here. We've not seen much of him at all,' she shivered, wrapping her shawl around her large belly. The wind was blowing fiercely this morning and the air it swept around was bitter. 'He does come and sleep here sometimes, but not often.'

'Oh,' Edela sighed in disappointment. She was desperately worried about Aleksander, and despite all her fears over his family's increasingly dubious past, she needed to know how he was. He had been part of her family for so many years now, and she'd always thought of him as another grandchild, but recently, he had become her closest friend. 'Well, when you next see him, please tell him that I'd like to speak to him. Very much.' She blinked away the tears that had been threatening all day and turned to leave.

***

'Tarak?' Thorgils looked concerned. 'Was about to kill Jael?'

'Yes,' Eydis said seriously, taking a sip of the hot tea that Fyn had carefully handed her.

'I suppose that means he'd already disposed of me?' Thorgils said wryly.

'But the contest is not a fight to the death,' Jael insisted, ignoring Thorgils.

'Well, he definitely doesn't like you,' Thorgils muttered.

'No, but he's not going to try and kill me in front of Eirik, is he? He would be killed for that, surely?' Jael looked around, noticing that Fyn's shoulders were up around his ears as he sat there silently. He wouldn't meet her eyes.

'When I went to sleep, I asked to see who was in danger,' Eydis said quietly. 'All the things I've seen lately have been confusing. I wanted to find out what was real, who I needed to help. I saw you and Tarak. It was a true vision, Jael, I'm certain of it.'

'And he had me on the ground?' Jael asked.

'Yes, he had you pinned there, and you couldn't breathe.' Eydis' eyes bulged in fear. 'In my dream, I was you, and I knew

I couldn't move. He was too heavy, and his hand was across my throat, and I couldn't breathe, and I couldn't move my arms or legs. He had a blade in his hand, and he brought it down, and there was nothing I could do.' Eydis shuddered, tears springing to her eyes as she relived the memory.

Fyn shook his head. 'You can't fight him, Jael! If what Eydis has seen comes true, he's going to kill you. You can't put yourself in that position. You won't survive!'

Jael stared at his anxious face, but she didn't feel particularly concerned at all. Tarak was huge, and his weight could break her if he managed to get her onto the ground like that, but in front of everyone on Oss? The fight would be stopped if it came to that. She'd heard the rules. It was not to be a fight to the death. But still, when she saw Eydis' troubled face, she knew there might be something in it. 'Well,' she said firmly, 'now we know what we're going to work on first this morning.' Finishing off her tea, Jael stood, leaving her cup on Fyn's tiny kitchen shelf, which was somehow still attached to the wall. 'Thorgils, let's go and lie down in the snow!'

***

Aleksander placed the bundle of furs under the shelter he'd made from branches and leaves, and a large piece of cloth he'd helped himself to from Kayla and Aedan's cottage. It was not enough to protect everything from a heavy snowfall, he knew, but it would keep much of the bad weather at bay.

He had been coming here on his daily ride since Hanna's warning, secreting an ever-growing pile of supplies and essentials into his shelter, which lay well hidden off the main road in a thick knot of trees. Aleksander didn't necessarily think he was in danger, but he was keen to leave Tuura as soon as he'd spoken to Edela, and it was better to be prepared. He sighed. He didn't want to have a conversation with her, but no matter how angry he felt, he wouldn't just abandon her here without a word. And, of course, there was always that nagging question of what if Edela was right? He shook his head. He could never let that thought linger for long. The implications were too unimaginable.

Aleksander took one last look at his little store, hidden away under a scattering of leaves, and hoisted himself up onto Sky, the only one who knew his secret hiding place.

The only friend he had left now.

***

Jael laughed as she walked into the house, which was not the reaction Eadmund had been hoping for.

He stood by the fire dressed in his mail, helmet, and arm guards, his arm-rings pushed high up his arms. He'd even managed to squeeze himself into his padded tunic. In truth, it was all a tight squeeze, but it wasn't too far off, and although everything looked a little rusty, despite his and Biddy's concerted efforts, Eadmund felt more like himself than he could remember feeling in years.

'Is there a war on that I don't know about?' Jael wondered, crouching down to pat the wailing puppies. 'Are we off to Hest already?' She straightened up and walked over to Eadmund, trying not to smile. He looked slightly impressive in his armour; she could definitely see the shape of a warrior starting to emerge.

'Well, no,' Eadmund admitted, removing his helmet. 'We were just going through my chest, so I thought it was time to sort all this out. Especially if I'm going to be using it.'

Jael looked horrified. 'You're not entering the contest, are you?'

'No, but thank you for your confidence,' he grinned, leaning towards Jael, intending to exchange some form of affection.

Jael walked right past him, heading for the back room. 'Is the bath ready?' she yawned, handing Biddy her cloak. Her hair was wet, and she shook from the cold. The thought of hot water had spurred her on during their ride home.

'Ahhh, well...' Biddy squirmed. 'I filled the bath for Eadmund this morning, so there's nothing there now.'

Jael looked furious, and the triumphant smile on Eadmund's face only made her fury double. 'I see,' she growled, stomping back to the fire, hoping to get a little warmth from the flames, her eyebrows pinched together in an angry scowl.

Eadmund tried not to laugh as he squeezed out of his armour, piece by piece. He bent over, shrugging off his mail, which eventually fell to the floor with a loud thump. 'Come on, grab your cloak,' he said. 'Let's go.'

Jael eyed him crossly. 'Into the cold again? I don't think so.'

Biddy brought Jael's cloak over as Eadmund slipped an arm around her shoulder.

'For once, Jael, don't argue, just come!'

***

She was waiting in the stables when he returned.

Aleksander didn't know where to look. He certainly didn't want to look into those eyes again. 'Edela, I have nothing to say to you. Not about my mother, at least.'

Edela stepped away from the stall as he led Sky in. He closed the gate behind them and started removing her saddle and bridle, not looking up.

'I understand, and we don't need to discuss that again,' Edela said, shaking. She had been waiting in the stables for some time and was frozen solid. 'I'm just glad to see you. To see that you haven't left yet.'

'But I want to,' Aleksander said coldly, coming towards her now. 'I can't help you anymore. I know Aedan or Aron would be happy to take you back to Andala. Even Kormac would.'

'Yes, of course, I understand,' Edela said. 'And you should go, whenever you wish. I'll be fine here. Alaric has decided to step in as my assistant, it seems.' She tried to smile, but it was forced. She wanted to cry because Alaric was not Aleksander, and she had come to rely on Aleksander's strength and friendship.

He hung Sky's bridle over a peg and grabbed a towel. 'Well, I hope Alaric knows what he's getting himself into,' he muttered, briskly rubbing the towel over Sky's back. 'He doesn't look the most adventurous man to me.'

Edela smiled. 'No, but he does know a few people who can help. And there's always Marcus.'

Aleksander stared at her sharply. 'I thought you were supposed to stay away from him?'

'Well, he ordered me to the temple the other day,' she said quietly. 'I had no choice but to go.'

'Oh.' Aleksander looked worried as he continued rubbing. He wanted to know more, but he just nodded his head. 'Well, I'm sure you know how to look after yourself after all these years.'

'Yes, I'll be alright, of course,' Edela shivered. 'Perhaps I will see you back in Andala in the spring, then?'

Aleksander hung up the damp towel and came to stand behind the gate. 'Perhaps.' His eyes were dark holes in the dim light of the stables. They gave no clue as to his true feelings, which was precisely what he wanted.

'Well, goodbye, then,' Edela said softly. She tried to smile, but she could feel herself starting to cry, so she ducked her head and hurried out of the stables before he could say another word.

Aleksander wanted to call out to her, to warn her about the ice. It had rained during the day, and the streets were deadly. But he said nothing. He just stood there, watching her go. She was wrong, he kept telling himself. It was the only thing he wanted to hear right now, that Edela was wrong. She had grabbed hold of the wrong dream this time, and he simply couldn't forgive her for it.

***

'Where are we going?'

Eadmund had hold of Jael's hand and she was not happy about being pulled along like a goat to milking.

'Sssshhh,' he turned and growled at her. 'Be quiet, woman. Just follow me. Quietly.'

Jael frowned, hurrying along behind him, wanting to rip her hand out of his, despite the fact that it was almost pleasant to be touching him.

It was dark but early enough that there were still people packing up for the night; bringing in their tools, securing their animals, shooing their red-faced children inside. Eadmund navigated them all with his head bent, slipping down a side alley, skirting the main streets of the fort.

Jael was getting colder and crosser the further they went, but eventually, he stopped beside a high, thickly wattled fence. She looked up to see that they were at the back of the hall, and she stared at Eadmund, utterly confused. He ignored her, feeling around for the gate, which was mostly hidden beneath creeping bushes. He'd used it many times before, though, so he found it quickly. And grabbing Jael's hand, Eadmund pulled her through the gate, closing it quietly behind them.

The moon was almost at its fullest as they stood there on glistening slabs of stone that led towards... a pool? Jael's mouth gaped open as she stared at Eadmund, who smiled and started ripping off his clothes in a furious burst of freezing cold energy. Quickly naked, he stood there wearing nothing but a ridiculous grin, before tip-toeing across the slick stones and hopping into Eirik's very own private hot pool.

Jael watched as Eadmund slipped into the water, a look of extreme bliss relaxing his face. He slid under, until the water was up to his beard, then lay his head back on the stones surrounding the small pool, looking up at the moon.

Jael glanced around. There were no windows in the back of the hall. There was one door, though. Perhaps that came off the kitchen? She wasn't sure, but it was very secluded here, and the water did look hot, she noticed as the steam rose all around Eadmund's head. So, stripping off her clothes, she raced to join him as the evening air froze the hairs on her arms. Sliding into the warm liquid, her eyes closed, and she felt the most wonderful sense of bliss as her aching body started unwinding.

Opening her eyes, Jael came face to face with her smug-looking husband. 'You're a bit close, don't you think?' she whispered crossly.

'I don't, no, not for what I have in mind,' Eadmund smiled, sliding even further forward. 'I'm not close enough at all. And right here, Wife, there's nowhere for you to run to. You're my prisoner.'

Jael laughed too loudly and Eadmund quickly clamped his hand over her mouth. Her eyes bulged as they both looked towards the kitchen door. They waited a moment, but no one came out. Eadmund removed his hand just as Jael turned back around to him, replacing it with his lips.

'You're very annoying,' she grumbled, moving her head away.

But Eadmund had absolutely no intention of letting her move at all. 'Stop running away from me,' he breathed. 'I'm your husband, and if I have to, I'll lock you up and keep you prisoner in our house, in our bed, and you'll have to stay there with me all day and all night, until you beg for mercy.' He kissed her again.

'*Beg* for mercy?' Jael said, pushing him away. 'You don't know me very well, do you?'

'No,' Eadmund whispered into her ear, his hands exploring her body beneath the surface. 'But I very much want to.'

Jael closed her eyes as his hands rested between her thighs. 'Well, if you insist,' she sighed. 'Just for a moment.'

CHAPTER FIFTY FIVE

They were not ready.

Jael worried that they were not ready, and she wanted to be as ready as they could be. She thought of Aleksander for the first time in days. What would he have had done to them? Defeated them, most likely, but he was surely smarter than Tarak, so perhaps they had a chance. If they could get through the handfuls of men standing in their way. They had to. They had to defeat Tarak.

For Fyn.

Eirik was on to his second speech now. He was starting to sound drunk, and happily so. '...and the winner will become Champion of Oss!' he called over the raucous cheering. 'And that winner will be gold-rich, fame-rich, and depending on who wins, of course,' he nodded at Jael, 'rich in women too!'

'I'd like to watch that,' Eadmund winked, squeezing his scowling wife's knee. He liked it when she scowled; something about the way her nose crinkled made him smile.

Eirik was busy toasting the contenders, but Jael had stopped listening. She was thinking of Fyn. This was their chance to avenge him, to destroy the man who had destroyed his life. She saw Eydis and remembered her dream. It was hard not to believe in the power of a dreamer's visions, but she couldn't, not this time. Still, she would have to ensure that she didn't end up on her back if she wound up fighting Tarak.

Just in case.

'If only Ivaar were in the contest,' Eadmund whispered in Jael's ear. 'That would make it much more interesting, don't you think?'

'For you, maybe, if you could remember how to use a sword,' she smirked. 'Perhaps next time?'

Eirik's speech was over at last, and the serious drinking was beginning. Jael watched Eadmund as he got up, walking over to his friends, cup in hand. She wasn't especially worried. He had drunk ale, wine, and mead since Edela's tincture but no more than a cup here or there, and so far there had been no sign that he craved more. It was impossible to rest easy, though. The Eadmund that was here now was not one she wanted to let slip through her fingers, despite the fact that she was still plagued by a regular urge to run away.

Eadmund had yet to wake up next to her, and the parcel continued to sit unopened by their door.

'Are you nervous? About tomorrow?' Isaura asked quietly as she sat down beside Jael. 'They are all so big and strong.' She looked at the huddles of large, thick-necked men who stood around the fires, loudly teasing and insulting each other. Bragging about the humiliation they would bring down upon the heads of their friends and enemies alike. 'Do you not feel scared at all?'

'Not scared, no,' Jael murmured, almost to herself. 'I think there's always some fear going into a fight. Fear of humiliation or pain or death. But no, I don't feel scared. I haven't felt scared since I was ten-years-old.'

They had not developed a friendship. Jael was far too uninterested in babies and dresses to be bothered fostering such a thing, and Isaura was far too intimidated to have anything much to say to her. But tonight, before the contest, Isaura needed Jael to get a message to Thorgils. Ivaar was head to head with Tarak now, far away from them, so she took her chance. 'Can you warn Thorgils to be careful,' she whispered, her eyes fixed on Ivaar. 'I know how he'll feel about trying to defeat Tarak, but I've heard

Tarak talking to Ivaar, and he says that he's the strongest he's ever felt. I fear that he'll hurt Thorgils badly to try and impress Ivaar. And because it's in the contest, Eirik will let it happen.'

'I'll warn him, of course. I doubt he'll listen, though,' Jael muttered, turning towards Isaura. 'But you shouldn't worry about Thorgils. He's trained hard. He's prepared for Tarak.'

Isaura didn't look convinced, but she nodded and tried to smile before slipping away.

Eirik took her place. 'I hope you're ready for them,' he smiled, nodding towards his warriors as they lurched loudly around the hall, full of ale and pre-battle bravado.

'I hope they're ready for me,' Jael said without a hint of a smile. 'I'm looking forward to winning my prize of gold and fame and women.'

Eirik laughed, draining his cup. 'Well, I'll have to change the prize if you become my champion, won't I? I don't imagine you're after any of those?'

'No, not really, but perhaps there is something you could give me...'

Eirik raised a bushy eyebrow, swaying towards her. 'Tell me.'

'Make Eadmund your heir again,' she said simply. 'If I win, I want to be the Queen of Oss one day. Eadmund's queen.' She wasn't sure she meant it, but Eirik didn't need to know that part.

Eirik blinked in surprise. 'Ha! I can't do that,' he laughed, then frowned. 'You wouldn't want that, would you? To be stuck here, being a queen? I thought you'd ask me to send you back to Brekka. Grant you a divorce. Isn't that what you really want?' He peered at Jael, shaking his head as a serving girl tried to offer him more ale.

'Brekka?' Jael mused as she found Eadmund, standing next to Torstan. He turned and smiled at her. 'No, my wish is that you make Eadmund your heir. Not Brekka.'

Eirik frowned, following her eyes.

He saw the way Eadmund was smiling at his wife, looking almost like the Eadmund he remembered from so long ago. He hadn't wanted to raise his hopes again, but so far, nothing was bringing them down. But the fall would come, he was certain it would come. 'I can't do that, Jael,' Eirik insisted firmly. 'I've chosen Ivaar. Ivaar will make a good king.'

Jael could hear the lack of conviction in his voice. She could see that he didn't believe that. But he wasn't ready to believe in Eadmund again either. Not yet. 'Ivaar will not make a good king,' she whispered hoarsely, narrowing her eyes. 'But Eadmund will. That tincture cured him. You just have to have faith in him again.'

Eirik shook his head. 'I don't need to have faith in him at all, that's where you're wrong. I've chosen Ivaar.'

'And you can sleep at night knowing he'll end up killing Eadmund and Eydis? Knowing that he'll destroy everyone here who remains loyal to Eadmund? Me? Any child Eadmund and I might have, if we live long enough under his rule?' She glared at Eirik. 'You might not have had a choice once, but you do now. And if you're worried about Eadmund, then look to me because I'll be beside him, whether he's standing or on the ground. Have faith in me. If I win the contest, have faith in *me*.' Jael stared into Eirik's fading eyes one last time, before getting up and walking away.

There was nothing more she could say to convince him.

***

'He's still here?' Edela looked surprised but relieved. 'I thought he would have gone by now.'

'No, Kayla said that Aleksander stayed with them last night,' Branwyn murmured, turning down her bed. 'Which is a good thing, I think. He mustn't be as mad as you imagine.'

Edela smiled as she rolled over, trying to find a comfortable spot, which was difficult with hips that ached as much as hers did, and a mattress that needed more stuffing. 'Well, I don't know about that,' she sighed. 'But I'm glad he's still here.'

Kormac came back from checking on the animals. Another storm was blowing through Tuura, and he'd spent much of the evening outside, securing everything for the night. 'There are soldiers everywhere at the moment,' he grumbled. 'I don't understand it. Are we facing an attack? Who is this mysterious enemy we don't know about?' He huffed and puffed his way over to the bed, sitting down to remove his damp cloak and mucky boots.

'Perhaps Marcus just likes to keep order?' Branwyn suggested. 'He's not from here, is he, so maybe he just sees everything differently than we do?'

'Then how did the elders let an outsider become their leader in the first place? Our leader? A leader who wants to change everything we've been and turn us into something we don't wish to become.' Kormac slipped under the furs, rustling his feet around, trying to warm them up.

'Perhaps he's only doing what is necessary?' Branwyn yawned, moving towards him. 'The dreamers must have told him that we need protecting.'

'Mmmm,' Kormac murmured, his head sinking into the pillow, his arms heavy after another long day at the smithy.

Edela listened as they whispered away to one another. She thought of Marcus and her body clenched in fear. She had spent every moment she could find studying the book, trying to absorb its knowledge as quickly as possible, but much of it was confusing and hard to read. True mastery of its texts would take months and much practice, and she wasn't sure if there was time for that. But at least Aleksander was still here, she smiled sleepily.

There was some hope after all.

***

'How are your dreams coming along?' Ayla wondered softly as she sat down next to Eydis. 'Have you been feeling stronger?'

Eydis frowned. Her dreams were still tying her up in knots. 'No, not stronger at all, just more frustrated,' she sighed, shaking her head. 'I keep asking to see one thing, the same thing, but it never comes.'

'Ahhh, well, that is when you must change what it is you're asking for,' Ayla smiled, sipping her wine. She watched Ivaar out of the corner of her eye. He had insisted she go and talk to his sister again. He was still desperate to know what she was seeing in her dreams, but so far, Eydis had revealed absolutely nothing. 'As I said before, the gods will only show you what they want you to see. If they don't believe what you're asking for will help you or someone else, you'll see nothing.'

Eydis looked ready to cry. 'But I need to see what will happen to my father,' she whispered. 'I need to see how he will die so that I can stop it, so that he can stay king, and then there will be no need for Ivaar.' She gasped, her head spinning anxiously, suddenly realising that she had no idea where Ivaar might be.

'It's alright,' Ayla assured her quickly, patting her arm. 'Ivaar is not near us. It's alright.'

Eydis sighed. 'I'm sorry. I shouldn't have said anything. No doubt you have to tell Ivaar everything I say.'

Ayla felt guilty as she faced those tear-filled eyes. 'Well, I am supposed to,' she whispered. 'But I won't. Besides, what is there to tell when you're dreaming of nothing but clouds?'

Eydis reached out for Ayla's hand. 'Are you sure you haven't seen it? My father's death?' she asked hoarsely. 'Truly?'

'Truly, I haven't,' Ayla promised her. 'If I had, I would tell you. Your father asked me the same thing, but I'm afraid it remains a secret for the gods alone to know.'

***

Ivaar pulled Tarak into a quiet corner. He'd watched Jael and Eadmund all night; their eyes constantly finding each other, the little touches that seemed insignificant, but were the mark of an intimate couple. He'd watched as they'd laughed with Thorgils and his father, barely acknowledging that anyone else was there. The frustration had crawled under his skin until it lay there, hot, and ready to burst. 'Tomorrow...' he breathed quietly, 'don't just beat them. Whoever you end up against, destroy them. Crush them into the earth. I want them in little pieces, too broken to stand.'

Tarak couldn't have been happier as he stood back and smiled; a smile that curled itself high up onto his scarred cheeks, right up into his menacing eyes. He could only hope that the bitch managed to make it through the rounds.

He was desperate to wrap his hands around her throat.

***

It was completely silent.

Eirik couldn't even hear the fire as he lay in his enormous bed. Three wives had lain at his side in this bed, and countless women he had cared little for, but he didn't remember their names. He lay in the middle these days. Somehow it made him feel less lonely, and there wasn't such an obviously empty space beside him.

He thought about Ayla.

She'd often been on his mind of late. Just thinking of her made him feel younger than he had in many years. He sighed wistfully. Perhaps, if he wasn't about to die, perhaps...

He laughed at the thought.

Why would a beautiful young woman want to lie with a shrivelled-up old man? Well, because he was the king, of course, and he could get most people to bend to his will. But a woman? No, he'd never tried that, or had he?

The wine was still in his head, making him dizzy, making him feel lighter than he had in a while. He thought of his conversation with Jael. Was he so blind that he didn't see what everyone else did?

Ivaar was nobody's favourite, that was the truth of it.

Even Ivaar's own mother had called him a strange boy.

But he was his son; Eadmund and Eydis' brother, and his son. Eirik could see the fire in his eyes, he could understand his bitter anger and resentment of Eadmund, but Ivaar wouldn't kill him, surely?

Closing his eyes, Eirik saw a vision of his own father. He'd been a gaunt, iron-eyed man, much like Ivaar. There had been no warmth in him, not a solitary flicker of it.

Grim Skalleson had taken Eirik's mother by the hair one night and slit her throat in front of the entire hall, in front of twelve-year-old Eirik too, just because he'd looked at him without respect. Eirik rolled onto his side, pulling his knees up to his chest. He still remembered the shock of it; the thin, red, bloody line as it crept across his mother's pale throat. The life fading from her eyes as they stared imploringly at him.

Grim had given him a choice.

Come and apologise, he'd bellowed to his captive audience of drunken slavers. Come and lick my boots, he'd laughed. Come and do that or your mother will die. And Eirik hadn't moved. He'd had enough of being humiliated in the hall, in front of everyone on Oss. He stood there, his legs like tree trunks, making a stand, trying to fight back against his father's tyranny, never believing for one moment what would happen next.

Somehow, despite his evil ways, he'd believed that his father had been capable of feeling love, but he'd been proven wrong.

Could he, would he, take the same risk again?

***

'Are you worried?' Eadmund asked, looking worried.

'About what?' Jael mumbled sleepily.

'Tomorrow, of course!' he laughed.

'If you don't stop talking and go to sleep, it will never *be* tomorrow,' she grumbled. 'And yes, I will be worried if I have to fight after a sleepless night with you blubbering in my ear till dawn!'

'So you tend to get quite angry when you're worried, then?'

'Eadmund!' Jael punched his arm and rolled over, pushing Ido, who had just found a good spot, away with her legs. 'Go to sleep, or you can go out and lie with Biddy.'

'Well, perhaps Biddy would be a more agreeable bed companion than you?' Eadmund muttered, rolling over, appreciating the unbelievable comfort of the bed again. Lying on his side had never even been possible in his old bed, but this... this was worth all the grumbles in the world.

'I'm sure she would,' Jael said softly. 'And no, I'm not worried, not about me. I just hope that Thorgils will be alright. Isaura thinks Tarak will try to destroy him.'

Eadmund frowned. 'I think Tarak is going to try and destroy everyone, and if he gets through Thorgils, that might mean you.'

'Mmmm, well I've an idea of how that might go, but I've faced worse than Tarak. If it comes to that, don't worry about me.'

'Perhaps I need to give you your gift in the morning, then, just in case I don't see you again?'

'Ha! Perhaps... now go to sleep!' Jael growled, pulling the furs over her head.

Eadmund smiled, but it faded quickly. This feeling, this new sense of being alive, it was like catching the sun inside his chest. It was a warm glow of unexpected happiness, and the fear of losing it too quickly made his throat tight. Jael could fight, he had no doubt about that, but so could Thorgils, and Tarak had crushed him over and over again.

He closed his eyes, hoping that this time Thorgils would get lucky, that he would finally have his victory over Tarak so that Jael would never have to face him.

CHAPTER FIFTY SIX

'Who will you put your coins on today?' Ivaar smiled cheerfully, joining his father by the fire.

'Is the weather fair?' Eirik croaked. He'd drunk more than he'd realised, and his head and throat were thick because of it.

'Fair enough, I'd say. A few clouds, but nothing threatening. They're already out clearing the Pit. We should be able to get in a full day.'

'That's good to hear. Thank you,' Eirik nodded to the servant who'd brought him a cup of ale.

'I can't wait,' Ivaar said, rubbing his hands together.

Eirik glanced at his son's happy face. 'I imagine you're hoping Tarak will cause some damage?'

'Well, not hoping,' Ivaar laughed. 'He will. We both know that, surely? I don't see anyone who could stop him. I've been watching them all train, and no one has impressed me yet, besides Tarak.'

'What about Thorgils?' Eirik moved over to his chair, sitting down with a groan. 'Or Jael? You don't think they can offer him a fight?'

Ivaar felt his shoulders tense, uncomfortable at the mention of those names. 'That I couldn't say. I've never seen Jael fight. Thorgils, I doubt it, but Jael? If I were to put her and Tarak next to each other, I'd say the tale of that defeat is already being sung.'

'You don't think a small man can beat a big man? You've

never seen that?'

'Of course, but a big man and a woman? That I haven't seen.' Ivaar shook his head, stopping in front of the fur-covered dais, eyeing his frowning father. 'So, my coins will be on Tarak. I have complete faith that he'll become your champion once more.'

'Mmmm, and then one day yours, I suppose?' Eirik said, leaning forward, studying his son's face, trying to see beyond what Ivaar wanted to show. 'You and Tarak will rule Oss. Is that how it will be?'

Ivaar squirmed, narrowing his eyes. 'Every king needs a champion, Father.'

'Of course, and Tarak has been a very loyal and effective one for me, but what if Jael were to win, or Thorgils?' Eirik suggested. 'Would you keep them as your champion? Have them beside you when this is your hall?'

Ivaar's smile had gone now. His father was testing him, and it made him irritable. 'It's hard to say. That might not be for many years yet, and who knows what the future holds for any of us.'

'How true that is,' Eirik muttered. 'As for me, I shall be placing my coins on Jael.' He stared at Ivaar, challenging his son. 'It's time that Oss had a new champion.'

***

Jael glanced around the bedchamber, wiggling her toes. She'd been awake for some time, and although she didn't feel the urge to run away from Eadmund, she was desperate to feel the wind on her face and Tig beneath her. She wanted to blow away all the tension that was festering in her head and twitching her limbs. So, with one quick look at Eadmund, she slipped out from under the furs, shivering her way to her clothes as silently as possible, heading for the door without looking back.

'You're not *leaving*?' Biddy whispered sternly, bent over her cauldron as Jael emerged from the bedchamber with a guilty look.

Jael walked quickly towards her pile of armour and weapons, nodding.

'Not without something to eat, you're not,' Biddy grumbled, ladling a big lump of porridge into a bowl.

Jael cringed. Her stomach was in knots. She might not have felt overly worried, but she had no appetite at all. She shook her head, but Biddy walked up to her, pushing the bowl into her chest.

'Eat, or I'll wake him up,' she hissed, nodding towards the bedchamber door.

Jael frowned but saw she had no choice.

She tried not to inhale the porridge, spooning as much as she could stand into her mouth before gagging and handing it back. 'I have to go. I'm going to see Fyn before it starts,' she said, whispering in Biddy's ear. 'I thought he might like to help me get ready.'

Biddy stared into Jael's eyes, worried. She grabbed hold of her arm. 'You be careful today. Don't do anything silly. Look after yourself.'

Jael looked away. She had to go.

Scooping up her pile of armour as quietly as possible, she smiled at the gift which was still gathering dust by the door. If she got through the day in one piece, perhaps Eadmund would have a reason to give it to her tomorrow?

***

Eadmund rolled over, his eyes still closed. He smiled. He felt almost warm and so completely comfortable. He felt the licking on his cheek, and his eyes flew open. It was Vella, with her familiar morning greeting. He frowned angrily, looking past the furry face to the empty pillow beside him.

***

Biddy hurried through her tidying, trying not to let worry consume her morning. She still had a lot of washing and burning to sort out for Eadmund, which she was glad of, grateful for anything that would take her mind off Jael.

'That woman!' came the furious bellow from the bedchamber.

Biddy almost dropped the cup she was carrying to the kitchen, unable to stop the smile that relaxed her anxious face.

***

'Jael!' Fyn came rushing out of his hut. 'What are you doing here? What about the contest?' He grabbed Tig's bridle as Jael dismounted.

'Well, nothing's happened to the contest, I just thought I'd go for a ride first. Clear my mind before it starts,' she smiled, unpacking Tig's saddlebags. She was already wearing her helmet, and she took it off, tucking it under one arm. 'I've brought my armour. I thought you could help get me ready. Good practice for when we go to Hest together.'

Fyn frowned but he put his arms out to take the heavy mail tunic she handed to him. In truth, it wasn't that heavy. Arnna had worked with Andala's Master Blacksmith to have it specially made for Jael. It was light enough for her to move easily but dense enough to prevent any weapon from getting through.

So far, at least.

'Do you want to put it on now?' Fyn wondered nervously. He wasn't sure who he was nervous for, but he'd hardly slept thinking about Eydis' dream.

'Now? No,' she laughed, walking Tig over to his shelter. 'There's plenty of time, and I could use a hot drink after that ride.' She slipped Tig a stale flatbread and walked towards the door in the hill without waiting for Fyn, who appeared to be in a complete muddle. 'Well, come on!' she called to him.

Jael was already sitting in front of the fire when Fyn came through the door.

'I have some dandelions,' he muttered sheepishly. 'That's about it.'

'Sounds fine.' Jael's eyes darted around the hut; the ride had done little to ease her tension.

'The weather is good,' Fyn said, preparing two cups.

'Seems to be,' Jael said distractedly. 'It's a pity you can't come and watch. It would feel good to witness Tarak's humiliation, don't you think?'

Fyn cringed, his shoulders hunching up to his ears, his eyes dark with discomfort. 'I'm not as confident as you about that, so no, I wouldn't want to watch him hurt you or Thorgils.'

'Truly?' Jael looked shocked. 'You don't think we have *any* chance?'

Fyn froze as he reached for the cauldron. He couldn't meet her eyes.

'Fyn –' she started.

'You heard what Eydis said. What happened in her dream.' He looked at her imploringly. 'Why don't you believe her? She's a dreamer!'

'She's a child dreamer,' Jael said firmly. 'She's wrong. I'm not going to let him kill me.'

Fyn poured hot water over his dandelion crumbles. 'Well, I've seen what he does to people. It's worse than a fight. It's humiliation.'

'But *I* know what he did to you, and I'm going to defeat him if Thorgils doesn't. I promise you that, Fyn,' Jael insisted. 'And when I'm done, you're going to come back to Oss and Tarak will be the one who's banished.'

'No!' Fyn yelled, hanging the cauldron back over the fire. 'No, Jael! No!' He was shaking, his eyes full of fear. 'I've told you before that it won't happen. Eirik won't banish Tarak, and he won't let me return. So please, leave it alone! It won't happen. He will never lose! He will always win! Just leave it alone, Jael. You don't understand! You will *never* understand!'

Jael shivered as she sat there, hearing the pain in his voice, feeling the spittle from his mouth, seeing the terror in his eyes.

And she remembered.

She bit her lip, wishing it away, but it kept coming with such force that she knew she couldn't ignore it.

'When I was ten-years-old...' she said quietly, her voice suddenly so far away, it sounded lost in a storm. She cleared her throat and began again. 'When I was ten, my mother took me to Tuura...'

***

'What's happened to your wife?' Thorgils wondered with a tight grin. He was not usually troubled by nerves, but he'd woken up with a dry throat, and a griping belly and both were getting worse. 'Has she run off already?'

'Well, yes, of course,' Eadmund laughed. 'She always does. Every morning, without fail.'

Thorgils raised an eyebrow, but he didn't pursue it further; Eadmund seemed happy enough. 'Well, hopefully, she'll be back in time for the start.'

'She will be. She's just gone for a ride.'

'Oh?' Thorgils wondered if she'd gone to see Fyn. He stared up at the pale-blue early morning sky. 'Nice day for it, then?'

'To smash Tarak's face into the dirt? A perfect day for that. Whoever does it, I'll enjoy watching.'

'I still remember when you did it all those years ago', Thorgils said wistfully as they walked to the hall. 'If only it had been a fight to the death, we wouldn't have had to suffer through eight more years of him.'

'Well, save a few pieces of him for me,' Eadmund muttered. 'I'd like to have a go at that bastard when I get back to myself again.'

Thorgils smiled confidently, but his insides felt like slush. 'Ahhh, here's the man who stands between Jael and the final battle,' he laughed as Torstan approached, his face looking much like Thorgils' insides.

'Well, I hope not,' Torstan squirmed uncomfortably. 'Hopefully, someone will stop her before she gets to me.'

'For your sake, I hope so,' Eadmund smiled.

They entered the hall, which was heaving with contestants and their families. Axes and swords were being hastily sharpened by edgy-looking warriors who were trying to hide their tension behind insults and puffed-up chests. The fires were high, and the servants were bustling around with trays of ale, smoked fish, and cheese.

Thorgils took one look at the drink and food on offer and felt ready to vomit. Torstan, however, reached for the first cup to come his way, and after that, quickly took another.

'Is that the best idea?' Eadmund wondered doubtfully, his own nerves starting to jangle as he looked around the hall. These men were hard. He'd fought against and alongside most of them. They were going to rip Jael to pieces, weren't they?

'That's coming from you, is it?' Torstan said smartly, wandering off in search of food.

Ivaar came striding towards them. Thorgils cringed and farted.

This was the last thing he needed.

'Wishing you were joining your friends today?' Ivaar asked coldly, his eyes resting on his brother's face.

'Me?' Eadmund had no intention of letting Ivaar have any fun at their expense. 'No, not in the slightest. I get a nice warm seat and a good view of everything, maybe a drink of ale. Sounds much better than rolling around on the ground with someone's arse in my face.'

Ivaar wanted to reach out and grab his brother by the throat. He looked too well, too healthy, too happy. It made him sick. 'And what about your wife? Has she changed her mind about the contest? Decided she'd rather stay home and cook something for you?' he smiled, watching Eadmund's eyes twitch.

Eadmund laughed, nudging Thorgils, who stood in great discomfort next to him. Thorgils grimaced, caught between wanting to make sure that Eadmund didn't get into any trouble, and his urgent need to go outside for a quick shit.

'Well, perhaps after she defeats Tarak, you'd like to come to our house for a meal?' Eadmund smiled.

'What a kind offer,' Ivaar said, his lips set in a thin line. 'I suppose you must enjoy this time with her before she goes back to Brekka. Back to Aleksander.'

Thorgils froze, eyes popping open.

Here was the twist that Ivaar always managed to deliver.

'Oh, you didn't know about Aleksander? About how Jael wants to go back to Brekka to be with him again?' Ivaar could barely contain himself. 'Well, I suppose she didn't want to break your fragile little heart. We've all seen what happens to you when you get that feeble heart of yours broken.' And with one final, triumphant look, he turned and strode away, happier than he'd felt in a long time.

Eadmund didn't know what to think. He completely ignored the servant who stood, holding out a cup of ale, turning instead to Thorgils, who suddenly gripped his belly.

'I need the shitter,' he tried.

Eadmund grabbed his arm. 'What is he talking about? Who's Aleksander?'

***

Jael had only just begun, but she didn't know if she could continue. She took a deep breath. 'My aunt was getting married...' she said quietly. 'I was so excited to go... I couldn't wait to see my cousins. My father stayed behind. I don't know why,' she frowned, listening to the crack of the fire as it spat angrily at them. She glanced down at her hands, rubbed them together, then looked up again. 'We had been there a few nights, all together in a large cottage, all of us children sleeping in the same bed, whispering all night. My brother was a nuisance, though. He was only two, and he'd never sit still. That night he was making such a fuss that my mother took him for a walk, trying to calm him down. I ran after them.'

Fyn sat on a stool, his eyes on Jael's face. She had drifted far away. Her body was rigid as she sat there, lost in the fire.

'There were a lot of men suddenly. On horses. Carrying torches. Flames everywhere. The sound of swords and screams. My mother screamed. One of my father's men was there. He pushed us into a cottage, told my mother to bar the door. He stayed outside. She hid us under the bed, but we heard it, the sound of the sword as it killed him. It was wet... stabbing, and then the door was kicked in. Four men.' She stumbled then. The images were so vivid now. 'Four men burst in, some covered in blood. All had swords. They took my mother, ripping her dress. She screamed so loudly. I had my hand over Axl's mouth, but I wanted to rush out and stop them, stop what they were doing to her. They shoved her dress up, forced themselves on her. Laughing. They all took turns raping her. And all I could do was watch. Silently. Not even moving, just watching. I couldn't close my eyes. I thought they would kill her...' She looked into Fyn's eyes, and he saw the tears in hers. 'And then my brother banged his head on the bed. He wouldn't lie still. I'd tried to hold him down, but he kept wriggling. He was so upset. And they found us.' She started shuddering. 'They found me...'

And Jael was there again, in that place, remembering the smell of them, and the pain of it, and her mother's screams disappearing into the night. Where had she gone? Why didn't she stop them? Why didn't she make it stop?

'My mother had run out. It seemed like forever that she was gone. She came back with Gant, and he sliced all four of them to pieces, right there in front of me. He took all their heads off, one by one. So quickly. There was nothing but blood, everywhere,' she sighed. 'And they were dead, but so was part of me. They took a part of me with them. And I can never get it back.' Jael grabbed Fyn's hand, her tear-filled eyes suddenly sharp again. 'But my revenge was taken. They did not survive what they did to me. What they did to my mother. And if I'd been there when Tarak raped you, I would have taken his head for you, Fyn, because you're wrong... I do know,' she cried. 'I do know...'

***

'What do you know, Thorgils?' Eadmund demanded crossly. 'Tell me!'

Thorgils grimaced. 'Can't I tell you after I've been for my shit?'

Eadmund grabbed his arm. 'Tell me, or you can shit in your trousers for all I care!' He pulled Thorgils towards the doors, dragging him outside, away from Ivaar's gloating eyes which were eagerly following them.

They hurried down the steps and through the square, Eadmund leading Thorgils towards the latrines before stopping just short.

'Eadmund, I don't really know anything,' Thorgils began. 'I don't know this Aleksander, but I assume it's the name of the man Jael left behind in Brekka.'

'She told you this?'

'Sort of,' Thorgils frowned. 'There was definitely someone. How could there not have been? She's a desirable woman. She was bound to have someone warming her bed all these years, wasn't she?'

Eadmund grumbled crossly. Of course, it made sense, but why hadn't she told him? Was that why she kept running away? Because she still loved this Aleksander?

Thorgils raced off and squatted behind the wattle fence, unable to hold it in any longer.

***

Fyn took one of his stools outside to stand on while he slipped Jael's mail over her head. It was sleeveless and fell between her hips and her knees. She wore a padded black tunic underneath it which fitted snugly over her chest and arms. Fyn hopped off the stool and rushed to help strap the leather guards around each of Jael's forearms. They were fringed with mail to protect her wrists. She took the belt he handed her, wrapping it around her waist twice, making sure it was tight enough to stay up, but loose enough to move comfortably when she did. Jael checked her two knives as she slotted them into her belt. She slipped *Toothpick* into his scabbard, and lastly took the two, smaller knives that Fyn held out to her, tucking one into each of the straps she'd tied around her ankles, covered by her socks and boots.

'You have a lot of weapons,' Fyn smiled, trying to blink away his worry as he handed over her helmet.

Jael smiled wryly. Her father had given her that helmet after he'd nearly taken her eye with his sword; it was the last time he'd ever fought her. She touched her scar, remembering the horror on his face when he'd seen the mess he'd made of hers. Its prominent nose guard and cheek plates were heavily engraved with wrestling wolves; two axes crossed on the back of the helmet for Furia. It had saved Jael's life on more than one occasion, and every dent was a reminder of how careful she needed to be. Never overconfident; always looking for that which she couldn't see coming. 'One or two,' she smiled, her eyes swollen now. She placed the helmet over her braids, strapping it firmly under her chin.

'You should go,' Fyn urged.

'I should,' Jael agreed, walking to where Tig stood, skipping about, desperate to leave. He was in a frisky mood, and despite her additional weight, he would get her back in time, she was sure. She led Tig back to Fyn. 'If I'm still standing, I'll be back. I'll be back for you, Fyn Gallas,' she said firmly, stepping into the stirrup and reaching for the saddle. 'Best you get your things together.'

Fyn blinked at her, wanting to believe she could do it, but his stomach fluttered more with nerves than any certainty that she could defeat Tarak. 'Good luck, Jael,' he wished her, reaching out to take her hand. 'Just remember, don't let him get you on your back.'

Jael stared at him sternly, her mind already at the contest now. 'I've worked very hard not to let any bastard get me on my back, believe me, Fyn!' She let go of his hand and pulled the reins to her waist. 'Come on, Tig! Let's go! Go! Go!'

Fyn watched as they flew up the snowy rise as one, wondering if he was ever going to see her again.

CHAPTER FIFTY SEVEN

Eirik was getting nervous.

Where was she?

He frowned, glancing at Eadmund who looked more angry than worried. 'She's taking her time coming back from this ride,' Eirik muttered crossly, fidgeting with his cloak pin. 'Are you sure she hasn't just decided to run away?'

Eadmund peered at his father in no mood to discuss Jael and her endless desire to run away. 'She'll be here soon,' he said sharply.

Eirik sighed, ignoring Ivaar, who sat gloating on his other side. Isaura perched nervously on the edge of her chair to Ivaar's right, Ayla sitting next to her. Eydis shivered beside Eadmund and looked as though she'd changed her mind about being there.

The Pit had been thoroughly cleared and divided up into four areas: one for each group of contestants. Eirik wasn't confident that they were going to fit all the battles in, though. Without Morac's help, he wasn't sure he'd organised everything properly. But Sevrin and Otto had stepped in, and were out in the Pit, ready to patrol the fights, along with two other men Eirik had selected.

The warriors in each group stood waiting, looking towards their king for the signal to begin.

Their king ignored them.

Eirik's eyes skirted the Pit, inhaling the ripe stench of nerves as the morning brightened around them all. He stared at the gates.

Again. They were open, waiting. He looked to the first men who were poised, waiting.

He could only give Jael moments more.

***

Tig flew faster than Jael had ever thought possible in so much snow. He must have sensed that she was going to battle, for he rode with a desperation she remembered. His hooves pounded down into the thick snow, and he brought them out powerfully, then down, again and again, thundering up the hill towards the fort. Jael heard nothing but the sound of crunching snow, and the steady beat of her heart. Inside her helmet, her mind was quiet and focused. She'd never had the chance to hurt those men for what they did to her. She'd watched as they died, hacked up pieces of who they once were, but there'd been little satisfaction in that. She felt grateful to Gant, but it had not been his revenge to seek.

Not for her.

Jael was tired of sitting back and watching as men in crowns, and men with swords took what they wanted. She'd had enough. This was no fight to the death, she knew, but whatever she did today, there would be no mercy. And if the gods favoured her, Tuuran and Oster alike, then they would be with her today while she fought.

For she was Furia's daughter, and she was ready for war.

***

All eyes turned towards the gates, listening to the rumble of hooves in the distance. They got louder as they rushed inside, echoing like drums around the silent fort.

Tig whinnied as Jael yanked hard on his reins, skidding to a stop just before the Pit. She could see that they were waiting on her, and thankfully, so was Askel. Sliding off Tig, she grabbed her red shield, handed the reins to her stable hand, and strode towards the Pit, one eye on Eirik, not looking for Eadmund, her face hard and ready for battle.

Jael found her group quickly. They had drawn straws, it seemed, and she was first to fight. There were smiles on the men's faces as they crowded around her, pushing her out into the centre.

There was no smile on hers.

Jael slid *Toothpick* from his scabbard, tightened her grip on her shield and took a deep, frosty breath as she strode towards her opponent, a thick-necked man called Niklas. He grinned, almost toothlessly at her, happy to think that she'd been drawn against him first. There was some fun to be had with her, he knew. Of course, he'd seen her fight Thorgils, but for all the show she'd put on, Thorgils had beaten her. He didn't imagine he'd have much of a problem, no matter how fancy she had dressed for the occasion.

Jael saw her father's face. She heard his voice booming in her ears. 'Don't rush,' he called to her. 'Use that clever head of yours, Jael. See everything. Wait. Wait.' She pushed her boots into the earth, eased her shoulders down and centred herself, taking in everything about her opponent. Watching the way he carried himself, his brand-new axe, his lack of a shield, his bloodshot eyes, his casual stance, his ale-sour breath as it drifted gently towards her.

Eirik blew on a small horn, and they began.

Niklas was confident, young, and arrogant as he sauntered around before her. That's what Jael saw in the brief glimpse she caught of his eyes as she ran at him, slashing her sword straight across his unprotected chest. She brought her leg up quickly, kicking him firmly in the place she'd just hit him, sending him flying, his head banging into the hard ground with a loud crack.

Niklas lay there blinking in surprise, his ears ringing, his axe well out of reach. Jael dropped down, leaning her weight on his chest, her arm across his throat, her sword tip at his eye.

There was no show today. Jael wanted Tarak. Only Tarak.

Everyone else was in her way, and the quicker she disposed of them, the better.

'Over!' Sevrin yelled, stepping into the ring. 'Jael wins!'

Jael stood up without smiling, nodded her acknowledgement to Sevrin, and walked to the back of the line.

Ivaar blinked. Jael looked ready to kill someone.

'Well, there's a fine start for me,' Eirik smiled confidently, finally relaxing. 'Gurin!' he called to his servant. 'Bring us something to warm our bellies! Some milk for Eydis, too.'

Eadmund was more worried than cross now as he tried to catch Jael's eye. She had her back to him, though, ignoring everyone as she stood there waiting for her next turn.

'Is Jael alright?' Eydis asked urgently.

'She is,' Eadmund murmured. 'So far.' He noticed how worried his sister looked. 'Are you alright, Little Thing? Here, take some of my furs.'

'No, no, I'm warm enough.' Eydis tried to smile, her breath puffing out in front of her. 'It's just that...'

'Just that, what?'

'I had a dream about Jael. About Tarak fighting her,' Eydis sighed. 'Jael couldn't move. She was lying on the ground. He was about to kill her.'

Eadmund felt the shiver as it charged up his spine. He grabbed Eydis' hand. 'Do you believe it? Was it a real dream?'

Eydis blinked, her mouth gaping open. She didn't know what to say, but in the end, there was only the truth. 'Yes.'

She hoped she was wrong.

Thorgils was not having much luck. His fight had been going for a while now, and he was impatient to move on. He was fighting an energetic, long-necked man named Povel, who bounced about like an excited dog, swaying this way and that, darting about, making little bursts of attack, then retreating.

Thorgils sighed. He stood back and waited, reminding himself of what Jael had taught him about fighting a battle with your mind. He could see what Povel was trying to do: play with him, confuse him, make him doubt himself. But as Thorgils waited, he realised that the only one with doubts was his opponent.

It was time to end things.

He strode forward, shield high, his sword extended, eyes hard. And shunting his shield in quick bursts, hard and fast, he fought off the wild blows of Povel's axe, smashing the rim into his chin, releasing his sword and bringing it down on Povel's arm guard. Povel scrambled to control his axe and shield at the same time, but the shock and force of the double blow overloaded his senses, and he dropped both, scrambling backwards, blood gushing from his gaping chin.

Otto was stalking around the perimeter of the ring, but he didn't stop the fight, even though Povel was now weaponless and injured.

Thorgils was in no mood to be generous.

Generous Thorgils would have thrown down his weapons and finished it with fists, but this Thorgils was only thinking of Tarak. He had a chance to meet him today, and he couldn't wait to get there. He lunged, slamming his shield into Povel's narrow chest, knocking its iron boss into his nose. Povel tumbled backwards this time, his face a bloody mess. And as Thorgils jammed his foot down on Povel's pulsing throat, Otto called it. 'Over! Thorgils wins!'

There was no smile from him either.

Not until Tarak was sucking dirt through his nostrils, would there be any smile on Thorgils' face.

***

Aleksander didn't know why he was still in Tuura.

All of his belongings were now hidden away in the forest, and he'd said goodbye to Edela. Nothing was keeping him here. Nothing but his own nagging questions. Edela had seen something, and he wanted to find an explanation for it. He knew that if he could find out what his mother had actually been doing, and who had really sent the men to Tuura, then Edela would have to see that she had just chosen the wrong dream.

He was certain of it.

He had gone to Alaric's, but there had been no one home. No doubt he was somewhere with Edela, looking for more information to help Jael.

Aleksander sighed.

He was supposed to help Jael, but he'd abandoned her grandmother and then broken his vow to wait for her. The thick clouds that hung around Tuura's walls matched his morose mood.

Looking up, he saw Alaric scurrying ahead of him. He was moving much faster than usual, and Aleksander had to hurry, pushing his way through a throng of people who had gathered near the gates to watch a fight being broken up by a thick swarm of soldiers. Whatever the argument had been over, small or large, the perpetrators were being crushed with force. Aleksander grimaced, looking away. He was yet to find anything to like about this place.

'Alaric!' He was close enough now to make himself heard, and indeed, Alaric spun around in surprise.

'Oh, it's you,' the old man frowned, his eyes darting up and down the street. 'What do you want?'

Aleksander laughed. 'You're not happy to see me, then?'

Alaric looked momentarily embarrassed, but his eyes remained sharp. He had become increasingly troubled by Aleksander's family history. Edela might have trusted him, but perhaps she was blinded by loyalty, and by the memory of the boy she knew many years ago. Alaric had no such loyalty. He was able to look at Aleksander with both eyes open. 'Well, you've hardly made yourself popular around Tuura, from what I hear,' he said sharply. 'And as for Edela... I think you abandoned her quite harshly. She needed your help and guidance, and you left her all alone.'

'I can't deny any of that,' Aleksander admitted with a guilty shrug, as aware as Alaric that they were standing in a very public place. 'But I need to speak with you. Please. I have some questions.'

Aleksander snatched his arm. 'Please, Alaric. I'm still here for a reason. I don't know what that reason is, but I need some answers. I'm sure you can help me. For Edela's sake,' he tried.

Alaric turned back with a weary sigh.

He could never resist doing anything to help Edela.

***

They were all through to the third round, Tarak noticed happily, hardly caring who he was facing next. There were only two people he wanted to break into pieces for Ivaar, and neither of them were within touching distance yet. He smiled as he walked to the back of his dwindling group. His fights had been relatively short, and the wait in between had him bored and thirsty, itching to move things along.

'We should break before the next round,' Ivaar suggested to his father. 'I can't feel my face, and I think we could all do with something to eat and drink if we're going to keep sitting out here much longer.'

Eirik was already out of his chair, grabbing hold of Eydis' hand. He smiled happily, frozen but elated. 'We take a break!' he called loudly to the contenders. 'Go warm yourselves up and get something in your bellies!'

Jael was as numb as anyone, but she just wanted to keep

going. It was her turn to fight again, and she was eager to put her sword to the idiot who was waiting for her. He'd watched her send two of his friends off quickly, but his expression hadn't changed one bit. He still appraised her with the same cocky smile, grabbing his crotch, thrusting it in her direction. Jael didn't even frown as she walked off. She looked right through him, her mind empty of everything but her desire to reach Tarak.

Eadmund watched Jael coming towards him, knowing that he couldn't say anything about Aleksander. He had calmed down a little, and as much as he wanted to throw that name in her face and demand she explain her feelings, he could see how focused she was. He couldn't break into that and distract her. Not after what Eydis had revealed to him. The thought of Tarak killing Jael tightened his chest, and when he looked at her, he only saw the fact that he loved her. There was no way he was going to let Tarak try to kill her. They would all be watching the fight. It couldn't happen.

Jael didn't smile as she approached Eadmund. She removed her helmet, tucking it under her arm as she walked him into the hall, suddenly noticing how cold she was. 'What's wrong?'

'Nothing,' Eadmund lied, trying to look less annoyed. 'You've done well so far.'

'Mmmm,' she mumbled, grabbing a piece of bread and a slice of cold meat. She wasn't hungry at all, but there was a lot more of the day to be had yet. 'So far doesn't mean much.'

'No.' Eadmund was starving but distracted. He reached for a cup of ale and drank it without thinking. 'Tarak is looking good. So is Thorgils.'

Jael looked up at him. 'What's wrong?'

Eadmund ducked his head, hoping to escape her piercing stare. 'I'm just... worried about you. Not many men watch their wives fight, do they? And, well... Eydis told me about her dream.'

'Oh.' Jael relaxed. That made sense of his face. 'Well, that's not going to happen. Now, if you'll excuse me, I shall join the long line of men going to piss.' She walked off without another word, as distant as if she were still in Brekka.

Eadmund watched her go, worried. He wasn't mad at all now.

He just wanted her to stay safe.

'Eydis thinks a storm is on its way, and by the look of the clouds up there, I think she may be right,' Eirik frowned, stopping beside his son.

'What do you want to do?' Eadmund wondered, trying not to look at Ivaar as he joined their discussion.

'I say we keep going to the end,' Ivaar suggested.

'No,' Eadmund said firmly, turning to his brother. 'There won't be enough light. The last two will be fighting in the dark, which won't make for much of a spectacle, will it?'

Eirik frowned. 'We'll have to see how we go, but we can't hold the last battle if we're reaching the end of the light, Eadmund's right. Things might have moved along quickly, but now we're getting down to the better fighters, so I anticipate longer battles. Let's just take a breath, and see how things unfold after the break.'

Eadmund glared at Ivaar, and Eirik could almost feel the hate between his two sons. It saddened and worried him. His father had killed his mother. He had killed his father.

Surely that was enough murder for one family?

***

'What is it that you wish to know?' Alaric sighed, perching on the edge of his cold, grim fireplace. He'd not wanted to be overheard discussing anything in the street, so he'd led Aleksander back to his cottage.

'I want to know what Edela found out,' Aleksander began.

'You mean about your grandmother?'

'My grandmother?' Aleksander shook his head, confused.

'No, my mother.' He paused, noticing the look of horror on Alaric's face at the slip of his tongue. 'What do I need to know about my *grandmother*?'

Alaric's mouth hung open while he thought of what to say. In the end, he knew that Aleksander was not a man about to be brushed aside with flimsy lies. 'I found a scribe who worked for the elderman at the time your grandmother and Edela entered the temple as dreamers.'

'My mother's mother?'

'Yes.'

'She was a dreamer?'

'She was, yes,' Alaric muttered impatiently. 'Though she was removed from the temple not long after she'd begun her training. This scribe knew the reason why, which is why I sought her out... for Edela.' Alaric puffed out his sunken chest.

Aleksander frowned, helping himself to Alaric's solitary stool. 'Do I want to know the reason why?'

'I suspect not, but you cannot run from what has happened in your family. Only be informed.'

'And?' Aleksander leaned forward reluctantly. 'What had she done?'

'She'd visited the Widow,' Alaric breathed. 'She bragged about it. About how her mother had taken her. How she had consulted with her, learned from her.'

Aleksander's face froze in horror. 'The Widow? And she was banished from the temple for that?'

'Of course!' Alaric's eyes popped open. 'The Widow was a woman of true evil. A dreamer witch. Blessed with greater gifts than almost anyone, but she used them all as weapons. She hurt, maimed, injured, killed for gold. She was merciless. A true mercenary of dark magic.' He shook his head. 'But how she was still alive when your grandmother was a child, I do not know. The Widow's name is one from the pages of history, from hundreds of years ago, but I suppose dark magic has many secrets...'

'If it was the Widow at all,' Aleksander suggested carefully.

'Maybe it was just a woman pretending to be her? Or perhaps my grandmother was a girl who liked to make up stories?' He felt a desperate need to defend his family, to cling to the belief that there was goodness there; not wanting their connections to the Widow to mark them as evil.

'A possibility, of course,' Alaric murmured, rubbing his chapped hands together. 'But according to Merya, the dreamers saw the truth in her tales, which is why she was banished.'

Aleksander thought back to his own visit to the Widow.

Why *had* she helped him in the end?

Why had she said nothing to him about his mother or his grandmother? He shuddered, and not just from the frigid chill in Alaric's cottage. Nothing good was going to come from following this path, he realised, but somehow, there had to be a way to show Edela that his mother had done nothing wrong; nothing to try and hurt Jael.

There had to be.

CHAPTER FIFTY EIGHT

Round three.

'I can't wait to feel those tits of yours when you're lying beneath my giant cock!' Reinar called to the amusement of the returning crowd.

Jael frowned, ignoring the cheers and jeers, wishing she hadn't eaten anything. She felt sick. And... was there any man on this island who wasn't a complete arse? She didn't respond to his posturing, except to tighten the line of her lips and sharpen the focus of her eyes.

Reinar was the next nothing in line, and she needed him gone. Fast.

Eirik blew his horn, and Reinar lunged. He came at Jael with an axe and a shield, and she could tell that he was skilled with both. Jael didn't move her feet. She just swayed to one side as he sailed past. There was a loud cheer. When Jael was fighting the crowd tended to be much larger than anywhere else.

She hadn't noticed. Her attention was only on her opponent.

He turned around, and so did she. Shields up, they came together.

Jael lashed out, *Toothpick* glinting as he flew through a burst of sunlight. She clenched her teeth, stretching forward, bringing her blade towards Reinar's arm, away from his shield. He spun out of her reach, his axe high, his mouth empty of insults now as he grimaced, ready to go again.

Jael had to think. Let him defeat himself or get it done?

Beating Tarak would require a lot of strength and energy. There was no point wasting it now. Jael turned, exposing her back to Reinar, much to the surprise of the gasping crowd.

Much to the surprise of Eadmund, who stood up.

'What is it?' Eydis asked anxiously.

'It's alright,' her brother muttered, his eyes fixed on Jael, his stomach tightening into a knot.

Eirik turned to follow his gaze, frowning. What was she doing?

Jael was listening.

The noise around her hushed as everyone held their breaths. She could hear Reinar's footsteps. He was coming for her, but slowly. He was uncertain. Not sure what she had planned.

Jael waited.

One heartbeat, two, three, and then she spun, snapping around, her right leg slicing through the air like a blade, straight into the side of Reinar's face. She heard the crack of his jaw as it hit the knife she'd strapped to her ankle, inside her boot.

He went down and didn't move.

Jael was on him quickly, whipping her knife out of its scabbard, bringing it up to Reinar's broken jaw, her chest over his face. 'How do you like my tits now?' she growled.

'Over!' Otto shouted. 'Jael wins!'

There was no sound from the crowd as she lifted herself off Reinar's motionless body and walked to the back of the line. No one said a thing. Watching from two groups away, Thorgils shook his head, smiling.

'Well, into the fourth round go my two,' Eirik smiled at Ivaar. 'My coins are looking in good shape.'

'Perhaps,' Ivaar admitted grudgingly. 'Although, now it will get much harder. This is where Jael will struggle.'

'If you say so,' Eirik said confidently. 'But she seems to know what she's doing.' He turned and winked at Eadmund. 'A good wife you have there, my son.'

'Well, if you're looking for someone to protect you, I suppose so, though, I haven't tried her cooking.'

***

Tarak glanced around, pleased to see that both Thorgils and Jael were still standing. He puffed out his bare chest, flexing his fist, eager to get through this last round before the four groups became two, and then one. He had no doubt that he'd be in that final battle, not a single doubt as he glared at the two men who were waiting for the signal. Their eyes were wide and jumping about. He could smell the fear on them.

Tarak had no concerns at all as he nodded at Ivaar and smiled.

Jael didn't look Torstan's way as she tightened her grip on *Toothpick*. She was left with Torstan and a man named Yari, who looked as though he'd drunk too much in the break. He stood, swaying gently next to Torstan. Despite that, she didn't discount him. He'd made it this far.

She would have to defeat both of them at once to get through to the next round.

Jael closed her eyes, taking a deep breath, hoping for her father's advice, but instead, she heard Gant's. 'Two opponents,' came his soft rasping voice in her ear. 'Easier than you'd think. Keep your back clear and get one down to the ground as quickly as possible. No time for showing off. Finish it fast.'

Jael had seen everything Torstan had. It would be easier to take him first.

Yari could wait.

Eirik blew his horn and Jael pounced on Torstan. He was in the middle of nervously readjusting his shield grip when she ran at him, lunging with her foot, smashing it into his shield with every bit of strength she had. Torstan lost his balance and stumbled backwards, falling to the ground. Through the cheers of the crowd, Jael could hear Yari coming up behind her. She threw herself down onto Torstan, who was busy trying to grab his sword which had slipped out of his hand. She landed on his shield, rested on her forearms, and whipped her right leg around sharply, taking Yari's legs out from under him. The cheers were loud now but Yari, despite his shock, didn't stay down for long.

Torstan had managed to get his fingers around his sword, but his grip was not strong. Jael raised herself up, smashing her shield into his face, getting up to kick his sword away, her sword tip at his throat.

'Torstan's out!' Sevrin yelled to the crowd.

Yari came at her again, slashing his axe towards Jael's back as she stood. She spun out of his path, quickly darting around his side. *Toothpick* twitched in her hand, and she lunged at Yari, slashing his shield repeatedly, swaying back and forth, avoiding his oncoming blade. He had a wild look in his eye; the look of a man who had drunk enough to dull his fear, but killed his good sense at the same time.

He was not going to make smart decisions.

He was just going to slash until he ran out of breath.

Jael stepped back, dropping her head to one side. She smiled, and it was ice-bright. Yari didn't wait to see what that meant. He came at her again, his axe in the air, his shield flat to his chest. Jael turned away as he ran past her, slipping *Toothpick* into his scabbard. She turned back around, both hands gripping her shield.

'What is she doing?' Eadmund growled, standing up again, scratching his frozen beard.

'Eadmund? What is it?' Eydis panicked beside him.

'It's alright, don't worry,' Eirik reassured her, blinking furiously, his eyes not leaving the fight. 'Jael is fine.'

But Eydis could hear their voices, and she held her breath, wringing her hands.

It was Yari's turn to smile as he came again, his axe cutting through the cold air, his breath billowing in front of him. He roared as he swung the axe down towards Jael. She lifted her shield high and caught the blade next to the iron boss, her hands on the furthest edges of the rim, her head to one side.

The blade stuck.

Jael jerked her shield backwards, as hard and fast as she could, yanking the axe out of Yari's hand. She threw the shield to the ground and slid *Toothpick* out of his scabbard before Yari had a chance to think, bringing the glinting, deadly tip towards his face, just before one of his glazed eyes.

'Over!' Sevrin called. 'Jael wins!'

Eadmund let out a smoky sigh, but he couldn't sit down. He was too tense. He tried to catch his wife's eye. She was getting closer. He only hoped that Thorgils would stop Tarak from getting anywhere near her. She was good, he couldn't deny that, but he didn't doubt Eydis' dream, or the determination on Tarak's face every time he looked Jael's way.

***

There was a short break before the start of the last two battles which would determine who would face each other in the final.

Thorgils' dream had come true.

Tarak was standing in the middle of the Pit, chest beating, frothing at the mouth, waiting for him. Jael had a man called Mikkel, who looked like a challenge. He reminded her of her father: large and brooding, not at all showy, full of quiet intent and experience. He wasn't about to be fooled by anything she'd produced so far. But they were fighting after Tarak and Thorgils, and Jael's focus, for now, was solely on her friend.

'Are you hurt anywhere?' she asked quickly. There was little time. She needed to get Thorgils ready in a hurry. As much as she wanted Tarak, she didn't want Tarak to have his fun at Thorgils' expense.

'Just a cut on my elbow, that's all,' Thorgils grunted. 'Nothing to trouble me. You?'

'No, nothing,' Jael said as they stood huddled to one side of the Pit. Ivaar and Tarak were talking in the distance, occasionally glancing their way. 'Now listen, the best thing you can do is get in charge of that bullish head of yours. Tarak's going to be caught up in trying to play with you, wanting to humiliate you for Ivaar's enjoyment. He wants to impress Ivaar, so he'll tease you and taunt you. He'll want to make it a game, but you can't play it.'

Thorgils didn't speak or even look at her.

He was imagining the feeling of his hands around Tarak's throat.

'Don't let his strength be a factor. Tire him out. Don't move unless you need to. Let him run around. Don't talk. Whatever you do, don't talk! Watch his eyes. And don't let him get you on the ground,' Jael said, worried by the distracted look on Thorgils' face. 'Remember, Eydis' dream won't come true if you finish him now.'

Thorgils nodded, barely listening. He glanced up at Isaura, not caring if Ivaar saw. He didn't care if anyone saw. That was his woman up there, and he would look at her if he wanted.

Isaura shivered. She held Thorgils' stare for a moment, willing him on, wanting him to be alright. She didn't care if Ivaar was watching, she would happily suffer any punishment for Thorgils to know that she was with him.

Jael moved towards the railings. 'If it starts to go wrong, look for me and you'll remember the things we practised.' She saw Tarak coming and gripped Thorgils' arm, staring into his eyes. She saw uncertainty there, but also fire, and that gave her some confidence. 'Go and shove that bastard's face in the dirt!'

Thorgils nodded, breathing heavily, beating his sword against his shield, wishing he'd used the break to head for the latrines, before quickly shutting it all out of his head.

Tarak was coming.

Ivaar took his seat next to Isaura. 'Are you sure you want to watch this?' he asked cheerfully. 'It might get very messy for poor Thorgils.'

'Well, that's confident of you,' Eirik grinned at his son, noticing the terror on Isaura's face. 'Too confident, I fear. Thorgils has been training with Jael, you know. Everyday. And you've seen what she can do.' He caught Isaura's eye and smiled reassuringly.

'Indeed, and I've seen what Thorgils has done,' Ivaar said grudgingly. 'But neither of them have faced anyone like Tarak. If Jael tried to kick him, he'd snap her leg in two.'

Eadmund frowned, wishing he could snap his brother in two. He hoped more than anything that Thorgils could do it. He didn't want Tarak anywhere near Jael. Next to him, Eydis shuddered. 'Here, Little Thing,' he said, handing her his fur. 'Take this. Go on.'

Eydis didn't argue this time as he draped it over her shaking arms. 'Thorgils won't win,' she whispered hoarsely, so their father couldn't hear. 'Tarak will defeat him. You know that.'

Eadmund tried to smile as he shook his head. 'I know what you've seen, but I know Thorgils, and he's not about to let Tarak get anywhere near Jael. He wants him all to himself.'

They had removed the extra railings from the Pit. There was more room for the contestants now. More room for Tarak to run around and tire himself out, Thorgils decided as he stood there waiting for Eirik's signal.

Tarak smiled as he strutted into the middle of the Pit, his scuffed blue shield held firmly to his bare chest, his sword, which was the longest and heaviest on Oss, straight out in front of him. He didn't wear a helmet and had no use for mail. The only armour he wore was a pair of boiled leather arm guards. His trousers, also leather, were slim-fitting, tucked into a pair of long black boots. He stopped just in front of Thorgils, his eyes barely blinking as he rolled his thick, corded shoulders, waiting to begin.

Jael held her breath as she stood by the railings, wrapping

her cloak tightly around her shoulders. The wind was picking up, and the clouds had started rushing overhead. She wondered if the gods were coming to watch.

Eirik stood and with a quick smile at Thorgils, blew his horn.

Thorgils panicked and attacked first.

He rushed at his opponent, sword flashing, aiming for Tarak's arms but Tarak was faster, hitting Thorgils back with his shield, meeting every slash of his sword with double the power Thorgils could manage. Thorgils cursed his rashness and stepped away, imagining the look on Jael's face. He stopped himself from shaking his head, though. Tarak didn't need to know that he was rattled. He took a deep breath, trying to focus on what he was trying to achieve.

Tire. Tarak. Out.

Thorgils snorted a burst of white smoke through his nostrils.

Time to start again.

Isaura wanted to leave, as much as she wanted to stay. It had not started well. Thorgils looked nervous, she thought, and who could blame him with that naked animal bearing down on him. She turned to Ayla, who had not said a word all day, desperate to ask what she saw, but Ayla's face looked as terrified as her own.

That was not a good sign.

Tarak came hard at Thorgils. He led with his shield, banging it into Thorgils' chest, slicing his sword towards his face. Tarak's reach was much longer than Thorgils was used to, and he had to jump back to avoid the sword's deadly tip as it approached his cheek. He stepped back, time and time again, as Tarak kept coming, butting out with his shield, defending himself, letting Tarak do all the work.

Tarak smiled, sensing Thorgils' plan. He swung his arm back as hard as he could, his sword almost touching the clouds in the sky. It took so long that Thorgils had time to slip out of the way and Tarak hit nothing but dust. He growled furiously, turning to pursue his opponent. 'Running away already?' he laughed, stalking quickly after Thorgils, who kept moving backwards, keeping away from Tarak, irritating him further. 'I suppose when you know you're beaten, it's all you can do!' Tarak boomed, bringing his sword down onto Thorgils' shield. Hard. The shield jarred sharply against his arm, and Thorgils' teeth slammed together. Tarak came again, bludgeoning Thorgils' shield over and over with his massive sword.

Thorgils slipped to one side, leaving Tarak fighting the dust again.

'Have you forgotten where you placed your sword, Thorgils?' Tarak laughed, enjoying the cheers from the crowd. 'Or is it that you're so nervous, fighting in front of your long lost love? Worried that she'll see you for the man you truly are?' He came rushing towards Thorgils again, chasing him. 'I'm sorry, did I say man? I meant coward!'

Thorgils turned around, standing his ground.

He wasn't sure that Tarak was tiring at all, and he was tired of running. He couldn't win like that. His palm was sweaty on his sword's grip as he lunged at Tarak's middle, but Tarak was taller than Thorgils, and he elbowed him in the side of the head as he came forward. Thorgils was knocked sideways, straight into the dirt, his head ringing so loudly that he couldn't hear anything except a high-pitched squeal that pierced his ears. He rolled away from Tarak's jab, and this time it was Tarak scrambling in the dirt.

That made him wild.

Throwing away his shield, Tarak ran at Thorgils, his sword in both hands now, his face twisting into a violent scowl.

'I wonder how that will work out for your Thorgils,' Ivaar smiled at Isaura.

'I imagine it's Tarak you need to be worried about,' Eirik said. 'He's the fool without a shield.'

Tarak herded Thorgils into the railings, and all Thorgils could do was defend with his shield. He butted it at Tarak's face, catching him on the cheek, which enraged him even more. Tarak smashed his sword on the shield, over and over, striking it as hard as he could until it broke. Thorgils slipped his hand out of the shieldless grip, throwing it away, ducking under Tarak's arm and coming around behind him with his sword, but Tarak spun and slashed with speed and power, his much heavier sword slicing straight across Thorgils' shieldless middle.

'No!' Jael yelled in horror as Thorgils staggered backwards, his eyes bursting open in shock. He wasn't wearing mail and Tarak's sword had sliced straight through his leather armour. Jael's eyes flashed to Isaura who had grabbed her throat, her face washed of any colour.

Eadmund was on his feet again. 'Father...' he urged.

'I'm watching,' Eirik said calmly. 'He's still standing. Let him fight, Eadmund. This is no fight to the death. Tarak knows that. Give Thorgils a chance.'

Thorgils stumbled away, shaken by the force of Tarak's blow. Tarak was after him, though, the smell of blood in his nostrils now. Thorgils looked to Jael; saw his fear reflected in her eyes. He shook his head, his ringing, pounding head, trying to think of what they had practised; trying, but his thoughts were jumbled, and the stinging pain in his middle was hard to ignore.

That was of no concern to Tarak who came again, aiming for the same spot. The crowd was roaring now, those who were supporting Tarak, at least. Thorgils' friends had gone quiet, worried about what was going to happen.

Again.

Tarak slashed his sword at Thorgils' stomach, but Thorgils jumped back, cutting Tarak's arm. A cheer went up, which infuriated Tarak. He glanced up at Ivaar, whose demanding eyes urged him to finish it.

Thorgils stood slightly slumped, gripping his sword close to his body, one arm resting against his wound, hoping to stem the gushing blood. It didn't seem to be working. His ears were buzzing. He had to blink to clear his vision. Tarak kept coming, though, and Thorgils had no choice but to lean forward to meet him. He swung his sword, making contact with Tarak's but Tarak leaned back and kicked him hard, right in his stomach. Thorgils' eyes bulged open as the pain hit; white, flashing shards of agony shooting before his eyes.

His sword flew out of his hand as he toppled to the ground.

'Thorgils!' The cry went up all around.

Jael could see Odda Svanter on the opposite side of the Pit, terror in her eyes. She saw Isaura, out of her chair, and Eadmund rushing down to the railings.

Tarak couldn't stop smiling as he threw himself onto Thorgils' bleeding body, shoving his knee into Thorgils' stomach, throwing his sword away. His arm was bleeding, but he didn't notice. He pulled it back and punched Thorgils in the face as hard as he could, again and again until Thorgils' eyes and nose matched the mess of blood coming out of his stomach.

'Over!' Eirik yelled loudly and reluctantly. 'Tarak wins.' He didn't even look at the gloating face of his eldest son as he sat back down.

Isaura couldn't stop the tears that slid down her face as Ivaar reached out and grabbed her hand. Ivaar couldn't stop the smile on his face as he watched Tarak raising his arm in victory.

Eadmund ran into the Pit to help Jael and Torstan lift Thorgils off the ground. He was unconscious, his head drooping onto his chest; a fleshy, bloody, Tarak-inflicted mess.

Biddy was standing at the railings waiting for him. Askel had rushed to find her when he saw how things were going for Thorgils. She pressed a rolled-up cloth against his stomach wound. 'Hold onto this,' she barked at Eadmund. 'Take him to the house quickly. I have everything waiting.'

Jael let go of Thorgils' arm, watching Torstan and Eadmund carry him away.

CHAPTER FIFTY NINE

Tuura's tavern was nothing more than a poorly lit, stinking hut hidden down a narrow series of alleyways in the middle of the fort, where men came to drink, and women came to tempt them to part with any coins they had left over.

It was where he'd met Hanna.

He wondered if that was why he kept coming back?

Aleksander sat at a table in the darkest corner he could find, slowly sipping the watery ale he'd bought with his last silver coin, Alaric's words spinning around his head.

What was his family's connection to the Widow?

His grandmother had been taken to her by her mother. His own mother had gone to see her, and even he had been there. Why? How did they know where to find her? And what was it about her that made her so deadly? She killed, they said, with dark magic; lived, even though she must have been hundreds of years old. Or were they all just tales made up to scare children before they went to sleep?

He didn't think so, but somehow he had to find out the truth.

Aleksander turned as the door creaked open, watching as Hanna and another woman entered the tavern. There were a few cheers at the sight of fresh offerings. Aleksander could hear the clinking sound as hands rustled in pockets.

He turned back around, confused.

'Hello,' Hanna murmured as she came to sit beside him,

ignoring the disappointed calls of the men holding up their coins, who quickly turned their attention towards her friend. 'I had a feeling you might be here again.'

'Did you?' Aleksander stared at his cup, trying to ignore the effect her voice was having on him. He wasn't drunk enough to be able to blame ale for any choice he made today. 'Would you like something to drink?' he asked quietly, glancing at her. She looked cold; her round cheeks were flushed, matching the pink tip of her nose.

'That would be nice,' she said, surprised by how sober he appeared. She had expected to find him in another messy state.

Aleksander filled his empty cup with the remainder of the jug and passed it to Hanna.

'Thank you,' she smiled.

His shoulders relaxed, and he smiled back. He was so tired of feeling lonely and sad. It would be nice to forget it all for a while.

Aleksander waved his hand at the serving girl, motioning for another cup and turned to Hanna, staring into her kind blue eyes, realising that he had no urge to run away at all.

***

Jael ran up to Eadmund, searching his face. 'How is he?'

Eadmund grabbed her arms, looking her over. 'How are *you*?'

'Fine.' She shook his words away. 'I'm fine.'

'You won?'

'I did.'

Eadmund hung his head. 'Already? They didn't wait?'

'No.' She looked up at the sky, which was darkening ominously. 'Eirik decided to hold the final fight today. The weather looks as though it will only get worse. They say a storm is coming.'

'Jael...' Eadmund looked at her with fear in his eyes. 'Thorgils is a mess. Biddy has stitched his wounds, and he's woken up, but he's a mess. You can't fight Tarak. As good as you are, you can't fight him. You're not as strong as Thorgils, and look at what happened to him!'

'Do you think I'm going to let what he did to Thorgils be the way it ends?' Jael growled. 'That Tarak gets away with hurting more people because no one can beat him? Stand up to him? Destroy him?' She shook her head, her whole body vibrating with fury. 'He has more to answer for than you know,' she spat. 'Nobody deserves to be defeated more than that bastard.'

'But Eydis...' Eadmund tried to remind her. 'She dreamed about this. About what Tarak would do to you.'

'So what?' Jael said coldly, her eyes already focusing on what she was about to do. 'What do I care about Eydis' dream? It's a *dream*. You can change a dream. The gods can change a dream. *I* can change this dream!' She grabbed Eadmund's arm. 'If it makes you feel better, stop the fight. If it comes to that and I'm on my back, and he's lowering his sword towards my throat, stop the fight. Easy.'

Eadmund didn't look convinced.

'Contestants to the Pit!' Sevrin yelled. 'We need to begin now before we lose the light!'

Eadmund reached for Jael's hand, panic in his eyes, wishing he could step into the Pit for her. He felt ashamed that he couldn't. 'He'll snap your legs. He'll shatter your shield. He will keep coming. You have to take out his foundations, remember?'

Jael nodded impatiently. She didn't want to hear any more. She had to go. She had to lock herself away now and find what she needed to defeat Tarak. Reaching up, she held Eadmund's face in her hands, kissing him quickly, then letting him go. With one final look, Jael turned and walked away, shutting him out of her head, feeling the thud of her heart as she strode towards the centre of the Pit.

'Eadmund!' Eydis called. 'Eadmund, you have to stop Jael!'

'Eydis,' Eirik soothed, moving to sit beside his anxious daughter. 'Come here, come here.' He wrapped an arm around her shoulder, giving her a squeeze. 'I've watched Jael fight all day. She is going to be just fine. I have all my coins on her now. She promised me that she'd be my champion, so you have to believe in her.' Eirik shivered, his eyes following Jael as she walked to meet Tarak, his stomach fluttering with nerves.

Jael blinked slowly. Everything had to be about defeating Tarak now. Every movement and breath, every look, everything she did had to be focused on undoing his confidence, breaking his belief, beating him any way she could. She let the memory of what he did to Thorgils float out of her mind.

Jael remembered standing in front of Aleksander, preparing to fight him.

He could have beaten Tarak, and she had beaten Aleksander. It could be done.

'Father?' Ivaar leaned across to interrupt Eirik's conversation with Eydis. 'We're all waiting.'

Eirik straightened up, looking at the Pit. He took a deep breath, asking Furia to protect her daughter, in this, surely her toughest test. He glanced at Tarak, whose eyes were trained on Jael, dripping with bloodlust. 'Otto!' he called.

Ivaar frowned as Otto turned from the railings and walked up to Eirik's chair.

'I will call this fight,' Eirik said quietly. He picked up his horn and walked down to the railings. Above his head, he could sense the afternoon light diminishing as the clouds swept in, thicker and more threatening than before. The wind chilled his face, but there was no sign of rain or snow yet. 'This,' Eirik began loudly, 'this is not a fight to the death, and you will both remember that! This is a fight to become my champion! The Champion of Oss! I have already spoken of the prizes on offer to the winner, but let it be known that another prize is waiting to be claimed if Jael is victorious. A prize that only she and I know about, but one which I now agree to!'

Jael's head snapped around in surprise.

Eirik nodded at her briefly. 'Prepare yourselves now, for victory will offer you everything you have always wanted!'

Eadmund wondered what prize Jael had asked for, but it was a fleeting thought, quickly replaced by a sick feeling of utter dread. The look on Tarak's face told him that Jael had no chance.

Jael took a quick breath, pushing back her shoulders.

How was she going to do it?

She'd thought about this moment for weeks, practising many different strategies, but as Thorgils had shown, practice meant nothing when you were facing Tarak in the naked flesh. She thought of Fyn, remembering what Tarak had done to him. Remembering what those men had done to her. She held onto that feeling of rage as it flew through her body, demanding to be released.

Eirik blew his horn.

This did not need to look good, Jael knew.

She also knew that she had to stay off the ground.

Jael ran straight at Tarak and threw herself to the ground, sliding towards him, kicking out at his ankle as hard as she could. She kept going, rolling, jumping to her feet, moving away. It had only taken a moment, but Tarak was frowning, shaking his ankle as she stood there in front of him, crouching, sheathing *Toothpick* and grabbing her knife from its scabbard, ready to go again.

Eadmund stood, hands over his mouth.

The crowd gasped, surprised by that as a beginning.

His foundations were thick, Jael could see. The knife down her boot would have hurt most men, broken a bone in many, but he hadn't even stumbled.

Tarak was well balanced as he came towards her, a frown digging itself into the small space between his thick eyebrows. Jael ran at him, sliding through the dirt again, this time slashing the back of his left leg with her knife. She felt pleasure in the sound of his tearing flesh and the bellow that rolled up from his naked chest as she slid past him.

Jael was quickly up again, crouching, ready.

Tarak turned on her, furious now. Furious and ready to make her bleed. He didn't even look down at his leg. He could feel the blood flowing steadily; not deep enough to slow him down, though, and soon the cold would freeze it. He squeezed his fists until his knuckles turned white, pulled his shield to his chest and smashed his sword on it in a thunderous burst of fury.

He would kill the slippery bitch now.

Tarak rushed at her, viciously hacking with his giant sword. Jael dropped one shoulder and twisted away, leaving Tarak cursing the dirt as he spun around to look for her. She was dancing about now. Now it *was* time to dance. He was big, too big for her to defeat with swords or knives alone. The power in his arms was far more than anything Jael could counter, but she could dance.

And she did.

Tarak chased her around the Pit.

Jael would come near him, he would lunge, and she would slip and twist away, just out of his reach. The crowd laughed at the sight of Oss' champion chasing a woman around the Pit as if she were a little rabbit.

Tarak's face was red, his blood was boiling.

He had to change things quickly.

Ivaar scowled in frustration as he walked down to the Pit, banging his hands on the railings.

It was not going well.

'Worried?' his father smiled at him. 'You should be.'

Ivaar looked straight ahead. 'No, I think it's Jael who should be worried,' he said coldly. 'A fly may buzz about and annoy a man, but eventually, the man will snap and kill the fly.'

Jael wanted to launch herself at Tarak now, but she knew he could hurt her if she didn't weaken him first. And the way he was surging towards her, there appeared nothing weak about him yet. She slipped her knife into her belt and slid *Toothpick* out of his scabbard.

Jael let him come, waiting for him this time. Tarak was

surprised, and that lessened the power he put into his swing. His sword was slow as it sliced towards her, giving Jael enough time to duck down, dropping into a crouch as fast as she could, throwing one leg out with speed, smashing her ankle into his once again. She rolled away, listening to his scream of frustration. That was a good sign, she thought to herself as she jumped up and lunged at him. Pulling her shield up near her chin and swinging back her sword, she aimed to hit him high on the shoulder. He raised his shield to meet her strike, swinging his sword back to counter-attack, but as he did so, Jael lashed out with her leg and caught him hard in the balls.

The crowd groaned, feeling Tarak's pain. His face turned even redder as he screamed, veins pulsing at his temples, his head dropping forward. Jael pounced, slamming her shield boss into the side of his face, watching the blood fly, splattering out of his torn cheek. Spinning away before he could recover, Jael dropped to the ground, slashing the backs of his legs with *Toothpick*, lifting her shield up to protect herself from Tarak's sword as it came clanging down with all his weight behind it. She absorbed the blow, then rolled away and was up, facing him, running at him, ready to finish him. His teeth were bared with pain, his legs bleeding, his balls breaking, and his cheek hanging open.

He was weak enough now.

Eirik looked back at Eadmund. There was nothing but tension on his son's face as he stood there, mouth open, eyes wide.

'Eadmund, please,' Eydis begged anxiously. 'Is she alright?' Eydis could tell by the noise of the crowd that Jael was still going. She could hear jeers and boos at Tarak, but she knew that the fight would not be over, that Jael would not be safe until her father called an end to it.

Tarak would never give in until the end.

He was still fighting, still slashing at Jael, heaving his giant sword towards her with his giant arm, but pain was on his face now, and blood was leaking out of him. *Toothpick's* iron-strong blade held off each blow. Jael's arm was getting tired, though, and she was struggling to breathe. The sheer weight behind his blows was weakening her. He cut her on the arm, just below her mail, and she screamed, jerking back, much to his amusement.

Tarak was not done yet, but nor was she.

Jael pulled away, stepping back with speed, far away, urging the bitter air into her lungs, into her head. She needed to think. Tarak wasn't going to let her have the time she sought, though, as he came for her again, but as he lunged, his leg gave way, and he stumbled, momentarily losing his balance. Jael saw the path then and ran towards it with everything she had. Her shield in front of her, her sword back, ready to release, her eyes fixed on him, Jael dropped to the ground and slid, kicking both feet into the side of his leg, the one she had cut twice, the one that had given way. She rolled away and was up, crouching as he fell, a giant, bleeding, screaming tower, thudding to the earth.

The gasp that weaved its way through the crowd was almost breathless.

'Who fell?' Eydis called to Eadmund. 'Who's on the ground?'

'Tarak.'

Eydis stood up. On the ground, but it wasn't over.

If he was on the ground, so was Jael, surely?

Jael rushed to Tarak before he could roll away.

That was a mistake.

He lunged for her throat, catching the top of her tunic with one hand, yanking her towards him. She fought against him, but he was too strong, and he pulled her on top of him, their faces almost touching.

Jael was on the ground.

Eadmund hurried down to Eirik. 'Watch him,' he croaked to his father. 'End it if he rolls her over. He will try to kill her. Eydis has seen it. Eydis thinks he'll kill her.'

Eirik's eyes popped open in surprise. He leaned forward anxiously.

Jael tried to pull herself back, ducking as Tarak threw a fist at her, his other hand still gripping her tunic. She spat in his face.

'You fucking rapist! You fucking rapist!' And she ripped her tunic out of his grasp and smashed her elbow into his nose, feeling the pain as her bone met his. She screamed, punching him hard in the open wound on his cheek. She hit him again and again until his eyes filled with blood and her hands were numb, and she could hear the gurgle in his throat as he tried to breathe.

No one said a word as Jael stood up, wiped the blood out of her eyes, and kicked Tarak as hard as she could in the balls.

She stood there, her body heaving as she watched him.

But Tarak didn't move.

There was no sound at all, from anyone. Every mouth hung open, heads turning towards Eirik, who seemed just as dumbstruck as everyone else.

'Over!' he called, finally, his voice heavy with relief. 'Jael wins!'

The cheers started then, dulled by shock at first, but the realisation of what Jael had done started to sink in, and they grew louder and louder. Eirik watched the faces as shock was replaced by disbelief, and then joy, and they rushed towards Jael as she stood there, breathing heavily, bleeding, her arms aching, vibrating all over, ready to drop to the ground.

Eadmund was the first to her. He grabbed Jael by the shoulders and wrapped himself around her, squeezing her as hard as he could, feeling the pounding of her heart against his chest, closing his eyes in relief.

Jael grimaced as he let her go, as the crowds came, patting her on the back, congratulating her. Not Ivaar though; he stayed where he was for a moment before walking away.

Jael's mouth was full of blood. She spat it on the ground as Eirik came up to her, his eyes filled with tears. He took her in his arms, his face breaking into a smile so wide his cheeks hurt. 'I have faith,' he laughed in her ear. 'I have faith in you, Jael! It's yours, all yours!'

CHAPTER SIXTY

Thorgils wouldn't meet her eyes.

His face looked much like Tarak's must have: a bulging, bruised, swollen mess. His lips were too thick to speak clearly, and his heart was too heavy to say much. 'You did it, then.'

'So they say.' Jael winced as she sat down on the bed next to him. Every part of her hurt, and she was grateful to be home. She hadn't wanted to stay long in the hall, but Eirik had insisted. She was his champion now. He'd wanted to show her off, and she had endured it for a while, before Eadmund insisted on taking her home, and for once, she hadn't argued.

'I wish I'd seen it,' Thorgils mumbled. 'I truly wish I had. And Fyn. He would have been so proud of you.'

Jael smiled at him, listening to the blizzard as it battered the house. It had felt better than she could have imagined, finishing Tarak as she had. Jael didn't care what became of him now. As soon as she could, she would talk to Eirik and bring Fyn back, and then there would be no more Tarak. She yawned, feeling the relief of the day being at an end. 'How are you?' she wondered.

Biddy had stitched Thorgils' stomach and refused to let him leave, despite his mother's insistence that he belonged with her. In the end, to Thorgils' relief, Odda been no match for Biddy's determination. Thorgils was more than happy to stay in the warmth and quiet of the house, and, when his stomach and face had healed, he was looking forward to enjoying a good meal.

'I'm embarrassed,' was all he could say. 'I'm better than I showed. I lost my head, as you no doubt knew I would. *I* should have been the one to finish Tarak.' Thorgils closed his eyes, grimacing at the pain in his belly, feeling the shame of his defeat.

Jael sighed. 'Well, one of us did, and in the end, that was all we really wanted, wasn't it?' She groaned, standing up. 'Just get better, and forget everything else. I'm going to my bed, but tomorrow we can talk about all the reasons you have to smile that you don't even know about yet.'

***

They filtered out slowly.

It had been a night to remember for many, and none had been in a hurry to leave the hall. Most of Tarak's supporters hadn't been afraid to show their faces. They were as keen to take part in the feast as any, and their allegiance had appeared to shift seamlessly over to Jael, Eirik noticed.

That was a good sign for the future.

As for Tarak... he wasn't sure what had happened to him. Ivaar had arranged for some of his friends to have him taken away, seen to, cared for. Eirik didn't know or particularly care. He was delirious with hope for Oss again; relieved to have found a way out of the hole he had dug for them all; thrilled to have secured a new future for his people that was better than he could have imagined.

He walked towards the high table where Ivaar sat, head down, drinking by himself. There were things Eirik needed to say to his son, things he wouldn't take well. He wondered if it were better to wait until morning? Then he spied Ayla. He turned, swaying towards her, enjoying the feeling of drunk happiness that still flowed through his sagging limbs.

'My lord.' She dropped her eyes.

'I'm surprised to see you here, still.'

'I was just leaving,' she said softly.

'That's a shame,' Eirik smiled. 'I thought perhaps we could have spoken about the future? About what you saw for me?'

Ayla frowned. 'We have had that talk, my lord.' She knew that Ivaar was watching and she kept her face blank.

'True, but I wondered if it was all bad?' Eirik murmured, moving closer. 'Whether you thought there was any chance I might snatch a last piece of happiness for myself?' He reached out to brush a loose strand of hair out of her eye.

'I...' Eirik's meaning was uncomfortably clear, and Ayla tried to ease herself away from him, hoping not to offend. 'I am Ivaar's, my lord. My loyalty is to him.'

'Ahhh,' Eirik sighed, turning to raise an eyebrow at his sullen son. 'I had assumed as much, but,' he murmured, leaning towards her again, his face breaking into a silly grin, 'it didn't hurt to ask, I thought, even at my age and with death stalking me as it does!'

Ayla couldn't help but smile. For all the dark things she saw coming, it was impossible not to feel the smallest amount of joy, especially when she looked at Eirik's face. But when she turned and saw Ivaar approaching, her smile ran away, out into the storm. 'I must go,' she whispered. 'I wish you luck.'

Eirik turned to watch his son approach.

Now? Should he do it now?

***

'I'm not sure what my favourite part of the day was,' Eadmund smiled as he held Jael's bruised body, warming her with his chest, wanting to keep her close. 'Tarak's bloody face when you kicked him in the balls, or Ivaar's miserable face in the hall tonight,' he laughed softly.

Jael wasn't listening. She was lost in the sound of the wind as it howled past the house; in the roar of Tarak as she knocked him down; the screams of her mother as she was raped; her own as a child, and as a woman, bloodied and bruised.

She had survived Tarak, despite Eydis' dream, but there was nothing to smile about. Not yet.

She needed to see Fyn.

'So,' Eadmund whispered. 'Tell me about Aleksander...'

***

The screams were growing louder, more terrifying. Aleksander ran into the night, lost, desperate to find his mother who had raced out after his father.

No one had noticed him.

There was too much screaming. Too much panic.

Flames lit the thatched roofs of some of the houses, horses whinnied in terror, swords clanging loudly. Aleksander ran as fast as he could in the darkness. But where was he going? A riderless horse came charging from out of nowhere, rising up on its hind legs, screeching to the moon. Aleksander ran to the side of the nearest cottage, his back pressed against it, his heart beating loudly. He didn't want to die. The screams and sounds he heard meant death was coming, but he didn't want to die.

Where had his mother gone?

He heard her scream, then. Frowning, listening again, he started running towards the sound of her voice, the screaming, keening, wailing of her voice. He ran through a huddle of cottages and out the other side, and there she lay, his mother, her hair blowing around her, as dark as the sky above.

Lying on the ground, over a body.

Aleksander froze. He recognised the hair, the shape of the back, the tunic. The sobs that rose up in his chest would not come out. His screams caught in his throat, and his mouth fell open as his shoulders rose and fell with every terrifying moment.

He couldn't move.

And then Fianna bent down over the slain body of her husband, and when she lifted herself up again, Aleksander saw the knife in her hand. His eyes grew wider, and his heart beat faster, and he started running, but she didn't see him.

Did she?

He called to her, but nothing came out of his mouth as he ran. Nothing.

But she saw him, didn't she?

As she put the blade to her throat, the tears flowing down her face, Aleksander ran, but a man ran in front of him, grabbing him, stopping him.

'Where are you going?' Gant asked angrily. 'You'll get yourself killed!' Then he turned, following the look of sheer horror on Aleksander's face and he let go of the small hand and ran. 'Fianna! No! No!'

But it was too late.

'I'm sorry,' she mouthed towards them. And then she was gone.

Gant kept running, but Aleksander stopped.

The line across her neck was thick with blood now; red and wet as it glistened under the soulful gaze of the moon. And Fianna Lehr pitched forward onto the dead body of her husband, her eyes filled with despair.

***

Jael had told him everything and nothing, but hopefully, enough to keep Eadmund from asking her any more, at least for now. Enough to comfort him, she hoped. She hurt everywhere but most of all inside, where the wounds of Tuura had lain hidden for so long. She needed sleep. She needed to go and shut that door again. Lock it back up, keep those men where they belonged: in the farthest reaches of her darkest places.

Jael sighed, and her whole body shuddered, sinking into the bed, soothed by the rise and fall of Eadmund's chest, so steady and calm beside her. She closed her eyes, at last, seeking peace and sleep, but all she saw was blood, and Tarak, and Aleksander, and those men, and her mother, and everything in between.

And the storm grew louder.

**

Eirik glanced around the hall.

Was this how he would die? *Where* he would die?

He looked towards Ivaar.

Would Ivaar truly try to kill his father as he had killed his own?

Eirik had no sword, but he had hands, he could find knives. There were many ways to get it done.

'Jael asked me for something else if she won,' Eirik started. 'I have to say, for all my talk, I didn't think it possible that she would. I thought she'd put on a show, as she did with Thorgils. But with Tarak?' He shook his head. 'No, I didn't think it would go that way.' He paused, pulling on his beard. 'She asked me to make Eadmund my heir again.'

Ivaar's morbid face froze in shock. 'What?' He laughed, shaking his head. 'Eadmund? Did she now. And you said yes?'

'No, I didn't. No, Eadmund is better, but that will not last. I don't believe it will.'

'I'm glad to hear it,' Ivaar sighed, relieved.

'But then she asked me... if I couldn't believe in Eadmund, that I should believe in her. If she were to win, become Champion of Oss, then she wanted me to choose Eadmund *and* her as the King and Queen of Oss. Together,' Eirik went on, taking some small amount of satisfaction in Ivaar's pinched face. 'And then she won. So I have given her what she asked for.'

Ivaar looked horrified. 'But... but you brought me back after all these years. *I* am your rightful heir. Eadmund will make a fool of you! A mess of Oss!'

'Possibly, but Jael won't,' Eirik said, suddenly sober, his face stern. 'And it is her prize. She earned it.'

'But I'm your *son*! Your eldest son!' Ivaar leaned forward, his lips mean and his eyes hard. 'You cannot do this to me again, Father! Eydis has seen it. Ayla has seen it! I will be the king here!' He didn't care who heard.

'Oss is important to me, Ivaar,' Eirik said with feeling. 'It is mine. I turned it from a prison into a kingdom. It means almost everything to me. But it doesn't mean everything. Not everything. It could burn and sink into the sea, and I would still have everything I needed if I had Eadmund and Eydis beside me. But you...' He looked at the angry man in front of him. 'You would destroy them. Eydis has seen that. She has seen how thirsty you are for your revenge. And I will not go to my pyre leaving them in your desperate hands.'

'You think that little of me?' Ivaar's face twisted painfully. 'You think I could hurt my own family? Eadmund had you banish me when I didn't kill his wife! That I have ill feeling towards him is understandable, but Eydis?' he implored. 'That is too much, Father. That is too hard a thing to hear.' He looked away, shaking with rage. 'Your dreamer is a child who has not learned to master her dreams yet. Mine sees no such thing, but she does see me as the King of Oss one day. You should believe her, because I certainly do.'

'You will take your family and leave when the storm is over,'

Eirik said coldly. 'And you will return in spring with your men, for all of the islands will be going to war against Hest, and I expect to see the men of Kalfa standing behind their lord, as the men of Oss will stand behind their king.'

Ivaar clamped his teeth together, his face clear of all emotion now. He was seething but not about to make it any worse. Like Tarak, another day would come, and bring with it another chance for revenge.

And he would be ready to take it.

***

Edela padded across the floor, her feet numb in cold socks. It was dark, early, and the fire had burned down to nothing. She bent over the bed and prodded Kormac. He jerked awake, staring at her, confused, trying to catch his breath.

'I need your help,' she whispered.

CHAPTER SIXTY ONE

Jael opened her eyes to see Eadmund standing in the doorway. She groaned, squinting at him in the barely-there light. She couldn't hear a thing, apart from Biddy and Thorgils mumbling in the distance. The storm appeared to have blown away, and finally, after spending two days snowbound, she could go to Fyn's.

It was time he knew what had happened.

Jael sat up, grimacing, yawning, thinking that perhaps another day spent in bed wasn't such a bad idea at all. She could only imagine how Tarak must be feeling. That made her smile. 'Are you just going to stare at me all morning?' she grumbled at her husband.

'No, I'm barring the door to stop you running away,' Eadmund smiled.

'Ha! Well, I didn't run away yesterday, or the day before, did I?'

'You couldn't move, so that doesn't count!' he grinned, coming forward, his hands behind his back. 'Besides, the blizzard meant you couldn't go anywhere, even if you'd wanted to. But today... today I think you've actually chosen not to run away.'

Jael frowned as he brought the gift out from behind his back and handed it to her. She smiled. 'Ahhh, the long-awaited present. And you think I've finally earned it, do you?'

'Perhaps. Or perhaps Biddy told me that she'd throw it in the fire if I didn't move it!'

Jael laughed, which hurt, as she unwrapped the dust-covered linen sheet the present was wrapped in. She laughed again as she pulled out a thick furry cloak. Bear fur, by the look of it. 'A warm cloak! At last!'

'Well, I thought you might need it if you were going to be staying here a while. Which you seem to be quite keen on.'

'I seem to be,' Jael admitted. 'Especially since your father has made us both his heirs. I can hardly leave now, can I?'

'True.' Eadmund still couldn't believe that she'd convinced Eirik to change his mind. 'You may as well put it on if you're going out.'

'I am,' she grimaced, easing herself onto the floor. 'I'm going riding.'

'Not without me, you're not,' Eadmund said, glaring sternly at her.

'Yes, without you. Go and say goodbye to Isaura and the children or something. I need a ride.' She patted him on the shoulder. 'Alone.'

***

Eydis woke with a start.

There was so much noise in her head. She tried to silence it but still keep hold of the dream. It had been so very clear just then, but now?

Now... it was gone.

She sighed, feeling annoyed as she sat up.

It had felt like an important dream to remember, of that she was certain.

***

'Aleksander! Wake up!' Hanna hissed in his ear, her hand clamped over his mouth. 'I have your clothes. You must get dressed quickly. Soldiers are coming!'

Aleksander blinked himself awake. He looked at her, frowning.

'Hurry!' Hanna whispered again, her eyes full of terror as she shook his shoulder. 'Get dressed. Your cousin is waiting outside.' She took her hand away from his mouth, pointing to his clothes.

Aleksander slid out of bed, heart racing, rushing to put them on, his eyes barely open. It was freezing in the room, and his fingers were so numb that he fumbled endlessly. Eventually, he managed to wrap his cloak around himself, grabbing his weapons and moving quietly to the door. He turned to look at Hanna, feeling an unexpected pang of loss, and, smiling quickly, he slipped outside.

***

Jael yawned as she wandered towards the gates, smiling at the warmth of her new cloak, then grimacing at the pain in her elbow, convinced that something was broken in there. She wanted to check for ice before heading off. The blizzard had been fierce, but she hadn't heard any rain. Still, she didn't want to take any risks with Tig.

The snow looked fresh and soft, the clouds pale and non-threatening as she wandered back to the stables, imagining Fyn's face when she told him what had happened to Tarak.

Jael saw something out of the corner of her eye, and she spun around, the hairs on her arms prickling.

Tiras.

She ran for him, lunging, catching the flap of his cloak as it trailed behind his escaping figure. He knew that she'd seen him and he'd run.

Why?

Jael yanked him towards her, throwing him against the wall of the nearest shed. 'Hello, worm,' she spat, then frowned. He was smiling at her so confidently that a shiver ran the length of her spine. 'What have you done?' she demanded, her face close to his. He didn't stop smiling. 'What have you *done*?' Jael whipped her knife out of its scabbard, pressing it to his throat. 'Tell me, you fucking bastard!'

'You won't kill me, Jael,' Tiras rasped. 'You won't kill me. You've shown that already. You're too weak. Weak like your father!'

Jael pricked Tiras' neck, making him bleed just enough to terrify him, to show him her intent. 'Tell me or don't but either way, I'll find out, and you'll be too dead to worry. I won't make the same mistake twice.'

Tiras did look worried, yelping at the pain in his neck, so Jael pressed the tip of her knife in again, harder, twisting it. He screamed, feeling his warm blood trickling down his cold neck. 'Wait! No! Wait!' he hissed desperately.

'What. Did. You. Do?' Jael screamed, leaning on the knife some more.

'Tarak...' Tiras managed to get out. 'I... told him... about your... friend. He's gone... find him.'

Jael frowned, momentarily confused, then her face froze.

She brought the knife screaming across Tiras' throat, dropped his spurting, dying body to the ground, and ran.

***

'Where are we going?' Aleksander asked as he raced to keep up with Aedan. They were taking the back streets, trying not to be seen.

'Sssshhh, keep your voice down,' Aedan whispered, turning around, his eyes only just visible. 'We have to get you out of here before the alarm is raised. We're going to get your horse.' He was wrapped in a black cloak. His hood was over his face, as was Aleksander's. They looked almost identical.

'If we're seen,' Aedan said hoarsely, 'I'll lead them away. It should confuse them. You find your horse.'

'Is she still in the stables?' Aleksander tried to keep up, but his head was so muddled that he kept stumbling.

'No, Aron took her nearer the gates. She's saddled and waiting. You just have to get on her and ride. Don't let them catch you.'

'Who?'

'Sssshhh,' Aedan whispered, putting his hand up as a group of soldiers ran past the buildings they were slipping between. 'It may be too late.' He paused, popping his head out into the street.

The soldiers were running in the opposite direction.

'Come on! Quick!' Aedan called and ran, keeping as far to the left of the street as possible, ducking under porches, trying to stay out of sight.

'There!' yelled a voice. 'Those men! Grab them!'

Aleksander looked to see that the soldiers had turned around and were now chasing them.

'Go!' Aedan yelled as he peeled away, running down an alley, leading half the soldiers in the opposite direction.

The other half followed Aleksander, and they were running fast, screaming at him to stop. The shadowy streets of Tuura all started to look the same.

He glanced around desperately.

Which way to the gates?

***

'Tarak's gone after Fyn!' Jael yelled, throwing open the door before disappearing back outside, running to the stables. There was no one around, only Biddy. 'Find Thorgils! Eadmund! Hurry!'

Tig was waiting, saddled and eager as she threw herself up onto his back. He could sense the tension in her. She knocked her heels into him, hard, and he whinnied, his head flying around angrily. They burst out of the stables together, already galloping by the time they reached the open gates.

Jael had her sword but no shield.

She should've grabbed a shield.

***

Biddy didn't even stop for her cloak as she raced across the square. Ketil was setting up his stall, but there was no sign of Eadmund or Thorgils anywhere. Surely Thorgils couldn't have walked too far in his condition?

She ran up the steps to the hall, pulling on one of the heavy doors, searching the surprised faces that turned in her direction.

Eadmund was already on his way to her. 'What's happened?' he called, his jaw clenching tightly.

Something was wrong.

Biddy gasped for breath. 'Jael... Tarak has gone after Fyn,' she breathed heavily. 'Jael said to get you quickly.'

Eadmund looked confused, turning to Thorgils who had more understanding, but almost as much confusion.

'I'll get Vili,' Thorgils grimaced and moved as quickly as he could, leaving Eadmund to follow him. 'You get Leada. Have you got your sword?'

'Thorgils, you're in no state –'

'Eadmund!' Eydis burst through the green curtain, still in her nightgown, her head swivelling with speed, trying to sense where her brother was. 'Eadmund! My dream!' Her face was horror-stricken. 'I had it again. Tarak will kill Jael! It's not over! It was the same dream. He will kill her!'

Eadmund turned and ran towards the doors, Thorgils stumbling after him.

***

Fyn had heard her coming.

He'd been waiting for the weather to clear. Hoping to see Jael. His fire was ready, water was heating in the cauldron, but when he'd rushed outside, he'd seen Tarak riding down the hill towards him instead.

He'd frozen in terror, then raced back inside to grab his sword.

The sword lay broken beside him now, and in his bleeding hand he held his eating knife, small in comparison to Tarak's giant sword as he circled him, taunting him, licking his swollen lips, cursing him. Fyn tried to think, but he was eleven-years-old again, shaking in his boots, unable to move.

He tried to remember what Jael had trained him to do.

Everything was a weapon. Everything.

His eyes darted around, and he could see a rock peeking out of the snow, not far from where Tarak stood. If he could get him near it, perhaps there was a chance it could do more damage than his small knife?

Tarak laughed, enjoying Fyn's terror. '*You* put that bitch up to it? It was *your* revenge that she was carrying out? Ha!' His smile turned into a snarl as he lurched forward, baring his teeth.

'My special, special friend. How I have missed our time together.' And reaching out with his sword, he pointed it at Fyn's heaving chest. 'Don't say you haven't missed me! I can see it in your eyes.' He ran the sword lightly over Fyn's tunic, down to the top of his belt, his eyes full of something other than anger now.

Fyn's arm was cut in three places. He could only see out of one eye. He was numb everywhere. But he knew those eyes. He knew what that look meant.

He turned his head away, gagging.

That was never going to happen again. Never.

Fyn kept the rock in one corner of his eye and lunged, trying to push Tarak over, towards the rock, his knife in his hand.

Tarak's legs were weak, injured after his fight with Jael, and he fell easily, pulling Fyn with him, rolling, avoiding Fyn's knife as it came towards his thick neck. He bellowed in agony at the pain in his legs as he hit the ground, his giant sword lost in the snow. Tarak was up on his knees quickly, though, smashing his fist into Fyn's face. Fyn tried to crawl away, towards the rock but Tarak grabbed him by the hair, tugging him back.

'It didn't have to be this way,' he hissed into Fyn's ear, one thick hand stroking his cheek, while the other held him down. 'But now you've made me so angry... I'm going to have to punish you.'

***

Jael's heart thudded in time to Tig's hooves as he ploughed through the snow. She dug her knees into him, urging him to go faster, following tracks in the fresh, white powder. Tarak had come this way, but how long ago? Then she heard it, a terrified scream echoing around the silent valley.

Fyn.

Jael swallowed, bending lower. 'Come on, Tig! Ha! Ha!'

She drove Tig down the slope as fast as she dared. Before he'd stopped, Jael slipped out of the saddle, dragged *Toothpick* out of his scabbard and ran. She could hear Fyn shrieking and sobbing as he lay face down in the snow, Tarak's hand on his back. 'Get off him!' Jael screamed, her voice breaking with anger. She couldn't look to see if Fyn was alright; there was no time.

She ran for Tarak, lunging at him with her sword.

Tarak ducked and scooped up his own sword, turning to face her.

'Fyn! Go! Take Tig and go!'

Fyn rolled away, groaning, sniffing, struggling to stand. 'Jael, no!' He wanted to stay and help. She couldn't stop him alone. He needed to help her.

'Fyn, I need you to keep Tig safe! Take him back to the fort! Now! Please!'

There was nothing else to say. Fyn knew how much she loved her horse.

He stumbled to his feet, running for Tig who was whinnying, skittering around anxiously, the smell of blood in his nostrils. Fyn grabbed hold of the reins, trying to soothe him enough to hop up into the saddle.

Tarak moved to go after them, but Jael blocked his path. 'No! Not him. Me again, you fucking bastard!' And she swung *Toothpick* at him.

Tarak was a swollen, bloody, limping mess, but he looked just as capable as ever as he brought his sword down to meet hers. The vibration of their blades meeting nearly had *Toothpick* out of Jael's hand. She shuddered backwards, her boot sinking into the snow. This was no flat dirt surface, carefully cleared and prepared for battle. This was a thick mess of trouble that promised death for someone.

Fyn urged Tig up the slope as fast as he could, turning back as they reached the rise just in time to see Tarak lunging at Jael, his face stretched into a maniacal grin.

Fyn gritted his teeth, shook his head and rode away.

***

'Where's the gate? Where's the gate?' Aleksander repeated to himself as he raced away from the soldiers.

Then he saw a guard tower. At last.

But where was Aron? Where was he waiting with Sky?

His head spun as he ran, but there was barely anyone around and certainly no horses.

Aleksander was running out of breath. The soldiers were getting closer. He shuddered, fearing they would catch him. He imagined what they'd do to Aedan and Aron if they did. Aleksander didn't want to put them in danger; he didn't want anything to happen to Sky.

He ran harder then, harder than he believed he could.

But the gates were shut.

He pulled up sharply, his eyes darting around. Where was Aron?

What did he do?

'Here!' came the hoarse whisper from behind him.

Aleksander turned to see Aron sitting on a horse, holding onto Sky's reins. Somehow he'd squeezed both horses into the tight space between two houses.

He was dressed like Aedan. Like Aleksander.

Aron dropped his hood over his face, handing Sky's reins to Aleksander. 'Get ready.'

'But the gates!' Aleksander squeezed between Sky and the house, managing to get a foot in the stirrup and his leg over the saddle.

'Wait,' Aron said calmly, his eyes fixed straight ahead.

The soldiers that had been chasing Aleksander ran past.

'Wait.' Aron watched the gates, not even blinking.

Aleksander held the reins tightly in numb hands, his stomach twisting nervously. The guards on the tower were talking to someone over the wall. Aleksander held his breath, glancing at

Aron, who tightened his grip on the reins.

'When I go, follow me as fast as you can,' Aron whispered. 'Don't stop.'

One guard walked up to the gates and lifted the heavy wooden beam, grumbling away to himself. He called on his companion to help him, and together they lifted it off completely, placed it against the wall, and pulled open one of the gates.

'Now!' Aron called, kicking his boots into his horse's flanks, urging him forward.

Aleksander followed on Sky, and together they burst across the street and out through the open gate before the guards had had a chance to move. Aron didn't even glance at his mother and father who stood to one side of the gates, waiting to get in.

***

'Aarrghh!' Jael screamed as Tarak's sword ripped open the wound on her arm. She blinked, trying to focus. Her limbs felt as heavy as boulders. She spun away from him, gulping in air, blood soaking her tunic.

She wasn't wearing mail.

Tarak ran at her, both hands wrapped around his giant sword as he lifted it above his head. Jael slipped to the side, turning, sweeping *Toothpick* across his back. She was losing her balance, though, and the cut she made was not as deep as it needed to be. Tarak grunted but barely broke stride as he turned on her again.

Jael growled, throwing *Toothpick* at Tarak's sword, and the clanging of iron echoed all around Fyn's hidden valley. This was going to tire her out, she realised. There was nothing clever in fighting like this, not with an elbow that was barely working. She had to get him to the ground.

Eydis' dream flashed before her eyes, but Jael blinked it away.

The power of Tarak's arm was going to kill her if she didn't weaken him somehow. Slipping *Toothpick* into his scabbard, Jael grabbed her knife and ran for him.

***

They were coming.

In the flat, white meadow there was nothing but the sound of their horses' hooves, and then the sound of more, coming behind them.

'We separate here!' Aron called. 'Go to your hiding place! Don't let them follow you. They won't find you there!' And he tugged on his reins, turning his horse to the left. 'Good luck!'

Aleksander had ridden these snowy fields for weeks now, and he knew where he was. He turned to count how many men had gone after Aron.

Four.

There were three still following him.

He knew Sky now. She would ride for him.

And Aleksander tapped her firmly with his boots, bending low over her neck, the wind biting at them both as they flew across the whiteness, three Tuuran soldiers chasing them down.

***

Fyn could tell Thorgils' bright-red mop of hair anywhere. 'Come on! Come on, Tig!' he called, his aching body urging Jael's horse forward. The snow was so deep, and they had been riding at such a pace that he could feel the big horse tiring beneath him.

Thorgils was struggling too.

His stomach wound had opened up, and he could feel the ooze of it seeping through his tunic. He looked up and saw a horse and rider coming towards them. He squinted. It looked like Tig, but not Jael. 'It's Fyn!' he called to Eadmund. 'You go! Hurry! He'll show you the way!'

Eadmund stared at Thorgils' pained face, saw the blood on his friend's hands and nodded. Tapping his boots against Leada's flanks, he urged her towards Fyn, who almost fell off Tig in relief.

'Jael!' was all he could croak, his swollen mouth thick with blood as he spun Tig around. 'Help Jael!'

Eadmund slapped the reins onto Leada's back, following Fyn. He hadn't ridden in years, and Leada didn't know him, but there was no time for any of it to matter now. Eydis' terrified screams rang in his ears, and Eadmund gritted his teeth, hoping he wasn't too late.

***

Aleksander pulled on Sky's reins, jumping down into the deep snow. He couldn't outride the soldiers, and he couldn't get to his hideout with them still following him. He slapped Sky on the rump. 'Go on! You go! Go!' Thankfully, she whinnied loudly and ran off.

He pulled out his sword and stood waiting.

It had been a long time.

He hoped he still remembered how to use it.

***

Jael kicked Tarak in the chest, dropped lower and smashed him in the groin with her boot. He yelled and stumbled, collapsing forward, the pain of his wounds starting to take a toll now. Jael didn't stop. She ran at him again, pulling the knife out of her mouth, stabbing him in the side. She yanked it out, ducking his scything blade and ran away.

He was wounded. Let him do the chasing.

Breaths came in strained gasps as she turned, watching Tarak, her body heaving. He came lumbering towards her, sword raised, shoulders hunched, and she knew that he was weak now. Jael stuck the knife between her teeth again and ran for him, launching herself up onto his chest, wrapping her arms around his thick neck. She pulled herself up as he bellowed, his sword flying uselessly, unable to reach her. He threw it away as Jael's hands tightened around his throat, choking him.

Jael released one hand, grabbing her knife.

Tarak hit her repeatedly, swinging her about as she tried to hold on and bring the knife to his throat. She was losing her grip, but she lashed out and stuck him in the side of the neck, jerking the blade down through his pulsing veins.

Tarak screamed. 'You fucking bitch! You're going to die now!' He roared, spinning around with speed.

Jael tried to hold on but the blood coursing down his neck was so slippery that she couldn't grip anything. It slid down his neck like a waterfall, and as he spun, she flew away, landing with a scream on her back, on top of the rock that had been sticking up out of the snow.

Tarak came for her, and Jael couldn't move.

Her knife had gone in the fall. She glanced around quickly, trying to free her legs. The rock was somewhere, lodged into her, and she couldn't escape its grip. Jael slid *Toothpick* out of his scabbard, but Tarak came with all his weight and smashed his knee down onto her arm.

Her sword fell out of her hand.

'Aarrghh!' She heard a snap, the pain blazing up her arm.

Eydis' dream. No. No.

Tarak lay his weight on her, and her chest was crushed. No breath would come. No weapons in reach. No air. Jael curled forward, smashing her head into his broken nose, jerking her body around underneath him.

It was useless. She couldn't move him.

She couldn't breathe.

Tarak shook his head, trying to ignore the pain. He was bleeding all over her, his neck was gaping open, but he was smiling. He had her now. 'Time to say goodbye, cunt,' he growled, bringing his sword up to her throat.

***

Two had gone down quickly, their blood dying the snow red. But the third knew how to use a sword better than most, and that man had shown Aleksander just how long it had been since he'd trained.

Since Jael.

Aleksander shook his head crossly.

Jael.

He wasn't going to be able to help her if he joined the two dead men in a bloody heap. He rushed at the remaining soldier, his sword ready to swing, then stopped, remembering Jael's favourite move. He smiled and spun, kicking the soldier in the side of the head. He'd never been as good at it as Jael, but he had a bigger foot, and the impact of it smashing into an unsuspecting jaw was enough to bring the soldier down. The man fell sideways, his senses dulled, his sword gone, and Aleksander rushed to finish him, stabbing his sword through his chest until he was sure he was dead.

He checked the other two. Both dead.

And sheathing his sword, Aleksander searched their bodies for anything useful. There were a few knives. One had a tinderbox, which would come in handy.

He whistled for Sky, who came back quickly, and without another thought for the bloody mess he'd made, he mounted her, and they raced across the snow, making sure to create confusion with their tracks.

Certain he would be followed.

***

Jael saw Eadmund's face. She heard Eydis' voice warning her that she was about to die. She couldn't breathe. Everything was going black. Her ears were buzzing. She remembered her new cloak, Aleksander, the puppies, Biddy, Thorgils. Her father. All within a blink, and then... and then... Tarak fell on top of her, his sword falling harmlessly into the snow, his head lolling lifelessly to one side.

And then, Eadmund.

Eadmund standing over her with *Toothpick*.

And *Toothpick* was thick with Tarak's blood.

Eadmund tried to pull Tarak's dead body off Jael. He could see her eyes closing, but moving Tarak was like trying to lift a horse. He pushed and pulled, and with Fyn's help, they eventually managed to roll him off her.

Eadmund dropped down to Jael's side. Her eyes were closed now, her face pale, her chest wasn't moving. 'Jael!' He shook her. 'Jael!' he screamed. 'No! Please, no!'

Thorgils was there, then, stumbling towards them. 'Jael! Jael!' he roared, his eyes full of tears.

Jael gasped, a sharp, desperate, straining sound, her eyes fluttering open. 'There's a fucking rock in my back,' she groaned, closing her eyes again.

***

Aleksander felt confused, and despite his warm cloak, he couldn't stop shaking.

Why had they come for him? Where would he go now?

He frowned, the clouds in his head finally parting.

Aron, Aedan, Branwyn and Kormac had all risked their lives to save him.

Why?

He thought of his mother and the cold reality of what she'd done lay about his bruised shoulders like a death shroud.

He glanced around. It was still just him and Sky. He'd made a mess of their tracks, riding all over the valley, every way he could think of to confuse his pursuers, but now he needed food, and warmth, and his supplies.

He needed to get back to Andala.

Sky whinnied loudly, coming to a stop just before the grove where he'd hidden everything. Aleksander stilled his breathing, listening. Someone was there. He could hear a horse. So could Sky.

'Well, you took longer than I'd imagined,' Edela grumbled, emerging from the trees, leading Deya and their pack horse. 'I thought we would have been away by now, but never mind. I have some dried fish you can nibble on while we're riding. It's not very nice, but it will do.'

Aleksander was stunned, his mouth flapping open. 'But... you...' He smiled suddenly. 'Of course. You. You saw it all.'

'Finally,' Edela smiled wearily. 'Yes, I did. And I wasn't about to let you ride away without me. You need me, you know. And I need you. We have to save Jael, don't we? Together.'

Aleksander slid off Sky, enclosing her shivering body in his weary arms. 'We do. Yes,' he sighed, feeling better than he had in days. 'We do.'

***

Runa stood next to Fyn, her eyes swollen from sobbing. She couldn't believe she had her son back again. She couldn't believe that Morac had been the one to convince Eirik to send him away. 'You saved my son,' she said again, her head bobbing towards the broken figure lying in bed, her bottom lip quivering.

Jael shrugged awkwardly. 'Not really. But at least now you can give him a proper home again. Feed him a decent meal or two.' Talking hurt. She was growing tired of visitors now.

Eirik saw Jael's discomfort, and he glanced at Runa. 'Let's leave Jael in peace. She needs to rest.' He winked at her.

Jael smiled gratefully at him as he ushered Runa outside.

Fyn stayed behind for a moment. 'Thank you, Jael,' he mumbled, unable to stop the tears from falling down his bruised and swollen face. 'Thank you for what you did. You nearly died for me. Twice.'

'Ahhh, well,' Jael said with a weary smile, 'I can't think of many better reasons to die, Fyn. It would have been worth it.'

'Fyn!' Eirik called from the main room. 'Hurry up, now!'

Fyn gave her a lop-sided smile and disappeared.

Jael closed her eyes, stroking Ido's soft black head as he lay firmly wedged into her side.

'I'm going to go and say goodbye to Isaura and the children,' Eadmund murmured, poking his head in the doorway. 'They're all finally leaving now.'

'I'm jealous,' Jael yawned. 'I'd love to watch Ivaar scurry away, back to his little pebble.'

'For now.' Eadmund came into the room, placing a hand on her head. 'He'll be back.'

'Yes, he will. And you'll need to be ready.'

'Me?' Eadmund laughed. 'I'm not the one who's too broken to move!' He leaned down and kissed her. 'We'll both need to be ready for whatever Ivaar brings.'

'Mmmm,' Jael murmured, enjoying his kiss enough to ignore the pain for a moment. 'Ivaar. And the rest of them.'

THE END

EPILOGUE

'They found the book, my lord.'

Jaeger Dragos spun around, his amber eyes blinking in surprise. 'They found the book?' His mouth hung open, a smile slowly winding its way around his handsome lips. 'They found the book! Really? Where is it?' He came rushing towards his trusted servant, grabbing his hands. 'Tell me, Egil, where is it?'

'It's on its way, my lord.'°

'Here? In Hest?'

'Yes, my lord, they found it hidden, not far from the castle.'

Jaeger shook his head in disbelief. He had spent years looking for that book.

The darkest, most powerful book ever written.

The Book of Raemus. The Book of Darkness. And now it was his.

Lost for centuries, he was finally going to have its power in his hands.

'Soon it will be spring, Egil, and they will launch their ships and send their men to try and destroy us,' Jaeger smiled, his mind wandering, his eyes bright with thoughts of what was to come. 'And my father thinks he knows how to protect us. But little does he know how ready we will be to destroy them all.'

For he who possessed the book would bring darkness to the entire world.

WHAT TO READ NEXT

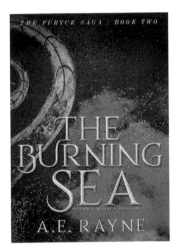

Available on Amazon

ABOUT A.E. RAYNE

I survive on a happy diet of historical and fantasy fiction and I particularly love a good Viking tale. My favourite authors are Bernard Cornwell, Giles Kristian, Robert Low, C.J. Sansom, and Patrick O'Brian. I live in Auckland, New Zealand, with my husband, three children and three dogs.

I promise you characters that will quickly feel like friends and villains that will make you wild, with plots that twist and turn to leave you wondering what's coming around the corner. And, like me, hopefully, you'll always end up a little surprised by how I weave everything together in the end!

***

Sign up to my newsletter for pre-sale and new release updates
www.aerayne.com/sign-up

Contact me:
a.e.rayne@aerayne.com
www.aerayne.com/contact

For more information about A.E. Rayne and her books visit:
www.aerayne.com
www.facebook.com/aerayne